'What's the problem?'

'Well, at the risk of sounding embarrassingly ridiculous, I'd like you to understand it's just dinner…not a date.'

Mac's eyes twinkled—and her stomach churned.

'I don't date, you see,' Izzy added, hoping to stop the churning with practicality. 'Well, not at the moment.'

'So dinner…not a date. That's okay.'

The smile playing around his words only added to the stomach-churning!

She sighed again, shrugged, and finally said, 'I can't be late home.'

And if he thought she hadn't noticed the satisfied expression on his face as she finally agreed he was wrong.

Used to getting his own way, was he?

A sure sign this was a man to be wary of.

Dear Reader,

In this book you'll meet Izzy, a foster child brought up by an extraordinary couple who have opened their home and their hearts to waifs and strays, fostering many children over a long period of time.

The house is quiet now, the children all grown up, though Izzy remains living in The Old Nunnery with her foster parents and daughter Nikki. But because of the love they received from their foster parents, Hallie and Pop Halliday, the children are all close, and in the next three books you'll meet more of them—Lila, Stephen and Marty—and follow their lives and their loves as they meet the people who will help them create their own families.

These stories—Lila's in particular—have been in my head for a long time, and somehow this seemed the right time to tell them. I hope you enjoy meeting 'the Halliday Mob', as they were always known around town, and following their lives as they seek families of their very own.

Meredith Webber

A FOREVER FAMILY FOR THE ARMY DOC

BY
MEREDITH WEBBER

Published in Great Britain 2017
By Mills & Boon, an imprint of HarperCollins*Publishers*
1 London Bridge Street, London, SE1 9GF

© 2017 Meredith Webber

ISBN: 978-0-263-92631-6

Printed and bound in Spain
by CPI, Barcelona

Meredith Webber lives on the sunny Gold Coast in Queensland, Australia, but takes regular trips west into the Outback, fossicking for gold or opal. These breaks in the beautiful and sometimes cruel red earth country provide her with an escape from the writing desk and a chance for her mind to roam free—not to mention getting some much needed exercise. They also supply the kernels of so many stories it's hard for her to stop writing!

When my sister and brother-in-law discovered they were unable to have children they began adopting babies and fostering older children, eventually adopting six of them. The family they blended together became very special—not only to each other but to our wider family—and brought fun and joy and laughter to all our lives. This particular sister has been my greatest support as a writer, and the first reader of all my books, so to Jenny, and all her family, this book and those that follow it are for you.

Praise for
Meredith Webber

'The romance is emotional, passionate, and does not appear to be forced as everything happens gradually and naturally. The author's fans and everyone who loves Sheikh romance are gonna love this one.'

—*Harlequin Junkie* on
The Sheikh Doctor's Bride

CHAPTER ONE

Izzy PACED HERSELF on the run along the coastal path, which, right now, bordered a small sheltered beach. Ahead, the path rose high over headland cliffs, and further on it wound through coastal scrub. A truly beautiful part of the world—the place she loved, the place she belonged.

She'd been working nights, so this early-morning run was in the nature of a reward. A little treat before returning to her real world—making sure Nikki was ready for the start of the new term, catching up with her parents to get the latest family news, walking the dogs across the lush paddocks around the house—relaxing!

Nikki!

Her daughter would be thirteen next month—thirteen going on thirty—sensible, loving, doing well at school. So why was there always a little knot of worry tucked beneath Izzy's sternum where Nikki was concerned?

Izzy stopped—well, jogged on the spot—peering down onto the beach where an unidentifiable lump of something lay just beyond the lapping water.

Too big to be a body, she told the lurch in her stomach, but best she check.

Scrambling down over lumpy rocks from the path to the sandy beach, she caught a glimpse of movement up ahead.

Someone else heading towards the unknown object?

Or someone leaving the—

No! It was definitely too big for a body; besides, the movement had now resolved into a person, tall, dark-haired—lots of dark hair—definitely heading for the lump.

Izzy was the first to reach what was now apparent as a beached mammal, and knelt beside it, speaking quietly, touching it gently—a baby whale? Surely it must be because dolphins were a different shape, sleeker, their faces pointed, beaked…

Although the sun was not yet high in the sky, the animal's skin was hot. Izzy ripped off her T-shirt, dunked it in the waves and spread it over the animal's back.

'Good idea,' a deep voice said. 'I've a towel in my pack, I'll get that.'

He'd turned and was gone before Izzy could get a good look at him, nothing but an impression of a very unkempt man with a lot of facial hair and plenty more in a tangled mess all over his head.

'Bring something like a bottle or a cup if you've got one, and clean water, too.'

She yelled the order after him then returned to studying the animal, trying to remember things she'd learned when she and Nikki had visited Sea World some years ago.

Sea mammals usually stranded themselves on their side.

Tick!

This one certainly had.

The stranger returned.

'Porpoise,' he said in an authoritative voice.

'You think? I thought maybe baby whale.'

A shout of laughter made her look up, and up, to the tousled-haired man standing above her.

'Whale calves are three times the size of this fellow and weigh a ton or more.'

'Know-it-all,' Izzy muttered to herself, but as the man had dunked his towel in the water and was efficiently covering the animal she could hardly keep arguing with him.

And why *was* she arguing?

Did it matter?

'I think the first thing is to get it onto its belly.'

Bit late now to tell him she'd already thought of that.

'But the fresh water?'

Ha, something she knew that he didn't!

Deep inside she wondered at the petty thoughts flashing through her head but hopefully he wouldn't have noticed the momentary pause before she answered.

'Just pour a little over each eye, like where he'd have an eyebrow, so it will run down. I seem to remember you need to keep the eyes moist but—'

'The salt gets encrusted on them if you use sea water,' he finished for her, smiling, so white teeth flashed in the mess of dark hair.

And something gave a tiny tug in the pit of Izzy's stomach…

No! Not that! No way!

Carefully he poured water to a point above first one eye, then the other, allowing the water to run down over both eyes.

'I'm Mac,' he said, screwing the lid back on the bottle to preserve the rest of the water.

'Izzy,' Izzy replied, lifting her hand towards his so they shook above the body of what was apparently a porpoise. 'We'll have to roll him this way, towards the sea, to get him on his belly and I think if we dig a hole along this side, he might turn easily.'

'You've done this before?' Mac asked, joining Izzy on the seaward side of the animal, and digging into the sand.

'Nope, but I once went to a lecture about beached mammals. Big ones you shouldn't roll because you can break their ribs, and, oh, you should keep the tail and flippers and this fin on the back wet because they cool themselves through these thinner bits of their body.'

Mac, who'd brought a billycan as well as the bottle of water, began filling it and tipping it carefully onto the fins and tail while Izzy kept digging, focused on what she was doing so the tremor of—what? Aware-ness?—that tickled through her body when Mac settled beside her again, scraping sand away, almost passed unnoticed.

Almost!

What malign fate had brought him to this precise spot at this exact moment in time? Mac wondered as he knelt far too close to the half-naked woman and pulled sand away from the stranded animal.

A three-week trek down the coast path had been an opportunity to clear his head and prepare him-self for the new job that lay ahead—literally ahead, for this particular section of the coastal path ended at Wetherby, not far from Wetherby District Hospital, currently awaiting its new director.

'Director' was a glorified title when the hospital, from what he'd learned, only boasted two doctors, with a private practice of four GPs in support—

'I think he's tilting this way.'

He glanced towards the speaker, who was completely oblivious to the effect she was having on his libido. She was kind of golden—like he imagined a sprite might be. She had golden skin, reddish-gold hair pulled ruthlessly back into a knot at the back of her head, but already escaping its confinement with damp little corkscrew curls flopping around her face. And golden eyes—well, probably brown, but with golden glints in them...

Better to think of the whole of her than individual bits, like the soft breasts, encased in a barely-there bikini top that brushed his arm as they dug—

He stood up, too aggravated by his wayward thoughts—not to mention the apparent return of his libido—to remain beside her.

'I'll lift the towel and shirt off it so we can replace them when it rolls,' he said, and congratulated himself on sounding practical and efficient.

'Good idea,' the sprite said, stopping her digging and scraping for a moment to smile up at him.

Oh, for Pete's sake, she had a dimple...

Fortunately for his sanity, the porpoise rolled into the hole they'd dug and now lay, snug on its belly, the rising tide sending wavelets splashing onto it.

The sprite had leapt away just in time, but she'd caught the full brunt of the splash, so water and sand were now splattered across her skin as she danced up and down in delight, clapping her hands and telling the uncaring animal how clever he was.

'Why do you assume it's a male?' Mac demanded, his reaction to the sight of her capering happiness making the words come out grouchier than he'd intended.

Golden eyes lifted to his.

'Honestly,' she said, a smile barely hidden on her lips, 'do you think a girl porpoise would be stupid enough to get into a fix like this?'

'Hmmph!'

He couldn't recall ever making a 'hmmph' noise before but that was definitely how it came out, but it was time to be practical, not argue over male versus female in the stupidity stakes. He'd certainly been the stupid one in his marriage, assuming it had meant things like love and fidelity on both sides…

Annoyed by the thought, he concentrated on the porpoise.

'What do we do next?'

Izzy studied the still stranded animal. At least it was right way up now, but was she keeping her eyes on it, so she didn't have to look at the man—Mac?

She'd been so delighted when their plan had worked, she'd looked up at him to share the success—straight into the bluest eyes she had ever seen. Right there, deep in the tangled mess of dark hair, was a pair of truly breathtaking blue eyes. She was pretty sure her heart *hadn't* stood still, even for an instant, but it sure had seemed like it…

Think about the porpoise!

'Maybe if we dig a trench, kind of extending our hole towards the sea, he might be able to slide forward as the tide rises.'

'Or perhaps we should get help,' the man with the

blue eyes said, giving the impression he was done with the animal rescue business.

Or maybe he was just being practical.

'We're three kilometres from town and I don't have a phone—do you?'

He looked put out as he shook his head, as if admitting he didn't have a phone was some kind of weakness, but who in their right mind would want to carry a phone on a wilderness walk? There were small fishing and holiday villages along the route and anyone walking it was obliged to report each day's destination so a search could be mounted if the walker didn't turn up. And at this time of the year there'd be other people on the path—

She looked up towards it—hopefully...

No people right now.

'So, it's up to us,' she said, hoping he'd stay so there'd be an 'us'. 'I don't suppose you're carrying a sleeping bag?'

'A sleeping bag?'

He seemed confused so she added quickly, 'Thing you sleep in—the nights have been cool, I thought you might—'

'I *do* know what a sleeping bag is,' he growled, 'I just can't see why you're asking.'

Grouchy, huh?

'For a sling,' she explained, although the bemusement on his face suggested he still wasn't with her. 'Can you get it?' she asked, very politely, and smiling as she spoke because she needed this man's help and didn't want to upset him any more than she already had.

'We'll try to slip it under him,' she explained. 'We

probably should have done it before he rolled but it's too late now, so we'll just have to build a little pool for him. I don't think we could lift him with the sleeping bag, but once the water rises and takes some of the weight, we'll be able to guide him into deeper water.'

'You want me to put my sleeping bag into the water for this animal?'

The disbelief in his voice stopped all thoughts of politeness.

'Oh, stop complaining and go get it. This part of the track ends at Wetherby. I'll buy you a new sleeping bag there.'

He didn't move for a moment, simply looking at her and shaking his head, as if she, not the stranded porpoise, was the problem.

Muttering something under his breath—something that could have been about bossy women—he turned and strode away, long, strong legs eating up the distance back to the track.

Izzy realised she was staring after him, shook *her* head in turn, and returned to digging with renewed determination.

Better by far than thinking of the blue eyes or strong legs or the fact that the rest of him, now his T-shirt was wet and clung to a very well-developed chest, wasn't too bad either.

Aware that he was behaving like a loutish imbecile, Mac returned to his already diminished pack and pulled out his sleeping bag, unrolling and unzipping it so it was ready when he reached the water.

Her idea was a good one—he should have thought of it himself.

Was he annoyed because he hadn't?

Or because of his inexplicable awareness of the woman who *had*?

Wasn't he done with that kind of attraction?

Not with women in general—he had several good women friends, some of whom, from time to time, he had taken to bed.

Until that had become awkward—more than physical attraction creeping in—though not on his side.

And the one thing he'd learned from his marriage was that physical attraction was dangerous. It messed with a man's head, leading him to make rash decisions.

And wasn't his head holding enough mess already? The Iraq posting, then finding out about his wife and *her* physical attractions…

Ex-wife!

He shook his head to free it of the past and studied the animal as he approached, determined to take control of this situation.

Wasn't that what ED specialists did?

'I'm deepening the hole—not easy because the sand just washes back in with the next wave but I think if we persist we can do it,' the woman, Izzy, said. 'Do you mind wetting his eyes again?'

So much for taking charge!

But as the tide rose and the water in their porpoise paddling pool grew deeper, he forgot about messy heads and wars and women, determined now to get this creature back into the deeper water where it belonged. He dug until his arms ached, pushing the sleeping bag beneath the heavy body, reaching for Izzy's fingers, grasping towards his from the other side.

By the time the water in the hole was knee deep they had their sleeping bag sling in place, each holding one

side, lifting as the waves came in and easing the docile creature inch by inch into deeper water.

'Look, he's floating now,' Izzy said, and Mac was surprised to realise the weight had gone from their sling.

'You're right,' he said, feeling a surge of relief for the animal. 'But just keep the bag underneath him. We need to roll him back and forth so he gets the feel of his body moving in the water. Well, I think that's the idea. I just know when you catch, tag, and release a big fish, you have to ease it back and forth in the water until it swims away.'

He pushed at the huge body and Izzy pushed back, the pair of them moving into deeper and deeper water until, with a splash of his tail, the rescued animal took off, diving beneath the surface and appearing, after an anxious few minutes, further out to sea.

'He's gone! We did it—we did it!' Izzy yelled, leaping towards Mac and hugging him so the sloppy, wet sleeping bag she was still holding wrapped around him like a straitjacket and he sank beneath the waves.

But once untangled and in shallower water, he returned the hug, the success of their endeavour breaking the reserve of strangers.

He was beginning to enjoy the armful of woman and wet sleeping bag when Izzy eased away, hauling the sleeping bag out of the water and attempting to fold it.

'I don't usually hug str—' she began, then frowned as if something far more important had entered her head.

'Oh, I do hope he doesn't come back,' she said anxiously. 'I hope the rest of the pod are somewhere out there looking for him and he can find them. Do you

know that when a whole pod is beached, and rescued, they try to let them all go at once so they can look after each other?'

Well, that got us over the awkwardness of the 'stranger hug'.

He'd have liked to reply, *Not our problem*, but now she'd mentioned it, he did feel a little anxious that the porpoise—*their* porpoise—would be all right.

Nonsense—he wasn't even certain porpoises swam in pods, and probably neither was she. The job was done and he needed to resume his walk—without his sleeping bag and without drinking water.

Alone?

'I don't suppose you'd like to walk with me as far as Wetherby, or as far along the track as you're going?'

She looked up at him and he noticed surprise in the gold-flecked eyes.

Noticed it because he'd felt it himself, even as he'd asked the question. Wasn't he off women?

Taking a sabbatical from all the emotional demands of a male-female relationship?

Not that it mattered because she was already dismissing the idea.

'Oh, no,' she was saying—far too quickly, really. 'I have to run. I'm just off nights and I've got to check my daughter's ready for school on Monday and my sister's up from Sydney for the weekend, and I think my brother might be in town—'

'Okay, okay!' he said, holding up his hands in surrender, then he smiled at the embarrassment in her face, and added, 'Although in future you might like to remember something my mother once told me.

Never give more than one excuse. More than one and it sounds as if you're making them up on the spot.'

'I *was* not! It's all true.'

Indignation coloured her cheeks and she turned to go, before swinging back to face him.

'There's a fresh water tap just a few hundred metres along the track; you can refill your bottle there.'

After which she really did go, practically sprinting away from him along the track—

For about twenty paces.

'Oh, the sleeping bag,' she said, pointing to the wet, red lump on the beach. 'You can't carry it wet, so hang it on a tree. I'll be back this way in a day or two and collect it so it's not littering the track, and if you tell me where you'll be staying I'll get you a new one.'

Izzy was only too aware that most of her parting conversation with the stranger had been a blather of words that barely made sense, but she *did* need to get back, or at least away from this stranger so she could sort out just what it was about him that disturbed her.

Had to be more than blue eyes and a hunky body— *had* to be!

'I won't be needing the sleeping bag.'

The shouted words were cool, uninterested, so she muttered a heartfelt, 'Good,' and turned away again, breaking stride only to yell belated thanks over her shoulder. Duty done, she took off again at a fast jog, hoping she looked efficient and professional, instead of desperate to get away.

By the time she slowed to cool down before reaching the car park, she'd decided that the silly connection she'd felt towards the man had been nothing more than

the combined effects of night duty and gratitude that there had been someone to help her with the porpoise.

Which, hopefully, would not re-beach himself the moment they were out of sight!

Mac resumed his walk with a lighter pack.

But vague dissatisfaction disturbed the pleasure he'd been experiencing for the past three weeks. Maybe because his solitude had been broken by his interaction with the woman, and it had been the solitude he'd prized most. It was something that had been hard to come by in the army, even when his regiment had returned from overseas missions and he'd been working in the barracks.

Strange that it had been the togetherness of army life, the company of other wives and somewhat forced camaraderie, that had appealed to Lauren—right up to his first posting overseas.

'But you're a doctor, not a soldier,' she'd protested, although she'd seen other medical friends sent abroad. 'What will happen to me if you die?'

He could probably have handled it better than promising not to die, which he didn't on his first mission. But by the second time he was posted to Afghanistan she'd stopped believing—stopped believing in him, and in their marriage—stopped believing in love, she told him later, while explaining that the excitement of an affair gave her a far bigger thrill than marriage could ever provide.

On top of the disaster that had been his second deployment, this news had simply numbed him, somehow removing personal emotion from his life. He knew this didn't show, and he had continued to be a compe-

tent—probably more than competent—caring doctor, a cheerful companion in the officers' mess and a dutiful son to both his parents and whichever spouses they happened to have in their lives at the time.

He'd always been reasonably sure that his parents' divorce, when he was seven, hadn't particularly affected him. He'd seen both regularly, lived with both at various times, got on well with his half-siblings, and had even helped them, at different times, when their particular set of parents had divorced. Walking the coastal path, he'd had time to reflect and had realised that perhaps it had been back then that he'd learned to shut his emotions away—tuck them into something like a memory box and get on with his life.

Had this shut him away, prevented him from seeing and understanding what had probably been Lauren's very real fear that first time he'd been sent abroad?

She'd contacted him, Lauren, when she'd heard he was back this time—an email to which he hadn't replied.

He'd wondered if the thrills she'd spoken of had palled, but found he didn't want to know—definitely didn't want to find out. In fact, their brief courtship and three-year marriage seemed more like some fiction he'd read long ago than actual reality.

A dream—or maybe a nightmare...

Not wanting his thoughts to slide back into the past where there were memories far worse than that particular nightmare, he shut the lid on his memory box and turned his thoughts to what lay ahead.

Inevitably, to the golden girl—woman—who'd popped into his life like a genie from a bottle, then jogged right back out again.

She must live in Wetherby, he realised, but the seaside town and surrounding area had a population of close to ten thousand, probably double that in holiday time.

It was hardly likely they'd run into each other...

And he'd be far too busy getting used to his new position, getting to know his colleagues and learning his way around the hospital and town to be dallying with some golden sprite.

Besides which, she had a child to get ready for school so was probably married, although he *had* checked and she didn't wear a ring.

Not that people did these days, not all the time, and there were plenty of couples who never married, and women, and men, too, he supposed, who had a child but weren't necessarily in a relationship.

But she *had* a child, and even if she wasn't partnered, he was reasonably certain that women with children would—and should—be looking for commitment, for security, in a relationship.

Not that he did relationships.

He was more into dallying, and since he'd been a single man again, the only dalliances he'd had were with women who felt as he did, women who were happy with a mutually enjoyable affair without any expectation of commitment on either side.

The path had wound its way to the top of a small rise and he halted, more to stop his rambling, idiotic thoughts than to look at the view.

But the view was worth looking at, the restless ocean stretching out to the horizon, blue and green in places, fringed with white where the surf curled before rolling up the beach.

Off the next headland he could see surfers sitting on their boards, waiting for the next good wave, and beyond that what must be the outskirts of the town.

Wetherby!

CHAPTER TWO

THE KITCHEN TABLE at the Halliday house could have seated twenty people quite comfortably, but Izzy and her sister Lila were under orders to set it for eight.

'I thought it was just us—how did we get to eight?' Izzy asked, as she obediently laid placemats while Lila added cutlery.

'Uncle Marty's coming and he'll probably have a new girlfriend,' Nikki, who was arranging a bowl of flowers for the centre of the table, volunteered.

'But that's you and me, two, and Lila, Hallie and Pop, five, then Marty and presumably his latest flirt, that's seven.'

'Plus the new doctor from the hospital. As chairman of the hospital board it seemed only right I get to know him,' the woman her foster children all called Hallie explained.

'She's matchmaking again,' Lila whispered to Izzy.

'Hopefully for you, not me,' Izzy retorted.

'But Lila doesn't live here,' Nikki pointed out. 'And, anyway, Mum, he might be The One.'

Izzy groaned. Thirteen-year-olds—*nearly* thirteen-year-olds—shouldn't be acting as marriage managers for their mothers!

'Now, don't start that again. I am perfectly happy with my single state, besides which he's the new doc and I'll be working with him, and while some people seem to manage to combine their work and social lives, it's always been a disaster for me.'

'It was only a disaster once,' Hallie reminded her, 'and that was probably my fault. He seemed like such a nice man when the board interviewed him. How was I to know he had two ex-wives he didn't happen to mention?'

'Two ex-wives and a jealous lover who damned near shot our Izzy.'

They all turned towards the back door and chorused Marty's name as he spoke. Nikki was first into his arms for a hug.

But Izzy hung back, shuddering at the memory of that ill-fated relationship, only looking up when Marty added, 'Okay, I'm home and it's great to see you all but just stand back, girls, because I found this bloke out in the garden, looking a little lost, and apparently he's come for dinner. Hallie's latest stray, I'd say, the new doc in town. Says his name's Mac.'

Izzy could feel her face heating while her body went stiff with shock. A long drawn out *no-o-o-o* was screaming somewhere inside her, while her hitherto reliable heart was beating out a little tattoo that had more to do with how the stranger looked than who he was.

Clean-shaven, with his long shaggy hair trimmed and slicked neatly back, his blue eyes framed by dark arched brows, he was possibly the most attractive man she'd ever seen.

Any woman's body would react to him, she told herself, glancing at Lila to see if she was similarly struck.

But, no, her beautiful, dark-haired, doe-eyed sister was shaking hands with the man called Mac and asking where he'd come from, where he'd trained, doctor-to-doctor questions.

Not that Mac had time to answer them, for Hallie had taken charge and was introducing him to the family.

'Marty you've met—he doesn't live here, just arrives from time to time, though usually not alone...'

Hallie frowned and looked around as if realising for the first time that Marty hadn't brought a woman.

'I took Cindy straight upstairs,' he explained. 'She wanted a shower before dinner, then I went out to see Pop in the shed and met Mac on the way back.'

'Ah,' Hallie said, nodding as if the world was now back in its rightful place. 'So, Mac—you do like to be called Mac, don't you? Isn't that what you said at the interview?'

The poor bewildered man nodded, and before Hallie could go off on another tangent—something they were all only too used to—Marty stepped in.

'Mac, the smallest of the women in the room is Nikki, and the redhead cowering in the corner is her mother, Izzy. It's not your fault that the last hospital director had a mad ex-lover who tried to shoot Izzy.'

Marty waved his arm.

'Come on over, Iz, and say hello to your new boss.'

'We've already met,' Izzy said bluntly, her anger at Marty for singling her out overcoming all her weird reactions to Mac.

'And I'm Lila.'

Bless her! She'd read the tension in the room, had

probably felt it emanating in waves from Izzy, and had stepped in to defuse things.

Now she was doing doctor talk again with the newcomer, smoothing over the earlier awkwardness and giving Izzy time to recover.

Mac tried to make sense of the place and people around him. He'd been directed to walk up the hill from the hospital and the only place on the hill was a big, old, stone-built building that looked as if it could house the hospital as well as all the staff.

He'd walked around it, wondering if the chairman of the hospital board might have a real house hidden somewhere behind it, and had ended up in a huge vegetable garden.

The man called Marty had rescued him, leading him into the old building through a cave-like back entrance and directly into a kitchen where, amidst what seemed like a dozen chattering women, stood his sprite. She had clothes on now, stretch jeans that hugged her legs and lower body and a diminutive top that showed a flash of golden skin at her waist when she moved.

Mrs Halliday he recognised, and the young girl with long golden-brown hair—okay, that was the daughter—while the real beauty of the room, the exotic darkhaired, black-eyed Lila, was finding it hard to hold his attention so his replies to her questions were vague and disjointed.

The sprite rescued him.

'This is the man I was telling you about,' she said to the room at large. 'The man who helped me with the porpoise.'

After which she finally turned her attention to him.

'Sorry about the chaos here tonight, Mac, but with—'

'With your sister up from Sydney, and your brother might be home…yes, I know,' he teased.

He saw the colour rise in her cheeks, but the flash of fire in her eyes suggested anger rather than embarrassment.

Bloody man! Izzy muttered inwardly. Now the whole family was looking at her.

Waiting for her famous temper to flare up?

No way! She would *not* react to this man's teasing. Bad enough her body was reacting to his presence, sending messages along her nerves and excitement through her blood. If this kept up she'd have to leave— town, that is—given that a distracted nurse was no help to anyone.

But Nikki—school…

Pop saved her from total, and quite ridiculous, panic by appearing through the kitchen door with a long, and remarkably dangerous-looking spear in his hand.

It stopped both the conversation and the sizzle in her blood.

'This's the best I can do, Nik,' he said, passing the lethal weapon to Izzy's daughter. 'I don't know if the aboriginals in this area made ceremonial markings on their spears but old Dan at the caravan park will know. You can ask him, and he'll show you what it needs.'

'Put that away right now!' Izzy ordered as Nikki began to caper around the room, flourishing the spear dangerously close to several humans.

Nikki disappeared, Hallie introduced Mac to Pop, she and Lila finished setting the table, and peace reigned, if only momentarily, in the Halliday kitchen.

Pop was explaining to Mac the project Nikki would be doing when school resumed, and why she needed a spear.

'I've made so much stuff for so many kids over the years,' he added. 'Izzy, was it you who was the robot? That was probably my most ingenious design, although I did go through a lot of aluminium foil.'

Any minute now he was going to dig out the old photos and she'd be squirming with embarrassment all night!

'Okay, dinner is ready.'

Hallie saved the day this time. She set the roasted leg of lamb on the table and handed Pop the carving knife and fork, Lila brought over dishes filled with crisply roasted potatoes and sticky baked pumpkin, while Izzy did her bit, taking the jugs of gravy from the warming drawer in the big oven and setting them on the table.

'Right!' Hallie said. 'Guest of honour—that's you, Mac—at the head of the table. Izzy, you'll be working with him so you might as well get to know a bit about him. You sit on one side and Lila on the other, and no descriptions of operations of any sort, please, Lila. Pop, you sit next to Lila, and then Nikki, and on the other side Marty and Cindy, and I'll sit at the end because—'

'Because you have to get up and down to get things,' the family chorused, and Izzy began to relax.

This was home, this was family, this was where she was safe, so who cared if her body found Mac whoever he was—did he *have* a last name?—attractive? Of course she'd felt attraction before—although not for quite a while, now she thought about it.

'Are you going to sit?'

Heat crept up her neck and with her hair piled haphazardly on top of her head, the wretched man would see it! How was she to know he'd hold her chair for her?

She thumped down in the seat, too quickly for him to guide it into place, pulled it in herself and turned to offer a brusque thank you. She met the blue of his eyes and felt herself drowning.

This wasn't attraction, this was madness.

'So, why Wetherby?'

Lila saved her again, asking the question that had been in Izzy's mind, only hers had been phrased more as 'Why the hell Wetherby?'.

Now he was smiling at Lila—well, what man didn't smile at Lila?—and the kind of dark voice she remembered from the beach was explaining in short, fairly innocuous sound bites: army doctor, Middle East on and off over the last few years—

'—so when I decided to get out of the service I looked for somewhere green, and close to the surf, yet small enough to be peaceful.'

'Well, it's certainly that—I'm guessing a month here and you'll be bored to tears,' Cindy told him.

'Hey, Cindy, this is my home!' Marty protested.

'And this is only the second time you've been here, Cindy, and then only for a night,' Nikki pointed out.

'Are all small-town people as defensive as Wetherbyans?' Mac murmured to Izzy, who felt the heat of his body radiating towards her and the breath of his words brush against her skin so all she could do was look blankly at him.

'Of course,' Lila said briskly, and although she'd once again saved the day, she was also studying Izzy

closely. Probably trying to work out what was happening.

As if I know, Izzy thought desperately, passing the potatoes to their guest, while Lila piled slices of meat from the platter Pop had filled onto Mac's plate.

Mac took the offerings of vegetables as they arrived and passed them on, poured gravy on his meat, and when his hostess picked up her knife and fork, he began to eat.

He tried to make sense of this family—anything to forget the woman by his side and the effect she was having on him. But how big, blond, blue-eyed Marty could be related to the beautiful Lila, let alone the petite redhead by his side, was beyond him.

'We're foster kids.'

He wasn't sure whether he was more surprised by Izzy speaking to him or the fact that she'd read his thoughts.

'*All* of you?'

'Oh, yes, and there's heaps more of us. It was a nunnery, you see, and Pop bought it for a song when he and Hallie married, and they intended filling it with their own kids, but that didn't happen so they went out and found the strays that careless parents leave behind, or kids whose parents died, in Lila's case. And they gave us all unquestioning love, and stability, and the confidence to be anything we wanted to be. But more than that, they gave us the security of a home, a family.'

'It's true,' Lila said, nodding from his other side.

'And it's been the best thing that happened in all of our lives,' Marty put in, although Hallie was telling them to hush, it was nothing anyone else wouldn't have done.

But for some reason Mac's thoughts had stopped earlier in the conversation so although he'd heard the rest, and been impressed, the question that came out was, 'A nunnery?'

How could these beautiful women be living in a nunnery? Except it wasn't a nunnery, of course it wasn't, it was just that his brain wasn't working too well. There was nothing immodest about the sprite's clothing, but from where he was sitting he could see the tops of the soft roundness of her breasts, and blood that should have been feeding his brain was elsewhere.

'It was cheap,' the man they all called Pop offered. 'And not that hard to knock two or three of the little cells together into decent-sized bedrooms.'

'You're a carpenter? Builder?'

Pop smiled and shook his head.

'Truckie—mainly long haul. I've taught all the kids to drive trucks.'

'I'm learning now,' Nikki announced, adding, rather to Mac's relief, 'Though only in the paddocks behind the house at the moment.'

The talk turned to the animals kept in the paddocks—did Mac ride? That was Nikki. Hallie mentioned the vegetable garden—'Feel free to help yourself to any vegetable…we always have far too many!'—and with the simple, delicious meal, and the general chat, Mac found himself relaxing in the midst of this strange family.

'You've family yourself, Mac?' Pop asked.

'Parents, of course,' he said. 'Though I don't see much of them. The army, you know—you never know from one day to the next where you'll be.'

He didn't add that their regular divorces and re-

marriages had dulled any filial emotion he'd ever felt
for them.

'Married?'

This time the question came from the beautiful Lila
and he didn't miss the wink she sent to Izzy.

Best to get that sorted once and for all, and quickly.

'Was once,' he replied, forcing himself to speak normally, although what felt like a very unsubtle third degree had his temper rising.

'And once was more than enough,' he added, to un-
derline the point.

He glanced at Izzy, who was blushing furiously,
and realised the questions weren't so much for him
but to tease her.

Marty put a stop to it.

'Enough!' he said, directing the word at Lila. 'Pop
asked a normal, everyday question, but all you're doing,
Lila, is teasing Izzy.'

He turned to Mac.

'Izzy had an unfortunate experience with a doctor
we had here a few years ago and it's become a bit of
a family joke.'

The shrill tone of a mobile phone broke up the conversation, and it was Marty who pulled one from his
pocket, glancing at it and moving away.

'Work. I'll probably have to go,' he explained as he
moved into a small room off the kitchen.

'Marty's a pilot on the rescue helicopter,' Lila explained, as the whole family turned anxious eyes towards the small room.

He returned briskly, grabbing a jacket from the back
of his chair.

'Got to go! Cindy, you coming or staying? If you're coming there's no time to get your stuff.'

Cindy, too, pushed back her chair.

'Coming,' she said.

The pair had barely left the room when another mobile sounded, and, having been free of its tyranny for three weeks, it took Mac a moment to realise it was his.

He glanced at the message on the screen before he, too, stood up.

'Looks like I'm starting work early. I'm sorry, Mrs Halliday. The meal, what I managed to eat of it, was wonderful.'

'Wait, I'll come with you,' the sprite announced.

'I know the way.'

He didn't really snap, it just came out a bit sharp, images of the tops of her soft breasts still lingering in his head.

'Sure, but you only arrived in town this morning so I doubt you know your way around the hospital. Hallie might have given you the basic tour, but if it's an emergency—and it will be if Marty's flying someone in— then you need the best help you can get, and that's me.'

She paused, then added with a teasing smile, 'So, lucky you!'

She couldn't possibly have known what he was thinking—not possibly, but it was obvious she intended coming with him as she rushed around the table kissing Hallie, Pop, Nikki and Lila, before linking her arm through his and practically dragging him out the door.

Escaping?

It certainly seemed that way as she led him headlong down the hill to the small hospital.

'But aren't you just off night duty?'

Good, he'd not only remembered something she'd said this morning, but had also managed a question, so his brain must be back in gear.

'Yes, but in case you didn't notice there was a certain amount of conspiracy stuff going on around that table tonight.'

'Conspiracy?'

He didn't want to admit he'd been more than slightly distracted by his neighbour at the table.

'Never mind,' Izzy said. 'Silly family stuff! I was just glad to get away.'

She moved a little further from him now she had him out of the house.

Sitting next to him, conscious of every movement of his body, had been torture, especially since she'd noticed the silky hairs on his forearms.

Dark, silky hairs…

Mesmerising dark silky hairs…

She shook her head, glad of the darkness so he didn't see her shaking loose her thoughts.

They were going to work and this was actually a good opportunity to see if she could detach herself from the idiotic attraction and concentrate solely on whatever they had to get done.

Never in her twenty-six years with the Hallidays had she been diverted from the sheer gluttonous enjoyment of one of Hallie's roast dinners, yet there she'd been, her fork toying with a piece of pumpkin as she'd wondered if his arms would feel as silky as they looked.

'But you *have* just come off night duty?' Mac asked, successfully getting her mind off silky hairs—though only just…

'Yes, but I've had a good sleep today. It's why I jog.

The steady pace seems to get rid of any leftover work tension and I can sleep like a baby.'

'Some babies don't sleep all that well,' Mac muttered.

What babies did he know?

Not that it mattered...

'We can go in this way,' she told him, leading him to the kitchen door at the rear of the building. 'We've only eleven patients at the moment with another seven in the nursing home at the back, so there'll be two registered nurses and two aides on duty in the main hospital, with another RN on call. Actually, there should be one of the local GPs on call, but there's a wedding...'

She led him down a short corridor, waving to a woman sitting at a curved desk in a room to the left.

'That's Abby,' she told him. 'Abby, Mac, Mac, Abby.'

'Good thing you had your phone on,' Abby told him. 'I wouldn't have known where to find you otherwise. I know you haven't officially started work but there's been an RTA on the highway, helicopter will bring in one patient for stabilisation and onward transport, and there are two ambulances also on the way.'

A patient requiring stabilisation was a tough introduction, but Mac was intrigued.

'And how do you get this information? Know to be prepared?'

He'd asked the question into the air between her and Abby, so Izzy answered him.

'First on scene is almost always police. They radio for ambulance support, a paramedic with the ambulance team assesses the injured and organises everything until the patients are safely removed.'

'He can order a helicopter?' Mac asked.

'Providing one can land,' Izzy responded. 'And Marty can land just about anywhere. Roads are great if they're flat and straight, but around here it's been dairy country since for ever, and there are fields close to the roads even in the hills.'

Izzy was leading him towards the large room that was their 'emergency department', as she explained. The room had a desk, curtains that could be drawn to allow privacy for patients and on the far side, three small rooms.

'The first one is the resus room,' Izzy told him. 'Next to it is a quiet room for mental health patients who sometimes find other people disconcerting, then a kind of all-purpose room, used for everything from resus to upset kids, to talking quietly to relatives when necessary.'

Mac heard a hitch in her voice and knew that talking to relatives—usually with grim news—wasn't one of her favourite things. In a small town, a death would probably be someone she knew...

He wanted to touch her shoulder, say he was sorry, but why?

An excuse to touch her?

To feel that golden skin?

Fortunately, while totally irrational and unmedical thoughts flashed through his mind he heard the *whup, whup, whup* of the helicopter.

Not a big army helicopter carrying injured troops— a smaller chopper, light, one patient. He was fine, but as sweat broke out on his forehead he wondered why he hadn't considered rescue helicopters when he'd chosen Wetherby.

Because he'd thought it was too small?

Or because he'd doubted the noise of the little dragonfly helicopters he'd encounter in civilian life would affect him?

'You okay?'

He shook his head, then realised she'd probably take it as a negative reply, so he said, 'Of course,' far too loudly and followed her out the door, presumably to meet their patient.

The rotors were still moving when a crewman ducked out to open the door wider so they could access the stretcher. Marty appeared from the front cabin to help and Mac was left to follow behind as his patient was rushed with admirable efficiency into the hospital.

Following behind, in the lights that surrounded the landing circle, he could see the patient was in a neck brace and secured onto a long spine board, with padded red supports preventing any head movement. One arm was in a temporary splint, and a tourniquet controlled blood loss from a messy wound on his left leg.

Mac's mind was on procedure, automatically listing what had to be done before the patient was transferred on to a major trauma centre.

'No obvious skull fracture,' the paramedic reported, 'but the GCS was three.'

So, some brain damage! A subdural haematoma with blood collecting inside the skull and causing pressure on the brain?

A CT scan would assess head injury, but would moving him for the scan cause more complications?

This was a patient with spine and head secured and moving on to a major hospital.

Leave the CT scan to them!

Intubation?

Definitely!

A young woman, presumably the paramedic, was using a manual resuscitator to help his breathing.

'The paramedic is intubation trained,' Izzy explained, somehow picking up on his thoughts once again, 'and I know the literature is divided about whether or not to intubate at the scene, but if we're doing the main stabilisation here, the paramedics tend not to intubate as that way they get the patients to us faster.'

Mac nodded. The patient's worst enemy, with severe trauma, was time. The sooner he or she had specialised help, the better the outcome.

So, intubation first, Izzy already checking for any obstruction in the mouth, before passing Mac what he needed for rapid sequence intubation. While he checked the tube was in place, she attached it to the ventilator.

The medical personnel from the helicopter were assisting, one taking blood for testing, the other setting up for an ECG.

'We coordinate our rosters,' Izzy explained as she set up the portable X-ray machine. 'Ambulance, helicopter and hospital, so we always have emergency-trained personnel to assist in a crisis. These two both work at Braxton Hospital when they're not rostered on ambulance or helicopter duty. The helicopter is based at Braxton, an hour and a half away, but the patient was brought here for stabilisation because we're closer.'

Mac wanted to ask why the helicopter pilot was in Wetherby if he was on call, but the screen was in place, the picture showing a shadow that suggested a

subdural haematoma and, anyway, he had other things to worry about.

Do a CT scan to be sure?

It meant moving the patient to the radiography room, maybe doing further damage to his spine—

No time!

Mac had already decided he'd have to drill a small hole into the patient's skull and insert a catheter to drain off some blood to relieve the pressure before he could be sent on.

Apparently Izzy had also read the situation correctly and had already shaved and prepped the area of scalp the shadow indicated.

The two paramedics—Mac had decided that's what they must be—had been making notes of all the findings, although all the information would also go directly into the computer. Mac knew the notes would travel with the patient in case of computer glitches.

'Are you okay in helicopters? Did Hallie ask you that?' The gold-flecked eyes were fixed on his face as Izzy asked the questions.

'Practically never out of one,' he told her as he carefully drilled through the patient's skull. 'Why?'

He sounded confident but Izzy was sure he'd gone pale and sweaty when the helicopter had come in.

'Well,' she said, 'another statistic shows better outcomes for serious trauma patients if a physician travels with them. I can stay here and Roger—have you even met our other resident doctor, Roger Grey?—he'll come if I need him. Would you be okay with going along?'

She paused, watching for any hint of a reaction, but Mac's attention was on the delicate job of inserting a catheter into the wound he'd created.

That done, he looked up at her, his eyes fixed on a point somewhere above her head so she couldn't read any reaction in them.

'Of course,' he said, but so shortly, so abruptly she guessed he'd rather poke a needle in his eye. 'We'll start a drip, and make sure there's saline, swabs and dressings available on the chopper. I'll look at his leg on the way.'

She went off to check, returning in time for Mac to give the order to return the patient to the chopper. However, a grim set to the new doctor's face made her wonder just what horrors he had seen in the helicopters that were used to ferry casualties in war zones.

A wailing ambulance siren recalled her to the other casualties coming in. Megan, the most experienced of the two paramedics, had given up her place in the helicopter for Mac and stayed at the hospital to help with the incoming patients.

There were three, none too serious, but two needing limbs set and the other slightly concussed. Izzy and Megan began the initial assessment, GCS and ECG, palpated skulls for signs of injury, set up drips with analgesia. One by one they were wheeled through to the radiography room for X-rays, and for the concussion patient a CT scan, Izzy blessing the radiography course she'd completed.

It was painstaking work, but needed to be completed swiftly in case some major problem showed up, so time passed without them realising that dawn was breaking outside the hospital, the sun rising majestically out of the ocean.

They were studying the films of the second of the

limb injuries, a compound fracture of the ankle, when they heard the helicopter returning.

'That's your lift home,' Izzy told Megan. 'And I think you should take Mr Anderson back to Braxton with you. That ankle will need pins and plating, and you've got an orthopod on tap up there.'

'Good idea. Of course we'll take him. I'll get Marty and Pete in to give a hand loading him.'

Izzy started on the paperwork for admitting the other two patients, one for observation, the other to have further X-rays then a temporary cast fitted on his leg, which would keep the bone stable until the swelling went down and a firmer cast could be used.

'And now we're all done, here comes the cavalry.' Megan nodded to the door where Roger Grey had appeared, accompanied by two of the day-shift nurses.

'Big night, do you need a hug?' Roger said, heading for Izzy with every intention of providing one.

She ducked away. Not that there was anything remotely sexual or untoward in Roger's hugs—he was just a touchy-feely kind of man, and there were often times when a member of the staff appreciated a quick hug.

But ducking away had her backing into someone else—someone who'd come in through the patient entrance, someone with a rock-solid body who steadied her with his hands, holding her in such a way she could see those dark silky hairs...

Moving hurriedly—escaping, really—she made the introductions, gave Roger a brief précis of what they'd already done for the two new patients, explained the third would go to Braxton, then, as exhaustion suddenly struck her, she turned towards the cloakroom.

There'd be a bikini, shirt, shoes and socks in her locker. She would run off the tension of the night, then swim, before heading home to sleep.

She peeled off the scrubs she'd been wearing since the ambulances had come in and threw them into the bin by the door—the opening door.

Mac's head poked around it.

'Sorry,' he said, though in bra and pants she was quite respectable. 'I wondered if you were going for a run. It's definitely what I need and we'd look silly running separately along the path.'

She'd have liked to say she was taking the path south but that would sound petty; besides, she wanted to collect the sleeping bag.

So she nodded, in spite of knowing that she was making a rash decision.

'I imagine you'll have to go home and change. I'll wait by your gate.'

CHAPTER THREE

I'LL WAIT BY your gate!

How stupid could she be?

This man, Mac, was causing her enough problems without her agreeing to go jogging with him—actually making arrangements to be *with* him instead of as far away from him as possible, which would have been the really sensible decision.

Although they'd be colleagues so she couldn't escape him forever.

She began some routine stretching so she wouldn't have to think about him—well, not as much…

He emerged in shorts and a faded T-shirt, his hair loose and tangled again, hanging just long enough to hide his ears.

Her body reacted with the little flutters and zings, but she was getting used to them now.

Nearly!

'Sorry to keep you waiting, and sorry to barge in on your run as well, but there were things I wanted to know.'

He brushed against her as he shut the gate, and, yes, the hairs were just as silky as they looked, and, no, she was *not* going to touch them…

'Such as?' she said instead.

'If your brother was on duty last night, shouldn't he have been in Braxton where the helicopter is based?'

They were walking briskly through the town and fortunately it was too early for many of the locals to be around.

'He has his own—his own helicopter, I mean. He can be back in Braxton as quickly as if he'd driven from his house there to the hospital. The paramedics load any extras he might need while his crewmate checks the machine. All he really does is get in and fly the thing, although he was a trained paramedic as well as the pilot.'

She paused, wanting to ask her own question about helicopters, but realised it was probably far too personal.

So she stuck with Marty.

'Even when he was young he had a passion for them. Pop made him a little model one that had some string around the rotor stem and you wound it up then pulled and the helicopter took off. But most of the time he just ran around with it in the air, making helicopter noises, diving, and rising, and chasing the rest of us.'

They'd reached the track and set out in a slow jog.

'You were a happy family, then?' he asked, turning to look at her as he asked the question, his eyes studying her face.

Looking for a lie?

'Very,' she said firmly. 'Oh, we had our fights like any family and there were always kids who found it hard to fit in.'

She faltered, paused, looked out to sea before add-

ing, 'Some of them had been so traumatised, so badly abused, they hated being happy, I guess.'

Mac nodded. You couldn't get through training as a doctor without seeing the horrific things people could do to one another—could do to children. At least, that was what he'd thought until he'd gone to war.

'Hallie and Pop must be remarkable people,' he said, forcing his mind back to the present as they resumed their jog, speeding up slightly.

'They are,' Izzy agreed, and the simple confirmation, the love in her voice, told him far more than the words.

They jogged in silence, and he breathed in the sea air and marvelled at the might of the waves crashing against the cliffs, the beauty in the scraggly, wind-twisted trees along the path, the little cove...their porpoise cove?

'The helicopter bothered you last night?'

He'd been so lost in his contemplation of the scene—concentrating on the details of the beauty around him to avoid his reactions to the woman beside him—that the question startled him.

He didn't have to answer it, he decided, but within a minute realised his companion—colleague, as he should be thinking of her—wasn't so easily silenced.

'Just the sound of it coming in made you go pale, yet you agreed to accompany the patient to the city.'

She was stating a fact, not asking a question, so now he didn't have to...

Except...

Except he wanted to!

For some reason, in this beautiful place, with this

woman he barely knew by his side, he *did* want to talk about it.

'It wasn't fear so much as memory,' he said, stopping to look out to sea while he found the words.

Not the words for the unimaginable horror—no words could cover that—but enough words to explain, to her and to himself.

'On my last tour one crashed—not a medical evac chopper but a big Chinook, carrying troops. One guy died and the others were badly injured. Getting them out of there was surreal, like living a nightmare. We weren't in much danger, weren't under direct attack, but putting men who'd been through what they'd been through into another bird, well, some of them just couldn't handle it.'

A hand slid into his and small fingers squeezed his.

'Were you able to sedate them?'

He nodded, then admitted, 'Only some.'

She removed her hand, stepped away to look more closely at him, folded her arms—to stop her hand straying again?—and shook her head.

'Well, I think given that experience, plus all the other things you've seen, you were remarkably brave going off last night.'

He had to smile at her fierce defence of him, a man she barely knew, but smiling at her brought a smile to her face, too, and the dimple peeped from her cheek.

And there was no way he couldn't touch it—just reach out and brush his forefinger against it.

She lifted *her* hand. To smack his away? But, no, all she did was brush her fingers across his forearm, then she beckoned with her head so once again they began to jog.

But the touches, unexpected yet somehow intimate, had changed something between them. It was acknowledgement certainly, but was it also acceptance of the attraction that had inexplicably sprung up between them, right back when they'd first met?

Or was he being fanciful?

Did she feel it or was her touch nothing more than a casual gesture?

Did it matter when he'd decided he didn't do attraction any more?

And he certainly didn't dally with colleagues...

He shook his head—he didn't do fanciful thinking either. Somewhere along the coast path to Wetherby he'd lost his common sense.

But glancing towards her, her strides lengthening now, the golden limbs moving with such grace, he felt a tightening in his gut, *and* in his groin if he was honest—

Tricky when they worked together.

Especially tricky when he knew the danger of physical attraction...

He lengthened his own stride, catching up and keeping pace with her, but they were beyond casual conversation now; it was a sprint, an unspoken challenge, and when she muttered, 'To the she-oak,' in laboured tones, he understood the challenge.

They sprinted, and male pride made sure he won, although she wasn't far behind, collapsing against the rough bark of the tree, fighting for her breath, while he was bent, hands on knees, dragging air into his depleted lungs.

'Well, if that doesn't help us sleep, nothing will,' Izzy finally had breath enough to say.

Mac, still bent, turned his head towards her.

'That was torture. I'm a walker, not a runner.'

But he was smiling as he spoke, and Izzy knew for certain she was lost. It had been bad enough when he'd touched her cheek and she'd reacted by feeling those silky hairs, but bent over, smiling up at her—a teasing smile—she understood that whatever it was she was feeling it was mutual.

And dangerous!

Especially now, when getting involved with a man was the last thing she needed—well, wanted...

And as for attraction, that was just a fleeting thing, and too easily confused with love, and love would be downright impossible just now.

Ignoring it seemed the best option, so she stood up straight, pulled off her shirt, kicked off her runners, and headed for the beach.

'It's a safe swimming spot if you don't go out too far, where there could be rips and undertows.'

Mac had straightened up and now he looked around.

'Isn't this our beach?'

Dear heaven, surely they weren't going to have an 'our' beach! Not yet, not already—this was moving far too fast and she wasn't even sure what 'this' was...

Although she knew for sure she didn't want it.

'No,' she said firmly. 'The porpoise cove—' no *our beach* from her! '—was the last one we passed, and someone had already removed your sleeping bag.'

But he'd stripped the T-shirt off his chest, and the sight of his upper body, a six-pack, no less, left her too breathless to say more.

She raced down the beach and dived beneath the

first wave, the cold water providing a cooling balm to her overheated body.

Not that he was going to let it go, she realised as he, too, dived in and emerged beside her.

'A cold swim is as good as a cold shower, I guess,' he said, smiling down at her, and while she was deciding that the man was just a flirt who went for any woman within reach and she should steer very clear of him, he tucked a strand of hair back behind her ears, then licked his fingers.

'Mmm...salty,' he murmured, before diving beneath the water again.

Well, that was weird, but didn't it prove that he was *definitely* a flirt who went for any woman within reach, and she *definitely* should steer clear of him?

More chilled by her thoughts than the water, she headed for the beach, crossed the rocks that guarded it, then pulled on her shirt. She'd carry her runners back to the fresh-water tap and clean her feet of sand before putting them on.

Mac was still in the water, swimming strongly back and forth across the little cove, but heeding her warning not to go too far out.

Realising he couldn't stay there for ever, Mac reluctantly left the water, walked up the beach, and along the path to join Izzy at the tap. That touch on her errant curl had been a mistake, and given that he *was* attracted to the woman, such touches were to be avoided in the future.

They barely knew each other, and he really should be putting all his efforts into getting this, his first civilian job, sorted. He'd managed the emergency situation

the previous evening satisfactorily—even managed the helicopter flight—but responding to an emergency was automatic. It was the rest of the job he had to get on top of, things like who did what, and when, and where.

There'd be rosters and staff duty statements and daily, weekly and monthly targets—all the bumf so beloved of bureaucrats everywhere, not only those in the army.

He eyed the woman standing waiting for him. It was a wonder she hadn't jogged away, but as she hadn't…

Keep your distance? suggested his sensible self. But surely the thought in his head would count as sensible!

'I don't officially start work until tomorrow, but you obviously know your way around the hospital, so I wondered if, after we've both had a sleep, you'd mind showing me around and telling me how things work and who's who, and how the GPs fit in and—'

'Who's good and who isn't, who's lazy and who's great?'

'No, no, I'm sure they're all great but it's more about—I don't know. I've an appointment with the hospital manager tomorrow morning but I have a feeling that will be all facts and figures and paperwork, not patients and staff and—'

He halted suddenly, mainly because those brown-gold eyes were fixed on his face.

Studying him or drinking in every silly word he was muttering?

'More to get a feel for the place,' she offered politely, and he laughed, not so much at the mock politeness but that she'd picked up on what he'd been trying to ask.

Not that she'd said yes…

'Four o'clock?' she suggested, and he felt a surge of pleasure—well, he was pretty sure it was just pleasure.

'Great! Maybe we could even have dinner after-wards—you can show me the best places to eat in town.'

Had he gone too far? She hesitated.

She had a daughter.

A partner as well?

'Okay,' she said, 'but I can't be late home. Nikki goes back to school tomorrow and she can twist Hallie and Pop around her little finger and they'll let her stay up as late as she likes.'

She paused then added, with a smile, 'They never let *us* stay up late before a school day!'

And in spite of the complaint, Mac read the love for the people who'd brought her up in her voice and saw it shining in her eyes.

Was she out of her mind?

Her body was already attracted to this man, so what would happen if she got to know him better?

Did he read her hesitation in her agreement that he asked, 'What's the problem?'

'Well, at the risk of sounding embarrassingly ri-diculous, I'd like you to understand it's just dinner, not a date.'

His eyes twinkled—and her stomach churned.

'I don't date, you see,' she added, hoping to stop the churning with practicality. 'Well, not at the moment.'

'So dinner, not a date, that's okay.' A smile playing around the words only added to the stomach churning!

'Although at the risk of *my* sounding ridiculous,

why don't you date? Not that I expected it to be. A date, you know—'

Of course he wouldn't—a guy who looked like him could have any woman he wanted, so why waste time with a scrawny redhead, especially one encumbered with a daughter?

So she'd made a complete fool of herself even mentioning dates.

And had a question to answer!

She looked at him and sighed.

'Long story but I'll definitely take you over the hospital this afternoon.'

'And tell me the long story over dinner!' he said firmly. 'Stories are good over dinner, and it's *just* dinner!'

She sighed again, shrugged, and finally said, 'We'll see, but I still can't be late home.'

And if he thought she hadn't noticed the satisfied expression on his face as she finally agreed, he'd be wrong.

Used to getting his own way, was he?

A sure sign this was a man to be wary of.

The hospital tour turned out to be fun. Mac insisted on meeting all the patients, and had sat and talked to the men and women in the nursing-home section. It didn't take long for one of the men to winkle out the information that Dr Macpherson—'Please call me Mac'—was an ex-military man and as two of the residents had seen service in Vietnam, topics of conversation weren't hard to find.

The women were equally impressed by the fact that Mac's grandmother had belonged to the Country

Women's Association, and the conversation shifted to scones.

'Izzy here makes beautiful lemonade scones,' someone said, and Mac's eyebrows rose.

'Really? Well, those I'll have to try,' he said. 'But right now I've persuaded her to have dinner with me so she can tell me all about Wetherby, and the hospital, and probably you lot!'

One of the men chuckled.

'Is a good gossip all you want?' one of the men teased, and the rest laughed, although as she and Mac departed, her cheeks pink with embarrassment, another of the residents called out, 'Now you take care of her, mind. She's a special girl, our Izzy.'

Izzy expected Mac to laugh it off, but instead he walked slowly away, turning his head from time to time, as if to study her.

Searching for her specialness?

As if!

Interesting, Mac decided.

Were all the patients as protective of this one nurse as the nursing-home residents obviously were?

And what had someone said at that chaotic introduction to the Halliday family?

Something about someone trying to shoot her?

'As you left me to choose where to go for dinner, I decided the Surf Club. They have the best dining room in town as far as position goes, right by the beach, looking out over the ocean.'

Practical—she was practical, he decided, half listening while still following his train of thought.

'It only does basic stuff, like steak and fish and usually a roast, but it's quality food and well cooked.'

She didn't turn towards him as she spoke and he sensed she was still a bit put out about the man's remark.

He walked beside her, through quiet streets towards the beach, avoiding the centre of town, such as it was.

'Are there many restaurants in town?'

Her pace slowed and now she turned to look at him.

'You've really been thrust in at the deep end,' she said. 'You've barely had time to settle into the house, let alone see the town.'

'My own fault,' he told her, hoping his voice was steadier than he was feeling, because a ray of light from the streetlamp was lighting up the side of her face, and the curls he now realised would always escape her attempts to tame them, glowed red-gold against the paler gold skin of her cheeks.

Or was it the line of her profile that had started attraction stirring again? A clean line, smooth forehead, straight nose and soft pink lips above a chin that, while not too obvious, suggested determination.

What would it take to break her determination not to date?

He swung back towards the sea.

What on earth was he thinking?

His head was still a mess, and anger over Lauren's behaviour still simmered somewhere deep inside.

He knew the anger was more to do with humiliation than infidelity, an army base being such a hotbed of gossip, but that didn't make it easier.

And marriage definitely wasn't on the cards—not again. But dating—provided they both knew that was

all it was—was different. Dating, and a dalliance, on a short-term basis, could be fun.

Except he didn't dally with colleagues.

Or with women who had children...

Izzy was talking about the town—had been for some minutes, he suspected—while his mind bounced between the present and the past.

'So recently we've had all kinds of new places spring up—offering Paleo and vegan food, as well as more exotic fare from the Middle East and North Africa. It's a result of people making what they call a "hill change" and coming to live in the country outside the town, growing weird and wonderful new fruit and vegetables, and refugees from other countries settling here.'

Fortunately, they'd reached the beach and there, on the right, was the Surf Club. But out in front was the ocean, and above it a nearly full moon, marking a path of silver out to the horizon.

'Magical, isn't it?' Izzy breathed, stopping to admire the view.

'Magical indeed,' Mac agreed, but he was including the moonlit woman beside him in his reply.

Maybe he was bewitched!

Didn't witches have red hair?

Or maybe black—

'Come on, we can see it from the restaurant,' the witch was saying, and he turned and followed her, dragging his thoughts from the mystical to the practical.

All the business of his discharge from the army, getting a job, the three-week walk—it had been a while since he'd been with a woman, that's all it was...

She should have chosen the Moroccan restaurant in the back street of the town, Izzy decided as the young waiter showed them to a table on the front veranda. The view out over the ocean, the white curl of the waves crawling up the curving beach, the surf crashing on the rocky headlands made it far too romantic a backdrop for what was 'just dinner'.

Studying the menu, deciding what to eat, these were helpful, practical things to get romance out of her head.

She didn't date!

Not at the moment anyway...

Not until...

Fortunately Mac seemed similarly intent on the offerings and choices so conversation was avoided until the waiter departed, leaving them a bottle of iced water and taking their orders with him.

'So,' Mac said, as the waiter disappeared, 'why don't you date?'

She frowned at him.

'Is that really any of your business?'

'Nope!' A cheeky smile accompanied the word and undid the little scrap of common sense she'd managed to regain with the decisions about eating.

'But you did say you'd tell me over dinner,' he reminded her.

She wasn't sure she *had* said any such thing, but she'd already realised this was a very persistent man, so she might as well get it over with.

'Nikki isn't mine,' she began, then realised that hadn't come out the way she'd meant it to. 'Well, she is but she wasn't.'

This was getting worse and heat was rising in her traitorous cheeks.

'I mean, I'm not her birth mother. Her birth mother was one of our sisters. She came to live with us when she was seven and not even the love Hallie and Pop gave so freely could make up for the horrific abuse she'd suffered as a young child. It was as if there was something broken inside her, too broken to ever be fixed...'

She'd been playing with her fork as she spoke but now glanced up at Mac, worried she'd begun this story in the wrong place and was boring him.

But his expression held interest, and also understanding, so, encouraged by a slight nod of his head, she ploughed on.

'Nikki was drug addicted when she was born. Her mother died soon after, asking me to care for her baby. As if she needed to ask—the baby was family. But drug-addicted babies are sick and fractious and Nikki demanded so much attention that any relationship was out of the question. In fact, I gave up my pre-med course and spent two years just looking after Nikki. Hallie and Pop were wonderful, of course, but she needed...'

The words dried up, and a lump the size of Ayers Rock had formed in her throat as she remembered that time.

'A mother,' Mac said quietly. 'I can understand that.'
Izzy nodded.

'Anyway, she got better, and life settled down. I decided I'd do nursing—I had credits from the pre-med course—and Hallie and Pop were happy to babysit.'

'So then you were too busy studying to date?'

Izzy returned the smile that accompanied his words,

although exchanging smiles was dangerous when even a smile could knot her stomach.

'Go on,' he encouraged, and she shrugged.

'There's not much more to it,' she said.

'Nikki's nearly thirteen years old,' he pointed out.

This time it was a sigh, not a shrug—a huge sigh!

'You know, I'd never thought about it before I had Nikki, but it's darned hard for a single mother to have normal relationships. Not only because you have to cancel if the child throws a fever, or starts coughing, or falls over and needs stitches, but because you start to worry about introducing strange men into her life.'

'*Strange* men?'

Another smile and this time a tweak along Izzy's nerves!

'I mean different men—not family. And what happens if she gets to know and like one of them, then the relationship falls apart and he's gone? There was no way I was going to bring a string of men into Nikki's life—not that I've ever had a string of men—but somehow it seemed easier not to bother.'

'So you never dated?'

Blue eyes dared her not to answer.

'Are you always this persistent?' she demanded, 'But if you must know, yes, I did—well, occasionally. Then—'

'Then? And, yes, I am always this persistent.'

Izzy had to smile, although memories of her last disastrous almost-relationship made her shiver.

'Someone with a gun?'

She looked up into the blue eyes.

'How did you—? Oh, dinner last night—bloody Marty opening his big mouth. Yes, another doctor,

a couple of years ago—since him we've had agency doctors. Nikki was ten, and somehow I had decided I needed a man in my life—well, in both our lives. She'd been asking questions about her father but I had no answers, then I began to worry what might happen if she *did* have a father.'

She put down the fork, straightened it carefully, fiddled with the knife, then continued, 'Well, of course she'd have a father, everyone does, but what if he suddenly appeared from nowhere? What if he took her?'

Mac heard what sounded very like panic in her voice and reached out to cover her restless fingers with his hand.

'I thought if she already had a father—a stepfather, but someone she might come to consider a father—then—'

'She'd be safer?'

Mac was rewarded with a blinding smile, although he suspected the shine in her eyes was from unshed tears.

'Exactly,' she said, her voice stronger now. 'I mean, Nikki's always had male role models in her life with Pop and all the brothers, but I kept thinking maybe if we were a family—a mother, father and daughter— she'd be safer.'

Mac could see a kind of weird logic in this, but he was caught up in the story and wanted to know more.

'So?' he prompted.

The gold-brown eyes met his, clear now but dubious, then she shrugged and continued.

'The man—the new doctor—came. Hallie matchmaking, I suspect. Anyway, he asked me out, and we… we got on well. We'd dated exactly four times when

his ex-girlfriend turned up. She threatened Nikki as well as me.'

Now her eyes held memories of the horror and he tightened his hold on her hand, while anger at a man he'd never met gripped his gut.

'So, the man you went out with thinking it might end up being a good thing for Nikki ended up putting you both in danger?'

Her eyes widened with surprise and a small smile replaced the tension around her lips.

'That's exactly how I felt! Talk about an idiot! Anyway, it put me off all thoughts of relationships, at least until she's away at university or travelling overseas.'

Their meals arrived, barramundi for him and lamb cutlets for Izzy, and tackling the tantalising offerings brought the conversation to a halt.

But Mac couldn't help considering the things he'd just learned as he ate his fish—delicious fish. Izzy was busy cutting the meat from her cutlets so he could watch her as he ate.

Not obtrusively, but glances, checking out that she was as attractive as he'd first thought, but also wondering what else was going on inside her head, because she certainly hadn't told him *all* the not-dating story.

Not that he was interested in dating either—well, not a colleague anyway. Far too incestuous somehow! Small hospital, small town—very like an army base— far too easy for stories to spread.

And the attraction thing bothered him. He knew he was attracted to her, and suspected it was mutual, but he knew only too well how attraction could blind a man to other facets of the 'attractee's' personality. Hadn't he and Lauren met and married within eight weeks?

And wasn't he determined not to make the same mistake again—the getting-married mistake? Attraction was fine. Short, mutually enjoyable affairs could be fun, although he doubted that would be possible in a town this size.

'The problem was…'

He was so lost in his own thoughts it took a moment to realise Izzy was speaking to him.

Well, who else could she be speaking to?

He lifted his head, raising his eyebrows.

'The problem was?' he repeated.

She sighed, looked out to the ocean for inspiration, before eventually meeting his eyes.

'Losing Nikki!'

He could hear the tears clogging her voice and reached out to touch her lightly on the arm.

Maybe not a good idea as she flinched and drew her arm away, swallowed hard and finally looked at him again.

'She's not legally mine, you see, so for the last few years—since then—I've been trying to adopt her, which isn't easy when I'm not a blood relative, I'm single, no one knows who or where her father is, and the law says both parents have to agree. I don't even have a formal agreement from her mother—all I have is a note on a piece of grubby paper, asking me to look after her.'

Mac felt his gut tighten in empathy for this woman's fears for the child she so obviously loved.

'I'd been vaguely looking into adoption when the other doctor came along and I knew if I was married it would be easier.'

She frowned, but possibly more at her thoughts than at him.

'I thought if it worked—with the doctor—we'd be a family. Not like our big family, though that's essential to both of us, but a kind of regular family...'

'Mother, father, children kind of family?' Mac asked, wanting to tease with the words but sensing she was very serious about this.

'Exactly!' she said, her smile lighting up her face, obviously delighted he'd somehow understood.

Not that he had!

Although he was reasonably sure it was all to do with Nikki and her safety.

Protection in case some drop-kick birth father turned up and wanted to take her away?

'So I went out with him, the other doctor, had those four dates and we got on okay, but then the gun thing happened and—'

He waited, sure there was more.

And there was...

'The woman threatened Nikki as well—the both of us, in the flat—and the thought I might have lost her, well, I went back to pushing the adoption idea. To adopting her as a single parent.'

'But surely in this day and age, adoption isn't all that hard, even for single women.'

Bewitching golden eyes met his.

'Don't kid yourself! Quite apart from the fact that Nikki's father appears to be untraceable, and she has never formally been handed over to the state for adoption, there are formidable background checks on all adoptive parents, on their homes, their friends, their social life.'

'Ah,' Mac said, as the penny dropped. 'So a string of lovers in your life could rule you out?'

'Even one could, because that would show there could be a string in the future and would that be in the child's best interests? Not to mention the invasion of privacy that the one lover might suffer.'

She sighed, then added, 'So...'

'It's easier not to bother,' Mac finished for her.

He considered this for a moment.

'But isn't that hard on you?'

His answer was a brilliant smile.

'Not really,' she said, shaking her head. 'You get out of the way of it, dating I mean, and I have heaps of men in my life with my brothers and their friends and friends at the hospital, so there's always someone who'll take me along to anything that needs a partner. In fact, I'm very happy with my life.'

Hmm, Mac thought, but he didn't say it, although Izzy's story had affected him deeply.

But not deeply enough to stop the attraction?

As if that mattered. If she did get involved with a man, he'd need to be committed both to her and to a future with her—to marriage—and apart from the fact that the helicopter ride had proven to him he wasn't over the effects of PTSD, he'd decided that he was probably genetically unsuited to marriage, given his parents' and his own failures.

And why was he considering marriage at all? It was a first date—well, not even a date...

CHAPTER FOUR

Izzy STARED OUT at the limitless ocean, wondering why on earth she'd told this man—this virtual stranger—things she'd never voiced to anyone, not even Lila.

The family knew she'd talked about a formal adoption, but although they may have guessed, she'd never voiced her fear of losing Nikki.

'Does this happen with all the women you take out to dinner?' she asked, turning back to her companion. 'Do they all pour out their deepest, darkest secrets to you?'

She hoped the words came out lighter than they felt inside her head, because inside her head was a mess, what with having to resist the attraction and then the unguarded conversation, and the totally unnecessary moon over the ocean.

'Not usually on the first d—dinner,' he said, a smile in the words, eyes twinkling, although he was serious when he added, 'but I do understand how you must feel. I've seen drug-addicted babies before so those first years must have been hell, and having fought for her to stay alive, to be well at the end of the withdrawal time, it would make her extra-special to you.'

'I had good teachers in Hallie and Pop. Most of the

kids they took in had problems, some of them horrendous ones, yet they showered us all with love.'

'And you, did you have problems?'

The question was so unexpected, she answered automatically.

'Not really. My mum dumped me on Gran when I was about three—we never quite figured out when—then Gran died when I was six, and after a while in temporary foster homes I was lucky enough to be given to Hallie and Pop.'

'You make is sound like an ideal childhood, which it can't possibly have been.'

He was frowning, but Izzy couldn't help smiling at his words.

'Compared to some it was, and the love we all got from Hallie and Pop made us a happy family and our world a very happy place.'

She checked the moon again—still there—*and* the ocean, silvered in its light, and sighed.

'We should probably go.'

Not that she wanted to, but the scene must have bewitched her and she'd already told Mac far too much about herself. Stay here and who knew what else might come out?

'I suppose we should. Will I see you at the hospital tomorrow?'

Izzy repeated the words in her head. Did he sound as if he wanted to?

Not that it mattered, of course! No dating!

'Not tomorrow. I'm still on days off, and with Nikki back at school it's a chance to do a big spring clean.'

'You do know it's autumn?' he teased, smiling at her again.

One smile, that's all it took to put her heart back into fibrillation! She had to get over this. Every fibre of her being was yelling at her to keep right away from him. He was a dangerous distraction and the less she saw of him the better.

Work would be okay—well, kind of okay—and unavoidable—but she could handle things at work.

'Autumn clean would sound stupid, but spring clean—well, people know what you mean.'

It was such an inane remark she wasn't surprised he raised his eyebrows at her.

But that was better than him smiling.

And he'd pushed back his chair so they were leaving.

Which meant she could get out of there without making an even bigger fool of herself.

She caught up with him at the bar and reminded him it was just dinner and they should go Dutch, but the beautiful surfie chick behind the bar had already taken his credit card and given him a dazzling smile.

He returned the smile with a pretty good one of his own, and Izzy walked away, reminding herself it didn't matter who Mac smiled at, they were colleagues, nothing more.

But that made walking along the esplanade towards the hospital, and Mac's house beside it, very uncomfortable, because the presence of moonlight and rolling surf and the old lighthouse on the hill was a scene for romance, and the presence of Mac's body, so close to hers, was an agonising distraction.

'I was looking at pictures of the old hospital when you were showing me around,' he said. 'I hadn't realised that the nuns had once run the place.'

Well, that tells me there will be no further personal

conversation, Izzy realised, *which isn't fair because he now knows far more than I'm comfortable with about me and I know zilch about him.*

'Yes,' she said, playing the game. 'The church used to be the other side of the hospital so the three—church, hospital and doctor's house where you live—formed a curve of the old brick and stone buildings. The church burned down and there was damage to the rear of the hospital so it was all rebuilt, keeping the old façade. Your house was saved, and although it's been renovated from time to time, it's pretty much as it was when it was built.'

'It's certainly a lovely old building,' Mac confirmed. 'I'm lucky to be able to live in it.'

Tension tightened Izzy's body. This matter-of-fact, almost tourist talk felt wrong after all they'd shared.

Well, after all she'd shared…

Somehow during their dinner—during most of the time they'd spent together—Mac had shown he was a kind and caring man, not a robot mouthing platitudes about old buildings.

It's just attraction, Mac reminded himself, when his determined discussion of the old hospital buildings had failed to distract him from thoughts of the woman by his side.

And she's a colleague…

And she doesn't date, let alone dally—

The stupid thoughts were brought to an abrupt halt as the blare of a horn split the night air, and a roaring sound filled his ears.

Some sixth sense made him grab Izzy and together they rolled back onto the road, while a massive semi-trailer ploughed straight past where they'd been stand-

ing and crashed into the massive fig tree that was a feature of the hospital's grounds.

'Are you all right?' he asked, as he helped Izzy to her feet, steadying her for a moment as tremors of fear, or perhaps relief, ran through them both.

'Fine!' she said, 'But whoever was behind the wheel of that rig isn't.'

But Mac was already on his way, running towards the crushed cab, as staff came hurrying from the hospital.

The driver's-side door was jammed, but he could see the driver slumped sideways in the seat, his hand still on the steering wheel, on the horn that had warned them of danger.

Then Izzy was there, climbing into the cab from the passenger side, gesturing him to join her.

Not altogether easy, as the tree prevented him from going around the front of the vehicle, and getting around the back would take too long.

He went over the top, using broken branches of the tree to steady himself, sliding off the bonnet and into the cab.

'Faint pulse at first, but I lost it. His feet are trapped,' Izzy said, as she pumped the man's chest, counting her compressions.

'I'm too big to get down there, but I'll do the CPR if you can edge your way in and maybe release them.'

He watched her squirm her way down into the compressed foot space.

'It's no good.'

Her voice was muffled by the sound of the engine. Engine!

'Can you reach up and turn off the engine?'

The silence was almost more deafening than the noise had been.

'Now, tell me exactly what's holding his feet in place.'

A nurse Mac hadn't met had arrived from the hospital with a resus bag, and a siren told Mac that help was on the way—hopefully a fire truck with cutting equipment.

'It's the engine block, I'd say—come back with the impact. I can see his feet, just can't budge them.'

Mac's mind flashed through dozens of road accidents he'd seen, some caused by carelessness, others by the dreaded IEDs.

'Try taking off his shoes,' he suggested, as he slipped a mask over the man's nose and mouth while the nurse attached the tube to the small oxygen tank in the bag.

You try taking off his shoes! Izzy wanted to retort, but she could see it was a good idea—just not easy to do. She wriggled and squirmed, finally getting one shoe off the size-twelve foot, and, like magic, the foot was free.

The other was harder, but by now she could hear voices outside the cabin, and knew more help was at hand. Metal shrieked as some kind of tool was used in an attempt to pry the driver's door open, and although the door remained shut there must have been some movement, because now she could reach the other shoe—well, steel-capped boot, in fact—and pulling a boot off was far harder than removing a shoe, something she must remember to tell Mac.

'Who's in there?' she heard someone ask.

'Driver and a nurse,' Mac replied. 'Driver's feet are trapped.'

'Get her out. We have to start cutting and although we've got foam to cover the cab, if there's spilt fuel, the welding torch could still spark a fire.'

'You hear that, Izzy? Out now!'

It was an order, but—

'One minute. Give me one minute,' she said, as fear for the trapped driver gripped her. She grabbed the boot with both hands and gave an almighty tug, crashing backwards into Mac as the boot came off.

Her held her for a moment, then lifted her bodily out of the cab, passing her to a fireman as if she was a weightless bundle of skin and bones. The fireman set her on her feet, grinning as he recognised her.

'Seen you looking better, Iz!' he teased, passing her over to Roger, who was on call for the night.

'You okay?' he asked, and she nodded, easing away from his side so the comforting arm he'd put around her shoulders fell away. Roger's hugs were fine, but if she'd wanted a hug right now it wasn't from him.

Dangerous thoughts!

She walked back towards the crash site, keeping out of the way of the ambos now lifting the driver onto a trolley. Mac was there beside it, keeping the resuscitator tube free from kinks, checking oxygen flow and the rise and fall of the patient's chest.

'Have you brought some kind of curse down on us?' Roger was asking Mac. 'Two nights here and two accidents! We can go months without an emergency!'

Mac shrugged, passed the tube and oxygen bottle to Roger, then stepped back, looking around, his gaze coming to rest on Izzy.

Remembering the ambo's comments, she realised she should have gone straight home once the cavalry had arrived. Now Mac was going to see her in whatever state she must be in.

And just *why* was that bothering her?

She wasn't interested in Mac.

Attracted to him, yes, but interested?

Definitely not!

'I'll walk you home,' the person in whom she was *not* interested was saying, and although she'd have liked to refuse, her legs were suddenly shaky and the hand that took her firmly by the elbow was comforting.

'Had he had a heart attack, do you think?' she asked, to distract herself from comforting.

'I'd say so.'

'He must have known something was wrong,' Izzy suggested. 'Big rigs don't usually come through town but he was headed for the hospital and he was giving everyone warning that he was on the way. His hand was definitely on the horn.'

She hesitated, then added, 'It could have been Pop! We all keep telling him it's time to retire and he's not driving as much these days, but when you see something like that...'

Mac heard the tremor in her voice and shifted his hand from her elbow to put his arm around her shoulders—comforting her, nothing more.

Although when the fireman had mentioned fire, he'd felt his lungs seize up.

'Thanks,' she said to him when they'd climbed the path behind the hospital and reached the nunnery. 'And thanks for dinner. I'm sorry I talked so much. You

know my entire life story and I know nothing more about you.'

It was too dark in the shadow of the building to see the flush of embarrassment he was sure was colouring her cheeks, and he knew, for certain, that he should let things go right there.

So what prompted him to speak again?

To say, 'Well, we could fix that. You could show me one of the other restaurants tomorrow night—and I'd let you pay half to prove it's not a date. I have meetings at the hospital in the morning but if I know anything at all about hospital meetings, mine will probably go on all day and I'll have no time to shop. So, shall we say six o'clock? Helping out a new colleague, nothing more. Please?'

He heard her sigh and held his breath. Though every functioning cell in his brain was telling him he needed to see less of her, not more, he wanted her to come, wanted to get to know more about the woman to whom he was so inexplicably—and inconveniently?—attracted.

'Okay,' she finally agreed, 'six o'clock.'

And with that, she vanished.

Well, she probably hadn't vanished, there was obviously a door somewhere along the wall that he hadn't noticed and certainly couldn't make out in the darkness.

Izzy escaped into the building, heading quietly up to the small suite of rooms that Pop had turned into a flat for her and Nikki. She looked in on her daughter, thankfully sound asleep, then headed for the bathroom, turning on the light and seeing her dirt-streaked face

and scratches here and there where she'd obviously rubbed against something.

At least the path home, mostly in the shadow of the nunnery, had been dark so Mac might not have noticed.

Mac might not have noticed?

The question shrieked in her head. She wasn't interested in Mac. It was attraction, nothing more, and right now, with the adoption process under way, the last thing she needed was a man making things difficult.

She stripped off her clothes, showered, and went to bed. In five hours she'd have to be up, getting Nikki organised and off to school.

Life would return to normal, whatever normal was.

Mac woke bathed in sweat and shivering uncontrollably. The nightmares he thought he'd left behind somewhere on the coastal track had returned, possibly because of the near miss he and Izzy had suffered when the big rig had crashed.

He closed his eyes and breathed deeply, murmuring the words he'd adopted as a mantra—'truthfulness, compassion, forbearance.'

He'd first heard them used at a meditation session his psychologist had suggested he attend, and for some reason they had made sense to him. Now they helped to clear his mind and calm his body so meditation could be followed by dream-free sleep.

Sometimes!

Tonight his mantra didn't work.

Concern over a new job?

He didn't think so.

Regret over the mess his marriage had been because

surely Lauren wouldn't have gone looking for excitement if their marriage had been better?

No, he'd been down that track so many times he'd accepted it was just one of those things.

Which left Izzy.

Hearing her story—he'd seen drug-addicted babies and knew just how much they suffered and how big a task it must have been for her to take on—had added admiration for the person she was to the attraction that had sprung between them in the beginning.

But he also understood just how important her daughter was to her, and he had to be careful not to cross any lines that might put Nikki's adoption into danger.

And apart from that, the nightmare had been a reminder that he hadn't fully recovered—another reason not to get involved with an attractive redhead!

Who definitely didn't want a man in her life!

Just now, or any time?

'Get over it, Mac, get back to truthfulness, compassion and forbearance, breathe in, breathe out, breathe…'

Izzy was slipping a casserole into the oven when Nikki returned from school.

'Yum,' her daughter said, sniffing the air in their small flat. 'Chicken Marsala. Pity I'm going out. Sorry, Mum, I forgot to tell you. Shan and I need to work on our new media assignment so I'm sleeping over at her place.'

'The new media assignment you were going to do in the holidays?'

Nikki laughed.

'We *did* make a start—we decided on a topic. Has the rise in the ocean temperature contributed to the increasing number of great white sharks off east coast beaches?'

'That's media, not biology?'

'Oh, Mum, of course it is. What makes the biggest headlines in a newspaper these days? Four people injured in a traffic accident or a surfer bitten by a shark?'

'Shows how much I know,' Izzy said. 'Well, the casserole will do for our dinner tomorrow night, because I'm showing Mac around town tonight and thought we might end up at the new Moroccan place.'

'Mac? Two nights running? You're dating! And another doctor! Oh, Mum!'

Izzy knew she should have kept quiet, but when did she not react to Nikki's teases?

'I am *not* dating the man,' she said firmly, although the disbelief in her daughter's blue eyes suggested it hadn't been firmly enough. 'If and when I decide to go on a date with a man, I will let you know.'

'Well, if and when you do decide, I hope you know not to go too far on a second date—that's coming on too strong, Mum.'

'Coming on too strong?' Izzy growled. 'It is *not* a date and, anyway, who made you an expert?'

'It's in all the magazines, Mum, and people talk about it in online chat rooms—the ones you let me join.'

Izzy smiled. This was an easier conversation—her daughter's grievance that she had limited online options was a common argument. And one in which she'd held the line—so far!

But tonight Nikki wasn't going to air it, flitting

away with, 'I've got to change and pack a few things,' and popping her head back into the combined kitchen and living room to say, 'Just check there's no mad ex-lover in his life.'

Cheeky brat! Izzy thought, but she was still smiling, pleased that she could have these conversations with her daughter—pleased Nikki could have them with her.

She knocked on the bathroom door, and opened it a crack.

'Do you want me to run you down to Shan's?' she asked.

'No, Hallie and Pop are going to the restaurant for dinner, so they'll drive me, but thanks.'

Izzy was closing the door when Nikki spoke again.

'Do *they* know about your non-date?'

'Well, no, but that's only because I haven't seen them today. There's no reason not to tell them.'

'Good,' Nikki called after her, 'because everyone in town will know, probably before you get to his house.'

Brat indeed, but she was right.

Izzy sighed. How on earth had she got herself into this situation? *Why* on earth had she said yes? He was a grown man, ex-army, he could find his way around a small town!

So this would be the last time they had a—what?

A rendezvous?

And to ensure he couldn't use the 'no time to shop' excuse again, she'd take the car, and they could do his shopping either before or after dinner.

Which was possibly one of the stupidest ideas she'd ever had, she realised later as she pushed the trolley around the supermarket while he threw in things he wanted.

Too domestic by far!

Too intimate somehow, especially as she kept running into people she knew and having to introduce Mac.

Which was when she realised that shopping together—although they weren't *really* shopping together—made them look like a couple. She couldn't keep adding 'I'm just pushing the trolley' to the end of every introduction, now, could she?

'What kitchen paper do you use?'

She was so lost in her 'couple' conundrum it took a moment to realise he was talking to her.

'Whatever's on special usually, although I do like it to be three-ply.'

'Kitchen paper comes in different plies?'

'Of course—the more plies, the thicker it is.'

'Well, what do you know?'

Mac was shaking his head, but now searching each pack for the little sign that gave the ply.

And Izzy, looking into the trolley for the first time and seeing the random selection of goods, forgot her worries over how shopping with him would look to the town and began to sort the contents.

'You've not shopped much?'

'Hardly ever,' he admitted. 'Maybe for coffee, or some biscuits for my quarters, but the army does meals rather well.'

'So you can't cook either?' Izzy demanded, and saw the hesitation on his face.

'Maybe just a little—bacon-and-egg sandwich and that kind of thing,' he said. 'But I've bought some books and one of my stepsisters said that if you can

read you can cook, because cookbooks have very clear instructions.'

Izzy shook her head.

'So did you read the book before you came shopping? Write down a list of what you might need in order to cook something you'd read in your book?'

Mac grinned at her.

'Books—I bought two, and, yes, I read one of them on the walk and it all seemed easy enough, but I didn't know until you arrived that we were going to shop.'

'Heaven save me from a helpless male,' Izzy muttered. 'Is there any food at all in your house?'

Mac nodded.

'I've got bread, butter, honey, tea bags and coffee, biscuits, and some milk—most of it left over from the walk, although the milk's fresh.'

'Great start! But to even get the basics, we need time and a list, so what say we abandon this trolley and get some dinner? We can make a list of basics while we're eating and come back later.'

CHAPTER FIVE

SOUNDED GOOD TO MAC. Wandering around the supermarket with Izzy had been a weird experience, but one he'd found himself enjoying more and more. It felt comfortable—right, somehow—and it was impossible to drop things into the trolley without the occasional brush of skin on skin, which added sizzle to the exercise.

Not that he should be thinking of sizzle—not with Izzy. She was definitely off limits!

'So, where shall we eat?'

'Do you like Moroccan food?'

They were walking out of the store, and she'd turned to look at him.

'Love it,' he said, glad for it to be true. 'In fact, one of the cookbooks I bought was a Moroccan one because we had a cook at one time whose family was Moroccan and it was some of the best food I ever tasted in the army.'

She smiled and shook her head.

'Most men would have stuck to steak and sausages—barbeque stuff—but, no, you go for something that a lot of women wouldn't try! At least that will make writing the list easier.'

She was still smiling, and there was something about a smiling sprite that did weird things to his intestines, but he manned up.

'It will?'

'It will,' she confirmed, leading him to the right, along what was obviously the main street in town. 'We'll know what spices to get, and things like dates, and dried apricots, and couscous, and rose water—'

'Rose water? You've got to be kidding!'

This time she laughed, and that felt good—good that he could make her laugh.

But it was treading on very dangerous ground, this being pleased about something so trivial.

Not that making someone laugh was trivial, but it all felt too...

Domestic?

'It's here—not very imaginatively named but great food.'

Izzy pushed through a curtain of glass beads then held them for him to enter the Marrakesh.

He eased past her, careful not to touch—well, not too much—and breathed in the odours of spice and sauces.

'Wonderful!' he said, as Izzy greeted a man who was obviously the owner, dressed in a smart suit with a dazzlingly white shirt.

'This is Hamid,' she said to Mac, and introduced the two of them. 'Hamid's son, Ahmed, is going to be Australia's next great surfing champion. He's still only young, but beating professionals quite regularly in local competitions.'

Hamid waved away the compliment with eloquent hands but his chest had puffed out and Mac knew he

was secretly delighted. Once settled at the table, menus in hand, he realised the scope of Moroccan food.

'I might need guidance,' he said.

Izzy glanced up and smiled.

'No menus in the army?'

'Certainly not this size!'

So she explained the different dishes, asked if he wanted something before the main meal.

'Hamid's mezze plate is wonderful, although it's not specifically Moroccan, more a general Arabic dish, with dips and lovely breads, olives and other bits and pieces.'

'Sounds good, and after that I'll have the chicken with prunes and apricots. Apricots seem to grow wild in Afghanistan and there's nothing as wonderful as a fresh one plucked from a tree. We even had them growing in our compound in Iraq.'

Izzy shook her head.

'We see war as such a terrible thing, and I know it is, but the pictures in the media here show things being blown up, or ruined vehicles or buildings, not a soldier reaching up to pluck an apricot from a tree and biting into it. That's so normal!

Mac grinned at her, something she wished he wouldn't do as grins seemed to make people complicit—as if they shared a secret.

'Actually,' he admitted, 'there's more time than you'd believe for things like apricots. "Hurry up and wait" is an old army saying. Yes, things are unbelievably hectic at times but in between…'

He shrugged, drawing far too much attention to broad shoulders in a blue shirt that stretched across a well-muscled chest.

She closed her eyes momentarily, mainly to banish an image of the chest beneath the shirt. Was there a god or goddess way back in ancient history or maybe a wise woman spirit guide on a tropical island she could call on to banish attraction? Or maybe a spell—some potion she could take…

She couldn't think of any kind of help so opened her eyes to find Hamid had arrived to take their orders.

That part was easy, but sharing a mezze plate meant inevitable touches of fingers. Izzy could feel tension spiralling along her nerves, tightening every sinew.

This had to stop!

She would help him shop, then cut all ties outside work hours. Even at work she could probably avoid him, and surely she was professional enough to handle things when she couldn't.

She was sufficiently distracted that she didn't see Hamid remove the much-depleted mezze plate, but when he returned with the chicken for Mac and a couscous and baked vegetable dish for her, she knew she'd have to pull herself together and make polite conversation.

Or perhaps a list!

A list would be much easier.

She dug a pen from her handbag, pinched a paper serviette from the table next to them and folded it into note-size.

'So,' she said, brightly, 'exactly what do you have in the way of supplies already?'

His eyes narrowed slightly as if maybe he'd guessed she needed a distraction.

'You can eat your dinner first,' he said, spooning

food into his mouth. A pause while he chewed and swallowed, then, 'Mine's delicious.'

Izzy obediently ate a few mouthfuls.

'There,' she said, 'now we can both eat and talk. Basics are bread, butter, milk, tea and coffee, which you seem to have covered.'

'The bread's going a bit green.'

'Okay, so bread...'

She wrote it down.

'Now, breakfast—what do you eat for breakfast?'

Mac held up a hand, obviously giving his full attention to his food.

'It's wonderful,' he eventually said. 'Maybe I can persuade Hamid to give me some small containers of this dish and I could have it for breakfast, lunch and dinner.'

'You'd grow to hate it,' Izzy suggested, and he smiled.

Smiles affected her, but it was, she decided, better than the grin.

'Probably,' he admitted. 'What do you have for breakfast?'

'Totally boring,' Izzy told him. 'Cereal, yoghurt, fruit.'

Another smile.

'That would do me. Write it down.'

Izzy sighed.

'You can't possibly be this hopeless,' she grumbled. 'You must know there are choices. There must be hundreds of types of cereals alone, not to mention plain and flavoured yoghurts—'

'And all kinds of fruit,' he finished for her, shaking his head and laughing. 'Don't look so serious. I can

make those choices in the shop. I'll just grab something that looks good and if I don't like it, I'll get something different next time.'

She didn't want to smile at him but a laughing Mac was hard to resist. The problem was that smiling at him arrested the laughter and something passed between them—nothing more than a quick clash of gazes—but it worried Izzy more than all the other sensations that being with Mac caused.

'Lunch?'

She spoke firmly, wanting to bring things back to normal between them. 'A sandwich? Cheese, ham, tomato, lettuce?'

And suddenly he was as decisive as she was.

'Ham and cheese—they'll last longer.'

Mac wasn't sure what had just happened, but something had—something that had been more than attraction—something dangerous, although not darkly so...

He scooped more of his meal onto his spoon and ate in silence, only half listening as Izzy added practical things—dishcloths, soap, washing powder—to his list.

Mac used her concentration on the list to study the woman across the table from him, a little frown drawing her eyebrows together. She wasn't a classic beauty, or even stunningly attractive, yet his body responded to every move she made, and every word she spoke. It was as if they were attached to each other with invisible wires—which was such a ridiculous fantasy he couldn't believe he'd thought it.

He had to get his head straight.

He had to keep things light between them. He knew her well enough by now to know she wasn't a dallying

kind of woman, even without the vulnerability of her position in regard to Nikki's adoption.

And there were still too many dark places in his psyche to think beyond dalliance with any woman.

They finished their meals—and apparently the list—he wiping his plate clean with some thick, fresh-baked bread, though Izzy seemed too distracted to have eaten all of hers.

But she pushed her plate away and said, 'Come on, let's go. You paid last night so it's my turn.'

He protested that she was doing him a favour but she ignored him, handing her credit card to Hamid to stop any further argument.

But back in the supermarket—shopping with her—it seemed dangerous again.

She had to get out of here, Izzy decided. Finish this as quickly as possible and get out—get home. For some obscure reason an ordinary wander around a supermarket was beginning to feel like a date—more like a date than dinner had.

She knew it wasn't, of course, but—

'That should keep you going,' she finally declared, heading resolutely towards the checkouts.

'That's if I can pay for it and don't end up in debtors' prison.'

'What, this little lot?' she teased, waving her hand at the almost full trolley. 'Back when we were young, we'd have Hallie pushing the lead trolley with three or four of us trailing along behind, each with a trolley.'

'The mind boggles,' Mac said, easing Izzy away from the handle and taking over the pushing, his body still close and warm.

'Oh, I need some toothpaste!' She dashed away,

grabbing two tubes, although she knew there was plenty at home.

Anything to get away from that warmth—that closeness—that somehow, even when he hadn't been near her, she'd been feeling.

'Throw them in with mine as thanks for all the help, not to mention the lift you're going to give me,' Mac suggested, and rather than argue—and get close again—she threw them in.

Once back at his house, she helped him unload the bags.

'I'll leave you to unpack so you know where you've put everything,' she said, backing towards the door as escape finally beckoned.

'None of this will go off if left for a few minutes, so I'll walk you home.'

'I've got a car,' Izzy reminded him. 'But thanks for the offer.'

'Then I'll walk you to your car,' he said, and did just that, opening the driver's door for her so their heads were close. She met his eyes and knew something was passing between them…like the promise of a kiss that couldn't be…

CHAPTER SIX

Izzy was still muttering, 'Promise of a kiss, indeed…' to herself when she reported to work the next morning. The walk down from home had been pleasant, dawn breaking, the first rays of the sun peeking from below the horizon.

She loved the town when it was like this, barely awake, and the early shift, beginning at six, was her favourite.

Abby, still on nights, was waiting for her in the ED.

'Ambulance on its way in—four-year-old with febrile convulsions. Little Rhia Watson—Sally and Ben's daughter. I've written down all the handover stuff—it's on the desk—and the other night nurse will do a proper handover to Chloe, who's on with you today—I think an agency nurse is coming for the swing shift.'

The conversation ended as the ambulance pulled up outside, and both women hurried out to meet it.

'She woke up crying in the night,' Sally explained as Ben carried his daughter into the room. 'Her temperature was up so I gave her some children's paracetamol and sponged her down, but nothing seemed to help. We stayed with her, trying to keep her cool, and she drifted

off to sleep then about half an hour ago she cried out and when we went in she was all stiff and shaking.'

'I called the ambulance,' Ben added, as he carefully laid his listless daughter on the examination table. 'She'd stopped shaking by the time they got there.'

The ambo was handing over his report to Abby, and although Izzy knew it would have all the details of Rhia's temperature, pulse, and oxygen saturation she knew she'd have to do it all again.

After she'd examined the little girl.

She took Rhia's hand. 'I'm Izzy and I'm a nurse and I'm going to look after you. Mum and Dad are still here. Now, can you tell me if you're hurting anywhere?'

'My head hurts…and my neck.'

'Get a doctor in here,' Izzy said quietly to Abby. She didn't want to alarm Rhia's parents but with neck pain or stiffness in a child this age there was always the possibility of meningococcal.

'Now, I'm just going to look at your tummy, is that okay?'

Dark brown eyes dulled by pain or fatigue looked blankly at her as Izzy checked the little girl's skin for any sign of a rash.

None, but that didn't mean anything at this stage.

'I'd like to give her an antibiotic injection just to be sure,' she said to the parents, who nodded, willing to go along with anything to make their little girl better.

'You're thinking meningococcal?' Mac asked quietly.

He had appeared from nowhere, but had obviously heard her.

'Or not,' Izzy said, 'but we usually start with an antibiotic just in case, then do the tests.'

He nodded, and she went off to get the penicillin while Mac introduced himself to the family and began his examination of their patient.

'Has she been vaccinated against meningococcal?' he asked, and Sally held out her hands in a helpless gesture.

'I think she had a needle for that when she was one but I'd have to check.' Fear brought a quaver to the words. 'Do you think that's what it is?'

Mac reached out and touched Sally's shoulder.

'We don't know but the fever means an infection and starting antibiotics straight away will help no matter what it turns out to be.'

He nodded to Izzy, who told Rhia about the needle, and waited until Ben had lifted his daughter into his arms before swabbing the skin, using deadening lotion, then slowly administering the antibiotic.

Rhia cried, but it was a half-hearted effort, and her listlessness made Izzy fear the worst.

Mac was explaining that he would need to take blood and some cerebrospinal fluid for testing, and Izzy suggested they move to the small room that was sometimes used as a second resus room.

Mac nodded, then smiled down at Rhia.

'Do you mind if *I* carry you instead of Daddy?'

There was no objection so he lifted her and carried her gently into the more private space. Izzy asked Ben to wait and with his help she filled in the admission form before leading him to join the others.

Mac had settled Rhia on a high table and with Izzy's help secured an IV port in their patient's little hand. He handed Izzy a vial of blood to be sent off for test-

ing, then explained to Rhia that he needed her to lie on her side so he could put another needle in her back.

'I'm sorry sweetheart,' he said, smiling at the little girl, 'but we need to find out what's making you sick. I'll do my best not to hurt you.'

But Rhia was beyond caring, she simply stared at Mac with those big blank eyes, while Sally cried quietly on her husband's shoulder.

So Izzy held their patient curled on her side on the table while Mac numbed the site with local anaesthetic, then inserted the needle to test CSF pressure before withdrawing a sample. Izzy cleaned and covered the site with a dressing before gently rolling Rhia onto her back.

Mac was putting details on the chart, so Izzy labelled and packed the fluid container, added the blood sample to the package and passed it to the courier she had phoned earlier.

'Now we wait,' Mac said quietly, as Rhia's parents moved closer to their daughter, one on either side, holding her hands and talking quietly.

Mac followed Izzy out of the room.

'If it's confirmed as meningococcal we'll have to find out who's been in contact with her for the last week and give them all a dose of clearance antibiotics—starting with her parents. And if it *is* meningococcal there'll be a run on the vaccine. Is it subsidised by the government or will people have to pay for it?'

'If she had the vaccine, and she probably did, it would have been Type C. Since that's been on the free list the most common strain in Australia is B and although there's now a vaccine for it, you have to buy it.'

Mac nodded.

'We'll have to admit her, if only for observation—at least until the test results come back.'

'She could go into the family room, and that way her parents could stay with her. She's an only child and Sally's a stay-at-home mum so she could be here all the time and Ben go to work from here.'

Mac grinned at her.

'Family room, huh? I did wonder why one of the rooms had a double bed.'

Was it the grin or the mention of a double bed that raised Izzy's heart rate?

'It's a very useful room to have,' she said reprovingly. 'Apart from making it easier for hospitalised children to have their parents with them, it's been great for elderly people especially. Imagine being married for sixty years and suddenly your spouse is hospitalised twenty miles away. It's too much to expect them to visit for an hour or two each day.'

Mac's smile was back and with it Izzy's heightened pulse.

'I'm still back at the imagining being married sixty years part—I didn't make it to three.'

'Didn't work out?'

She remembered him saying he'd been married—back at that embarrassing dinner. And something else—that he wouldn't marry again?

His marriage must have been bad.

And the wretch was still smiling.

'I think you'll find in your statistics that something like forty percent of marriages fail.'

'You're wrong, it's one in three marriages fail so that's thirty-three percent,' Izzy muttered, disturbed by the conversation, although she couldn't work out why.

Mac's life, former, present, or future, had nothing to do with her.

Mac watched her walk along the passage that gave entry to the rooms that made up the ward. He liked the design of the hospital, with an enclosed courtyard garden on the other side of the passage. And along the outside of the patient rooms was a long veranda so those well enough could sit outside, enjoying the sunshine and the view over the town to the ocean.

Halfway down was the nurses' station, well set up with computers, monitors and light boxes. Someone had taken the trouble to make the new hospital, in the damaged part of the old building, into a relaxed and pleasant place for patients, and a great working environment for the staff.

'You're Mac, I believe,' a voice said from behind him, and he turned to greet a young Asian woman, the crisp white coat and the stethoscope slung around her neck a dead giveaway that she was a doctor.

'I'm Aisha Narapathan,' she introduced herself, holding out a slim hand for him to shake. 'I've a patient in Room Fourteen, and I pop in to see her most mornings.'

Mac introduced himself, and smiled.

'You're from the local GP group?'

Aisha nodded.

'We act as on-call doctors when you and Roger are off duty and although our patients are happy with the treatment they get in hospital, I like to check up on them myself. At times when there's been only one doctor employed at the hospital, and we've been rostered on for morning rounds. It might seem a clunky system at first but it works.'

She smiled again, and added, 'Most of the time. You've had a busy weekend, I hear. Normally one of us would have been on call—we cover weekends as well—but Saturday night was our receptionist's wedding and, it being a country town, we were all invited.'

'We managed,' Mac assured her.

'I'm sure you did,' Aisha said. 'With Izzy around, even the most helpless of the contract doctors we've had at the hospital can manage.'

She moved on but not before Mac caught the flash of a bright diamond on the ring finger of her left hand.

Was she the doctor engaged to Roger Grey?

His thought was confirmed when he saw her as she was leaving.

'You must come to dinner one day. Roger and I would love to have you. I'll tell him to arrange it with you.'

An aide arrived with a message. There was a phone call for him in his office.

He headed in that direction, pausing only to say goodbye to Aisha.

Was this job going to turn into a deskbound one? Surely not—and not if the weekend was anything to go on.

But interaction with people—with patients and their relatives—was the part of medicine he enjoyed the most.

The voice on the phone introduced himself as the pathologist at Braxton Hospital.

'I've emailed the results to you but thought it would be good if we spoke.'

He introduced himself, asked the usual questions

about where Mac had trained, seeking acquaintances in common, then explained.

'It's meningitis meningococcal for sure. The bacteria are present in the spinal fluid but none in the blood.'

'Thanks, mate,' Mac said. 'I owe you one for getting it done so quickly.'

But as soon as he'd hung up he wondered if the hospital would have ceftriaxone on hand, or whether he should have ordered some for Braxton.

There were optional drugs, but lately it had been the one of choice for meningococcal attacks on the brain.

He looked up from doodling the name on his desk pad to see Izzy flash past the door.

'Izzy!'

She turned, stopping in the doorway. For the first time he realised just how horrible the dark blue uniform tunic looked on a redhead, although he still felt his groin tighten just looking at her.

'Ceftriaxone?' he asked.

'So it *is* meningitis,' she said, her voice flat with the anxiety she felt for the child. 'We've some in stock. I'll set up a drip.'

'I'll do it,' he said, 'but come with me while I tell Rhia's parents. They'll feel better with someone they know in the room.'

Will they? Izzy wondered, but she accompanied Mac back to the family room, where Mac explained the result.

He did it well, she realised, listening to his explanation of what was happening inside their daughter's body, then moved swiftly on to treatment.

'We've got it early,' he told them. 'You were right to get help immediately she had the seizure. There

are good drugs to treat it and we'll start a drip straight away so the antibiotic is going directly into her bloodstream. I'll also give the pair of you antibiotics and later the vaccine.'

He turned his attention to the small patient in the big single bed in the family room.

'I know you're feeling bad right now,' he said, stroking strands of pale brown hair off her face, 'but we're going to get you better.

'She'll be here for a few days, probably longer,' he said quietly to Ben on his way out the door. 'You might want to get some toys she's familiar with and her own pyjamas and a few clothes for her and the pair of you.'

'And books. I'll get books—she loves us reading to her.'

Hmm…Izzy thought to herself when she heard Ben's voice strengthen at the thought of having something to do to help. She knew already that Mac was a good doctor, he'd shown that in the emergencies over the weekend, but he was also a good psychologist.

Or perhaps just a caring man, sensitive to how Ben must have been feeling?

Whatever! She didn't need to be seeing these compassionate sides of him, they would add depth to the silly attraction she was already feeling.

But right now at least she could get away from him—she had a job to do in the pharmacy.

Except he caught up with her on the way and it was hardly a pharmacy, just a room where drugs were kept.

A very small room!

She paused outside the door.

She didn't *have* to go in!

Of course she did, she knew where it was kept.

He'd stopped beside her and she was so conscious of him her skin itched.

This was crazy—there was no other word for it. She'd been attracted to The Rat, as her family now called the last man in her life, but not like this—not as if the attraction was a tangible thing, not only causing responses inside her body but in her skin as well.

'What's the protocol?' she asked, forcing her mind to matters medical, fumbling with her keys to find the right one as if that, and not her disinclination to be in a very small room with him, was the hold-up.

'Seven days' IV for Rhia, in saline, not Ringer's, because it doesn't mix well with anything that has calcium in it. Then we'll have to give antibiotics to any people who've been in close contact with her in the last week, and check all of their statuses as far as vaccination goes. We'll get a list of friends and relations from her parents. Was she at childcare of any kind that you know of?'

Whatever was affecting her couldn't be affecting him that he was being so practical.

She could do practical!

'She's four. She'd be at the local pre-school probably three days a week. I'll get our secretary to phone the director and get a list.'

'Of teachers, too,' Mac reminded her as she finally got the key to fit into the keyhole and unlocked the door of the pharmacy.

They stepped inside together—close—and without turning to face her Mac said, 'I understand your reluctance to be going out with men because of the adoption business, and I know it's bizarre, but I've never felt an attraction like the one I feel for you. I thought maybe

if we gave in to it, say for a week or two, it might go away. That's if you feel it, too, of course...'

His voice was only slightly strangled, but Izzy knew any words she said would come out far worse—if at all.

He'd touched her lightly and somehow they turned to face each other, not touching, not close enough to cause a scandal should anyone walk past, but Izzy could feel the shape of him in her skin, catch the warmth of his breath on her lips.

'You *must* feel it,' he said. 'Something this strong can't be one-sided.

She almost nodded—no way could she deny it. But caution, memory of the last disaster—and somewhere in her head and heart concern for Nikki—held her back.

'The ceftriaxone should be in here,' she said, moving towards a cupboard where she knew the powder was kept. It would be dissolved in the saline solution and dripped slowly into Rhia.

Then Mac was right behind her, peering into the cupboard, examining its contents, taking his cue from her—now totally professional.

'I have had a look inside these cupboards and the refrigerators but, as yet, couldn't put my hand on anything.'

'Which is why you have staff,' Izzy told him, so rattled by his presence she was shaking.

'Staff I can put my hand on?' he teased, touching her lightly on the shoulder. Not *quite* professional!

Was he another Rat or just another touchy person like Roger?

Izzy doubted it—this was something they both felt.

'We can't talk here,' she said desperately, a vial of the yellowish powder in her hand.

'Then later?' he asked, his breath now warming her neck.

'Sometime!' she said, almost shouting, desperate to get out of the room, away from Mac, if only so her body could settle down and her brain regain some thinking power.

He moved away, finding a bag of saline for all he'd said he didn't know his way around.

Izzy glanced at her watch—it had been less than five minutes since they'd left the corridor, yet it had seemed like a lifetime.

But was he right? Could a short—short what? Affair? Liaison?—kill the attraction?

She had no idea but as it was impossible to think while he was in such close proximity, she chose escape.

'I'll leave you to mix it if that's okay? I've other patients I need to check. They'll be thinking no one cares about them.'

And she fled, although her excuse hadn't been entirely true. Patients in a small hospital knew the staff could become caught up in emergencies and they bore it well, knowing it could be them or one of their loved ones who needed urgent attention next time.

And Mac was probably intuitive enough, from what she'd seen of him, to know it, too.

Was he avoiding her as assiduously as she was avoiding him? Izzy wondered later, when she was sitting in the secretary's room, working out how she could juggle the rosters for the week.

They would need more nursing staff on duty to han-

dle vaccinations and antibiotics for adults and children who'd been in contact with Rhia, and the budget didn't have much wriggle room.

'Here's the list from Sally and Ben. They've included phone numbers where they knew them.'

She looked up to see Mac hovering over her desk, a piece of paper in his hand.

'One of the aides could have delivered that,' she said, disconcerted to have him back in her space when she'd thought she'd escaped.

She'd been looking up at him so saw from a half-smile that he was about to say something silly, then he glanced towards Belle at the desk at the back of the room and must have thought better of it.

Instead he tilted his head to see what she'd been doing. 'Have we enough staff to help out with the vaccinations when people hear about it and start coming in?'

Izzy pointed at the sheet.

'It's a juggling act, but staffing at small hospitals always is so, yes, we'll manage.'

A soft chime told them they had a patient in the ED and the enrolled nurse on duty there needed help.

'I'll go,' Mac said. 'You keep juggling, and maybe Belle can start on the phone calls.' He took his list from Izzy and passed it over to Belle, talking to her in a quiet voice, suggesting what she might say, emphasising it was a precautionary move but it was better to be safe than sorry.

As he whisked out of the room, Izzy let out the breath she'd been holding. What *was* it about this man that had her so uptight? So dithered and confused?

Another soft chime and she knew she was needed.

The rosters would have to wait, and as for unanswer-able questions—well, those she had to put right out of her mind.

What was quite a large room for a country ED was filling up rapidly—filling up with worried-looking mothers or fathers, each clutching a small child by the hand.

'Dr Mac told me to phone the pre-school earlier,' the enrolled nurse on duty told her, 'and they must have started contacting parents straight away.'

Izzy could see Mac in a curtained alcove already, speaking to an anxious father. He saw Izzy, excused himself, and came across to her.

'We'll do antibiotic jabs today and ask parents to check their child's immunisation schedule and come back if they need the vaccine.'

'Sounds good,' Izzy said. 'I'll rustle up a few more nurses or aides to organise this scrum.'

As the day wore on, the trickle of people who'd been in contact with Rhia became a flood. Mac had con-tacted Braxton for more antibiotic and warned they could also be needing vaccine.

He was, Izzy realised when they had a break in cus-tomers late afternoon, the most organised doctor she'd ever worked with, and his efficiency seemed to make the whole process move more smoothly.

Swing shift nurses and aides had come in, taking over from anyone who had to go off duty on time to collect children or meet appointments, but the flood was once again a trickle and all but Izzy had returned to normal duties.

Mac was sitting behind the reception desk, eating a sandwich that had grown stale enough to have the

edges of the bread curling up in a most unappetising manner.

'Want some?' he said.

'Eugh! No way! I did grab something earlier but I'm going to make a cuppa while the place is quiet. Do you want one?'

He shook his head, lifting a can of soda that was sitting on the desk.

But the image of him, sandwich in one hand, soda in the other, stayed with Izzy as she hurried to the tea room.

He was just a man, an ordinary man—good doctor, though—but still just a man!

So why was he affecting her the way he was?

Why so instantly?

Why him when other men roused no emotion whatsoever?

It must be, she finally decided, just one of life's mysteries to which there was no answer—no logical explanation.

CHAPTER SEVEN

MAC WATCHED HER disappear out the door and wondered about attraction. Why one woman and not another?

He looked at the curling edge of the sandwich and decided she'd been right—it wasn't worth eating. Dumping it and the empty can in the bin, he picked up the ED admissions book, looking back through the pages, seeing more than one night a week when they had no patients at all.

Had he brought the rush of emergencies to this small town?

That was nearly as ridiculous a thought as the attraction one he'd had earlier!

But forcing himself to focus—so as not to think about the other matter—he could see that this time of the day was always quiet. Patients, it seemed, came into the ED late afternoon, three to five, then the numbers dropped off until six-thirty when another trickle might arrive.

With the news about Rhia spreading, tonight's trickle would more likely be a flood.

'Will we have extra staff on this evening in case the people Belle phoned start coming in?' he asked Izzy, who was coming through the door with her cup of tea.

'Yes, we will,' a voice that wasn't Izzy's answered, and he realised Roger was right behind her. 'But I mean "we", not "you". Time the pair of you were off. The hospital can't afford overtime, you know.' He smiled, then added, 'Well, not the amount of overtime you've racked up over the weekend. Izzy doesn't count as she wasn't even on duty so how could she possibly claim overtime?'

As a nurse Mac had met, but whose name he couldn't remember, had followed Roger into the room, it was hard to argue.

'I'm happy to leave you to it,' Mac said, then turned to Izzy. 'And as I've just thrown my lunch into the bin and I know you haven't eaten, how about we duck into town for an early dinner at that Thai restaurant you mentioned? I've a few things to go over with Roger, so you'd have time to slip home and change.'

He hesitated, then added, 'Nikki might like to come, too—save you having to feed her.'

Was it nothing more than a friendly gesture, or was it a test? Izzy wondered. She'd told him she hadn't dated because she didn't want men coming in and out of Nikki's life, so asking Nikki made it just a casual dinner.

Didn't it?

And asking in front of other staff, that was casual, too—or had he done *that* to make it hard for her to refuse?

'Go and change, the man said.' Roger's voice broke into her muddled thoughts. 'No one in their right mind wants to be seen eating in town with someone in that appalling uniform.'

'It's practical and not that appalling!' She automati-

cally defended the uniform Hallie had chosen, although Izzy had never yet met anyone it suited.

'Just go!' Roger ordered, and she went.

Befuddled, that was what she was.

And tired now the let-down after a busy day was seeping into her body.

Better tiredness than the things she felt when she was with Mac.

So why was she going to dinner with him?

Again!

With him and Nikki—that sounded better, and felt better, too, the tiredness leaving her as she wondered whether the two would get on well.

'Fab!' was Nikki's reaction. 'Shan and I can get on with the project.'

'After you've eaten,' Izzy told her firmly. 'Mac was good enough to ask us both so you'll sit and eat with us. It's an early dinner so if you like Shan could come back here with us and stay over if you've work you'd like to do.'

Nikki surprised her with a warm hug.

'You're the greatest, Mum!'

And Izzy's heartbeats went erratic again, although a very different kind of erratic from the way it reacted to Mac.

Enough! Shower and change, go downtown and eat with the man, then home to bed.

Inviting Nikki to dinner was nothing more than kindness.

As for the attraction—well, that was nothing but chemistry, a reaction.

Like a nuclear explosion?

Ridiculous, but that was how it felt—sudden and totally inexplicable, but so powerful…

She *really* shouldn't be seeing him again tonight!

She left the shower and dressed quickly, pulling on a long shift that swirled about her ankles.

Hair!

Always a problem, but tonight there was no time to fight it so she rammed combs into each side to hold the rebellious curls back off her face. If she hadn't spent so long in the shower, pondering imponderables, she could have put it up, but it was too late for regrets.

She grabbed a shawl to put around her shoulders in case the night turned cool, and walked into the living room, calling to her daughter.

Rather to her surprise, Nikki's clothes were, for her, remarkably conservative—jeans and a blue and white striped top.

'What, no holes or rips in your gear?' Izzy teased, and Nikki laughed.

'I didn't want to embarrass your doctor friend on our first family date.'

'He is not my friend and it's not a date,' Izzy retorted, then plunged into further trouble. 'Well, he is a friend the way colleagues become friends but it definitely isn't a date.'

They were walking down the path to the doctor's house by now, so Izzy couldn't see Nikki's face when her daughter asked, 'Why not a date, Mum? Is it because of me?'

Izzy sighed.

'Not really, although probably, early on, yes, I worried you might get to like a man I was seeing then he'd disappear, then later I worried—'

'About me being affected by you having someone else? Shared love? Possible abuse?'

'You're too smart for your own good,' Izzy said, putting her arm around Nikki's shoulders and giving her a hug.

'Not really,' Nikki told her. 'You can't help hearing and reading about all that kind of thing, but it's time you had someone special in your life, Mum. I'm old enough and we're close enough for me to tell you if I thought anyone was creepy. I mean, I know Roger's always giving me a pat but he's not creepy, not like that cleaner you had at the hospital a few years back. He was an old man—'

'At least forty,' Izzy put in.

'Old!' Nikki reiterated. 'He used to give Shan and me lollies and then we'd run away.'

Sheesh! Izzy knew exactly who Nikki meant but this was the first she'd heard of the lollies. The man hadn't been there long, mainly because other staff members were uneasy about him, but if she hadn't known *that* about her daughter what else might she not know?

'Mum, we're here, and there's Mac waiting at his gate and I know you're thinking bad mother thoughts but, really, we were fine and if we'd told you, you'd have put a stop to it and we liked the lollies.'

'You okay?' Mac asked, touching Izzy lightly on the shoulder.

Fortunately she was so numbed by what Nikki had just told her that the electricity that flashed through her body was only a half-charge, although her knees felt wobbly and she was pleased when he hooked his arm through hers, his other arm through Nikki's, and led them down towards the town.

'Not often I get to take *two* beautiful women out to dinner,' Mac said.

Then he laughed when Nikki retorted with, 'Flatterer!'

She then asked him about the meningococcal, having heard about it at school.

'I've had the vaccine—actually, I've had every vaccine ever developed, thanks to an over-anxious mother.'

She was teasing Izzy, Mac knew, but there was a gentleness in it that suggested a maturity beyond her age.

Growing up in a house with grandparents, as Hallie and Pop surely were?

Not that he had time to ponder the question, for she was speaking again.

'Sorry, miles away, what did you ask?' he said.

'Do you know anything about global warming?'

'Nikki!' Izzy protested, 'Let's just have a nice peaceful dinner without any debates on the problems of the world.'

'It's for my project, and he's a doctor—he'd know a lot of science.'

Time to intervene, Mac decided, though he'd far rather just keep walking, feeling the warmth of Izzy by his side, imagining how things could be—might be?

Probably wouldn't be...

'But not how to cure global warming, Nikki,' Mac told her. 'It's something that's going to take a lot of research and there still won't be a vaccine for it, but what, apart from sharks and global warming, do you do at school? You're in high school, right?'

Nikki listed off her subjects, gave character sketches—not always good but none too bad—of her

teachers, and by that time they'd reached the restaurant and he had to relinquish his hold on Izzy.

Which was just as well, because seeing her in the bright advertising lights outside, his body tightened, his lungs seized, and he rather thought he might be shaking.

This was ridiculous!

Or was it, when she looked so ravishing? Red hair pushed back so it was a mass of rioting curls behind her head. A long dress with swirling patterns of what looked like autumn leaves, skimming across her lithe figure, emphasising pert breasts, a slim waist and hips that were designed to be held, in order to draw her closer.

'Are we going in, or are you going to stand there all night, staring at Mum?'

Had he been staring?

Surely not—he wasn't some schoolboy seeing his first woman.

Besides, the last thing she wanted in her life right now was a man…

He shuffled the pair of them in front of him into the restaurant, although it was an effort not to feel the silky material of that miraculous dress.

Miraculous dress?

He was losing it!

Or maybe he'd spent so many years seeing women in camouflage or uniform or khaki fatigues that the dress had affected him.

The dress or the woman inside it?

Nikki was introducing him to Shan's mother, who ran the front of house at the restaurant. She led them

to a table in a quiet alcove, leaving them with menus and a bottle of cold water.

'You've had too big a day,' Izzy said to him. 'You look punch-drunk!'

'You've had a bigger day and you look magnificent!'

'She does, doesn't she?' Nikki said, adding, with the candour of youth, 'That's Mum's favourite dress.'

Izzy blushed and shook her head, then filled her water glass and drank deeply, thankful she didn't have a coughing fit or embarrass herself in some other way, given that her daughter had already mortified her.

Mac's head was bent over the menu, Nikki's close to his as she pointed out the best dishes, and seeing the pair of them Izzy felt a pang of conscience.

Maybe she should have done something about finding a father for Nikki earlier. Back when she was little—starting at pre-school where other kids had fathers—she'd sometimes asked about hers, but as none of them had a clue who'd fathered her sister's baby, Izzy could only tell the truth, that not even her sister had known.

At four, Nikki had accepted it, but Izzy knew that any day now Nikki would begin to wonder about a mother who hadn't known who her baby's father was. She knew her mother had been sick and died, but not about the drugs—something else that would have to be a conversation soon.

Izzy sighed, and Mac turned towards her.

'You don't have a favourite? It's too hard to choose?'

He smiled and her toes curled obligingly and she was glad they were sitting, with her feet tucked safely under the table, so no one could see *that* reaction. Per-

haps in future she should wear shoes, not sandals, when out with Mac.

Although there was no real reason why she should be out with Mac again, and plenty of reasons why she shouldn't.

'I'm having the chicken pad Thai and coconut prawns,' Nikki announced, and, too bamboozled by her emotions, Izzy took the easy way out.

'I'll have the same,' she said, then caught Nikki's questioning look.

'You're going to eat noodles in front of Mac? And in your favourite dress?' her daughter said, in a voice that couldn't have been more incredulous. 'You know what a mess you always get into with noodles.'

'Not always,' Izzy said weakly, but with Mac now looking at her she wasn't about to back out.

She got into a mess with the noodles. For reasons beyond her comprehension, where other people could manipulate their spoons and forks to get them neatly into their mouths, the best she could manage was to get one end in and slurp the rest, leaving the juice all down her chin.

Or the whole lot fell out of the spoon as she lifted it towards her chin and she splattered herself, the table-cloth and anyone within arm's length of the disaster.

Nikki refrained from saying 'I told you so', and Mac was super-helpful with extra napkins, but if she'd thought her daughter's mention of her favourite dress was mortifying, this was fifty times worse and probably had a special name but she didn't know it.

The meal was delicious, and Shan's mother insisted it was on the house, but as they left Izzy realised that suggesting Shan return with them to stay the night

hadn't been such a good idea. The pair went on ahead, way ahead, and the chatter and laughter drifting back grew fainter and fainter.

'Are they making sure we're left on our own for the walk home?' Mac asked.

'I'm afraid so,' Izzy answered gloomily. 'It seems Nikki's decided I need a man in my life and as long as you don't have a demented ex-lover then you'll do!'

'I'm flattered. And, no, no demented ex-lover.'

Their stroll had slowed so much they were dawdling and as they reached the deep shadows of the old fig tree he paused, touching her lightly on the shoulder to turn her towards him.

'And what about you?' he asked quietly. 'Would I do for you?'

It was too dark to see any reaction on her face but he watched her shake her head.

'It's all too hard just now,' she murmured. 'And you really don't want this either, for all the attraction there is between us.'

'So you do feel it?'

His voice was rough with some emotion he didn't understand, but the kiss he dropped on her lips was nothing more than a breath of air—the brush of a butterfly's wing.

Yet he felt the tremor that ran through her body, felt it in her shoulder where his hand still rested lightly.

He wanted her in a way he'd never felt before, yet knew it couldn't be. She wouldn't—couldn't—take the risk of losing her child, although how realistic that risk was he wasn't sure.

Neither was she a woman he could dally with—she was too fine, too caring, too loving and the way he was,

his head still in a mess, nightmares roaring through his sleep—he'd end up hurting her.

Yet he couldn't let her go—couldn't ease her away when she leant into him—couldn't *not* kiss her when she raised her face to his, her lips an unseen invitation in the gloom beneath the tree.

Long and deep, this kiss! He probed her lips, tasted them with his tongue, felt her mouth open to the unspoken invitation and was lost. His arms wrapped around her, clamping her body to his, and his heart beat with a frenzied tattoo against his ribs.

She breathed his name, her fingers on his face now, moving across his cheeks, his temple, learning him through touch while he learnt the secrets of her mouth, the taste of her, her soft shape against his hardness.

It knew no bounds, this kiss, until the need to breathe, to replenish empty lungs with air, forced their heads apart. Knees weak, he stepped back to rest against the massive trunk of the tree, Izzy moving with him, still in his arms.

And with her hands now framing his face, which he knew would be nothing more than a faint oval in the darkness, she whispered, 'Do you really think a short affair would cure this? Do you think it would ever be enough?'

He drew her close again, his lips moving against her hair, kissing as he answered.

'I have no idea,' he said, because honesty was suddenly important. 'I'd be willing to find out, but you're the one with most at stake, my lovely one, so it's up to you.'

He felt her slump, as if her bones had melted, felt her head shake against his chest.

'I don't know!'

The plaintive response cut into him, as painful as a knife wound.

'Then let's just wait until you do,' he told her, straightening up from the tree, steadying her with his hands, brushing his fingers over her hair, then his thumb across her lips.

'We'll wait,' he repeated, then took her hand and led her out of the darkness, seeing the redness of her well-kissed lips, the glow of colour in her cheeks, and the doubt that shadowed the happiness in her eyes.

Back on the footpath, hands unlatched, they walked briskly up past the hospital and onto the path to the old nunnery.

'I'm sorry to be such a wuss about this,' she muttered as they reached the place where she'd disappeared before. 'But I really don't know where I stand and whether the adoption could be threatened and—well, I don't know anything at all right now—my brain's stopped working.'

'It's been a long day,' Mac told her, although what he really wanted to do was kiss away the hopelessness he knew she was feeling.

'Too long,' she agreed, then straightened up and actually smiled at him.

'Thank heavens I invited Shan back for the night. It means the two of them will be shut away in Nikki's room and I can sneak in without a post mortem of the evening and an inquisition on why it took us so long to get home.'

He smiled and touched her dimple.

'Good luck with that,' he said, and watched as she

did the disappearing thing again, although this time he did see the door through which she vanished.

Izzy made her way slowly up to the flat. She knew her hair would be a mess but hoped, in case she did run into Nikki or Shan, she didn't look as well kissed as she felt.

It had been a mistake, kissing Mac, but that oh-so-light touch of his lips on hers had weakened her to such an extent she could do no more than slump against him, and lift her lips…

For more?

Of course for more!

The man was right, this attraction—or chemical re-action—that had sizzled between them from that first meeting on the beach was too strong to be ignored.

Yet ignore it she should.

Unless he was right, and having a quick affair might let it fizzle out…

How quick was a quick affair?

Nikki probably knew more about relationships than she did—from second-hand experience admittedly.

Not that she could discuss this with Nikki…

Or anyone really…

Although—

She ran her mind quickly over the much-loved people she considered sisters and brothers. Lila had absolutely no experience with men, determined to find out who she was before she became someone else as part of a pair. Marty was an expert on affairs and would undoubtedly say, *Go for it, Iz!* because that was how he lived his life.

Stephen, now…

Sir Stephen they'd always called him when they

wanted to tease, because of all of them he had family that actually wanted him—two families, in fact—wealthy ones at that—two sets of grandparents fighting for the right to bring him up, in and out of courts, while Steve fitted himself awkwardly into Hallie and Pop's chaotic family.

She had no idea about Steve's love life. Nikki's mother had always been the one closest to Stephen, living with him in Sydney off and on, infuriating him with her behaviour, her addictions, her irresponsibility. Yet he'd always taken her in whenever she'd needed a bed, helped her when she'd needed help.

Perhaps that's why he'd been so good to her, Izzy, when she'd struggled with Nikki as a baby. And remembering that, she knew he'd say don't jeopardise the adoption!

She sighed. Fat lot of help her family were!

She showered, ran a comb through her hair, and climbed into bed, exhausted by the day and the emotions but unable to sleep because the kiss played over and over in her head, remembered ripples and tremors of desire tormenting her body.

CHAPTER EIGHT

MAC FELT AT a loss, arriving at the hospital the next morning to find it an Izzy-free zone. A quick check of the rosters showed she wouldn't be on until two, which was, he decided, probably a good idea.

But a recent idea?

He checked again and, yes, there'd been a shuffle in the rosters.

Was she avoiding him?

Had she spent the night reminding herself of all the reasons why getting involved with him could harm her adoption plans?

His night had been tortured not by nightmares but by thoughts of a single kiss, and by images of where that kiss might lead in the future.

Not that he had reason to be optimistic. He was well aware just how important Nikki was to her, and understood her reluctance to jeopardise the adoption process.

But even if they had to wait—surely what was just paperwork couldn't take too long…

'Are you with us or off with the fairies?'

He looked up from his desk where he'd been staring blankly at Izzy's name on the roster, and assured Abby he was all present and correct.

'Very army,' she said. 'Anyway, there are people stacking up in the ED for antibiotic shots and although Aisha—a local GP, have you met her?—is helping out, it's getting hectic.'

'Yes, I've met Aisha and, yes, I'll come,' he said, pushing himself up from the chair, pushing away memories of a splinter of time beneath the huge old tree, and turning his mind to what lay ahead.

At least he'd checked on Rhia and the Watsons when he'd first arrived, pleased to see the little girl was no worse.

Somehow he and Aisha got through the flood of panicky residents, many of whom, he guessed, hadn't had any contact with the Watsons, and by the time they stopped for a late lunch things had settled down. But Izzy's arrival coincided with the local ambulance, bringing in a ten-year-old boy who'd fallen in the school playground, suspected broken arm.

Izzy heard the ambulance approaching as she walked down to work. No flashing lights and sirens but she knew its noise as well as that of her own car.

Would Mac be in the ED, alerted ahead of the new arrival?

She'd woken in a stupid panic, unsure how to face a man with whom she'd shared such a fiery kiss the night before, and, given how the rosters had been disrupted the previous day, it had been easy to switch her shift time.

But she had to face him sometime—face him in daylight or the bright lights of the hospital—and put the kiss behind her. Behind them both.

The ambulance attendant was bringing a small boy through the doors, a white-faced, frightened small

boy clutching at his right arm, which was stabilised in a sling.

Izzy went to him immediately, all thoughts of kisses gone from her head.

'And what have you done to yourself, Kurt Robson?' she teased, kneeling beside him and putting her arm around his shoulder.

'Fell over, that's all, but it hurts.'

'Of course it does.'

She looked up at the ambo.

'Have his parents been contacted?'

'His mum's on the way.'

'That's great, isn't it, Kurt?'

Kurt's face suggested it might not be that great.

'Mum might be angry,' he muttered. 'When I hurt my foot she was. She said I was playing too roughly, but this time, truly, I just fell over.'

'That's okay, we'll sort things out with Mum.'

'We gave him seven mils of paracetamol for the pain but that's all he's had,' the ambo said, handing the paperwork over to Izzy and heading for the door, and probably a late lunch.

Kurt's mother and Mac arrived at the same time, one through the front ED entrance, the other from the hospital.

'He had a fall,' Izzy told Mac, trying desperately to remind her body that this was work and she could handle colleague-to-colleague stuff for all that her blood was singing through her veins at the mere sight of him.

Who knew what a casual touch might do?

Turn her brain to mush, that's what, she realised when he brushed against her as he, too, knelt to talk to the boy.

Okay—enough's enough!

She breathed deeply and moved away to greet Mrs Robson, then Mac was by her side, speaking quietly to her.

'It should just be a simple X-ray; we do that here, don't we?'

Izzy nodded, the deep breath not quite stabilising her yet.

'I can actually do a bit more than that. With my pre-med degree I added a thirteen-week radiography course—before Nikki. We don't have an MRI machine but we can most other radiography.'

'Wonder Woman!' Mac teased softly, undoing the small amount of good that deep breathing had effected.

'Not really,' Izzy responded, letting a little of the irritation she was feeling because of him seep into her voice. 'You're probably just as capable of most radiography stuff as I am. Every doctor can do a simple X-ray.'

He grinned at her but she refused to be charmed.

Colleagues, they were colleagues! She'd work out the rest later.

Much later…

But thoughts of charm and singing blood disappeared when Izzy shoved the X-ray film into the light box. The same picture would be on the screen at the ED's front desk and she knew Mac was looking at it there.

'Mac!'

He came immediately and she wondered if he'd seen what she'd seen and realised it wasn't something to discuss in front of the Robsons.

'What are you seeing?' he asked, and she pointed to the fine line that showed a break in the humerus.

'That's the obvious one, but look at the elbow joint—isn't it slightly distorted?'

Mac ran his finger over the picture then turned his attention to the shoulder joint.

'That seems loose as well. Has the boy had other fractures, do you know?'

'None that have been reported here, but he said Mum got angry when he hurt his foot.'

'Okay, let's get him back in here and look at the foot,' Mac said, leaving with a touch on her shoulder that was so light she might have imagined it.

She heard him talking to Mrs Robson and Kurt, explaining they wanted to do some more checking.

'Is there anyone in your family that's had broken bones before?' he was asking Mrs Robson.

'Well, most kids do, don't they?' she said. 'I know I had a broken leg when I was younger.'

'And you went mad at me when I hurt my foot!' Kurt put in, and his mother laughed.

'Mothers worry,' she said, patting down his unruly brown hair.

Mac lifted Kurt onto the X-ray table while Izzy focused the camera over the foot he'd hurt earlier. Mac escorted Mrs Robson from the room while Izzy checked she'd get what she wanted.

'Hold still again,' she said, slipping into the side room and pressing the button to activate the camera.

She took different angle shots, propping the little foot with foam pads, and when she was satisfied she returned him to his mother, who by this time was get-

ting anxious, although someone had given her a cup of tea and plate of biscuits.

This time they studied the shots on the computer in the radiography office, enlarging details so they could easily see the two metatarsals that had thickened areas where breaks had healed.

'Brittle bones?' Izzy asked. 'I've heard of it but wasn't sure it existed as a condition.'

'OI,' Mac replied. 'Osteogenesis imperfecta—there are eight levels of it, with the first four being the most common. OI One is the best to have, and probably what young Kurt has, and often people can go through all their lives without knowing they have it.'

'Genetic?' Izzy asked, so absorbed in learning something new that the fact that she was shoulder to shoulder with Mac wasn't bothering her at all.

'Usually, but not always. The problem is, we could set his arm but with OI I'm not sure that it shouldn't be pinned. I think someone said the other day that there's an orthopaedic specialist in Braxton.'

'Paul Kent,' Izzy told him. 'Very good. Should we get the ambulance back to take them?'

Mac had straightened and now turned towards her, a slight smile greeting her question.

'I think that's best, don't you? Although it leaves Mrs Robson stuck there without a vehicle.'

Colleagues, Izzy reminded herself, ignoring the effect of that slightest of smiles.

'If Paul decides to operate, Mrs Robson will want to stay anyway, and her husband has a ute so he can take over anything they need when he finishes work.'

Mac nodded and left the room, leaving Izzy to turn off machines and tidy up.

He was on the phone to the specialist when she returned to the ED and the ambulance was pulling in.

'Can I phone someone to pick up your car?' she asked Mrs Robson, who shook her head.

'I've called my sister—she only lives down the road, she'll walk up and get it. She has the extra set of keys to it and the house so she can pack things for me and Kurt—better than my husband would.'

She smiled and Izzy realised that however Mac had explained the situation it had left the woman at ease, not anxious and distracted as many mothers would be.

'Osteogenesis imperfecta—I like learning new things,' she said to Mac as the ambulance departed. 'I know we covered something about brittle bones in the course I did but I'm sure I didn't hear that name.'

'It's not that common,' Mac told her, 'but learning new things—well, that happens all the time.'

She knew he was teasing—suggesting—but also knew she had to ignore it. That kiss last night—and where it might lead—was something she had to think seriously about.

'Then I'd better go and learn new things about what's been happening at the hospital all day. I haven't even signed on for my shift, let alone had any kind of handover.'

'Of course,' he said, and something in his voice told her he understood she was backing off, trying to ignore what had happened between them.

Mac headed for his office, only too aware that there was paperwork multiplying on his desk, pleased to have a really boring distraction.

Seeing Izzy—a far from boring distraction—had reminded him that a relationship with a colleague was

not a good idea. In fact, it was a dreadful idea! Especially when he was new to the job of being a civilian doctor, and really needed to concentrate on doing that job well.

Belle came in with a message for him. Paul Kent had received the X-rays and would phone him after he'd seen Kurt.

He thought of Izzy repeating the diagnosis, her face alight with learning something new, and his gut knotted.

The thought of *not* having a relationship with that particular colleague was far too depressing to even contemplate. Somehow they had to make this work—not only the being colleagues part of it but the hesitation they both felt about involvement.

Very reasonable hesitation!

'Are you sighing over the paperwork?' Belle asked, bringing in a sheaf of more bumf. 'One thing I can tell you, if you don't get onto it, it just multiplies. Worse than rabbits, paperwork.'

He laughed but knew what she said was true, so he set aside all thoughts of the redhead beetling around somewhere in the building and concentrated on sorting the urgent from the non-urgent, the notices of new procedural policy from the important things that needed a response.

Izzy started her catching up with a visit to Rhia. As Mac had said, she was holding her own, although she was still pale and from the chart slightly feverish. Ben was in the room with her.

'I've sent Sally home to get some sleep.'

He twisted his hands together as he spoke then looked up at Izzy.

'She *will* get better, won't she?' he asked, and the desperation in his voice touched Izzy's heart.

'We'll do everything we can to make sure she does,' she promised. 'She's getting the best of care, the drugs we're giving her will be fighting the infection, and...'

She hesitated, mainly because she hated making promises she couldn't keep.

'They usually win,' she finished, hoping he had missed the pause. 'It just takes time,' she told him, 'so you and Sally have to look after yourselves because even after she's out of here, she could need a long convalescence.'

'We'll make sure we're there for her,' Ben promised. Then his head lifted again and his dark eyes met Izzy's. 'I know all parents think their kids are special, but she's especially precious to us. Sally had a couple of miscarriages before Rhia and hasn't been able to get pregnant since. We've thought about IVF because we'd love another child, but we'd have to go to the city, and it's so expensive.'

'It's becoming more affordable, so who knows,' Izzy told him, not mentioning that her brother Steve was already talking about setting up a private IVF clinic right here in Wetherby.

She smiled as she thought about his grandiose plan of building a relaxing seaside resort where couples could stay while they underwent fertility treatment or IVF programmes. He believed that the failures in IVF conception were often brought on by stress and his clinic resort could alleviate a lot of that.

So Steve was in her mind when she ran into Mac in the tea room.

'Shouldn't you be at home, cooking up a Moroccan delicacy? Your shift's long finished.'

'Paperwork,' he said succinctly, turning from the urn where he was making a coffee to offer to make one for her.

'No, tea for me at this time of the evening,' she said. 'I don't need any stimulants to keep me from sleep tonight.'

He found a teabag and made her a tea, raising a milk bottle in silent query.

She shook her head and he passed her the rather battered mug.

Inevitably their fingers touched, and he raised his eyebrows as he asked, 'Something keep you from sleep last night? Stimulation?'

Izzy gave a huff of laughter.

'Not that so much as where it could lead,' she told him as one of the enrolled nurses came looking for Izzy.

'It's Mrs Warren in bed nine,' she said. 'Says she's feeling right poorly, whatever that might mean.'

'I'll see to her,' Izzy said quietly, setting her tea down on the table and leaving the room. Mrs Warren should really be in a hospice, but the nearest one was in Braxton and she didn't want to leave her friends and family.

She *was* poorly, her skin sagging around her bones, her old eyes clouded with pain and confusion. Three months earlier she'd been an extremely fit and spritely ninety-three-year-old living by herself, capable of managing her house and garden, getting a little help with shopping and occasional visits from a social worker.

An accident in the bathroom, a fall that had left her

with a broken hip, bruised ribs and a bang on the head
had changed all that. Lying in bed, she was a prime
victim for pneumonia, and although she seemed to have
fought that off, she was still far from well, her organs
slowly closing down.

Izzy slipped into the chair beside her and took her
hand, talking quietly to her.

'I see someone's brought you flowers from your
garden,' she said, nodding towards the big bunch of
colour on a shelf on the wall.

'Jimmy,' Mrs Warren whispered. 'He's a good lad.
He comes every day and often brings a mate so we can
have a laugh, but I don't want to laugh any more, Izzy.
I've had enough.'

'I know, love,' Izzy soothed. 'I know.'

Mrs Warren's health directory had been explicit that
she didn't want measures taken to keep her alive, but
her heart refused to give in, still beating strongly in
the old woman's skeletal body.

Izzy sat with her until she drifted off to sleep, then
she checked the other patients under her care. With everything quiet she returned to Mrs Warren, sitting with
her through the night until, at four, her heart finally
gave in, and the old woman passed away.

Technically, one of the GPs was on call for the night
shift, but why wake him just to certify death when
Mac would be here at six? Possibly earlier, knowing
Mac. Declaring Mrs Warren dead could wait, as could
breaking the news to her family.

Izzy had wanted to call them earlier, but Mrs Warren had insisted she didn't want wailing relatives sitting around her bed.

'I'm happy to go,' she'd told Izzy, 'so there's no reason for tears.'

She was phoning Mrs Warren's eldest daughter when Mac arrived.

'What are you doing here?' he demanded. 'Have you done a double shift?'

Izzy held up a hand to silence him as someone answered the phone and she began her explanation.

Mac shook his head and left the nurses' station, but when he returned it wasn't to chide her. Instead, he touched her lightly on the arm.

'You sat with her all night?'

Izzy nodded.

'She didn't want the family, just someone to be there.'

'You should have had the coffee,' Mac said, but the glint in his eyes and the smile tugging at his lips told her he approved.

Probably would have done the same, Izzy realised, and the warmth his light touch had generated blossomed into appreciation.

He was a good man.

It was a refrain that stayed with her as her feet pounded on the coastal path. She'd had to run to clear her head and have any hope of sleep but the 'good man' thought stuck and she knew it tipped the scales in his favour in the matter of any relationship between them.

Mac got on with his working day with a certain sense of relief. Relief because he'd see much less of Izzy while she was on the swing shift from two till ten, but qualifying the relief was a touch of let-down.

Damn it all, he *liked* seeing her at work! Enjoyed a

glimpse of her red curls as she flashed past a door, enjoyed the feel of her by his side as they studied notes or discussed a patient.

The worst of it was he'd see even less of her out of working hours. It was unlikely she'd want to try his Moroccan tagine at ten-thirty at night.

He fought an urge to check the nursing rosters again—he'd checked twice already today and she was definitely on the swing shift. And today he wouldn't see her come on duty. He had a district hospital meeting—some kind of meet and greet the new guy, he guessed—at Braxton Hospital at two this afternoon.

Belle had booked him into a motel in Braxton for the night as apparently there was always an informal dinner held after these meetings.

The paperwork following Mrs Warren's death diverted him for a few minutes and a visit to the nursing home took up a little more time, but the day still loomed as a very long one without Izzy.

Until a very attractive blonde bounced into his office.

'I'm Frances, I'm your physiotherapist—well, not yours particularly but the hospital one. I do two days a week in Wetherby, one here at the hospital and tomorrow in a private practice. I'm based in Braxton, so some of the patients here I've already seen at the hospital there.'

'Like the young man whose ankle was pinned and plated in Braxton last weekend? I heard he was coming back to us today.'

'And you've got another man from the same accident—simple tib and fib break who'll be seeing me here as an outpatient.'

Mac nodded. He'd discharged the patient with the simple break after fitting a full cast and had talked to him about needing physio once the cast came off, but apparently Frances would have exercises he could do now.

He walked with her as she visited the occupied rooms, introducing the Watsons and little Rhia, pleased that Frances spoke mostly to Rhia, telling her she'd be back to give her some toys that would help her stay strong in hospital.

'You probably haven't explored the physio cupboard,' Frances said as they left the room.

'I've seen a room that looked to be full of toys, and I did wonder just how many children might ever be here at any one time to warrant so many.'

Leaving Frances to go about her work, Mac returned to his office, aware of how much he didn't know about the hospital he was supposedly running. What other visiting therapists might they have? How did he contact one if he needed someone for a specific patient? An OT for a stroke patient, for instance?

All the information he needed would be here in his office somewhere, but he'd avoided being in it, doing only the absolutely necessary paperwork—and then only when bullied into it by Belle.

True, there had been emergencies to be dealt with in his first few days, and Rhia's diagnosis had led to a flood of outpatients, but now things had quietened down, it was time to learn his job—his real job—especially as the other district doctors would expect him to know *something* at this afternoon's meeting.

'Let's start at the beginning,' he said to Belle when he'd summoned her to his office. 'Tell me everything I

need to know about how the place runs. I know who's in charge of Housekeeping, and I have met the cooks, but apart from Frances what other visiting profession-als do we have? Where do I find their information?'

He smiled at her.

'I fear I've been leaving everything to you.'

'Not your fault,' Belle assured him. 'You've hardly had a moment to breathe since you arrived.'

But she ran him through the normal weekly and monthly routines, through the visiting profession-als, and volunteers who worked mainly in the nursing home, playing board games and doing craft projects with the residents.

'It's all in there somewhere,' she said, waving her hand at the filing cabinets banked against one wall, 'but generally you only need to ask me and I'll either find it for you or find out what you want to know.'

'In fact, you really run the place,' Mac said, smiling at her. 'I had a sergeant like that in the army.'

They talked a little longer, Mac realising just how much was involved in running even a small hospital.

Frances appeared at the door, greeted Belle like an old friend, then handed Mac a knobby ball.

'Stress ball,' she said. 'You just squeeze it in your hand—one hand at a time—you'll be surprised how much it will relieve that tension in your neck and shoul-ders.'

What tension in my neck and shoulders? Mac wanted to ask, but with Belle there…

And Frances was right, although how she'd noticed it he didn't know.

'Thanks,' he said, taking the ball and squeezing it in his right hand then throwing it across the table to

Belle, wanting to make light of it—to not have people thinking he couldn't cope.

'Want a go?' he said, but Belle only tossed it back.

'I've got one of my own,' she said, 'only mine's hot pink. Frances keeps an eye on all of us.'

Enough of an eye to see tension in his neck?

Tension that was part of his PTSD, or new tension caused by his attraction to a certain redhead?

He wondered if the visiting professionals included a psychologist...

Mac kept squeezing, one hand and then the other, while Belle and Frances were now discussing a barn dance to be held that weekend at a property out of town.

'It's to raise money for the animal shelter,' Frances explained. 'Do come, I'll email you the directions. They have a kind of auction and you can bid on the different animals and if you win the bid your money goes towards its keep for the year.'

He agreed it sounded fun and was about to ask if he could take Izzy along when he realised that being linked with him was probably the last thing she wanted.

Or needed...

'It's very casual,' Frances was explaining, while he squeezed hard on his stress ball.

Because he was thinking of Izzy?

'It really *is* in a barn out on the animal refuge,' Belle added.

'As long as I don't have to wear a hat with corks dangling off it,' Mac told them, and the laughter broke up the meeting.

So, off to Braxton! *And it will probably do you good not to see Izzy for a whole day*, he thought. *That* situation was getting way out of control...

CHAPTER NINE

'WHY ARE YOU doing the swing shift?' Nikki demanded the next morning while Izzy was packing her lunch for school. 'You never do it because it's a quiet one, and working at the weekend means you won't be able to take me to the barn dance.'

'Hallie and Pop will take you,' Izzy said firmly, not answering the real question because she didn't want to admit she'd changed shifts to avoid Mac.

'There's no need because I'm going with Shan and her older brothers and sister,' Nikki informed her, but Izzy barely listened, her mind back to trying to work out why one kiss had affected her so badly.

Badly enough to change shifts in an effort to avoid the man causing her mind and body so much trouble!

Not that she could avoid him for ever. But she'd hoped the break would give her time to work out what was happening—to rationalise the feelings in her body and remind herself that her first priority was getting through the three- to six-month process of officially adopting her daughter.

Not that it was working—the shift change. She missed seeing Nikki after school, although now she had mornings to catch up with her and hear the latest

school news, and she could make sure Nikki was taking a nutritious lunch, but Mac's absence from her life wasn't helping her sort out her thoughts or her feelings.

Even thinking about the kiss sent tremors down her spine, and she couldn't think about the situation without thinking about the kiss so, in truth, she was in a muddle.

A muddle made worse when she saw him as she came on duty that afternoon!

'You avoiding me?' he asked, just enough edge in his voice to tell her it wasn't really a joke.

'Trying to,' Izzy answered honestly, if weakly, as her brain lit up like a fireworks display and her body was rattled by more reactions than it could handle.

'Working, is it?' he asked, so genially she wanted to hit him. How could he be so composed?

Because he was a man?

Because he was used to kissing women he barely knew?

'How was the meeting?' Izzy managed to ask, determined to get her mind focused on work. She'd leave her body till later and run it to exhaustion…

'Very educational.'

Izzy raised her eyebrows, sure he was being facetious.

'No, I mean it,' he assured her, with a smile she really, really didn't need. 'I had no idea of the complexities of coordinating health services in regional areas. Whoever set this all up was a genius. The army couldn't have done it better.'

'High praise indeed,' Izzy said drily.

'No, I mean it. The way they manage to coordinate the staffing of the emergency services, like the am-

bulance and helicopter, with staffing at the hospitals so there's always a paramedic available to go out to accidents—that alone must take endless fiddling and adjustments.'

'It's a lot of paperwork,' Izzy agreed, and won another unnecessary smile.

'Which most doctors and, I imagine, nurses hate. Yet it all gets done.'

'Because the office staff know the system and have their own procedures in place,' Izzy told him. 'It took quite a while, but at the moment it's working. Most of the time!'

'I'm still mightily impressed,' Mac said.

'Good, but I've got to get to work. Rhia's drip will need changing and apparently the chap who had his ankle fixed in Braxton is complaining about cramps.'

She turned away but not quickly enough to miss Mac's last words, quietly spoken but sneaking into her ears and, damn it, into her heart.

'I've missed you, Izzy!'

The shift was quiet, a few visitors to the ED that Izzy could handle on her own—a footballer with a strained wrist, X-rayed to make sure it wasn't broken, and just before she went off duty, an older man with chest pain but no history of heart problems or angina.

Roger was on call, but by the time he arrived Izzy had ascertained that the ECG was normal, blood pressure and oxygen sat both good, but a blood test showed high troponin levels.

'That's ringing a bell for me,' Roger said. 'We'll admit him anyway and do half-hourly obs but I'll check back through his file.'

Izzy started the process of admitting the man, chatting to him in between the questions she needed to ask.

Yes, he'd been before, feeling the same way, and had stayed three days while the doctors did tests. He'd been to a cardiologist in Braxton who had done more tests, but found nothing.

'And how are you feeling now?' Izzy asked, as a wardsman arrived to move the patient to a hospital bed.

'The pain's gone but I just don't feel well,' the man explained. 'Just not right.'

Scary, was Izzy's first thought. With no symptoms to treat apart from giving him the blood thinners, there was little they could do but wait and see.

Roger returned as she was accompanying the trolley to a patient room.

'I've found the records of past blood tests. Turns out his blood tests always show a higher level of troponin than is normal. He's had every test under the sun, but the cardiologist found nothing.'

'But we keep him here?'

'My word we do,' Roger said. 'And keep him hooked up to the monitors so we can see if there's the slightest change in his status. High troponin levels could be an indicator of an imminent heart attack, but there've been no studies done on abnormally high levels in an otherwise well person.'

Izzy settled the man into what they considered their 'cardiac ward', a room with monitors already set up so it was only a matter of attaching the leads to their new patient's legs, chest and arms, slipping a blood oxygen monitor onto one finger, and watching information come up on the monitor screen.

'You should be gone,' the night shift nurse told her.

'I've called in an extra nurse so we can keep an eye on him, and Roger's staying awhile, just to be sure.'

Izzy glanced at her watch and realised it was after eleven. Tiredness swamped her suddenly. Adrenalin seeping out, she knew that, but it wasn't helping her put one foot in front of the other as she collected a jacket and headed out the back door for the short walk home.

'Izzy!'

She muffled the shriek that the soft murmur of his voice had caused and turned to see Mac standing in the light shed from the hospital's kitchen window.

'I thought I'd walk you home.'

The moment the words were out of his mouth Mac knew it was probably the lamest thing he'd ever said, but he'd been lurking around the back of the hospital for over an hour, wondering if this constituted stalking, feeling incredibly stupid but needing to see the woman who had him tied in knots.

'May I walk you home?'

She was standing on the path, apparently bemused by his sudden appearance, but then she smiled and he forgot his doubts about stalking, and all but forgot his name.

'That would be nice,' she said, 'although it's quite stupid for you to be doing this. You've got an early shift tomorrow and I imagine the district meeting went on to a dinner and a few drinks last night and you didn't get to bed till all hours.'

But she hadn't said no, so he took her arm and drew her close, felt her warmth, while the effect her body had on his sent blood racing under his skin.

They reached the shadows of the old nunnery and stopped of one accord, turning to each other as if there

was nothing else to do, kissing gently at first, touches of lips on lips, remembering, revelling in their own restraint.

But restraint couldn't hold back the attraction, and the kiss deepened, until Mac heard a low groan from Izzy and she pressed closer, slid her arms around his back, pulling him into her, or her into him, the kiss saying things for which there were no words.

'I want you, Iz,' he murmured when they paused for breath. 'My body aches for you, and I'm sure you feel the same. I know you've got real reservations— that you could be risking the adoption—but surely we could work that out if something happened.'

She stopped his words with kisses, but he pulled away again, smitten by a wild idea.

'We could even get married if things were dicey,' he said, 'and you'd have that family you thought you might get with that other doctor. Mother, father, daughter—a family.'

Izzy sighed but this time didn't kiss him, leaning her head against his chest instead.

'You don't want to get married,' she reminded him.

'Only because the Macphersons, or my branch of them, seem to be genetically challenged when it comes to marriage. My parents have both had plenty of practice at it—the getting married part—but don't seem able to make it stick, and I was obviously a hopeless husband, but if it made things right for you and Nikki we could do it. It wouldn't have to last for ever.'

'Go home,' Izzy told him, stepping backwards so she couldn't touch him again—kiss him again— weaken...

She didn't add that they were just the words every

woman wanted to hear—the 'wouldn't have to last for ever' ones.

As if!

She opened the door and slipped inside, without another word to the man she'd been kissing. No way could she tell him that beyond her dream for Nikki had always been another, buried deep because for so long it had seemed impossible—a dream of love and happiness and a marriage that *would* last for ever...

Aware he'd said something wrong, Mac took himself home. Unfortunately, his disappointment at the abrupt end to the kisses wasn't enough to cool his blood or release him from the tension the kisses had caused.

Izzy's body seemed to have imprinted itself on his, so he could feel her pressed against his chest, a ghost lover...

Perhaps the nightmare was inevitable, the roar of planes, the thud of bombs landing, the explosive roar of the devastation that followed.

And he'd mentioned *marriage*?

Expected some woman to put up with the movies that mangled his head at midnight?

His shrink had suggested a relationship might help, hence the dallying, which did seem to stop them.

But would it work for ever?

Could he take the chance?

And why was he even considering it, given how hurriedly Izzy had shied away from the suggestion?

Unable to sleep, he found solace in a book, an easy-to-read mystery he'd found in the house's book-shelves when he'd moved in, so when sleep did come, his thoughts were turning over clues, seeking an an-

swer to the mystery, not thinking of the past, or of a red-headed woman with skin like silk and kisses like magic.

No sign of Mac when Izzy went to work the next afternoon, but it was Saturday, he was off duty although probably on call.

She hoped she didn't need him!

She went about her work, calmly and efficiently, spending some time with Rhia while her parents went out for a walk. The little girl had recovered so quickly Izzy was surprised Mac hadn't discharged her so she could spend the weekend at home, but maybe he feared a relapse.

The young man with the pins and plates in his ankle was complaining about pain, but after checking he'd had pain relief only an hour earlier, she decided it was probably boredom and found one of the 'toys' in the physio cupboard that would test his skill—tipping a board to get little balls to run into holes.

It was totally frustrating and she'd only ever seen one patient do it successfully, but she knew that because it *looked* easy most patients, young men in particular, refused to be beaten by it, so it would occupy him for a few hours.

And help him forget his pain…

She caught up with paperwork, told Shan and Nikki they both looked fabulous when they popped in to show off their barn dance outfits—battered jeans, hardly unusual these days, and checked shirts, while the tattered straw hats over cute pigtails completed the look.

'Behave yourself,' she said as Nikki kissed her

goodbye, not really worried that her daughter would get up to mischief. All that lay ahead!

But as she handed over to the night shift and prepared to leave work, she was looking forward to getting home and a good night's sleep—undisturbed by memories of kisses from a—

Non-for-ever-and-ever man?

Was that what she could call him?

Definitely a non-marrying type.

He'd spelt that out.

So walking out the back door and hearing the whispered 'Izzy' sent her blood pressure soaring.

'What *are* you doing here?' she demanded. 'You're supposed to be at the dance. They're taking bets at the nursing home on you and Frances getting together.'

'They're what?'

Mac sounded so horrified, Izzy had to laugh.

'They're easily bored,' she said. 'But you should be at the dance. It's expected of the local doctor.'

'I went but you weren't there.'

The words tingled down Izzy's spine.

You can't let him affect you, she told herself, but her body was beyond listening, especially to anything that might be common sense.

'I did leave some money with Belle to buy an animal. I rather fancied the three-legged goat.'

'That's Arthur,' Izzy responded, hoping some normal chit-chat might settle her nerves. 'I kept him a couple of years ago.'

'Lucky Arthur,' Mac murmured, and Izzy knew no amount of chit-chat would work. Her shoulder was already leaning towards his and when he took her hand,

her fingers gripped his, joining, intertwining—together...

They walked up the hill, their immediate future as inevitable as it was unspoken. He'd seen her family at the dance, would know—because Nikki was a loudmouth—that the flat would be empty, and suddenly she didn't want to fight this any more. She wanted him in a way she'd never felt before—never even imagined she *could* want someone.

And at this moment for ever was a foreign land, it was the now, and what lay ahead, the now she wanted—needed.

'It's this way,' she said, her voice shaking as, fingers still linked, she led him through the door...

And into her bedroom...

The hospital grounds were well lit so some light came through the windows, enough for Izzy to see Mac's face as he sought her lips.

She raised her hands and ran them through his hair, holding his head to hers—wanting, needing the kiss to last.

His hands explored her body, her back, her breasts, passing softly over her as if to imprint her on his memory. But as the kiss deepened, the touches, hers and his, became more urgent, more demanding, her fingers tugging at his shirt so she could feel his skin, his easing open the buttons on her uniform to hold one breast in his palm.

A brush of thumb across the nipple and she could feel it peak, moaned softly, then slid her hand between them to find his hardness.

Restraint fled, and hands tore at clothes until they stood naked, close, not touching anywhere but with

their lips. Kissing, breathing heavily, his hand between her legs now, hers holding his length in her hand.

'Bed?'

One whispered word, yet she knew he was asking, not suggesting—asking her if it was really what she wanted.

It was to be her decision!

'Bed!' she confirmed, and they fell together, finding each other's bodies close, touching, kissing, prolonging the anticipation, increasing the level of desire to near explosion point.

Mac held her close, felt the moisture in the softness between her legs, heard the gasp of breath, the whisper of need—and knew this wasn't dalliance, though dalliances in the past had left him prepared.

A brief pause, long enough to ensure safe sex but also to wonder why it *wasn't* dalliance, why it felt different. But the moment passed, Izzy's body arching up to his, her pleas for more, for proper contact, inflaming his desire.

Too quickly over, lying together, panting slightly, drained but content to simply lie, touching, breathing.

No words, but stirrings, too soon surely, but slowly now, with teasing fingers and gentle touches, they drew more pleasure from each other, until Izzy's cry of release was echoed by his own groan of enjoyment, a confirmation of some kind, but of what, he didn't know.

Relaxed together, their talk was general—lovers' talk, of pleasure given and received, widening to talk of their lives, so different, hers made great by the love of strangers, his not really settled until he'd found a home in the army.

How had Wetherby come up?

Later he would ask himself that question a hundred times, but it had, and they talked of the town, the locals, the incomers seeking respite from city life, the refugees rebuilding lives shattered by oppression and war.

So for her to ask, 'How did you come to choose the town?' was almost inevitable, and for him to answer— no problem at all.

She was lying on her side, pressed against his chest, held in the half-circle of his arm, her golden skin asking for the occasional kiss, a light brush of fingers— eyelids, nose, ears.

'Long ago, so far back it seems like another life,' he told her as he touched, 'I'd just finished my degree, felt freed at last from books and studies and responsibilities. I had leave before I went back to the army, and, like a couple of million other young Aussies do every year, I went to Bali. Have you been?'

He felt her head shake a no against his chest.

'I've heard it's beautiful.'

'It is, a kind of magical place where the real world no longer exists—it's all about the now, and fun, and laughter—beautiful beaches, great surf, nightclubs, and dancing, and gentle people smiling at your antics. It was so relaxing, as I said, another world, with everyone living for not even the day but for the moment.'

Izzy had snuggled closer, and even when he continued, 'I met a girl,' she seemed unbothered.

In fact, she laughed and teased, 'Of course.'

'We spent our time together—two short weeks, two Aussies having fun—until we walked into the hotel one day and one of the receptionists called out to me. "You're Nicholas Macpherson?" she said, and when I agreed she told me that my father had been hospital-

ised with a major heart attack and the family wanted me back home.'

He was remembering that time—that moment—so didn't realise Izzy had pulled away, until in the dim light he saw she was sitting on the bed.

'*What* did you say your name was?' she demanded.

Mac stared at her, puzzled by the abrupt change in the mood and by something in her voice.

Should he make light of it?

'Hey, you know me. I'm Mac—we've just made love. Twice.'

'I meant your other name, your whole name?'

This wasn't light—not at all.

Mac sat up, reaching out for her, wanting to hold her, to see her face, but she scrambled off the bed.

'Izzy, what's up?' he asked, totally bamboozled.

'Just tell me your name, your whole name!'

He heard an edge of hysteria in the words, and responded to it.

'Nicholas Edward Macpherson.'

If he'd thought this might calm her down he was totally wrong. Instead, she scrambled around the room, picking up items of clothing and pulling them on, whispering, 'I've got to go, I've got to go. I've got to get out of here, I've got to think.'

He stood up, found his own shorts and pulled them on, then walked tentatively towards her, touching her shoulder to calm her down.

'Iz,' he said gently, 'you live here. It's your place, not mine. But let me help you, tell me what the problem is. Surely there's nothing we can't talk about.'

She turned away from him, shoulders slumped,

pressed her head against the window pane and whispered, 'Just go, please, just go!'

He went, although he worried about leaving her alone.

Should he call someone?

Hallie?

And tell her he'd just made passionate love to her daughter but now she seemed to have cracked?

Hardly.

And if there was one word that described Izzy it was sensible. She wouldn't do anything silly.

Would she?

He walked down to his house, poured a whisky, and sat down with it to think.

But where to start?

It was his name that had upset her, but she'd always known his name.

The Macpherson part anyway.

He went back over the conversation and, yes, it was definitely his name that had upset her, but why...

No amount of thinking answered that one so he sent a text, saying he was there for her and please to contact him, any time, because he really needed to know she was okay.

No point in telling her he loved her, although somewhere along the way, maybe halfway through the whisky, it had occurred to him that that was what he felt for her.

Love!

Could it really be?

It felt like love...

A whole new kind of love...

CHAPTER TEN

NIKKI MAC... NIKKI MAC... The words pounded in Izzy's head as she ran the coast path.

Stupid really when only yesterday—*was* it yesterday?—the refrain had been, 'He's a good man...'

But maybe she was wrong, maybe she should have asked him when he was in Bali, although the sums all added up in her head. She knew his age, and could work back to when he'd got his degree and, anyway, she knew she wasn't wrong.

Nikki Mac. Her sister had texted almost daily about the glory of this Nikki Mac—and of the holiday romance that had no future, although why, she'd never said. She'd been well when she'd gone, had been through a detox programme in Sydney, then given herself the holiday as a reward.

And she'd come back clean, they'd known that, and had stayed clean for months, or so they'd thought because she'd returned straight to Sydney, at first staying with Stephen, then finding a flat and working for a web designer, her dream job.

Until the sleaze bag, as Stephen called her on-again off-again boyfriend, had come back into the picture,

tempting their fragile sister with promises of fame—
singing in a night club where drugs were plentiful…

Izzy sighed, remembering the lost soul they'd all
loved so much. As well as drugs, there'd been a brush
with anorexia, and episodes of cutting, so no one had
been surprised that Liane, their lovely Liane, hadn't
realised she was pregnant.

And hooked again on drugs!

Hallie had flown to Sydney, Stephen had tried to
step in, and everyone had forgotten Nikki Mac until
the baby came, and with her a grubby piece of paper on
which she'd asked Izzy to look after her baby, Nikki.

Izzy's even stride faltered and she brushed tears
from her eyes.

Now she knew, it was so obvious—Nikki's blue
eyes, the same dark, clear blue…

She shook away the useless thoughts and ran on.
She had to think, to work out what to do.

Did she tell?

She *had* to tell?

But who first?

Nikki?

Izzy's usual easy stride faltered again.

What if Nikki chose her father…?

What if Mac *wanted* her?

Mac didn't *do* for ever…

What if Mac *didn't* want her?

Wouldn't that be worse for Nikki?

Worse than not knowing?

Squelching down the howl of agony the thought of
losing Nikki caused, Izzy pounded on.

She wouldn't think about it now!

She'd think about it tomorrow…

And having decided that, she turned and headed back towards town, forcing herself to blank out the turmoil in her head, looking at the ocean, drinking in the beauty of her surroundings, smelling the salt in the air, the faint scent of eucalyptus from the scrub, thinking nothing, nothing, nothing…

She heard the ambulance before she saw it, and as she came over the last headland, realised it was heading down to the beach.

A crowd of surfers, boards slung across the sand in a far too haphazard way—Nikki and Shan's project—sharks!

Her feet flew towards the now stationary ambulance, although she knew they'd do everything she'd be able to. She pushed through the gathering crowd, saw the anonymous figure in a full black wetsuit, one leg showing torn, lacerated fabric, skin, blood—

'It's Ahmed,' someone told her. 'Luckily the jet ski had been taking surfers out to the big point break and the rider saw it happen and headed straight over, frightening off the shark and bringing Ahmed in to the beach.'

As she left the beach, Izzy took out her phone to call his family, then saw Hamid heading down from the esplanade—someone else had already called.

So she went to the hospital instead, showered and pulled on some scrubs, coming out of the staffroom as Mac was asking the ambos to take the trolley through to the resus room.

'Shark bite,' he said to Izzy, as if this was just another day, another crisis, fully expecting her to be there to lend a hand. 'Could you cut off his wetsuit? The pressure of it could be worsening the blood loss. Start

with the arms so we can get a drip in. Abby, you set up a cannula as soon as you can.'

They worked in silence except when Mac requested help, stripped the fit young man then laid warmed blankets over his body to help fend off shock. Mac handed tweezers to Izzy.

'Just pick out any neoprene you can see, or anything else that shouldn't be there. Abby, can you flush the wound as Izzy works, flush it hard. I want to X-ray the foot to make sure there are no broken bones, because if there aren't I think we can put him back together again without sending him to Braxton.'

Izzy picked at bits of black material from the tattered skin and flesh and wondered at Mac's confidence.

But he'd no doubt seen worse, the results of bombs or IEDs and had learned to put body parts back together again.

So if anyone could save Ahmed's foot, Mac could.

The X-ray showed no bone damage, and Mac sent for Roger to handle the anaesthesia before giving instructions to the nurses about the instruments and sutures he'd need.

It took three hours, but eventually the young man had what looked like a patchwork but recognisable foot.

'I'd like to keep him here for his parents' sake,' Mac said, turning his attention to Izzy, one professional to another. 'He'll need strong IV antibiotics and at least twenty-four hours of intensive care to monitor him. Can we handle that?'

She knew he'd asked because it was a nursing question and as nurse manager it would be her decision.

'Yes,' she said, no hesitation. 'We'll have to juggle

rosters but we can have someone with him for twenty-four hours, and you can review things after that.'

'Good,' he said, nodding at her, although a little frown that she knew had nothing to do with Ahmed now creased his brow.

'I'll sort out the rosters,' she said. 'Abby, will you take the first shift?'

She left the room, not needing a reply, and not wanting to spend any more time with Mac now the emergency situation was easing and it would be harder to pretend they were nothing more than colleagues.

Though perhaps after her behaviour last night, he'd be pleased to return to just being colleagues, perhaps thinking he'd had a lucky escape...

Izzy covered Abby's shift, knowing it was Sod's Law that they had an unusual number of ED visitors, a small boy with a fish hook in his foot, needing Mac to cut it out and stitch it up; a pregnant woman complaining of feeling sick, her blood pressure far too high, protein in her urine test, all signs of pre-eclampsia.

'Do you usually admit a pre-eclampsia patient for bed rest?' Mac asked Izzy.

'When the blood pressure is this high, we do,' she said. 'We can monitor the baby's well-being as well as hers.'

'I'll give her a series of magnesium sulphate injections—latest studies seem to indicate it can stop it developing to full-blown eclampsia.'

Izzy sent an aide to organise a bed, and prepared the first of the injections Mac wanted while he talked quietly to the patient, explaining what was happening in her body, why it sometimes happened, and how

resting and the medication could help her through the pregnancy.

'But the other kids?' she wailed, as Mac gave her the injection.

He looked helplessly at Izzy.

'Three,' she said, 'one at school, two still at home with Mum.'

She turned her attention to their patient.

'Where are the children now?' she asked.

'Their dad's with them but he's back to work tomorrow.'

Izzy touched her lightly on the shoulder.

'Don't worry. I'll talk to Hallie, she'll organise something then go and see your husband and explain it all to him.'

The woman looked relieved, but Mac was obviously puzzled.

'Does Hallie run the entire town?' he asked, and their patient smiled.

'Just about,' she said, 'and if it comes to organising things she's the best so I know whatever she does for the kids, they'll be okay.'

'What *does* she do in cases like this?' Mac asked Izzy as the patient was wheeled away.

Unable to look directly at him, Izzy busied herself cleaning up the room.

'There are a lot of groups—Country Women's Association, church groups, Girl Guides—they all have people who love to volunteer. You'll find she'll soon have a roster of babysitters and probably a cook and a gardener as well, making sure the family is well cared for.'

Mac nodded slowly.

'I suppose to some extent the army is the same, only

there it would be a welfare officer organising it all. And possibly not as efficiently. She'd have made general in the army, your Hallie.'

And Izzy couldn't help but smile at the compliment, but smiling at Mac reminded her of all the reasons she shouldn't, reminded her of all the stuff she had to sort out before she could talk to him—or Nikki for that matter.

Just the thought of it made her feel ill.

'I'd better get on to the general, then,' she said, and slipped away, the ED suddenly quiet, and therefore a dangerous place to be with Mac...

Mac drifted through the hospital, physically there and doing his job, but a part of his mind still struggled with the truly weird experience he'd had the previous evening, when Izzy had gone from a lively and generous lover to a—

Madwoman?

Was she bipolar?

Had some other personality disorder?

But why would his name have triggered such an extreme reaction—so extreme she'd momentarily forgotten they were in her house, not his?

His heart felt heavy with...

What?

Love unspoken?

Despair that whatever it had been between them was now over?

No, there had to be a rational explanation. It was just a matter of getting some time alone with her, and the two of them talking.

Sensibly, rationally.

But he remembered the feel of her skin against his, heard the little noises she'd made as she'd writhed on the bed beneath him.

Could he really be rational about this when just thinking of the previous night had him hard?

At work?

What had happened to common sense?

Professionalism?

He grabbed a roomy white coat from the laundry, although he rarely wore one on the wards, and did a round, not seeing her, but checking all their patients.

He had notes to write up about the district meeting, figures to get ready for the district director, plenty of work to keep him in his office *and* to block a certain red-haired nurse completely from his mind.

Not easy when Hallie arrived, wanting a bit of information about how long he expected the woman with pre-eclampsia to be in hospital.

'Just so I have some idea of how long she'll need help, although she'll still need someone to lend a hand when she gets out, won't she?'

Mac told her what he thought, agreed she'd need help even when he let her go.

'It will depend on whether her blood pressure comes down and stays down,' he explained. 'If not, I'll keep her in until the baby's due. If it goes into full eclampsia—'

'She'll need a Caesar,' Hallie finished for him. 'I started nursing here in the days when the doctors did the lot—well, doctors and nurses—we had a great midwife.'

Mac had to smile. This woman took everything in

her stride—much like Izzy, he supposed, although he
didn't really know, Izzy, did he?

Had it all been just too sudden?

Was that what lay behind the panic?

'Are you settling in?' Hallie asked, and he hoped
she couldn't read what he'd been thinking on his face.

'Yes, fine, thank you.'

She laughed!

'That's far too polite given you've had one crisis
after another from the moment you arrived. I hope
Izzy's been some help. She's got a good head on her
shoulders, that one. I sometimes think of all the children I've had over the years, she's—well, parents
shouldn't have favourites—but Izzy's close. Lila, of
course, is Pop's little gift from God. He saved her,
you know, from a burning car and she's clung to him
ever since.'

And, having delivered these scraps of information,
Hallie departed, off to organise her army of volunteers,
small-town spirit at its best.

Which was when he realised he *was* settling in, beginning to see how small towns worked...

Feeling at home here?

Well, he *had* been...

Izzy shuffled the nursing rosters, phoned around to
see who was available, then drew up a list of those
who'd special Ahmed, checking for symptoms of delayed shock or infection, looking after his parents who
were taking turns beside his bed.

She put herself down for Ahmed duty for the night
shift—doing double shifts had never worried her—but

now she'd sneak off home and have a sleep before she began her regular shift at two.

Sneak off?

Well, not exactly, although she crossed her fingers that she wouldn't see Mac as she made her escape.

Crossing fingers—what a childish thing to do—but somehow that was how she felt: as bewildered as she'd sometimes been as a child, having to make a decision that seemed far too complex for her brain.

More than one decision...

Of course she could ignore it—say nothing?

Not to Nikki—

Not to Mac—

And be haunted for the rest of her life?

Once safely home she showered again, feeling new sensitivity in her body, thinking of Mac's hands, his kisses, the joy she'd been feeling.

But she had to sleep, so in the end put all thoughts and memories resolutely from her mind and did sleep, waking just in time to change into a uniform, make a sandwich to eat on the walk down the hill, and arrive at work on time.

She'd just grabbed a sticky bun from the kitchen and was heading for the nurses' station for handover when she ran into Mac.

Inevitably ran into Mac!

'I saw you've put yourself down for the night shift, specialling Ahmed,' he said, very colleague-to-colleague, pure professional.

Well, she could do professional—or would have been able to if she couldn't feel the bit of pink icing from the bun on her cheek.

'I don't mind doing a double shift. And if he's rest-

less, it's better for him to have someone he knows with him rather than one of the agency nurses we have available. He's been trying to teach me to surf—not having much success, but we have a laugh together.'

She wanted to swipe her finger across her cheek, but didn't want to draw attention to the icing.

Some hope! It was Mac's finger that did the swiping, Mac's finger that held up the tell-tale smear before licking it, smiling, and saying, 'Delicious,' in a tone that made her cheeks burn.

Mac saw the colour rise beneath her skin, waited, hoping she'd say something, hoping—

Well, he didn't know what he hoped, except that he'd been keeping an eye on the back entrance to the hospital for the last ten minutes, wanting to catch her, hoping perhaps they could talk.

But when he saw her, iced bun half-eaten in her hand, a smear of pink icing on her cheek, he'd had no words.

He'd lost the questions he wanted to ask—couldn't remember even the basic one—what had happened last night—

Now she whisked away, into the bathroom, no doubt to clean her sticky fingers and check for icing on her face.

How could she think of such mundane things when he burned to know what was going on between them?

When he wanted to know if there *was* anything between them?

Oh, for Pete's sake, what was he doing, maundering around like this?

He didn't do love, he reminded himself, he dallied,

and if the initial meeting in a dalliance didn't work, he moved on.

So move on now!

Right now!

Phone Frances to apologise for leaving the barn dance early, find out whether he was keeping a three-legged goat fed for a year, maybe ask her over to try his Moroccan tagine, which he hadn't actually made just yet, still surviving on toast and packet soup, and a nourishing lunch the kitchen supervisor insisted he eat.

But he didn't phone Frances, instead he checked on Ahmed, talking to his gentle mother, calming down.

Ahmed's condition remained stable through the night, although Izzy was worried about the swelling in his foot. Had they missed a bit of foreign matter, or had infection set in? His temperature was a little raised, but otherwise he seemed to be sleeping peacefully, still dopey from the anaesthetic.

Her relief came in—it would be up to Mac or Roger, whoever was on duty later this morning, to decide if he still needed someone with him.

Weariness descended like a cloud, but aware the arguments going on in her head would keep her from sleep, she changed from her uniform to jogging clothes and set off along the path.

The physical exertion might help her sleep later, but it did little for the muddle in her mind. She tried to narrow it down, to decide what was the worst thing that could possibly happen, and knew the answer—losing Nikki—either Nikki's choice or Mac's, which brought her back to not telling...

Finally realising that after a double shift nothing

was making any sense, she turned her attention to the world around her, seeing what looked like someone sitting by the fresh-water tap.

A walker coming from the other direction?

Another jogger, although now the mornings were getting colder not many were out this early.

By the time she was close enough to realise it was Mac, she was too close to him to suddenly turn tail and run.

Besides which, she had to talk to him sometime, if only to apologise for her behaviour the other night.

'Thought I might see you here,' he said, and she tried desperately to hear something in his voice, or to see a clue as to what he was thinking in his eyes, his face.

'I need to apologise,' she said. 'I behaved stupidly. I'm sorry.'

'More panic than stupidity, I'd have thought.'

Still no hint of thoughts or feelings, while her own body was alive with sensation just being close to him.

Although maybe his coolness made things easier?

Perhaps he'd met to tell her it was all a mistake and they could forget what had happened and just be colleagues.

Except she couldn't forget—couldn't not tell—

'I'm sorry,' she said. 'Really sorry. You must have thought I was mad.'

He didn't answer, studying her instead, then a hint of a smile quirked one corner of his lips and her heart flipped in her chest.

'Not mad but definitely upset about something. Can you talk about it?'

If only he hadn't smiled. She sighed, and shook her head.

'Not just yet,' she said miserably. 'I really want to but I need to think it through, need to get *my* head around it before I can discuss it rationally.'

He reached out and took her hand, drew her closer, almost close enough to kiss, but no kiss, just his hand with a firm grip on hers.

'Maybe I can help,' he said quietly. 'I'm not a total idiot. I knew something I'd said, however inadvertently, had completely thrown you.'

He squeezed her fingers almost as if he didn't mind she'd been so weird.

'It took a while to make sense of it—in fact, it wasn't until last night I had time to actually sit down and go over the conversation we'd been having. And found no clues, until you asked my name.'

'Nicholas!' Izzy breathed the word.

'Nicholas indeed, and that's when I remembered! I'd been telling you about this girl—well, woman— I'd been seeing over in Bali, and when I remembered telling you my first name I also remembered what she used to call me—'

'Nikki Mac?'

Izzy asked it as a question but she already knew the answer.

He nodded, face grave.

'Nikki?'

Izzy shrugged helplessly.

'I don't know—it's what I think. The whole time she was away her texts to me were of no one else—just Nikki Mac. I wanted details. Was it serious? "Not me, not ever!" she replied. It was just a lovely fling with a

wonderful, intelligent man, and they both knew that was all it was. She went straight to Sydney to a job Steve had got for her—her dream job, she said.'

'Art,' Mac said, his voice dark, sober...

'She was brilliant,' Izzy remembered, brushing tears from her eyes. 'Drawing, painting, photography, she could make three lines on a piece of paper look like a scene, a few more and it would be a person.'

Mac stood up and drew her close enough to put his arm around her shoulders, holding her, comforting her.

'I saw her work,' he said quietly. 'And she had such plans, such dreams.'

He let her go, turned away, staring out to sea.

'I killed them for her, didn't I? Carelessness on my part, her getting pregnant.'

Now Izzy went to him, touched his shoulder, moved closer.

'We don't know for sure, Mac. Health issues meant she was never regular, so I doubt she knew or even suspected for quite a few months. She knew she'd have support from all of us, but I think the tortured memories of her own childhood came back to haunt her when she realised she was pregnant, and it never took very much to turn Liane back to drugs. It was the only escape she knew and the slightest blip in her life would have her reaching for their oblivion.'

'I had to leave early. I should have found her, I should have checked she was okay.' Mac's own demons were now haunting him. 'She'd talked of Wetherby—that's where I heard the name—but had told me she was going back to Sydney. Told me she was sterile, but still I should have checked. My father was ill, and I'd been

posted to Townsville to begin my intern year. I thought about her often, but—'

'You weren't to know. Liane had told the truth as she knew it. She *had* been told she'd never have a child— her body too damaged in childhood, and long-term drug use on top of that.'

Mac knew Izzy's words were meant to comfort him, but the wound went too deep.

How could he not have found her?

How could he not have known he had a child?

How careless he had been back in those joyous holiday days, revelling in the magic that was Bali, and the beautiful woman who called him Nikki Mac?

He took a deep breath and turned back to Izzy.

'Nikki?' he said.

Izzy shook her head.

'I'm not up to that yet. I haven't worked it out. It frightens me, Mac—all the ifs and buts and maybes. I can't talk about it yet.'

She hesitated, then added, 'And in spite of the name and Nikki's blue eyes, she might not be your child. Wouldn't you want to be sure?

Mac knew the words made sense—of course they should make sure—but he also felt as if the night— and all his thinking—had given him something precious. A child...

Did he want to risk losing that?

'I'd be happy to accept her as mine. We could get married,' he said, trying hard to sound sensible and practical when inside he was a gibbering mess. 'Wouldn't that solve all the problems?'

'Get married?'

She almost yelled the words at him. '*You* don't want

to get married, and *I* don't want to marry someone who isn't a for-ever-and-ever person, and how would Nikki feel? She's not stupid. She'd know we were doing it for her and that would be a terrible burden for her to bear.'

'It was just a thought,' Mac said, slightly staggered that she'd been so adamant. He'd thought it quite a good idea. In fact, the more it moved around in his head now, the better it got.

Which just went to show how little he understood women, he supposed, although now the thought was there it wasn't going to go away.

Marrying Izzy had become a very attractive proposition…

All he had to do was work out how to do it—how to persuade her…

Start with a kiss?

CHAPTER ELEVEN

IZZY MOVED AWAY, totally befuddled—by the conversation, by her body's traitorous reaction to Mac's closeness, and by the ridiculous proposal.

Possibly the ridiculous proposal should have come first.

'I'm going back,' she said. 'I need to run, to clear my head.'

And she set off at a brisk jog, pausing only to turn back.

'We should check,' she said. 'Steve had Nikki's DNA taken when she was a baby, wanting to be sure the sleaze bag Liane hooked up with for drugs wasn't the father. If I get a copy to you, can you ask someone to compare them?'

Mac frowned at her.

Had he been serious when he'd said testing didn't matter—that he was happy to accept Nikki as his child?

'Well, could you?' she demanded, as tiredness, confusion and being close to him combined to make standing there any longer almost impossible.

He nodded, nothing more, and she jogged away, turning back a second time.

'You won't say anything to anyone?'

She'd meant to sound firm, in control, but knew it had come out as a wimpy, pathetic plea.

'As if I would,' Mac muttered at her, and she turned back to her run, racing now, as if demons snapped at her heels.

She had to talk it through with someone, try to get her head around it all.

Hallie would be the ideal listener, and would probably offer sage advice, but to tell her about Mac's business—well, about his part in it, if he'd had a part in it—when she'd asked him not to say anything…?

She'd sleep on it, then maybe talk to Mac again, be sensible about the test, so they could decide together how to go forward with it.

But being within a two-metre radius of Mac—forget that, being in the same postcode as him—caused so many physical reactions that battling them left little brain space for common-sense discussions.

Except she'd have to do it.

Maybe after a sleep she'd feel better, think better…

Mac walked slowly back to town, still taking in the fact he was a father, maybe, still obsessing that he should have done something earlier, kept in touch with Liane for all she'd kept reminding him that it would only ever be a holiday fling—a dalliance.

Had she used that word?

Was that where he'd picked it up?

Surely not! He'd moved on, worked, met and married Lauren, been divorced and worked some more.

Then Izzy!

He sighed and walked up to the hospital. Roger was on duty but Mac wanted to see Ahmed, and check on

Rhia, *and* the pregnant woman they'd admitted with pre-eclampsia. For some reason seeing her safely through the rest of her pregnancy was suddenly very important.

Because he was a father?

Might be a father?

Nonsense!

Anyway, being a father was far more than the accident of conception. Being a father was a whole new world of learning.

He stopped at the bottom of the ramp leading into the hospital and turned to look out at the ocean, the revelation so strong it had stolen his breath.

It was what he wanted!

He wanted to be a father, to learn to be a father to Nikki—at least Nikki first. Somehow he and Izzy had to sort this out.

And he and Nikki?

Izzy was right, he had to compare their DNAs, to know for certain, for Nikki's sake as much as his.

He turned back towards the hospital, the exhilaration of his revelation leaving a far more frightening question in his head.

What if Nikki didn't want a father—or want him as a father?

Hell's teeth, no wonder Izzy was in a muddle…

Sleep brought no answers for Izzy, if anything it made her feel more woolly-headed than ever. She made a cup of tea and stared at her much-changed roster on the door of the refrigerato.. Next to it was Nikki's monthly calendar of the school and social events.

Rehearsals seemed to figure large in after-school

activities for Nikki and it took a moment for Izzy to recall they must be coming up to the school concert. This was Nikki's first year in the high-school concert, held every second year, the primary school having a similar event in between.

But what was Nikki's group doing? A music video? Well, an onstage performance of a music video, all the year seven students involved either singing and dancing on stage, or making and shifting props around.

Nikki was singing, but then she always did, right from her first year at school.

Could Mac sing?

The thought stopped Izzy dead.

She *had* to do something and do it now!

Not right now as she had to go to work, but today, or tomorrow.

But right now she could contact Steve, get him to email a copy of the DNA results. Until they knew for sure, there was no point in upsetting Nikki with all of this.

But once they knew?

'Oh, help!'

She hadn't realised she'd said the words aloud until Hallie walked in, a tin of freshly baked biscuits in her hands.

'Help what?' Hallie demanded. 'I did knock and when you didn't answer, I thought you'd gone to work.'

'On my way,' Izzy said, grabbing a couple of biscuits.

'And the help?' Hallie asked gently.

'Oh, Hallie, I don't know if anyone can help.'

And with that she departed.

Although maybe Mac and she could talk to Hallie

together. Her mother had seen the best and worst that people could do to each other, and had wisdom that Izzy could never hope to acquire. And Hallie knew children, and relationships, and a lot of psychology...

Fortunately Mac wasn't at the hospital when she arrived, having gone in the ambulance to Braxton with the pre-eclampsia patient whose blood pressure had failed to stabilise and who would probably need a Caesar.

But tomorrow Mac was off, Nikki had early rehearsals, she'd ask Hallie to have a late breakfast with her and Mac in the flat, make pancakes—

She got that far in the planning before panic set in so maybe that was a good thing. The panic usually came much earlier in her plans.

Mac returned as she finished giving out evening medications and the hospital was quietening down for the night.

'We should have DNA results in a couple of days. I forwarded that copy you emailed me of Nikki's along with mine—I had mine done when I joined the army— to a mate who'll fast-track it.'

The couple of days turned into a week, a week of sleepless nights and tortured days as far as Izzy was concerned. Her mind refused to function when it came to anything personal—Nikki, her, Mac—so she changed the hospital rosters yet again, putting herself on night duty to avoid at least one of the problems as much as possible.

But eventually the results came back, positive as she'd been sure they would be, and another weekend lay before them.

'It's Nikki we have to think about,' Mac said, slipping into a chair across the desk where she was writing up the night report, sliding the confirmation email across the desk towards her.

Izzy looked up at the man she'd been avoiding so assiduously, into the clear blue eyes, and felt her heart weep.

'I know,' she whispered. 'And it terrifies me!'

'Should we find someone to talk to first—a child psychologist?' Mac suggested, and Izzy realised he was as anxious about Nikki as she was.

'I was thinking Hallie,' she said. 'If anyone knows children, it's her. And Pop of course, but he's not one for words, but I thought if we talked to Hallie...'

Mac reached out and took her hand, squeezing her fingers gently.

'We'll work it out,' he said.

She gave a little huff that was half despair, half laughter.

'Will we?'

Mac left her to finish her shift, walking downtown to the promenade where he sat, looking out to sea, soothed by the sound of the surf.

And the answer came to him, so suddenly he was suspicious of it. He turned it this way and that, studying it from all directions, from his, Nikki's and Izzy's points of view and decided, yes, he was right.

Excited now, he hurried back to the hospital to catch Izzy as she came off duty.

'Walk you home?' he said, and whether it was the lightness of his words, or the smile that followed them, Izzy stopped dead and stared at him.

'What is it?' she demanded. 'You've won lotto?'

He shook his head and took her hand.

'No, far better. I've thought of how to do it.'

He probably shouldn't have taken her hand as it had set all the nerves in his body atwitch, registering this was Izzy he was touching, reminding him just how attracted to her he was.

But he held tight and they walked together up the hill, bodies touching, hers bombarding his with silent messages that almost made him forget the purpose of the walk.

'You've thought of how to do it?' she finally prompted, no doubt battling her own awareness of him.

Remembering them naked together, as he'd been?

'*I'll* talk to Nikki,' he announced, then wondered why this brilliant solution didn't seem to have affected Izzy as much as he'd thought it would.

'Why? What about?'

He stopped, turned to face her, and took her face between his palms so he could look into her dark eyes, run his thumb across her soft lips.

'I'll talk to her about Liane, about our holiday together, tell her about the Liane I knew, explain why we parted—different life paths for each of us—and how I didn't know about the pregnancy, didn't know I had a child, a daughter.'

He felt the smile as her cheeks moved in his hands.

'And then?'

He dropped his hands and drew her close, slipping his arms around her to hold her loosely in front of him.

'I haven't quite got that far, but she'll have stuff to say, questions, opinions. I thought we'd take a walk, maybe to the lighthouse, and you'd come, too, but be a bit apart, but she'll need you, I know she will.'

He leaned forward and kissed her lightly on the lips.

'What do you think?'

How could she think?

Standing here so close to Mac, his words whirling in her head while emotion whirled in her body.

Instinctively, it felt right what he'd said, or what she'd understood of what he'd said.

And outside, walking, that was good, less formal and more relaxed.

Well, Nikki might be relaxed, at least to start with, but Izzy could feel tension building in her body just thinking about the situation.

She leaned into Mac, and his arms tightened about her.

'We'll work it out, you'll see,' he said, and he sounded so convinced she almost believed him.

Almost because even fuzzy-headed, she could imagine so many scenarios that wouldn't be right—

Or was she over-thinking?

Mac was rubbing his hands up and down her arms, warming and reassuring at once.

'It will be a start,' he finally said. 'We both know this will be a huge emotional mess to dump on Nikki, but together, all three of us, I'm sure we can work through it.'

Izzy nodded, wanting nothing more than to stay there in his arms—for the moment to continue for ever.

'Go get some sleep,' Mac whispered. 'We'll talk later, maybe go out, the three of us, tomorrow afternoon.'

And maybe tomorrow wouldn't come...

But tomorrow did come, and the rush to get Nikki off to another rehearsal with the necessary props meant

there was little time for explanations, although Izzy did mention Mac had asked if they'd both like to walk up to the lighthouse with him later in the day.

'Can Shan come?'

Izzy shook her head. She should have expected the question. Since the pair had first met in primary school, Shan had been included in most of their excursions, trips and even holidays.

'Not today.'

Izzy hoped her tone was light enough for Nikki not to ask the inevitable why, but apparently Nikki had already put her own interpretation on the outing.

'Is he going to ask my permission to marry you?' Nikki teased, and Izzy chased her out the door.

But he *had* asked, Izzy remembered, only because of Nikki and family, though, not because he loved her.

Before the thought could settle in her heart, she got busy, doing the spring clean she'd been promising to do, decluttering and cleaning the little flat with ferocious energy.

Anything to stop her thinking about what lay ahead.

About Nikki and how she would take it, what it would mean to her, and the big one—where did they all go from there...?

Mac had arranged to meet them at three, and with no little trepidation Izzy walked with Nikki down to his house.

'I thought we'd drive to the parking area at the bottom of the hill,' he said, stowing a backpack into the boot of the car.

'Is that food?' Nikki asked, and Mac laughed.

'Food and drink—all kinds of stuff that's bad for you, like chips, and cake, and soft drink.'

'So we'll have a picnic, that's great. We haven't been up there for ages, have we, Mum?'

Which was when Izzy realised that her nerves were so taut she was beyond even the simplest conversation. She made a noise she hoped would be taken for agreement and climbed into the car, where Mac's presence was nearly as overwhelming as her tension.

But once walking up through the coastal scrub towards the top of the hill, she relaxed. Mac, with his loaded backpack, was walking with Nikki, asking her about the concert, about her singing, whether she enjoyed it.

Seeing the two of them together, there was no way Izzy couldn't ask herself about what might have been, although she knew it was time to look to the future, not dwell on the past.

But a tear for Liane slid down her cheek.

Finding a sheltered spot where they'd be out of the wind but still able to look out at the ocean, Mac spread the picnic blanket he'd purchased that morning, then brought out his goodies.

As they settled down, drinks in hand, Nikki raised her glass to him, grinned, and said, 'Well, if we're not here so you can ask my permission to marry Mum, why are we here?'

'Nikki!' Izzy protested, but Mac had to laugh. The cheeky question had broken the tension that had been building in him all day.

'No, I've already asked her that and she didn't think it *is* a good idea, but this *is* a family thing, Nikki, and something that's hard for me to tell and maybe going to be even harder for you to hear. I want to talk to you

about Liane, your birth mother. You see, I knew her once, a long time ago.'

'You *knew* Liane! But that's amazing, and it's not hard to hear at all. I'm always asking the family about her, poor woman. What chance did she have after such an appalling childhood? And even when she came to live with Hallie she was never happy—running away, getting into trouble, on and off drugs.'

'Exactly,' Mac said, 'but I didn't know about that— she never talked about it—never mentioned the past at all. We were both on holiday, I'd just finished at university and she—well, Izzy tells me Liane had been in detox and the holiday was her reward for being off the drugs.'

'Was this in Bali?'

Mac hesitated. Somehow Nikki was leaping ahead of all his carefully prepared sentences. Had she already guessed where this was going? He looked at Izzy who was looking steadfastly out to sea—no help at all.

'It was,' he told Nikki, and he took her hand. 'And it was magical! The beautiful place, the smiling people, the beaches and the surf, we had such fun. We went up into the mountains, climbing to the very top of a peak that looked out over all the island, we wandered around temples where monkeys played, and bought flowers to weave in Liane's hair—hair like yours, that golden-brown colour.'

He paused, uncertain how this was going, Nikki's eager face suggesting she was taking it all in.

'Go on,' she whispered, so he did.

'She was special, your mother. She laughed and sang—that must be where you get it—and everywhere she went people smiled at her. She was like a beautiful

bird or a brilliant butterfly, you had to look at her all the time, to watch her for the extra shine she seemed to bring to everything around her.'

He hesitated, but then added, 'And I loved her.'

Nikki was sitting very still, Izzy apparently turned to stone, but once he'd started, he knew he had to keep going.

'The trouble was it was a holiday—two weeks—and at the end we both knew we'd be parting. I was in the army—they'd trained me as a doctor and I'd been posted to Townsville way up in North Queensland—and she had a fabulous job waiting for her in Sydney. So we'd told ourselves all along it was just for now, and living for the moment, for the day, probably what made it so special.'

He paused, remembering that fateful moment in the hotel.

'As it turned out, we didn't even get two weeks!' he said. 'Two days before our holiday finished I had a message from home. My father was seriously ill and I had to go home. The army gave me leave but it was weeks before he was out of danger, and by then I had to get to Townsville.'

'You didn't keep in touch, didn't email, text, even read each other's social media pages?'

Mac took a deep breath.

'We'd agreed not to, but leaving the way I did, I tried to get in contact with her, but it was as if she'd been nothing but a dream. When she didn't return my calls or emails, I understood she'd meant what she'd said but I cannot tell you how deeply I regret not persevering. I should have contacted her, if only to make sure she'd

got to Sydney safely—but we'd promised not to spoil what we'd had by trying to make it last long distance.'

He took Nikki's other hand and waited until she looked up at him.

'I'm sure you've guessed where this is going, and I know this must be terribly hard for you, but I had no idea. Liane said she had been told by doctors that she could never have children. We lived and loved and laughed because we knew our time together was so limited. If I'd known, if I'd even suspected—but I didn't, and what happened happened, and I cannot say how sorry I am.'

The silence was so loud it hammered in Mac's ears as he waited for a reaction.

'So you're my dad?' Nikki said at last, studying his face as if she might recognise it. 'Are you sorry about that?'

'Good grief, no, it's the most amazing thing that's ever happened to me, apart from meeting Liane. Izzy worked it out kind of by accident, but we've checked and it's true. I'm still getting used to it and I don't know if I can be called a dad when you've gone all this time without me to do dad things with you, but I'd like to start, if that's okay with you, and maybe if we start small and get to know each other, eventually it will seem right to both of us.'

'You can walk me down the aisle when I get married!'

The remark was so unexpected that Mac could only gape, but Izzy burst out laughing and reached out to hug her daughter.

'Oh, Nikki, you do bring everything back to basics.'

She pushed the long golden-brown hair off Nikki's face and looked into her eyes.

'I know this is all a huge thing for you to take in. It's been pretty huge for Mac and me as well, but we'll both be there for you, to answer questions or talk about the situation. As Mac said, he can't become an instant father but I think he's a good man and he'll soon learn the job.'

'It's really weird,' Nikki responded, shaking her head as if that might help all the information settle. 'To think I've got a dad. Just wait till I tell Shan and the girls at school.'

And hearing that, Izzy relaxed, smiling at Mac across what was suddenly *their* daughter.

Silence fell between them, punctuated occasionally by a question or remark.

'You really loved her?' Nikki asked.

'I really did,' Mac said, with such conviction Izzy knew it was true.

More silence, then, 'Does this mean we can shift into the doctor's house with Mac? It's a great house, I've always loved it.'

'It does *not*,' Izzy said firmly.

'But you could come for sleepovers,' Mac replied.

'But if we moved in, then you and I would get to know each other better. You said we'd have to do that before we could love each other like a dad and daughter, and if we were living there you and Mum could grow to love each other, too, and then get married and we'd be a family.'

'Pushing things, Nikki!' Izzy warned, well aware of how the girl could tease, and embarrassed that Mac should be put in such a delicate position.

But she'd underestimated Mac.

'It's a great idea, but we needn't rush things,' he told Nikki. 'And I don't need your mother living in my house to fall in love with her because that's already happened.'

Izzy simply stared at him, her lips moving in protest but no sound coming out, and when they did come out they made no sense.

'You can't—you don't—that's silly—'

Nikki, however, was ignoring her, her gaze riveted on Mac.

'You're kidding me, right? You've come down here, found a daughter and fallen in love with her mother— that's fairy-tale stuff, not real life.'

Mac smiled.

'Sounds like it, doesn't it, but it wasn't entirely magical. I had some rough times in the army and needed somewhere peaceful, and I remembered Liane mentioning Wetherby, just once. It was a place, she said, where nothing ever happened. That was exactly what I was looking for so, really, it was your birth mother who brought me here and that's how I found you.'

'Shan will *never* believe this!'

Izzy smiled at Mac and said, 'It's okay, that's a normal reaction from a nearly thirteen-year-old. And I think the days of nothing ever happening in Wetherby are over—if you think Nikki's excited about talking to her friends, wait until the town gossips get hold of this.'

Mac groaned, but he was smiling, and somehow the awkwardness that had stopped the conversation with his love declaration was gone.

Fortunately!

Gone but not forgotten. They lingered on the hill

until the sun began to sink over the rolling hills to the west, then packed up their picnic and walked back to the car.

'Can you drop me at the restaurant so I can tell Shan?' Nikki asked, excitement shimmering in her voice.

Mac looked at Izzy who shrugged, and said, 'Might as well get it over and done with,' she told him. 'The sooner the story starts on the rounds, the sooner it will die. But I need to go home and talk to Hallie and Pop before they hear it from someone else.'

'I'll come with you,' Mac said quietly, and Izzy groaned, but inwardly.

It was the right thing to do, but what she really needed was time away from him.

Not that she believed the love thing he'd said. How could he be in love with her, he who dallied rather than loved?

But having him with her to see Hallie and Pop was a good idea so she'd think about the love business later.

The couple she considered her parents were in the kitchen, sharing a rare bottle of wine.

'Good,' Hallie said, 'you can each have a glass. Pop and I don't ever finish the bottle. It always seems like a nice idea but one glass does us.'

Izzy and Mac joined them at the kitchen table, accepted their wine from Pop, sipped and—

'Something you want to tell us?' Hallie asked.

'Yes, but it's more Nikki than us. Well, us in some ways, or more precisely Mac, but—'

'Perhaps you should let Mac tell us,' Pop said gently,

moving his chair closer to Izzy and putting his arm around her shoulders.

So Mac did, leaving little out, explaining that they'd told Nikki, and she was already spreading the news.

'How did she take it?' Hallie asked, and Mac looked to Izzy to answer.

'Okay so far, but there'll be questions and it will take time for it all to sink in. It's not every day you find your father.'

'Nor every day a father finds his daughter either,' Hallie reminded her, looking at Mac with raised eyebrows.

'In truth, I'm lost,' he said, 'so many conflicting emotions churning inside me. Regret I wasn't there for Liane, that I wasn't there for Nikki when she was born, then worry—or more probably terror—that I might not be any good at this dad business. And now I've found her, what if she decides she doesn't want me? Not immediately—there'll be novelty value for a while, I imagine—but down the track. What if she blames me for her mother going back onto drugs? For her mother's death?'

Hallie smiled and poured him another drink.

'Do you think all parents don't go through that list of doubts and many, many more, every day of their lives? You just hang in there, do your best, be yourself, be as truthful as you can, and hope it all works out.'

'You make it sound so easy,' he said, and Pop shook his head.

'We all know it's not, but worrying about what might be never got anyone anywhere. It's like the holiday you took with Liane, take each day as it comes and get as much joy as you can from it. That's how Hallie

and I always worked. Yes, there'll be tears and probably tantrums and you'll do or say the wrong thing, but with love, and patience, things usually come right at the end.'

Having made a speech far longer than she could remember ever hearing from Pop, Izzy was surprised when he turned to her.

'Are you all right with all of this, lass?' he asked, and Izzy felt tears prick at her eyelids.

'Just about,' she admitted. 'Though it will take time for all of us. I think it's the most wonderful thing for Nikki and, really, that's all that matters.'

'Humph!' Pop said. 'That's the way you always think, but it's time you put yourself first, Izzy. Think of what *you* want and how you would like this to work for you.'

'Pop's right,' Hallie put in, and Izzy held up her hands in surrender.

'Okay, but like we've all been saying it'll take time. It's a big change in all our lives, a huge change for Nikki and Mac—so we all need time to work out where we fit.'

And suddenly the energy that expectation and concern had built in her all day drained away, leaving her in a state of total exhaustion.

'In fact, if you'll all excuse me, I really need to have a hot shower and a wee rest before I can even begin to think about the future.'

Mac was on his feet immediately.

'I'll walk you up to the flat,' he said, but Hallie held up her hand.

'Let her go, Mac,' she said gently. 'It's been a lot for

her to handle as well, and do you think she doesn't have
a list of doubts and what-ifs as long as yours?'

Mac subsided into his chair once more, and Izzy
beat a hasty retreat.

Her mind was blank—overloaded, she knew—and
much as she'd have liked to have Mac's arms around
her, she was so emotional she knew where it would
lead.

Which was another complication she'd think about
later, along with that strange declaration.

How could he love her when he didn't do love?

CHAPTER TWELVE

HE WAS WAITING at the fresh-water tap again the next morning, appearing like a wraith in the light sea mist.

'So, shall we get married?' he said as she bent over to catch her breath.

Catch her breath when he'd just made what sounded very like an extremely casual but probably serious proposal?

She straightened cautiously, and looked into the now-familiar blue eyes.

'Why?' she asked.

He kind of smiled and kind of shrugged, and reached out to touch her cheek.

'It just seems like a good idea,' he finally replied, no smile now, deadly serious.

'For you, for Nikki, or for me?' Izzy asked, the hammering of her heart against her sternum telling her just how important his answer would be.

Wishing…

Hoping…

'For all of us,' he said.

Wrong answer!

Her head dropped, her eyes watered, her body trembled in reaction and he reached out and put his hands

on her shoulders, drawing her slightly closer but not close enough for body contact.

Just close!

'And…' he said, and she could read stress in his face, feel tension in his hands.

'And…' she prompted.

Wrong prompt!

'Damn it, Izzy, you know why. I told you yesterday that I love you.'

'You told Nikki that you love me,' Izzy reminded him gently, although her heart had stopped hammering and was doing a little skipping thing in her chest. 'Not the same thing.'

'But you heard me say it,' he protested, and she wondered if she should give him a break.

No way!

'Not to me!'

He drew her close, clasped his arms around her back and rested his chin on her head.

'Oh, Izzy, I have no idea why it's so hard. Perhaps because I've thought for a long time that people say it too readily, too often, and the words lose their meaning. But I've known for days now, probably weeks, yet putting how I feel into words—'

'You're doing okay,' Izzy whispered, feeling the love through the lips in her hair, the hands on her back.

'I love you, Izzy. There, I've said it, but it wasn't just words, it was a pledge of my heart, my life, my love for ever. All for you, my for-ever-and-ever woman!'

She raised her head to his for the kiss to seal the declaration, but put her finger to his lips before they touched hers.

'Isn't it my turn now?' she asked, then had to laugh at the astonished look on his face.

'But of course you love me,' he said. 'You must! We're meant to be together. Even without Nikki it would have been you and me. Besides, you have to marry me, because being with you, loving you has stopped my nightmares.'

'Well, there's a good reason,' Izzy teased.

But Mac was serious again.

'Not as good as love,' he said quietly. 'I think we both knew there was something special between us from our first meeting at the beach that morning. It was as if a whole new world had started—for me anyway.'

'For me, too,' Izzy agreed, and now she did kiss him, revelling in the sense of belonging that filled every cell in her body.

'I love you, Mac,' she whispered as they pulled apart.

'And I you,' he confirmed, and he took her hand to walk back along the track—to a daughter, to marriage, to a family…and to happy ever after.

* * * * *

If you enjoyed this story,
check out these other great reads
from Meredith Webber:

A SHEIKH TO CAPTURE HER HEART
THE MAN SHE COULD NEVER FORGET
THE ONE MAN TO HEAL HER
THE SHEIKH DOCTOR'S BRIDE

All available now!

MILLS & BOON®

EXCLUSIVE EXTRACT

Secret royal prince Dr Elias Santini is stunned
when he rushes to an emergency delivery.
The patient is Beth Foster… and she's
having his baby!

Read on for a sneak preview of
THEIR SECRET ROYAL BABY

'How pregnant is she?' Elias asked.

'Twenty-nine weeks. Her waters broke as we got her
onto the gurney. Elias, this baby is coming and very
rapidly.'

They had reached the cubicle and Elias took a steadying breath.

'What's her name?'

Before Mandy could tell Elias he was already stepping
into the cubicle.

And before Mandy said the name, he knew it.

'Beth.'

She was sitting up, wearing a hospital gown, and
there was a blanket over her. Her stunning red hair was
worn up tonight but it was starting to uncoil and was
dark with sweat. Her gorgeous almond-shaped eyes were
for now screwed closed and she wore drop earrings in
rose gold and the stones were rubies.

They were the same earrings she had worn the night
they had met.

He could remember vividly stepping into her villa

and turning the light on and watching the woman he had seen only in moonlight come into delicious colour—the deep red of her hair, the pale pink of her lips and eyes that were a pure ocean blue.

Now Valerie had her arm around Beth's shoulders and was telling her to try not to push.

For Elias there was a moment of uncertainty.

Could Mandy find someone else perhaps? Could he swap with Roger?

Almost immediately he realised there was no choice. From what Mandy had told him this baby was close to being born.

His baby?

Don't miss
THEIR SECRET ROYAL BABY
by Carol Marinelli

Available March 2017
www.millsandboon.co.uk

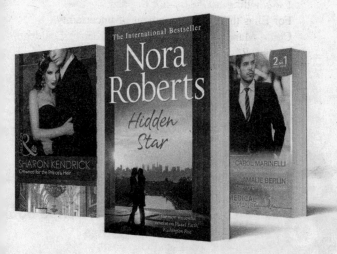

Join Britain's BIGGEST Romance Book Club

50% OFF your first parcel

- **EXCLUSIVE offers** every month
- **FREE delivery dire** to your door
- **NEVER MISS a titl**
- **EARN Bonus Bool** points

Call Customer Services
0844 844 1358*

or visit
millsandboon.co.uk/subscriptio

* This call will cost you 7 pence per minute plus your phone company's price per minute access charge.

ÉMILE ZOLA

NANA

TRANSLATED WITH AN INTRODUCTION
BY GEORGE HOLDEN

PENGUIN BOOKS

Penguin Books Ltd, Harmondsworth, Middlesex, England
Viking Penguin Inc., 40 West 23rd Street, New York, New York 10010, U.S.A.
Penguin Books Australia Ltd, Ringwood, Victoria, Australia
Penguin Books Canada Limited, 2801 John Street, Markham, Ontario, Canada 13R 1B4
Penguin Books (N.Z.) Ltd, 182–190 Wairau Road, Auckland 10, New Zealand

—

This translation first published 1972
Reprinted in this edition 1982
Reprinted 1983, 1985, 1986

—

—

Made and printed in Great Britain by
Hazell Watson & Viney Limited,
Member of the BPCC Group,
Aylesbury, Bucks
Set in Intertype Baskerville

Introduction

ALTHOUGH the modern reader can enjoy *Nana* as the masterpiece it is without having read any of Émile Zola's other novels, and indeed without knowing of their existence, it is in fact one of the most important elements in the grandiose twenty-novel saga which he published between 1871 and 1893 under the generic title of *The Rougon-Macquarts: the Natural and Social History of a Family under the Second Empire*.

As that title indicates, the saga was planned as a study of the effects of heredity and environment on the members of a single family, tracing the passage of madness and disease from the dread ancestress Adelaïde Fouque down the legitimate line of the Rougons and the illegitimate line of the Macquarts, against a wide variety of backgrounds, from the Provençal countryside, where Zola grew up with friends such as Cézanne and Baille, to Paris, where he was born in 1840 and spent the greater part of his life. In his theoretical work *The Experimental Novel* (1880), published at the same time as *Nana* and inspired by Claude Bernard's *Introduction to the Study of Experimental Medicine*, Zola tried to establish an analogy between literature and science, arguing that imagination had no place in the modern world, and that the novelist, like the scientist, should simply observe and record, introducing characters with specific hereditary peculiarities into a given environment – just as the chemist places certain substances in a retort – and then noting down the progress and results of his 'experiment' for the attention of legislators and the ultimate benefit of mankind. As Zola's sharp-witted disciple and friend Henry Céard was quick to protest, this analogy is untenable, for while the chemist can stand back and take no further part in his experiment, the novelist cannot do likewise, or his novel will never be written. It is more than likely that Zola was well aware of the flaws in his argument before Céard pointed them out, and he may well have

used the theory of the experimental novel, like the term 'naturalism', which he applied to the literary movement of which he was the acknowledged leader, largely in order to impress a public easily over-awed by pseudo-scientific terminology. But although he never allowed his much-publicized theories to limit his poetic imagination or cramp his most unscientific style, his fascinated interest in the workings of heredity and environment did inspire him with the idea of composing a complex family saga which should also be a carefully documented picture of every part of French society under the Second Empire.

The importance of prostitution at every level of the pleasure-loving society of Napoleon III's France made it inevitable that one of the novels of the Rougon-Macquart series should be devoted to a courtesan, and in the plan for the saga which Zola submitted to the publisher Lacroix in 1869 he listed: 'A novel set in the world of pleasure and prostitution with Louise Duval, the daughter of a working-class couple, as the heroine. ... Louise is what is known as a "high-class *cocotte*". Picture of the world in which these women live. Poignant drama of a woman's life ruined by the appetite for luxury and facile pleasures.'

Zola was convinced that nobody had yet had the courage or the ability to paint a true-to-life portrait of the modern courtesan – the rich, powerful *demi-mondaine* or 'high-class *cocotte*', who during the Second Empire had succeeded the poor sentimental, consumptive *grisette* of Louis-Philippe's reign and Henry Murger's novels. Admittedly there existed a large number of titillating novels, often anonymous, about the courtesans of Paris, but Zola not unreasonably dismissed these barely literate productions as 'stupid, mediocre books which can tempt only schoolboys on holiday', and declared in an article published in 1866: 'I await the true story of the *demi-monde*, if somebody one day dares to write that story.' In the projected story of Louise Duval – later to become Anna or 'Nana' Coupeau – Zola planned to become that somebody.

It could scarcely be said that he was well equipped for the task: at that time he was leading a chaste, hard-working life,

and although his work as a journalist took him to the theatres, art galleries and boulevard cafés, he had neither the money, the time nor the inclination to mix with the courtesans of the *demi-monde*. However, he studied them and their admirers from a distance, writing caustically in various newspaper articles about the Théâtre des Variétés, 'where two years ago [in 1867] all the princes of this world went to pay homage before even visiting the Universal Exhibition'; of actresses such as the notorious Hortense Schneider who hypnotized a stupid public with 'an obscenity underlined by a wiggle of the hips'; or of the young men of good family who 'applaud the trite productions of Messrs Offenbach and Hervé and make queens of wretched tight-rope dancers who frolic on the boards like fairground artistes.' And, in a reference to the famous scene of the masochistic senator in Otway's *Venice Preserved*, which was to inspire a no less famous scene in *Nana*, Zola wrote in 1868 that replicas of Otway's character were to be found in Second Empire Paris : 'Look around and you will find him among us. Oh, how many sinister comedies you can see, how many men who toss aside their dress-coat like a theatrical costume and roll on the carpet, playing the dog and begging to be kicked !'

In 1870 the defeat and capture of Napoleon III at Sedan, and the collapse of the Second Empire, provided Zola with a splendid final curtain for his family saga, and enabled him to point to the moral corruption of the period as the principal cause of the country's humiliation. He was not alone in holding this view : Dumas *fils*, in his plays, blamed France's defeat on prostitution, while Paul de Saint-Victor stigmatized the courtesans who 'filled the novels of the period, monopolized the stage, and reigned in the Bois, at the races, at the theatre, wherever crowds assembled', and asked : 'Who can say how much energy was destroyed, strength enervated and spirit debilitated by that laxity of morals? Who can measure the degree to which it contributed to our fearful misfortunes?' But in fact the overthrow of the Second Empire had changed nothing but the form of government obtaining in France, and in 1872 Charles Yriarte reported that 'the

7

whores have returned to the Bois. ... People are supping again at the Helder and betting again at the races, there are mashers as there used to be, fools as there always have been, and tarts to suit every pocket.'

This was fortunate for the future author of *Nana*, for he was able to continue studying, at first or second hand, aspects of the 'world of pleasure and prostitution' which had remained virtually unchanged since before the Franco-Prussian War. He was in no hurry as yet to document himself for *Nana*, since his novel of the 'high-class *cocotte*' was now scheduled to follow some time after the story of Nana's mother, Gervaise Macquart, *L'Assommoir*, which did not appear in book form until 1877. But in the meantime, for nearly a decade, he took notes on theatre life behind the scenes, on police raids on shady hotels, on society scandals and Longchamp races, usually publishing his material in newspapers such as *La Cloche* or *Le Sémaphore de Marseille*, but always storing it away for his novel.

Early in 1878 Zola began documenting himself in earnest for *Nana*. By now his attitude to the subject had changed radically from the puritanical disapproval of 1869 to a more human, balanced and sympathetic interest. His appetite for financial gain and literary fame had also been whetted by the recent appearance of two novels about prostitutes: *Marthe, the Story of a Prostitute*, by a promising young writer called Joris-Karl Huysmans, published in Brussels in September, 1876, and *The Whore Élisa*, by the veteran novelist Edmond de Goncourt, published in Paris in March 1877. Neither book had obtained any success – Huysmans's because it was an impressionistic study by an unknown author, and Goncourt's because it was primarily an earnest protest against the treatment of inmates in women's prisons – but both novels had escaped the prosecution for obscenity the authors had expected, and Zola's instinct told him that the more ambitious, less esoteric work he planned to write would win the popular acclaim his colleagues had missed, yet still succeed in avoiding official condemnation. If he needed any further encouragement, it was provided by his friend Manet, who, full of admiration for *L'Assommoir*,

which he read in serial form in 1876, and captivated by Zola's sketch in Chapter Eleven of Gervaise Macquart's precociously immoral daughter, gave the title *Nana* to his portrait of the courtesan Henriette Hauser – a portrait of a plump young woman *en déshabillé* standing in front of a mirror, which, innocuous though it may seem to modern eyes, was nonetheless rejected by the hanging committee for the Paris Salon of 1877.

One of Zola's first documentary forays of 1878 was into the Café Anglais, that great haunt of the *jeunesse dorée* of the Second Empire, where he lunched with an old habitué of the house and questioned him at length about the exploits of his younger days and the courtesans he had entertained on those same premises. He took detailed notes of his informant's account of the lives and deaths of the great *demi-mondaines*, particularly Blanche d'Antigny, whom he was to take as his principal model for Nana, and Cora Pearl, alias Eliza Emma Crouch, the English courtesan who had been Prince Napoleon's mistress and who, like Nana, had had a brief but sensational career on the stage. On the men who had provided the *grandes cocottes* with their wealth and power, Zola wrote : 'A whole society clinging to the skirts of those women. The pressure of the males. Old men debauching themselves and breathing their last away from home. Bestiality, an old man sniffing in slippers. Young idiots ruining themselves, some to keep in fashion, some out of infatuation. Middle-aged men with high positions falling genuinely in love.' On Cora Pearl (Lucy Stewart in the novel) he noted : 'She used to go hunting with Prince Napoleon at Meudon. Prince Napoleon puts all his louis in his boots. They played bezique together, using beans instead of louis.' And in a note which looked forward to the final scene of his novel he wrote : 'Caroline Letessier installing d'Antigny at the Grand Hôtel. Death provides d'Antigny with friends for one evening ...'

Zola had decided that Nana's career should be closely associated with the theatre, and that the novel should open with a first night at the Variétés. He himself had come to know the world of the theatre at close quarters, not only as a journalist and critic but also as a playwright, for in 1873 he

9

had presented an adaptation of his novel *Thérèse Raquin* at the Théâtre de la Renaissance and in 1874 a comedy called *The Rabourdin Heirs* at the Théâtre de Cluny. But he did not know enough as yet about theatrical life in general and the Variétés in particular; and for the information he wanted he turned to Ludovic Halévy, Offenbach's brilliant librettist, who was an ardent admirer of *L'Assommoir* and had offered to help him to the best of his ability. Halévy not only told him anecdotes about Blanche d'Antigny but took him on 15 February 1878 to the Variétés, to see an operetta called *Niniche* by Alfred Hennequin and Albert Millaud. At the theatre he entertained Zola with the story of the marital and amorous life of the star, Anna Judic, whose husband, a some-time shop-assistant, had once fought her lover Millaud in the wings of the Bouffes, but now winked at the liaison and devoted his life to managing her affairs and caring for their two children. Zola avidly noted down the details of this *ménage à trois*, which would be presented in *Nana* in the characters of Mignon, his wife Rose and her lover Faucherey; and he looked and listened just as eagerly during the intervals, when Halévy took him backstage and showed him the dressing-room where in 1867 Hortense Schneider, dressed as the Grand Duchess of Gerolstein, had ceremoniously received the Prince of Wales.

Next he decided that he needed to see the interior of a 'high-class *cocotte*'s' house, and his disciple Léon Hennique persuaded the young and beautiful Madame Valtesse de la Bigne to show him over her mansion on the Boulevard Males-herbes. Zola was even invited to stay to dinner, but his hostess was too intelligent and cultured to accord with his preconceived ideas of a courtesan, and nothing of her conversation or personality went to the making of Nana. On the other hand, her house was everything Zola had hoped for, and he made detailed notes as he was taken on a conducted tour of the premises. He was particularly impressed by Madame Valtesse de la Bigne's bed – a splendidly ornate conglomeration of naked Cupids, erotic bas-reliefs, birds and butterflies – which he would make Nana's field of operations in his novel.

During the summer of 1878 Zola prepared the preliminary outline, or *ébauche*, of *Nana*, summarizing the career of his heroine as seen in his novel, from the theatrical sensation which would make her name to 'a conclusion, death or something else', and specifying the theme of the book : 'The philosophical subject is as follows : A whole society hurling itself at the cunt. A pack of hounds after a bitch, who is not even on heat and makes fun of the hounds following her. *The poem of male desires*, the great lever which moves the world. There is nothing apart from the cunt and religion.' By July 1878 he was able to write to Céard : 'I have established the plan of *Nana*, and I am very pleased.' In the same letter he thanked Céard for some notes his disciple had sent him about courtesans' dinner-parties and conversations : 'A thousand thanks for your notes. They are excellent, and I shall use them all. The dinner-party in particular is astounding. I should like to have a hundred pages of such notes – I would write a magnificent book ...'

He now proceeded to draw up a list of the characters for his novel, filling up a descriptive card for each one. Some of the characters were explicitly based on people Zola knew personally or about whom he had been informed : Fontan on the actor Coquelin *cadet*, the Mignons on the Judics, Faucherey on Albert Millaud, Lucy Stewart on Cora Pearl, La Tricon on a notorious procuress called La Guimond and Steiner on Blanche d'Antigny's lover the banker Bischoffsheim. But other characters were simply inventions to suit the author's purpose, or, if they were drawn from life, amalgams of several people : thus Nana herself was not based only on Blanche d'Antigny, but also on Anna Deslions, Delphine de Lizy, Lucie Lévy, Hortense Schneider and a host of other *cocottes* on whom Zola's friends and disciples had provided information. The card on his heroine read as follows :

Nana. Born in 51. In 67 (end of the year, December) she is seventeen. But she is very big, anybody would think she was at least twenty. Blonde, pink, Parisian face, very wide-awake, her nose slightly turned up, her mouth small and laughing, a dimple on her chin, her eyes blue and very bright, with golden lashes. A few freckles which come back every summer, but very few,

five or six on each temple like flecks of gold. The nape of her neck an amber colour, with a tangle of little hairs. Smells of woman, very much a woman. Light down on the cheeks.

Must tell the story of her previous life. See *L'Assommoir* for all the first period: played as a child in the Goutte-d'Or district, served her apprenticeship as a flower-girl at Titreville's in the Rue du Caire, ran away to live with an old man (see whether she gave herself first to a man of her own class), left her old man to run around; ups and downs; returned to her parents' home several times, ran away again, finally didn't reappear. That's where I left her. Her father and mother dead. I'll pick her up again there, without giving many details. She has had her ups and downs. At the first night certain men, Cartier and the young men, may recognize her from having seen her in haunts of ill fame. She appears in an operetta with Rose Mignon. She is already well known in certain circles. At that time she may be the mistress of Bordenave, the manager of the theatre, who says this: 'I know perfectly well she hasn't any voice, she can't sing well, and she acts very badly; but what does that matter? ... Wait till you see her. I know her.' One part of the audience knows her, the other doesn't; tremendous curiosity! Those who know her and those who don't. Nana has a flat on the Boulevard Haussmann, in a new building behind the construction site of the Opéra. A lover, a Russian, has left her, her rent hasn't been paid, troubles everywhere. At the time she has a sweetheart, Paul Daguenet; she knows Arsène Labordette, Juillerat. Cartier has seen her at the Casino, very drunk, picked up by the police. Vandeuvres has met her in a high-class house of call where she was passed off as a young widow from the provinces. That's the starting-point.

Her character: good-natured above all else. Follows her nature, but never does harm for harm's sake, and feels sorry for people. Bird-brain, always thinking of something new, with the craziest whims. Tomorrow doesn't exist. Very merry, very gay. Superstitious, frightened of God. Loves animals and her parents. At first very slovenly, vulgar; then plays the lady and watches herself closely. – With that, ends up regarding man as a material to exploit, becoming a force of Nature, a ferment of destruction, but without meaning to, simply by means of her sex and her strong female odour, destroying everything she approaches, and turning society sour just as women having a period turn milk sour. The cunt in all its power; the cunt on an altar, with all the

men offering up sacrifices to it. The book has to be the poem of the cunt, and the moral will lie in the cunt turning everything sour. As early as Chapter One I show the whole audience captivated and worshipping; study the women and the men in front of that supreme apparition of the cunt. – On top of all that, Nana eats up gold, swallows up every sort of wealth; the most extravagant tastes, the most frightful waste. She instinctively makes a rush for pleasures and possessions. Everything she devours; she eats up what people are earning around her in industry, on the stock exchange, in high positions, in everything that pays. And she leaves nothing but ashes. In short a real whore. – Don't make her witty, which would be a mistake; she is nothing but flesh, but flesh in all its beauty. And, I repeat, a good-natured girl.

Ups and downs. In the end she has to die at the height of her youth, at the height of her triumph.

The question of heredity in Nana. An extreme case of the Rougon-Macquarts. The product of Gervaise and an alcoholic, Coupeau.

About 20 August 1878 Zola finally began the actual writing of his novel, writing to Flaubert : 'Just now I can feel that little quivering of the pen which has always foreshadowed the happy delivery of a good book.' But it was to prove a long-drawn delivery : it was 19 September before Zola had finished the first chapter, and although he worked away on the novel throughout the autumn and winter, he had only completed a quarter of the book by January 1879, when he had to return to Paris to supervise the rehearsals of a stage version of *L'Assommoir* at the Ambigu. In that same month the *Voltaire* announced with a great flourish that despite the competition of ten other newspapers it had secured exclusive rights to publish *Nana* in serial form, and in May the first instalment was promised for early October. 'Ridiculous rumours are circulating here about *Nana*,' Céard told Zola at the end of May. 'In a Franco-Russian salon where I set foot the other evening, a gentleman was maintaining in all seriousness that *Nana* was Valtesse, and he also cited the names of three or four other women highly priced on the Parisian market, who were also supposed to figure in your next novel ...'

13

However, not only was the novel in question far from being complete, but Zola had not even finished documenting himself for the latter part of the story. On Sunday 8 June he went to Longchamp with the publisher Marpon to see the Grand Prix and refresh his memories of the racing scene for the great racecourse episode in *Nana*; and during the months to come, he would go on appealing to friends and disciples, Céard above all, for help with the background to scenes such as the reception for Estelle Muffat's wedding or Nana's death in a fourth-floor bedroom in the Grand Hôtel.

On 5 October 1879 he delivered the first three chapters of *Nana* to the editor of the *Voltaire*, and within days the newspaper launched the biggest publicity campaign ever mounted so far to advertise a novel. 'There is enormous curiosity about *Nana*,' Céard wrote to Zola on 15 October. 'That name is repeated *ad infinitum* over all the walls of Paris. It is becoming an obsession and a nightmare.' The first instalment of the novel appeared on 16 October, and for a few days the story of the Second Empire courtesan was accompanied in the same newspaper by extracts from *The Experimental Novel*, fiction and theory together sending the more conservative critics into paroxysms of rage. During the last months of 1879 Zola had not only to write at a furious rate to keep ahead of the *Voltaire* printers, but had to spend his mornings correcting the newspaper instalments for the definitive version due to be published in book form in 1880. At last, on 7 January 1880, he was able to write to Céard : 'I finished *Nana* this morning' – before taking to bed for three days in utter exhaustion.

On 15 February Charpentier published the novel in a first edition of 55,000 copies which sold out the same day. But almost the only expressions of praise and admiration came in letters from a few friends, chief among them Gustave Flaubert, who in a letter to the author enthused over 'a beautiful book, and a new book, absolutely new in your series and in everything that has been written so far', while he wrote to Charpentier : 'What a book ! It's bold and daring, and our good friend Zola is a man of genius ...' In complete contrast, polite society was shocked by what it

called the crudity of Zola's novel; the pious were outraged by the author's portrait of sanctimonious Monsieur
Venot and the analogy between sexual and religious fervour;
while the monied classes frowned at the reference in the
penultimate chapter to workers slaving night and day in the
mills to provide the wealth to satisfy Nana's caprices. As for
the critics, disappointed in the hopes aroused by Zola's last,
somewhat insipid novel, *A Page of Love*, that the wild beast
of modern literature had been tamed, they launched a
furious onslaught on *Nana*. Pontmartin, in the *Gazette de
France*, pointed out the 'harmony between this literary orgy
and the radical saturnalia' and condemned *Nana* as 'the
last word of demagogy in the novel'. Chapron, in the *Événe-
ment*, declared that the book was 'so utterly worthless that
the obscenities with which it is sprinkled are obviously just
an attraction for libidinous old men and inquisitive women
of all ages'. And Ulbach, in *Gil Blas*, dismissed the novel as a
product of 'the incipient erethism of an ambitious and impotent brain maddened by its sensual visions'.

None of the critics of the time seems to have noticed the
careful symmetry Zola had achieved between the two halves
of the novel – the balance attained between the rise and fall
of Nana the actress in the first part and the triumph and
death of Nana the courtesan in the second – or his brilliant
use of animal imagery throughout the book – the games
Muffat and Nana play as dog and bear, Fauchery's comparison of the courtesan to a golden fly, and the supreme confusion in the minds of everybody watching the Grand Prix
between Nana the woman and Nana the horse. The only
point which all the more thoughtful critics made, and which
some of them laboured relentlessly, was the improbability of
a basically vulgar prostitute such as Nana ever reaching the
summit of the *demi-monde*. Thus Georges Ohnet wrote : 'A
goose like Nana would do very bad business and would be
promptly abandoned by her lovers. In this age of competition
it requires more intelligence to succeed in being a whore
kept in luxury than to make a fortune in a respectable business.' And Paul de Saint-Victor asked how Zola could possibly show his readers 'the most crude and bestial sort of

whore' as 'the sole authentic type of a world that is so complex and variegated, so rich in rare eccentricities and unexpected exceptions'.

This was missing the point. It is true that Nana is a vulgar creature as far removed as possible from distinguished courtesans such as Madame Valtesse de la Bigne; after all, it was Zola's intention to show her rising from the gutter to take a savage revenge on the rich on behalf of her class. She also has an instinctive, if sporadic, kindliness which goes hand-in-hand with her vulgarity, behaving at times with almost motherly tenderness and pity to her principal victim, the Comte Muffat; as Zola repeatedly remarked in his notes, she is fundamentally good-natured, *une bonne fille*. But the explanation of her triumph in the *demi-monde* is that she is more than a mere street-walker with surprising luck : just as the book is not simply a realist novel but 'the poem of male desires', so Nana is not simply a successful courtesan but a superhuman sex-symbol.

Only two of Zola's readers seem to have realized this fully at the time of the book's appearance. One was Gustave Flaubert, who in the letter quoted above remarked that 'Nana is something of a myth, without ceasing to be real'; and the other was Paul Arène, who wrote that

Monsieur Zola, more of a poet than he believes, more Romantic than he wants to admit, and who fortunately does not always take care to reconcile his works with his theories, has, perhaps quite unconsciously, employed a very old technique : just as the Greeks attributed to a single Hercules all the exploits of fifty strong men, so he credits Nana with a series of achievements and crimes for which the entire immoral army of Paris would not be sufficient, even supported by Lesbos and Corinth.

In this context it is significant that nowhere in Zola's book are we given a detailed portrait of Nana, and that no portrayal of Nana on stage or screen, even by the most talented and beautiful of actresses, has ever conveyed a tenth of the overwhelming impression made by Zola's heroine in the novel. For Nana is an incomparable literary creation, both reality and myth, both courtesan and monster, both woman and goddess.

GEORGE HOLDEN

TRANSLATOR'S NOTE

THE French text used for this translation was the first edition published by Charpentier in 1880.

I would like to thank Dr Robert Baldick for patiently answering my questions on points of detail which arose while I was making this translation, and for kindly allowing me to consult in advance of publication the relevant chapters of his forthcoming biography of Zola.

G. H.

THE French text used for this translation was the first edition published by Charpentier in 1890.

I would like to thank Dr. Robert Baldick, for patiently answering my questions on points of detail which arose while I was making this translation, and for kindly allowing me to consult in advance of publication the relevant section of his forthcoming bibliography of Zola.

AT nine o'clock the auditorium of the Théâtre des Variétés was still virtually empty; a few people were waiting in the dress circle and the stalls, lost among the red velvet armchairs, in the half-light of the dimly glowing chandelier. The great red patch of the curtain was plunged in shadow, and not a sound came from the stage, the extinguished footlights, or the desks of the absent musicians. Only up above in the gallery, around the rotunda of the ceiling, on which naked women and children were flying about in a sky turned green by the gas, shouts and laughter emerged from a continuous din of voices, and rows of heads in caps and bonnets could be seen under the wide bays framed in gold. Every now and then an attendant bustled in with tickets in her hand, driving in front of her a lady and gentleman who sat down, the man in tails, the woman slim and erect, sweeping the theatre with a leisurely gaze.

Two young men appeared in the stalls and stood there, looking around.

'What did I tell you, Hector?' exclaimed the elder of the two, a tall fellow with a little black moustache. 'We've come too early. You could just as well have let me finish my cigar.'

An attendant was passing.

'Oh, Monsieur Faucherry,' she said familiarly, 'it won't be starting for another half-hour.'

'Then why do they announce it for nine o'clock?' murmured Hector, his long thin face taking on a vexed expression. 'Why, only this morning Clarisse, who is in the show, swore to me that it started on the stroke of eight.'

For a moment they fell silent, gazing up into the darkness of the boxes. But the green wallpaper with which they were decorated made them darker than ever. Down below, under the circle, the ground-floor boxes were lost in pitch darkness. In the boxes in the dress circle there was nobody but a fat lady slumped on the velvet rail. To the right and left, be-

tween lofty pillars, the stage-boxes remained empty, draped with long-fringed pelmets. The gold and white auditorium, set off with pale green, was only dimly visible, as if filled with a fine dust by the tiny flames of the huge crystal chandelier.

'Did you get your stage-box for Lucy?' asked Hector.

'Yes,' his companion replied, 'but it wasn't easy. . . . Oh, there's no danger of Lucy, of all people, coming too early !'

He stifled a slight yawn, then continued after a pause :

'You're lucky, never having seen a première before. . . . *The Blonde Venus* is going to be the theatrical event of the year. Everybody has been talking about it for the past six months. Oh, my dear fellow, the music ! And the verve ! . . . Bordenave, who knows what he's doing, has saved it up for the Exhibition.'

Hector listened eagerly. He asked a question.

'And what about Nana, the new star, who's going to play Venus – do you know her?'

'Oh, dear, here we go again !' cried Fauchery, throwing up his hands. 'Ever since this morning, everybody has been asking me about Nana. I've met over a score of people, and it's been Nana here and Nana there. What do they expect me to tell them? Do I know all the girls in Paris? . . . Nana is something invented by Bordenave. I don't need to say more than that.'

He calmed down. But the emptiness of the auditorium, the half-light of the chandelier, the church-like gloom full of whispering voices and banging doors irritated him.

'Oh, no,' he said all of a sudden, 'this place makes you feel too old. I'm not staying here. We may find Bordenave downstairs. He'll give us some details.'

Downstairs, in the big marble-paved vestibule where the ticket-barrier was installed, the audience was beginning to arrive. Through the three open gates could be seen the vibrant life of the swarming boulevards, ablaze with light in the fine April night. The rumbling of carriages stopped short, doors slammed, and people entered in little groups, waiting at the barrier before climbing the double staircase behind, where the women, their hips swaying, lingered for a moment. In the crude gaslight, on the pale bare walls skimpily decor-

ated in the Empire style to form a peristyle like a cardboard temple, tall yellow posters were boldly displayed with Nana's name in thick black letters.

Some gentlemen were reading them, as if accosted on the way; others were standing about chatting together, blocking the doors; while near the box-office a thickset man with a broad, clean-shaven face was curtly rebuffing people who were pressing him to let them have seats.

'There's Bordenave,' said Fauchery, coming down the staircase.

But the manager had already stopped him.

'You're a fine one!' he called out to him from a distance. 'So that's how you write an article for me. . . . I opened the *Figaro* this morning. Not a thing.'

'Now wait a minute!' replied Fauchery. 'I have to know this Nana of yours before I can talk about her. . . . Besides, I haven't promised anything.'

Then to cut the conversation short, he introduced his cousin, Monsieur Hector de la Faloise, a young man who had come to Paris to complete his education. The manager weighed up the young man with a single glance, but Hector examined him with a certain emotion. So this was Bordenave, the notorious exhibitor of women who treated them like a slave-driver, the man who was forever hatching some new advertising scheme, shouting, spitting, slapping his thighs, a shameless character with a coarse sense of humour. Hector thought it encumbent on him to make a polite remark.

'Your theatre . . .' he began in a piping voice.

Bordenave calmly interrupted him with a vulgar correction, like a man who prefers to call a spade a spade.

'You mean my brothel.'

Fauchery promptly gave an approving laugh, while la Faloise stood there with his compliment stuck in his throat, deeply shocked, but trying to look as if he appreciated the remark. The manager had rushed away to shake hands with a theatre critic whose notices had considerable influence. When he came back, la Faloise had almost recovered his composure. He was afraid of being dismissed as a provincial booby if he showed how taken aback he was.

'They tell me,' he started again, determined to find something to say, 'that Nana has a delightful voice.'

'That girl?' exclaimed the manager, shrugging his shoulders. 'Why, she's tone-deaf!'

The young man hurriedly added:

'At any rate, she's an excellent actress.'

'Her? ... She's a great lump of a girl! She doesn't know what to do with her hands and feet.'

La Faloise blushed slightly. He no longer knew what to say. He stammered:

'I wouldn't have missed this première for anything. I knew that your theatre ...'

'You mean my brothel,' Bordenave interrupted once more, with the cold obstinacy of a man of conviction.

Meanwhile Fauchery, who was perfectly collected, was looking at the women coming in. He came to his cousin's rescue when he saw him gaping foolishly, not knowing whether to laugh or lose his temper.

'Oh, do try to please Bordenave, and call his theatre whatever he likes, seeing that it amuses him. ... As for you, my dear fellow, don't you try to fool us. If this Nana of yours can't sing or act, you'll have a flop on your hands, that's all. To tell the truth, that's what I'm afraid is going to happen.'

'A flop? A flop!' shouted the manager, turning red in the face. 'Does a woman need to be able to sing and act? Don't be stupid, my boy. ... Nana has something else, dammit, and something that takes the place of everything else. I scented it out, and it smells damnably strong in her, or else I've lost my sense of smell. ... You'll see, you'll see; she'll only have to appear and the whole audience will be hanging out their tongues.'

He had held up his big hands which were trembling with enthusiasm, and now, having relieved his feelings, he lowered his voice and muttered to himself:

'Yes, she'll go far! Oh, yes, so help me, she'll go far! ... A skin! Oh, what a skin she's got!'

Then, as Fauchery began questioning him, he consented to go into details, using such crude expressions that Hector de la Faloise was embarrassed. He had got to know Nana and

decided to put her on the stage. As it happened, he had been looking for a Venus at the time. He wasn't the sort who let a woman encumber him for any length of time; he preferred to let the public have the benefit of her straight away. But he had a lot of trouble on his hands at his theatre, which had been turned topsy-turvy by the girl's arrival. Rose Mignon, his star, a good actress and an adorable singer, was daily threatening to leave him in the lurch, for she was furious and guessed that she had a rival. As for the bill, good God, what a rumpus that had caused! In the end he had decided to print the names of the two actresses in the same-sized type. He didn't like being pestered. Whenever one of his little women, as he called them – Simonne or Clarisse, for instance – didn't toe the line, he just gave her a kick in the arse. Otherwise life was impossible. After all, he sold them, and he knew what the little tarts were worth!

'Look,' he said, breaking off short. 'There's Mignon and Steiner. They're always together. You know, Steiner's getting sick of Rose; that's why the husband never lets him out of his sight, in case he does a bunk.'

On the pavement outside, the row of gas-jets blazing along the cornice of the theatre cast a patch of brilliant light. Two small trees stood out sharply, a crude green colour, and a column shone white, so brightly lit that you could read the notices on it at a distance, as if in broad daylight, while the dense night of the boulevard beyond was dotted with lights above the vague mass of an ever-moving crowd. Many men were not entering the theatre straight away, but staying outside to chat while finishing their cigars under the line of gas-jets, which gave their faces a livid pallor and silhouetted their short black shadows on the asphalt.

Mignon, a very tall, broad-shouldered fellow, with the square-shaped head of a strong man at a fair, was pushing his way through the midst of the groups, dragging on his arm the banker Steiner, a small pot-bellied man with a round face framed in a beard which was turning grey.

'Well,' said Bordenave to the banker, 'you met her yesterday in my office.'

'Ah! So that was her, was it?' exclaimed Steiner. 'I

thought as much. Only I was coming out as she was going in, and I scarcely caught a glimpse of her.'

Mignon was listening with half-closed eyelids, and nervously twisting a big diamond ring round his finger. He had understood that it was Nana they were talking about. Then, as Bordenave was drawing a portrait of his new actress which lit a flame in the eyes of the banker, he ended up by joining in the conversation.

'Oh, come now, my dear fellow, she's a slut! The public will soon send her packing. Steiner, old man, you know that my wife is waiting for you in her dressing-room.'

He wanted to take possession of him again. But Steiner refused to leave Bordenave. In front of them a stream of people was crowding around the box-office, and there was a din of voices, in the midst of which Nana's name sounded with all the lilting vivacity of its two syllables. The men standing in front of the playbills spelt it out aloud; others uttered it in a questioning tone as they passed; while the women, at once uneasy and smiling, repeated it softly with an air of surprise. Nobody knew Nana. Where had Nana come from? And stories and jokes, whispered from ear to ear, went the rounds. The name was a caress in itself, a pet name which rolled easily off every tongue. Merely by pronouncing it thus, the crowd worked itself into a state of good-natured gaiety. A fever of curiosity urged it forward, that Parisian curiosity which is as violent as a fit of brain-fever. Everyone wanted to see Nana. A lady had the flounce of her dress torn off; a man lost his hat.

'Oh, I've had enough of your questions!' shouted Bordenave, whom a score of men were besieging with queries. 'You'll see her for yourselves. ... I'm off: they need me backstage.'

He disappeared, delighted at having fired his public. Mignon shrugged his shoulders, reminding Steiner that Rose was waiting for him, to show him the costume she was going to wear in the first act.

'Why, there's Lucy out there, getting down from her carriage,' said la Faloise to Fauchery.

It was indeed Lucy Stewart, an ugly little woman of about

24

forty, with a long neck, a thin, drawn face and a heavy mouth, but so lively and gracious, that she was really very charming. She had brought along Caroline Héquet and her mother – Caroline a woman of a cold type of beauty, the mother a dignified creature who looked as if she were stuffed.

'Come along with us : I've kept a place for you,' she said to Fauchery.

'Not on your life ! I wouldn't see a thing !' he replied. 'I prefer being in the stalls, and I've got a seat there.'

Lucy looked cross. Didn't he dare show himself in her company? Then, suddenly calming down, she jumped to another topic.

'Why didn't you tell me that you knew Nana?'

'Nana? I've never set eyes on her.'

'Honestly? Somebody assured me you'd slept with her.'

Standing in front of them, Mignon put his finger to his lips, motioning them to be quiet. And when Lucy questioned him, he pointed out a young man who was passing, and murmured :

'Nana's fancy man.'

Everyone looked at him. He was a good-looking fellow. Fauchery recognized him : it was Daguenet, a young man who had thrown away three hundred thousand francs on women, and was now playing the stock market in order to treat them to occasional bouquets and dinners. Lucy thought he had beautiful eyes.

'Ah, there's Blanche !' she cried 'It was she who told me you'd slept with Nana.'

Blanche de Sivry, a plump fair-haired girl, whose pretty face was getting pudgy, had just arrived with a thin, well-groomed, very distinguished man.

'The Comte Xavier de Vandeuvres,' Fauchery whispered in la Faloise's ear.

The Count and the journalist shook hands, while Blanche and Lucy started a lively argument. One of them in blue, the other in pink, they blocked the way with their flounced skirts, and Nana's name kept recurring so shrilly in their conversation that people started listening to them. The Comte de Vandeuvres carried Blanche off. But by this time Nana's

name was echoing more loudly than ever in every corner of the foyer, in the midst of a curiosity sharpened by delay. Why didn't the show begin? The men pulled out their watches, late-comers jumped out of their carriages before they had stopped, and groups of people came in from the pavement, where the passers-by, slowly crossing the now empty gas-lit area, craned their necks to see inside the theatre. A street-urchin came up whistling, planted himself before a playbill at the door, and cried out: 'Hey, Nana!' in a tipsy voice, before slouching away, shuffling his old boots. This raised a laugh. Gentlemen of unimpeachable appearance repeated : 'Nana! Hey, Nana!' People were crushed together, a quarrel broke out at the box-office, and there was a growing clamour caused by the hum of voices calling for Nana, demanding Nana in one of those accesses of silly facetiousness and crude sensuality which take hold of crowds.

Then, above the din, the bell announcing the rising of the curtain sounded. Shouts of 'They've rung, they've rung!' reached the boulevard; and there followed a stampede, with everyone wanting to go in, while the theatre attendants increased their forces. Mignon, looking rather uneasy, finally managed to get hold of Steiner again, who had not been to see Rose's costume after all. At the very first sound of the bell, la Faloise had pushed his way through the crowd, pulling Fauchery with him, so as not to miss the opening scene. All this eagerness on the part of the public irritated Lucy Stewart. What brutes these people were, pushing women about like that! She hung back, with Caroline Héquet and her mother. The foyer was now empty, while in the background the long-drawn rumble of the boulevard could still be heard.

'It's not as if these shows of theirs were always amusing!' Lucy kept repeating as she climbed the stairs.

In the auditorium Fauchery and la Faloise, standing in front of their stalls, were gazing about them again. By now the house was resplendent. Tall jets of gas lit the great crystal chandelier with a blaze of pink and yellow flames, which rained down a stream of light from gallery to pit. The scarlet velvets of the seats were shot with tints of lake, while all the

gilding shone brightly, the pale green decorations softening its brilliance beneath the crude paintings on the ceiling. The footlights were turned up, and with a sudden flood of light set fire to the curtain, whose heavy crimson drapery had all the richness of a fairy-tale palace, and contrasted sharply with the shabbiness of the proscenium arch, where cracks showed the plaster under the gilding. It was already warm in the theatre. At their music-stands the orchestra were tuning their instruments with a delicate trilling of flutes, a muffled tooting of horns and a lilting sound of violins, which rose above the increasing uproar of voices. All the spectators were talking, jostling and settling down in a general assault on the seats; and the crush in the passage was now so great that every door into the house was laboriously admitting an inexhaustible flood of people. There were signals, rustlings of fabrics, an endless procession of skirts and coiffures, broken now and then by the black of a dress-coat or a frock-coat. All the same, the rows of seats were gradually filling up, while here and there a light-coloured dress stood out from its surroundings, or a head with a delicate profile bent forward under its chignon, in which there flashed the lightning of a jewel. In one of the boxes a bare shoulder gleamed like snowy silk. Other women sat languidly fanning themselves, following with their gaze the movements of the crowd, while young gentlemen, standing up in the stalls, their waistcoats open, gardenias in their button-holes, pointed their opera-glasses with gloved fingertips.

The two cousins began looking for faces they knew. Mignon and Steiner were together in a ground-floor box, sitting side by side with their arms resting on the velvet balustrade. Blanche de Sivry seemed to be in sole possession of a stage-box on the level of the stalls. But la Faloise fixed his attention on Daguenet, who was in a stall two rows in front of his own. Next to him a very young man, seventeen years old at the most, who looked as if he were playing truant from school, was gazing around with big, beautiful, innocent eyes. Fauchery smiled as he looked at him.

'Who is that lady in the dress circle?' la Faloise asked suddenly. 'The one with a girl in blue beside her.'

He pointed out a stout, tight-laced woman whose once fair hair had turned white and been dyed yellow, and whose round face, heavily rouged, looked puffy under a rain of little childish curls.

'That's Gaga,' was Fauchery's only reply, and as this name seemed to astonish his cousin, he added :

'You don't know Gaga? She was the delight of the early years of Louis-Philippe's reign. Nowadays she drags her daughter about with her wherever she goes.'

La Faloise never once glanced at the girl. The sight of Gaga moved him, and he did not take his eyes off her. He found her still very attractive, but he did not dare to say so.

Meanwhile the conductor raised his violin-bow and the orchestra launched into the overture. People were still coming in; the bustle and noise were on the increase. Among that unchanging audience peculiar to first nights, groups of old acquaintances gathered welcoming one another warmly. Old first-nighters, hat on head and perfectly at ease, kept exchanging greetings. The whole of Paris was there, the Paris of letters, of finance and of pleasure. There were a great many journalists, a few authors, a number of speculators, and more courtesans than respectable women. It was a singularly mixed world, composed of all the talents, and tarnished by all the vices, a world where the same fatigue and the same fever appeared in every face. Fauchery, in replying to his cousin's questions, showed him the boxes reserved for the newspapers and the clubs, and then named the dramatic critics – among them a lean, dried-up individual, with thin spiteful lips, and, above all, a stout fellow with a good-natured expression, lolling against the shoulder of his neighbour, a young lady over whom he brooded with a tender, fatherly eye.

But he broke off when he saw la Faloise bow to some people in a box facing the stage. He appeared surprised.

'What !' he said. 'You know the Comte Muffat de Beuville?'

'Oh, I've known him for a long time,' replied Hector. 'The Muffats used to have an estate near ours. I often go to their

house. The Count's with his wife and his father-in-law, the Marquis de Chouard.'

And with some vanity – for he was flattered by his cousin's astonishment – he entered into particulars : the Marquis was a Councillor of State and the Count had just been appointed Chamberlain to the Empress. Fauchery, who had picked up his opera-glasses, looked at the Countess, a plump brunette with white skin and fine dark eyes.

'You must introduce me to them in one of the intervals,' he said at last. 'I've already met the Count, but I'd like to go to their Tuesday receptions.'

Loud cries of 'Hush' came from the upper circle and the gallery. The overture had begun, but people were still coming in. Late arrivals were forcing whole rows of spectators to rise, the doors of boxes were banging, loud voices could be heard arguing in the passage. And the sound of conversations continued, a sound similar to the twittering of a host of talkative sparrows at the close of day. The auditorium was a confused mass of people, heads and arms moving about, as some people sat down and tried to make themselves comfortable, while the others insisted on remaining standing so as to have a final look round. A shout of 'Sit down, sit down !' came from the dark depths of the pit. A shiver of expectation went round the house : at last they were going to see this famous Nana, whom Paris had been talking about for a whole week !

Little by little, however, the buzz of talk died down among occasional fresh outbursts of loud speech. And in the midst of this languid murmur, these dwindling sighs, the orchestra struck up the lively notes of a waltz with a cheeky rhythm full of roguish laughter. The audience were titillated, and began smiling. Then the claque in the front rows of the pit broke into frantic applause. The curtain was going up.

'Hullo !' exclaimed la Faloise, who was still talking. 'There's a man with Lucy.'

He was looking at the stage-box on the second tier to his right, the front of which was occupied by Caroline and Lucy. At the back of this box could be seen the worthy countenance of Caroline's mother, and the profile of a tall young man, with a fine head of hair and immaculate attire.

'Do look,' la Faloise insisted. 'There's a man there.'

Fauchery reluctantly levelled his opera-glasses at the stage box. But he turned back straight away.

'Oh, that's Labordette,' he murmured in a casual tone of voice, as if everyone should find that gentleman's presence both natural and immaterial.

Behind the cousins people called out : 'Silence !' They had to stop talking. The audience now froze into immobility, and lines of heads, all erect and attentive, rose from stalls to the gallery. The first act of *The Blonde Venus* was set on Mount Olympus, a cardboard Olympus, with clouds in the wings and Jupiter's throne on the right of the stage. First of all Iris and Ganymede, supported by a troupe of celestial attendants, sang a chorus while they arranged the gods' seats for their council meeting. Once again the pre-arranged applause of the claque broke out all alone; the audience, a little puzzled, sat waiting. But la Faloise had applauded Clarisse Besnus, one of Bordenave's little women, who was playing Iris in a soft blue dress with a great sash in the seven colours of the rainbow tied round her waist.

'You know she has to take her chemise off to put that on,' he said to Fauchery, loud enough to be heard by those around him. 'We tried it this morning. You could see her chemise under her arms and on her back.'

Then a slight shiver ran through the house. Rose Mignon had just come on stage as Diana. Although she had neither the face nor the figure for the part, being thin and dark, with the adorable ugliness of a Parisian street-urchin, she none the less appeared charming, as if she were a satire on the character she was playing. Her first song, an idiotic complaint about Mars, who was getting ready to desert her for Venus, was sung with a chaste reserve so full of spicy implications that the audience warmed up. Her husband and Steiner, sitting side by side, laughed complaisantly and the whole house roared when Prullière, a great favourite with the public, appeared as a general, a comical Mars, sporting a gigantic plume, and dragging along a sword which reached up to his shoulder. He explained that he had had enough of Diana; she was too stuck-up for his liking. Thereupon Diana swore she was going

to keep a sharp eye on him and to take her revenge. The duet ended with a comic yodelling which Prullière carried off very amusingly with the voice of an angry tom-cat. He had about him all the entertaining fatuity of a juvenile lead with a successful love-life, and he rolled his eyes with a roguish air which drew shrill feminine laughter from the boxes.

Then the audience cooled down, for the following scenes struck them as tiresome. Old Bosc, an imbecilic Jupiter, with his head crushed beneath the weight of a huge crown, only just succeeded in raising a smile, when he had a domestic quarrel with Juno on the subject of their cook's accounts. The march-past of the gods – Neptune, Pluto, Minerva and the rest – nearly spoiled everything. The audience grew impatient, an ominous murmur slowly arose, and as the spectators lost interest in the performance they started looking round the house. Lucy was laughing with Labordette; the Comte de Vandeuvres was craning his neck over Blanche's sturdy shoulders, while Fauchery, out of the corner of his eye, took stock of the Muffats – the Count looking very serious, as if he had not understood the jokes, and the Countess smiling vaguely, her eyes lost in reverie. But all of a sudden, in the midst of this lull, the applause of the claque rattled out like a volley of shots. Was it Nana at last? The girl was certainly keeping them waiting.

It was a deputation of mortals whom Ganymede and Iris had brought along, respectable bourgeois who were all deceived husbands. They had come to see the master of the gods to lodge a complaint against Venus, who was firing their wives with excessive ardour. The chorus, in simple doleful tones, broken by eloquent silences, caused great amusement. A neat phrase went round the house : 'The cuckolds' chorus, the cuckolds' chorus', and it caught on, for there was a cry of 'Encore !' The singers had funny faces which everybody thought suited their role, especially that of a fat man which was as round as the moon. Meanwhile Vulcan arrived in a towering rage, asking for his wife, who had run away three days before. The chorus resumed their plaint, calling on Vulcan, the god of cuckolds. Vulcan's part was played by Fontan, a comic actor of a talent at once vulgar and original, with a

swaggering gait of the wildest whimsicality; and he was got up as a village blacksmith, with a fiery red wig and bare arms tattooed with arrow-pierced hearts. A woman's voice exclaimed very loudly : 'Oh, isn't he ugly !' and all the other women laughed and applauded.

Then followed a scene which seemed interminable. Jupiter looked as if he would never finish assembling the Council of the Gods, in order to submit the deceived husbands' request to it. And there was still no sign of Nana ! Were they keeping her for the final curtain? Such a long wait had ended up by annoying the audience. Their murmuring began again.

'It's going badly,' a radiant Mignon said to Steiner. 'They'll give her a fine reception, you'll see !'

At that very moment the clouds at the back of the stage parted, and Venus appeared. Very tall and well-built for her eighteen years, in her goddess's white tunic, and with her long fair hair hanging loosely over her shoulders, Nana came down towards the footlights with quiet self-assurance. Greeting the audience with a laugh, she launched into her big song :

'When Venus roams at eventide . . .'

From the second line on, people looked at each other inquiringly. Was this some joke, some wager on Bordenave's part? Never had anybody heard a more tuneless voice, or one less skilfully controlled. Her manager had been right : she certainly sang like a trombone. What is more, she didn't even know how to deport herself on the stage : she thrust her arms out in front, swaying her whole body in a manner which struck the audience as vulgar and ungraceful. Cries of 'Oh, oh !' were already coming from the pit and the cheap seats, and there was some whistling, when a voice in the stalls suggestive of a moulting cockerel called out enthusiastically :

'Jolly good !'

The whole audience looked to see who had spoken. It was the cherub, the truant from boarding-school, with his magnificent eyes wide open, and his fair complexion flushed at the sight of Nana. When he saw everyone turning towards him, he went very red at the idea that he had spoken aloud with-

32

out meaning to. Daguenet, his neighbour, looked at him smilingly; the public laughed, as if disarmed, and no longer thought of hissing; while the young gentlemen in white gloves, fascinated in their turn by Nana's shapely figure, broke into rapturous applause.

'That's it! Jolly good! Bravo!'

Nana, in the meantime, seeing the audience laughing, began to laugh herself. The general gaiety increased. There was no denying she was an amusing creature, this lovely girl. Her laughter made a delightful little dimple appear in her chin. She stood there waiting, not in the least embarrassed, on good terms with the audience straight away. She herself seemed to be admitting with a wink that she had no talent at all, but that that didn't matter, because she had something else. And then, after a gesture to the conductor which signified: 'Let's go, old fellow!' she began her second verse:

' 'Tis Venus who at midnight passes ...'

It was still the same shrill voice, but now it tickled the audience so deftly in the right place that it sent a slight shiver through them now and then. Nana was still smiling her smile, which lit up her little red mouth and shone in her great bright blue eyes. When she came to certain rather spicy lines, she tilted up her nose with pleasure and her pink nostrils quivered, while a bright flush coloured her cheeks. She still swayed backwards and forwards, for that was all she knew how to do. And the audience no longer considered this ugly; on the contrary, the men pointed their opera-glasses at her. When she came to the end of the verse, her voice failed her completely, and she realized that she would never get through the whole song. So, without getting flustered, she thrust out one hip which was roundly outlined under a flimsy tunic, bent backwards, so that her breasts were shown to good advantage, and stretched out her arms. Applause burst forth on all sides. In the twinkling of an eye she had turned round and was going upstage, revealing the nape of her neck to the audience, a neck on which her reddish hair looked like an animal's fleece. Then the applause became positively frantic.

The rest of the act was not so exciting. Vulcan wanted to

33

box Venus's ears. The gods held a consultation, and decided to go and hold an inquiry on earth before giving the deceived husbands satisfaction. It was then that Diana surprised a tender conversation between Venus and Mars, and vowed that she would not take her eyes off them during the journey. There was also a scene in which Cupid, played by a little twelve-year-old girl, answered every question put to her with 'Yes, mamma! No, mamma!' in a whining voice, with her fingers in her nose. Then Jupiter, with the severity of an angry schoolmaster, shut Cupid up in a dark closet, telling him to conjugate the verb 'I love' twenty times. The finale proved more popular : it was a chorus which both company and orchestra carried off very well. But once the curtain had come down, the claque tried in vain to whip up a call, for the whole audience were already on their feet, making for the doors.

Stamping and jostling, jammed as they were between the rows of seats, they exchanged impressions. One phrase summed up what everyone thought :

'It's idiotic.'

A critic was saying that it needed cutting down to size. Not that the operetta mattered, for people were talking about Nana above all else. Fauchery and la Faloise, who had been among the first to come out, met Steiner and Mignon in the passage outside the stalls. In this gas-lit gut of a place, which was as narrow and low-ceilinged as a gallery in a mine, the atmosphere was suffocating. They stopped for a moment at the foot of the stairs on the right of the theatre, protected by the curve of the banisters. The spectators in the cheap seats were coming downstairs with a continuous tramp of boots; a stream of black dress-coats was passing by, while an attendant was doing her best to protect a chair on which she had piled coats and cloaks from the pushing of the crowd.

'But I know the girl,' cried Steiner, as soon as he caught sight of Fauchery. 'I'm certain I've seen her somewhere ... At the Casino, I think, and she got herself picked up there, she was so drunk.'

'As for me,' said the journalist, 'I don't know where it was; like you, I've certainly met her before ...'

He lowered his voice and added with a laugh :

'At La Tricon's, perhaps.'

'Of course, it *would* be that sort of place,' Mignon declared. He seemed exasperated. 'It's disgusting that the public should give a reception like that to the first slut that comes along. Soon there won't be any decent women left on the stage. ... Yes, I'll end up by forbidding Rose to act any more.'

Fauchery could not help smiling. Meanwhile the downward tramp of boots on the steps went on, and a little man in a cap could be heard drawling :

'Oh, she's got some flesh on her, and no mistake! Something to get your teeth into!'

In the passage two young men, spick and span with curled hair and turned-down collars, were quarrelling. One of them kept repeating the words 'Beastly, beastly!' without giving any reasons; the other replied with the words 'Stunning, stunning!' and also disdained all argument.

La Faloise thought she was very good; he simply ventured to say that she would be better still if she cultivated her voice. Then Steiner, who was no longer listening, seemed to awake with a start. In any case they would have to wait and see. Perhaps everything would go wrong in the following acts. The audience had been very kind, but they hadn't been won over yet. Mignon swore that the show would never finish, and when Fauchery and la Faloise left them to go up to the foyer, he took Steiner's arm, leant hard against his shoulder, and whispered in his ear :

'My dear fellow, you must see my wife's costume in the second act ... it's really spicy!'

Upstairs in the foyer, three crystal chandeliers were burning with a brilliant light. The two cousins hesitated for a moment, for the open glass door revealed a sea of heads filling the whole gallery, with two currents moving in a continuous eddy. They went in all the same. Five or six groups of men, talking loudly and gesticulating, were standing firm in the midst of all the jostling; the others were filing up and down, with their heels tapping on the waxed floor as they turned round. To right and left, between pillars

of mottled marble, women were sitting on benches covered with red velvet, watching the crowd go by with weary eyes, as if the heat had made them languid. In the lofty mirrors behind them you could see the reflections of their chignons. At the end of the room, in front of the bar, a man with a huge paunch was drinking a glass of fruit-syrup.

Fauchery had gone on to the balcony to get some fresh air. La Faloise, who was studying photographs of actresses hung in frames alternating with mirrors between the columns, ended up by following him. They had just extinguished the line of gas-jets on the façade of the theatre. It was dark and cool on the balcony, which they took at first to be unoccupied. There was just a young man, enveloped in shadow, leaning on the stone balustrade in the recess to their right. He was smoking a cigarette, the tip of which shone in the dark. Fauchery recognized Daguenet. They shook hands.

'What are you doing here, my dear fellow?' asked the journalist. 'Hiding yourself in nooks and crannies – you, a man who never leaves the stalls on a first night !'

'But I'm smoking, you see,' replied Daguenet.

Then Fauchery, to embarrass him, went on :

'Well, what do you think of the new actress? ... They're being rather unkind about her in the corridors.'

'Bah !' murmured Daguenet. 'They must be men she's refused to have anything to do with !'

That was his only judgement on Nana's talent. La Faloise leant forward and looked down at the boulevard. On the other side of the street, the windows of a hotel and a club were brightly lit up, while on the pavement a dark mass of customers occupied the tables of the Café de Madrid. Despite the lateness of the hour, crowds were still moving slowly along the boulevard; a throng was continuously emerging from the Passage Jouffroy; people were having to wait five or six minutes before they could cross the road, the string of carriages stretched so far.

'What a bustle ! What a noise !' la Faloise kept repeating, for Paris still astonished him.

A bell rang for some time and the foyer emptied. People

hurried along the corridors. Whole groups of spectators came in after the curtain had gone up, to the annoyance of those who were already in their seats. Everyone settled down again with an expectant face and renewed attention. La Faloise's first glance was for Gaga, and he was dumbfounded to see by her side the tall fair-haired man who had previously been in Lucy's stage-box.

'What did you say that man's name was?' he asked.

Fauchery didn't see him to begin with.

'Oh, yes, it's Labordette,' he said at last, in the same casual tone of voice.

The setting of the second act came as a surprise. It was a cheap dance-hall, the Boule Noire, at carnival time. Masqueraders were singing a round, accompanying the chorus with a tapping of their heels. This glimpse of low life, which nobody had expected, caused so much amusement that the house encored the round. It was to this dance-hall that the group of gods, led astray by Iris, who boasted untruthfully that she knew the Earth well, were to come in order to proceed with their inquiry. They had put on disguises so as to remain incognito. Jupiter came on stage as King Dagobert, with his breeches inside out and a huge tin crown on his head. Phoebus appeared as the notorious postilion of Longjumeau, and Minerva as a Normandy nursemaid. Loud bursts of merriment greeted Mars, who was dressed in a comical uniform as a Swiss admiral. But the laughter became uproarious when Neptune appeared, clad in a smock with a tall, bulging cap on his head and love-locks glued to his temples. Shuffling along in his slippers, he said in an oily voice :

'What the hell! When you're a good-looker, you've got to let 'em love you!'

There were cries of 'Oh! Oh!' while the ladies raised their fans a little higher. Lucy, in her stage-box, laughed so noisily that Caroline Héquet silenced her with a tap of her fan.

From that moment the operetta was saved, and indeed promised to be a great success. This carnival of the gods, this dragging of Olympus in the mud, this mockery of a whole religion, a whole world of poetry, struck the audience as rich

entertainment. A fever of irreverence took hold of the literary first-nighters : legend was being trampled underfoot, the ancient images were being shattered. Jupiter looked a fool, and Mars was too funny for words. Royalty had been turned into a farce and the Army into a joke. When Jupiter, suddenly falling in love with a little laundress, began dancing a mad can-can, Simonne, who played the part of the laundress, kicked out at the master of the immortals, and addressed him so amusingly as 'My big daddy!' that an explosion of laughter shook the whole house. While they were dancing, Phoebus treated Minerva to salad-bowls of punch, and Neptune sat in state among seven or eight women, who regaled him with cakes. Allusions were seized upon by the audience, indecent meanings were suggested, and inoffensive phrases were given obscene twists by exclamations from the stalls. It was a long time since the theatrical public had wallowed in such irreverent nonsense. It made a change for them.

Nevertheless the plot moved on amid these fooleries. Vulcan, smartly got up in a yellow suit with yellow gloves and a monocle in one eye, was still pursuing Venus, who finally turned up dressed like a fishwife, with a kerchief round her head, and her bosom, covered with big gold trinkets, prominently displayed. Nana was so white and plump, and looked so natural in this part which called for big hips and a loud mouth, that she immediately captivated the whole house. As a result Rose Mignon was forgotten, though she was got up as a delightful baby, with a wickerwork harness and a short muslin frock, and had just sighed out Diana's plaints in a charming voice. The other girl, that hefty wench who slapped her thighs and clucked like a hen, gave off an odour of life, a potent female charm, which intoxicated the audience. From the second act onwards she was allowed to get away with anything. She could hold herself awkwardly, sing every note out of tune, and forget her lines – it didn't matter : she had only to turn round and laugh to raise shouts of applause. When she gave her special thrust of the hip, the stalls lit up, and a glow of passion rose from gallery to gallery, until it reached the gods. So it was a triumph when she

led the dance. She was at home in this final romp : with her hand on her hip, she brought Venus down to street level and sat her in the gutter. And the music seemed made for her plebeian voice – shrill piping music, reminiscent of the Saint-Cloud fair, with squeaks from the clarinets and trills from the little flute.

Two numbers were encored again. The opening waltz, that waltz with the roguish beat, had returned to carry the gods away. Juno, dressed as a farmer's wife, caught Jupiter with his laundress and boxed his ears. Diana, surprising Venus in the act of making an assignation with Mars, lost no time in passing on the hour and place to Vulcan, who cried : 'I have a plan !' The rest of the act was not very clear. The inquiry ended in a final gallop, after which Jupiter, out of breath, streaming with perspiration, and minus his crown, declared that the women on earth were delightful and that all the blame lay with the men.

The curtain was falling when a few voices, rising above the cheers, shouted :

'Everybody ! Everybody !'

Thereupon the curtain went up again and the artistes re-appeared hand in hand. In the middle of the line Nana and Rose Mignon stood side by side, curtseying. The audience applauded, the claque cheered. Then, little by little, the house half-emptied.

'I must go and pay my respects to the Comtesse Muffat,' said la Faloise.

'That's right – and you can introduce me,' replied Fauchery. 'We'll come downstairs afterwards.'

But it was no easy matter getting to the first-tier boxes. In the corridor at the top of the stairs there was an absolute crush. To get through the groups of people, you had to make yourself small and elbow your way along. Standing under a copper lamp, in which a gas-jet was burning, the portly critic was passing judgement on the operetta in the presence of an attentive circle. People who were passing mentioned his name to each other in an undertone. He had laughed all the way through the second act, according to the rumour going round the corridors; all the same, he was now being very

severe, and speaking of taste and morals. Farther off, the thin-lipped critic was displaying a benevolence which had an unpleasant after-taste, like curdled milk.

Fauchery glanced into one box after another through the round openings in the doors. Then the Comte de Vandeuvres stopped him with a question, and when he learnt that the two cousins were going to pay their respects to the Muffats, he pointed out Box Seven, from which he had just emerged. Then, bending down, he whispered in the journalist's ear:

'I say, my dear fellow, this Nana – surely she's the girl we saw one evening on the corner of the Rue de Provence?'

'By jove, you're right!' cried Fauchery. 'I knew I'd seen her before!'

La Faloise introduced his cousin to the Comte Muffat de Beuville, who was very cool. But on hearing Fauchery's name the Countess had raised her head, and with a few discreet words she complimented the journalist on his articles in the *Figaro*. Leaning on the velvet-covered ledge in front of her, she turned half round with a pretty movement of the shoulders. They chatted for a short time, and the conversation turned to the Universal Exhibition.

'It's going to be splendid,' said the Count, whose square-cut face with its regular features retained a certain gravity. 'I visited the Champ-de-Mars today, and came away completely wonder-struck.'

'They say it won't be ready in time,' la Faloise ventured to remark. 'There's such a muddle ...'

But the Count interrupted him with his severe voice:

'It will be ready. That's the Emperor's wish.'

Fauchery gaily recounted how one day, when he had gone there in search of a subject for an article, he had come close to being locked in the aquarium, which was then in course of construction. The Countess smiled. Now and then she glanced down into the auditorium, raising an arm covered to the elbow in a white glove, and fanning herself languidly. The house, almost deserted, was in a doze. A few gentlemen in the stalls had opened out newspapers, and were receiving friends, very much at ease, as if they were in their own

houses. Only a well-bred whispering could be heard beneath the great chandelier, the light of which was softened by the fine cloud of dust raised by the exodus at the beginning of the interval. At the doors men had gathered in groups to see the ladies who had remained seated. They stood there motionless for a minute, craning forward and displaying the white expanse of their shirt-fronts.

'We are counting on you next Tuesday,' said the Countess to la Faloise.

She invited Fauchery, who bowed. Not a word was said about the operetta; Nana's name was not so much as mentioned. The Count was so icily dignified that he might have been at a sitting of the Legislative Body. In order to explain their presence that evening, he simply remarked that his father-in-law was fond of the theatre. The door of the box must have been left open, for the Marquis de Chouard, who had gone out in order to leave room for the visitors, stood there with his tall old figure erect, his face soft and white under a broad-brimmed hat, and his misty eyes following the women who passed by.

As soon as the Countess had issued her invitation Fauchery took his leave, feeling that it would be unseemly to talk about the operetta. La Faloise was the last to leave the box. He had just noticed the fair-haired Labordette, comfortably installed in the Comte de Vandeuvres's stage-box, and chatting at very close quarters with Blanche de Sivry.

'Dammit,' he said, catching up with his cousin, 'does that fellow Labordette know every woman in Paris? He's with Blanche now.'

'Of course he knows them all,' replied Fauchery calmly. 'Where have you been all these years, my dear chap?'

The corridor was a little less crowded, and Fauchery was about to go downstairs when Lucy Stewart called him. She was right at the other end, at the door of her stage-box. It was terribly hot inside, she said, and she was occupying the whole width of the corridor, together with Caroline Héquet and her mother, all three nibbling burnt almonds. An attendant was chatting with them in a motherly way. Lucy scolded the journalist; he was a fine fellow, dropping in on other

women, and not even coming to ask if they were thirsty! Then, changing the subject, she said :

'You know, my dear, I think Nana's very good.'

She wanted him to stay in the stage-box for the last act, but he made his escape, promising to meet them at the door afterwards. Downstairs, outside the theatre, Fauchery and la Faloise lit cigarettes. The pavement was blocked by a crowd of men who had come down the theatre steps and were inhaling the fresh air out on the boulevard, where the noise had died down a little.

Meanwhile Mignon had dragged Steiner off to the Café des Variétés. Seeing Nana's success, he had started talking enthusiastically about her, while watching the banker out of the corner of his eye. He knew him well; twice he had helped him to deceive Rose, and then, when the caprice was over, had brought him back to her, faithful and repentant. In the café there were too many customers for comfort crowded round the marble-topped tables. A few were standing up, drinking in a great hurry. The wide mirrors reflected this mass of heads to infinity, and greatly magnified the narrow room with its three chandeliers, its benches covered with imitation leather, and its winding staircase draped with red. Steiner went and sat down at a table in the first room, which opened onto the boulevard, its doors having been removed rather early for the time of year. As Fauchery and la Faloise were passing, the banker stopped them.

'Come and have a beer with us.'

But he was preoccupied by an idea : he wanted to have a bouquet thrown to Nana. At last he called a waiter whom he addressed familiarly as Auguste. Mignon, who was listening, looked at him so sharply that he got flustered, and stammered :

'Two bouquets, Auguste, and deliver them to the attendant. A bouquet for each of the ladies, at the right moment.'

At the other end of the room, her head resting against the frame of a mirror, a girl of eighteen at the most was sitting motionless in front of her empty glass, as if dazed by a long and fruitless wait. Under the natural curls of her beautiful ash-blonde hair, she had a virginal face with velvety eyes

42

which were soft and innocent. She was wearing a dress of faded green silk, and a round hat which had been dented by blows. The cool night air had made her very pale.

'Why, there's Satin,' murmured Fauchery when he caught sight of her.

La Faloise questioned him. Oh, she was just a street-walker, a common tart. But she was so vulgar that people amused themselves by getting her to talk. And the journalist, raising his voice, asked her :

'What are you doing here, Satin?'

'Twiddling my bloody thumbs,' Satin replied calmly, without budging.

The four men were delighted, and started laughing.

Mignon assured them that there was no need to hurry; it took twenty minutes to put up the scenery for the third act. But the two cousins had finished their beer and wanted to go back to the theatre; they were feeling cold. Mignon, left on his own with Steiner, put his elbows on the table and spoke to him quietly.

'It's all agreed, then? We'll go to her house, and I'll introduce you. ... You know, it's between the two of us – my wife needn't know.'

Back in their seats, Fauchery and la Faloise noticed a pretty, quietly dressed woman in the second tier of boxes. She was with a serious-looking gentleman, a chief clerk at the Ministry of the Interior, whom la Faloise knew from having met him at the Muffats'. As for Fauchery, he was under the impression that her name was Madame Robert : a respect-able woman who had only one lover at a time, and that always a respectable man.

But they had to turn round, for Daguenet was smiling at them. Now that Nana had scored a hit, he had come out of hiding; indeed he had just been lording it in the corridors. By his side was the truant schoolboy, who had not left his seat. Nana had plunged him into such a state of stupefied admiration. She was a real woman, he thought to himself; and he blushed scarlet, mechanically pulling his gloves off and on. Then, since his neighbour had spoken of Nana, he ventured to question him.

'Excuse me, Monsieur, but that lady in the operetta – do you know her?'

'Yes, slightly,' murmured Daguenet, with some surprise and hesitation.

'Then you know her address?'

The question, addressed as it was to him, sounded so crude that he felt inclined to respond with a box on the ear.

'No,' he said curtly.

And with that he turned his back. The fair-haired boy realized that he had just been guilty of some breach of good manners. He blushed more than ever and looked bewildered.

The traditional three knocks were given, and in the midst of the returning throng, attendants laden with cloaks and overcoats made determined attempts to return people's things. The claque applauded the scenery, which represented a grotto on Mount Etna, hollowed out of a silver mine and glittering like newly minted coins. In the background Vulcan's forge glowed like a setting sun. As early as the second scene Diana came to an understanding with the god, who was to pretend to go on a journey, so as to leave the way clear for Venus and Mars. He had scarcely left Diana alone before Venus appeared. A shiver went round the house. Nana was naked, flaunting her nakedness with a cool audacity, sure of the sovereign power of her flesh. She was wearing nothing but a veil of gauze; and her round shoulders, her Amazon breasts, the rosy points of which stood up as stiff and straight as spears, her broad hips, which swayed to and fro voluptuously, her thighs – the thighs of a buxom blonde – her whole body, in fact, could be divined, indeed clearly discerned, in all its foamlike whiteness, beneath the filmy fabric. This was Venus rising from the waves, with no veil save her tresses. And when Nana raised her arms, the golden hairs in her arm-pits could be seen in the glare of the footlights. There was no applause. Nobody laughed any more. The men's faces were tense and serious, their nostrils narrowed, their mouths prickly and parched. A wind seemed to have passed over the audience, a soft wind laden with hidden menace. All of a sudden, in the good-natured child the woman stood revealed, a disturbing woman with all the im-

pulsive madness of her sex, opening the gates of the unknown world of desire. Nana was still smiling, but with the deadly smile of a man-eater.

'God!' was all that Fauchery said to la Faloise.

In the meantime Mars, in his plumed helmet, came hurrying to the trysting-place, and found himself between the two goddesses. There followed a scene which Prullière played with subtlety. Caressed by Diana, who wanted to make a final attack on his feelings before handing him over to Vulcan, and cajoled by Venus, who was excited by the presence of her rival, he gave himself up to these tender delights with the blissful expression of a fighting cock. Finally a grand trio brought the scene to a close, and it was then that an attendant appeared in Lucy Stewart's box and threw two huge bouquets of white lilac onto the stage. The audience applauded, and Nana and Rose Mignon bowed, while Prullière picked up the bouquets. A good many people in the stalls turned smilingly towards the ground-floor box, occupied by Steiner and Mignon. The banker's face was flushed, and his chin was twitching convulsively, as if he had an obstruction in his throat.

What followed gripped the audience completely. Diana had gone off in a rage, and immediately afterwards Venus, sitting on a mossy bank, called Mars to her. Never before had any theatre dared to put on such a passionate seduction scene. With her arms around Prullière's neck, Nana was drawing him towards her when Fontan, with comical gestures of rage and an exaggerated imitation of the face of an outraged husband surprising his wife *in flagrante delicto*, appeared at the back of the grotto. He was holding the famous net with the iron meshes. For a moment he swung it, like a fisherman about to make a cast: and then, by an ingenious trick, Venus and Mars were caught in the snare, the net wrapping itself round them and holding them motionless in their amorous posture.

A murmur arose, swelling like a growing sigh. There was some hand-clapping and every pair of opera-glasses was fixed on Venus. Little by little Nana had taken possession of the audience, and now every man was under her spell. A wave

of lust was flowing from her as from a bitch on heat, and it had spread further and further until it filled the whole house. Now her slightest movements fanned the flame of desire, and with a twitch of her little finger she could stir men's flesh. Backs arched and quivered as if unseen violin-bows had been drawn across their muscles; and on the nape of many a neck the down stirred in the hot, stray breath from some woman's lips. In front of him Fauchery saw the truant school-boy half lifted out of his seat by passion. Curiosity led him to look at the Comte de Vandeuvres, who was very pale, with his lips pursed; at fat Steiner, whose face was apoplectic; at Labordette, ogling away with the astonished air of a horse-dealer admiring a perfectly proportioned mare; and at Daguenet, whose ears were blood-red and twitching with pleasure. Then a sudden instinct made him glance behind him, and he was astounded at what he saw in the Muffats' box. Behind the Countess, who looked pale and serious, the Count was sitting bolt upright, his mouth agape and his face mottled with red, while beside him, in the shadows, the misty eyes of the Marquis de Chouard had become cat-like, phosphorescent, speckled with gold. The audience were suffocating, their very hair growing heavy on their perspiring heads. In the three hours they had been there, their breath had filled the atmosphere with a hot human scent. In the flickering glare of the gaslight, the cloud of dust in the air had grown denser as it hung motionless beneath the chandelier. The whole house seemed to be swaying, seized by a fit of giddiness in its fatigue and excitement, and possessed by those drowsy midnight urges which fumble between the sheets. And Nana, in front of this fascinated audience, these fifteen hundred human beings crowded together and overwhelmed by the nervous exhaustion which comes towards the end of a performance, remained victorious by virtue of her marble flesh, and that sex of hers which was powerful enough to destroy this whole assembly and remain unaffected in return.

The operetta drew to a close. In answer to Vulcan's triumphant summons, all the gods filed past the lovers with ohs and ahs of stupefaction and amusement. Jupiter said : 'I think it is frivolous of you, my son, to summon us to see such

46

a sight as this.' Then a reaction took place in favour of Venus. The chorus of cuckolds was ushered in once more by Iris, and begged the master of the gods not to grant their request, for since their wives had taken to staying at home, life had become impossible for the men; the latter preferred being deceived and happy, which was the moral of the operetta. So Venus was set free, Vulcan obtained a legal separation from her, Mars was reconciled with Diana, and Jupiter, for the sake of domestic peace, packed off his little laundress into a constellation. And finally Cupid was released from his dungeon, where, instead of conjugating the verb 'to love', he had been busy making paper darts. The curtain fell on an apotheosis, with the cuckolds' chorus on their knees singing a hymn of gratitude to Venus, who stood there smiling in all the splendour of her sovereign nudity.

The audience, already on their feet, started making for the exits. The authors' names were given, and there were two curtain-calls in the midst of thunderous applause and frenzied shouts of 'Nana! Nana!' Then, even before the house was empty, darkness fell. The footlights went out, the chandelier was turned down, long strips of grey canvas slipped from the stage-boxes and swathed the gilt decorations on the galleries; and the auditorium, lately so full of heat and noise, suddenly fell into a heavy sleep, while a musty, dusty smell began to rise into the air. In the front of her box, very erect and muffled up in furs, stood the Comtesse Muffat; and as she waited for the crowd to disperse, she gazed into the darkness.

In the corridors people were jostling the attendants, who were losing their heads among the tumbled heaps of clothing. Fauchery and la Faloise had hurried out to see everyone leaving. Men were lining the foyer, while two endless rows of people came slowly down the double staircase, in a compact, regular formation. Steiner, following in Mignon's wake, had been among the first to leave. The Comte de Vandeuvres took his departure with Blanche de Sivry on his arm. For a moment or two Gaga and her daughter seemed at a loss, but Labordette hurried off to find them a carriage, and gallantly closed the door on them. Nobody saw Daguenet go by. As the

truant schoolboy, determined to wait at the stage-door, was running with burning cheeks towards the Passage des Panoramas, the gate of which he found closed, Satin, standing on the pavement, moved forward and brushed him with her skirts; but in his despair he pushed her away roughly and vanished into the crowd, tears of impotent desire in his eyes. Men coming out of the theatre were lighting cigars and walking off, humming : 'When Venus roams at eventide . . .' Satin had gone back in front of the Café des Variétés, where Auguste let her eat the sugar left over from the customers' orders. A stout man, who had come out in a very excited condition, finally took her off into the shadows of the boulevard, which was gradually going to sleep.

Yet people were still coming downstairs. La Faloise was waiting for Clarisse. Fauchery had promised to meet Lucy Stewart, with Caroline Héquet and her mother. They finally arrived, and were taking up a whole corner of the foyer, laughing very loudly, when the Muffats passed by with icy expressions. Bordenave had just appeared through a little door, and was exacting the promise of an article from Fauchery. He was dripping with perspiration, his face flushed as if he were drunk with success.

'You're good for two hundred nights,' la Faloise said to him politely. 'The whole of Paris is going to come to your theatre.'

But Bordenave took umbrage at this remark; and indicating with a jerk of his chin the audience filling the foyer, a herd of men with parched lips and ardent eyes, still burning from the enjoyment of Nana, he snarled :

'You mean my brothel, you stubborn idiot !'

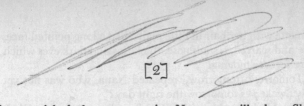

[2]

At ten o'clock the next morning Nana was still asleep. She occupied the second floor of a large new house on the Boulevard Haussmann, whose landlord let flats to single ladies so that they should suffer the first inconveniences. A rich merchant from Moscow, who had come to spend a winter in Paris, had installed her there, paying six months' rent in advance. The rooms were too big for her, and had never been completely furnished. The vulgar luxury of consoles and gilded chairs formed a sharp contrast with junk-shop furniture such as mahogany tables and zinc candelabra trying to pass as Florentine bronze. All this smacked of the courtesan deserted too soon by her first serious protector and falling back on shifty lovers, and suggested a bad start handicapped by refusals of credit and threats of eviction.

Nana was sleeping on her stomach, hugging in her bare arms a pillow in which she had buried a face pale with sleep. The bedroom and the dressing-room were the only two rooms which had been properly furnished by a local upholsterer. A ray of light filtering under a curtain revealed the rosewood bedstead, and the hangings and seats of figured damask with a pattern of big blue flowers on a grey ground. In the humid atmosphere of this bedroom Nana suddenly awoke with a start, as if surprised to find an empty place beside her. She looked at the other pillow lying next to hers; there was the hollow of a human head among its flounces which was still warm. Groping with one hand, she pressed an electric bell by the bed.

'He's gone, then?' she asked the maid who came in.

'Yes, Madame, Monsieur Paul went off less than ten minutes ago. ... As Madame was tired, he didn't want to wake her. But he asked me to tell Madame that he'd come tomorrow.'

While she was speaking, Zoé, the maid, was opening the Venetian shutters, and the daylight poured in. Zoé, a dark

brunette with her hair in little plaits, had a long pointed face, pale and scarred, a snub nose, thick lips and dark eyes which were forever moving.

'Tomorrow, tomorrow,' repeated Nana, who was not yet fully awake; 'is tomorrow the right day?'

'Yes, Madame, Monsieur Paul has always come on Wednesday.'

'No, I remember now!' exclaimed the young woman, sitting up. 'Everything's changed. I wanted to tell him so this morning. . . . He'd clash with my dago, and then we'd be in a pretty pickle!'

'Madame didn't warn me; I couldn't know,' murmured Zoé. 'When Madame changes her days, she'll be well advised to tell me, so that I may know . . . Then the old skinflint isn't coming on Tuesday any more?'

'The old skinflint' and 'the dago' were the nicknames they applied between themselves, without any humorous intent, to their two paying visitors, one of whom was a thrifty tradesman from the Faubourg Saint-Denis, while the other was a Wallachian, a self-styled count, whose money, always paid at irregular intervals, never looked as if it had been honestly come by. Daguenet had reserved for himself the mornings after the old skinflint's visits, and as the tradesman had to be home by eight o'clock the young man would watch for his departure from Zoé's kitchen, and then take his place, which was still quite warm, till ten o'clock. Then he too would go about his business. Nana and he considered this a very convenient arrangement.

'Never mind!' said Nana; 'I'll write to him this afternoon. And if he doesn't get my letter, then tomorrow you'll stop him coming in.'

In the meantime Zoé was walking quietly around the room, talking about the previous night's triumph. Madame had shown such talent, she sang so well! Oh, Madame didn't need to worry any more!

Nana, propping herself up on her pillows, only shook her head in reply. Her nightdress had slipped down, and her hair, unfastened and tousled, flowed over her shoulders.

'I suppose you're right,' she murmured thoughtfully: 'but

how am I going to hold out? I'm going to have all sorts of trouble today. ... Now, let's see, has the concierge been up yet this morning?'

Then the two women put their heads together for a serious talk. Nana owed three quarters' rent, and the landlord was talking of seizing the furniture. Then, too, there was a positive landslide of creditors, with a livery-stable keeper, a draper, a dressmaker, a coal merchant, and others besides, who came every day and installed themselves on a bench in the hall. The coal merchant especially was a dreadful fellow who shouted on the stairs. But Nana's greatest cause of distress was her little Louis, a child she had had when she was sixteen, and who had been left in the care of a nurse in a village near Rambouillet. This woman was demanding three hundred francs before she would agree to give little Louis back. Since her last visit to the child Nana had been seized with a fit of maternal love, and was desperate at the thought of being unable to carry out a plan which had now become an obsession with her. This was to pay off the nurse and to place the boy with her aunt, Madame Lerat, at Les Batignolles, where she could go and see him as often as she liked.

Meanwhile the maid kept hinting that her mistress ought to have told the old skinflint of her needs.

'Oh, I told him everything,' cried Nana, 'and he replied that he had too many liabilities. He won't go beyond his thousand francs a month. ... The dago's broke just now; I think he's lost some money at the tables. ... As for my poor Mimi, he seems to be in need of a loan himself; a fall in share prices has cleaned him out, and he can't even afford to bring me flowers any more.'

She was referring to Daguenet. In the unconstraint of her awakening she had no secrets from Zoé, and the latter, accustomed to such confidences, received them with respectful sympathy. Since Madame deigned to speak to her of her affairs, she would make so bold as to say what she thought. For one thing, she was very fond of Madame; she had left Madame Blanche for the express purpose of entering her service, and Heaven knew that Madame Blanche was straining every nerve to get her back! There was no lack of situations,

and people knew her well enough, but she would have stayed with Madame even in straitened circumstances, because she believed in Madame's future. And she concluded by spelling out her advice. When you were young, you often did silly things. But now it was time to look alive, for men only thought of having their fun. Oh, there'd be plenty of them from now on! Madame would only have to say the word to quieten her creditors and find all the money she needed.

'All that doesn't give me three hundred francs,' Nana kept repeating, as she plunged her fingers into the rebellious locks of her chignon. 'I've got to have three hundred francs today, straight away. . . . It's ridiculous not knowing anybody who'll give you three hundred francs.'

She racked her brains. She had intended to send Madame Lerat, whom she was expecting that very morning, to Rambouillet. The thwarting of her whim spoilt the previous night's triumph for her. Among all those men who had cheered her, to think that there wasn't one who would bring her fifteen louis! Besides, you couldn't accept money like that! Heavens, how unlucky she was! And she kept harking back to her baby – he had blue eyes like a cherub's, and he lisped: 'Mama' in such a funny voice that you could die laughing!

At that moment the electric bell at the outer door rang with its urgent, tremulous vibration. Zoé returned, murmuring with a confidential air:

'It's a woman.'

She had seen the woman in question a score of times before, but she always pretended not to recognize her, and to be ignorant of the nature of her relations with ladies in financial difficulties.

'She gave me her name . . . Madame Tricon.'

'La Tricon!' cried Nana. 'Why, that's right! I'd forgotten her. . . . Show her in.'

Zoé ushered in a tall old lady who wore her hair in ringlets and looked like the sort of countess you see haunting lawyers' offices. Then she withdrew, disappearing noiselessly with the lithe serpentine movement with which she usually left a room on the arrival of a gentleman. However, she might just as

well have stayed. La Tricon did not even sit down. There was only a brief exchange of words.

'I've got someone for you today. ... Are you agreeable?'

'Yes. ... How much?'

'Twenty louis.'

'At what time?'

'Three o'clock. ... It's agreed then?'

'It's agreed.'

Straight away La Tricon started talking about the state of the weather. It was dry and pleasant for walking. She still had four or five people to see. And off she went, consulting a small notebook. Left on her own, Nana looked relieved. A slight shiver shook her shoulders, and she snuggled down again in the warm bed, with the laziness of a cat afraid of the cold. Little by little her eyes closed, and she lay smiling at the thought of dressing little Louis prettily the following day; while in the slumber into which she sank once more, the feverish dream of endless applause which she had had all night returned like a sustained accompaniment and gently soothed her weariness.

At eleven o'clock, when Zoé showed Madame Lerat into the room, Nana was still asleep. But she awoke at the noise, and said at once :

'Oh, it's you. ... You must go to Rambouillet today.'

'That's what I've come for,' said her aunt. 'There's a train at twenty past twelve. I've got time to catch it.'

'No, I shan't have the money till later,' replied the young woman, stretching herself and throwing out her chest. 'You can go and have lunch, and then we'll see.'

Zoé brought a dressing-gown.

'The hairdresser's here, Madame,' she murmured.

But Nana did not want to go into the dressing-room. She called out herself :

'Come in, Francis.'

A neatly dressed man pushed open the door and bowed. At that moment Nana was getting out of bed, her bare legs in full view. But she did not hurry, and held out her hands to let Zoé draw on the sleeves of the dressing-gown. As for Francis, very much at ease, and without turning away, he

53

waited with a serious expression on his face. Then, when she had sat down, and he had begun combing her hair, he spoke.

'Perhaps Madame hasn't seen the papers. There's a very nice article in the *Figaro*.'

He had bought a copy of the newspaper. Madame Lerat put on her spectacles and read the article out loud, standing in front of the window. She had the build of a policeman, and she drew herself up to her full height, while her nostrils narrowed whenever she read out a gallant epithet. It was a notice by Fauchery, written immediately after the performance, and it consisted of a couple of glowing columns, full of witty sarcasm about the artiste and of open admiration for the woman.

'Excellent!' Francis kept repeating.

Nana didn't care if she was teased about her voice. He was a nice fellow, that Fauchery, and she wouldn't forget the good turn he had done her. Madame Lerat, after reading the article again, roundly declared that men all had the devil in their shanks; and she refused to explain herself further, satisfied with this spicy comment, which only she understood. Francis finished putting up Nana's hair. He bowed and said:

'I'll keep my eye on the evening papers. Half-past five as usual, eh?'

'Bring me a pot of pomade and a pound of burnt almonds from Boissier's!' Nana called out to him across the drawing-room just as he was shutting the door.

Then the two women, alone once more, remembered that they had not embraced, and they planted big kisses on each other's cheeks. The notice had excited them. Nana, who till now had been half asleep, was again seized with the fever of her triumph. Rose Mignon must be having a bad morning, and no mistake! Her aunt had refused to go to the theatre, because, so she said, powerful emotions played havoc with her stomach, so Nana started describing the events of the evening, growing intoxicated at her own account, as if the applause had rocked Paris to its foundations. Then, breaking off all of a sudden, she asked with a laugh if anyone could have imagined all that when she had been a kid playing in the Rue de la Goutte-d'Or. Madame Lerat shook her head.

No, no one could ever have foreseen it. And she began talking in her turn, assuming a serious expression, and calling Nana her daughter. Wasn't she a second mother to her, since the first had gone to join Papa and Grandmama? Nana was touched and almost burst into tears. But Madame Lerat declared that the past was the past, and a dirty past at that, with things in it which it didn't do to stir up every day. She had left off seeing her niece for a long time, because the rest of the family accused her of ruining herself along with the girl. As if that were possible, for heaven's sake! She didn't ask her for any confidences; she believed that Nana had always lived decently, and now it was enough for her to have found her again in a fine position, and to see that she felt the right way about her son. Virtue and hard work were still the only things that mattered in this world.

'Who is the baby's father?' she asked all of a sudden, her eyes alight with an expression of intense curiosity.

Nana was taken by surprise, and hesitated for a moment.

'A gentleman,' she replied.

'There now!' said her aunt. 'They maintained you'd had him by a stone-mason who was forever beating you. Well, you'll tell me all about it some day; you know how discreet I am! ... And I'll look after him as if he was a prince's son.'

She had given up her business as a florist and was living on her savings, which she had got together sou by sou, till now they brought in an income of six hundred francs a year. Nana promised to rent some pretty little rooms for her, and to give her a hundred francs a month besides. At the mention of this figure, her aunt forgot herself, and shrieked at her niece, urging her to bleed them white, now she had them in her power : by 'them', of course, she meant men. Then they both embraced again, but in the midst of her joy, Nana's face, as she brought the conversation back to little Louis, seemed to cloud over at a sudden recollection.

'Isn't it a bore? – I've got to go out at three o'clock,' she murmured. 'What a nuisance!'

Just then Zoé came in to say that lunch was served. They went into the dining-room, where an old lady was already sitting at the table. She had not taken her hat off, and she

was wearing a dark dress of an indecisive colour somewhere between puce and brown. Nana did not seem surprised to see her there. She simply asked her why she hadn't come into the bedroom.

'I heard voices,' replied the old lady. 'I thought you had company.'

Madame Maloir, a respectable-looking, well-mannered woman, acted as an old friend and companion to Nana. Madame Lerat's presence seemed to worry her at first. Then, when she learnt that she was Nana's aunt, she looked at her with an amiable expression and a faint smile. In the meantime Nana, declaring that she was as hungry as a wolf, threw herself on the radishes, eating them without bread. Madame Lerat, who had turned very formal, refused the radishes, saying that they gave her indigestion. When Zoé brought in some chops, Nana picked at the meat, and contented herself with sucking the bones. Now and then she examined her old friend's hat out of the corner of her eye.

'Is that the new hat I gave you?' she asked.

'Yes, I did it up,' Madame Maloir murmured with her mouth full.

The hat was a fantastic affair, with a deep brim in front, and adorned with a lofty feather. Madame Maloir had a mania for doing up all her hats; she alone knew what suited her, and with a few touches could make a workman's cap out of the most elegant headdress. Nana, who had bought her this particular hat so as not to be ashamed of her any more when she took her out, nearly lost her temper.

'Take it off, at any rate!' she cried.

'No, thank you,' the old lady replied with dignity. 'It doesn't get in my way : I can eat very comfortably with it on.'

After the chops came cauliflower and the remains of a cold chicken. But as each successive dish arrived, Nana made a little face, hesitated, sniffed, and then left her plateful untouched. She finished her lunch with a little jam.

Dessert took a long time. Zoé did not clear the table before serving the coffee; the ladies simply pushed their plates away. They went on talking about the triumph of the previous

evening. Nana kept rolling cigarettes, rocking backwards and forwards on her chair as she smoked them. As Zoé had remained behind and was lounging idly against the sideboard, the company ended up listening to her life-story. She said she was the daughter of a midwife in Bercy who had lost all her money. First of all she had gone into service with a dentist, and after that with an insurance agent, but neither position suited her; and then, not without a certain pride, she listed the names of the ladies she had served as personal maid. Zoé spoke of these ladies as somebody who had held their fate in her hand. Without her it was certain that more than one of them would have had trouble on their hands. For instance, one day when Madame Blanche was with Monsieur Octave, along came an old man. What did Zoé do? She pretended to fall as she was crossing the drawing-room; the old man rushed to her assistance, ran to the kitchen to fetch her a glass of water, and Monsieur Octave made his escape.

'Oh, that's a good one!' said Nana, who was listening to her with affectionate interest, a sort of submissive admiration.

'Now, I've had my troubles ...' began Madame Lerat. And drawing closer to Madame Maloir, she started confiding in her. Both ladies kept sucking lumps of sugar dipped in cognac. But if Madame Maloir listened to other people's secrets, she never revealed anything about herself. People said that she lived on a mysterious allowance in a room which no one had ever entered.

All of a sudden Nana flared up.

'Don't play with the knives, Auntie. ... You know it upsets me.'

Without thinking, Madame Lerat had crossed a couple of knives on the table in front of her. In spite of her outburst, the young woman denied that she was superstitious. Thus spilling salt didn't matter, and even Fridays didn't count; but when it came to knives, she couldn't help it, she knew that that was a sign. There could be no doubt about it, something unpleasant was going to happen to her. She yawned, and then said with an air of profound boredom:

'Two o'clock already. ... I must go. ... What a bore!'

The two old women looked at each other. All three shook their heads without speaking. To be sure, life wasn't all beer and skittles. Nana tilted her chair back again and lit another cigarette, while the others sat pursing their lips discreetly and thinking philosophic thoughts.

'While we're waiting for you, we'll play a game of bezique,' said Madame Maloir after a short silence. 'Does Madame play bezique?'

Certainly Madame Lerat played it, and to perfection. There was no need to bother Zoé, who had vanished; a corner of the table would do quite well. And they folded back the tablecloth over the dirty plates. But as Madame Maloir was going to get the cards out of a drawer in the sideboard, Nana said that, before she sat down to her game, it would be very nice of her if she would write a letter for her. Nana found it a bore writing letters; besides, she wasn't sure of her spelling, while her old friend could turn out the most touching epistles. She ran to fetch some good notepaper from her bedroom. A bottle of cheap ink stood on one of the pieces of furniture, with a rusty pen beside it. The letter was for Daguenet. Madame Maloir herself wrote in her fine Italian hand : 'My darling man'; and she went on to tell him not to come the next day, because 'that was impossible', but added that 'she was with him in her thoughts every moment of the day, whether she was near or far away'.

'And I end up with "A thousand kisses",' she murmured.

Madame Lerat had nodded her approval of every phrase. Her eyes were sparkling; she loved to find herself involved in a love affair. So, putting on a tender expression, and cooing like a dove, she suggested an addition of her own :

'"A thousand kisses on your beautiful eyes."'

'That's it : "A thousand kisses on your beautiful eyes",' Nana repeated, while a blissful look passed over the faces of the two old women.

Zoé was rung for, and told to take the letter down to a commissionaire. As it happened, she was chatting just then to the theatre messenger, who had brought her mistress the daily bulletin, which he had forgotten in the morning. Nana had this man shown in, and told him to deliver the letter to

Daguenet on his way back. Then she asked him a number of questions. Oh yes, Monsieur Bordenave was very pleased; the theatre was already fully booked for a week to come; and Madame had no idea how many people had asked for her address since the morning. When the man had gone, Nana announced that she would only be away for half an hour at the most. If there were any callers, Zoé would make them wait. As she spoke, the electric bell rang. It was a creditor, the livery-stable keeper. He had installed himself on a bench in the hall, and the fellow could twiddle his thumbs there for the rest of the day; there was no hurry.

'Come along now, let's go!' said Nana, still drugged with laziness, and yawning and stretching all over again. 'I ought to be there already.'

Yet she did not budge, but went on watching the play of her aunt, who had just declared four aces. Chin on hand, she became engrossed in the game, but gave a violent start on hearing three o'clock strike.

'Christ!' she exclaimed.

Then Madame Maloir, who was counting the tricks she had won, said encouragingly to her in her soft voice :

'It would be best, dearie, to get your business over with straight away.'

'Be quick about it,' said Madame Lerat, shuffling the cards. 'If you're back here with the money before four o'clock, I can take the half-past four train.'

'Oh, it won't take me long,' she murmured.

Within ten minutes Zoé had helped her on with a dress and a hat. She didn't care if she looked badly dressed. Just as she was about to go downstairs, there was another ring at the door. This time it was the coal merchant. Well, he could keep the livery-stable owner company – that would amuse the two of them. Only, not wanting a scene, she crossed the kitchen and made her escape by the backstairs. She often went that way : all she had to do was lift her skirts so as not to dirty them.

'When a woman's a good mother, anything's excusable,' Madame Maloir said sententiously when she was alone with Madame Lerat.

'Eighty in kings,' replied the latter, with whom cards were an obsession.

And the two of them settled down to an interminable game.

The table had not been cleared. The smell of the meal and the smoke from the cigarettes filled the room with a misty fog. The two women had just started sucking brandy-soaked lumps of sugar again. They had been playing and drinking for twenty minutes when the bell rang for the third time. Zoé bustled into the room and chivvied them just as if they had been her own friends.

'Look here, the bell's ringing again. ... You can't stay here. If a lot of people arrive I'll need the whole flat. ... So off you go, off you go!'

Madame Maloir wanted to finish the game; but Zoé looked as if she were going to pounce on the cards, so she decided to carry them off just as they were, while Madame Lerat moved the brandy bottle, the glasses and the sugar. They both hurried into the kitchen, where they installed themselves at a corner of the table, between the dishcloths, which were spread out to dry, and the bowl, which was still full of dishwater.

'We said three hundred and forty. ... It's your turn.'

'I play hearts.'

When Zoé returned she found them absorbed in their game once more. After a long pause, while Madame Lerat was shuffling the cards, Madame Maloir asked :

'Who was it?'

'Oh, nobody to speak of,' the maid replied casually. 'Just a boy. ... I was going to send him packing, but he's such a pretty lad, without a hair on his chin, and blue eyes, and a girl's face! So I told him to wait after all. He's holding a huge bouquet which he wouldn't let out of his hands. He needs a good hiding – a brat like that who ought to be at school still!'

Madame Lerat went to fetch a jug of water to mix herself a toddy, for the lumps of sugar had made her thirsty. Zoé muttered something to the effect that she wouldn't

mind if she had a toddy too. Her mouth, she said, was as bitter as vinegar.

'So where did you put him?' asked Madame Maloir.

'Oh, in the room at the back, the little one that isn't furnished. ... There's only one of Madame's trunks there and a table. That's where I always put the stingy ones.'

She was pouring sugar into her toddy when the electric bell made her jump. To hell with them! Wouldn't they even let her have a drink in peace? This peal of bells promised well. All the same, she ran to open the door. When she came back, Madame Maloir gave her a questioning glance.

'It's nothing,' she said; 'just a bouquet.'

All three refreshed themselves, nodding to one another before they drank. Then, while Zoé was finally clearing the table, bringing the plates out one by one and putting them in the sink, two other rings followed close after each other. But it was nothing important, for, keeping the kitchen informed of what was going on, she twice repeated her disdainful remark:

'It's nothing – just a bouquet.'

All the same, between two tricks, the old woman laughed to hear her describe the expressions on the faces of the creditors in the hall when the flowers arrived. Madame would find her bouquets on her dressing-table. What a pity it was that they cost such a lot, and that you couldn't get so much as ten sous for them! They were a terrible waste of money.

'Speaking for myself,' said Madame Maloir, 'I'd be quite content if every day I got what the men in Paris spend on flowers for the women.'

'You aren't hard to please, are you!' murmured Madame Lerat. 'Why, if you had just the money spent on the wire round the stalks. ... Sixty in queens, dearie.'

It was ten to four. Zoé could not understand why her mistress was out so long. Usually when Madame was obliged to go out in the afternoon she got it over in no time. But Madame Maloir declared that you couldn't always arrange things just as you wished. There was no denying that life was full of snags, said Madame Lerat. The best course was to

wait. If her niece was late, that must be because her business had delayed her. Besides they couldn't complain : it was nice and comfortable in the kitchen. And as she had no hearts left, Madame Lerat played a diamond.

The bell rang again, and when Zoé reappeared she was flushed with excitement.

'My dears, it's fat Steiner!' she announced from the doorway in a loud whisper. 'I've put *him* in the little sitting-room.'

At this point Madame Maloir explained who the banker was to Madame Lerat, who didn't know the gentleman. Was he getting ready to drop Rose Mignon? Zoé shook her head : she knew a thing or two. But once again she had to go and answer the door.

'Here's a fine kettle of fish!' she murmured when she came back. 'It's the dago! It wasn't any good telling him Madame had gone out : he settled down in the bedroom. We didn't expect him till tonight.'

At a quarter past four Nana still hadn't returned. What could she be up to? It didn't make sense! Two more bouquets were delivered, and Zoé, growing uneasy, looked to see if there was any coffee left. Yes, the two ladies would be glad to finish off the coffee; it would wake them up. Hunched up on their chairs, they were beginning to fall asleep from constantly taking cards from stock with the same gesture. The half-hour struck. There was no doubt about it : something must have happened to Madame. They began whispering to each other.

All of a sudden Madame Maloir forgot herself, and in a deafening voice announced :

'I've got the five hundred! Quint major in trumps!'

'Shut up, for God's sake!' Zoé said angrily. 'What will all those gentlemen think?'

In the silence which followed, broken only by the whispered muttering of the two old women quarrelling over their game, the sound of rapid footsteps came from the backstairs. It was Nana at last. Before she had opened the door, they could hear her panting. She burst in, looking very red in the face. Her skirt, the strings of which must have been broken,

was trailing on the steps, and the flounces had just been dragged through a pool of something unpleasant which had trickled under the door of the first-floor flat, where the maid was a regular slut.

'So here you are – and about time too!' said Madame Lerat, pursing her lips, for she was still vexed at Madame Maloir's five hundred. 'You certainly know how to keep people waiting!'

'Madame really has been rather naughty,' added Zoé.

Nana was already in a bad temper, and these reproaches infuriated her. Was this the way to welcome her after all the trouble she'd had?

'Leave me alone, will you?' she shouted.

'Hush, Madame, there are some people waiting to see you,' said the maid.

Lowering her voice, the young woman stammered breathlessly:

'Do you suppose I've been having a good time? Why, I thought I'd never have done. I'd have liked to see you there in my place! I was so furious, I felt like slapping somebody's face. And then I couldn't find a cab to come home in! Luckily it's only a stone's throw from here, but all the same, I had to run like mad.'

'Have you got the money?' asked the aunt.

'What a question!' retorted Nana.

She sat down on a chair next to the stove, for her legs had failed her after so much running; and without stopping to draw breath, she pulled out of her bodice an envelope containing four hundred-franc notes. They were visible through a large rent she had made with a savage finger in order to make sure of the contents. The three women around her stared at the envelope, a crumpled, dirty piece of coarse paper in her small gloved hands.

It was too late now – Madame Lerat would not be able to go to Rambouillet till the next day. Nana entered into lengthy explanations.

'There are some people waiting to see you,' the maid reminded her.

But Nana flared up again. They could wait: she'd go to

them in a minute, when she'd finished her business. And as her aunt put her hand out for the money, she said :

'Oh, no! Not all of it. Three hundred francs for the nurse, and fifty for your journey and expenses, makes three hundred and fifty. . . . I'm keeping fifty francs for myself.'

The big difficulty was finding change. There weren't ten francs in the house. They didn't even bother to ask Madame Maloir, who never had more than her bus fare on her, and was listening in a disinterested manner. Finally Zoé went out of the room, saying that she would go and look in her box, and she came back with a hundred francs in hundred-sou pieces. They were counted out on a corner of the table, and Madame Lerat took her leave at once, after promising to bring little Louis back with her the following day.

'You say there are some people waiting to see me?' continued Nana, still sitting on the chair and resting.

'Yes, Madame, three people.'

Zoé mentioned the banker first. Nana made a face. Did that fellow Steiner think she was going to let him have his way with her just because he had thrown her a bouquet the night before?

'Besides, I'm fed up,' she declared, 'I shan't see anybody. Go and say you don't expect me back today.'

'Madame will think the matter over, and Madame will see Monsieur Steiner,' Zoé murmured gravely, without budging, annoyed to see her mistress on the point of committing another foolish blunder.

Then she mentioned the Wallachian who was probably getting bored by now in the bedroom. At that, Nana flew into a rage and became more obstinate than ever. She wouldn't see anybody, anybody at all! Who the devil had landed her with such a leech of a man?

'Chuck 'em all out! I'm going to play a game of bezique with Madame Maloir, that's what I'm going to do.'

The bell interrupted her. That was the last straw. Another bore! She forbade Zoé to go and open the door, but the latter had left the kitchen without listening to her. When she reappeared she handed over a couple of visiting cards, saying with an authoritative air :

'I told them Madame was receiving visitors. ... The gentlemen are in the drawing-room.'

Nana had sprung to her feet in a rage, but the names of the Marquis de Chouard and the Comte Muffat de Beuville, which were inscribed on the cards, calmed her down. She remained silent for a moment.

'Who are these two?' she asked at last. 'Do you know them?'

'I know the old one,' replied Zoé, discreetly pursing her lips.

And as her mistress continued to question her with her eyes, she added simply:

'I've seen him somewhere.'

This remark seemed to make up the young woman's mind for her. She regretfully abandoned the kitchen, that snug refuge where you could chat and relax amid the pleasant fumes of the coffee-pot while it was warming on the embers. She left Madame Maloir there playing patience; the old woman still had not taken her hat off, but now, to make herself more comfortable, she had at least undone the strings and tossed them back over her shoulders.

In the dressing-room, where Zoé rapidly helped her on with a tea-gown, Nana revenged herself for the trouble people were causing her by cursing the male sex under her breath. Her foul language saddened the maid, for she saw to her distress that her mistress was not rising above her origins as quickly as she had hoped. She even begged Madame to calm down.

'Why the hell should I?' was Nana's crude retort. 'They're filthy pigs, and they like that sort of thing.'

All the same, she put on her royal airs and graces, as she called them. Just as she was making for the drawing-room, Zoé held her back, and of her own accord introduced the Marquis de Chouard and the Comte Muffat into the dressing-room. It was better like that.

'I am sorry to have kept you waiting, gentlemen,' said the young woman with studied politeness.

The two men bowed and sat down. A blind of embroidered tulle kept the little room in a sort of twilight. It was the most

65

elegant room in the flat, for it was hung with a light-coloured material and contained a large marble-topped dressing-table, a cheval glass framed in inlaid wood, a chaise longue, and some armchairs upholstered in blue satin. On the dressing-table the bouquets of roses, lilacs and hyacinths looked like a crumbling floral ruin. Their perfume was strong and penetrating, while through the humid air, full of the insipid exhalations of the washstand, came occasional whiffs of a more pungent aroma, the scent of a few grains of dry patchouli ground to powder at the bottom of a bowl. And as she curled up, pulling together her dressing-gown, which had been carelessly fastened, Nana gave the impression of having been surprised at her toilet : her skin was still damp, and with a smile on her lips, she looked shy and startled in the midst of her lace frills.

'Madame, you will pardon our insistence, I feel sure,' said the Comte Muffat gravely. 'We have come collecting. Monsieur and I are members of the Charity Committee for this district.'

The Marquis de Chouard hastened to add gallantly :

'When we learnt that a great artiste lived in this house, we resolved to make a point of putting the needs of our poor people before her. Talent never goes without a heart.'

Nana put on a show of modesty. She answered with little nods, thinking fast at the same time. It must have been the old man that had brought the other one : he had such lecherous eyes. And yet the other wasn't to be trusted either : the veins in his temple were swelling fit to burst. He could quite well have come by himself. Now she saw what had happened : the concierge had given them her name, and they had egged one another on, each man for himself.

'Gentlemen, you were quite right to come up,' she said, very graciously.

The electric bell made her start again. Another call, and that Zoé always opening the door ! She went on :

'One is only too happy to be able to give.'

At bottom she was flattered.

'Oh, Madame,' the Marquis continued, 'if only you knew about the poverty here ! Our district has over three thousand

people in it, and yet it's one of the richest parts of Paris. You cannot imagine what such distress is like – children with nothing to eat, women ill, without any help at all, dying of cold ...'

'The poor souls!' cried Nana, deeply moved.

She was so touched that tears filled her beautiful eyes. No longer studying her gestures, she leant forward with a quick movement, and her open dressing-gown revealed her neck, while the bent position of her knees emphasized the rounded contours of her thighs under the thin material. A slight flush tinged the Marquis's grey cheeks. The Comte Muffat, who was on the point of speaking, lowered his eyes. The air in the little room was stifling: it had the close heavy warmth of a greenhouse. The roses were withering, and an intoxicating scent was rising from the patchouli in the bowl.

'One would like to be very rich on occasions like this,' added Nana. 'Still, we each do what we can. Believe me, gentlemen, if I had known ...'

She was on the point of saying something foolish, she was so moved, so she did not finish her sentence. For a moment she was worried at not being able to recall where she had put her fifty francs on changing her dress. But then she remembered: they must be on the corner of her dressing-table under an inverted pot of pomade. As she was getting to her feet, there was a long ring on the bell. Another one! It would never end. The Count and the Marquis had stood up too, and the latter seemed to have pricked up his ears; no doubt he knew that kind of ring. Muffat looked at him; then they averted their eyes. They were embarrassed by each other's presence, and resumed their frigid attitudes, the one square-set and solid with his thick head of hair, the other straightening his thin shoulders, over which fell his locks of scanty white hair.

'Upon my word,' said Nana, bringing the ten big silver coins, and treating the whole thing as a joke, 'I'm going to give you a heavy load, gentlemen. .... It's for the poor ...'

And the adorable dimple in her chin deepened. She assumed her ingenuous childlike expression, as she held the pile of five-franc pieces on her open palm and offered it to the two men, as if she were saying to them: 'Well then, who

wants some?' The Count was the quicker of the two. He took the fifty francs, but left one coin behind, and, in order to retrieve it, had to pick it up off the young woman's skin, a warm supple skin which sent a thrill through him. She was in a gay mood and went on laughing.

'There you are, gentlemen,' she continued. 'Another time I hope to give more.'

The two men no longer had any pretext for staying, and they bowed and went towards the door. But just as they were about to go out, the bell rang again. The Marquis could not conceal a faint smile, while a frown made the Count look graver than before. Nana detained them for a few moments, to give Zoé time to find yet another corner for the newcomer. She did not like callers to meet in her flat, but this time the place must be packed. So she was relieved when she found the drawing-room empty. Had Zoé stuffed them into the cupboards, she wondered?

'Good-bye, gentlemen,' she said, pausing on the threshold of the drawing-room.

She enveloped them in her smile and her limpid glance. The Comte Muffat bowed. Despite his great social experience, he had lost his composure. He needed air, and was leaving with a dizzy feeling produced by that dressing-room, a scent of flowers and female flesh which choked him. And behind his back the Marquis de Chouard, sure that he could not be seen, made so bold as to wink at Nana, his face suddenly distorted and his tongue touching his lips.

When the young woman came back into the dressing-room, where Zoé was waiting for her with letters and visiting-cards, she cried out, laughing louder than ever:

'There's a couple of beggars for you! They've got away with my fifty francs!'

She wasn't annoyed: it struck her as a great joke that *men* should have got money out of *her*. All the same, it was mean of them, because she hadn't a sou left. But at the sight of the cards and letters her bad temper returned. The letters weren't too bad: they were from fellows who, after applauding her the night before, were now making protestations of passion. But the callers could go to the devil.

Zoé had stowed them away all over the place, and she pointed out that the flat was very convenient, since every room opened onto the corridor. It wasn't like Madame Blanche's, where everyone had to go through the drawing-room. Madame Blanche had had a lot of trouble because of that.

'Send them all away,' continued Nana, who was pursuing her own train of thought. 'Starting with the dago.'

'Oh, as for him, Madame, I sent him packing a long time ago,' Zoé said with a smile. 'He only wanted to tell Madame that he couldn't come tonight.'

Nana was overjoyed to hear this news, and clapped her hands. He wasn't coming! What a stroke of luck! She would be free! She heaved a sigh of relief, as if she had been spared the most abominable of tortures. Her first thought was for Daguenet. Poor dear, she had just written to tell him to wait till Thursday! Madame Maloir must write a second letter straight away. But Zoé announced that Madame Maloir had slipped away unnoticed, as she usually did. Whereupon Nana, after talking of sending someone with a message, began to hesitate. She was very tired. A whole night's sleep would be so wonderful. The thought of such a treat finally carried the day. For once she could afford it.

'I'll go to bed as soon as I get back from the theatre,' she murmured gleefully, 'and you mustn't wake me before noon.'

Then, raising her voice:

'Now, get a move on, and shove the others downstairs!'

Zoé did not budge. She would never have dreamt of giving Madame advice, but she usually found a way to give Madame the benefit of her experience when Madame seemed to be letting her temper run away with her.

'Monsieur Steiner as well?' she asked curtly.

'Certainly,' replied Nana. 'Him first of all.'

The maid waited a little longer, to give Madame time for reflection. Wouldn't Madame be proud to get such a rich gentleman away from her rival, Rose Mignon, especially as he was known in all the theatres?

'Hurry up, my dear,' said Nana, who understood her perfectly, 'and tell him I can't stand him.'

But suddenly she changed her mind. The next day she might feel like having him. So she laughed, winked, and with a mischievous gesture cried :

'After all, if I want him, the best way is still to chuck him out.'

Zoé seemed impressed. She looked at Madame with sudden admiration, and then went and chucked Steiner out without any further hesitation.

Meanwhile Nana waited patiently for a few minutes, to give her time to sweep the place out, as she put it. What an onslaught the flat had suffered ! She poked her head into the drawing-room, and found it empty. The dining-room was empty too. But as she was continuing her inspection in a calmer frame of mind, feeling sure that there was nobody left, she opened the door of a closet and suddenly came upon a very young man. He was sitting on top of a trunk, holding a huge bouquet on his knees, and looking very quiet and well-behaved.

'Good Lord !' she cried. 'There's one still here !'

The young fellow had jumped down at the sight of her, blushing red as a poppy. He did not know what to do with his bouquet, which he kept shifting from one hand to the other, choking with emotion. His youth, his confusion and the comical figure he cut with his flowers melted Nana's heart, and she burst out laughing. So now she had children after her ! Men were coming to her in baby-clothes ! She relaxed and became familiar and maternal, slapping her thighs and asking jokingly :

'Do you want me to blow your nose for you, baby?'

'Yes,' the boy replied in a low supplicating voice.

This answer made her merrier than ever.

He was seventeen years old, he said. His name was Georges Hugon. He had been at the Variétés the night before, and now he had come to see her.

'And these flowers are for me?'

'Yes.'

'Then give them to me, you great booby !'

But, as she was taking the bouquet, he seized her hands and kissed them with all the eagerness peculiar to his time

of life. She had to slap him to make him leave go. For a baby, he certainly didn't beat about the bush! But as she scolded him, she turned pink and started smiling. Then she sent him off, telling him that he might call again. He staggered away, scarcely able to find the way out.

Nana went back into her dressing-room, where Francis arrived almost at once in order to do her hair: she only dressed properly in the evening. Sitting in front of the mirror, and bending her head beneath the hairdresser's nimble fingers, she remained silent and thoughtful. Suddenly Zoé came in to announce:

'There's one of them, Madame, who refuses to go.'

'Well then, leave him,' she answered calmly.

'And more of them keep arriving.'

'Oh, tell them to wait. When they start feeling hungry, they'll go.'

Her mood had changed, and now she was delighted to keep a string of men waiting. An amusing idea occurred to her: she escaped from Francis's hands and ran to bolt the door herself. Now they could crowd into the other rooms as much as they liked: after all, they were scarcely likely to break through the wall. Zoé could come in and out through the little door leading to the kitchen. Meanwhile the electric bell went on ringing more than ever. Every five minutes a clear, shrill ring recurred as regularly as if it were produced by some well-adjusted machine. And Nana counted these rings to while away the time. But suddenly she remembered something.

'I say, where are my almonds?'

Francis too had forgotten about them. But now he took a paper bag out of one of the pockets of his frock-coat, with the discreet gesture of a man of the world, offering a lady a present: all the same, whenever he presented his accounts, he always put the almonds down on his bill. Nana put the bag between her knees, and started munching away, turning her head from time to time under the hairdresser's gentle touch.

'Christ,' she murmured, after a silence. 'There's no end to them.'

71

The bell had sounded three times in quick succession. Its summonses were becoming more urgent. There were modest rings, which seemed to stammer like a first declaration of love; there were bold rings which vibrated under a brutal finger; and there were hasty rings which sent a rapid shudder through the air. It was a regular peal, as Zoé said, a peal loud enough to set the entire neighbourhood by the ears, a whole mob of men, jabbing at the ivory button, one after another. That old joker Bordenave had really been far too generous with her address. Why the whole of the previous night's audience would be there before long!

'By the way, Francis, have you got five louis?' Nana asked. He drew back, examined her hair, and then said calmly: 'Five louis? That depends.'

'Oh, you know, if you want security . . .' she went on.

And without finishing her sentence, she indicated the adjoining rooms with a sweeping gesture. Francis lent her the five louis. Whenever she had a moment's respite, Zoé came in to get Madame's things ready. Soon she had to dress, while Francis waited in order to put the finishing touch to her coiffure. But the bell kept interrupting the maid, who left Madame with her corset half-laced and only one shoe on. Despite her long experience, Zoé began losing her head. After putting men all over the place, and in every nook and cranny, she had been forced to stow them away in threes and fours, which was contrary to all her principles. So much the worse for them if they ate each other up: it would make more room! And Nana, safe behind her bolted door, began making fun of them, saying that she could hear them panting. They must look a sight in there with their tongues all hanging out, like a lot of doggies sitting around on their behinds. The previous night's success was not over yet, for this pack of men had followed up her scent.

'I only hope they don't break anything,' she murmured.

She began to experience a certain uneasiness, imagining she could feel their hot breath coming through the chinks in the door. But then Zoé showed Labordette in, and the young woman gave a little cry of relief. He wanted to talk to her

about an account he had settled for her at the court of conciliation, but she would not listen, and said :

'I'm taking you with me. .... We'll have dinner together. ... Afterwards you'll come with me to the Variétés. I don't go on till half-past nine.'

Dear Labordette, how lucky it was he had come ! He never asked for any favours. He was just a friend, doing little services for the women he knew. Thus, on the way in, he had dismissed the creditors in the hall. Not that those good fellows wanted to be paid; on the contrary, if they had insisted on waiting, it was in order to pay their compliments to Madame, and to renew their offers of service to her in person after her wonderful success the night before.

'Let's go !' said Nana, who was now dressed.

At that moment Zoé came in again, crying :

'Madame, I refuse to open the door any more. .... They're waiting in a queue on the stairs.'

A queue on the stairs ! Even Francis, despite his affectation of English imperturbability, began laughing as he put away his combs. Nana, who had taken Labordette's arm, pushed him into the kitchen, and made her escape. At last she was free of men and could relax, for she knew that she could be alone with Labordette anywhere without fear of any nonsense.

'You'll see me home tonight,' she said, as they went down the backstairs. 'Like that I'll feel safe. .... Just imagine, I'm going to sleep all night – yes, a whole night by myself ! It's a crazy idea I've had, darling ...'

THE Comtesse Sabine, as it had become customary to call Madame Muffat de Beuville, in order to distinguish her from the Count's mother, who had died the year before, held a reception every Tuesday in her house in the Rue Miromesnil, at the corner of the Rue de Penthièvre. It was a huge square building, and the Muffats had lived in it for a hundred years or more. The street front, in its melancholy, seemed to be asleep, lofty and dark and convent-like, with its great shutters nearly always closed. And at the back, in a little damp garden, some trees had grown up, and were straining towards the sunlight with such long slender branches that they could be seen above the slates of the roof.

This particular Tuesday, about ten o'clock in the evening, there were scarcely a dozen people in the drawing-room. When she was expecting only close friends, the Countess opened neither the little drawing-room nor the dining-room. It was cosier like that, with everyone chatting around the fire. The drawing-room, in any case, was very large and very lofty; it had four windows looking out on the garden, from which, on this rainy evening in late April, there came a sensation of damp, despite the great logs burning in the fireplace. The sun never shone down into this room; in the daytime it was dimly lit by a faint greenish light, but in the evening, when the lamps and the chandelier were burning, it looked merely solemn, with its massive mahogany Empire furniture, and its hangings and chair coverings of yellow velvet stamped with bold designs. Entering it, one was in an atmosphere of cold dignity, of ancient manners, of a bygone age breathing an air of piety.

However, opposite the armchair in which the Count's mother had died – a square armchair with a stiff frame and inhospitable upholstery which stood on the other side of the fireplace – the Comtesse Sabine was seated in a deep easy-chair, whose red silk padding was as soft as eiderdown. It was

the only piece of modern furniture there, a touch of whimsy introduced amid the prevailing severity, and clashing with it.

'So we shall have the Shah of Persia,' the young woman was saying.

They were chatting about the crowned heads who were coming to Paris for the Exhibition. Several ladies had formed a circle in front of the fireplace, and Madame Du Joncquoy, whose brother, a diplomat, had held a post in the East, was giving some details about the Court of Nazr-ed-Din.

'Are you feeling unwell, my dear?' asked Madame Chantereau, the wife of an iron-master, seeing the Countess shiver slightly and turn pale.

'Oh, no, not at all,' the latter replied with a smile. 'I felt a little cold. This drawing-room takes so long to warm up.'

And with that she swept the walls with her melancholy gaze, from floor to ceiling. Her daughter Estelle, a slight, insignificant girl of eighteen, at the awkward age of life, left the footstool on which she was sitting, and silently came and propped up one of the logs which had rolled from its place. But Madame de Chezelles, a convent friend of Sabine's, and her junior by five years, exclaimed :

'Well, I wouldn't mind having a drawing-room like yours ! At least you can receive guests here. ... They only build boxes nowadays. ... Oh, if I were in your place !'

She chattered on, explaining with lively gestures how she would alter the hangings, the seats – everything in fact. Then she would give balls to which all Paris would come running. Behind her seat her husband, a magistrate, stood listening with a serious air. It was rumoured that she deceived him quite openly, but people forgave her and received her just the same, because, they said, she was such a featherbrain.

'Oh, that Léonide !' murmured the Comtesse Sabine, smiling her faint smile and saying nothing more.

A languid gesture expressed her meaning. After living there seventeen years, she certainly would not alter her drawing-room now. It would henceforth remain just as her mother-in-law had wished to preserve it during her lifetime. Then, returning to the subject of the conversation, she said :

'I have been assured that we shall also have the King of Prussia and the Emperor of Russia.'

'Yes, we have been promised some splendid festivities,' said Madame Du Joncquoy.

The banker Steiner, recently introduced into this circle by Léonide de Chezelles, who knew the whole of Parisian society, was sitting chatting on a sofa between two of the windows. He was questioning a deputy, from whom he was trying to elicit news about a fluctuation on the Stock Exchange which he had got wind of, while the Comte Muffat, standing in front of them, was silently listening to their talk, looking even greyer than usual. Four or five young men formed another group near the door, round the Comte Xavier de Vandeuvres, who in a low voice was telling them an anecdote. It was presumably a very spicy one, for they were shaking with suppressed laughter. All alone in the centre of the room, a stout man, a chief clerk at the Ministry of the Interior, sat solidly in an armchair, dozing with his eyes open. But when one of the young men appeared to doubt the truth of the anecdote, Vandeuvres raised his voice.

'You are too much of a sceptic, Foucarmont; you'll spoil all your pleasures that way.'

And he returned to the ladies with a laugh. The last scion of a great family, with feminine manners and a witty tongue, he was at this time running through a fortune with a voracious appetite which nothing could appease. His racing stable, one of the most famous in Paris, cost him the earth; his betting losses at the Imperial Club amounted monthly to an alarming sum of money, while year in, year out, his mistresses cost him a farm and a few acres of arable land or forest, a whole slice in fact of his vast estates in Picardy.

'You're a fine one to call other people sceptics when you don't believe a thing yourself,' said Léonide, making room for him beside her. 'It's you who spoil your own pleasures.'

'Exactly,' he replied. 'I wish to give others the benefit of my experience.'

But she imposed silence on him : he was shocking Monsieur Venot. And, the ladies having drawn aside, a little old man

of sixty, with bad teeth and a subtle smile, was revealed in the depths of an easy-chair. There he sat as comfortably as in his own house, listening to everybody's remarks and not uttering a word. With a slight gesture he indicated that he was not shocked at all. Vandeuvres had resumed his dignified manner and added gravely :

'Monsieur Venot is well aware that I believe what it is one's duty to believe.'

This was an act of faith, and even Léonide appeared satisfied. The young men at the end of the room had stopped laughing : the company were very strait-laced, and there was no amusement to be found here. A cold breath had passed over them, and in the ensuing silence Steiner's nasal voice became audible. The Deputy's discreet answers had ended up by driving him to desperation. For a moment the Comtesse Sabine looked at the fire; then she resumed the conversation.

'I saw the King of Prussia at Baden-Baden last year. He's still full of vigour for his age.'

'Count Bismarck is due to accompany him,' said Madame Du Joncquoy. 'Do you know the Count? I lunched with him at my brother's ages ago, when he was the Prussian envoy in Paris. There's a man now whose latest successes I find it hard to understand.'

'But why?' asked Madame Chantereau.

'Good gracious, how can I explain? He doesn't appeal to me. His appearance is boorish and ill-bred. Besides, as far as I'm concerned, I find him stupid.'

With that everybody started talking about Count Bismarck. Opinions differed considerably. Vandeuvres knew him, and assured the company that he was a good drinker and a good gambler. When the discussion was at its height, the door opened, and Hector de la Faloise appeared. Fauchery, who followed in his wake, went up to the Countess, and bowing, said :

'Madame, I remembered your gracious invitation.'

She smiled, and made an amiable reply. The journalist, after bowing to the Count, stood for a moment in the middle of the drawing-room. Steiner was the only person he recog-

nized, so he looked rather at a loss. But then Vandeuvres turned round, and came and shook hands with him. Delighted at this encounter, and seized by a sudden desire to be expansive, Fauchery buttonholed him, and said in a low voice :

'It's tomorrow. Are you going?'

'Of course.'

'At midnight, at her house.'

'I know, I know. I'm going with Blanche.'

He tried to escape and return to the ladies in order to put forward another good argument in Monsieur de Bismarck's favour. But Fauchery detained him.

'You'll never guess whom she has asked me to invite.'

And, with a slight nod, he indicated the Comte Muffat, who was just then discussing an article in the budget with Steiner and the Deputy.

'Impossible !' said Vandeuvres, astounded and amused.

'My word on it ! I had to swear that I'd bring him along. Indeed that's one of my reasons for coming here.'

Both laughed silently, and Vandeuvres, hurriedly rejoining the circle of ladies, exclaimed :

'I declare that on the contrary Monsieur de Bismarck is extremely witty. For instance, one evening he made a delightful joke in my presence . . .'

La Faloise meanwhile had heard the few rapid words that had been exchanged in an undertone, and he gazed at Fauchery in the hope of an explanation which was not granted him. Of whom were they talking, and what were they going to do at midnight the next day? He did not leave his cousin's side again. The latter had gone and taken a seat. He was especially interested by the Comtesse Sabine. Her name had often been mentioned in his presence, and he knew that, having been married at the age of seventeen, she must now be thirty-four, and that since her marriage she had spent a cloistered existence with her husband and her mother-in-law. In society, some spoke of her as a woman of frigid piety, while others pitied her, recalling her charming bursts of laughter and the fiery glances of her great eyes in the days before she was imprisoned in this old town house. Fauchery

scrutinized her and hesitated. A friend of his, a captain who had recently died in Mexico, had, after dinner on the very eve of his departure, made him one of those coarse confessions of which even the most discreet men are occasionally guilty. But he retained only a vague recollection of that confession : the two men had dined all too well on the evening in question; and when he saw the Countess in her black dress and with her quiet smile, seated in that old-world drawing-room, he had his doubts. A lamp which had been placed behind her threw into relief her dark, full-cheeked profile, in which only the somewhat thick lips indicated a sort of imperious sensuality.

'What bores they are with their Bismarck !' murmured la Faloise, who always made a show of finding society life tedious. 'It's like the morgue here. A fine idea of yours it was to want to come !'

Fauchery questioned him abruptly :

'Tell me, has the Countess a lover?'

'Good heavens, no ! My dear fellow !' he stammered, visibly taken aback, and quite forgetting his pose. 'Where do you think you are?'

Then it dawned on him that his indignation was rather old-fashioned, and lying back on the sofa, he added :

'Dammit, I say no, but I can't be sure. There's a little chap over there, that fellow Foucarmont, who's always around. And I suppose odder things than that have been known to happen. It's no concern of mine, in any case. . . . All I know is that if the Countess plays around, she's pretty sly about it, for the thing never gets about, and nobody talks about it.'

Then, without Fauchery taking the trouble to question him, he told him all he knew about the Muffats. In the midst of the ladies' conversation, which still continued in front of the fireplace, the two of them lowered their voices, and, seeing them there with their white ties and white gloves, one might have supposed them to be discussing serious topics in carefully chosen terms.

It turned out that old Madame Muffat, whom la Faloise had been well acquainted with, was an insufferable old lady

always hand in glove with the clergy. She had a grand manner too, and the sort of authoritative gestures which bent everybody to her will. As for Muffat, he was an old man's child; his father, a general, had been created a count by Napoleon I, and naturally he had found himself in favour after the Second of December. He wasn't a very light-hearted individual either, but he passed for a decent individual with an upright character. Add to that an old-fashioned code of conduct, and such a lofty conception of his duties at Court, his dignities and his virtues, that he behaved as if he were always in church. It was Mama Muffat who had given him this splendid upbringing : daily visits to the confessional, no pranks or escapades, and indeed nothing of a young man's normal life. He was a practising Christian, and had attacks of faith of such violence that they might be compared to attacks of fever. Finally, to add a last touch to the picture, la Faloise whispered something in his cousin's ear.

'You don't say so !' said the latter.

'On my word of honour, I had it on the best authority. . . . He was still a virgin when he got married.'

Fauchery chuckled as he looked at the Count, whose face, with its fringe of whiskers and lack of moustaches, seemed to have grown squarer and harder now that he was quoting figures at the reluctant Steiner.

'Upon my word, he looks as if he might have been,' murmured Fauchery.

'A fine present he made his wife ! . . . Poor little thing, how tedious she must have found him ! I'll wager she doesn't know the first thing about it !'

Just then the Comtesse Sabine happened to say something to him. He did not hear her, he was so preoccupied with the amusing and extraordinary case of Muffat. She repeated her question.

'Monsieur Fauchery, you have published an article on Monsieur de Bismarck, haven't you? . . . So you have spoken to him?'

He leapt to his feet and approached the circle of ladies, trying to collect his wits, and finding an answer almost immediately :

'Dear me, Madame, I must admit that I wrote that article with the help of biographies which had been published in Germany. ... I have never so much as set eyes on Monsieur de Bismarck.'

He remained near the Countess, and, while talking with her, pursued his train of thought. She did not look her age; one would have put her down as twenty-eight at the most; her eyes above all, steeped in blue shadow by her heavy eyelids, retained a glow of youth. Brought up in a divided family, so that she used to spend one month with the Marquis de Chouard, and another with the Marquise, she had married very young, shortly after her mother's death, probably urged on by a father eager to get her off his hands. The Marquis was said to be a dreadful man, about whom strange tales were beginning to be told, in spite of his great piety. Fauchery asked if he was going to have the honour of meeting him. Yes, her father was coming, but very late; he had so much work to do! The journalist, who thought he knew where the old gentleman spent his evenings, kept a straight face. But a mole, which he noticed on the Countess's left cheek, close to her mouth, suddenly attracted his attention. The curious thing was that Nana had precisely the same mole, with the same curly hairs on it; only they were golden in Nana's case, and as black as jet in the Countess's. And this woman didn't have any lovers.

'I've always wanted to meet Queen Augusta,' she was saying. 'They say she is so good, so devout. ... Do you think she will accompany the King?'

'It isn't considered likely, Madame,' he replied.

She had no lovers : that was obvious. One had only to look at her beside that daughter of hers, so stiff and insipid on her footstool. That sepulchral drawing-room of hers, smelling like a church, revealed plainly enough the iron hand, the austere existence, which weighed upon her. There was no trace of her own personality in that ancient abode, black with damp. It was Muffat who reigned supreme there, who dominated the household with his devout upbringing, his penances and fasts. But the sight of the little old gentleman with the black teeth and subtle smile, whom he suddenly

81

discovered in his armchair behind the ladies, provided him with an even more convincing argument. He knew the man well. It was Théophile Venot, a sometime lawyer who had made a speciality of church cases. He had retired with a handsome fortune, and now led a rather mysterious existence, for he was received everywhere, treated with great deference, and even somewhat feared, as if he represented a mighty force, an occult power which was felt to be behind him. All the same, his behaviour was very humble. He was a churchwarden at the Madeleine, and had only accepted the post of deputy mayor of the Ninth Arrondissement in order, so he said, to have something to do in his spare time. No, the Countess was well protected; there was nothing to be done in that quarter.

'You're right, it's deadly boring here,' Fauchery said to his cousin, once he had escaped from the circle of ladies. 'Let's go.'

But Steiner, whom the Comte Muffat and the Deputy had just left, came up in a fury, sweating and muttering under his breath:

'All right, if they won't talk, they won't talk. ... I'll find somebody who will.'

Then, pushing the journalist into a corner, and changing his tone of voice, he said triumphantly:

'So, it's tomorrow, eh? I'll be there, my boy!'

'Really?' murmured Fauchery, taken aback.

'You didn't know? ... Oh, I had a lot of trouble finding her at home! And Mignon stuck to me like a limpet.'

'But the Mignons are going to be there.'

'Yes, she told me so. ... Still, she saw me in the end, and she invited me. ... On the stroke of midnight, after the show.'

The banker was radiant. He winked at Fauchery and added meaningly:

'You're all right, eh?'

'What do you mean?' said Fauchery, pretending not to understand. 'She wanted to thank me for my article, so she came to see me.'

'Yes, yes. ... You fellows don't know how lucky you are.

You get paid for services rendered. ... Incidentally, who's paying the piper tomorrow?'

The journalist spread out his hands, as if to say that nobody had any idea. Just then Vandeuvres called to Steiner, who knew Monsieur de Bismarck. Madame Du Joncquoy had almost admitted defeat, and concluded :

'He made an unpleasant impression on me, and I think he had an evil face. ... But I'm quite willing to believe that he has a nice wit. That would account for his success.'

'Without doubt,' said the banker with a faint smile. He was a Jew from Frankfurt.

Meanwhile la Faloise had finally plucked up courage to question his cousin. Catching up with him, he hissed into his ear :

'So there's going to be a supper-party at some woman's place tomorow night, is there? ... But who's the woman, eh? Who's the woman?'

Fauchery motioned to him that people were listening to them, and that they had to behave themselves. The door had just opened again, and an old lady had come in, followed by a young man, whom the journalist recognized as the truant schoolboy who had made a memorable impression by voicing approval of Nana at the first night of *The Blonde Venus*. This lady's arrival caused a stir among the company. The Comtesse Sabine had risen briskly from her seat to go and greet her, taking both her hands in hers, and addressing her as her 'dear Madame Hugon'. Seeing that his cousin watched this little incident inquisitively, la Faloise tried to ingratiate himself with him by telling him about the newcomer in a few brief phrases. Madame Hugon, the widow of a notary, lived quietly at Les Fondettes, an old estate of her family's, in the neighbourhood of Orléans, but also kept up a small establishment in Paris, in a house she owned in the Rue de Richelieu, and was now spending a few weeks there in order to settle in her youngest son, who had just begun studying law. She had been a close friend of the Marquise de Chouard, and had been present at the birth of the Countess, who, before her marriage, used to stay at her house for

months at a time, and was still treated almost as a member of the family.

'I have brought Georges to see you,' Madame Hugon said to Sabine. 'He's grown up, I hope.'

The young man, with his bright eyes and the fair curls which made him look like a girl dressed up as a boy, bowed gracefully to the Countess and reminded her of a bout of battledore and shuttlecock they had played together, two years before, at Les Fondettes.

'Philippe isn't in Paris?' asked the Comte Muffat.

'Dear me, no!' replied the old lady. 'He's still garrisoned at Bourges.'

Taking a seat, she began talking proudly about her eldest son, a strapping big fellow, who, after enlisting on an impulse, had recently been promoted to the rank of lieutenant. All the ladies spoke to her with respectful sympathy, and the conversation continued in a tone at once more pleasant and more refined. And Fauchery, at the sight of the respectable Madame Hugon, her motherly face lit up with such a kindly smile between her broad tresses of white hair, decided that he had been utterly ridiculous to suspect the Comtesse Sabine even for a moment.

All the same, the big chair with the red silk upholstery in which the Countess was now sitting down had just attracted his attention. Its style struck him as crude, not to say strangely suggestive, in this dull drawing-room. It was obviously not the Count who had introduced this voluptuous piece of furniture into the house. It gave the impression of being an experiment, of marking the birth of an appetite for enjoyment. Then he forgot where he was and began musing, harking back in spite of everything to that vague confidence imparted to him one evening in a private room in a restaurant. Impelled by a sort of sensual curiosity, he had always wanted to gain admittance to the Muffats' circle, and, now that his friend was in Mexico for all eternity, who could tell what might happen? Possibly he was being foolish but the idea tormented him; he felt drawn on, his animal nature aroused. The big chair had a rumpled look, its back a suggestive slant which now amused him.

'Well, are we going?' asked la Faloise, mentally vowing that, once outside, he would find out the name of the woman at whose place everybody was going to have supper.

'All in good time,' replied Fauchery.

But he was no longer in any hurry, excusing himself on the basis of the invitation he had been asked to give, an invitation which was far from easy to deliver. The ladies were chatting about a taking of the veil, a very moving ceremony which had touched the hearts of the whole of Parisian society during the last three days. It was the eldest daughter of the Baronne de Fougeray, who, at the bidding of an irresistible vocation, had just entered the Carmelite Order. Madame Chantereau, a distant cousin of the Fougerays, was saying that the Baroness had been obliged to take to her bed after the ceremony, she was so exhausted from weeping.

'I had a very good place,' declared Léonide. 'I found the whole thing very interesting.'

All the same, Madame Hugon felt sorry for the poor mother. How sad to lose a daughter in such a way!

'I am accused of being excessively pious,' she said, in her quiet frank manner, 'but that does not prevent me from thinking that children who obstinately commit suicide in that way are very cruel.'

'Yes, it's a terrible thing,' murmured the Countess, shivering a little as if she were cold, and snuggling further down in her big chair in front of the fire.

Then the ladies started a discussion. But they kept their voices very low, while the light trills of laughter occasionally interrupted the gravity of their talk. The two lamps on the mantelpiece, which had shades of rose-coloured lace, cast a feeble light over them, and there were only three other lamps on distant pieces of furniture, so that the vast drawing-room remained in a soft shadow.

Steiner was getting bored. He was describing to Fauchery an escapade attributed to little Madame de Chezelles, whom he referred to simply as Léonide – 'a regular bitch', he said, lowering his voice behind the ladies' armchairs. Fauchery looked at her as she sat quaintly perched, in her voluminous dress of pale blue satin, on one corner of her armchair. She

looked as slight and impudent as a boy, and he ended up by feeling astonished at seeing her there : people behaved themselves better at Caroline Héquet's, whose mother had organized her house on strict moral principles. There was a subject for a whole article here. What a strange world Parisian society was ! The most exclusive circles found themselves invaded. Obviously that silent Théophile Venot, who contented himself with smiling and showing his ugly teeth, must be a legacy from the late Countess. So must be such ladies of mature years as Madame Chantereau and Madame Du Joncquoy, besides four or five old gentlemen, sitting motionless in corners. The Comte Muffat had brought along with him a few high officials, distinguished by that immaculate appearance which was required at that time of the men of the Tuileries; they included the chief clerk, who was still all alone in the middle of the room, with his clean-shaven face, his vacant gaze, and his coat buttoned so tightly that he could scarcely dare to move. Almost all the young men and a few individuals with distinguished manners had been brought along by the Marquis de Chouard, who had maintained close relations with the Legitimist party after rallying to the Empire by joining the Council of State. There remained Léonide de Chezelles, Steiner and indeed a whole shady-looking bunch against which Madame Hugon, with her amiable, elderly serenity, stood out in sharp contrast. And Fauchery, seeing how his article was going to work out, named this last group 'the Comtesse Sabine's little bunch'.

'On another occasion,' continued Steiner in a low voice, 'Léonide got her tenor down to Montauban. She was living in the Château de Beaurecueil, five miles away, and she used to come in daily in a carriage and pair to visit him at the Lion d'Or, where he was staying. The carriage used to wait at the door, and Léonide would stay for hours inside the hotel, while a crowd gathered and looked at the horses.'

There was a pause in the talk, and there followed a few moments of solemn silence in the high-ceilinged room. The two young men went on whispering, but then they too fell silent, and nothing could be heard but the quiet footsteps of the Comte Muffat as he crossed the floor. The lamps seemed

to have grown dimmer; the fire was going out; an austere shadow shrouded the old friends of the family where they sat in the chairs they had occupied in that house for forty years. It was as if, in a momentary pause, the invited guests had suddenly sensed the approach of the Count's mother, with her icy, haughty manner. But the Comtesse Sabine had already resumed the conversation :

'You know, there was a rumour. . . . The young man was said to have died, and that explained the poor child's decision to take the veil. Besides, they say that Monsieur de Fougeray would never have given his consent to the marriage.'

'They say a lot of other things too,' Léonide exclaimed without thinking.

She started laughing and refused to say any more. Sabine was infected by this gaiety, and put her handkerchief to her lips. And in the vast and solemn room the laughter of the two women took on a sound which struck Fauchery's imagination : the sound of crystal breaking. Undoubtedly this was the first sign of a crack. Everyone began talking again. Madame Du Joncquoy demurred; Madame Chantereau knew for certain that a marriage had been planned, but that matters had gone no further; even the men ventured to express their opinions. For a few minutes the conversation was a babble of opinions, in which the various elements of the company, whether Bonapartist, or Legitimist, or worldly and sceptical, jostled one another simultaneously. Estelle had rung to order wood to be put on the fire; the footman turned up the lamps; it was like an awakening. Fauchery smiled, as if he had been put at ease.

'The fact is that they marry God when they haven't been able to marry their cousin,' muttered Vandeuvres, who found the whole subject a bore. Joining Fauchery, he went on :

'My dear fellow, have you ever seen a woman who had a man to love her become a nun?'

He did not wait for an answer, for he had had enough of the topic, but asked in an undertone :

'Tell me, how many of us will there be tomorrow? . . . There'll be the Mignons, Steiner, yourself, Blanche and I. . . . Who else?'

'Caroline, I believe ... Simonne ... Gaga in all probability. ... You can never tell for certain, can you? At a party like that you expect to find twenty people, and thirty turn up.'

Vandeuvres, who was looking at the ladies, turned abruptly to another subject.

'She must have been very good-looking, that Du Joncquoy woman, fifteen years ago. ... Poor Estelle has grown lankier than ever. What a plank of wood to take to bed with you.'

But he broke off to return to the subject of the supper-party the next day.

'What's so tiresome about those affairs is that there's always the same set of women. ... A chap wants a little novelty. So do try and dig up a new girl. ... Good Lord, I've just had an idea! I'll ask that fat fellow over there to bring the woman he was trailing about the other night at the Variétés.'

He was referring to the chief clerk, who was fast asleep in the middle of the drawing-room. Fauchery amused himself by following this delicate negotiation from a distance. Vandeuvres had sat down beside the stout man, who remained very much on his dignity. For a while the two of them appeared to be discussing with great propriety the question of the hour, namely how to discover the real feelings which lead a young girl to take the veil. Then the Count returned to report:

'It's incredible. He swears she's a respectable woman. She'd refuse to come. ... Yet I'd have sworn that I've seen her at Laure's.'

'What, you mean to say you go to Laure's!' Fauchery said with a chuckle. 'You dare to set foot in places like that! I was under the impression that it was only we poor devils who ...'

'Oh, my dear chap, a fellow has to see every side of life.'

They all sniggered, and with sparkling eyes began comparing notes about the *table d'hôte* in the Rue des Martyrs, where fat Laure Piédefer served dinner at three francs a head for women in difficulties. A nice place it was, where all the women used to kiss Laure on the lips! And as the Com-

tesse Sabine, overhearing a word or two, turned her head towards them, they drew back, huddling together in excited merriment. They had not noticed that Georges Hugon was near them, listening to them, and blushing so hotly that a rosy flush had spread from his ears to his girlish neck. The boy was full of shame and ecstasy. From the moment his mother had turned him loose in the drawing-room, he had been hovering around Madame de Chezelles, the only woman present who struck him as being *chic*. And even then she wasn't a patch on Nana!

'Last night,' Madame Hugon was saying, 'Georges took me to the theatre. Yes, we went to the Variétés, where I can't have set foot for the last ten years. That child simply adores music. ... As for myself, I can't say that I enjoyed it very much, but he was so happy! .. They put some extraordinary things on the stage nowadays. Besides, I must admit that I have no great enthusiasm for music.'

'What, you don't love music, Madame?' cried Madame Du Joncquoy, lifting her eyes to heaven. 'Is it possible for anybody not to love music?'

There was a general exclamation of surprise. Nobody uttered a word about the operetta at the Variétés, at which virtuous Madame Hugon had failed to understand any of the allusions. The ladies knew about it, but refused to discuss it. Instead they promptly plunged into an orgy of sentiment, expressing refined and ecstatic admiration for the masters. Madame Du Joncquoy liked nobody but Weber, while Madame Chantereau stood up for the Italians. The ladies' voices had become soft and languorous, and instead of a fireside conversation one might have been listening, in an atmosphere of religious piety, to the quiet, ecstatic music of a little chapel.

'Now, let's see,' murmured Vandeuvres, bringing Fauchery back into the middle of the drawing-room; 'we really must find a new woman for tomorrow. Shall we ask Steiner to help?'

'Oh, when Steiner's got a woman,' said the journalist, 'it's because Paris has done with her.'

Meanwhile Vandeuvres was looking all around him.

'Wait a minute,' he continued. 'The other day I met Foucarmont with a charming blonde. I'll go and tell him to bring her.'

And he called to Foucarmont. They quickly exchanged a few words. Some sort of complication must have arisen, for both of them, walking carefully and stepping over the ladies' skirts, went off to find another young man, with whom they continued the discussion in a window recess. Fauchery was left on his own, and had just decided to go over to the fire, where Madame Du Joncquoy was declaring that she could never hear Weber played without immediately seeing lakes, forests and sunrises over dew-drenched landscapes, when a hand touched him on the shoulder and a voice behind him said :

'It isn't very sporting of you.'

'What isn't?' he asked, turning round and recognizing la Faloise.

'Why, that supper tomorrow. . . . You could easily have got me invited.'

Fauchery was finally going to explain when Vandeuvres came back to tell him :

'It appears she isn't one of Foucarmont's women. She's living with that gentleman over there. . . . And she won't be able to come. What rotten luck ! . . . But I've pressed Foucarmont into service, and he's going to try to get Louise of the Palais-Royal.'

'Is it not true, Monsieur de Vandeuvres,' asked Madame Chantereau, raising her voice, 'that Wagner's music was hissed last Sunday?'

'Oh, it was given a frightful reception, Madame,' he replied, coming forward with his usual exquisite politeness.

Then, as the ladies did not detain him, he moved away and whispered in the journalist's ear :

'I'm going to press some more of them into service. . . . Those young fellows must know some likely girls.'

Soon he was to be seen accosting various men in every corner of the drawing-room, and engaging them in conversation in his usual amiable and smiling way. He joined one group after another, whispered something to everybody, and

looked back as he moved away with a sly wink or a meaning nod. It was as if he were giving out a password in that casual way of his. Details of the party were exchanged and the meeting-place announced, while the ladies' sentimental dissertations on music served to drown the low, excited sound of these recruiting operations.

'No, don't talk to me about your Germans,' Madame Chantereau was saying. 'Singing should be all gaiety and light. Have you heard Patti in the *Barber*?'

'She was delicious!' murmured Léonide, who picked out nothing but operatic airs on her piano.

Meanwhile the Comtesse Sabine had rung. When there were only a few visitors on Tuesday, tea was served in the drawing-room itself. While directing a footman to clear the small table, the Countess followed the Comte de Vandeuvres with her eyes. She was still smiling that vague smile of hers which revealed something of her white teeth. As the Count was passing by, she questioned him.

'What are you plotting, Monsieur de Vandeuvres?'

'I, Madame?' he answered calmly. 'I'm not plotting anything at all.'

'Really? ... You seem so very busy. ... But if you have nothing to do, you can make yourself useful.'

She placed an album in his hands, and asked him to put it on the piano. But on the way he found an opportunity to inform Fauchery in a whisper that they were going to have Tatan Néné, the best-developed girl that winter, and Maria Blond, the actress who had just made her first appearance at the Folies-Dramatiques. Meanwhile la Faloise kept stopping him at every step in the hope of receiving an invitation. He ended up by offering his services, and Vandeuvres engaged him straight away; only he made his promise to bring Clarisse with him, and when la Faloise affected to show certain scruples, he reassured him by saying:

'Since I'm inviting you, that should be enough.'

All the same, la Faloise would have liked to know the name of the hostess. But the Countess had recalled Vandeuvres, and was questioning him as to the way in which the English made tea. He often visited England, where his horses took

part in the races. According to him, the Russians were the only people who knew how to make tea; and he gave the Countess their recipe. Then, as if he had been following a lengthy train of thought while he had been speaking, he broke off to ask:

'By the way, what has become of the Marquis? Weren't we going to see him?'

'Yes, and I'm sure you will,' replied the Countess. He promised me faithfully that he would come. But I'm beginning to be a little worried. ... His work must have kept him.'

Vandeuvres smiled to himself. He too seemed to have his suspicions as to the exact nature of the Marquis de Chouard's work. He had been thinking of a pretty woman whom the Marquis occasionally took into the country with him. Perhaps they could have her too.

In the meantime, Fauchery decided that the moment had come to risk giving the Comte Muffat his invitation, for it was getting late.

'Are you serious?' asked Vandeuvres, who thought that he was joking.

'Perfectly serious. ... If I don't carry out my commission, she'll tear my eyes out. It's a caprice of hers, you know.'

'Then I'll give you a helping hand, my dear chap.'

Eleven o'clock struck. Assisted by her daughter, the Countess was pouring out the tea. As nearly all the guests were old acquaintances, the cups and platefuls of little cakes circulated informally. Even the ladies did not leave their armchairs in front of the fire, and sat sipping their tea and nibbling the cakes which they held between their fingers. From music the conversation had descended to the subject of caterers. Boissier was the only person for bon-bons, and Catherine for ices, although Madame Chantereau stood up for Latinville. The ladies' speech grew more and more indolent, as a sense of lassitude started lulling the company to sleep. Steiner had begun working once more on the Deputy, whom he had trapped in one corner of the settee. Monsieur Venot, whose teeth must have been ruined by sweet things, was eating biscuits, one after the other, with a mouselike nibbling sound,

while the chief clerk seemed to have his nose stuck in his teacup for good. The Countess moved in a leisurely way from one guest to another, never pressing them, but pausing for a few moments to look at the men with an air of silent inquiry before smiling and passing on. The fire had brought a flush to her face, and she looked as if she were the sister of her daughter, who seemed so gawky and dried-up beside her. As she approached Fauchery, who was chatting with her husband and Vandeuvres, she noticed that they suddenly fell silent; consequently she did not stop, but walked past them to hand the cup of tea she was carrying to Georges Hugon.

'There's a lady who would like to have you for supper,' the journalist said gaily, addressing the Comte Muffat.

The latter, whose face had looked tired and grey all evening, seemed extremely surprised. 'What lady?'

'Why, Nana!' said Vandeuvres, to get the invitation out of the way.

The Count assumed a more serious expression. His eyelids fluttered almost imperceptibly, while a look of discomfort, as at the onset of a headache, passed over his forehead.

'But I am not acquainted with that lady,' he murmured.

'Come now, you've been to see her,' Vandeuvres pointed out.

'What's that? I've been to see her? ... Oh, yes, the other day on behalf of the Charity Committee. I had forgotten about that. All the same, I am not acquainted with her, and I cannot accept.'

He had adopted an icy manner to make them understand that this joke struck him as being in very poor taste. A man in his position did not sit down at the table of a woman like that. Vandeuvres protested that it was going to be a supper-party for people in the arts, and talent excused everything. But without listening any more sympathetically to the arguments advanced by Fauchery, who spoke of a dinner at which the Prince of Scotland, the son of a queen, had sat down beside a former music-hall singer, the Count repeated his refusal. In spite of his great politeness he even gave vent to a gesture of irritation.

Georges and la Faloise, who were standing opposite each other drinking their tea, had overheard the brief exchange of remarks between their neighbours.

'Ah, so it's at Nana's!' murmured la Faloise. 'I should have guessed as much.'

Georges said nothing, but he was all aflame. His fair hair was in disorder and his blue eyes shone like candles, the vice which had surrounded him for the past few days had stirred his blood so fiercely. At last he was going to experience all the things he had dreamt of!

'The trouble is, I don't know the address,' la Faloise continued.

'It's a third-floor flat on the Boulevard Haussmann, between the Rue de l'Arcade and the Rue Pasquier,' said Georges, all in one breath.

And when the other looked at him in some astonishment, he added, turning bright red, and bursting with conceit and embarrassment:

'I'm going to the party. She invited me this morning.'

But just then there was a great stir in the drawing-room, and Vandeuvres and Fauchery had to stop pressing the Count. The Marquis de Chouard had just come in, and everybody was crowding around him. He had moved painfully forward, his legs almost giving way beneath him, and now he stood in the middle of the room, pale-faced and blinking, as if he had just come out of some dark alley, and were blinded by the brightness of the lamps.

'I had given up hope of seeing you tonight, Father,' said the Countess. 'I should have been worried till the morning.'

He looked at her without answering, as if he did not understand. His nose, which seemed disproportionately large on his clean-shaven face, looked like a swollen pimple, while his lower lip hung down. Seeing him in such a pitiful state, the kindly Madame Hugon said compassionately to him:

'You work too hard. You ought to rest more. .... At our age we should leave work to the young people.'

'Work? Ah, yes, work,' he stammered at last. 'Always a lot of work.'

Pulling himself together, he straightened up his bent figure,

passing his hand, in a gesture he often made, over his grey hair, which hung in scanty locks behind his ears.

'What are you working on as late as this?' asked Madame Du Joncquoy. 'I thought you were at the Minister of Finance's reception.'

The Countess broke in to say:

'My father had to examine a draft law.'

'Yes, a draft law,' he said, 'that's it, a draft law. ... I had shut myself up to study it. ... It concerns the factories. ... I would like them to observe the Sabbath. ... It's really shameful that the government is unwilling to take firm action on that matter. The churches are growing emptier every Sunday; we are heading towards catastrophe.'

Vandeuvres had exchanged glances with Fauchery. They both happened to be behind the Marquis, and they were sniffing at his clothes. When Vandeuvres found an opportunity to take him aside, to speak to him about that lovely creature he was in the habit of taking to the country, the old man put on a great show of surprise. Perhaps they had seen him with the Baronne Decker, at whose house at Viroflay he sometimes spent a few days. Vandeuvres's only revenge consisted of asking him abruptly:

'I say, where on earth have you been? Your elbow is covered with cobwebs and plaster.'

'My elbow?' he murmured, looking a little worried. 'Why, yes, you're right. ... There's a little dirt on it. ... I must have picked that up when I was coming downstairs from my study.'

Several people were taking their leave. It was nearly midnight. The two footmen had begun silently removing the empty cups and the plates of cakes. In front of the fireplace the ladies had changed places and drawn closer together, and were chatting more freely than before in the languid atmosphere peculiar to the close of a party. The drawing-room itself was going to sleep, and shadows were slowly creeping from its walls. Fauchery said he must be going, but once again forgot his intention at the sight of the Comtesse Sabine.

She was resting from her duties as hostess, and sitting silently in her usual seat, her eyes fixed on a log which was

turning into embers, her face appeared so white and impassive that he felt a sudden pang of doubt. In the glow of the fire the black hairs on the mole at the corner of her lips looked almost fair. It was Nana's mole, down to the colour of the hairs. He could not refrain from whispering something to that effect in Vandeuvres's ear. It was true; the other had never noticed it before. And both men pursued this comparison between Nana and the Countess. They discovered a vague resemblance in the chin and the mouth, but the eyes were not at all similar. Then, too, Nana had a good-natured look about her, while you couldn't tell with the Countess : she gave the impression of a cat sleeping with its claws drawn in and its paws stirred by a barely perceptible nervous quiver.

'All the same, she'd be all right in bed,' declared Fauchery.

Vandeuvres undressed her with his eyes.

'Yes, I suppose she would,' he said. 'But I'm a bit dubious about her thighs, you know. I'm willing to bet you that she has no thighs !'

He stopped, for Fauchery had touched him sharply on the elbow, nodding in the direction of Estelle, who was sitting in front of them on her footstool. They had raised their voices without noticing her, and she could not have avoided overhearing them. Nevertheless she remained sitting there stiff and motionless, without a hair stirring on her neck, the thin neck of an overgrown schoolgirl. They moved a few feet away, Vandeuvres insisting that the Countess was a perfectly respectable woman. Just then voices were raised in front of the fireplace. Madame Du Joncquoy was saying :

'I granted you that Monsieur de Bismarck might have a nice wit. ... But if you are going so far as to call him a genius ...'

The ladies had returned to their original subject of conversation.

'Not Monsieur de Bismarck again !' murmured Fauchery. 'This time I'm going for good !'

'Wait a minute,' said Vandeuvres, 'we must get a definite reply from the Count.'

The Comte Muffat was chatting with his father-in-law

96

and a few serious-looking men. Vandeuvres drew him aside and repeated Nana's invitation, backing it up with the information that he was going to be at the supper himself. A man could go anywhere; nobody would think of suspecting evil where at most there could only be curiosity. The Count listened to these arguments with downcast eyes and an expressionless face. Vandeuvres could feel that he was hesitating when the Marquis de Chouard came up with an inquiring look on his face. And when the latter was informed of the question at issue, and Fauchery had invited him in his turn, he looked at his son-in-law furtively. There followed an embarrassed silence, but both men encouraged one another, and they would probably have ended up by accepting if the Comte Muffat had not caught sight of Monsieur Venot staring hard at him. The little old man was no longer smiling; his face was cadaverous, his eyes as sharp and bright as steel.

'No,' the Count replied at once, in so decisive a tone that further insistence was out of the question.

Then the Marquis refused even more sternly than his son-in-law. He talked morality. The upper classes had a duty to set a good example. Fauchery smiled and shook hands with Vandeuvres. He couldn't wait for him, but had to leave straight away, for he was expected to drop in at his newspaper office.

'At Nana's at midnight then?'

La Faloise was going too. Steiner had just taken his leave of the Countess. Other men followed them, and the same phrase – 'at midnight, at Nana's' – was repeated again and again as they went to collect their overcoats in the anteroom. Georges, who could not leave without his mother, had stationed himself at the door, where he gave everybody the exact address : 'The third floor, the door on your left.' However, before going out, Fauchery gave a final glance around the room. Vandeuvres had resumed his position among the ladies, and was joking with Léonide de Chezelles. The Comte Muffat and the Marquis de Chouard were joining in the conversation, while the kindly Madame Hugon was falling asleep with her eyes open. Lost behind the ladies' skirts,

Monsieur Venot, an insignificant figure once more, was smiling again. Midnight struck slowly in the vast solemn room.

'What's that?' Madame Du Joncquoy exclaimed. 'You think that Monsieur de Bismarck is going to make war on us and beat us? ... Oh, that's too ridiculous for words!'

Everybody, in fact, was laughing around Madame Chantereau, who had just repeated this prophecy which she had heard made in Alsace, where her husband owned a factory.

'Fortunately we have the Emperor to protect us,' said the Comte Muffat in his grave official way.

This was the last remark Fauchery was able to catch. He closed the door, after casting one more glance in the direction of the Comtesse Sabine. She was talking sedately with the chief clerk, and seemed to be taking a considerable interest in that stout individual's conversation. He must have been mistaken: there was no crack, no flaw there at all. It was a pity.

'Are you coming down, or aren't you?' la Faloise shouted to him from the entrance-hall.

And out on the pavement, as they took leave of each other, they repeated once more:

'Tomorrow, at Nana's.'

SINCE that morning Zoé had handed over the flat to a *maître d'hôtel* who had come from Brébant's with a staff of assistants and waiters. Brébant was to supply everything, from the supper, the plates, the cutlery, the glasses, the linen and the flowers, down to the chairs and the footstools. Nana could not have produced a dozen napkins out of all her cupboards; and not having had time to fit herself out after her recent success, and scorning to go to a restaurant, she had decided to make a restaurant come to her. This struck her as being more *chic*. She wanted to celebrate her triumph as an actress with a supper which would set people talking. As her dining-room was too small, the *maître d'hôtel* had set up a table in the drawing-room, a table with twenty-five covers, placed rather close together.

'Is everything ready?' asked Nana, when she came home at midnight.

'I've no idea,' Zoé replied roughly, looking beside herself with worry. 'I've got nothing to do with it, thank the Lord. They're making a terrible mess in the kitchen and all over the flat! . . . And on top of that I've had a bit of trouble to deal with. Those two came here again. You should have seen me chuck them out!'

She was referring to her employer's former 'gentlemen', the tradesman and the Wallachian, whom Nana, sure of her future and wanting to shed her old skin, as she put it, had decided to dismiss.

'There's a couple of leeches for you!' she murmured. 'If they come back, tell them you're going to set the police on them.'

Then she called Daguenet and Georges, who had remained behind in the hall, where they were hanging up their overcoats. The two men had met at the stage-door, in the Passage des Panoramas, and she had brought them home with her in a cab. As there was nobody there yet, she shouted to them

99

to come into the dressing-room while Zoé was getting her ready. Hurriedly, and without changing her dress, she had her hair done up, and stuck some white roses in her chignon and her bodice. The little room was littered with the drawing-room furniture, which the caterers had been obliged to trundle in there, a pile of side-tables, sofas and arm-chairs with their legs in the air; and just when Nana was ready she caught her dress on a castor and tore it. At this she swore furiously; things like that only happened to her! She angrily pulled off her dress, a very simple affair of white foulard, so fine and supple that it clung to her like a long shift. But she put it on again straight away, for she could not find another to her taste, on the verge of tears and com-plaining that she looked an absolute fright. Daguenet and Georges had to patch up the tear with some pins, while Zoé did her hair all over again. All three fussed around her, especially the boy, who was kneeling on the floor with his hands among her skirts. She finally calmed down when Daguenet assured her that it could not be later than a quarter past twelve, seeing that she had got through the third act of *The Blonde Venus* at breakneck speed, scamping her lines and skipping whole couplets.

'It's still too good for that bunch of idiots,' she said. 'Did you see them tonight? There were some ugly mugs and no mistake. ... Zoé, my girl, you'll wait in here. Don't go to bed, because I may need you. ... Ah, there's the bell. And about time too.'

She ran off, while Georges stayed where he was with the tails of his coat brushing the floor. He blushed as he saw Daguenet looking at him. All the same, they had taken a great liking to each other. They rearranged their ties in front of the big cheval-glass, and brushed each other down, for they were all white from rubbing against Nana.

'Anybody'd think it was sugar,' murmured Georges, gig-gling like a greedy child.

A footman, hired for the evening, was showing the guests into the small drawing-room, a narrow room in which only four armchairs had been left in order to squeeze everybody in. From the large drawing-room next door came the clatter

of plates and cutlery, while a bright ray of light shone under the door. When she came in, Nana found Clarisse Besnus, whom la Faloise had brought along, already installed in one of the armchairs.

'What! You've got here first!' said Nana, who since her success spoke to her as an equal.

'Oh, it's his fault,' replied Clarisse. 'He's always afraid of arriving late. ... If I'd taken him at his word, I wouldn't have waited to take off my paint and my wig.'

The young man, who was meeting Nana for the first time, bowed, paid her a compliment, and spoke of his cousin, hiding his agitation behind exaggerated politeness. But Nana, not listening to him, and not knowing who he was, merely shook hands with him, and then moved swiftly towards Rose Mignon, with whom she promptly assumed a distinguished manner.

'Ah, dear Madame, how nice of you to come! ... I was so anxious to have you here!'

'It's I who am delighted, I assure you,' said Rose with equal amiability.

'Do sit down. ... Do you require anything?'

'No, thank you. ... Ah, yes, I've left my fan in my pelisse. Steiner, look in the right-hand pocket, will you?'

Steiner and Mignon had come in behind Rose. The banker turned back and reappeared with the fan, while Mignon gave Nana a brotherly kiss and forced Rose to do the same. Didn't they all belong to the same family in the theatre? Then he winked as if to encourage Steiner, but the latter was daunted by Rose's steely gaze, and contented himself with kissing Nana's hand.

Just then the Comte de Vandeuvres appeared with Blanche de Sivry. There was an exchange of deep bows, and Nana ceremoniously led Blanche to an armchair. Meanwhile Vandeuvres laughingly told the company that Fauchery was engaged in an altercation at the foot of the stairs because the concierge had refused to allow Lucy Stewart's carriage to come into the yard. They could hear Lucy in the hall calling the concierge a filthy boor. But when the footman opened the door, she came forward with her laughing grace of manner,

announced her name herself, and took both Nana's hands in hers, telling her that she had liked her straight away and considered her wonderfully talented. Nana, puffed up by her novel role of hostess, thanked her, genuinely embarrassed by Lucy's compliments. However, she had seemed preoccupied ever since Fauchery's arrival, and as soon as she could get near him, she asked in an undertone :

'Is he coming ?'

'No, he didn't want to,' the journalist answered abruptly, taken off his guard, although he had thought up some sort of a story to explain the Comte Muffat's refusal.

Seeing the young woman's sudden pallor, he realized how stupid he had been, and tried to retract his words.

'He couldn't come : he's taking the Countess to the ball at the Ministry of the Interior tonight.'

'All right,' murmured Nana, who suspected him of letting her down, 'you'll pay for that, my lad.'

'Oh, come now,' he said angered by the threat, 'I don't like that sort of errand. Ask Labordette the next time you want something done.'

They angrily turned their backs on each other. Just then Mignon was pushing Steiner up against Nana, and when Fauchery had left her, he said to her in a low voice, and with the good-natured cynicism of an accomplice who wants to do a friend a good turn :

'He's just longing for it, you know, only he's afraid of my wife. But you'll stick up for him, won't you ?'

Nana did not appear to understand. She smiled, and after looking at Rose, the husband and the banker, she finally said to the latter :

'Monsieur Steiner, you will sit next to me.'

At that moment a sound of laughter and whispering came from the hall, the noise of gay, chattering voices, as if a whole convent of runaway nuns were on the premises. And Labordette appeared with five women in tow, his boarding-school, as Lucy Stewart maliciously put it. There was Gaga, majestic in her tight-fitting blue velvet dress ; Caroline Héquet, clad as usual in black silk trimmed with Chantilly lace ; Léa de Horn, looking as dowdy as ever ; fat Tatan Néné, a good-natured

blonde with the bosom of a wet nurse, whom everybody teased; and finally little Maria Blond, a girl of fifteen, as skinny and corrupt as a street arab, who was making her début at the Folies. Labordette had brought the whole lot in a single carriage, and they were still laughing at the way they had been squeezed in with Maria Blond on their knees. But then they pursed their lips, shook hands and exchanged greetings with perfect decorum. Gaga put on childish airs, trying so hard to be well behaved that she developed a lisp. Tatan Néné alone let them down. They had been telling her on the way that six stark naked Negroes would wait on them at Nana's supper party, and after looking around anxiously, she asked to see them. Labordette called her a little silly, and begged her to be quiet.

'And Bordenave?' asked Fauchery.

'Oh, you can imagine how upset I am,' cried Nana. 'He won't be able to join us.'

'Yes,' said Rose Mignon, 'his foot got caught in a trap door, and he sprained his ankle badly. . . . If only you could hear him swearing, with his leg tied up and laid out on a chair!'

At this everybody deplored Bordenave's absence. Nobody ever gave a good supper-party without Bordenave. Ah, well, they would try to do without him. And they were already chatting about something else when a booming voice was heard:

'What's this? What's this? Is this the way you're going to bury me?'

There was a shout, and everybody looked round. It was Bordenave, huge and crimson-faced, standing in the doorway with one leg held stiff, and leaning for support on Simonne Cabiroche's shoulder. Simonne, a little creature who had had a certain amount of education, and could play the piano and speak English, was his mistress for the time being. She was a tiny, dainty blonde, so delicately built that she seemed to be bending under Bordenave's huge weight. Yet she remained smilingly submissive. He posed there for a few moments, conscious that the two of them made a striking picture.

'Shows how fond I am of you, eh?' he continued. 'Fact is, I was afraid I'd get bored, and I said to myself : "I'm going." '

But he interrupted himself with an oath. 'Hell and damnation!'

Simonne had stepped forward too quickly, and his foot had just taken his full weight. He gave her a shove, but she went on smiling, and, ducking her pretty head like an animal afraid of a beating, held him up with all the strength a dimpled little blonde can command. At the same time, in the midst of exclamations, everybody rushed to help him. Nana and Rose Mignon trundled up an armchair, into which Bordenave gently lowered himself, while the other women slid a second one under his leg. And all the actresses present kissed him as a matter of course. He kept on grumbling and sighing.

'Hell and damnation! Hell and damnation! ... Ah, well, my stomach's all right, as you'll see soon enough.'

More guests had arrived, and by now nobody could move any more in the room. The noise of plates and cutlery had ceased, and now a quarrel could be heard going on in the big drawing-room, where the *maître d'hôtel*'s voice was growling angrily. Nana was growing impatient, for she did not expect any more guests, and could not understand why supper was not served. She had just sent Georges to find out what was going on, when she was astonished to see more men and women arriving. She did not know any of them at all. Feeling somewhat embarrassed, she questioned Bordenave, Mignon and Labordette. They did not know them either. But when she asked the Comte de Vandeuvres, he suddenly remembered: they were the young men he had recruited at the Comte Muffat's. Nana thanked him. That was very good of him. Only they would be terribly crowded; and she asked Labordette to go and have seven more covers set. He had scarcely left the room before the footman showed in three newcomers. No, this time the whole thing was becoming ridiculous; there couldn't possibly be room for them all. Nana was beginning to grow angry, and in her loftiest manner declared that such behaviour was scarcely in good taste. But when she saw two more people arrive, she began laughing; it really was too funny for words. Never mind; they would have to fit in as best they could. Everybody was standing except for

Gaga and Rose, and of course Bordenave, who had two arm-chairs all to himself. There was a buzz of voices as the company chatted in low voices, occasionally stifling a slight yawn.

'Look here, lass,' said Bordenave, 'why don't we all sit down at table? . . . Because we're all here, aren't we?'

'Oh, yes, we're all here, I can tell you that!' she answered with a laugh.

She looked around her, but suddenly grew serious, as if she were surprised at not seeing somebody she expected. Probably there was a guest missing whom she chose not to mention. They would have to wait a little longer. A few minutes later the company noticed in their midst a tall gentleman with a noble face and a splendid white beard. The surprising thing was that nobody had seen him come in; he must have slipped into the little drawing-room through the bedroom door, which had remained ajar. Silence reigned, broken only by the sound of whispering. The Comte de Vandeuvres certainly knew who the gentleman was, for they had exchanged a discreet handshake; but the questions the women asked him were answered only with a smile. Thereupon Caroline Héquet wagered in a low voice that it was an English lord, who was on the eve of returning to London to get married; she knew him well; indeed she had had him. This story went the rounds of the ladies present; but Maria Blond, for her part, insisted that she recognized the stranger as a German ambassador who often spent the night with a friend of hers. Among the men he was summed up in a few rapid phrases. A responsible citizen, to judge by his looks. Perhaps he was going to pay for the supper. That was quite on the cards. He looked the sort who would. And anyhow who cared, provided the supper was a good one? In the end the company remained undecided, and indeed they were already beginning to forget the white-bearded old gentleman, when the *maître d'hôtel* opened the door of the big drawing-room.

'Supper is served, Madame.'

Nana had already accepted Steiner's arm without appearing to notice a movement on the part of the old gentleman, who started to walk behind her by himself. In any case it was impossible to organize any formal procession, and men and

women entered anyhow, joking with homely good humour about this lack of ceremony. A long table stretched from one end to the other of the vast room, which had been completely cleared of furniture; but even so this table was not long enough, for the plates on it were touching one another. The room was lit by four candelabra with ten candles apiece, the most striking being one in silver plate with sheaves of flowers to both right and left. The luxury was the sort to be found in a restaurant : china with a thin gold edge but no monogram, silverware worn and tarnished by constant washings, and crystal glasses of the kind of which an odd dozen can be made up in any cheap store. The scene suggested a premature house-warming in a *nouveau-riche* establishment where nothing had yet found its place. There was one chandelier missing, and the candles had scarcely begun burning properly, casting a pale yellow light above the dishes and stands, on which fruit, cakes and preserves alternated symmetrically.

'Sit where you like, you know,' said Nana. 'It's more amusing that way.'

She remained standing half-way down the room. The old gentleman whom nobody knew had placed himself on her right, while she kept Steiner on her left. Some guests were already sitting down when the sound of oaths came from the little drawing-room. It was Bordenave. Everybody had forgotten him, and he was having all the trouble in the world to hoist himself out of his two armchairs, cursing and swearing, and calling for that little bitch Simonne who had gone off with the rest. The women ran in to him, full of commiseration, and Bordenave eventually appeared, supported or rather carried by Caroline, Clarisse, Tatan Néné and Maria Blond. But then he had to be installed at the table, and that proved no easy matter.

'In the middle, facing Nana !' somebody shouted. 'Bordenave in the middle ! He'll preside over the meal !'

The ladies accordingly seated him in the middle. But he needed a second chair for his leg. When it was in place, two of the women raised his leg and carefully stretched it out. He didn't mind : he'd eat sideways.

'Hell and damnation,' he growled, 'but I'm in a bit of a fix tonight ! ... Ah, well, my darlings, Papa commends himself to your tender care !'

He had Rose Mignon on his right and Lucy Stewart on his left, and they promised to take good care of him. Everybody was now getting settled. The Comte de Vandeuvres placed himself between Lucy and Clarisse, Fauchery between Rose Mignon and Caroline Héquet. On the other side of the table, Hector de la Faloise had rushed to sit next to Gaga, and that despite appeals from Clarisse opposite; while Mignon, who was sticking close to Steiner, was only separated from him by Blanche, and had Tatan Néné on his left, with Labordette next to her. Finally, at the two ends of the table, young men were seated indiscriminately with women such as Simonne, Léa de Horn and Maria Blond. It was in this region that Daguenet and Georges found themselves drawn closer together as they both gazed smilingly at Nana.

However, two of the women were left standing, and there was a great deal of joking about their plight. The men offered to accommodate them on their knees. Clarisse, who could not move her elbows, told Vandeuvres that she was counting on him to feed her. And then that fellow Bordenave took up so much room with his chairs ! There was a final effort, and at last everybody was seated; but, as Mignon loudly remarked, they were like herrings in a barrel.

'Purée d'asperges comtesse or consommé à la Deslignac,' murmured the waiters, carrying platefuls of soup behind the guests' chairs.

Bordenave was loudly recommending the consommé when a shout went up, followed by protests and indignant exclamations. The door had opened, and three late arrivals, a woman and two men, had just come in. Oh, no, there was really no room for them ! Nana, however, without getting up from her chair, screwed up her eyes in an attempt to find out whether she knew them. The woman was Louise Violaine, but she had never seen the men before.

'This gentleman, my dear,' said Vandeuvres, 'is a friend of mine, a naval officer called Monsieur de Foucarmont. I invited him.'

Foucarmont bowed, very much at ease, adding:

'And I took the liberty of bringing along a friend of mine.'

'Splendid! Splendid!' said Nana. 'Do sit down. ... Let's see. ... Clarisse – move up a little. You've got lots of room down there. That's it – where there's a will ...'

Everybody crowded together more than ever, and Foucarmont and Louise got a little piece of the table for the two of them, but the friend had to sit some distance from his plate, and reached for his food between his neighbours' shoulders. The waiters took away the soup plates, and started serving *crépinettes de lapereaux aux truffes* and *gnochis au parmesan*. Bordenave stirred up the whole company by announcing that at one moment he had had the idea of bringing along Prullière, Fontan and old Bosc. At this Nana put on a haughty look and remarked curtly that she'd have given them a pretty warm reception. If she'd wanted any of her colleagues, she'd have asked them herself. No, no, she didn't want any third-rate actors there. Old Bosc was always drunk; Prullière was too stuck-up; and as for Fontan, he was insufferable in company with his loud voice and his stupid antics. Besides, third-rate actors were always out of place when they found themselves in the company of gentlemen such as those around them.

'Yes, yes, that's true,' said Mignon.

Around the table the gentlemen in question looked irreproachable, with their white ties and evening coats and their pale features, the natural distinction of which was further refined by fatigue. The old gentleman was as deliberate in his gestures and wore as subtle a smile as if he were presiding over a diplomatic congress. Vandeuvres, with his exquisite politeness towards the ladies next to him, might have been at one of the Comtesse Muffat's receptions. That very morning Nana had said to her aunt that, as far as the men were concerned, they could not have done better: they were all either well born or wealthy, in other words out of the top drawer. And, as for the ladies, they were behaving very well. Some of them, such as Blanche, Léa and Louise, had come in low dresses, but only Gaga was perhaps showing a bit too much,

particularly in view of the fact that at her age she would have done better not to have shown anything at all. Now that the company had finally settled down, the laughter and the jokes began to fail. Georges reflected that he had been at merrier dinner-parties in middle-class houses in Orléans. There was scarcely any conversation. The men who were not mutually acquainted stared at one another, while the women sat quietly and decorously; and it was this which surprised Georges most of all. They seemed positively respectable, and he had imagined that everybody would start kissing straight away.

The third course, consisting of a Rhine carp *à la Chambord* and a saddle of venison *à l'anglaise* was being served when Blanche remarked :

'Lucy, my dear, I met your Olivier on Sunday. . . . How he's grown !'

'Why, yes ! After all, he's eighteen,' replied Lucy. 'Which doesn't make me feel any younger. . . . He went back to school yesterday.'

Her son Olivier, whom she always spoke of with pride, was a pupil at the Naval Academy. There followed a conversation about children, during which all the ladies waxed sentimental. Nana described her own great happiness. Her baby, little Louis, was now taken care of by her aunt, who brought him round to see her every morning at eleven o'clock. She would take him into her bed, where he played with her griffon terrier, Lulu. It was enough to make you die laughing to see the two of them hiding under the clothes at the bottom of the bed. They had no idea how cunning little Louis had already become.

'Oh, I had such a day yesterday !' Rose Mignon said in her turn. 'Just imagine, I went to fetch Charles and Henri from their boarding-school; and then I simply had to take them to the theatre at night. . . . They jumped about, clapping their little hands and shouting : "We're going to see Mama act ! We're going to see Mama act !" . . . Oh, they were so excited!'

Mignon smiled complacently, his eyes moist with paternal tenderness.

'And at the theatre,' he went on, 'they were so funny! They

were as serious as grown men, eating Rose up with their eyes, and asking me why Mama's legs were all bare like that.'

The whole table roared with laughter, and Mignon looked radiant, flattered in his pride as a father. He worshipped his children, and had only one object in life, which was to increase their fortune by investing the money earned by Rose at the theatre and elsewhere with the scrupulous care of a faithful steward. When, as conductor of the orchestra in the *café-concert* where she used to sing, he had married her, they had been passionately in love with each other. Now they were good friends. There was an understanding between them: she worked as hard as she could, using her talent and beauty to the best advantage, while he had given up his violin in order the better to watch over her interests as an actress and as a woman. One could not have found a more united or down-to-earth couple anywhere.

'What age is your eldest?' asked Vandeuvres.

'Henri's nine,' replied Mignon, 'but a big fellow for his years!'

Then he started chaffing Steiner, who was not fond of children, and with quiet audacity informed him that, if he were a father, he wouldn't waste his money so stupidly. While he was talking, he watched the banker over Blanche's shoulders to see if it was coming off with Nana. But for the last few minutes Rose and Fauchery, who were talking very close together, had been getting on his nerves. Surely Rose wasn't going to waste her time on a fellow like that? In that sort of case, dammit all, he put his spoke in. And making a great show of his fine hands, with the diamond flashing on his little finger, he finished off a fillet of venison.

Meanwhile the conversation about children was still going on. La Faloise, excited by the immediate proximity of Gaga, asked after her daughter, whom he had had the pleasure of noticing in her company at the Variétés. Lili was quite well, but she was still such a tomboy! He was astonished to learn that Lili was entering her nineteenth year. Gaga became even more imposing in his eyes, and when he tried to find out why she had not brought Lili with her:

'Oh, no, no, never!' she said huffily. 'It's less than three

months ago that she absolutely insisted on leaving boarding-school. .... I was thinking of marrying her off straight away. ... But she's so fond of me that I had to take her home, though very much against my will!'

Her blue eyes with their blackened lashes blinked repeatedly while she talked about the problems of finding a husband for her little darling. If, at her time of life, she hadn't a single sou put by, but was still hard at work pleasuring men, especially very young men who might almost be her grandsons, it was simply because she considered a good match far more important. And with that she leant closer to la Faloise, who reddened under the huge bare shoulder plastered with powder with which she was almost crushing him.

'You know,' she murmured, 'if she goes the same way, it won't be my fault. .... But young people are so peculiar.'

There was a lot of movement around the table, as the waiters bustled to and fro. After the third course, the *entrées* had just appeared; they consisted of *poulardes à la maréchale, filets de sole sauce ravigote* and *escalopes de fois gras*. The *maître d'hôtel*, who till then had been serving Meursault, now offered a choice between Chambertin and Léoville. Amid the slight hubbub caused by the change of plates, Georges, who was growing more and more astonished, asked Daguenet if all the other ladies present also had children; and the other, amused by this question, provided him with some further details. Lucy Stewart was the daughter of an English-born workman, a greaser at the Gare du Nord: she was thirty-nine years old and had a face like a horse, but was absolutely adorable, and though she was consumptive positively refused to die. In fact, she was the most *chic* of all the women there, with three princes and a duke to her credit. Caroline Héquet, born at Bordeaux, the daughter of a little clerk who had since died of shame, was lucky enough to have an intelligent mother, who, after cursing her at first, had made it up with her after a year of reflection, telling herself that at least she would help her daughter to save a fortune. The daughter, twenty-five years old and very cold, was considered to be one of the finest women you could buy, at a price which never varied. The mother, a model of orderliness, kept the

books, recording income and expenditure with strict precision. She ran the whole household from a small flat she occupied two stories above her daughter's where she had also established a workroom for dressmaking and sewing. As for Blanche de Sivry, whose real name was Jacqueline Baudu, she came from a village near Amiens. A splendid creature, but stupid and untruthful, she claimed to be the granddaughter of a general, and never admitted to her thirty-two summers. She was a great favourite with the Russians on account of her *embonpoint*. Then Daguenet added a few brief words about the rest. There was Clarisse Besnus, whom a lady had brought back from Saint-Aubin-sur-Mer as her maid, only for the husband to launch her into a different profession. There was Simonne Cabiroche, the daughter of a furniture dealer in the Faubourg Saint-Antoine, who had been brought up in a large boarding-school with a view to becoming a governess. And then there were Maria Blond, and Louise Violaine, and Léa de Horn, who had all been reared in the gutters of Paris, not to mention Tatan Néné who had been a cowherd in the poorer part of Champagne till she was twenty. Georges looked at the ladies as he listened, dazed and excited by the brutal judgements being whispered in his ear, while behind him the waiters kept repeating in respectful tones:

'*Poulardes à la maréchale . . . Filets de sole sauce ravigote . . .*'

'My dear fellow,' said Daguenet, giving him the benefit of his experience, 'don't take that fish: it's no good at all at this time of night. . . . And have the Léoville: it's less treacherous than the other.'

Waves of heat were rising from the candelabra, from the dishes being handed round, and from the whole table round which thirty-eight people were suffocating; and the waiters kept forgetting themselves and running across the carpet, so that it was spotted with grease. Yet the supper failed to get any livelier. The ladies toyed with their meat, leaving half of it uneaten. Tatan Néné alone helped herself greedily to every dish. At that advanced hour of the night, the guests' appetites were only nervous cravings, the capricious desires of dis-

ordered stomachs. The old gentleman next to Nana refused every dish offered him; he had only taken a spoonful of soup, and now he sat in front of his empty plate gazing silently around him. There were some discreet yawns, and occasionally eyelids closed, and faces turned haggard. It was a dreadful bore – as it always was, according to Vandeuvres. This sort of supper ought to be a naughty affair, he said, if it was to be amusing. Otherwise, if it was too decent and respectable, you might as well eat in good society, where it wasn't any more boring. If it hadn't been for Bordenave, who was still bawling away, everybody would have fallen asleep. Bordenave himself, with his leg duly stretched out on its chair, was letting his neighbours, Lucy and Rose, wait on him as if he were a sultan. They were giving him their entire attention, looking after him, pampering him, and watching over his glass and plate; but that did not prevent him from complaining.

'Who's going to cut up my meat for me? ... I can't, the table's miles away.'

Every few minutes Simonne got up and stood right behind him to cut his meat and his bread. All the women took a great interest in what he was eating. The waiters were constantly recalled, and he was stuffed to suffocation. When Simonne wiped his mouth, while Rose and Lucy were changing his plate, he found this a charming attention, and condescending at last to express his appreciation, he said:

'That's right, my girl, that's as it should be. ... That's what all women are made for!'

Everybody woke up a little, and the conversation became general as the company was finishing some orange sherbets. The hot roast was a fillet served with truffles, and the cold roast a galantine of guinea-fowls in jelly. Nana, annoyed by the lack of spirit displayed by her guests, had begun talking very loudly.

'You know the Prince of Scotland has already reserved a stage-box to see *The Blonde Venus* when he comes to visit the Exhibition.'

'I very much hope that all the princes will come and see it,' Bordenave declared with his mouth full.

'The Shah of Persia is expected on Sunday,' said Lucy Stewart.

Whereupon Rose Mignon began talking about the Shah's diamonds. He wore a tunic entirely covered with gems; it was a wonderful thing, a flaming star worth millions of francs. And the ladies, with pale faces and eyes glittering with covetousness, craned forward, listing the names of the other kings and emperors who were expected. All of them were dreaming of some royal caprice, some night of love to be paid for with a fortune.

'Now, tell me,' Caroline Héquet asked Vandeuvres, leaning forward as she did so, 'how old is the Emperor of Russia?'

'Too old for you,' the Count replied with a laugh. 'Nothing doing there, I warn you.'

Nana made a pretence of being offended. The witticism struck most of the guests as rather too cutting, and there was a murmur of protest. But then Blanche gave a description of the King of Italy, whom she had seen once in Milan. He could scarcely be described as handsome, but that didn't prevent him from having all the women he wanted. She was slightly piqued when Fauchery assured her that Victor Emmanuel could not come to the Exhibition. Louise Violaine and Léa favoured the Emperor of Austria, and all of a sudden little Maria Blond was heard to say:

'What an old stick the King of Prussia is! ... I was at Baden last year, and you were always meeting him with Count Bismarck.'

'Bismarck?' Simonne broke in. 'Now I knew him once ... a charming man.'

'That's what I was saying yesterday,' exclaimed Vandeuvres, 'but nobody would believe me.'

And, just as at the Comtesse Sabine's, there followed a lengthy discussion about Bismarck. Vandeuvres repeated the same phrases, and for a moment or two he might have been back in the Muffats' drawing-room, the only difference being that the ladies were different. Then, just like the company the previous evening, they passed on to a discussion about music. After that, Foucarmont having let slip some mention of the taking of the veil which had caused such a stir in

Parisian society, Nana showed considerable interest and insisted on having some details about Mademoiselle de Fougeray. Oh, the poor child, burying herself alive like that! Still, when it was a question of vocation! All round the table the women seemed deeply moved. Georges, bored at hearing these things a second time, was beginning to ask Daguenet about Nana's personal life, when the conversation reverted inevitably to Count Bismarck. Tatan Néné bent towards Labordette to ask him in a whisper who this Bismarck might be, because she didn't know him. Whereupon Labordette, keeping a perfectly straight face, told her some fantastic stories: this fellow Bismarck was in the habit of eating raw meat, and when he met a woman near his lair he would carry her off on his back; the result was that at the age of forty he had already had thirty-two children.

'Thirty-two children at forty!' Tatan Néné exclaimed in credulous astonishment. 'He must be pretty worn out for his age.'

There was a roar of laughter, and it dawned on her that Labordette had been making fun of her.

'That's unfair! How am I to know if you're joking or not?'

Meanwhile Gaga had got no further than the Exhibition. Like all the ladies present she was eagerly getting ready for what promised to be an excellent season, with provincials and foreigners pouring into Paris. Perhaps, after the Exhibition, if business had gone well for her, she would be able to retire at last to a little house at Juvisy which she had had her eye on for a long time.

'What else can I hope for?' she said to la Faloise. 'Life is full of disappointments. ... Oh, if only I still had somebody to love me!'

Gaga was turning sentimental because she had felt the young man's knee pressing gently against her own. He was blushing hotly. Lisping away, she weighed him up at a glance. Not much of a catch to be sure; but then she wasn't hard to please any more. La Faloise obtained her address.

'Just look at that,' Vandeuvres murmured to Clarisse. 'I think Gaga's pinching your Hector.'

'A lot I care,' replied the actress. 'The fellow's an idiot. ... I've already chucked him out three times.... And it makes me sick to see little boys running after old women.'

She broke off, and jerked her head in the direction of Blanche, who ever since the beginning of the meal had been sitting hunched up in a most uncomfortable position, in order to show off her shoulders to the distinguished old gentleman three seats away from her.

'You're being ditched as well, my dear,' she said.

Vandeuvres smiled shrewdly and shrugged his shoulders. He was the last person to want to prevent poor Blanche from scoring a success. He was more interested in the spectacle which Steiner was presenting to the table at large. The banker was noted for his sudden passions. That terrible German Jew, that powerful financier who handled millions of francs, became an absolute idiot when he fell for a woman. And he wanted them all : not one could appear on the stage but he bought her, however expensive she might be. Vast sums were quoted, and on two occasions his furious appetite for women had ruined him. The whores, as Vandeuvres used to say, avenged public morality by emptying his money bags. A big speculation in the salt mines of the Landes had made him a power once more in the financial world, and for the past six weeks the Mignons had been eating into the profits from that transaction. But people were beginning to lay wagers that the Mignons would not finish the meal, for Nana was showing her white teeth. Once again Steiner was caught, and so badly this time, that as he sat by Nana's side, he seemed stunned, eating mechanically, his lower lip hanging down, his face mottled. She had only to name her price, yet she did not hurry, playing with him instead, giggling into his hairy ear, and enjoying the little twitches which kept passing over his heavy face. She could fall back on him any time if that skinflint of a Comte Muffat really meant to play Joseph with her.

'Léoville or Chambertin?' murmured a waiter, poking his head between Nana and Steiner, just as the latter was addressing her in a low voice.

'Eh? What?' he stammered, losing his head. 'Whatever you like – I don't care.'

Vandeuvres gently nudged Lucy Stewart, who had a spiteful tongue and a ferocious wit once she got going. That evening it was Mignon she found exasperating.

'He'd cheerfully hold the candle for them, you know,' she remarked to the Count. 'He's hoping to repeat the trick he pulled off with little Jonquier. ... You remember Jonquier, who was with Rose but suddenly fell for big Laure. ... Mignon procured Laure for Jonquier, and then brought him back to Rose, as if he were a husband who'd been allowed a little escapade. ... But this time it won't work. Nana doesn't look as if she hands back the men who are lent to her.'

'Why on earth is Mignon glaring at his wife like that?' asked Vandeuvres.

He leant forward, and saw Rose who was becoming extremely affectionate towards Faucherey. So this was the explanation of his neighbour's anger. He said with a laugh :

'Well, well, are you jealous?'

'Jealous!' said Lucy in a fury. 'Good heavens, if Rose wants Léon, she's welcome to him, for what he's worth! ... One bouquet of flowers a week, if that! ... Look, my dear, these actresses are all the same. Rose cried with rage when she read Léon's article on Nana; I know she did. So now, you see, she's got to have an article too, and she's earning it. ... As for me, I'm going to chuck Léon out, you see if I don't!'

She paused to say : 'Léoville' to the waiter standing behind her with his two bottles, and then went on, lowering her voice :

'I'm not going to make a scene : that isn't my style. ... But she really is a filthy slut. If I were in her husband's place I'd lead her a pretty dance. ... And she'll regret it too. She doesn't know my Faucherey : he's a nasty character too, sucking up to women like that to get on in the world. ... Oh, a nice lot they are, and no mistake !'

While Vandeuvres was doing his best to calm her down, Bordenave, neglected by Rose and Lucy, suddenly lost his temper, and complained that they were letting Papa die of hunger and thirst. This produced a timely diversion, for the

party was flagging; the guests had stopped eating, and were simply toying with their platefuls of *cèpes à l'italienne* and *croustades d'ananas Pompadour*. The champagne, however, which they had been drinking ever since the soup course, was gradually beginning to fill the guests with a nervous intoxication. They ended up by behaving less decorously than before. The women began leaning on their elbows in the midst of all the plates and glasses, while the men, in order to breathe more easily, pushed their chairs back; dress-coats mingled with light-coloured bodices, and bare shoulders, half turned towards the table, took on a silky gleam. It was too hot, and the glow of the candles above the table grew yellower and duller. Now and then, when a woman bent forward, the nape of her neck shone like gold under a rain of curls, and the glitter of a diamond clasp lit up a lofty chignon. There was a touch of fire too in the occasional jest, in the sparkle of laughing eyes, in the glimpse of white teeth, and in the reflection of the candelabra in a champagne glass. The guests were telling jokes at the tops of their voices, gesticulating wildly, asking questions which nobody answered, and calling to one another from one end of the room to the other. But the loudest din was being made by the waiters; they imagined that they were in the corridors of their restaurant, jostling one another, and serving the ices and dessert to an accompaniment of guttural exclamations.

'Children,' shouted Bordenave, 'you know we've got a performance tomorrow. . . . Be careful! Not too much champagne!'

'As far as I'm concerned,' said Foucarmont, 'I've drunk every imaginable sort of wine in all the four quarters of the globe. . . . Extraordinary liquids some of them were, strong enough to kill a man on the spot. . . . Well, none of them ever had the slightest effect on me. . . . I can't make myself drunk. I've tried and I can't.'

He was very pale and calm, lolling back in his chair and drinking without stopping.

'All the same,' murmured Louise Violaine, 'leave off: you've had enough. . . . A fine thing it would be if I had to look after you the rest of the night.'

Intoxication was giving Lucy Stewart's cheeks a red consumptive flush, while Rose Mignon was growing moist-eyed and sentimental. Tatan Néné, stupefied from over-eating, was laughing vaguely at her own stupidity. The others, Blanche, Caroline, Simonne and Maria, were all talking at once, telling each other about their private affairs, an argument with their coachman, plans for a picnic in the country, and complicated stories of lovers stolen and restored.

A young man near Georges tried to kiss Léa Horn and got a slap for his pains, accompanied by a 'Look here, let me go!' uttered in a tone of fine indignation. Georges himself, very tipsy and very excited by the sight of Nana, had been solemnly nursing a plan to get on all fours under the table, and go and curl up at Nana's feet like a puppy. Nobody would have seen him, and he would have stayed there in the quietest way. But when, at Léa's request, Daguenet told the young man to behave himself, Georges suddenly felt utterly heartbroken, as if he had just been scolded himself. Everything was stupid and wretched, and there was nothing worth living for. Daguenet, however, started teasing him, and made him swallow a big glassful of water, asking him what he would do if he found himself alone with a woman, seeing that three glasses of champagne were enough to bowl him over.

'Why, in Havana,' Foucarmont went on, 'they make a brandy from a certain wild berry which tastes as if you're swallowing fire. . . . Well, one evening I drank over a litre of it, and it didn't affect me one little bit. . . . Better than that, another time when we were on the coast of Coromandel, some savages gave us heaven knows what sort of a mixture of pepper and vitriol; and that didn't affect me either. . . . I can't make myself drunk.'

For the last few minutes la Faloise's face opposite had been getting on his nerves. He began sneering at the young man and making unpleasant jokes. La Faloise, whose head was swimming, kept shifting about in his seat and snuggling up against Gaga. But then his agitation had been increased by a new source of anxiety: somebody had just taken his

handkerchief, and with drunken obstinacy he demanded it back again, questioning his neighbours and bending down to look under people's chairs and feet. And when Gaga tried to calm him down, he muttered :

'It's very embarrassing. .... There are my initials and my coronet in the corner. ... It could compromise me.'

'I say, Monsieur Falamoise, Lamafoise, Mafaloise!' shouted Foucarmont, who thought it extremely witty to disfigure the young man's name *ad infinitum*.

But la Faloise grew angry and stammered something about his ancestors. He threatened to throw a decanter at Foucarmont's head, and the Comte de Vandeuvres had to intervene to assure him that Foucarmont was really very funny. And indeed, everybody was laughing. This shook the bewildered young man, who agreed to resume his seat; and he obeyed with childlike submissiveness when his cousin ordered him in a loud voice to eat up. Gaga had put her arm round him again; but every now and then he cast a sly and anxious glance at the other guests, still looking for his handkerchief.

Then Foucarmont, who was now in the mood for joking, attacked Labordette right at the other end of the table. Louise Violaine tried to make him hold his tongue, saying that when he started teasing other people like that, it always turned out badly for her. He had hit on the idea of addressing Labordette as 'Madame' and he must have found it very funny, for he kept on doing it, while Labordette calmly shrugged his shoulders, replying every time :

'Do shut up, my dear fellow – you're just being silly.'

But as Foucarmont persevered, and even became insulting, without anybody knowing why, he gave up answering him and appealed to the Comte de Vandeuvres.

'Monsieur, kindly make your friend hold his tongue. ... I don't want to become angry.'

He had fought a couple of duels, and was treated with respect and admitted into every circle. There was therefore a revulsion of feeling against Foucarmont. The company liked his wit and found him very funny; but that was no reason why the evening should be spoilt. Vandeuvres, whose delicate features were darkening with anger, insisted on his restoring

his sex to Labordette. The other men, Mignon, Steiner and Bordenave, who were all very tipsy by now, also intervened with shouts which drowned his voice. Only the old gentleman, sitting forgotten next to Nana, retained his distinguished air and his weary, silent smile, as with lack-lustre eyes he watched the dessert degenerate into a shambles.

'What do you say to our taking coffee in here, my dear?' said Bordenave. 'We're all very comfortable.'

Nana did not reply at once. Ever since the beginning of the supper party she had had the impression of no longer being in her own home. All these people had overwhelmed her and bewildered her, calling the waiters, talking at the tops of their voices, and making themselves comfortable, just as if they were in a restaurant. She herself had forgotten her duties as hostess, busying herself exclusively with the portly Steiner, who was bursting with apoplexy beside her. She listened to his propositions, turning them down every time with a shake of the head and that provocative laughter which is peculiar to full-bodied blondes. The champagne she had been drinking brought a flush to her cheeks; her lips were moist, her eyes sparkling; and the banker offered more with every coy movement of her shoulders, with every voluptuous swelling of her throat when she turned her head. Close to her ear, he could see a patch of delicate, satiny skin, which drove him crazy. Occasionally Nana was interrupted, and then, remembering her guests, she tried to be gracious in order to show that she knew how to receive guests. Towards the end of the meal she was very tipsy; much to her annoyance, champagne made her tipsy straight away. Then an infuriating idea occurred to her. Her lady guests were behaving badly as part of a dirty trick on her. Oh yes, she could see it all! Lucy had given Foucarmont a wink to egg him on against Labordette, while Rose, Caroline and the others were doing their best to stir up the men. Now there was such a din you couldn't hear yourself speak, because they thought they could do as they pleased when they came to supper at Nana's. Well, they'd soon learn different. She might be tipsy, but none of them could teach her anything about lady-like behaviour.

'Do tell them to serve the coffee here, my dear,' repeated Bordenave. 'I'd prefer it here, on account of my leg.'

But Nana had sprung to her feet, hissing into the astonished ears of Steiner and the old gentleman :

'Serves me right. . . . That'll teach me to go and invite such a filthy mob.'

Then she pointed to the door of the dining-room, and added loudly :

'If you want any coffee, it's in there.'

The company left the table and crowded towards the dining-room, without noticing Nana's anger. And soon nobody was left in the drawing-room but Bordenave, who advanced cautiously, leaning against the wall, and cursing away at those confounded women, who didn't care a damn about Papa once their bellies were full. Behind him the waiters were already busy clearing the table, following the loudly voiced orders of the *maître d'hôtel*. Jostling one another, they rushed to and fro, and made everything vanish like a pantomime backcloth at the sound of the stage-manager's whistle. The ladies and gentlemen were due to return to the drawing-room after drinking their coffee.

'Crikey, it's a bit nippy in here,' said Gaga with a slight shiver, as she entered the dining-room.

The window here had been left open. Two lamps illuminated the table, where coffee and liqueurs were set out. There were no chairs, and the guests drank their coffee standing, while the noise the waiters were making in the next room grew louder and louder. Nana had disappeared, but nobody worried about her absence. They managed perfectly well without her, helping themselves to coffee, and rummaging about in the drawers in the sideboard in search of spoons, which had not been provided. Several groups had formed as people separated during supper joined one another; and there was an exchange of glances, knowing laughs and witty remarks which summed up the state of affairs.

'Monsieur Fauchery ought to come to lunch with us one of these days, don't you agree, Auguste?' said Rose Mignon.

Mignon, who was toying with his watch-chain, fixed the journalist for a moment with his stern gaze. Rose was out of

her mind. As a good manager, he would have to put a stop to this nonsense. Payment had to be made for an article, but that should be the end of the matter. However, he was well aware how self-willed his wife could be, and as he made it a rule to wink paternally at the odd escapade when it was necessary to do so, he answered amiably:

'Certainly, I'd be delighted if he would. ... Do come to-morrow, Monsieur Fauchery.'

Lucy Stewart, who was chatting with Steiner and Blanche, heard this invitation, and, raising her voice, she said to the banker:

'It's a mania all these women have got. One even went so far as to steal my dog. ... But is it my fault, my dear, if you drop her?'

Rose turned round, deathly pale. Sipping her coffee, she gazed hard at Steiner, and all the suppressed anger she felt at his abandonment of her flamed out in her eyes. She saw more clearly than Mignon; it was stupid of him to try to repeat the Jonquier trick – that sort of dodge never succeeded twice running. Well, never mind: she would have Fauchery. She had been mad about him since the beginning of the supper-party, and if Mignon didn't like it, he had only himself to blame.

'You aren't going to fight, are you?' Vandeuvres asked Lucy Stewart.

'No, never fear. Only she'd better keep her mouth shut, or I'll tell her a few home truths.'

Then, summoning Fauchery with an imperious gesture, she said:

'I've got your slippers at home, darling. I'll send them over to your concierge's lodge tomorrow.'

He tried to joke about it, but she swept away majestically. Clarisse, who had propped herself against a wall in order to drink a quiet glass of kirsch, shrugged her shoulders. What a fuss over a man! Wasn't it inevitable that the moment two women found themselves together in the presence of their lovers, their first idea was to do each other out of them? It was only natural. Take her own case, for instance. If she had wanted to, she would have scratched Gaga's eyes out on

Hector's account. But he wasn't worth it. And as la Faloise was passing by she contented herself with saying to him :

'You like them pretty far gone, don't you, love ! Not just ripe, but positively mushy !'

La Faloise looked very annoyed. He was still on edge, and his suspicions were aroused by Clarisse's mockery.

'It was you who took my handkerchief, wasn't it !' he murmured. 'Give it back !'

'What a bore he is with that handkerchief of his !' she cried. 'Look, you idiot, why should I have taken it from you ?'

'That's easy,' he said suspiciously. 'To send it to my people, of course, and compromise me.'

Meanwhile Foucarmont was diligently setting to work on the liqueurs. He continued to gaze sneeringly at Labordette, who was drinking his coffee in the midst of the ladies. And he gave vent to a series of disjointed comments on the other man : he was the son of a horse-dealer – some said the bastard son of a countess; he had no income, but always had twenty-five louis in his pocket; he danced attendance on all the whores, but never slept with any of them.

'Never, never !' he repeated, growing angrier every minute. 'No, dammit all, I've got to box his ears.'

He drained a glass of Chartreuse. Chartreuse didn't have the slightest effect on him, not even that much – and he tapped his thumbnail against the edge of his teeth. But all of a sudden, just as he was advancing on Labordette, he turned white and fell like a log in front of the sideboard. He was dead drunk. Louise Violaine cursed her luck. She had known all along that things would turn out badly; and now she would have to spend the rest of the night looking after him. Gaga reassured her. She examined the officer with the eye of a woman of experience, and declared that there was nothing the matter with him; he would sleep like that for anything from twelve to fifteen hours without any serious consequences. Foucarmont was carried out.

'I say, where's Nana got to?' asked Vandeuvres.

Yes, now they came to think of it, she had disappeared after leaving the table. Everybody suddenly remembered her

and wanted to know where she was. Steiner, who had been feeling anxious about her for some time, asked Vandeuvres about the old gentleman, for he too had disappeared. But the Count reassured him: he had just seen the old gentleman to his carriage. He was a distinguished foreigner whose name there was no point in mentioning, for he was a very rich man who paid for supper-parties without asking anything in return. Then, as Nana was being forgotten once more, Vandeuvres caught sight of Daguenet looking round a door and beckoning him. He found the lady of the house sitting in the bedroom, white-lipped and erect, while Daguenet and Georges stood gazing at her with dismayed expressions.

'What's the matter with you?' he asked in surprise.

She did not answer, or even turn her head, and he repeated the question.

'The matter with me,' she cried at last, 'is that I don't like people making a bloody fool of me!'

Then she proceeded to give vent to everything that came into her head. Oh, no, she wasn't a fool – she could see what they were up to. They'd taken no notice of her during supper, and said all sorts of frightful things, to show that they despised her. A lot of sluts who couldn't hold a candle to her! Well, they wouldn't catch her going to any trouble for them again, just to be pulled to pieces afterwards. She didn't know what was keeping her from chucking the whole filthy lot out of the house. And choking with rage, she burst into sobs.

'Come now, my dear,' said Vandeuvres familiarly, 'you've had far too much to drink. Be reasonable.'

No, she wouldn't budge. She meant to stay where she was.

'I may be tipsy – that's quite on the cards. But I want people to show me a bit of respect.'

For the past quarter of an hour Daguenet and Georges had been vainly begging her to return to the dining-room. She stubbornly refused. Her guests could do whatever they liked; she despised them too much to go back to them. Never! Never! They'd have to cut her in pieces before she'd leave her room.

'I ought to have had my suspicions,' she went on. 'It's that

cat Rose who cooked the whole plot up. And I bet it was Rose who stopped that respectable woman I was expecting from coming tonight.'

She was referring to Madame Robert. Vandeuvres gave her his word of honour that Madame Robert had declined the invitation of her own accord. He listened and argued unsmilingly, for he was accustomed to this sort of scene, and knew how women in such a state ought to be treated. But whenever he tried to take hold of her hands to lift her out of her chair and take her with him, she struggled free, growing angrier and angrier. Nobody, she said, would ever get her to believe that Fauchery hadn't deliberately discouraged the Comte Muffat from coming. He was a regular snake was Fauchery, an envious character who was capable of doing anything to destroy a woman's happiness. Because, after all, she knew for certain that the Count had fallen for her. She could have had him if it hadn't been for Fauchery.

'Him, my dear? Never!' cried Vandeuvres, forgetting himself and laughing out loud.

'Why not?' she asked, looking serious and sobering up slightly.

'Because he's absolutely in the hands of the priests, and if he so much as touched you with the tips of his fingers he'd go and confess it the day after.... Now listen to a bit of good advice. Don't let the other fellow get away.'

She remained silent for a moment, thinking over what he had said. Then she got up, and went and bathed her eyes. Yet when they tried to take her into the dining-room, she still shouted 'No!' furiously. Vandeuvres left the bedroom smiling, without pressing her any further; and the moment he was gone she burst into tears, and threw herself into Daguenet's arms, saying:

'Oh, Mimi, you're the only one for me.... I do love you, Mimi.... Oh, wouldn't it be wonderful if we could always live together. Heavens, how unlucky women are!'

Then she noticed Georges, who, seeing them kiss, was growing very red, and she kissed him too. Mimi couldn't be jealous of a baby! She didn't want Paul and Georges ever to fall out, because it would be so nice for them all three to

stay like that, knowing how fond they were of one another. But a peculiar noise disturbed them : somebody was snoring in the room. After hunting around, they finally came across Bordenave, who, after taking his coffee, must have made himself comfortable there. He was sleeping on two chairs, his head propped on the edge of the bed, and his leg stretched out in front. Nana thought him so funny with his mouth open and his nose moving with every snore, that she went into a fit of uncontrollable laughter. She left the bedroom, followed by Daguenet and Georges, and went through the dining-room into the drawing-room, laughing louder and louder.

'Oh, my dear,' she cried, almost throwing herself into Rose's arms, 'you've never seen anything so funny! Come and have a look.'

All the women had to come with her. She took their hands coaxingly, and took them along willy-nilly, in such a spontaneous outburst of mirth that they all began laughing on trust. The whole party vanished and then returned, after standing breathlessly for a minute around Bordenave's magisterial form. Then there was an explosion of merriment, and when one of the women told the rest to be quiet, they could hear Bordenave's snores continuing in the distance.

It was nearly four o'clock. In the dining-room a cardtable had just been set up, at which Vandeuvres, Steiner, Mignon and Labordette had taken their seats. Behind them Lucy and Caroline stood laying bets, while Blanche, half-asleep and dissatisfied with the night's entertainment, kept asking Vandeuvres every five minutes if they were going soon. In the drawing-room there was an attempt at dancing. Daguenet was at the piano, or the music-box as Nana called it. She had not hired a pianist, because Mimi could play as many waltzes and polkas as anybody could wish. But the dancing was half-hearted, and the ladies were chattering drowsily in the depths of the sofas. Suddenly, however, there was a tremendous din. A bunch of eleven young men had arrived and were laughing loudly in the hall as they jostled to get into the drawing-room. They had just come from the ball at the Ministry of the Interior, and were in evening dress

with the ribbons of various unknown orders. Nana was annoyed at this noisy incursion, and called the waiters who still remained in the kitchen, ordering them to throw these gentlemen out. She swore that she had never seen any of them before. Fauchery, Labordette, Daguenet and the rest of the men had all come forward to enforce respect for the lady of the house. Insults were exchanged, fists were shaken, and for a moment it seemed as if it were going to be a general set-to. However, a sickly-looking little fellow with fair hair kept insistently repeating :

'Come now, Nana, the other evening at Peters', in the big red room. . . . You invited us, remember?'

The other evening, at Peters'? She didn't remember at all. To begin with, which evening? And when the little fair-haired fellow named the day as Wednesday, she remembered that she had indeed supped at Peters' on the Wednesday; but she hadn't invited anybody, she was almost sure of that.

'But suppose you *did* invite them, my dear?' murmured Labordette, who was beginning to have his doubts. 'Perhaps you were a little merry.'

Then Nana burst out laughing. It was quite possible, she really didn't know. Anyway, seeing that these gentlemen were here, they had her permission to come in. Everything worked out amicably, several of the newcomers found friends in the drawing-room, and what had begun as an unpleasant scene ended in an exchange of handshakes. The sickly-looking little fellow with fair hair bore one of the greatest names in France. What is more, the eleven anounced that others were due to follow them; and sure enough, the door opened every few minutes to admit men in white gloves and full evening dress. They too had come from the ball at the Ministry. Fauchery asked jokingly whether the Minister was coming too, but Nana answered crossly that the Minister went to the houses of people who weren't a patch on her. What she did not say was that she had suddenly begun to hope that she might see the Comte Muffat come in among those latecomers. He might have changed his mind. So, while chatting to Rose, she kept an eye on the door.

Five o'clock struck. The dancing had stopped, and only

the card-players persisted with their game. Labordette had given up his seat, and the women had returned to the drawing-room. The air there was heavy with the somnolence of a party prolonged into the early hours; and a dull light came from the lamps, whose charred wicks glowed red inside their globes. The ladies had reached that vaguely melancholy hour when they felt it necessary to tell each other the story of their lives. Blanche de Sivry spoke of her grandfather, the general, while Clarisse invented a romantic story about a duke seducing her at her uncle's house, where he used to come to hunt wild boar. Both women, sitting with their backs to each other, kept shrugging their shoulders and asking themselves how the devil anybody could tell such thumping lies. As for Lucy Stewart, she quietly admitted her lowly origins, and spoke of her own accord of her childhood days when her father, the greaser at the Gare du Nord, used to treat her to an apple turnover on Sundays.

'Oh, there's something I really must tell you!' little Maria Blond exclaimed abruptly. 'Across the street from my place there's a Russian gentleman who's incredibly rich. Well, just imagine, yesterday I received a basket of fruit – but what a basket! Huge peaches and enormous grapes, extraordinary fruit for the time of year. . . . And in the middle of it all, six thousand-franc notes. It was the Russian. . . . Naturally I sent it all back, but I must say I felt a little sorry about the fruit.'

The ladies looked at one another and pursed their lips. Little Maria Blond had a cheek at her age. Besides, to think that things like that should happen to sluts like her!

They all felt a profound contempt for one another. Lucy in particular aroused their jealousy, for they were beside themselves at the thought of her three princes. Since Lucy had begun taking a ride in the Bois every morning, a habit which had made her reputation, they had all taken up riding in a frenzy of emulation.

Day was about to dawn. Nana turned her eyes away from the door, losing hope of seeing Muffat arrive. The company were bored to distraction. Rose Mignon had refused to sing *The Slipper* and sat curled up on a sofa, chatting in a low

voice with Fauchery and waiting for Mignon, who had already won about fifty louis from Vandeuvres. True, a fat gentleman with a decoration and a serious face had recited an Alsatian dialect version of *Abraham's Sacrifice*, a piece in which the Almighty exclaimed : 'By me !' whenever he swore, and Isaac always answered : 'Yes, Papa !' Nobody, however, had seen the jokes, and the recitation had fallen flat. The guests were at their wits' end as to what to do to make merry and finish the evening in a suitable fashion. For a moment Labordette nursed the idea of denouncing the women to la Faloise, who kept on prowling round each of them in turn, to see if she were hiding his handkerchief in her bosom. As there were still a few bottles of champagne in the sideboard, the young men had started drinking again. They shouted at one another and tried to whip up their spirits; but the whole company began to succumb to a dismal sort of stupid intoxication. Then the little fair-haired fellow, the one who bore one of the greatest names in France, at his wits' end, and desperate at the idea that he could not think of anything amusing, hit on a brilliant idea : he took his bottle of champagne and emptied it into the piano. The others were convulsed with laughter.

'I say ! Why is he putting champagne in the piano?' asked Tatan Néné, who had watched him in astonishment.

'What, my dear, you mean to say you don't know why?' replied Labordette solemnly. 'It's because there's nothing better than champagne for pianos. It gives them tone.'

'Oh, I see,' murmured Tatan Néné, completely convinced.

And when the others began laughing at her she grew angry. How was she to know? They were always making fun of her.

Things were definitely going badly. The night looked like ending in disaster. In one corner of the room Maria Blond had started squabbling with Léa de Horn, whom she accused of sleeping with men who weren't really rich. They were getting positively insulting, criticizing each other's looks. Lucy, who was plain to the point of ugliness, told them to shut up. Good looks were nothing, she said : a good figure was all that mattered. Farther off, on a sofa, an embassy

official had slipped his arm round Simonne's waist, and was trying to kiss her neck; but Simonne, tired out and grumpy, pushed him away every time, slapping him across the face with her fan and shouting : 'Stop it !' For that matter, none of the ladies would allow herself to be touched. Did the men take them for whores? However, Gaga had recaptured la Faloise, and was practically holding him on her lap; while Clarisse was lost from view between a couple of gentlemen, shaken by the hysterical laughter of a woman being tickled. The little game round the piano was still going on in a mood of playful silliness, with all the men jostling one another in their eagerness to empty the dregs of their bottles into the instrument. It was a nice, simple game.

'Here, old boy, have a drink. ... Lord, but he's a thirsty old piano ! ... Look out, here's another bottle ! We mustn't waste a single drop !'

Nana had her back turned and did not see them. She was now falling back on the portly Steiner, who was sitting next to her. So much the worse for that fellow Muffat, who hadn't taken the opportunity that was offered him. Sitting there in her white foulard dress, as light and crumpled as a shift, sitting there with her tired eyes and her cheeks pale with the slight intoxication from which she was suffering, she offered herself to him with the honesty of a good-natured whore. The roses in her hair and her bodice had lost their petals, and nothing remained but their stalks. Steiner drew back his hand sharply from the folds of her skirts, where he had just come in contact with the pins Georges had stuck there. A few drops of blood appeared on his fingers, and one fell on Nana's dress and stained it.

'Now the bargain's signed in blood,' Nana said.

It was growing lighter. A dull glow, full of poignant melancholy, was stealing through the windows. And with that the guests began to leave in a rush, in a sour, bad-tempered mood. Caroline Héquet, annoyed at having wasted a whole night, said that it was high time to be off unless you wanted to witness some pretty nasty scenes. Rose pouted as if to suggest that her honour had been compromised. It was always like that with courtesans like Caroline Héquet : they

didn't know how to behave, and were quite disgusting when they started on their careers. And Mignon having cleaned Vandeuvres out completely, the couple took their leave without bothering about Steiner, after repeating their invitation to Fauchery for the following day. Lucy thereupon refused to allow the journalist to take her home, and loudly told him to go back to his trashy actress. At this, Rose, who had turned round, promptly retorted with a muttered 'Dirty bitch !' But Mignon, who in feminine quarrels always adopted the superior attitude of a fatherly man of experience, had already pushed her out of the flat, at the same time telling her to be quiet. Lucy came downstairs in solitary state behind them. After her came la Faloise, whom Gaga had to carry off, ill, sobbing like a child, and calling for Clarisse, who had long since gone off with her two gentlemen. Simonne too had vanished. Indeed nobody was left but Tatan, Léa and Maria, whom Labordette obligingly took under his wing.

'You know,' said Nana, 'I don't feel a bit like going to sleep. We must find something to do.'

She looked at the sky through the windowpanes. It was a livid colour, and sooty clouds were scudding across it. It was six o'clock. Over the way, on the other side of the Boulevard Haussmann, the glistening roofs of the still-slumbering houses stood out sharply against the dawn sky, while along the deserted roadway a gang of street-sweepers went by with a clatter of wooden clogs. Faced with this dismal awakening of Paris, she was overcome by a sentimental girlish yearning for the country, for an idyllic excursion, for something pure and white.

'You know what?' she said, coming back to Steiner. 'You're going to take me to the Bois de Boulogne, and we're going to drink some milk there.'

She clapped her hands in childish glee. Without waiting for the banker's reply – he naturally agreed, although he had been thinking of something else and was rather annoyed – she ran to throw a pelisse over her shoulders. In the drawing-room there was nobody left with Steiner except the bunch of young men. By this time they had emptied even the dregs of the glasses into the piano, and were talking of going,

when one of their number ran in triumphantly, holding a
final bottle which he had found in the pantry.

'Wait a minute!' he shouted. 'Here's a bottle of Chartreuse! ... There, it needed some Chartreuse; that'll buck
it up. ... And now let's go. ... We've fooled around here
long enough.'

In the dressing-room Nana was obliged to wake up Zoé,
who had dozed off on a chair. The gas was still alight. Zoé
shivered as she helped her mistress on with her hat and her
pelisse.

'Well, it's over, dear. I've done what you wanted me to,'
said Nana, speaking familiarly to the maid in a sudden burst
of confidence, and relieved at the thought that she had made
up her mind. 'You were right; the banker's as good as anybody else.'

The maid was grumpy and still half-asleep. She muttered
that Madame ought to have come to a decision the first
evening. Then, following her into the bedroom, she asked
what she was to do with 'those two'. She was referring to
Bordenave, who was still snoring away, and Georges, who
had sneaked in to bury his head in a pillow and had finally
fallen asleep on the bed, where he was breathing as gently
as a cherub. Nana told her to let them sleep on. But seeing
Daguenet come into the room she grew misty-eyed again. He
had been watching her from the kitchen, and was looking
utterly miserable.

'Look, Mimi, be reasonable,' she said, taking him in her
arms, and kissing and caressing him. 'Nothing's changed;
you know that it's Mimi I still adore! ... I had to do it,
hadn't I. ... I promise you we'll have even nicer times now.
Come tomorrow, and we'll arrange about hours. ... Now,
quick, give me a kiss to show me you love me. ... Oh, harder
than that!'

Pulling herself away, she rejoined Steiner, feeling happy
and once more obsessed with the idea of drinking milk. There
was nobody left in the flat but the Comte de Vandeuvres and
the man wearing the decoration who had recited *Abraham's
Sacrifice*. The two men seemed glued to the card-table; they
had forgotten where they were, and had not noticed the

daylight outside while Blanche had decided to stretch out on a sofa to try and get a little sleep.

'Oh, Blanche must come with us!' cried Nana. 'We're going to drink some milk, dear. . . . Do come – you'll find Vandeuvres here when we get back.'

Blanche got up lazily. This time the banker's apoplectic face turned white with annoyance at the idea of taking this fat creature with him, who was sure to cause him embarrassment. But the two women had already got him by the arms, and were repeating:

'You know, we want them to milk the cow in front of us.'

AT the Variétés they were giving the thirty-fourth performance of *The Blonde Venus*. The first act had just finished, and in the green-room Simonne, dressed as the little laundress, was standing in front of the console-table, surmounted by a looking-glass, situated between the two corner doors which opened obliquely on to the dressing-room passage. All alone, she was examining her face, and rubbing her finger below her eyes to correct her make-up, while the gas-jets on either side of the mirror warmed her with their crude light.

'Has he arrived?' asked Prullière, entering the room in his Swiss Admiral's costume, with its big sword, enormous top-boots, and huge plume of feathers.

'Who?' said Simonne, without turning her head, and laughing into the mirror to see her lips.

'The Prince.'

'I don't know; I've just come down. . . . Oh, he's bound to turn up. He comes every night.'

Prullière had gone over to the fireplace opposite the console-table, where a coke fire was burning, and two more gas-jets were flaring brightly. He raised his eyes, and looked at the clock and the barometer on the left and right, which were decorated with gilded sphinxes in the style of the First Empire. Then he stretched himself out in a huge wing chair whose green velvet had been so worn by four generations of actors that it looked yellow in places; and there he stayed motionless, staring vacantly into space, in that weary, resigned posture of actors accustomed to waiting for the call to go on stage.

Old Bosc too had just come in, dragging his feet and coughing. He was wrapped in an old yellow box-coat, part of which had slipped off one shoulder to reveal the gold-spangled cloak of King Dagobert. He put his crown on the piano, and for a moment or two stood grumpily stamping his

feet, without saying a word. His hands were trembling slightly, with the beginnings of alcoholism, but he looked a good sort for all that, and a long white beard lent a venerable appearance to his crimson drunkard's face. Then, in the silence of the room, while a shower of hail was rattling against the panes of the big square window which looked out on the courtyard, he made a gesture of disgust.

'What filthy weather!' he growled.

Simonne and Prullière did not budge. Four or five pictures – landscapes and a portrait of the actor Vernet – hung yellowing in the heat of the gas, and a bust of Potier, one of the bygone celebrities of the Variétés, gazed into space with its vacant eyes. But just then the silence was broken by a loud voice. It was Fontan, dressed for the second act as a young dandy in a costume which was completely yellow, even to his gloves.

'You know what?' he shouted, gesticulating. 'Today's my name-day!'

'What?' asked Simonne, coming up to him with a smile, as if attracted by the huge nose and vast clown's mouth of the man. 'You mean to say your name's Achille?'

'Right! ... And I'm going to get Madame Bron to send up some champagne after the second act.'

For a little while a bell had been ringing in the distance. The long-drawn sound grew fainter, then louder, and when the bell stopped, a shout could be heard coming up and down the stairs until it was lost along the passages : 'On stage for Act Two! On stage for Act Two!' This shout came nearer, and a pale-faced little man passed the green-room doors, yelling at the top of his shrill voice : 'On stage for Act Two!'

'Champagne!' exclaimed Prullière, without appearing to hear the din. 'By heaven, you're doing well!'

'If I were you I'd have it sent up from the café,' old Bosc said slowly. He had sat down on a bench covered with green velvet, with his head against the wall.

But Simonne said that they had a duty to consider Madame Bron's little perquisites. She clapped her hands excitedly, and gazed in fascination at Fontan's goat-like face, in which eyes and nose and mouth were twitching continuously.

136

'Oh, that Fontan!' she murmured. 'There's nobody like him, nobody at all!'

The two doors of the green-room stood wide open to the corridor leading to the wings. Along the yellow wall, which was brightly lit by a gas-lamp just out of sight, there passed a succession of rapidly moving figures – men in costume and half-naked women wrapped in shawls, in other words, all the walkers-on in the second act, who would shortly make their appearance as carnival masks in the ball at the Boule Noire; and at the end of the corridor their feet could be heard clattering down the five wooden steps which led to the stage. As Clarisse went running by, Simonne called to her, but she said she would be back in a moment. And indeed she reappeared almost at once, shivering in the thin tunic and sash which she wore in the part of Iris.

'Lord, but it's cold,' she said, 'and I've left my furs in my dressing-room.'

Then as she stood toasting her legs, in their bright pink tights, in front of the fire, she added: 'The Prince has arrived.'

'Ah!' the others exclaimed inquisitively.

'Yes, that's what I was running for. I wanted to see. He's in the first stage-box on the right, the same he was in on Thursday. That's the third time he's been this week. Lord, but she's lucky, that Nana is! I was willing to bet he wouldn't come again.'

Simonne opened her mouth to say something, but her words were drowned by a fresh shout close to the green-room. In the passage the call-boy was yelling at the top of his shrill voice: 'They've knocked!'

'Three times!' said Simonne, when she was able to make herself heard. 'It's getting exciting. He won't go to her place, you know; he takes her to his. And it seems that it's costing him a pretty penny.'

'What else can he expect when he goes out on the town?' Prullière murmured wickedly, getting up to have a last look in the mirror at the handsome face beloved by the boxes.

'They've knocked! They've knocked!' the call-boy kept

repeating, in a voice which gradually died away as he ran along the corridors on one floor after another.

Then Fontan, who knew what had happened the first time the Prince had gone with Nana, told the two women the whole story, while they snuggled up against him, roaring with laughter whenever he bent down to whisper certain details in their ears. Old Bosc had not budged: he was totally indifferent. That sort of thing no longer interested him. He was happily stroking a big ginger cat, which was lying curled up on the bench; and he ended up by taking her in his arms with the good-natured tenderness of an ageing monarch. The cat arched its back, and then after a prolonged sniff at the big white beard, doubtless repelled by the smell of paste, it curled up again on the bench and went to sleep. Bosc remained grave and absorbed.

'You can do what you like, but if I were you I'd get the champagne from the café – it's better there,' he said suddenly to Fontan as the other was coming to the end of his story.

'The curtain's up!' cried the call-boy in a drawn-out, broken voice. 'The curtain's up! The curtain's up!'

The shout echoed on for a moment, and there was a sound of hurrying footsteps. The padded door at the end of the passage opened suddenly, letting in a burst of music and a distinct murmur of voices; and then it swung to again with a dull thud.

A sleepy calm once again reigned in the green-room, as if the place were a hundred miles from the auditorium in which a huge crowd was applauding. Simonne and Clarisse were still talking about Nana. Now *there* was a girl who never hurried! Why, the day before she had come on late yet again. But then they fell silent, for a tall girl had just poked her head round the door, and, seeing that she had made a mistake, had gone off to the end of the passage. It was Satin, wearing a hat and a little veil, and trying to look like a lady paying a call.

'A real little trollop she is!' murmured Prullière, who had seen her hanging around the Café des Variétés for the past year. And Simonne told the others how Nana had recognized

Satin as an old friend, had taken a fancy to her, and was pestering Bordenave to give her a part in the show.

'Good evening to you!' said Fontan, shaking hands with Mignon and Fauchery, who had just come in.

Old Bosc himself offered them the tips of his fingers, while the two women kissed Mignon.

'A good house tonight?' asked Fauchery.

'Splendid!' replied Prullière. 'You should see the way they're lapping it up!'

'I say,' remarked Mignon, 'aren't you on about now?'

Oh, all in good time! They were only at the fourth scene yet. Only Bosc got up with the instinct of an old trouper who could feel that his cue was coming. And sure enough, at that very moment the call-boy appeared at the door.

'Monsieur Bosc!' he called out. 'Mademoiselle Simonne!'

Simonne flung a fur-lined pelisse over her shoulders and went out. Without hurrying, Bosc went and got his crown, which he put on his head and tapped into place. Then, trailing his coat behind him, he tottered out of the room, grumbling and scowling like a man who has been rudely disturbed.

'You were very kind in your last notice,' continued Fontan, addressing Fauchery. 'Only why do you say that actors are vain?'

'Yes, my boy, why do you say that?' cried Mignon, bringing his huge hands down on the journalist's slender shoulders with such force as almost to double him up.

Prullière and Clarisse managed to refrain from bursting into laughter. For some time past the whole company had been deriving amusement from a comedy going on in the wings. Mignon, furious about his wife's caprice, and annoyed to see Fauchery giving the two of them only a dubious sort of publicity, had hit on the idea of revenging himself on the journalist by overwhelming him with marks of friendship. Every evening, when he met him at the theatre, he would slap him heartily on the back, as if carried away by feelings of affection; and Fauchery, who was a puny little man in comparison to that colossus, was obliged to accept the slaps with a forced smile so as not to fall out with Rose's husband.

'So you'd insult Fontan, would you, my lad?' continued Mignon, carrying the joke even further. 'On guard! One, two, and got you in the chest!'

He lunged and struck the young man so hard that the latter went very pale for a moment and could not speak. With a wink Clarisse showed the others Rose Mignon standing on the threshold of the green-room. Rose had witnessed the scene, and walked straight up to the journalist, as if she had failed to notice her husband; then, standing on tiptoe, bare-armed in her costume as the Baby, held her face up to him with a coaxing childish pout.

'Good evening, Baby,' said Fauchery, kissing her familiarly.

This was his revenge. Mignon did not even seem to notice this kiss, for everybody kissed his wife in the theatre. But he laughed, and gave the journalist a spiteful look. The latter would undoubtedly have to pay for Rose's bravado.

In the passage the padded door opened and closed again, blowing a storm of applause as far as the green-room. Simonne came in after her scene.

'Old Bosc has scored a hit,' she cried. 'The Prince was doubled up with laughter, and applauded with the rest as if he'd been paid to. ... I say, do you know the tall gentleman sitting by the Prince in the stage-box? A very dignified, good-looking man with splendid whiskers.'

'That's the Comte Muffat,' replied Fauchery. 'I know that the Prince, when he was at the Empress's the day before yesterday, invited him to dine with him tonight. ... He must have debauched him afterwards!'

'So that's the Comte Muffat! We know his father-in-law, don't we, Auguste?' Rose said to Mignon. 'You know – the Marquis de Chouard. I went to sing at his place, you remember. ... Well, he's in the house too. I noticed him at the back of a box. Now *there's* an old boy for you ...'

Prullière, who had just put on his huge plume of feathers, turned round to call her.

'Rose, let's be off!'

She ran after him, leaving her sentence unfinished. At that moment, Madame Bron, the concierge of the theatre, passed the door with a huge bouquet in her arms. Simonne asked

jokingly if it was for her; but the concierge did not bother to answer, merely jerking her chin towards Nana's dressing-room at the end of the passage. Oh, that Nana! She was always getting flowers. Then, when Madame Bron came back, she handed a letter to Clarisse, who let out a muffled oath. That nuisance la Faloise again! He just wouldn't leave her alone! And when she learnt that the gentleman in question was waiting in the concierge's lodge, she shouted:

'Tell him I'm coming down at the end of this act. ... I'm going to give him one right across the face.'

Fontan had rushed forward, shouting:

'Madame Bron! ... Just a minute, Madame Bron! ... Send up six bottles of champagne at the interval, will you.'

Meanwhile the call-boy had reappeared, panting for breath, to call out in a sing-song voice:

'Everybody on stage! ... You're on, Monsieur Fontan! Hurry up! Hurry up!'

'All right, all right, I'm on my way, Barillot,' replied a flustered Fontan.

And he ran after Madame Bron, saying:

'You've got that, have you? Six bottles of champagne in the green-room at the interval. ... It's my name-day, and I'm treating everybody.

Simonne and Clarisse had gone off with a great rustling of skirts. Everybody disappeared; and when the door at the end of the passage had swung to with its usual thud, a fresh hail shower could be heard beating against the window of the now silent green-room. Barillot, a pale-faced little old man who had been the theatre call-boy for thirty years, had gone up to Mignon with easy familiarity and offered him his open snuff box. This offering and accepting a pinch of snuff gave him a minute's rest in his interminable running up and down the stairs, and along the dressing-room passages. True, he still had to summon Madame Nana, as he called her; but she did as she pleased and didn't care a fig for fines; if she wanted to miss her cue, she missed it, and that was that. But he stopped short in amazement and muttered:

'Well, I never, she's ready: here she is! ... She must know that the Prince is here.'

Nana had indeed appeared in the corridor. She was dressed as the Fishwife, with her arms and face all white, and a couple of red spots under her eyes. She did not come into the green-room, but simply nodded to Mignon and Fauchery.

'Evening. How are things?'

Mignon alone shook her outstretched hand. Then Nana proceeded majestically on her way, followed by her dresser, who almost trod on her heels while stooping to adjust the folds of her skirt. Behind the dresser, bringing up the rear of the procession, came Satin, trying to look lady-like but already bored to death.

'And Steiner?' Mignon asked abruptly.

'Monsieur Steiner left yesterday for the Loiret,' said Barillot, leaving to go back into the wings. 'I believe he intends to buy a country house in those parts.'

'Oh, yes, I know, Nana's country house.'

Mignon had grown suddenly serious. Oh, that Steiner! He had promised Rose a town house in the old days! Still, it didn't do to fall out with anybody. They would just have to try all over again. Deep in thought, but maintaining his superior air, Mignon paced up and down between the fireplace and the console-table. There was nobody in the green-room now but Fauchery and himself. The journalist was tired, and had just stretched out in the depths of the big armchair. There he stayed quite still, with half-closed eyes, while the other glanced down at him as he passed. When they were alone Mignon scorned to slap his back all the time : what was the use, since nobody was there to enjoy the sight? He cared too little to be personally entertained by the jokes he perpetrated in his role as a facetious husband. Glad of this respite of a few minutes, Fauchery stretched his feet out languidly towards the fire, and let his eyes wander from the barometer to the clock. In the course of his pacing, Mignon planted himself in front of Potier's bust, gazed at it unseeingly, and then turned back to the window overlooking the dark pit of the courtyard. The rain had stopped, and a profound silence had fallen over the room, a silence made still more oppressive by the fierce heat of the coke fire and the glare of the gas-jets. Not a sound came from the wings. The

staircase and the passages were deadly still. It was one of those stifling silences at the end of an act when the green-room seems to be falling asleep in an asphyxiating murmur, while on the stage the whole company are creating the deafening uproar of a grand finale.

'The little fools !' Bordenave's hoarse voice could suddenly be heard exclaiming.

He had only just arrived, and he was already bawling out complaints about two chorus-girls, who had nearly fallen flat on the stage because they were playing the fool. When he caught sight of Mignon and Faucheryi, he called them to show them something : the Prince had just expressed a desire to compliment Nana in her dressing-room, during the interval. But as he was leading them into the wings, the stage-manager went by.

'Find those bitches Fernande and Marie for me !' Bordenave cried angrily.

Then, calming down, and trying to assume the dignified expression of a heavy father, he wiped his face with his handkerchief and added :

'I am going to receive His Highness.'

The curtain fell in the midst of a long-drawn salvo of applause. Straight away there was a frantic rush of people across the dusky stage, which was no longer lit by the foot-lights, and the walkers-on hurried to get back to their dressing-room, while the scene-shifters rapidly removed the set. Simonne and Clarisse, however, had remained upstage, talking together in whispers. On the stage, between two of their cues, they had just settled a little matter. On mature reflection Clarisse had decided that she preferred not to see la Faloise, who could not bring himself to leave her for Gaga, and so Simonne was simply going to go and explain to him that a man couldn't cling to a woman in that fashion. In short, she would settle his hash.

Accordingly Simonne, dressed in her laundress's costume, but with furs over her shoulders, ran down the greasy steps of the narrow spiral staircase with the damp walls which led to the concierge's lodge. This lodge, situated between the actors' staircase and that of the management, was shut in on both

sides, right and left, by large glass partitions, and resembled a huge transparent lantern, in which two gas-jets were blazing away. Letters and newspapers were piled up in a set of pigeon-holes, and on the table bouquets of flowers lay waiting beside dirty plates and an old bodice, the button-holes of which the concierge was busy mending. And in the midst of this filth and disorder, immaculately dressed, white-gloved men of the world sat with patient, submissive expressions on the four straw-bottomed chairs, turning their heads sharply every time Madame Bron came downstairs from the theatre with a reply to some message or other. As it happened, she had just handed a note to a young man who had hurriedly opened it under the gaslight in the vestibule, and who had gone slightly pale on reading the classic message, which so many others had read in that very spot : 'Impossible tonight, darling – I've an engagement.' La Faloise was sitting on one of the chairs at the back of the room, between the table and the stove. He seemed set on passing the entire evening there, yet he looked uneasy, and kept tucking up his long legs because a whole litter of black kittens were pestering him, while the mother cat sat staring at him with her yellow eyes.

'Oh, it's you, Mademoiselle Simonne! What can I do for you?' asked the concierge.

Simonne asked her to send la Faloise out to her. But Madame Bron was unable to oblige her straight away. Under the staircase, in a sort of deep cupboard, she kept a little bar, to which the walkers-on came for drinks in the intervals; and seeing that just then there were five or six big fellows there, still dressed as masked dancers at the Boule Noire, who were dying of thirst and in a tremendous hurry, she was a little flustered. A gas-jet was blazing in the cupboard, in which could be seen a tin-topped table and a few shelves filled with partly emptied bottles. Whenever the door of this coal-hole was opened, a strong whiff of alcohol came out which mingled with the smell of stale cooking in the lodge and the penetrating scent of the bouquets on the table.

'Well, now,' continued the concierge when she had served the walkers-on, 'is it the little dark chap over there you want?'

'No, don't be silly!' said Simonne. 'It's the thin one next to the stove – the one whose trousers your cat's sniffing at.'

And with that she took la Faloise off into the lobby, while the other gentlemen resigned themselves once more to their vigil in the stifling room, and the masked dancers drank on the stairs, pushing one another about and joking in the hoarse voices of drunkards.

On the stage, above, Bordenave was cursing the scene-shifters, who seemed to be taking all night changing the scenery. He accused them of dawdling on purpose, and felt sure the Prince was going to have a set-piece fall on his head.

'Push hard! Push hard!' shouted the foreman.

At last the backcloth went up into the air, and the stage was clear. Mignon, who had been keeping his eye on Fauchery, seized the opportunity to start his bullying again. He clasped him in his big arms, shouting:

'Look out! That pole nearly fell on you!'

And he carried him off, shaking him before putting him down again. At the sound of the scene-shifters' raucous laughter, Fauchery turned white; his lips trembled, and he seemed on the point of losing his temper as Mignon, putting on a good-natured air, slapped him on the shoulder with enough affectionate violence to break him in two.

'You see, I value your health,' he said. 'Dammit all, I'd be in a pretty pickle if anything happened to you!'

But just then there was a murmur of 'The Prince! The Prince!' and everybody turned and looked at the little door into the auditorium. So far nothing could be seen but Bordenave's round back and beefy neck, bobbing up and down in a series of obsequious bows. Then the Prince came into view. Tall and sturdy, with a fair beard and a pink complexion, he had the sort of distinction peculiar to a solidly built man of pleasure, his square shoulders clearly indicated beneath the impeccably cut frock-coat. Behind him walked the Comte Muffat and the Marquis de Chouard, but as this particular corner of the theatre was in darkness the group was lost from view amid huge moving shadows.

To speak to a queen's son, the heir to a throne, Bordenave had assumed the voice of a showman exhibiting a bear, a

voice tremulous with false emotion. He kept repeating:

'If His Highness will be good enough to follow me. . . . If His Highness would deign to come this way . . . His Highness must take care . . .'

The Prince was not hurrying in the least. On the contrary, he was very interested, and kept lingering to watch the scene-shifters' operations. A batten had just been lowered, and this row of lights, hanging in its iron mesh, illuminated the stage with a wide beam of light. Muffat, who had never yet been behind the scenes at a theatre, was even more astonished than the rest, filled with a feeling of malaise, a vague repugnance mingled with fear. He looked up into the flies, where more battens, on which the gas-jets had been turned down, gleamed like galaxies of little bluish stars amid the chaos of the upper flies and wires of all thicknesses, painters' cradles, and backcloths spread out in space, like huge sheets hung out to dry.

'Lower away!' the foreman shouted all of a sudden.

And the Prince himself had to warn the Count, for a back-cloth was descending. They were installing the scenery for the third act, which was the grotto on Mount Etna. Men were busy fixing poles in the sockets, while others were fetching the frames, which were leaning against the walls of the stage, and fastening them with strong ropes to the poles. At the back of the stage, in order to produce the blaze of light from Vulcan's glowing forge, a stage-hand had fixed a lampstand, and was now lighting the burners in their red glasses. The scene was one of apparent confusion, not to say chaos, but everything down to the slightest movement was in fact pre-arranged. And in the midst of all the hustle and bustle, the prompter was shuffling up and down to stretch his legs.

'His Highness does me too much honour,' Bordenave was saying, still bowing energetically. 'This isn't a big theatre, but we do what we can. . . . Now, if His Highness deigns to follow me . . .'

The Comte Muffat was already making for the dressing-room passage. The fairly steep slope of the stage had taken him by surprise, and some of his uneasiness was due to his awareness that he was standing on a hollow floor. Through

the open sockets gas could be seen burning down below and human voices and cellar draughts coming up from the gloomy depths bore witness to a whole subterranean existence. But just as the Count was going up-stage, a little incident halted him. Two women dressed for the third act were chatting by the peep-hole in the curtain. One of them, bending forward, and widening the hole with her fingers to get a better view, was scanning the auditorium.

'I can see him,' she suddenly said. 'Christ, what a mug!'

Deeply shocked, Bordenave had to restrain himself from giving her a kick in the behind. But the Prince smiled, and looked pleased and excited to have heard the remark. He gazed warmly at the little woman who did not give a damn for His Highness, and she, for her part, laughed cheekily. Eventually, however, Bordenave persuaded the Prince to follow him. The Comte Muffat was beginning to perspire and had just taken his hat off. What inconvenienced him most was the heavy, dense, over-heated air of the place, with its overpowering smell, a smell peculiar to the wings of a theatre, and combining the different scents of gas, of the glue used to make the scenery, of dirty nooks and crannies, and of the chorus-girls' grubby underwear. In the corridor the atmosphere was still more suffocating, full of the acrid scents of toilet-waters, the perfumes of soaps, and the stench of human breath. The Count raised his eyes as he passed and glanced up the staircase well, startled by the sudden flood of light and warmth which fell on the back of his neck. Up above there was a clinking of basins, the sound of laughter and shouting, and a banging of doors, which in their continual opening and shutting let out a variety of feminine smells, the musky scent of paint and powder mingling with the pungent odour of women's hair. He did not stop; on the contrary, he quickened his step, and almost took to his heels, his skin tingling with the thrill of this exciting glimpse of a world he knew nothing of.

'Fascinating place, a theatre, eh?' said the Marquis de Chouard, with the delighted expression of a man who feels thoroughly at home.

But Bordenave had at last reached Nana's dressing-room

147

at the end of the passage. He calmly turned the door-handle, then, standing back, said :

'If His Highness will be good enough to go in . . .'

They heard the cry of a startled woman, and saw Nana, bare to the waist, run behind a curtain, while her dresser, who had been drying her, stood with her towel still in the air.

'Oh, it's silly coming in like that,' cried Nana from her hiding-place. 'Don't come in; you can see that you can't come in.'

Bordenave seemed displeased by this flight.

'Do come out my dear,' he said. 'It doesn't matter. It's His Highness. Come now, don't be childish.'

And, when she refused to appear, still a little shaken though already beginning to laugh, he added in a gruff fatherly voice :

'Good heavens, these gentlemen know perfectly well what a woman looks like. They won't eat you.'

'I'm not so sure of that,' the Prince said wittily.

Everybody started laughing loudly to flatter him. It was an exquisite *mot*, a thoroughly Parisian witticism, as Bordenave remarked.

Nana made no further reply, but the curtain began moving : no doubt she was making up her mind. Meanwhile the Comte Muffat, his cheeks flushed, took stock of the dressing-room. It was a square room with a very low ceiling, entirely hung with a light brown material. A curtain of the same material hung from a copper rod, forming a sort of recess at the far side of the room, while two large windows opened on the courtyard of the theatre, three yards at the most from a leprous wall on which, in the darkness of the night, the panes cast squares of yellow light. A large cheval-glass stood opposite a white marble dressing-table, which was covered with a disorderly array of bottles and glass jars containing oils, essences and powders. The Count went up to the cheval-glass and saw that he was looking very flushed, with small beads of perspiration on his forehead. He lowered his eyes, and came and stood in front of the dressing-table, on which the basin full of soapy water, the little scattered ivory utensils

and the damp sponges seemed to absorb his attention for a moment. The feeling of vertigo which he had experienced when he had first called to see Nana on the Boulevard Haussmann overcame him once more. He felt the thick dressing-room carpet yielding underfoot, while the gas-jets burning by the dressing-table and the cheval-glass seemed to be shooting hissing flames around his temples. For a moment, afraid of fainting under the influence of this female scent which he was now encountering again, intensified tenfold by the low ceiling, he sat down on the edge of the upholstered couch between the two windows. But he got up again straight away and went back to the dressing-table, where he gazed unseeingly into space, thinking about a bouquet of tuberoses which had once faded in his bedroom, and had nearly killed him. When tuberoses rot, they give off a human smell.

'Hurry up!' Bordenave whispered, putting his head round the curtain.

In the meantime the Prince was listening obligingly to the Marquis de Chouard, who had picked up the hare's foot from the dressing-table and was explaining the way grease-paint was put on. In a corner of the room Satin, with her pure virginal face, was staring at the gentlemen, while the dresser, Madame Jules, was getting ready Venus's tights and tunic. Madame Jules was a woman of indeterminate age, with the parchment skin and changeless features peculiar to old maids whom no one ever knew when they were young. She had shrivelled up in the torrid atmosphere of the dressing-rooms, among the most famous thighs and bosoms in all Paris. She invariably wore a faded black dress, and on her flat and sexless chest a forest of pins was stuck in where her heart should have been.

'I beg your pardon, gentlemen,' said Nana, drawing aside the curtain, 'but you took me by surprise . . .'

They all turned round. She had not covered herself at all, but simply buttoned on a little cambric bodice which half revealed her breasts. When the intruders had put her to flight, she had scarcely begun undressing, and was stripping off her Fishwife costume. A bit of her chemise still poked out of her drawers behind. And there she stood, bare-armed,

bare-shouldered, bare-breasted, in all her adorable youthfulness and fair, fleshly beauty, still holding the curtain with one hand, as if ready to draw it again at the slightest provocation.

'Yes, you took me by surprise. ... I'll never dare ...' she stammered in mock embarrassment, while a rosy flush coloured her neck and a shy smile touched her lips.

'Get along with you,' cried Bordenave, 'seeing that these gentlemen approve of your looks!'

She ventured a few more hesitant, girlish expressions, wriggling as if somebody were tickling her, and saying:

'His Highness does me too great an honour. I beg His Highness to excuse me for receiving him like this ...'

'It is I who am being importunate,' said the Prince, 'but I was unable, Madame, to resist the desire to compliment you ...'

Thereupon, quite calmly, to reach her dressing-table, she walked in nothing but her bodice and her drawers through the midst of the gentlemen, who drew back to let her pass. Her drawers ballooned out over her full hips while, with swelling bosom, she continued to greet her visitors with her delicate smile. All of a sudden she appeared to recognize the Comte Muffat, and she held out her hand to him as an old friend. Then she scolded him for not having come to her supper-party. His Highness deigned to chaff Muffat about this, and the latter stammered a reply, shivering with excitement at the thought that for a second he had held in his own feverish grasp that little cool scented hand. The Count had dined extremely well with the Prince, who was a great eater and a heavy drinker. Both of them were even a little tipsy, but they were behaving very creditably. To hide his emotion, Muffat could think of nothing but a remark about the heat.

'Heavens, how hot it is here,' he said. 'How do you manage to live in such a temperature, Madame?'

The conversation was about to continue on this subject when noisy voices were heard outside the dressing-room door. Bordenave drew back the slide over a grated peep-hole of the sort used in convents. Fontan was outside with Prullière and Bosc, and all three had bottles under their arms and their

hands full of glasses. He knocked on the door, shouting that it was his name-day and that he was standing champagne all round. Nana glanced inquiringly at the Prince. Heavens, His Highness didn't want to spoil anybody's fun. He would be only too delighted. But without waiting for permission Fontan came in, lisping in a baby voice :

'Me not mean, me pay for champagne . . .'

Then all of a sudden he noticed the Prince, whom he had not known to be there. He stopped short, and assuming an air of comical solemnity, announced :

'King Dagobert is in the corridor, and wishes to drink the health of His Royal Highness.'

The prince smiled, so everybody voted Fontan's little joke charming. But the dressing-room was too small to hold everybody comfortably, and they had to crowd together, Satin and Madame Jules against the curtain at the back of the room, and the men clustered around the half-naked Nana. The three actors still had on the costumes they had been wearing in the second act. While Prullière took off his Swiss Admiral's cocked hat, the huge plume of which would have knocked against the ceiling, Bosc, in his purple cloak and tin crown, steadied himself on his tipsy old legs and greeted the Prince as became a monarch receiving the son of a powerful neighbour. The glasses were filled and the company clinked them together.

'I drink to Your Highness !' said old Bosc in regal tones.

'To the Army !' added Prullière.

'To Venus !' cried Fontan.

The Prince indulgently held his glass in the air, and waited until the end of the toasts, bowed three times, and murmured :

'Madame . . . Admiral . . . Sire . . .'

Then he emptied his glass at one draught. The Comte Muffat and the Marquis de Chouard followed his example. Nobody was joking any longer : they were at Court. The world of the theatre was re-creating the real world in a sort of solemn farce under the hot glare of the gas. Nana, forgetting that she was dressed only in her drawers, with a bit of her chemise poking out behind, began playing the great lady,

Queen Venus, opening her private apartments to the dignitaries of State. In every sentence she used the words 'Royal Highness', bowing with the utmost conviction, and treating her colleagues Bosc and Prullière as if the one were a sovereign and the other his attendant minister. And nobody dreamt of smiling at the strange contrast presented by this real prince, this heir to a throne, drinking a barn-stormer's champagne, and very much at ease in this masquerade of royalty, surrounded by whores, buskers and pimps. Bordenave, carried away with enthusiasm by the scene before him, began thinking of the money he would have taken if His Highness had agreed to appear like that in the second act of *The Blonde Venus*.

'I say,' he cried, becoming familiar, 'let's bring some of my girls down here.'

Nana would not hear of it. She herself, however, was beginning to unbend. Fontan attracted her with his comical face. She rubbed up against him, eyeing him with the sort of covetous glances a pregnant woman gives to some unsavoury piece of food she fancies, and suddenly spoke familiarly to him :

'Come on, now, you great booby, give us some more !'

Fontan filled the glasses again, and the company drank, repeating the same toasts.

'To His Highness !'

'To the Army !'

'To Venus !'

But then Nana called for silence. Raising her glass, she said :

'No, no ! To Fontan ! It's Fontan's name-day. To Fontan ! To Fontan !'

So they clinked glasses a third time, and drank to Fontan's health. The Prince, who had watched the young woman devouring the actor with her eyes, bowed to the latter and said with his usual politeness :

'Monsieur Fontan, I drink to your success !'

Meanwhile the tail of His Highness's frock-coat was sweeping the marble top of the dressing-table behind him. The place was indeed like an alcove or a small bathroom,

with the steam from the basins and sponges, and the strong scent of the essences, mingling with the sharp intoxicating fumes of the champagne. The Prince and the Comte Muffat, between whom Nana was wedged, had to raise their hands in the air so as not to brush against her hips or her breasts with the slightest movement. Madame Jules stood waiting stiffly, without a single drop of perspiration on her face, while Satin, astonished in her depravity to see a prince and gentlemen in evening dress going after a naked woman in the company of a bunch of actors, thought to herself that society folk weren't as particular as all that.

In the passage Old Barillot's bell could be heard approaching. When he reached the door of Nana's dressing-room he stopped short in amazement at the sight of the three actors still dressed in the costumes they had worn in the second act.

'Gentlemen, gentlemen,' he stammered, 'do hurry up. . . . They've just rung the bell in the foyer.'

'Oh, the public will have to wait,' Bordenave said calmly.

All the same, as the bottles were now empty, the actors went upstairs to dress after yet another exchange of courtesies. Having wetted his beard with champagne, Bosc had just taken it off, and from behind that venerable disguise the drunkard had suddenly reappeared, with the ravaged, empurpled face of an old actor who has taken to drink. At the foot of the stairs he could be heard remarking to Fontan in his husky voice, with reference to the Prince :

'I made him sit up, didn't I !'

In Nana's dressing-room nobody remained now but His Highness, the Count, and the Marquis. Bordenave had gone off with Barillot, whom he advised not to knock without first letting Madame know.

'Will you excuse me, gentlemen?' asked Nana, setting to work to make up her arms and face, over which she took especial care before her appearance in the nude in the third act.

The Prince sat down on the divan with the Marquis de Chouard. Only the Comte Muffat remained standing. In that suffocating heat the two glasses of champagne they had

drunk had increased their intoxication. Satin, seeing the gentlemen shutting themselves up with her friend, had thought it best to disappear behind the curtain, where she sat waiting on a trunk, annoyed at having to stay in one place, while Madame Jules went calmly to and fro, without a word or a look.

'You sang your number marvellously,' said the Prince.

With that a fresh conversation began, but in short snatches with frequent pauses. Nana was not always able to reply. After rubbing cold cream over her arms and face, she laid on the grease-paint with the corner of a towel. For a moment she stopped looking at her reflection in the glass, and glanced smilingly at the Prince, but without putting down the grease-paint.

'His Highness flatters me,' she murmured.

Her task was a very complicated one, and the Marquis de Chouard followed it with an expression of blissful enjoyment. He spoke in his turn.

'Couldn't the orchestra play more softly when accompanying you?' he asked. 'It drowns your voice, and that is an unforgivable crime.'

This time Nana did not turn round. She had picked up the hare's-foot, and was lightly dabbing at her face, giving all her attention to this operation. She was bending forward over the dressing-table so far that the white curves of her drawers stood out below the edge of her chemise. But she wanted to show that she appreciated the old man's compliment, so she wriggled her hips slightly.

Silence reigned. Madame Jules had noticed a tear in the right leg of the drawers. She took a pin from the cluster over her heart, and for a few moments knelt on the floor, busying herself about Nana's thigh, while the young woman, without seeming to notice her presence, covered herself with rice-powder, taking great care to avoid putting any on her cheekbones. But when the Prince declared that if she were to come and sing in London all England would want to applaud her, she laughed amiably, and turned round for a moment with her left cheek very white, in the midst of a cloud of powder. Then she suddenly turned serious, for it

was time for her to put on her rouge. With her face once again close to the mirror, she dipped her fingers in a jar and began applying the rouge below her eyes, gently spreading it back towards her temples. The gentlemen maintained a respectful silence.

The Comte Muffat indeed had not yet opened his lips. His thoughts had returned willy-nilly to his younger days. His bedroom as a child had been very cold. Later on, at the age of sixteen, after kissing his mother good night every evening, he used to take the icy sensation of that kiss with him into his sleep. One day, passing a half-open door, he had caught sight of a maidservant washing herself; and that was the only memory which had ever disturbed him from puberty until the day he married. After that, he had found his wife punctilious in carrying out her conjugal duties, but had himself felt a pious repugnance for them. He had grown up, and was now growing old, in ignorance of the flesh and in conformity to rigid devotional practices, having always ordered his life according to laws and precepts. And now, all of a sudden, he was thrown into this actress's dressing-room, into the presence of this naked courtesan. He, who had never seen the Comtesse Muffat putting on her garters, was witnessing the intimate details of a woman's toilet, in a chaotic disarray of jars, in the midst of that powerful perfume which he found so sweet. His whole being was in revolt: the way in which Nana had slowly been taking possession of him for some time past terrified him, reminding him of the pious stories of diabolic possession which he had read as a child. He believed in the devil; and, in a confused sort of way, Nana was the devil, with her laughter, her breasts and her crupper, which seemed swollen with vice. But he promised himself that he would be strong. He would know how to defend himself.

'Then it is agreed,' said the Prince, lounging comfortably on the divan. 'You will come to London next year, and we shall give you such a warm welcome that you will never return to France. ... Ah, my dear Count, you don't value your pretty women enough. We shall take them all from you!'

'That won't bother him,' the Marquis de Chouard

murmured maliciously, emboldened by the absence of strangers. 'The Count is virtue itself.'

Hearing his virtue mentioned, Nana looked at him so comically that Muffat felt intensely annoyed. The next moment, his reaction astonished him and made him angry with himself. Why should the idea of being virtuous embarrass him in the presence of this courtesan? He could have struck her. But Nana had just dropped a brush on the floor while picking it up from her dressing-table; and as she bent down to recover it he darted forward. Their breaths mingled for a moment, and Venus's loosened tresses flowed over his hands. He experienced a sense of pleasure mingled with remorse, the sort of pleasure peculiar to those Catholics whom the fear of hell spurs on to commit sin.

At that moment Old Barillot's voice came from behind the door.

'Madame, may I give the knocks? The audience is getting impatient.'

'All in good time,' Nana replied calmly.

She had dipped her paint-brush in a pot of kohl; then, putting her nose close to the glass, and closing her left eye, she passed it delicately between her eye-lashes. Muffat stood behind her, watching. He saw her reflection in the mirror, with her round shoulders and her breasts half hidden in a rosy shadow. And try as he might he could not turn away his eyes from that dimpled face, which seemed fraught with desire, and which the closed eye made so seductive. When she shut her right eye and passed the brush along it, he realized that he belonged to her.

'Madame, they're stamping their feet,' the call-boy shouted again in his breathless voice. 'They'll end up by smashing the seats. . . . May I give the knocks?'

'Oh, bother!' Nana said impatiently. 'Knock away – I don't care. . . . If I'm not ready they'll just have to wait for me!'

She calmed down, and turning to her visitors, added with a smile:

'Honestly, you can't even have a minute's conversation.'

Her face and arms were finished now, and with her finger

she put two broad strokes of carmine on her lips. The Comte Muffat felt more disturbed than ever. He was fascinated by the perverse attraction of Nana's powders and paints, and filled with a frantic longing for the young woman's painted charms, the unnaturally red mouth in the unnaturally white face, and the exaggerated eyes, ringed with black and burning fiercely, as if ravaged by love. Meanwhile Nana went behind the curtain for a moment to take off her drawers and slip on Venus's tights. Then, with calm immodesty, she came out and unbuttoned her little cambric bodice, holding out her arms to Madame Jules, who pulled the short sleeves of the tunic over them.

'Hurry up, since they're getting angry!' she muttered.

The Prince, his eyes half-closed, followed the swelling lines of her bosom with the air of a connoisseur, while the Marquis de Chouard gave an involuntary nod of the head. Muffat gazed at the carpet to avoid seeing any more. In fact Venus, with only her gauze veil over her shoulders, was ready. But Madame Jules went on circling around her, inspecting her with her bright vacant eyes, and looking like a little wooden doll. With sharp movements she pulled pins out of the inexhaustible pin cushion over her heart, and pinned up Venus's tunic, passing her shrivelled hands over all those plump, naked charms without any sign of emotion, as if completely uninterested in her sex.

'There!' said the young woman, taking a last look at herself in the mirror.

Bordenave came back looking worried and announcing that the third act had begun.

'All right, I'm coming,' said Nana. 'What a fuss about nothing! Why, it's usually me that waits for the others.'

The gentlemen left the dressing-room, but they did not take their leave of Nana, for the Prince had expressed a desire to watch the third act from the wings. Left alone, Nana looked all around her in surprise.

'Where on earth has she got to?' she asked.

She was looking for Satin. When she finally found her, waiting on her trunk behind the curtain, Satin calmly replied:

'I didn't want to get in your way, with all those men here.'

And she added that she was going now. But Nana held her back. What a silly thing to do, now that Bordenave had agreed to take her on! They were going to settle the whole thing after the show was over. Satin hesitated. It was all too complicated; she was out of her element. All the same, she stayed.

As the Prince was coming down the little wooden staircase, a strange sound of oaths and scuffling feet came from the other side of the theatre. An incident had occurred which had taken by surprise the actors waiting for their cues. For a few minutes Mignon had been teasing Fauchery again, smothering him with caresses. He had just devised a new game, flicking the other man's nose, in order, so he said, to keep the flies off him. But all of a sudden, carried away by his success, and acting on a whim, Mignon had given the journalist a slap in the face, a genuine, resounding slap. This time he had gone too far : Fauchery could not accept such a blow with a laugh, in the presence of so many people. Whereupon the two men, dropping their play-acting, had sprung at each other's throats, their faces livid with hate, and were now rolling about on the floor behind the framework of a flat, calling each other pimps.

'Monsieur Bordenave! Monsieur Bordenave!' hissed the stage-manager, coming up in a flutter.

Bordenave made his excuses to the Prince and followed him. When he recognized Fauchery and Mignon on the floor, he gave vent to a gesture of annoyance. They had picked a nice time, and no mistake, with His Highness on the other side of the scenery, and the whole audience able to hear them! To make matters worse, Rose Mignon had arrived, out of breath, at the very moment she was due on stage. Vulcan, in fact, was giving her her cue, but Rose stood rooted to the spot at the sight of her husband and her lover writhing at her feet, lashing out at each other, and tearing each other's hair out, their frock-coats covered with dust. They were barring her way; and indeed a scene-shifter had even stopped Fauchery's hat just as the wretched thing was going to roll on to the stage in the middle of the struggle.

Meanwhile Vulcan, who had been making up jokes to keep the audience amused, gave Rose her cue a second time. But she stood motionless, still gazing at the two men.

'Oh, never mind *them*!' Bordenave whispered to her furiously. 'Get on the stage, quick! ... It's no business of yours! You're missing your cue!'

And with a push from him, Rose stepped over the struggling bodies, and found herself in the glare of the footlights, facing the audience. She had failed to understand why the two men were fighting on the floor. Trembling from head to foot, and with a humming in her ears, she came down towards the footlights, Diana's sweet amorous smile on her lips, and launched into her duet with such warmth in her voice that the public gave her an ovation. Behind the scenery she could hear the punches the two men were giving each other. They had rolled down as far as the proscenium arch, but fortunately the music was drowning the noise their feet were making against the flats.

'Hell and damnation,' shouted Bordenave in exasperation, when at last he succeeded in separating them, 'why couldn't you fight at home? You know perfectly well I don't like this sort of thing. ... You, Mignon, will do me the pleasure of staying on this side of the stage, and as for you, Fauchery, if you leave the prompt side, I'll chuck you out of the theatre. You understand, eh? – you keep to your different sides, or I forbid Rose to bring you here at all.'

When he rejoined the Prince, the latter asked what was the matter.

'Oh, nothing at all,' he murmured blandly.

Nana was standing wrapped in furs, talking to her distinguished visitors while waiting for her cue. As the Comte Muffat was going to have a look at the stage between two of the flats, the stage-manager motioned to him to step softly. A drowsy warmth was descending from the flies, and in the wings, which were lit by glaring patches of light, one or two people stood about talking in low voices, or walked away on tip-toe. The gas-man was at his post beside an intricate arrangement of taps; a fireman, leaning against a frame, was craning forward, trying to catch a glimpse of the stage; while

on his seat, high up, the curtain-man was waiting with a resigned expression, ignoring the operetta, but constantly on the alert for the bell which would tell him to pull his ropes. And in this stifling atmosphere, amid all this shuffling and whispering, the voices of the actors on the stage sounded strangely muffled, surprisingly artificial. Farther off again, beyond the confused noises of the orchestra, something like a vast breathing sound was audible. It was the breath of the audience, which sometimes swelled up until it burst forth in exclamations, laughter or applause. Though invisible, the presence of the public could be felt distinctly, even in its silences.

'There's something open,' Nana said sharply, pulling her furs tighter around her. 'Go and have a look, Barillot. I bet that somebody's just opened a window. . . . Honestly, you can catch your death of cold here!'

Barillot swore that he had closed every window himself. Perhaps there were some broken panes. The actors were always complaining of draughts. Through the heavy warmth produced by the gas, blasts of cold air were constantly passing, making it a regular pneumonia trap, as Fontan called it.

'I'd like to see *you* in a low-cut dress,' Nana went on crossly.

'Hush!' murmured Bordenave.

On the stage Rose rendered a phrase in her duet so subtly that applause drowned the sound of the orchestra. Nana fell silent, and her face grew grave. Meanwhile the Count was venturing down a passage, when Barillot stopped him and warned him that if he went any further he would be visible to the audience. He had an oblique view from behind one of the flats, strengthened by a thick layer of old posters, and could also see a corner of the stage, the cave on Mount Etna hollowed out of a silver mine, with Vulcan's forge in the background. Battens lowered from the flies lit up the glitter dust which had been laid on heavily with a brush. Frames containing panes of red and blue glass were used in calculated opposition to produce the appearance of a fiery brazier, while in the background, gas-jets had been installed at floor-level to throw a line of dark rocks into relief. And there, on

a gently sloping platform, in the midst of those dots of light like fairy lamps scattered about in the grass on the night of a public holiday, old Madame Drouard, who played Juno, was sitting, dazzled and sleepy, waiting for her cue.

Suddenly there was a stir as Simonne, who was listening to a story Clarisse was telling her, cried out :

'Look ! It's La Tricon !'

It was indeed La Tricon, with her aristocratic manner and her hair in ringlets. When she saw Nana she went straight up to her.

'No,' said the latter after a rapid exchange of words, 'not now.'

The old lady looked grave. Prullière passed by and shook hands with her, while two little chorus-girls stood gazing at her in awe. For a moment she seemed to hesitate. Then she beckoned to Simonne, and there was another rapid exchange of words.

'Yes,' Simonne said at last. 'In half an hour.'

But as she was going back up to her dressing-room, Madame Bron, who was once more going the rounds with letters, handed her one. Lowering his voice, Bordenave angrily reprimanded the concierge for having allowed La Tricon into the theatre. That woman ! And that evening of all evenings ! He was full of indignation on account of His Highness. Madame Bron, who had been thirty years in the theatre, answered in a sour tone of voice. How was she to know? La Tricon did business with all the ladies in the theatre : Monsieur le Directeur had met her a score of times without raising any objections. And while Bordenave was muttering oaths La Tricon stood calmly scrutinizing the Prince with the air of a woman who can size up a man at a glance. A smile lit up her yellow face. Then she slowly walked away through the crowd of respectful women.

'Straight away, then?' she said, turning round to address Simonne.

Simonne looked extremely annoyed. The letter was from a young man whom she had promised to meet that evening. She gave Madame Bron a scribbled note which read : 'Impossible tonight, darling – I've an engagement.' But she

was still worried : the young man might wait for her in spite of everything. As she was not appearing in the third act, she wanted to leave straight away, and accordingly asked Clarisse to go and see if the coast was clear. Clarisse was only due on stage towards the end of the act, and so she went downstairs, while Simonne went back upstairs for a minute to the dressing-room they shared with each other.

In Madame Bron's bar downstairs a walker-on who played the part of Pluto was drinking by himself, draped in a great red robe embroidered with golden flames. The concierge had obviously been doing good business, for the hole under the stairs was wet with slops. Clarisse hitched up the tunic of her Iris costume, which was trailing on the slimy steps behind her, but she stopped cautiously at the turn of the stairs, and simply craned forward to peep into the lodge. Her instinct had been right, for that idiot la Faloise was still there, sitting on the same chair between the table and the stove ! He had made a pretence of going off in front of Simonne, but then he had come back. For that matter, the lodge was still full of gentlemen, who sat there, gloved and elegant, patient and submissive, inspecting each other gravely as they waited. There was nothing left on the table but the dirty plates, Madame Bron having just distributed the last of the bouquets. A single fallen rose was withering on the floor near the black cat, which had curled up to sleep while the kittens ran wild races and danced wild gallops between the gentlemen's legs. For a moment Clarisse was tempted to throw la Faloise out. The idiot didn't like animals, and that put the finishing touch to him. He was drawing in his elbows because of the cat, so as not to touch her.

'Mind out, or she'll nip you,' said Pluto, who was a joker, as he went upstairs, wiping his mouth on the back of his hand.

After that, Clarisse dropped the idea of creating a scene with la Faloise. She had seen Madame Bron give the letter to Simonne's young man, and he had gone out to read it under the gaslight in the lobby. 'Impossible tonight, darling – I've an engagement.'

And, doubtless accustomed to the formula, he had quietly

disappeared. There at least was somebody who knew how to behave. Not so the others, the fellows who stayed there stubbornly, on Madame Bron's decrepit straw-bottomed chairs, in that great glass cage, where the heat simply roasted you and the smell was anything but pleasant. The men must be keen to put up with all that! Clarisse went upstairs again in disgust, passed behind the stage, and nimbly climbed the three flights of the dressing-room staircase to tell Simonne what had happened.

In the wings the Prince had left the others and was talking to Nana. He had not taken his eyes off her and stood gazing at her intently between his half-closed eyelids. Nana did not look at him, but kept smiling and nodding. Suddenly the Comte Muffat, yielding to an overwhelming impulse, left Bordenave, who was explaining to him the working of the winches and rollers, and came over to break up this conversation. Nana looked up and smiled at him as she smiled at His Highness. But she had her ears cocked all the time, listening for her cue.

'The third act is the shortest, I believe,' said the Prince, embarrassed by the Count's presence.

She did not answer : her whole expression had altered, and suddenly she was completely absorbed in her work. With a rapid movement of the shoulders, she had slipped off her furs, and Madame Jules, standing behind her, had caught them in her arms. And then, after putting both hands to her hair as if to make it fast, she walked naked on to the stage.

'Hush! Hush!' whispered Bordenave.

The Count and the Prince had been taken by surprise. In the midst of a profound silence, a deep sigh became audible, like the distant murmur of a great crowd. Every evening when Venus entered in her divine nakedness the same effect was produced. Muffat suddenly wanted to see, and put his eye to the peep-hole. Beyond the dazzling arc formed by the footlights the dark auditorium looked as if it were full of a reddish smoke, and against this neutral background to which the rows of faces lent a vague pallor, Nana stood out white and gigantic, blotting out all the boxes from the balcony to the flies. He saw her from behind, standing with body erect

and arms outstretched, while on the floor, level with her feet, the prompter's head – an old man's head, with a humble, honest face – looked as if it had been severed from his body. At certain points in her opening number an undulating movement seemed to begin at her neck, descend to her waist, and die out in the trailing hem of her tunic. When she had sung her last note in the midst of a storm of applause, she bowed to the audience, the gauze floating about her, and her hair reaching down below her waist. And seeing her like that, bent in two with her hips broadened out, backing towards his peep-hole, the Count straightened up, looking very pale. The stage had disappeared and now he could see nothing but the back of the scenery, with its covering of old posters pasted up in every direction. On the sloping platform, among the lines of gas-jets, the whole of Olympus had joined Madame Drouard, who had fallen into a daze. They were waiting for the end of the act, Bosc and Fontan sitting on the floor with their knees drawn up to their chins, and Prullière stretching and yawning before going on. They were all tired and red-eyed, impatient to go home to bed.

Just then Fauchery, who had been prowling about on the prompt side ever since Bordenave had forbidden him the other, button-holed Muffat in order to keep himself in countenance, and offered to show him the dressing-rooms. A growing languor had left the Count without any will-power, and after looking around for the Marquis de Chouard, who had disappeared, he ended up by following the journalist. He experienced a mingled feeling of relief and uneasiness as he left these wings from which he could hear Nana singing.

Fauchery had already preceded him up the staircase, which was closed on the first and second floors by wooden swing-doors. It was one of those stairways to be found in shady tenement houses, such as the Comte Muffat had seen during his rounds as a member of the Charity Committee. It was bare and dilapidated; its walls were painted with yellow distemper, its steps had been worn by the constant tread of feet, and its iron balustrade had been polished by the rubbing of countless hands. On every landing, on a level with the floor, there was a low window like a square ventilator,

while in lanterns fastened to the walls gas-jets burned, shedding a crude light on the surrounding squalor, and giving off a heat which was trapped under the steps of the narrow spiral staircase.

When he reached the foot of the stairs, the Count once again felt a hot breath on the back of his neck, that odour of women which was wafted down in a flood of light and sound from the dressing-rooms above; and now, with every step he climbed, the musky scent of powders and the acrid perfume of toilet vinegars made his head swim the more. On the first floor two corridors branched sharply off, with yellow-painted doors numbered with big white figures, like the doors in a shady hotel. Some of the tiles on the floor had come loose, and as the old building had settled, they had been left sticking out above the rest. The Count ventured a glance through a half-open door, and saw a filthy room which looked like a barber's shop in a poor district. It was furnished with two chairs, a mirror and a small dressing-table blackened by the grease from brushes and combs. A great strapping fellow, with steam rising from his sweating shoulders, was changing his shirt there, while in a similar room next door a woman was pulling on her gloves before leaving, her hair all damp and limp, as if she had just had a bath. But just then Fauchery called the Count, and the latter had nearly reached the second floor when a furious 'Bloody Hell!' came from the corridor on the right. Mathilde, a little trollop who played *ingénue* parts, had just broken her washbasin, the soapy water from which was flowing out on to the landing. A dressing-room door slammed shut. Two women in their stays skipped across the passage, and another, with the hem of her chemise between her teeth, appeared for a moment, only to dash away. Then there came a sound of laughter, a quarrel, the first words of a song which was suddenly interrupted. All along the passage glimpses of naked flesh, white skin, and pale underwear could be seen through chinks in doorways. Two girls in high spirits were showing each other their birthmarks. Another, who was very young, almost a child, had pulled her petticoats up above her knees to sew up a tear in her drawers; while the dressers, catching sight of the

two men, drew curtains half to, for modesty's sake. The mad rush which follows the end of a performance had already begun, as white paint and rouge were removed, ordinary clothes were put on again in the midst of clouds of rice-powder, and the musky odour that wafted through the swing-doors smelt stronger than ever. On the third floor Muffat abandoned himself to the feeling of intoxication which was taking hold of him. The chorus-girls' dressing-room was there, with a score of women crowded together amid a litter of soaps and bottles of lavender water, in what looked like the living-room in a lower-class brothel. As he went by, he heard a fierce sound of washing behind a closed door, an absolute storm in a handbasin. And he was about to go up to the top floor when curiosity led him to venture another glance through an open spy-hole; the room was empty, and in the flaring gaslight all he could see was a chamber-pot forgotten among a heap of skirts on the floor. This sight was the last impression he took with him. Upstairs, on the fourth floor, he was almost suffocated. All the smells and all the heat in the theatre were concentrated there. The yellow ceiling looked as if it had been baked, and a lamp burned in the midst of a reddish mist. For a few moments he clung to the iron banister-rail, which had an almost living warmth, shutting his eyes and breathing in all the animal essence of woman, of which he was still ignorant but which was beating full in his face.

'Come along,' shouted Fauchery, who had vanished a little earlier. 'Somebody's asking for you.'

At the end of the corridor was the dressing-room shared by Clarisse and Simonne. It was a long, ill-built room under the roof, with cant walls and a sloping ceiling. There were two deep-set openings high up, but at that hour of the night the dressing-room was lit by gas-jets. The walls were covered with cheap wallpaper, with a pattern of pink flowers climbing up green trellis-work. A couple of planks placed side by side and covered with oilcloth did duty as dressing-tables; they were black with spilt water, and underneath were a number of dented zinc jugs, pails full of slops, and coarse yellow earthenware pitchers.

There was a whole collection of cheap articles in the room, twisted and soiled by use : chipped basins, toothless combs, all those odds and ends which, in their hurry and carelessness, two women will leave scattered about when they undress and wash together in a place where they spend only a little time, and whose squalor has ceased to worry them.

'Come on in,' Fauchery repeated, with the familiarity of men among whores. 'Clarisse wants to give you a kiss.'

Muffat finally decided to go in. But he stopped short in surprise at the sight of the Marquis de Chouard comfortably installed on a chair between the two dressing-tables. The Marquis had retired to this dressing-room some time before. He was sitting with his feet apart because a pail was leaking and letting a pool of whitish liquid foam spread over the floor. He was obviously quite at ease, with the air of a man who knew all the best places, and was revelling in this stifling bathroom atmosphere, amid this blatant feminine immodesty, which this filthy room both exaggerated and excused.

'Are you going with the old chap?' Simonne asked Clarisse in a whisper.

'Not likely,' the other replied loudly.

The dresser, a very ugly and very familiar girl, who was helping Simonne into her coat, doubled up with laughter. The three nudged each other, stammering out remarks which made them laugh more than ever.

'Come along, Clarisse, kiss the gentleman,' said Fauchery. 'You know he's rolling in money.'

And turning to the Count, he said :

'You'll see, she's very nice ! She'll give you a kiss.'

But Clarisse was disgusted with men. She spoke angrily about the filthy devils waiting in the porter's lodge down below. Besides, she was in a hurry to go back downstairs : they were going to make her miss her last scene. Then, as Fauchery barred her way out, she gave Muffat a couple of kisses on his side-whiskers, saying :

'That's not for you, you know ! It's because Fauchery's pestering me.'

And with that she slipped out. The Count felt embarrassed

in his father-in-law's presence, and the blood had rushed to his face. In Nana's dressing-room, in the midst of all those hangings and mirrors, he had not experienced the sharp excitement which the wretched poverty of this garret, full of the two women's disorder, aroused within him. Meanwhile the Marquis had gone off after Simonne, who had left the room in a hurry, whispering in her ear, while she shook her head in refusal. Fauchery followed them, laughing, and the Count found himself alone with the dresser, who was rinsing out the basins. Then he left too and went downstairs, his legs almost giving way beneath him. Once again, he saw half-dressed women running for cover and doors banging as he passed. But in the midst of all the girls scurrying about on the four floors, the only thing he saw clearly was a cat, the big ginger cat he had seen before, which, in that musky, oven-like atmosphere, was stalking upstairs, rubbing its back against the banisters, with its tail in the air.

'I do declare,' said a hoarse woman's voice, 'I thought they were going to keep us all night! ... What a bloody nuisance they are with their curtain-calls!'

It was all over: the curtain had just fallen. There was a positive stampede up the stairs, and the walls rang with the exclamations of people in a frantic hurry to dress and be off. As the Comte Muffat reached the last step, he saw Nana and the Prince walking slowly along the passage. The young woman stopped, then lowered her voice to say with a smile:

'All right then: I'll see you later.'

The Prince returned to the stage, where Bordenave was waiting for him. Left alone with Nana, Muffat gave way to an impulse of anger and desire. He ran up behind her, and, just as she was going into her dressing-room, planted a rough kiss on her neck, on the little golden hairs curling low down between her shoulders. It was as if he were returning the kiss which had been given him upstairs. Nana was furious, and raised her hand to slap him. But when she recognized the Count, she smiled.

'Oh, you frightened me!' she said simply.

And her smile was adorable in its embarrassment and

submissiveness, as if she had despaired of this kiss and was happy to have received it. But she could do nothing for him either that evening, or the next day. He would have to wait. Even if she had been free, she would have kept him waiting, to whet his desire. Her glance said as much. At length she went on :

'I'm a landowner, you know. . . . Yes, I'm buying a country house near Orléans, in a part of the world where you go yourself sometimes. Baby told me so – little Georges Hugon I mean. You know him? So come and see me down there.'

Frightened by his roughness – the roughness of a naturally timid man, and ashamed of what he had done, the Count bowed ceremoniously, promising to take advantage of her invitation. Then he went off, walking like a man in a dream.

He was going to join the Prince when, passing the foyer, he heard Satin yell :

'You dirty old man ! You bloody well leave me alone !'

It was the Marquis de Chouard, who had fallen back on Satin. The girl was sick to death of all these nobs. True, Nana had kept her promise and introduced her to Bordenave, but the necessity of keeping her lips sealed for fear of blurting out something stupid had been a terrible strain; and now she wanted to let herself go, the more so as she had come across an old flame of hers in the wings. This was the walker-on who played the part of Pluto, a pastrycook who had already treated her to a whole week of love and slaps. She had been waiting for him when the Marquis had annoyed her by talking to her as if she were one of those theatrical ladies. So finally she put on a dignified expression and said haughtily :

'My husband's coming ! You just wait !'

Meanwhile the actors and actresses were leaving one by one in their outdoor coats, looking tired out. Groups of men and women were coming down the little winding staircase, their battered hats and shabby shawls silhouetted in the half-light, their faces pale and ugly without their make-up. On the stage, where the side-lights and battens were being extinguished, the Prince was listening to an anecdote Bordenave was telling him. He wanted to wait for Nana, and

when at last she appeared, the stage was dark, and the duty fireman was finishing his round, lantern in hand. To save His Highness the trouble of going out by way of the Passage des Panoramas, Bordenave had given orders to open the corridor which led from the porter's lodge to the lobby of the theatre. Along this corridor women were racing pell-mell, delighted at the opportunity to avoid the men who were waiting for them in the other passage. They were elbowing their way along, glancing back over their shoulders, and only breathing freely when they got outside. Fontan, Bosc and Prullière, on the other hand, left the theatre at a leisurely pace, laughing at the figure cut by the well-to-do admirers who were pacing up and down the Galerie des Variétés while the women were making off along the boulevard with their sweethearts. Clarisse was particularly artful. She distrusted la Faloise, and, sure enough, he was still there in the lodge, among the gentlemen stubbornly waiting on Madame Bron's chairs. They all craned their heads forwards, and she walked straight past, hidden by a friend. The gentlemen blinked in bewilderment at the whirl of skirts eddying at the foot of the narrow stairs, appalled to think that they had waited so long only to see them all disappear like that without being able to recognize a single one. The litter of black kittens were sleeping on the oilcloth, nestling against their mother's belly. She was lying with her paws outstretched, in a state of perfect bliss, while the big ginger cat sat at the other end of the table, his tail stretched out behind him, and his yellow eyes following the flight of the women.

'If His Highness will be good enough to come this way,' said Bordenave at the foot of the stairs, pointing to the corridor.

A few chorus-girls were still crowding along it. The Prince began following Nana, while Muffat and the Marquis walked behind. It was a long passage between the theatre and the building next door, a sort of narrow alley-way which had been covered with a sloping glass roof. Damp oozed from the walls, and footsteps on the paved floor rang out as in an underground vault. It was cluttered up with the sort of rubbish usually found in an attic, a work-bench on which the

concierge did repairs to the scenery, and a pile of wooden barriers which were set up outside the theatre every evening to keep the queue in order. Nana had to hitch up her dress as she passed a drinking-fountain, for the tap had not been properly turned off and was flooding the paving-stones. In the lobby the party broke up. And when the Prince had left, Bordenave summed up his opinion of him with a disdainful shrug of the shoulders.

'He's a bit of a boor all the same,' he said to Fauchery, without explaining himself any further. Then Rose Mignon took the journalist off with her husband to try to effect a reconciliation between them at home.

Muffat was left alone on the pavement. His Highness had just calmly handed Nana into his carriage, and the Marquis had gone off after Satin and her pastrycook. In his excitement he was content to follow this depraved couple in the vague hope of being granted some favour. Muffat, feeling as if his head were on fire, decided to walk home. The struggle within him had completely ceased. The ideas and beliefs of the last forty years were being drowned in a flood of new life. While he was walking along the boulevards, the rumble of the last carriages deafened him with the name of Nana : the gas-lamps set naked flesh dancing before his eyes – the naked flesh of Nana's lithe arms and white shoulders. And he felt that he was completely hers : he would have abjured everything, sold everything, to possess her for a single hour that very night. His youth, the lustful puberty of adolescence, was awakening within him at last, flaring up suddenly in the frigidity of the Catholic and the dignity of the middle-aged man.

THE Comte Muffat, accompanied by his wife and daughter, had arrived the previous night at Les Fondettes, where Madame Hugon, who was staying there with her son Georges, had invited them to come and spend a week. The house, which had been built towards the end of the seventeenth century, stood in the middle of a huge square enclosure; it was a perfectly plain building, but the garden possessed some magnificent shady trees, and a series of pools fed by spring water. It lay beside the road from Orléans to Paris, a stretch of rich verdure and a clump of trees which broke the monotony of the flat countryside, where cultivated fields extended as far as the eye could see.

At eleven o'clock, when the second lunch-bell had brought everybody together, Madame Hugon, smiling in her kindly motherly way, gave Sabine two big kisses, one on each cheek, saying :

'This is a custom of mine in the country, you know. . . . Oh, seeing you here makes me feel twenty years younger. . . . Did you sleep well in your old room?'

Then, without waiting for a reply, she turned to Estelle :

'And has this little one had a good night too? . . . Give me a kiss, my child.'

They had taken their seats in the vast dining-room, the windows of which looked out on the park. But they only occupied one end of the long table, where they sat crowded together, for company's sake. Sabine, who was in high spirits, recalled various memories of her youth which had been just awakened – memories of months spent at Les Fondettes, of long walks, of a tumble into one of the pools on a summer evening, of an old romance of chivalry she had found on the top of a cupboard and read during the winter, beside a fire of vine branches. And Georges, who had not seen the Countess for a few months, thought there was something strange about her, something different about her face – whereas that stick

of an Estelle seemed more unobtrusive and silent and awkward than ever.

While they were eating a simple meal of boiled eggs and chops, Madame Hugon began complaining about her housekeeping problems. The butchers, she said, were becoming impossible; she bought everything in Orléans, yet they never brought her the cuts she asked for. Besides, if her guests had nothing worth eating, they had only themselves to blame; they had come too late in the season.

'It's absolutely absurd,' she said. 'I've been expecting you since June, and now we're half-way through September. As you can see, it isn't very nice outside.'

And she pointed to the trees on the lawn, the leaves of which were beginning to turn yellow. The sky was overcast, and the horizon was obscured by a bluish haze, which was full of a soft, peaceful melancholy.

'Oh, but I'm expecting company', she continued, 'to brighten things up a little. ... First of all two gentlemen Georges has invited – Monsieur Fauchery and Monsieur Daguenet : you know them, don't you? Then Monsieur de Vandeuvres, who has been promising me a visit these five years; this year, perhaps, he'll make up his mind to come !'

'Ah,' said the Countess with a laugh, 'if we've got nobody but Monsieur de Vandeuvres. ... He's too busy.'

'And what about Philippe?' asked Muffat.

'Philippe has applied for leave,' replied the old lady, 'but you will probably have left Les Fondettes by the time he arrives.'

Coffee was served. The conversation had turned to Paris, and somebody mentioned Steiner. This name drew a little cry from Madame Hugon.

'Monsieur Steiner?' she said. 'Isn't he that stout man I met at your house one evening – a banker, I believe? ... Now *there's* a dreadful man for you ! Why he's bought an actress an estate only a couple of miles from here, beyond the Choue, over Gumières way. The whole countryside's shocked. Did you know about it by any chance?'

'No, I didn't,' replied Muffat. 'So Steiner's bought a place near here, has he?'

Hearing his mother broach this subject, Georges had looked down at his coffee-cup, but in his astonishment at the Count's answer, he raised his eyes and stared at him. Why had he told such a blatant lie?

The Count, for his part, noticed the young man's movement, and gave him a suspicious glance. Madame Hugon was providing her guests with further details : the place was called La Mignotte, and to get there you had to go up the Choue as far as Gumières in order to cross by a bridge ; that added another couple of miles to your journey, but otherwise you got your feet wet and ran the risk of a ducking.

'And what is the actress's name ?' asked the Countess.

'Ah, they did tell me,' murmured the old lady, 'but it's slipped my mind. ... Georges, you were there this morning, when the gardener spoke to us ...'

Georges put on a show of searching his memory. Muffat waited, twirling a coffee-spoon between his fingers. Then the Countess said to her husband :

'Isn't Monsieur Steiner with that singer at the Variétés, that Nana ?'

'Nana, that's the name ! A horrible creature !' cried Madame Hugon, with growing annoyance. 'And they are expecting her at La Mignotte. I've heard all about it from the gardener. ... Didn't the gardener say they were expecting her this evening, Georges ?'

The Count gave a little start of astonishment, but Georges replied briskly :

'Oh, Mother, the gardener didn't know what he was talking about. Just now the coachman was saying the opposite. Nobody's expected at La Mignotte till the day after tomorrow.'

He tried to assume a natural expression, while watching the Count out of the corner of his eye to see the effect of his remarks. The latter was twirling the spoon again, as if reassured. The Countess, her eyes gazing dreamily at the blue haze in the far reaches of the park, seemed to have lost all interest in the conversation. With the shadow of a smile on her lips, she seemed to be following up a secret thought which had suddenly occurred to her ; while Estelle, sitting stiffly on

174

her chair, had listened to everything that had been said about Nana without a trace of emotion appearing on her virginal white face.

'Dear me,' murmured Madame Hugon after a pause, becoming her good-natured self once more, 'I've got no right to get angry. I should live and let live. ... If we meet that lady on the road, we shall look the other way, that's all.'

As they were leaving the table, she once again chided the Comtesse Sabine for having put off her visit so late that year. But the Countess defended herself, blaming the delay on her husband. Twice, on the eve of departure, when all the trunks had been locked, he had cancelled the journey on grounds of urgent business; and then he had suddenly decided to set off, just when the visit seemed to have been shelved. At this the old lady told her how Georges in the same way had twice announced his arrival without showing up, and had finally turned up at Les Fondettes two days before, when she was no longer expecting him. They had just come down into the garden, and the two men, walking on either side of the ladies, were listening to them in sulky silence.

'Never mind,' said Madame Hugon, kissing her son's fair hair, 'Zizi is a sweet boy to come and bury himself in the country with his mother. ... No, darling Zizi doesn't forget me !'

In the afternoon she was worried when Georges, who immediately after leaving the table had complained of a slight headache, seemed to be gradually overcome by a severe migraine. About four o'clock he decided to go up to bed; that was the only possible remedy. If he slept until the following morning he would be perfectly all right. His mother insisted on putting him to bed herself; but as she was leaving his room, he ran and locked the door, explaining that he was locking himself in so that no one should come and disturb him. Then he called out winningly : 'Good night ! See you tomorrow, Mother darling !' and promised to sleep like a log. He did not go back to bed, however, but, pale-faced and bright-eyed, silently put on his clothes. Then he sat on a chair and waited. When the dinner-bell rang, he listened to hear the Comte Muffat making his way towards the drawing-

room. Ten minutes later, when he was certain that nobody would see him, he climbed nimbly out of his window, which was on the first floor, and looked out on the rear of the house, and slid down a rainwater pipe to the ground. Extricating himself from the clump of shrubs in which he had landed, he left the park and galloped across the fields towards the Choue, his stomach empty and his heart pounding with excitement. Night was closing in, and a thin drizzle was beginning to fall.

It was in fact that evening that Nana was due to arrive at La Mignotte. Since Steiner had bought her this country house in May, she had occasionally felt such a longing to move in that she had cried; but each time Bordenave had refused to give her even the shortest leave, putting her off till September on the pretext that he did not intend to put on an understudy in her place, even for a single evening, as long as the Exhibition was on. Towards the end of August he spoke of October. Nana was furious, and declared that she would be at La Mignotte on 15 September. To show her defiance of Bordenave, she even invited a host of people in his presence. One afternoon, in her rooms, as Muffat, whose advances she was skilfully resisting, was begging her to grant him her favours, and shaking with emotion, she finally promised to be kind, but at La Mignotte, and to him too she named the middle of September. Then on the twelfth she was seized by a desire to go off straight away, with nobody but Zoé, for Bordenave might have been told of her plans and be about to discover some means of detaining her. She was delighted at the idea of putting him in a fix by sending him a doctor's certificate. Once the idea had entered her head of being the first to arrive at La Mignotte, and of living there for two days without anybody knowing about it, she hustled Zoé through the business of packing, and finally pushed her into a cab, where, in a sudden burst of emotion, she kissed her and begged her pardon. It was only when they got to the station refreshment-room that she thought of sending Steiner a letter to tell him what she was doing. She begged him to wait a couple of days before joining her, if he wanted to find her in good form. And then, hitting on

another idea, she wrote a second letter, in which she implored her aunt to bring little Louis to her at once. It would do baby so much good! And what fun they would have together under the trees! In the railway carriage between Paris and Orléans she spoke of nothing else; her eyes were full of tears; she mingled together flowers, birds and child in a sudden access of maternal affection.

La Mignotte was over eight miles from the station, and Nana lost a good hour hiring a carriage, a huge ramshackle barouche, which clanked and clattered along at a snail's pace. She had set to work straight away on the coachman, a silent little old man, plying him with questions. Had he often passed by La Mignotte? So it was behind that hill, was it? There must be lots of trees there, eh? And could you see the house from a distance? The little old man answered with a series of grunts. Inside the barouche Nana was dancing up and down with impatience, while Zoé, annoyed at having left Paris in such a hurry, sat stiff and sulky beside her. The horse suddenly stopped short, and the young woman thought they had reached their destination. She put her head out of the window and asked:

'Are we there?'

The driver's only answer was to whip up his horse, which began laboriously climbing a hill. Nana gazed ecstatically at the vast plain beneath the grey sky in which great clouds were banking up.

'Oh, look at all that grass, Zoé! Is that all corn, do you think? ... Heavens, how pretty it is!'

'One can see that Madame doesn't come from the country,' the maid said at last in a huffy tone of voice. 'Speaking for myself, I got to know the country all too well, when I was with my dentist. He had a house at Bougival.... And what's more, it's chilly tonight. It's damp too, in these parts.'

They were driving under some trees, and Nana sniffed the air like a puppy, breathing in the scent of the leaves. All of a sudden, at a turn in the road, she caught sight of the corner of a house among the trees. Perhaps that was it, and she struck up a conversation with the driver, who shook his

head again. Then, as they were driving down the other side of the hill, he simply pointed his whip and murmured :

'There it is, yonder.'

She got up and leant almost her whole body out of the window.

'Where? Where?' she cried, pale with emotion, and unable to see anything yet.

At last she caught sight of a bit of wall, and started squealing and jumping about with all the excitement of a woman overcome by a lively emotion.

'I can see it, Zoé! I can see it! ... Look out at the other side! Oh, there's a terrace on the roof, with bricks. And that's a hothouse over there! But the place is huge! ... Oh, how happy I am! Look, Zoé! Look!'

By this time the carriage had drawn up before the main gate. A small door was opened, and the gardener, a tall, gaunt fellow, appeared, cap in hand. Nana made an effort to regain her dignity, for the driver already seemed to be chuckling inwardly, behind his sealed lips. She refrained from breaking into a run, and listened to the gardener, who, in contrast to the driver, was extremely talkative, begging Madame to excuse the disorder everywhere, seeing that he had only received Madame's letter that morning. But despite all her efforts, she could scarcely keep her feet on the ground, and walked so fast that Zoé could not keep up with her. At the end of the drive she paused for a moment in order to take the house in at a glance. It was a large building in Italian style, flanked by a smaller construction, which a rich Englishman had built after two years' residence in Naples, and of which he had immediately tired.

'I'll take Madame over the house,' said the gardener.

But she had gone ahead of him, and she shouted back to him that he was not to bother, and that she preferred to go over the house by herself. And without removing her hat, she started exploring the different rooms, calling to Zoé, shouting her impressions from one end of a corridor to the other, and filling the empty house, which had been uninhabited for many months, with her cries and laughter. First there was the hall: it was a little damp, but that didn't matter – they

weren't going to sleep in it. Then came the drawing-room, which was very *chic* with its windows opening on the lawn, though the red suite of furniture was hideous; she would alter all that. As for the dining-room, what a beauty it was – and what feasts you could give in Paris if you had a dining-room as big as that! As she was going up to the first floor, she realized that she had not seen the kitchen, and she came downstairs again, to give vent to excited exclamations. Zoé was forced to marvel at the beauty of the sink and the width of the hearth, where you could have roasted a whole sheep. When she went upstairs again, it was her bedroom that especially enchanted her, a bedroom hung with Louis Seize cretonne in a delicate shade of pink by an Orléans upholsterer. You ought to be able to sleep like a log in such a cosy little nest! Next came four or five guest bedrooms, and then some magnificent attics, which would be very convenient for trunks and boxes. A sullen Zoé trailed along in Madame's wake, casting an icy glance into each room, and watching Madame disappear up the steep ladder leading to the attics. Madame could do as she pleased, but *she* had no desire to break her legs, thank you very much. But a voice reached her ears, sounding far away, as if it were coming down a chimney.

'Zoé, Zoé, where are you? Do come up. ... You've no idea! It's out of this world!'

Zoé went up grumbling. She found Madame on the roof, leaning on the brickwork balustrade, and gazing at the valley which spread out into the distance. The horizon was vast, but it was shrouded in grey mist, and a fierce wind was driving a fine drizzle before it. Nana had to hold her hat on with both hands to keep it from being blown away, while her skirts streamed out behind her, flapping like a flag.

'No, thank you!' said Zoé, pulling her head back straight away. 'Madame's going to get blown away ... what filthy weather!'

Madame did not hear what she said. Leaning over the balustrade, she was gazing at the grounds below her. They consisted of seven or eight acres of land, enclosed within a wall. Then the sight of the kitchen garden seized her atten-

tion. She darted back into the house and pushed past the maid on the stairs, stammering :

'It's full of cabbages ! ... You've never seen such big cabbages ! ... And lettuces, and sorrel, and onions, and everything ! Come quick !'

The rain was falling more heavily now. She opened her white silk parasol, and ran down the garden walks.

'Madame will catch cold !' shouted Zoé, who had stayed safely under the glass porch over the steps.

But Madame wanted to see, and at each new discovery there was an exclamation.

'Zoé, there's spinach ! Do come and see. ... Oh ! Artichokes ! They *are* funny. So artichokes have flowers, do they ? ... Now, what can that be ? I've never seen that before. ... Do come, Zoé, perhaps you know.'

The maid did not budge. Madame must be raving mad. For now the rain was coming down in torrents, and the little white silk parasol was already completely black; it didn't shelter Madame either, and her skirts were wringing wet. Not that that seemed to bother her. In the pouring rain she toured the kitchen garden and the orchard, stopping in front of every tree, and bending over every bed of vegetables. Then she ran and looked down the well, lifted up a frame to see what was underneath it, and became engrossed in the contemplation of a huge pumpkin. She felt an urge to go along every path in the garden, and to take immediate possession of all the things she had dreamt of in the old days, when she had been a poor working-girl in Paris. The rain was getting heavier, but she did not feel it, her only complaint being that the daylight was fading. She could not see clearly any longer, and had to touch things with her fingers to find out what they were. All of a sudden, in the twilight, she made out a bed of strawberries, and all the longings of her childhood burst forth.

'Strawberries ! Strawberries ! There are some here : I can feel them ! ... A plate, Zoé. Come and pick strawberries.'

And Nana squatted in the mud, dropping her parasol and exposing herself to the full force of the downpour. Her hands dripping with water, she began picking strawberries among

the leaves. Meanwhile there was no sign of Zoé with the plate. As the young woman was getting to her feet, she was suddenly gripped with fear. She imagined she had seen a shadow glide by.

'It's an animal!' she screamed.

But she stood rooted to the path in astonishment. It was a man, and she had recognized him.

'Heavens above, it's Baby! ... What are *you* doing here, Baby?'

'Why, I've come to see you, of course,' replied Georges.

She was still somewhat bewildered.

'So you heard from the gardener that I was coming? ... Oh, you poor child! You're soaking wet!'

'Yes, and I'll tell you why. The rain caught me on my way here, and then, as I didn't want to go upstream as far as Gumières, I crossed the Choue, and fell into a damned water-hole.'

Nana promptly forgot all about the strawberries. She was trembling and full of pity. Poor Zizi in a waterhole! And she led him towards the house, talking of lighting a big fire.

'You know,' he murmured, stopping her in the dark, 'I was in hiding because I was afraid of being scolded like in Paris, when I come and see you and you're not expecting me.'

She made no reply, but burst out laughing, and gave him a kiss on the forehead. Till then she had always treated him like a little boy, never taking his declarations seriously, and amusing herself at his expense, as if he were somebody of no consequence whatever. There was a great fuss about installing him in the house. She absolutely insisted on the fire being lit in her bedroom, as they would be most comfortable there. Georges had not surprised Zoé, who was used to all sorts of meetings, but the gardener, who was bringing the wood upstairs, was dumbfounded by the sight of this gentleman dripping with water, to whom he was certain he had not opened the gate. He was sent away as he was no longer needed.

A lamp lit the room, and the fire was burning with a great flame.

'He'll never get dry,' said Nana, seeing Georges beginning to shiver. 'He's going to catch cold.'

And there were no men's trousers in the house! She was on the point of calling the gardener back, when an idea occurred to her. Zoé, who was unpacking the trunks in the dressing-room, had brought Madame a change of linen, consisting of a chemise, some petticoats and a dressing-gown.

'But that's perfect!' cried the young woman. 'Zizi can put all that on. You don't mind wearing my things, do you, Zizi? ... When your clothes are dry, you can put them on again and go straight back home, so as not to have a scolding from your mama. ... Hurry up. I'm going to change too, in the dressing-room.'

Ten minutes later, when she reappeared in a tea-gown, she clasped her hands together in ecstasy.

'Oh, the darling! Doesn't he look sweet dressed like a woman!'

He had simply slipped on a long night-gown with a lace insertion, a pair of embroidered drawers, and the dressing-gown, which was a long cambric garment trimmed with lace. In these clothes with his bare young arms showing, and his wet tawny hair falling to his shoulders, he looked just like a girl.

'It's because he's as slim as I am!' said Nana, putting her arms round his waist. 'Zoé, come and see how it suits him. It's made for him, isn't it – except for the bodice, which is too wide. ... He hasn't got as much as I have, poor Zizi!'

'Yes, it's true I'm wanting a bit there,' murmured Georges with a smile.

All three roared with laughter. Nana had set to work buttoning the dressing-gown from top to bottom, so as to make him decent. Then she turned him round like a doll, patting him and puffing the skirt out behind. At the same time she asked him if he was comfortable and if he was warm enough. Good heavens, yes; nothing could be warmer than a woman's chemise: if he had been able to, he would always have worn one. He wriggled about inside it, enjoying the feel of the fine linen, the delightful scent of this loose-fitting

garment in which he thought he discovered something of Nana's own warm life.

Meanwhile Zoé had taken the soaked clothes down to the kitchen in order to dry them as quickly as possible in front of a fire of vine-branches. Then Georges, as he lounged in an easy-chair, ventured to make a confession.

'I say, aren't you going to have anything to eat this evening? *I'm* dying of hunger. I haven't had any dinner.'

Nana was cross with him. The great booby, to sneak out of his mama's house on an empty stomach, just to go and fall in a waterhole? But she was as hungry as a hunter too. Of course they must eat! Only they would have to make do with what they could get. And they set to work to improvise the oddest of dinners on a small table they rolled up in front of the fire. Zoé ran down to the gardener's, who had cooked a cabbage soup in case Madame didn't dine at Orléans before she arrived, because Madame had forgotten to tell him in her letter what he was to get ready. Fortunately the cellar was well furnished. So they had cabbage soup, with a piece of bacon. Then, rummaging in a bag, Nana found a whole heap of provisions which she had taken the precaution of stuffing into it: a *pâté de foie gras*, a bag of sweetmeats and some oranges. The two of them ate like wolves, with the healthy appetite of twenty-year-olds, not standing on ceremony with each other. Nana kept calling Georges 'my sweet', a form of address which struck her both as affectionate and familiar. At dessert, so as not to disturb Zoé, they used the same spoon in turn to empty a pot of jam they found at the top of a cupboard.

'My sweet,' said Nana, pushing back the table. 'I haven't had such a good dinner these past ten years!'

However, it was growing late, and she wanted to send the boy off for fear he should get into trouble. But he kept telling her he had plenty of time. Besides, his clothing was not drying well, and Zoé declared that it would take at least another hour; and as she was falling asleep on her feet after the fatigue of the journey, they sent her off to bed, after which they were alone in the silent house.

It was a delightful evening. The fire was dying out amid

glowing embers, and in the big blue room, where Zoé had made up the bed before going upstairs, the atmosphere was rather oppressive. Nana, overcome by the heat, got up to open the window for a moment, and uttered a little cry.

'Heavens, how beautiful it is! ... Come and look, my sweet.'

Georges joined her; and, as if considering the window-sill too narrow, he put his arm round Nana's waist and rested his head against her shoulder. The weather had suddenly changed; the sky was clearing, and a full moon was shedding a golden light over the countryside. Utter peace reigned in the valley, which could be seen broadening out into the vast expanse of the plain where the trees looked like dark islets in a bright and motionless lake. And Nana, her heart melting, felt herself a child again. She was sure that she had dreamt of nights like this during a period of her life which she could no longer recall. Since leaving the train, everything that she had experienced – the vast countryside, the grass with its strong scents, the house, the vegetables – had overwhelmed her to such a degree that she felt as if she had left Paris twenty years before. The life she had been living only the previous day was far away, and she was experiencing sensations she had never known before. Meanwhile Georges was giving her little coaxing kisses on the neck, unsettling her even more. With a faltering hand she pushed him away, as if he were a child whose affectionate embraces were fatiguing, and she kept telling him that he ought to go. He did not contradict her : all in good time – he would leave all in good time.

A bird burst into song and then fell silent. It was a robin, in an elder tree below the window.

'Wait a minute,' whispered Georges; 'the lamp's frightening it. I'll put it out.'

And when he came back and put his arm round her waist again, he added :

'We'll light it again in a minute.'

Then, as she listened to the robin, while the boy pressed against her, Nana remembered. Yes, it was in story-books that she had met all this before. In the old days she would

have given anything to have a full moon, like this, and robins, and a lovestruck boy beside her. Heavens, she could have wept, it all seemed so sweet and innocent! There was no doubt about it!' She had been born to lead a virtuous life. She pushed Georges away, as he was getting bolder.

'No, leave me alone. I don't want to. . . . It would be very wrong at your age. . . . Listen, I'll just be your mama.'

She was overcome with scruples of modesty and blushed scarlet. Yet nobody could see her; the room behind them was in darkness, while the countryside stretched out before them in still and silent solitude. She had never known such a feeling of shame before. Little by little, she felt her resistance melting, in spite of her embarrassment and her scruples. That costume of the boy's, that woman's chemise and that dressing-gown set her laughing again. It was as if a girlfriend were teasing her.

'Oh, it's not right, it's not right,' she stammered, after a last effort.

And with that, in face of the lovely night, she sank like a virgin into the child's arms. The house slept.

Next day, at Les Fondettes, when the bell rang for lunch, the dining-room table was no longer too big for the company. Fauchery and Daguenet had driven up together in one carriage, and now another had just arrived with the Comte de Vandeuvres, who had followed by the next train. Georges was the last to come downstairs, looking a little pale, with rings under his eyes. In answer to the others' inquiries he said that he was feeling much better, though he was still rather shaken by the violence of the attack. Madame Hugon looked into his eyes with an anxious smile, and adjusted his hair, which had been carelessly combed that morning, but he drew back as if embarrassed by this caress. During the meal she teased Vandeuvres affectionately, saying that she had been expecting him for the past five years.

'And here you are at last. . . . How did you manage it?'

Vandeuvres replied in the same joking vein. He told her that he had lost a fantastic sum of money at the club the night before, and left Paris with the intention of ending his days in the country.

'Heavens, yes, if you can find me an heiress in these parts. ... There must be some delightful women round here.'

The old lady thanked Fauchery too for having been so good as to accept her son's invitation, and then, to her surprise and delight, she saw the Marquis de Chouard enter the room. A third carriage had just brought him to the house.

'Good heavens,' she cried, 'there must be a rendezvous here this morning! You've passed the word round. ... But what's happening? For years I've never succeeded in bringing you together, and now you all drop in at once. ... Not that I'm complaining.'

Another place was laid. Fauchery found himself next to the Comtesse Sabine, whose liveliness and gaiety surprised him when he remembered how languid she had seemed in the austere Rue Miromesnil drawing-room. Daguenet, on the other hand, who was sitting on Estelle's left, seemed rather uneasy at his proximity to that tall silent girl, whose pointed elbows alarmed him. Muffat and Chouard had exchanged a sly glance, while Vandeuvres went on joking about his forthcoming marriage.

'Talking of ladies,' Madame Hugon said at last, 'I have a new neighbour whom you probably know.'

And she named Nana. Vandeuvres affected the liveliest surprise.

'What! You mean to say Nana's place is near here?'

Fauchery and Daguenet expressed similar astonishment, while the Marquis de Chouard went on eating the breast of a chicken without appearing to understand what the others were saying. Not one of the men had smiled.

'I do,' continued the old lady, 'and indeed the person in question arrived at La Mignotte yesterday evening, as I said she would. I learned that from the gardener this morning.'

At that the gentlemen could not conceal a very genuine astonishment. They all looked up. What was that? Nana had arrived? But they were not expecting her till the next day, and had thought they would arrive before her! Georges alone sat looking at his glass with downcast eyes and a tired

expression. Ever since the beginning of lunch he had seemed to be sleeping with his eyes open and a vague smile on his lips.

'Are you feeling ill, Zizi?' asked his mother, who had not taken her eyes off him.

He started, and blushed as he replied that he was perfectly all right now, but his face still wore the weary, insatiable expression of a girl who has danced too much.

'What's that on your neck?' asked Madame Hugon in alarm. 'It's all red.'

He stammered in embarrassment that he didn't know, that there was nothing on his neck. Then pulling his shirt-collar up, he added:

'Ah, yes, it's an insect that stung me.'

The Marquis de Chouard cast a sidelong glance at the little red mark. Muffat, too, looked at Georges. The meal was nearly over, and the company was planning various excursions. Fauchery was finding the Comtesse Sabine's laughter increasingly disturbing. As he was passing her a dish of fruit their hands touched, and for a second she looked at him so soulfully that he thought once again of that secret which had been confided to him one evening by a drunken friend. Then, too, she was no longer the same woman. Something about her was more pronounced than before, and her grey foulard gown, which fitted loosely over her shoulders, added a touch of unconstraint to her delicate, high-strung elegance.

When they left the table, Daguenet stayed behind with Fauchery to joke crudely about Estelle, whom he called 'a pretty broomstick to shove into a man's hands'. However, he grew serious when the journalist told him the size of the dowry she would bring her husband: four hundred thousand francs.

'And what do you think of the mother?' asked Fauchery. 'She's all right, eh?'

'Oh, I wouldn't say no to her! ... But it's no go, old fellow!'

'Who can tell? ... You'd have to try first ...'

It was impossible to go out that day, for the rain was still

falling in heavy showers. Georges had disappeared hurriedly and double-locked his door. The other gentlemen avoided mutual explanations, though none of them was deceived as to the reasons which had brought them together. Vandeuvres, who had lost heavily at the tables, had really had the idea of lying fallow for a season, and he was counting on Nana's presence in the neighbourhood to keep him from getting too bored. Fauchery, taking advantage of the holidays granted him by Rose, who was very busy just then, was planning to discuss a second article with Nana, if he found that the country made them both feel affectionate. Daguenet, who had been sulky with her since Steiner had come on the scene, was thinking of resuming their old relationship, or at least of enjoying a few pleasant moments, if the opportunity offered. As for the Marquis de Chouard, he was waiting for his time to come. But, among all these men who were following in the tracks of Venus – a Venus with the rouge scarcely washed from her cheeks – Muffat was both the most ardent and the most tortured by novel sensations of desire and fear and anger warring in his anguished heart. He had been given a definite promise : Nana was expecting him. Why then had she left Paris two days earlier than expected? He decided to go to La Mignotte after dinner that very evening.

At night, as the Count was leaving the park, Georges hurried after him. He left him to follow the road to Gumières, crossed the Choue, and arrived at Nana's house breathless, furious, and with tears in his eyes. Oh, yes, he understood everything! That old man on his way to the house was coming to keep a rendezvous. Nana, dumbfounded by this explosion of jealousy, and upset to see the way things were turning out, took him in her arms, and comforted him as best she could. No, he was completely wrong : she wasn't expecting anybody; if the gentleman came, it wouldn't be her fault. What a silly boy Zizi was to be taking on like that about nothing at all ! She swore on her child's head that she loved nobody but her Georges. And with that she kissed him and wiped away his tears.

'Now listen,' she went on, when he had calmed down a

little, 'I'm going to show you that I'm all yours. Steiner has arrived – he's up there now. And you know that I can't throw *him* out, darling.'

'Yes, I know, I'm not talking about *him*,' murmured the boy.

'Well, then, I've stuck him in the room at the end, telling him I was out of sorts. He's unpacking his trunk. . . . Since nobody's seen you, run upstairs and hide in my room, and wait for me.'

Georges threw his arms round her neck. So it was true after all that she loved him a little! And they would put the lamp out like yesterday and stay in the dark till daybreak! Then, as the door-bell sounded, he quietly slipped away. Upstairs in the bedroom, he took off his shoes straight away so as not to make any noise, and hid on the floor, behind a curtain.

Greeting the Comte Muffat, Nana was still shaken and rather embarrassed. She had given him her word, and would even have liked to keep it, since he struck her as a serious admirer. But really, who could have foreseen all that had happened the day before? There was the journey, and the house she had never set eyes on before, and the boy arriving soaked to the skin. How sweet it had all seemed to her and how delightful it would be to go on the same way! So much the worse for the gentleman! For three months past she had been keeping him waiting, posing as a respectable woman to excite him more and more. Well, he would have to go on waiting, and if he didn't like it he could lump it. She would give up everything rather than deceive Georges.

The Count had taken a seat with the ceremonious air of a country neighbour paying a call. Only his hands were trembling slightly. Lust, whipped up by Nana's skilful tactics, was at last wreaking terrible havoc in that sanguine, virginal nature. The grave-faced chamberlain, accustomed to crossing the state apartments of the Tuileries with dignified step, now bit on his bolster every night, sobbing with exasperation as he conjured up the same sensual vision. This time he was determined to have his way. Walking along the road, in the utter peace of the twilight, he had dreamt of taking brutal

action. And the moment he had finished his opening remarks he tried to seize hold of Nana with both hands.

'No, no, you mustn't,' she said, smiling at him and not losing her temper.

He took hold of her again, clenching his teeth, and as she struggled to get free, crudely reminded her that he had come to go to bed with her. At a loss as to what to do, but still smiling, Nana took his hands and spoke coaxingly to him in order to soften her refusal.

'Look, darling, do behave yourself. ... I can't, honest, I can't. ... Steiner's upstairs.'

But he was beside himself; she had never seen a man in such a state. She grew frightened, and put her fingers over his mouth to stifle the cries he was uttering. Lowering her voice, she begged him to be quiet and let go of her. Steiner was coming downstairs. He was being ridiculous. When Steiner entered the room, he found Nana lying back comfortably in her armchair, and heard her saying :

'I adore the country ...'

She looked round and broke off to say :

'It's Monsieur le Comte Muffat, darling. He saw a light on while he was strolling past, and came in to bid us welcome.'

The two men shook hands. Muffat, his face in the dark, remained silent for a moment. Steiner seemed in a peevish mood. Then they chatted about Paris; business was going badly, and some dreadful things had happened on the Stock Exchange. A quarter of an hour later, Muffat took his leave; and as the young woman was seeing him to the door he tried, but without success, to obtain a rendezvous for the following night. Steiner went up to bed almost immediately, grumbling about the everlasting ailments that seemed to afflict courtesans. With the two old men safely out of the way, Nana went to join Georges, whom she found still hiding dutifully behind his curtain. The room was in darkness. He pulled her down on to the floor, so that she sat beside him, and they began playfully rolling about, stopping their game and smothering their laughter with kisses whenever their bare feet hit some piece of furniture. Far away on the road to Gumières the Comte Muffat was walking slowly home, hat in

hand, bathing his burning forehead in the coolness and silence of the night.

During the days that followed, life was wonderful for Nana. In the boy's arms she became a girl of fifteen once more, and under the caressing influence of this new childhood the flower of love blossomed again in a nature jaded and disgusted by experience of men. She experienced sudden fits of blushing, flurries of emotion which left her trembling, urges to laugh and cry – all the symptoms of an uneasy virginity mingled with desires which made her feel ashamed. She had never felt anything comparable to this. The country filled her with tender emotion. As a little girl she had often wished to live in a meadow, looking after a goat, because one day, on the slopes of the fortifications, she had seen a goat bleating at the end of its tether. Now this estate, all this land which belonged to her, filled her heart to bursting, her childhood ambitions had been so greatly surpassed. Once again she tasted the novel sensations experienced by young girls; and at night, when she went upstairs dazed by her day in the open air, and intoxicated by the scent of the leaves, to join her Zizi behind the curtain, she felt like a schoolgirl having a holiday escapade, a love-affair with a young cousin to whom she was going to be married, trembling at the slightest noise, terrified lest her parents should hear her, and savouring the delicious novelty and the voluptuous terrors of a first affair.

Nana now found herself subject to the fancies of a sentimental girl. She would gaze at the moon for hours. One night she had an urge to go down into the garden with Georges when the whole household was asleep; and they strolled under the trees with their arms round each other's waists, finally lying down in the grass, where the dew soaked them to the skin. On another occasion, when they were in the bedroom, she was silent for a long time and then threw herself sobbing into the boy's arms, stammering that she was afraid of dying. She would often sing in a low voice a favourite ballad of Madame Lerat's which was full of flowers and birds. The song would move her to tears, and she would break off in order to clasp Georges in a passionate embrace,

begging him to swear vows of undying love. In short, she was utterly silly, as she herself admitted when the two of them had become good pals again and were sitting bare-legged on the edge of the bed, smoking cigarettes and tapping their heels against the wood.

But what utterly melted the young woman's heart was little Louis's arrival. She had an access of maternal affection which was as violent as a fit of madness. She took her son out into the sunshine to watch him kicking about; she dressed him like a little prince and rolled about with him in the grass. The moment he arrived she decided that he would sleep near her, in the room next to hers, where Madame Lerat, who was greatly impressed by the country, started snoring the moment her head touched the pillow. Little Louis's arrival did not hurt Zizi's position in the least. On the contrary, Nana said that she now had two children, and she treated them with the same capricious affection. At night, more than a dozen times, she would leave Zizi to go and see if little Louis were breathing properly, but on her return she would lavish what remained of her motherly caresses on Zizi, playing at being his mama, while he took a depraved pleasure in being dandled in the girl's arms and allowed himself to be rocked to and fro like a baby being put to sleep. It was all so delightful, and Nana was so charmed with this existence, that she seriously suggested that they never leave the country. They would send everybody else away, and he, she and the child would live alone. And they made a thousand plans till daybreak, without so much as hearing Madame Lerat as she snored loudly after the fatigue of picking flowers in the fields.

This charming life lasted nearly a week. The Comte Muffat used to come every evening, and go away again with a tear-stained face and burning hands. One evening he was not even admitted to the house. Steiner had been obliged to go up to Paris, and he was told that Madame was indisposed. Nana became more disgusted every day at the idea of deceiving Georges. He was such an innocent boy, and he had such faith in her. She would have regarded herself as the lowest of the low if she had betrayed him, and besides it would have sickened her to do so. Zoé, who watched the

progress of this affair with mute disdain, thought that Madame was going out of her mind.

On the sixth day a band of visitors suddenly broke into this idyll. She had invited a host of people under the belief that none of them would come. So, one fine afternoon, she was amazed and annoyed to see a charabanc full of people pulling up outside the gate of La Mignotte.

'It's us!' shouted Mignon, getting out of the vehicle first, and then extracting his sons, Henri and Charles.

Labordette appeared next, and began handing out an endless succession of ladies – Lucy Stewart, Caroline Héquet, Tatan Néné, Maria Blond. Nana was hoping that that was all, when la Faloise sprang down from the step in order to receive Gaga and her daughter Amélie in his trembling arms. That made a total of eleven people. Installing them in the house proved a difficult business. There were five guest rooms at La Mignotte, one of which was already occupied by Madame Lerat and little Louis. The largest was given to the Gaga and la Faloise establishment, and it was decided that Amélie should sleep on a camp-bed in the adjoining dressing-room. Mignon and his two sons had the third room, Labordette the fourth. There remained one room, which was turned into a dormitory, with four beds in it, for Lucy, Caroline, Tatan and Maria. As for Steiner, he would sleep on the divan in the drawing-room. At the end of an hour, when everybody had been settled in, Nana, who had begun by being furious, was thoroughly enjoying playing the role of lady of the manor. The ladies complimented her on La Mignotte – 'a simply marvellous place, darling' – and besides they brought her a whiff of Parisian air, giving her all the gossip of the past week, and all talking at once, roaring with laughter, shouting and slapping each other on the back. By the way, how about Bordenave? What had he said about her running away? Oh, nothing much. After bawling that he would get the police to get her back, he had simply put on an understudy in the evening. And the understudy in question, little Violaine, had actually scored quite a hit as the Blonde Venus. This piece of news made Nana rather thoughtful.

It was only four o'clock in the afternoon, and somebody suggested they should go for a stroll.

'You know what?' said Nana. 'I was just off to pick some potatoes when you arrived.'

At that they all decided to go and pick some potatoes without even changing their clothes first. It was quite a party. The gardener and two helps were already in the potato field at the end of the grounds. The ladies knelt down and began clawing the earth with their be-ringed fingers, giving cries of delight whenever they discovered a really large potato. It struck them as terribly amusing. Tatan Néné in particular was in her element; she had picked so many potatoes in her youth that she forgot herself and started giving the others advice, calling them absolute duffers. The gentlemen worked rather less energetically. Mignon, looking every inch the worthy father, took the opportunity afforded by his stay in the country to complete his sons' education, and told them about Parmentier.

Dinner that evening was tremendously gay. Everybody ate ravenously. Nana, who was in a very excited state, had words with her butler, who had been in service at the bishop's palace in Orléans. The ladies smoked with their coffee. An ear-splitting noise of merrymaking came from the open windows, and died away in the distance in the quiet of the evening, while the peasants belatedly going home along the lanes turned round to look at the house ablaze with lights.

'It's a shame, you're going back the day after tomorrow,' said Nana. 'Still, we'll arrange something all the same.'

They decided to go the next day, Sunday, to see the ruins of the old Abbey of Chamont, which were about five miles away. Five carriages would come from Orléans to pick up the company after lunch, and bring them back to dinner at La Mignotte about seven. It would be delightful.

That evening, as usual, the Comte Muffat climbed the hill to ring at the gate, only to be startled by the brightly lit windows and the shouts of laughter. When he recognized Mignon's voice, he realized what had happened, and went off, raging at this new obstacle, his patience utterly exhausted, and bent on taking violent measures. Georges,

entering by way of a side-door to which he had the key, went quietly upstairs to Nana's room, keeping close to the walls. However, he had to wait for her till after midnight. She appeared at last in a very tipsy condition, and even more motherly than on the previous nights; whenever she drank a lot she became so amorous that she was positively leechlike. Thus she absolutely insisted on his accompanying her to Chamont Abbey. He resisted as best he could, for he was afraid of being seen; if he were seen out driving with her there would be a terrible scandal. But she burst into tears, giving vent to the noisy despair of a slighted woman, so that to console her he promised faithfully to join the party.

'You really do love me, then?' she stammered. 'Say that you love me. ... Tell me, darling, if I died, would you be dreadfully upset?'

At Les Fondettes the proximity of Nana had thrown the house-party into confusion. Every morning over lunch the kindly Madame Hugon returned to the subject of 'that woman' despite herself, telling her guests the news the gardener had brought her, and revealing that obsessive fascination which courtesans exert on the worthiest of ladies. Tolerant though she was, she was revolted and exasperated, feeling a vague presentiment of disaster, which frightened her in the evenings as much as if she had known that a wild beast had escaped from some menagerie and was at large in the countryside. She started picking quarrels with her guests, accusing all of them of prowling round La Mignotte. The Comte de Vandeuvres had been seen laughing on the high road with a bare-headed lady : but he defended himself against the accusation and denied that it was Nana, the fact being that it was Lucy who had accompanied him a little way in order to tell him how she had just turned her third prince out of doors. The Marquis de Chouard also went out every day, but he maintained that this was on doctor's orders. Towards Daguenet and Fauchery Madame Hugon was being unjust. The former in particular never left Les Fondettes, for he had given up the idea of renewing the old connection, and was busy paying respectful attention to Estelle. Fauchery also stayed with the Muffat ladies. On one occasion only had

he met Mignon in a lane with an armful of flowers, giving his sons a lecture on botany. The two men had shaken hands, and given each other news about Rose. She was in excellent health; they had both received a letter from her that morning, in which she urged them to take advantage of the country air for a few more days. Of all her guests, therefore, the old lady spared only the Comte Muffat and Georges. The Count, who said he had serious business to attend to in Orléans, could obviously not be running after that woman : and as for Georges, the poor child was beginning to cause her considerable anxiety, seeing that every evening he was afflicted with an appalling headache which forced him to go to bed while it was still light.

Meanwhile Fauchery had become the Comtesse Sabine's faithful companion during the Count's absence every afternoon. Whenever they went to the end of the park, he carried her folding stool and her parasol. Besides he amused her with the sort of witticisms that come easily to a journalist, and gently coaxed her into one of those sudden intimacies which are permissible in the country. She had appeared to consent to it from the first, becoming quite a girl again in the company of a young man whose noisy teasing seemed unlikely to compromise her. But now and then, when they found themselves alone for a moment behind a bush, their eyes would meet, and they would pause in the midst of their laughter, growing suddenly serious and looking at each other sadly, as if they had seen into the depths of each other's heart.

On Friday a fresh place had to be laid for lunch. Monsieur Théophile Venot, whom Madame Hugon remembered having invited at the Muffats' the previous winter, had just arrived. He sat with his shoulders hunched, affecting the good-natured humility of a man of no importance, and did not seem to notice the uneasy deference with which he was treated. When he had succeeded in getting the company to forget his presence, he sat nibbling little lumps of sugar during dessert, watching Daguenet as the latter handed Estelle some strawberries, and listening to Fauchery, who was making the Countess laugh with one of his anecdotes. Whenever anyone looked at him, he smiled in his quiet way. When

everybody rose from the table, he took the Count's arm, and took him off into the park. He was known to have exercised great influence over the latter ever since his mother's death. Indeed strange stories were told about the dominion which the sometime lawyer enjoyed in that household. Fauchery, who doubtless found his arrival embarrassing, explained the origin of the man's wealth to Georges and Daguenet. It was an important lawsuit which the Jesuits had entrusted to him in the past; and in his opinion, the worthy man was a terrible fellow, despite his plump, gentle face, and nowadays had a finger in every priestly pie. The two young men had laughed at this, for they thought the little old man looked positively imbecilic. The idea of an unknown Venot, a gigantic Venot, acting for the whole body of the clergy, struck them as a comical notion. But they fell silent when the Comte Muffat reappeared, pale-faced and leaning on the old man's arm, red-eyed as if he had been weeping.

'I bet they've been chatting about hell,' Fauchery murmured jokingly.

The Comtesse Sabine overheard the remark. She turned her head slowly and their eyes met in one of those lingering glances in which they were accustomed to sounding each other cautiously before venturing any further.

After lunch it was the guests' custom to stroll along a terrace overlooking the plain, as far as the end of the lawn. On Sunday afternoon the weather was exquisitely mild. There had been signs of rain about ten in the morning, but although the sky had not cleared it had as it were melted into a milky fog which hung like a cloud of luminous dust in the golden sunlight. Madame Hugon accordingly proposed that they should go down through the little terrace gate and go for a walk in the direction of Gumières as far as the Choue; she was fond of walking, and still very active in spite of her sixty years. Besides all her guests declared that they had no need of a carriage. They reached the wooden bridge over the river in somewhat straggling order. Fauchery and Daguenet arrived first with the Muffat ladies; then came the Count and the Marquis, one on each side of Madame Hugon, while Vandeuvres, fashionably dressed and looking rather

bored on the high road, brought up the rear, smoking a cigar. Monsieur Venot, now slowing down and now quickening his step, passed smilingly from one group to another, as if determined to hear every word.

'And poor dear Georges is in Orléans!' Madame Hugon was saying. 'He wanted to consult old Doctor Tavernier, who never goes out now, about his headaches. . . . Yes, you weren't up, because he went off before seven o'clock. At least it will make a change for him.'

She broke off to say :

'Why, what's making them stop on the bridge?'

The fact was that the ladies and Daguenet and Fauchery were standing motionless on the crown of the bridge. They seemed to be hesitating as if some obstacle had made them uneasy, yet the road was open before them.

'Go on!' shouted the Count.

They did not budge, looking at something which was approaching and which the others could not see as yet, for the road wound about and was bordered by a thick screen of poplars. Meanwhile a dull sound was growing louder, in which the noise of wheels could be heard mingled with shouts of laughter and the cracking of whips. All of a sudden five carriages came into view, one after the other, full to bursting and bright with dazzling blue and pink dresses.

'What's that?' Madame Hugon asked in surprise.

Then she guessed, and exploded with indignation at such an invasion of her road.

'Oh, that woman!' she murmured. 'Walk on, walk on. Don't look as if you . . .'

But it was too late. The five carriages, which were taking Nana and her company to the Chamont ruins, rolled onto the narrow wooden bridge. Fauchery, Daguenet and the Muffat ladies were forced to retreat, while Madame Hugon and the others had to stop behind one another, in a line along the roadside. It was a magnificent parade. The laughter in the carriages had stopped, and faces turned with expressions of curiosity. The two parties examined each other in the midst of a silence broken only by the measured trot of the

horses. In the first carriage Maria Blond and Tatan Néné were reclining like a couple of duchesses, their skirts hanging out over the wheels, and cast disdainful glances at the respectable women who went about on foot. Next came Gaga, taking up a whole seat, and half smothering la Faloise beside her, so that nothing could be seen of him but his nose poking out anxiously. Then there followed Caroline Héquet with Labordette, Lucy Stewart with Mignon and his sons, and last of all Nana sharing a victoria with Steiner, with poor darling Zizi on a basket seat in front of her, his knees pressed against her own.

'That's the last of them, isn't it?' the Countess calmly asked Fauchery, pretending not to recognize Nana.

The wheel of the victoria almost brushed against her, but she did not step back. The two women exchanged a profound glance, one of those momentary scrutinies which are at once complete and definitive. As for the men, they behaved perfectly. Fauchery and Daguenet looked icy, and recognized nobody. The Marquis, who was very nervous, fearing some farcical reaction on the part of the ladies, had broken a blade of grass he was rolling between his fingers. Only Vandeuvres, who had remained somewhat apart from the rest, winked at Lucy, who smiled at him as she passed.

'Be careful!' Monsieur Venot had murmured, as he stood behind the Comte Muffat.

The latter, utterly dumbfounded, was gazing after Nana as she disappeared from sight. His wife had slowly turned round and was examining him. He looked down at the ground, as if to escape the sound of the galloping hooves which were carrying away both his flesh and his heart. He could have cried aloud in his agony, for catching sight of Georges nestling among Nana's skirts, he had just understood everything. A mere child! He was shattered at the thought that she should have preferred a mere child to him! Steiner he could accept, but that child!

Meanwhile Madame Hugon had not recognized Georges at first. As for him, he would have jumped into the river they were crossing if Nana's knees had not restrained him. So, white as a sheet, and icy cold, he sat rigid in his place. He

looked at nobody, thinking that it was just possible that he might go unnoticed.

'Heavens above!' the old lady said suddenly, 'that's Georges who's with her!'

As the carriages had passed by there had been an uncomfortable feeling among these people who recognized each other yet gave no sign of recognition. The brief, delicate encounter had seemed to go on for ever. And now the wheels were bearing away the carriage-loads of girls more gaily than ever through the sunlit countryside. The fresh air blew in their faces, bits of bright-coloured fabric fluttered in the breeze, and laughter broke out again as the people in the carriages started joking among themselves and glanced back at the respectable folk who remained at the roadside, looking annoyed. Turning round, Nana could see the strollers hesitate, and then return the way they had come, without crossing the bridge. Madame Hugon was leaning silently on the Comte Muffat's arm, looking so sad that nobody dared console her.

'I say, love, did you see Fauchery?' Nana shouted to Lucy, who was leaning out of the carriage in front. 'What a filthy look he gave me! He'll pay for that. ... And Paul, too, a fellow I've been so kind to! Not so much as a nod.... They're a polite lot, I must say!'

And she gave Steiner a terrible dressing-down when he expressed the opinion that the gentlemen's behaviour had been perfectly correct. So she and the other ladies weren't worth raising your hat to, were they? So any blackguard could insult them, could he? Thanks – he was as bad as they were! That put the lid on it! A man should always raise his hat to a woman.

'Who was the tall one?' asked Lucy at the top of her voice, above the noise of the wheels.

'That was the Comtesse Muffat,' answered Steiner.

'There now! I thought as much,' said Nana. 'Well, my dear, she may be a countess, but she's no better than she should be. ... Yes, she's no better than she should be.... I've got an eye for that sort of thing, you know! And now I know your Countess as well as if she was my own child.... I'm

willing to bet she sleeps with that snake Faucherty. . . . Yes, I tell you she's his mistress! A woman can always tell that sort of thing about another woman.'

Steiner shrugged his shoulders. Since the previous day his irritation had been steadily increasing. For one thing, he had received some letters which necessitated his leaving the following morning; and for another, it wasn't much fun coming down to the country just to sleep on the drawing-room divan.

'And this poor baby!' Nana continued, suddenly touched at the sight of Georges's pale face, as he sat in front of her, still rigid and breathless.

'Do you think Mama recognized me?' he stammered at last.

'Oh, that's for sure. Why, she cried out. . . . But it's my fault. He didn't want to come with us. I forced him to. . . . Listen, Zizi, would you like me to write to your mama? She looks such a respectable sort. I'll tell her I'd never seen you before, and it was Steiner who brought you along for the first time today.'

'No, no, don't write to her,' said Georges in great anxiety. 'I'll explain it all myself. . . . Besides, if she makes a fuss about it, I shan't go home again.'

But he remained very pensive, racking his brains for excuses he could make in the evening. The five carriages were rolling across flat country, along an interminable straight road lined with fine trees. The countryside was bathed in a silvery-grey atmosphere. The ladies continued shouting remarks from carriage to carriage behind the backs of the drivers, who chuckled at their unusual fares. Occasionally one of them would stand up to look out, and remain stubbornly leaning on her neighbour's shoulders until a sudden jolt threw her down on the seat again. Meanwhile Caroline Héquet was deep in conversation with Labordette; the two of them were agreed that Nana would sell her country house before three months were out, and Caroline was instructing Labordette to buy it quietly for her on the cheap. In front of them la Faloise, who was in a very amorous mood, unable to reach Gaga's apoplectic neck, was pressing kisses on her spine, through her dress, which was stretched to the point of

splitting, while Amélie, perched stiffly on the edge of the bracket-seat, kept begging them to stop, for it exasperated her to sit idly there watching her mother being kissed. In the next carriage Mignon, in an attempt to impress Lucy, was making his sons recite fables by la Fontaine; Henri, who was particularly good at this, was rattling his poems off without pause or hesitation. But Maria Blond, at the head of the procession, was beginning to feel bored; she was tired of fooling the credulous Tatan Néné, whom she had been persuading that Paris dairywomen manufactured eggs with a mixture of paste and saffron. The journey was taking too long; were they never going to get to their destination? Transmitted from one carriage to the next, the question finally reached Nana, who, after asking her driver, got up and shouted:

'A quarter of an hour at the most. . . . You see that church behind the trees over there . . .'

Then she went on:

'You know, it seems that the owner of the Château de Chamont is an old lady of Napoleon's time. . . . Oh, she was a wild one according to Joseph, who heard about her from the bishop's servants . . . the sort you don't find any more. Now, of course, she's turned religious.'

'What's her name?' asked Lucy.

'Madame d'Anglars.'

'Irma d'Anglars! I knew her!' cried Gaga.

Admiring exclamations burst forth from the line of carriages, only to be drowned by the sound of the horses' hooves as they quickened their pace. Heads were poked out to look at Gaga; Maria Blond and Tatan Néné turned round and knelt on the seat, with their hands on the open hood; and the air was filled with questions and spiteful witticisms, tempered by a grudging admiration. The idea that Gaga had known her filled them all with respect for that distant past.

'Mind you, I was very young at the time,' Gaga went on. 'All the same, I remember seeing her drive by. . . . They said she was disgusting in her own house, but sitting in her carriage, she looked terribly *chic*. And the tales they told about her! The dirty tricks she played and the cunning dodges she got up to! . . . I don't wonder that she's got a castle. Why, she

used to clean a man out just by looking at him. .... To think Irma d'Anglars is still alive! Why, my dears, she must be getting on for ninety.'

At this the ladies became suddenly serious. Ninety years old! There wasn't one of them, as Lucy loudly declared, who would live to that age. They were all worn out. Besides Nana said she didn't want to make old bones; it wouldn't be any fun. They were drawing near their destination, and the conversation was interrupted by the cracking of whips as the drivers urged their horses on. Yet in the midst of all the noise Lucy continued talking, changing the subject and urging Nana to go back with them all the next day. The Exhibition was going to close, and they really had to return to Paris, where the season was exceeding all their expectations. But Nana was obstinate. She loathed Paris, and she wasn't going to go back there in a hurry.

'We're going to stay here, aren't we, darling?' she said, giving Georges's knees a squeeze, and taking no notice of Steiner.

The carriages had pulled up abruptly, and in some surprise the company got out in a deserted spot at the bottom of a small hill. One of the drivers had to point out with his whip the ruins of the old Abbey of Chamont, where they lay hidden among the trees. They were a tremendous disappointment. The ladies thought it was ridiculous making such a fuss about a few heaps of stones covered with briars, and part of a tumble-down tower. It really wasn't worth coming five miles just to see that! Then the driver pointed out the way to the castle, the grounds of which began close to the abbey, and advised them to take a little path and follow the walls. They could go round the park while the carriages would go and wait for them in the village square. He assured them it was a delightful walk, and they agreed to follow his suggestion.

'Lord, but Irma's done well for herself,' said Gaga, halting in front of a gate at one corner of the park, leading on to the road.

All of them stood silently gazing at the enormous thicket which blocked the gateway. Then, following the little path,

they skirted the park wall, looking up now and then to admire the trees, whose lofty branches stretched out over them to form a dense vault of greenery. After three minutes they found themselves in front of a second gate; through this a wide lawn was visible, over which two venerable oaks cast vast shadows. Three minutes further on, yet another gate afforded them a view of an immense avenue, a corridor of shadows, at the end of which a bright spot of sunlight shone like a star. They stood there in astonished admiration, silent at first, but then giving vent to exclamations. So far they had tried to joke about it all with a touch of envy in their hearts, but this decidedly impressed them. What a marvel Irma was! A sight like this gave you some idea of the woman! The line of trees continued, and there were endlessly re-current patches of ivy on the wall, glimpses of roofs above it, and screens of poplars interspersed with dense masses of elms and aspens. Was there no end to it? The ladies would have liked to catch a glimpse of the castle, for they were weary of walking on and on, seeing nothing but leafy recesses through every opening they came to. They took the bars of the gate in their hands, and pressed their faces against the ironwork. Kept at a distance like this, and dreaming of the castle lost to view in this immensity, they were overcome by a feeling of respect. Soon, being unaccustomed to walking, they grew tired. And the wall did not stop; at every turn of the deserted path the same line of grey stones stretched ahead of them. Some of them, despairing of ever getting to the end of it, began talking of turning back. But the more the walk fatigued them, the more respectful they became, for at each successive step they were increasingly impressed by the calm, majestic dignity of the estate.

'This is getting ridiculous!' said Caroline Héquet, gritting her teeth.

Nana silenced her with a shrug. For a little while she had been rather pale and very serious, and had not spoken a single word. Suddenly the path took a final turn, the wall ended, and as they came out on the village square, the castle appeared before them, at the far end of a grand courtyard. All of them stopped, struck by the proud sweep of the wide

steps, the twenty windows of the façade, the spread of the three wings, which were built of brick framed in stone cordons. Henri IV had once lived in this historic building, and his great room, with its great bed hung with Genoa velvet, was still preserved there. Breathless with admiration, Nana gave a little childlike sigh.

'God Almighty!' she whispered to herself.

But just then everybody was deeply moved when Gaga suddenly declared that it was Irma herself who was standing in front of the church. She recognized her perfectly – as upright as ever, the old minx, despite her years, with the same flash of her eyes when she put on her high-and-mighty airs. The congregation was coming out of Vespers, and for a few moments Madame paused in the church porch. She was dressed in brownish-yellow silk, and looked very simple and very tall, her venerable face suggesting an old marquise who had survived the horrors of the Revolution. In her right hand a bulky missal shone in the sunlight, and very slowly she crossed the square, followed at a distance of fifteen paces by a footman in livery. As the church emptied, all the inhabitants of Chamont bowed respectfully to her; an old man kissed her hand, and a woman made as if to fall on her knees. She gave the impression of a powerful queen, loaded with years and honours. Going up the steps of the castle, she disappeared from sight.

'That's what you get when you lead an orderly life,' Mignon declared with an air of conviction, looking at his sons as if to teach them a lesson.

Then everybody had his say. Labordette thought she was extraordinarily well preserved. Maria Blond made a coarse remark, annoying Lucy, who declared that people ought to show respect for old age. All the women, in any event, agreed that she was an absolute marvel. Then the company got back into their carriages. All the way from Chamont to La Mignotte, Nana remained silent. She had turned round twice to look back at the castle, and now, lulled by the sound of the wheels, she forgot that Steiner was beside her and Georges in front of her. A vision appeared in the twilight, in which Madame continued to sweep past with all the

majesty of a powerful queen, loaded with years and honours.

That evening Georges returned to Les Fondettes for dinner. Nana, who had grown increasingly strange and off-hand, had sent him to ask his mama's forgiveness; it was his duty, she told him sternly, showing a sudden respect for the decencies of family life. She even made him swear not to come back to spend the night with her; she was tired, and he would be doing no more than his duty in obeying her. Extremely vexed by this moralizing, Georges nonetheless appeared before his mother with heavy heart and bowed head. Fortunately for him, his brother Philippe, a gay devil of a soldier, had arrived during the day, and this cut short the scene he had been dreading. Madame Hugon confined herself to looking at him with eyes full of tears, while Philippe, who had been put in possession of the facts, threatened to go and fetch him home by the scruff of his neck if he ever went back to see that woman. Greatly relieved, Georges began slyly planning to slip away about two o'clock the following day to arrange his future meetings with Nana.

Meanwhile at dinner-time the company at Les Fondettes seemed somewhat embarrassed. Vandeuvres had announced that he was leaving; he had decided to take Lucy back to Paris with him, amused at the idea of carrying off that girl whom he had known for ten years, yet never desired. The Marquis de Chouard bent over his plate, thinking about Gaga's young lady. He could remember dandling Lili on his knees, and marvelled at the way that children had of shooting up; that little thing was getting very plump too. The Comte Muffat in particular was silent, pensive and flushed. He had given Georges a long look, and after dinner he went upstairs, saying that he had a slight chill and intended to lock himself in his bedroom. Monsieur Venot had rushed after him, and upstairs an emotional scene ensued. The Count threw himself on the bed, stifling his hysterical sobs in the pillow, while Monsieur Venot softly called him his brother, and advised him to beg for divine forgiveness. But he heard nothing, choking with emotion. Suddenly he sprang off the bed and stammered :

'I'm going over there. . . . I can't stand it any longer. . .'

'All right,' murmured Venot, 'I'll come with you.'

As they left the house, two figures were vanishing into the shadows of a garden path, for every evening now Fauchery and the Comtesse Sabine left Daguenet to help Estelle make tea. Out on the high road the Count walked so fast that his companion had to run to keep up with him. Though out of breath, the latter never ceased lavishing on him the most powerful arguments against the temptations of the flesh. The other man never opened his mouth, but strode on through the darkness. When he arrived outside La Mignotte, he said simply :

'I can't stand it any longer. ... Go away.'

'God's will be done, then,' murmured Monsieur Venot. 'He uses many means to ensure his final triumph. Your sin will be one of his weapons.'

At La Mignotte there was some wrangling during the meal. Nana had found a letter from Bordenave waiting for her, in which he advised her to take a rest, and gave the impression that he did not give a damn for her; little Violaine, he said, was being encored twice every night. But when Mignon continued urging her to go back with them the next day, Nana lost her temper and declared that she did not intend to take advice from anybody. What is more, she was absurdly strait-laced at table. Madame Lerat having let out some expletive or other, she loudly announced that she'd be damned if she was going to let anybody, even her own aunt, use foul language in her presence. After which, in a fit of stupid respectability, she bored her guests with a display of virtuous sentiments, telling them all of plans for a religious education for little Louis and a whole scheme of good behaviour for herself. When the company began laughing she uttered some profound statements, nodding her head like an opinionated bourgeoise, saying that an orderly life was the only recipe for wealth, and declaring that she had no intention of dying in the poorhouse. The ladies were exasperated and protested. They couldn't believe it : Nana had changed ! But she sat motionless, lost in a reverie once more, her vacant eyes fixed on a vision of a very rich and greatly honoured Nana.

The company were going up to bed when Muffat appeared. It was Labordette who caught sight of him in the garden. He understood at once, and did him the service of getting Steiner out of the way and then leading him by the hand along the dark corridor as far as Nana's bedroom. In affairs of this kind Labordette always conducted himself with the utmost tact and skill, giving the impression that he was delighted to be making other people happy. Nana showed no surprise; she was only somewhat annoyed by the ardour of Muffat's passion for her. Life was a serious business after all. Loving somebody was ridiculous: it got you nowhere. Besides she felt certain scruples on account of Zizi's tender years; she really hadn't behaved very well. But now, dammit, she was going to get back on the right road; she was going to take on an old man.

'Zoé,' she said to the maid, who was enchanted at the idea of leaving the country, 'pack our bags when you get up to-morrow. We're going back to Paris.'

And she went to bed with Muffat, but without pleasure.

THREE months later, one December evening, the Comte Muffat was strolling along the Passage des Panoramas. It was a very mild evening, and a shower of rain had sent people pouring into the passage. There was a huge crowd there, moving slowly and laboriously along between the shops on either side. Under the glass panes, white with reflected light, the passage was brilliantly illuminated. A stream of light emanated from white globes, red lanterns, blue transparencies, lines of gas-jets, and gigantic watches and fans outlined in flame, all burning in the open; and the motley window displays, the gold ornaments of the jewellers, the crystal jars of the confectioners, the light-coloured silks of the milliners, glittered in the glare of the reflectors behind the clear plate-glass windows; while among the brightly coloured array of shop signs a huge crimson glove in the distance looked like a bleeding hand which had been severed from an arm and fastened to a yellow cuff.

The Comte Muffat had slowly returned as far as the boulevard. He glanced out at the roadway, and then came back at a gentle pace, keeping close to the shop-windows. The damp, warm atmosphere filled the narrow passage with a luminous mist. Along the flagstones, which had been moistened by dripping umbrellas, footsteps rang out continuously, but unaccompanied by any sound of voices. Passers-by elbowed him at every turn, and gazed inquisitively at his silent face, which looked ghastly pale in the gaslight. To escape from this curiosity the Count planted himself in front of a stationer's, where with profound attention he contemplated a display of paper-weights in the form of glass balls containing floating landscapes and flowers.

He saw nothing: he was thinking of Nana. Why had she lied to him again? That morning she had written and told him not to come round in the evening, explaining that little Louis was ill, and that she was going to spend the night

watching over him at her aunt's. But he had felt suspicious and called at her house, where he learnt from the concierge that Madame had just left for her theatre. He was astonished at this, for she was not acting in the new operetta. Why then had she told him that lie, and what could she be doing at the Variétés this evening?

Jostled by a passer-by, the Count unconsciously left the paper-weights, and found himself in front of a window full of knick-knacks, where he gazed with his absorbed expression at an array of notebooks and cigar-cases, all of which had the same blue swallow stamped on one corner. Nana had certainly changed. In the early days after her return from the country, she used to drive him wild with her kittenish caresses, kissing him on his whiskers all round his face, and swearing that he was her pet and the only man she adored. He was no longer afraid of Georges, whom his mother had kept at Les Fondettes. There remained fat Steiner, whom he thought he had ousted, although he did not dare provoke an explanation on his score. He knew that he was in extraordinary financial difficulties again, and on the verge of being hammered on the Stock Exchange, so that he was clinging like grim death to the shareholders of the Landes salt pits and trying to wring a final investment out of them. Whenever he met Steiner at Nana's she would explain, in a reasonable tone of voice, that she did not want to turn him out like a dog, after all he had spent on her. In any case, for the last three months he had been living in such a daze of sensual excitement that apart from the need to possess her, he had experienced no very distinct feelings. In the tardy awakening of his flesh he was filled with a childish greed for pleasure, which left no room for either vanity or jealousy. Only one distinct impression had struck him and that was that Nana was becoming less affectionate : she no longer kissed him on the beard. This made him uneasy, and as a man who knew nothing about women he wondered what he had done to offend her, especially as he was under the impression that he was satisfying all her desires. He kept harking back to the letter he had received that morning with its complicated lie, apparently invented for the simple purpose

of spending the evening at her own theatre. Pushed along by a fresh thrust of the crowd, he had crossed the passage and was racking his brains in front of the entrance to a restaurant, his eyes fixed on some plucked larks and a huge salmon laid out inside the window.

At last he seemed to tear himself away from this spectacle. He shook himself, looked up, and noticed that it was nearly nine o'clock. Nana would be coming out soon, and he would demand the truth from her. And he walked on, recalling the evenings he had already spent in this spot when meeting her at the stage-door. He knew all the shops, and in the gas-laden air, he recognized their different smells, the strong scent of Russian leather, the perfume of vanilla rising from a chocolate-dealer's basement, the savour of musk blown through the open doors of the perfumers. As a result he no longer dared to linger before the pale faces of the shop assistants, who gazed at him calmly as at a familiar figure. For a moment he seemed to be studying the line of little round windows above the shops, as if he had never noticed them before among the medley of signs. Then, once again, he went up to the boulevard, and stood there for a minute. A thin drizzle was now falling, and the cold feel of it on his hands calmed him. He thought of his wife who was staying in a country house near Mâcon, where her friend Madame de Chezelles had been ill ever since the autumn. The carriages in the roadway were rolling through a river of mud, and he reflected that the country must be unbearable in such vile weather. But suddenly he was seized with anxiety and went back into the hot, close passage, striding along among the idlers: the thought had struck him that if Nana were suspicious, she would slip out by way of the Galerie Montmartre.

From then on the Count kept watch at the stage-door itself, though he did not like this part of the passage, where he was afraid of being recognized. It was at the junction of the Galerie des Variétés and the Galerie Saint-Marc, a shady-looking corner full of obscure little shops – a shoemaker's without any customers, a few dusty furniture shops, and a smoky, somnolent reading-room whose shaded lamps cast a sleepy green light all evening. There was never anybody in

this corner but well-dressed, patient gentlemen prowling around among the drunken scene-shifters and ragged chorus-girls who always congregate about stage-doors. Outside the theatre a single gas-jet in a frosted-glass globe lit up the doorway. For a moment Muffat thought of questioning Madame Bron : then he grew afraid that Nana might be told that he was there and escape by way of the boulevard. So he started walking again, determined to wait until he was turned out when the gates were locked, something which had happened on two previous occasions; the thought of going home to his solitary bed wrung his heart with anguish. Every time that hatless girls and men in dirty shirts came out and stared at him, he returned to his post in front of the reading-room, where, looking in between two posters stuck on a window-pane, he was always greeted by the same sight : a little old man, sitting stiff and solitary at the vast table, and holding a green newspaper in his green hands under the green light of one of the lamps. But a few minutes before ten, another gentleman, a tall, fair, good-looking man with well-fitting gloves, also began walking up and down outside the theatre. After that, at each successive turn, the two of them treated each other to a suspicious sidelong glance. The Count walked as far as the corner of the two galleries, which was adorned with a high mirror, and when he saw himself reflected in it, looking grave and elegant, he felt a mixture of shame and fear.

Ten o'clock struck, and suddenly it occurred to Muffat that it would be very easy to find out whether Nana were in her dressing-room or not. He went up the three steps, crossed the little yellow-painted lobby, and slipped into the yard through a door which was simply left on the latch. At that hour of the night, the narrow courtyard, as damp as the bottom of a well-shaft, with its stinking water-closets, its drinking-fountain and the kitchen range, which the concierge had decorated with potted plants, was drenched in a dark mist; but the two walls on either side, both pierced with windows, were ablaze with light, which was streaming from the property store and the fireman's post on the ground floor, the manager's offices on the left, and the dressing-rooms up-

stairs on the right. It seemed as if the fire-holes of furnaces were opening on to the darkness from top to bottom of this well. The Count had immediately noticed the light in the window of the dressing-room on the first floor, and, relieved and happy, he forgot where he was, and stood gazing upwards in the midst of the slime and the insipid stench peculiar to the courtyard of any old Parisian building. Big drops were dripping from a broken water spout, and a ray of gaslight from Madame Bron's window was casting a yellow glow over a patch of moss-covered pavement, the base of a wall rotted away by water from a sink and a whole heap of garbage in which a green spindle tree in a cooking-pot was surrounded by old pails and broken crocks. A window-fastening creaked, and the Count fled.

Nana was certainly going to come down. He returned to his post outside the reading-room; in the slumbering shadows, broken only by the glimmer of a dim light, the little old man still sat motionless, his head bent over his newspaper. Then he set off again, going farther this time across the large gallery and along the Galerie des Variétés as far as the Galerie Feydeau, which was cold and deserted, sunk in miserable darkness. Coming back, he passed the theatre, turned the corner of the Galerie Saint-Marc, and ventured as far as the Galerie Montmartre, where a sugar-chopping machine in a grocer's shop held his attention for a while. But when he was taking his third turn, the fear that Nana might escape behind his back robbed him of all self-respect. He stationed himself beside the fair-haired gentleman, right outside the theatre, and the two men exchanged a glance of brotherly humility, mingled with a touch of distrust born of the suspicion that they might be rivals. Some scene-shifters, coming out for a smoke in the interval, jostled them, but neither one nor the other ventured to complain. Three tall girls with untidy hair and dirty dresses appeared on the doorstep, munching apples and spitting out the cores; the men bowed their heads, taken aback by their impudent stares and foul language, and feeling sullied and soiled by these trollops who thought it amusing to push each other against them.

Just then Nana came down the three steps. She went white when she caught sight of Muffat.

'Oh, it's you,' she stammered.

The sniggering girls took fright when they recognized her, and they stood stock-still, side by side, looking as stiff and serious as maidservants whom their mistress has caught doing something wrong. The tall fair-haired gentleman had moved away, at once reassured and sad at heart.

'Well, give me your arm,' Nana continued impatiently.

They walked slowly away. The Count had prepared some questions to ask her, but he now found nothing to say. It was she who, talking quickly, told a story to the effect that she had been at her aunt's as late as eight o'clock, and, seeing that little Louis was much better, had suddenly decided to drop in at the theatre for a few minutes.

'Some important business?' he asked.

'Yes, a new show,' she replied, after a slight hesitation. 'They wanted my opinion.'

He could tell that she was lying, but the warm feel of her arm, as it leant heavily on his own, left him powerless. He felt neither anger nor rancour after his long wait : his one thought was to keep her with him now that he had got hold of her. The next day he would try to find out why she had come round to her dressing-room. Nana, still hesitant and obviously a prey to the inner anguish of somebody trying to come to a decision, stopped in front of a window display of fans as they were turning the corner of the Galerie des Variétés.

'I say, that's pretty,' she murmured, 'that mother-of-pearl mount with those feathers.'

She added casually :

'So you're coming home with me?'

'Of course,' he said in surprise, 'seeing that your child's feeling better.'

She felt sorry that she had told him that story. Perhaps little Louis had taken a turn for the worse and she talked of returning to Les Batignolles. But when he offered to accompany her she dropped the idea. For a moment she was filled with the white-hot fury of a woman who is conscious of being

214

trapped and has to sing small. But in the end she grew resigned and decided to gain time; provided she could get rid
of the Count about midnight, everything would work out all
right.

'I'd forgotten that you're a bachelor tonight,' she murmured. 'Your wife doesn't come back till tomorrow morning,
does she?'

'No,' replied Muffat, a little embarrassed to hear her talking familiarly about the Countess.

But she pressed him further, asking the time of his wife's
train, and wanting to know whether he was going to the
station to meet her. She had slowed down more than ever, as
if she were fascinated by the shop-windows.

'Look at that!' she said, stopping again in front of a
jeweller's shop. 'What a funny bracelet!'

She adored the Passage des Panoramas, still obsessed by the
passion she had felt in her youth for fancy goods, fake jewellery, gilded zinc and cardboard made to look like leather.
She could not tear herself away from the shop-windows
any more than when she had been a street-urchin in
down-at-heel shoes, lost in wonder in front of a confectioner's
wares, or listening to a musical-box in a neighbouring shop,
and above all going into ecstasies over cheap, gaudy knick-
knacks, such as nutshell work-boxes, rag-pickers' baskets for
holding toothpicks, and thermometers mounted on obelisks
and Vendôme Columns. But that evening she was too agitated, and looked at things without seeing them. When all
was said and done, it irked her to think she was not free; and
in her mood of mute rebellion she felt a furious desire to do
something foolish. A lot of good it had done her to be the
mistress of men of wealth and position! She had cleaned out
the Prince and Steiner to satisfy her childish caprices, and yet
she had no idea where the money had gone. Even now her
flat on the Boulevard Haussmann was not entirely furnished;
the drawing-room alone was finished, all in red satin, and
looked thoroughly out of keeping, over-decorated and overcrowded as it was. Her creditors, moreover, were pestering
her more than they had done when she was penniless, something which caused her constant surprise, for she boasted of

being a model of economy. For a month past that thief Steiner had been hard put to it to find a thousand francs on the occasions when she had threatened to kick him out if he failed to bring them. As for Muffat, he was a fool : he had no idea what it was usual to give, so she couldn't blame him for his miserliness. She would have got rid of all these people long ago if she hadn't repeated her good resolutions to herself a score of times a day. You had to be sensible, as Zoé said every morning, and Nana herself was haunted by the queenly vision seen at Chamont, which had now become a religious memory with her, constantly recalled and magnified. And that was why, though trembling with repressed indignation, she now hung submissively on the Count's arm as they went from window to window among the fast-diminishing number of passers-by. The pavement was drying outside, and a cold wind blew along the gallery, sweeping away the warm air under the glass roof, and shaking the coloured lanterns, the lines of gas-jets and the giant fan blazing like a set piece in a firework display. At the door of the restaurant a waiter was putting out the gas-lamps, while the motionless assistants in the bright, empty shops looked as if they had fallen asleep with their eyes open.

'Oh, isn't that sweet !' exclaimed Nana, retracing her steps to the last of the shops and going into ecstasies over a porcelain greyhound, which stood with raised forepaw in front of a nest hidden among roses.

At last they left the passage, but she refused the offer of a cab. It was very pleasant out, she said; besides, they were in no hurry, and it would be charming to return home on foot. When they reached the Café Anglais she had a sudden longing to eat some oysters, and pointed out that because of little Louis's illness she had eaten nothing since morning. Muffat did not dare to thwart her. As yet, however, he was reluctant to be seen in public with her, so he asked for a private room, and hurried along the corridors. She followed him with the air of a woman who knew the place well, and they were on the point of being ushered into a room by a waiter who was holding the door open, when a man rushed out of a neigh-

bouring room, from which a tempest of shouts and laughter was coming. It was Daguenet.

'Good Lord, it's Nana!' he cried.

The Count had dashed into the private room, leaving the door ajar behind him. But as his hunched shoulders disappeared from sight, Daguenet winked and added teasingly:

'God, but you're doing nicely! You pick them up at the Tuileries nowadays!'

Nana smiled and put a finger to her lips to beg him to be quiet. She saw that he was in a very excited state, but she was glad to have met him there, for she still had a certain affection for him, in spite of his rudeness in cutting her when he had been with a party of respectable women.

'What are you doing nowadays?' she asked amicably.

'Settling down. It's true – I'm even thinking of getting married.'

She shrugged her shoulders with a pitying air. But he jokingly went on to say it was no sort of life, earning just enough on the Stock Exchange to buy flowers for the ladies and keep up a decent front. His three hundred thousand francs had lasted him only eighteen months; now he intended to be practical, and he was going to marry a girl with a huge dowry, and end up as a Prefect like his father. Nana went on smiling incredulously. She nodded in the direction of the room he had just left.

'Who are you with in there?'

'Oh, a whole gang,' he said, forgetting his plans in an access of drunken enthusiasm.

'Just imagine – Léa's telling us about her trip to Egypt. It's an absolute scream! There's a story about a bath ...'

And he told the story while Nana lingered indulgently. They had ended up by leaning against the walls of the corridor, facing each other. Gas-jets were burning under the low ceiling, and a vague smell of cooking hung about the folds of the hangings. Now and then, in order to hear each other's voices, when the din in the room became louder than ever, they had to lean forward. Every few seconds, a waiter laden with dishes found his way along the corridor barred, and had

to separate them. But without interrupting their conversation, they simply drew back against the walls, chatting as if they were in their own homes, in the midst of the din of the supper-parties and the jostling of the waiters.

'Look at that,' murmured the young man, pointing to the door of the private room into which Muffat had disappeared.

Both of them looked. The door was quivering slightly, as if a breath of air were shaking it. Finally, very slowly, and without the slightest sound, it closed. They exchanged a silent chuckle. The Count must look a comical sight all alone in there.

'By the way,' she asked, 'have you read Fauchery's article about me?'

'*The Golden Fly*? Yes,' replied Daguenet. 'I didn't mention it because I was afraid of upsetting you.'

'Upsetting me – why? It's a very long article.'

She was flattered that the *Figaro* should concern itself about her person, although if it had not been for the explanation of her hairdresser Francis, who had brought her the paper, she would not have understood that it was she who was the subject of the article. Daguenet examined her on the sly, sneering in his mocking way. Well, since she was pleased, everybody ought to be.

'Excuse me!' shouted a waiter, holding an ice pudding in both hands, as he walked between them.

Nana had stepped towards the little room where Muffat was waiting.

'Well, good-bye,' said Daguenet. 'Go back to your cuckold.'

She stopped short.

'Why do you call him a cuckold?'

'Because he is a cuckold, dammit!'

She came back and leant against the wall, her interest aroused.

'Ah,' she said simply.

'What, you mean to say you didn't know? Why, my dear girl, his wife is Fauchery's mistress. ... It must have started in the country. ... This very evening when I was coming here, Fauchery left me, and I suspect he's meeting her at his

place tonight. They've concocted some story about a journey, I believe.'

Overcome with surprise, Nana remained speechless.

'I knew it!' she said at last, slapping her thigh. 'I guessed it just from seeing her on the road that day. . . . To think of a respectable woman deceiving her husband, and with that blackguard Fauchery too! He'll teach her some nice things, and no mistake!'

'Oh, it isn't her first time,' Daguenet murmured spitefully. 'She probably knows as much as he does.'

At this Nana gave vent to an indignant exclamation.

'Really? . . . What a filthy lot they are! How disgusting!'

'Excuse me,' shouted a waiter laden with bottles, as he separated them.

Daguenet drew her towards him again, and held her hand for a moment. He adopted his crystalline voice, a voice with notes as sweet as those of a harmonica, which had won him enormous success with the ladies.

'Good-bye, darling. . . . You know, I still love you.'

She disengaged her hand from his, and while a thunder of shouts and cheers which made the drawing-room door shake almost drowned her voice, she said with a smile :

'It's all over, silly. . . . But that doesn't matter. Come up and see me one of these days, and we'll have a chat.'

Then she turned serious again, and went on in the tones of a respectable woman shocked to the core of her being :

'So he's a cuckold, is he? . . . Well, so much the worse for him. Because I've never been able to stomach a cuckold.'

When at last she went into the private room, she found Muffat sitting patiently on a narrow divan with pale face and nervously twitching hands. He did not reproach her at all, and in her agitation she was torn between feelings of pity and contempt. The poor man, so abominably deceived by a worthless wife! She felt like throwing her arms round his neck to comfort him. On the other hand it served him right; he was a fool with women, and this would teach him a lesson : however, pity carried the day. She did not leave him after eating her oysters, as she had planned to do. They stayed for scarcely a quarter of an hour in the Café Anglais,

and then went back together to the Boulevard Haussmann. It was eleven o'clock; by midnight she was sure to have found some means of gently getting rid of him.

In the ante-room she took the precaution of giving Zoé instructions.

'Watch out for him, and tell him not to make any noise if the Count's still with me.'

'But where shall I put him, Madame?'

'Keep him in the kitchen. That's the safest thing to do.'

In the bedroom Muffat was already taking off his over-coat. A big fire was burning in the hearth. It was the same room as before, with its rosewood furniture and its hangings and chair-coverings of figured damask with big blue flowers on a grey ground. On two occasions Nana had thought of doing it over again, the first time in black velvet, the second in white satin with pink bows; but as soon as Steiner agreed, she demanded the money the redecoration would cost, only to spend it on something else. All she had bought for her bedroom was a tiger-skin rug for the hearth and a hanging crystal lamp.

'I'm not sleepy; I'm not going to bed,' she said, when they were alone together.

The Count obeyed her with the meekness of a man no longer afraid of being seen. His only care was to avoid annoying her.

'Just as you wish,' he murmured.

All the same, he took his boots off too, before sitting down by the fire. One of Nana's pleasures consisted of undressing in front of the mirror on her wardrobe door, which reflected her from head to foot. She used to take off all her clothes and then stand stark naked, gazing at her reflection and oblivious of everything else around her. A passion for her body, an ecstatic admiration of her satin skin and the supple lines of her figure, kept her serious, attentive and absorbed in her love of herself. The hairdresser often found her standing like that, but she did not so much as turn her head as he came in. Muffat was always angry when this happened, much to her surprise. What had got into him? She did that to please herself, not other people.

That particular evening, wanting to have a better view of herself, she lit the six candles in the brackets. But while she was slipping off her chemise, she suddenly paused. She had been preoccupied for a little while, and a question was trembling on her tongue.

'You haven't read the *Figaro* article, have you? ... The paper's on the table.'

Daguenet's laugh had recurred to her memory, and she was troubled by a doubt. If that devil Fauchery had made fun of her, she'd have her revenge.

'They say it's about me,' she continued, affecting indifference. 'What do *you* think, darling?'

And letting go her chemise, she stood there naked, waiting for Muffat to finish Fauchery's article. Muffat read it slowly. Entitled *The Golden Fly*, it was the story of a girl descended from four or five generations of drunkards, her blood tainted by an accumulated inheritance of poverty and drink, which in her case had taken the form of a nervous derangement of the sexual instinct. She had grown up in the slums, in the gutters of Paris; and now, tall and beautiful, and as well made as a plant nurtured on a dungheap, she was avenging the paupers and outcasts of whom she was the product. With her the rottenness that was allowed to ferment among the lower classes was rising to the surface and rotting the aristocracy. She had become a force of nature, a ferment of destruction, unwittingly corrupting and disorganizing Paris between her snow-white thighs, and curdling it just as women, every month, curdle milk. It was at the end of the article that the comparison with a fly occurred, a fly the colour of sunshine which had flown up out of the dung, a fly which had sucked death from the carrion left by the roadside and now, buzzing, dancing and glittering like a precious stone, was entering palaces through the windows and poisoning the men inside, simply by settling on them.

Muffat raised his head and stared into the fire.

'Well?' asked Nana.

But he made no answer. It seemed as if he wanted to read the article again. A chill feeling was creeping from his scalp to his shoulders. The article had been written anyhow, with

extravagant phrases, unexpected witticism and odd juxta-
positions. Yet he was struck by what he had read, for it had
suddenly awakened within him everything he had been reluctant to think about for the last few months.

Then he looked up. Nana had grown absorbed in her
ecstatic contemplation of herself. She had bent her neck and
was gazing attentively in the mirror at a little brown mole
just above her right hip. She was touching it with the tip of
her finger, and by leaning backwards was making it stand out
more than ever; situated where it was, it presumably struck
her as both quaint and pretty. Then she studied other parts
of her body, amused by what she was doing, and filled once
more with the depraved curiosity she had felt as a child. The
sight of herself always surprised her, and she looked as
astonished and fascinated as a young girl who has just discovered her puberty. Slowly she spread out her arms to set
off her figure, the torso of a plump Venus, bending this way
and that to examine herself in front and behind, lingering
over the side-view of her bosom and the sweeping curves of
her thighs. And she ended up by indulging in a strange game
which consisted of swinging to right and left, with her knees
apart, and her body swaying from the waist with the continuous quivering of an almeh performing a belly-dance.

Muffat sat looking at her. She frightened him. The newspaper had dropped from his hands. In that moment of
clarity and truth, he despised himself. Yes, that was it : she
had corrupted his life, and he already felt tainted to the core
of his being, by undreamt-of impurities. Now everything was
going to rot within him, and for a moment he realized how
this evil would develop; he saw the havoc wrought by this
ferment, himself poisoned, his family destroyed, a section of
the social fabric cracking and crumbling. And, unable to take
his eyes away, he stared at Nana, trying to fill himself with
disgust for her nakedness.

Nana had stopped moving. With one arm behind her neck,
one hand clasped in the other, and her elbows far apart, she
had thrown back her head, so that he could see a fore-
shortened reflection of her half-closed eyes, her parted lips,
her face lit up with loving laughter, while behind, her mane

of loosened yellow hair covered her back with the fell of a lioness. Bending back with her hips thrust out, she displayed the solid loins and the firm bosom of an Amazon, with strong muscles beneath the satin texture of the skin. A delicate line, curving only slightly at the shoulder and thigh, ran from one of her elbows to her foot. Muffat's eyes followed this charming profile, noticing how the lines of the fair flesh vanished in golden gleams, and how the rounded contours shone like silk in the candle-light. He thought of his former dread of Woman, of the Beast of the Scriptures, a lewd creature of the jungle. Nana's body was covered with fine hair, reddish down which turned her skin into velvet; while there was something of the Beast about her equine crupper and flanks, about the fleshy curves and deep hollows of her body, which veiled her sex in the suggestive mystery of their shadows. She was the Golden Beast, as blind as brute force, whose very odour corrupted the world. Muffat gazed in fascination, like a man possessed, so intently that when he shut his eyes to see no more, the Beast reappeared in the darkness, larger, more awe-inspiring, more suggestive in its posture. Henceforth it would remain before his eyes, in his very flesh, for ever.

But Nana was hunching her shoulders. A little shiver of emotion seemed to have run through her limbs, and with tears in her eyes she was trying, as it were, to make herself small, as if to become more conscious of her body. She unclasped her hands and slid them down as far as her breasts, which she squeezed in a passionate grasp. Then, holding herself erect, and embracing her whole body in a single caress, she rubbed her cheeks coaxingly first against one shoulder and then against the other. Her greedy mouth breathed desire over her flesh. She put out her lips and pressed a lingering kiss on the skin near her armpit, laughing at the other Nana who was likewise kissing herself in the mirror.

Muffat gave a long, weary sigh. This solitary self-indulgence was beginning to exasperate him. Suddenly his self-control was swept away as if by a mighty wind. In a fit of brutal passion he seized Nana round the waist and threw her down on the carpet.

'Let go!' she cried. 'You're hurting me!'

He realized that he was powerless against her. He knew that she was stupid, vile and deceitful, yet he longed to possess her, despite all the poison in her.

'Oh, how stupid!' she said angrily, when he let her get up.

However, she soon calmed down. He would go now. She slipped on a nightdress trimmed with lace, and came and sat down on the floor in front of the fire. It was her favourite place. When she questioned him again about Fauchery's article, Muffat made a noncommittal reply, for he was anxious to avoid a scene. Besides she declared that she had a hold over Fauchery. Then she relapsed into a long silence, wondering how best to get rid of the Count. She would have liked to do it in a pleasant way, for she was still a good-natured woman and disliked hurting other people, especially in the present case where the man was a cuckold — a fact which had finally awakened her sympathy.

'So, it's tomorrow morning you expect your wife back,' she said at last.

Muffat had stretched out in the armchair, looking drowsy and feeling weary in every limb. He nodded. Nana looked at him with a serious expression on her face, thinking hard. Sitting among the folds of rumpled lace and resting her weight on one thigh, she was holding one of her bare feet in both hands and turning it mechanically this way and that.

'Have you been married long?' she asked.

'Nineteen years,' replied the Count.

'Ah! ... And is your wife nice to you? Do you get on well together?'

He was silent at first. Then, with some embarrassment, he said:

'You know I've asked you never to talk about that sort of thing.'

'And why not?' she cried, already beginning to lose her temper. 'Talking about your wife won't do her any harm, will it? ... After all, women are all the same ...'

But she stopped for fear of saying too much. She contented herself with assuming a superior expression, because she considered herself extremely kind. The poor fellow needed to be

treated gently. Besides an amusing thought had just occurred to her, and she smiled as she looked at him.

'I say,' she continued, 'I haven't told you the story that Fauchery's spreading about you. . . . Now, *there's* a viper for you! I don't bear him any ill-will, because his article may be all right, but he's a regular viper all the same.'

And laughing more than ever, she let go of her foot, and, crawling across the floor, came and rested her breasts against the Count's knees.

'Just fancy, he swears you'd still got it when you married your wife. . . . Well, had you? . . . Is it true?'

Her eyes pressed for an answer, and she raised her hands to his shoulders and began shaking him to make him own up.

'I suppose so,' he replied at last in a solemn voice.

At that she sank down again at his feet, stuttering in helpless laughter, giving him little pats and slaps.

'No, it's too funny for words. There's nobody like you; you're an absolute marvel. . . . My poor pet, you must have looked such a fool! When a man doesn't know, it's always so funny! I'd have given anything to see you, I really would! . . . And did it go off all right? Tell me about it – *please* tell me about it.'

She showered him with questions, asking about everything and insisting on all the details. And she laughed so much, with sudden bursts of gaiety which doubled her up with mirth, her nightdress hitched up and slipping off her shoulders, and her skin turned to gold by the light of the big fire, that, little by little, the Count described his wedding night to her. He no longer felt any embarrassment. He himself began to find it amusing to explain how – to use the accepted euphemism – 'he had lost it.' However, he chose his words carefully, from a last remaining feeling of modesty. The young woman, now thoroughly interested, questioned him about the Countess. According to him, she had a wonderful figure, but was a regular icicle for all that.

'Don't worry,' he murmured in a cowardly moment. 'You've no reason to be jealous.'

Nana had stopped laughing. She resumed her former position, with her back to the fire, bringing her knees up

under her chin and clasping her hands round them. Then, in a serious tone of voice, she declared :

'You know, it doesn't pay to look a fool with your wife the first night.'

'Why?' the Count asked in surprise.

'Because,' she replied slowly, with a solemn air.

She shook her head at him, looking very wise. After a while, however, she deigned to explain herself more clearly.

'You see, I know what happens. ... The fact is, my pet, women don't like a man to be helpless. They don't say anything, because there's such a thing as modesty, you know, but you can be sure they think about it a lot. And sooner or later, when a man hasn't known what to do, they go and make other arrangements. ... There, dearie.'

He did not seem to understand, so she became more explicit. She was teaching him this lesson in a motherly spirit, as a friend, out of the goodness of her heart. Ever since she had discovered that he was a cuckold, the secret had weighed upon her, and she had been longing to talk about it with him.

'Good heavens, I'm talking about things that are no concern of mine. ... But that's just because I think everybody ought to be happy. ... We're just having a chat, aren't we? Well, then, you're going to answer me frankly.'

But she broke off to change her position, for she was getting burnt.

'Lord, isn't it hot! My back's absolutely baking. ... Wait a minute, and I'll cook my tummy a bit. ... That's the best thing for aches and pains !'

And when she had turned round to face the fire, with her feet tucked under her, she went on :

'Look, you say you don't sleep with your wife any more?'

'No, I swear I don't,' said Muffat, dreading a scene.

'And you think she's an absolute icicle?'

He nodded.

'And is that why you love me? ... Answer me ! I shan't be cross.'

He nodded again.

'All right,' she concluded. 'I thought as much. Oh, you poor thing ! ... You know my aunt Lerat? The next time she

comes, get her to tell you the story about the greengrocer who lives across the street from her. .... Just imagine, that man. .... God, but this fire's hot! I've got to turn round. I'm going to toast my left side now.'

As she turned her hip to the blaze, a comical idea struck her, and she poked good-natured fun at herself in her pleasure at seeing herself looking so plump and pink in the light of the fire.

'I look like a goose, don't I? ... Yes, that's it, a goose on the spit! I'm turning round and round, and cooking in my own juice.'

She was roaring with laughter again when there was a sound of voices and slamming doors. Muffat was surprised, and gave her a questioning look. She turned serious again, and an anxious expression came over her face. It must be Zoé's cat, a wretched animal that broke everything. It was half-past twelve. Why on earth had she had the crazy idea of trying to make her cuckold happy? Now that the other man was here, she had better get him out of the way, and the sooner the better.

'What were you saying?' the Count asked indulgently, delighted to see her so good-humoured.

But in her desire to be rid of him, she suddenly changed her mood and turned brutal, not mincing her words any longer.

'Oh, yes, the greengrocer and his wife. ... Well, my dear, they never touched each other, not once! She was very keen on it, you understand, but he was a fool and didn't know what to do. .... He thought she was frigid and went elsewhere, taking up with tarts who treated him to all sorts of horrors, while she, for her part, did just the same with some fellows who were a lot craftier than her fool of a husband. .... And things always turn out that way when people don't get on together. I know!'

Muffat had turned pale. He had finally begun to understand her allusions, and tried to silence her. But she was in full spate.

'No, leave me alone! ... If you weren't fools, you'd be as nice to your wives as you are to us, and if your wives weren't

227

idiots they'd take as much trouble to keep you as we do to catch you. . . . Instead of behaving like they do. . . . There, my pet, now put that in your pipe and smoke it.'

'Don't talk about decent women,' he said harshly. 'You don't know what they're like.'

At that Nana rose to her knees.

'I don't know what they're like? . . . Why, they aren't even clean, your decent women aren't! No, they aren't even clean! I defy you to find a single one who'd dare show herself as I'm doing now. . . . Oh, you make me laugh with your decent women! Don't push me too far – don't force me to tell you things I might regret later.'

The Count's only answer was a muttered insult. Nana in her turn went white. For a few seconds she looked at him without speaking. Then she snapped:

'What would you do if your wife were deceiving you?'

He made a threatening gesture.

'Well, then, if I were deceiving you?'

'Oh, you,' he murmured, with a shrug of his shoulders.

Nana was not a spiteful woman by nature. Since the beginning of the conversation she had been resisting the temptation to throw his cuckoldry in his teeth. She would have liked to question him quietly on the subject, but now he had begun to exasperate her. She had had enough.

'In that case, sweetie,' she said, 'I don't know what the hell you're doing here. . . . You've been boring me stiff for the last two hours. . . . So go and find your wife, because she's at it with Fauchery. Yes, right now, in the Rue Taitbout, at the corner of the Rue de Provence. You see, I'm giving you the address.'

Then, as she saw Muffat get to his feet, swaying like a felled ox, she said triumphantly:

'If decent women are going to meddle in our affairs and take our lovers away from us! . . . Oh, they're a nice lot, those decent women are!'

But she was unable to say anything more. With a terrible movement he had hurled her full length on the floor, and he lifted his heel as if he meant to stamp on her head to silence her. For a moment she was filled with utter fear. Then,

blinded by rage, he began charging madly around the room, and his choking silence and the anguish tearing him apart moved her to tears. She felt a pang of regret, and curling up in front of the fire so as to toast her right side, she set about trying to console him.

'Honest, darling, I thought you knew. Otherwise I wouldn't have spoken, you can be sure of that. ... Anyhow, perhaps it isn't true. I'm not saying anything for certain. That's what I've been told, and that's what people are saying, but that doesn't prove anything, does it? ... Come on, you mustn't get all upset. If I were a man I wouldn't care a damn about women! They're all the same, you know, rich or poor – they're all a lot of sluts.'

She was attacking her own sex in an unselfish attempt to lessen the cruelty of the blow for him. But he was not listening to her and did not hear a word she said. While stamping around he had put on his boots and his overcoat. He strode round the room once again, and then, in a final rush, finding himself near the door, he dashed out. Nana was furious.

'Good-bye – and good riddance!' she said aloud, although she was now alone. 'He's nice and polite, I must say, when he's spoken to! ... And me doing my best for him too! I was the first to get my breath back, and I reckon I ate enough humble pie. ... Besides he'd been getting on my nerves.'

All the same, she was not pleased with herself, and sat scratching her legs with both hands. But then she decided to make the best of it.

'To hell with him! It isn't my fault if he's a cuckold!'

And cooked on every side, and as warm as toast, she went and buried herself under the bedclothes, after ringing for Zoé to show in the other man, who was waiting in the kitchen.

Once outside, Muffat set off at a furious pace. A fresh shower had just fallen and he kept slipping on the greasy pavement. When he looked up automatically at the sky, he saw some ragged, soot-coloured clouds scudding along in front of the moon. At this hour of the night the passers-by were becoming few and far between on the Boulevard Haussmann. He skirted the fences round the site of the new

Opéra, trying to remain in the dark, and muttering unconnected words. That woman was lying. She had invented her story out of stupidity and cruelty. He ought to have crushed her head when he had it under his heel. When all was said and done, the whole business was too shameful. He would never see her again or touch her again, or, if he did, it would mean that he was a wretched coward. And with that he breathed deeply, as if he had been set free. Oh, that naked, stupid monster, roasting herself like a goose, and slavering over everything that he had respected for forty years. The moon had come out, and the empty street was bathed in white light. He felt afraid, and he burst out sobbing, suddenly, maddened with despair, as if he had fallen into a tremendous void.

'Heaven's above!' he stuttered. 'It's all over! There's nothing left!'

People were hurrying home along the boulevards. He tried to regain his composure, making an effort to reason out the facts as the story that woman had told him kept returning to his burning head. It was the next morning that the Countess was due to return from Madame de Chezelles's country house. There was nothing, in fact, to have prevented her from returning to Paris that evening, and spending the night with that man. He now began to recall certain details of their stay at Les Fondettes. One evening, for instance, he had surprised Sabine under some trees, in a state of such agitation that she was unable to answer his questions. The man had been there. Why shouldn't she be with him now? The more he thought about it the likelier the whole story became, and he ended up by regarding it as natural and even inevitable. While he was taking off his clothes in a whore's apartment, his wife was undressing in a lover's room; nothing could be simpler or more logical! Reasoning in this way he endeavoured to keep cool. He felt as if there were a great downward rush in the direction of fleshly madness, which, as it grew and gained ground around him, was sweeping away the whole world. Warm images pursued him. A naked Nana suddenly evoked a naked Sabine. At this vision, which brought them together in a shameless relationship, under

the influence of the same desire, he stumbled into the road-way, and a cab nearly ran over him. Some women who had come out of a café jostled him and roared with laughter. Then, overcome once more, despite all his efforts, by a fit of weeping, and not wishing to burst out sobbing in front of other people, he plunged into a dark, empty street, the Rue Rossini, and wept like a child as he walked past its silent houses.

'It's all over,' he moaned. 'There's nothing left now, nothing left.'

He was weeping so hard that he had to lean against a door, burying his face in his wet hands. The sound of footsteps drove him away. He felt a shame and fear which made him flee from other people with the uneasy step of a night prowler. When passers-by met him on the pavement he tried to assume a casual manner, imagining that they could read his secret from the sway of his shoulders. He had followed the Rue de la Grange-Batelière as far as the Rue du Faubourg-Montmartre, where the bright lights took him by surprise, and he retraced his steps. For nearly an hour he roamed the district like that, always picking the darkest corners. No doubt he had some objective towards which his steps were patiently, instinctively, leading him through a maze of end-less turnings. At last he looked up at a street corner. He had reached his destination, the junction of the Rue Taitbout and the Rue de Provence. He had taken an hour, in the midst of his painful mental torments, to arrive at a place he could have reached in five minutes. One morning, the previous month, he remembered going up to Fauchery's rooms to thank him for a notice of a ball at the Tuileries, in which the journalist had mentioned him. The flat was on the *entresol*, with small square windows, half-hidden by a colossal shop-sign. The last window on the left was bisected by a brilliant band of lamplight coming between the half-closed curtains. And he remained with his eyes fixed on that shining line, apparently waiting for something.

The moon had disappeared in an inky sky from which an icy drizzle was falling. Two o'clock struck at the Trinité. The Rue de Provence and the Rue Taitbout grew darker, apart

from the bright patches of light from the gas-lamps, which in the distance were steeped in a yellow mist. Muffat did not budge. It was the bedroom : he remembered it now, hung with red cotton, with a Louis XIII bed at the far end. The lamp must be on the mantelpiece to the right. Presumably they were in bed, for not a single shadow passed across the window, and the bright streak shone as motionless as the light of a night-lamp. With his eyes still raised, he began forming a plan : he would ring the bell, go upstairs despite the concierge's protests, break down the doors with a thrust of his shoulders, and fall upon them in bed before they had time to loosen their embrace. For a moment the thought that he had no weapon with him gave him pause, but then he decided that he would strangle them. He returned to his plan, trying to improve it, while waiting for some sign, some indication, which would leave him no doubts.

If a woman's shadow had appeared at that moment he would have rung the bell. But the thought that he might be mistaken rooted him to the spot. What would he say if he were wrong? Doubts began to return. His wife couldn't be with that man : the idea was monstrous and impossible. All the same, he stayed where he was, gradually overcome by a sort of torpor, and sinking into a languid daze induced by this long wait, in which the fixity of his gaze was giving him hallucinations.

There was a sudden shower of rain. Two policemen were approaching, and he had to leave the doorway where he had taken shelter. When they had disappeared down the Rue de Provence, he returned to his post, wet and shivering. The bright line was still bisecting the window. This time he was going away for good when a shadow crossed it. It moved so quickly that he thought he had been mistaken. But then more shadows flitted past, one after another, as the whole room sprang to life. Riveted once more to the pavement, he felt an unbearable burning sensation in his stomach as he now decided to wait to find out the truth. Outlines of arms and legs darted after one another, and an enormous hand travelled about with the silhouette of a water-jug. He could make out nothing clearly, but he thought he recognized a

woman's chignon. He argued the point with himself; it looked like Sabine's hair, only the neck seemed too thick. By now he did not know what to think and could bear no more. In his appalling agony of uncertainty, his stomach was causing him such acute suffering that he pressed against the door to calm himself, shivering like a pauper. Then seeing that, in spite of everything, he could not turn his eyes away from that window, his anger changed into a moralistic fantasy. He pictured himself as a deputy haranguing an assembly, denouncing debauchery and prophesying disaster; and in a paraphrase of Fauchery's article on the poisoned fly he declared that morals such as these, reminiscent of those of the Roman decadence, meant an end to all society. This did him good. But in the meantime the shadows had disappeared. Presumably they had gone back to bed. He went on watching and waiting.

Three o'clock struck, then four. He could not tear himself away. Whenever a shower fell, he drew back into a corner of the doorway, his legs splashed with rain. Nobody passed by now, and occasionally his eyes would close, as if burnt by the line of light on which he kept them stubbornly fixed, with stupid persistence. On two subsequent occasions the shadows flitted about, repeating the same gestures and moving the silhouette of the same gigantic jug; and twice calm returned, and the lamp again cast its discreet nightlight glow. These shadows increased his uncertainty. Besides a sudden idea had just occurred to him which comforted him in that it put off the time for action : he had only to wait until the woman left the house. He would easily be able to recognize Sabine. Nothing could be simpler : there would be no scandal, and he would be certain of the facts. All he had to do was stay where he was. Among all the confused feelings which had been agitating him, he now felt only a dull longing to know the truth. But tedium was sending him to sleep in his doorway, and by way of distraction he tried to calculate how long he would have to wait. Sabine was due to be at the station about nine o'clock; that gave him roughly four and a half hours. He felt full of patience; he would even have been content not to move again, and he

found a certain charm in imagining that his vigil in the dark was going to last forever.

All of a sudden the streak of light vanished. For him this simple event was an unexpected catastrophe, something both worrying and disagreeable. Obviously they had just put the lamp out and were going to sleep. At that hour that was reasonable enough, but he was irritated by it, because now the darkened window ceased to hold any interest for him. He watched it for another quarter of an hour, but then he felt tired, and leaving the doorway took a turn along the pavement.

Until five o'clock he walked to and fro, looking up from time to time. The window remained blank and lifeless, and now and then he wondered if he had not dreamed that shadows had been dancing up there on those panes. A terrible sense of fatigue weighed him down, a dazed feeling in which he forgot what he was waiting for on that street corner. He kept stumbling over the paving-stones, starting into wakefulness with the icy shudder of a man who no longer knows where he is. Nothing was worth worrying about to such a degree. Since those people were asleep, let them go on sleeping! What was the good of meddling in their affairs! It was very dark, and nobody would ever know anything about the night's events. And with that, every feeling within him vanished, even curiosity itself, carried away by the longing to have done with it all and to find relief somewhere. The cold was increasing, and he was beginning to find the street insufferable. Twice he walked away and walked back slowly, dragging his feet, only to go farther next time. It was all over; there was nothing left. He went all the way down to the boulevard and did not return.

There followed a melancholy progress through the streets. He walked slowly, always at the same pace, and hugging the walls. The sound of his heels rang out, and he saw nothing but his shadow circling around, lengthening and shrinking with every gas-lamp. This lulled him and occupied him mechanically. He never knew afterwards where he had been; it seemed to him as if he had gone round and round for hours, like a circus horse. Only one memory remained, a distinct

recollection. Without being able to explain how it came about, he found himself with his face pressed against the gate at the end of the Passage des Panoramas, gripping the bars with both hands. He was not shaking them, but simply trying to see into the passage, his heart swelling with overwhelming emotion. But he could not make out anything clearly, for shadows were flooding along the deserted gallery, and the wind whistling down the Rue Saint-Marc was blowing a damp cellar-like breath into his face. He lingered stubbornly for a while, but then, awakening from his dream, he was filled with astonishment, and asked himself what he could possibly be looking for at that hour, pressing against the bars so fiercely that they had left their mark on his face. Then he had set off walking again, in utter despair, his heart full of infinite sadness, feeling alone and betrayed in the midst of all that darkness.

Day broke at last, that grey dawn that follows winter nights, and looks so melancholy from the muddy Paris pavements. Muffat had returned to the wide streets which were then being laid on either side of the new Opéra. Soaked by the rain and broken up by cart-wheels, the chalky soil had turned into a quagmire. Without looking to see where he was putting his feet, he walked on and on, constantly slipping and recovering his balance. The awakening of Paris, with its gangs of sweepers and the first groups of workmen, proved a fresh embarrassment as the light grew stronger. People stared at him in surprise, struck by his soaked hat, his muddy clothes and his dazed expression. For a long time he sought refuge against the palings, among the scaffolding, his empty mind haunted by a single remaining idea, the thought that he was miserably unhappy.

Then he thought of God. This sudden idea of divine help, of superhuman consolation, surprised him, impressing him as something unexpected and extraordinary. It conjured up for him the picture of Monsieur Venot, and he saw his plump little face and rotten teeth. Undoubtedly Monsieur Venot, whom he had been avoiding for months and thereby rendering miserable, would be delighted if he went and knocked on his door and fell weeping into his arms. In the old days

God had always been so merciful towards him. At the slightest sorrow, the smallest obstacle on the path of life, he had gone into a church to kneel down and humble his littleness in the presence of the Supreme Power; and had always left fortified by prayer, ready to give up the good things of this world, and uniquely preoccupied with a yearning for eternal salvation. But at present he only practised his religion by fits and starts, at times when the terror of hell came upon him; all kinds of weak inclinations had overcome him and the thought of Nana disturbed his devotions. And now the idea of God astonished him. Why had he not thought of God straight away, in this terrible crisis in which his feeble humanity was collapsing in ruins?

Meanwhile, with slow laborious steps, he looked for a church. But he had lost his bearings, the early hour had changed the appearance of the streets. Then, however, as he turned the corner of the Rue de la Chaussée-d'Antin, he caught sight of a tower looming vaguely in the fog at the end of the Trinité Church. The white statues overlooking the bare garden looked like so many chilly Venuses among the yellow leaves of a park. Under the porch he paused to get his breath back, for the ascent of the wide steps had tired him. Then he went in. The church was cold, for the boilers had been out since the previous evening, and the lofty vaults were full of a fine mist which had filtered in through the windows. The aisles were deep in shadow, there was not a soul to be seen, and the only sound audible in the sinister darkness was that of the old shoes of some half-awake verger or other sulkily dragging himself about. Muffat, however, heart-broken and forlorn, after bumping into a cluster of chairs, fell on his knees in front of the grille of a little chapel near to a font. Folding his hands together, he began searching within himself for prayers, his whole being yearning to abandon itself in a transport of devotion. But his lips alone shaped a few stammered words; his mind was still far away, returning to the outer world and restlessly roaming the streets again, as if under the lash of implacable necessity. And he kept repeating: 'O God, come to my assistance! O God, do not desert Thy creature, who abandons himself to Thy justice! O God,

I adore Thee : Thou wilt not leave me to perish under the blows of my enemies !' There was no answer; the shadows and the cold weighed upon his shoulders, and the noise of the old shoes continued in the distance, interfering with his prayers. Indeed he could still hear nothing but that irritating noise in the deserted church, where not even a little sweeping was done before the early Masses had somewhat warmed the air of the place. After that he rose to his feet with the help of a chair, his knees cracking as he did so. God had not arrived. Why should he have wept in Monsieur Venot's arms? The man could do nothing.

And then mechanically he returned to Nana's house. Outside he slipped and was conscious of tears coming to his eyes, but he did not feel angry against fate, merely weak and ill. When all was said and done, he was too tired, too drenched with rain, too chilled with cold, but the idea of going back to his great dark house in the Rue Miromesnil froze his heart. The outside door at Nana's was not open, and he had to wait for the concierge to appear. He smiled as he went upstairs, already penetrated by the languorous warmth of that cosy retreat, where he would be able to stretch himself out and sleep.

When Zoé opened the door to him, she gave a start of astonishment and alarm. Madame had had a terrible headache, and hadn't slept a wink all night. Still, she could always go and see whether Madame was still awake. And with that she slipped into the bedroom, while he slumped into one of the armchairs in the drawing-room. But Nana appeared almost at once. She had jumped out of bed, and had scarcely had time to slip on a petticoat. Her feet were bare, her hair tousled, and her nightdress all torn and crumpled by a night of love.

'What ! You here again !' she cried, flushing scarlet.

She had dashed out, stung with anger, to throw him out herself. But when she saw him in such a pitiful state, so utterly forlorn, she felt a final pang of pity.

'Well, you're a pretty sight, you poor thing !' she continued more gently. 'What on earth's the matter? ... Oh, I know ! You've been spying on them and it's riled you !'

He made no reply. He looked like a broken-down animal. However, she realized that he still lacked definite proof, and, to cheer him up, she added:

'You see, I was wrong after all. Your wife's a decent woman, that's for sure! And now, dear, you'd better go home to bed. You need it.'

He did not budge.

'Now then, off you go! I can't keep you here. ... You don't think you're going to stay here at this time of night, do you?'

'Yes, let's go to bed,' he stammered.

She repressed a violent gesture, for her patience was running out. Was the man going crazy?

'Come on now, off you go,' she repeated.

'No.'

At that she exploded with anger and irritation.

'No, this is too much! ... Don't you understand I'm sick and tired of you? ... Go back to your wife, who's doing the dirty on you. Yes, she's doing the dirty on you; it's me who's telling you this time. ... There! Is that enough for you? Now will you get out and leave me alone?'

Muffat's eyes filled with tears. He clasped his hands together.

'Let's go to bed.'

Nana suddenly lost all self-control, choking with nervous sobs. He was taking advantage of her, that's what he was doing. What had all this got to do with her anyway? She'd done her best to tell him the truth as gently as possible, out of sheer goodness of heart. And now he wanted to make her pay the piper! Well, he could think again! She had a kind heart, but not as kind as that!

'Hell, I've had enough of this!' she swore, smashing her fist down on the furniture. 'I tried my best, you know, I wanted to be faithful to you. ... But I could be a rich woman tomorrow, if only I said the word.'

He looked up in surprise. He had never given a thought to this question of money. She had only to express a wish and he would fulfil it straight away. His whole fortune was at her disposal.

'No, it's too late,' she retorted angrily. 'I like men who give without being asked. . . . No, if you were to offer me a million for just one time, I'd turn it down. It's all over : I've got something better. . . . So get out or I shan't answer for the consequences. I'll do something terrible.'

She advanced threateningly towards him, and in the midst of her anger, the anger of a good-natured girl driven to extremities but convinced of her rights and her superiority over tiresome respectable folk, the door opened suddenly and Steiner appeared. That was the last straw. She shrieked :

'Well, I'm damned ! Here's the other one !'

Taken aback by her piercing cry, Steiner stopped short. Muffat's unexpected presence annoyed him, for he was afraid that it might lead to the scene he had been trying to avoid for three months. Blinking his eyes, he shifted uneasily from one foot to the other, avoiding the Count's gaze. He was out of breath, and his face flushed and distorted, as was only natural in a man who had rushed across Paris with good news only to find himself in unexpected trouble.

'What do *you* want?' Nana asked harshly, ignoring the Count.

'What do I . . . I . . . ?' he stammered. 'I've brought you the . . . you know what.'

'The what?'

He hesitated. Two days before, she had given him to understand that if he could not find her a thousand francs to pay a bill with, she would never see him again. For two days he had been scouring the town for the money, and he had finally succeeded in making up the sum that very morning.

'The thousand francs,' he said at last, taking an envelope out of his pocket.

Nana had forgotten.

'The thousand francs !' she cried. 'Do you think I want your charity? . . . Look, here's what I think of your thousand francs !'

And, snatching the envelope, she threw it in his face. Prudent Jew that he was, he bent down laboriously to pick it up, and then looked at the young woman in bewilderment.

Muffat and he exchanged a despairing glance, while she put her hands on her hips to shout louder than before.

'Well, have the two of you finished insulting me? ... I'm glad you've come too, dearie, because now we can have a clean sweep. ... Come on now, out you go!'

Then, as they made no move, standing rooted to the spot, she went on:

'You think I'm acting like a fool, don't you! Well perhaps I am! But you've pushed me too far! ... And to hell with it – I've had enough of being on my best behaviour! If it kills me, what I'm doing now, then that's my affair!'

They tried to calm her down and begged her to listen to reason.

With a sudden movement she flung open the bedroom door, and in the middle of the rumpled bed, the two men saw Fontan. He had not expected to be displayed like that, for he was lying with his legs in the air and his nightshirt all awry, his skin showing dark against the crumpled lace on which he was wallowing. However, he did not bat an eyelid, for he was used to sudden surprises on the stage. Indeed, after the first shock, he hit upon a grimace to make the best of the situation, and 'played the rabbit', as he put it, pushing out his lips, wrinkling up his nose, and wiggling the whole of the lower half of his face. His leering, faun-like features exuded vice. It was Fontan whom Nana had gone to fetch at the Variétés every day for the past week, under the influence of the sort of fierce passion which courtesans often feel for a comedian's grimacing ugliness.

'There!' she said, pointing to him with a gesture worthy of a tragic actress.

Muffat, who had accepted everything till now, rebelled at this affront.

'Whore!' he stammered.

Nana, who was already in the bedroom, came back in order to have the last word.

'Me, a whore? Then what about your wife?'

And she slammed the door behind her, noisily pushing home the bolt. Left alone, the two men gazed at one another in silence. Zoé had just come into the room. She did not

hustle them out, but chatted very reasonably with them. As a sensible woman she thought that Madame was being too silly for words. All the same she defended her, declaring that this affair with the actor wouldn't last; they just had to wait for her to come to her senses. The two men left without saying a word. On the pavement outside, moved by fellow feeling, they exchanged a silent handshake. Then they turned their backs on each other, and shuffled away in opposite directions.

When Muffat finally got back to his house in the Rue Miromesnil, his wife was just arriving. The two met on the great staircase, whose walls exhaled an icy chill. As they raised their eyes, they saw each other. The Count was still wearing his mudstained clothes, and his face had the bewildered pallor of a man returning from a debauch. The Countess, looking as if she were exhausted by a night in the train, was dropping with sleep, her hair all tousled and rings under her eyes.

THE scene was a little fourth-floor flat in the Rue Véron in Montmartre. Nana and Fontan had invited a few friends round to share their Twelfth-Night cake with them. They had moved in only three days before, and this was their house-warming party.

The whole thing had happened suddenly in the first glow of their honeymoon, for they had had no fixed intention of setting up house together. After her grand outburst, when she had unceremoniously thrown out the Count and the banker, Nana felt the world crumbling about her. She took in the situation at a glance : the creditors would come crowding into her hall, interfere with her love affairs, and threaten to sell everything she possessed unless she behaved sensibly; there would be no end of quarrels and anxieties if she was to have any hope of saving her furniture from their clutches. She preferred to let everything go. Besides the flat on the Boulevard Haussmann was beginning to bore her. It was so ridiculous with its great gilded rooms. In her sudden affection for Fontan she started dreaming of a bright, pretty little bedroom, returning to the old ideal of her flower-girl days, when her highest ambition had been to have a rosewood wardrobe with a mirror on the door and a bed hung with blue rep. Within two days she sold what she could smuggle out of the house in the way of knick-knacks and jewellery, and then disappeared with about ten thousand francs, without saying a word to the concierge. It was a plunge into the dark, in which she vanished without trace. In this way she could prevent the men from hanging around her. Fontan was very nice. He did not say no to anything, but just let her do as she liked. He even displayed a real spirit of comradeship. He had nearly seven thousand francs of his own, and, despite the fact that people accused him of stinginess, he agreed to add them to the young woman's ten thousand. The sum struck them as a solid foundation on which to set up together. And

so they started from there, both drawing on their common hoard to rent and furnish the two rooms in the Rue Véron, and sharing everything like old friends. In the early days it was really delightful.

On Twelfth-Night, Madame Lerat was the first to arrive with little Louis. As Fontan had not yet come home, she ventured to express certain fears, for she trembled to see her niece giving up the prospect of wealth.

'Oh, Aunt, I love him so much!' cried Nana, pressing her hands to her heart in a pretty gesture.

This declaration produced an extraordinary effect on Madame Lerat, and tears came into her eyes.

'That's true,' she said with an air of conviction. 'Love comes before everything else.'

And with that she went into raptures over the prettiness of the rooms. Nana showed her the bedroom, the dining-room and even the kitchen. Heavens, it wasn't a big place, but then they had had it repainted and changed the wall-paper, and it all looked very gay in the sunshine.

Then Madame Lerat detained the young woman in the bedroom, while little Louis installed himself behind the char-woman in the kitchen to watch a chicken being roasted. If, said Madame Lerat, she was taking the liberty of making a few remarks, it was because Zoé had just been to see her. Zoé had gallantly remained in the breach, out of loyalty to her mistress. Madame would pay her later on; she had no worries on that score. And in the break-up of the Boulevard Hauss-mann establishment she was standing up to the creditors, beating a dignified retreat, saving what she could from the wreck, and telling everybody that Madame was travelling, without ever giving an address. Indeed, out of fear of being followed, she was even depriving herself of the pleasure of calling on Madame. However, that morning she had run round to Madame Lerat's, because matters had taken a new turn. The day before, some of Madame's creditors – the up-holsterer, the coal merchant and the laundress – had turned up, offered to give Madame an extension of time, and even proposed to advance Madame a considerable sum of money if only Madame would return to her flat and behave like a

sensible person. The aunt repeated Zoé's words. Presumably there was a gentleman behind it all.

'Never!' declared Nana in disgust. 'They're a nice lot, those tradesmen! Do they think I'm for sale just so they can pay their bills? ... Why, I'd rather starve to death than deceive Fontan.'

'That's what I told them,' said Madame Lerat. '"My niece", I said, "isn't that sort of woman."'

Nana, however, was extremely vexed to learn that La Mignotte was up for sale, and that Labordette was buying it for Caroline Héquet at a ridiculous price. The news sent her into a fury against the whole clique, who were a cheap lot, in spite of all their airs and graces. Yes, there was no doubt about it, she was worth more than the whole lot of them put together!

'They can laugh as much as they like,' she concluded, 'but money will never bring them real happiness. ... Besides, you know, Aunt, I don't even know now whether that lot are still alive or not: I'm too happy to care.'

At that moment Madame Maloir came in, wearing one of those peculiar hats which she alone could devise. It was a joy to see her again. Madame Maloir for her part explained that grand places put her off, and that henceforth she would come back now and then for her game of bezique. There was a second tour of the flat; and in the kitchen, where the cook was basting the fowl, Nana talked about the need for economy, saying that a maid would have cost too much, and that she wanted to look after her home herself. Little Louis was meanwhile gazing in fascination at the oven.

Then there was a loud burst of voices. Fontan had come in with Bosc and Prullière, and the company could now sit down to table. The soup had already been served when Nana showed off her flat for the third time.

'Ah, children, how comfortable you are here!' Bosc kept repeating, simply to please these friends who were treating him to dinner, for at bottom, talk about "the nest", as he called it, bored him.

In the bedroom he made an even greater effort to be amiable. Normally he referred to women as camels, and en-

cumbering himself with one of those filthy animals stirred him to the only sort of indignation of which, in his drunken disdain of the whole world, he was capable.

'Ah, the sly pair!' he went on with a wink. 'They did this on the sly. ... Well, you were right. It's going to be charming, and we'll come and see you – by God we will!'

Then when little Louis arrived on the scene, straddling a broomstick, Prullière remarked mischievously :

'Well, I'll be damned! So you've had a baby already?'

This struck everybody as tremendously funny and Madame Lerat and Madame Maloir shook with laughter. Nana, far from being annoyed, laughed tenderly, and said that unfortunately this wasn't the case. She would have liked it to be, both for the little boy's sake and for her own, but perhaps a baby would arrive all the same. Fontan, putting on a good-natured air, took little Louis in his arms, playing with him and lisping :

'Never mind! He loves his daddy, doesn't he. ... Call me Papa, you little beast!'

'Papa ... Papa ...' stammered the child.

Everybody smothered him with kisses, but Bosc was bored and suggested sitting down to table; that was the only thing that mattered in life. Nana asked her guests' permission to put little Louis beside her. The dinner was very merry, though Bosc suffered from the proximity of the child, against whom he had to defend his plate. Madame Lerat annoyed him too. She was in a maudlin mood, and whispered to him all sorts of mysterious confidences about high-born gentlemen who were still running after her. Twice he had to push away her knee, for she kept snuggling up to him and gazing at him with watery eyes. Prullière behaved very badly towards Madame Maloir, and never once helped her to anything. He was completely taken up with Nana, and seemed annoyed at seeing her with Fontan. Besides the turtle-doves were kissing so much they were beginning to be rather a bore. Contrary to all the rules they had insisted on sitting side by side.

'Dammit all, eat up!' Bosc kept repeating with his mouth full. 'You've got plenty of time for that sort of thing! Wait till we're gone.'

But Nana could not restrain herself. She was in an ecstasy of love, blushing like a schoolgirl, her looks and her laughter overflowing with tenderness. Gazing at Fontan, she overwhelmed him with pet names – 'my doggie, my duckie, my sweetie' – and whenever he passed her the water or the salt, she bent forward and kissed him at random on lips, eyes, nose or ear. Then, if she was reproved, she returned to the attack with the cleverest tactics, and with the submissiveness and suppleness of a beaten cat would catch hold of his hand when nobody was looking, to hold it and kiss it again. It seemed as if she had to touch some part of him. As for Fontan, he put on airs and condescendingly allowed himself to be worshipped. His great nose twitched with sensual joy, and his goat face, with its comically monstrous ugliness, positively basked in the devout adoration lavished on him by that superbly full-bodied, fair-skinned girl. Occasionally he gave a kiss in return, in the spirit of a man who is having all the pleasure but wants to show a little kindness.

'Oh, you two are getting on my nerves!' cried Prullière. 'Move up, you!'

And he pushed Fontan away, changing covers to take his place next to Nana. There were shouts and applause at this, together with some very crude jokes. Fontan made a great show of despair, putting on his comical act as Vulcan crying for Venus. Prullière promptly became very amorous, but Nana, whose foot he was groping for under the table, slapped his face to stop his antics. No, she certainly wasn't going to go to bed with *him*. A few weeks before, she had felt a certain attraction to him because of his good looks, but now she detested him. If he pinched her again under the pretence of picking up his napkin, she'd throw her glass in his face.

Nevertheless the evening went well. The company had naturally begun talking about the Variétés. Wasn't that bastard Bordenave ever going to kick the bucket? His filthy diseases were affecting him again, and causing him so much pain that you couldn't go near him without getting your head bitten off. The day before, during rehearsals, he had been yelling at Simonne all the time. Now *there* was a fellow they wouldn't shed many tears over when he went! Nana declared

246

that if he asked her to take another part she'd send him packing and no mistake. Besides she was thinking of leaving the stage; the theatre wasn't a patch on home life. Fontan, who was not in the present production nor the one they were rehearsing, also spoke enthusiastically about the joy of being completely free, and of spending his evenings with his little darling, toasting his feet by the fire. At this the others exclaimed at how lucky they were, pretending to envy them their luck.

The Twelfth-Night cake was cut and handed round. The bean fell to the lot of Madame Lerat, who dropped it into Bosc's glass. Then there were shouts of 'The King drinks! The King drinks!' Nana took advantage of this outburst of gaiety to go and put her arms round Fontan's neck again, kissing him and whispering in his ear. But Prullière, with a forced smile on his handsome face, objected that they were not playing the game. Meanwhile little Louis slept soundly on a couple of chairs. It was nearly one o'clock when the company separated, shouting their farewells as they went downstairs.

And for three weeks the two sweethearts led a really delightful life. Nana fancied she was back in her early days when her first silk dress had caused her indescribable pleasure. She went out little, affecting a desire for solitude and simplicity. One morning, when she had gone out early to buy some fish herself in the La Rochefoucauld Market, she was taken aback to meet her old hairdresser Francis face to face. He was as impeccably dressed as ever, in the finest linen and an irreproachable frock-coat; and Nana felt ashamed that he should see her in the street in her dressing-gown, with tousled hair and down-at-heel shoes. But he had the tact to be even more polite than usual towards her. He did not allow himself a single question, and affected to believe that Madame was on her travels. Madame, he said, had made so many people unhappy when she had decided to leave Paris. It had been a terrible loss for everybody. The young woman, however, ended up by asking him a few questions, for she was eaten up by a curiosity which made her forget her previous embarrassment. As the crowd was jostling them, she pushed

him into a doorway, and, holding her little basket in one hand, stood in front of him. What were people saying about her disappearance? Heavens, the ladies to whom he went were saying this, that and the other: altogether she had created a tremendous stir. And what about Steiner? Monsieur Steiner was in a bad way; he would come to a bad end if he couldn't come up with another success. And Daguenet? Oh, he was getting on famously: Monsieur Daguenet was settling down. Stirred by her memories, Nana opened her mouth to ask another question, but she hesitated at the idea of pronouncing Muffat's name. Francis, understanding her embarrassment, smiled and spoke first. As for Monsieur le Comte, it was pitiful to see how he had suffered since Madame's departure. He was like a soul in pain, and you could see him wherever Madame was likely to be found. Finally Monsieur Mignon had run into him, and had taken him home to his own place. This piece of news made Nana laugh, but there was something forced about her laughter.

'Oh, so he's with Rose now, is he?' she said. 'Well, you know something, Francis? – I don't care a damn! ... What a hypocrite, all the same! He's got used to it, and now he can't do without it for a week! And to think that he used to swear he'd never have another woman after me!'

Under the surface she was furious.

'Rose has got herself a nice bargain there,' she went on, '– my leftovers! Oh, I see it all now: she wanted her revenge because I took that brute Steiner away from her. ... Isn't she clever catching a man when I've chucked him out?'

'That isn't the way Monsieur Mignon tells the story,' said the hairdresser. 'According to him, it was Monsieur le Comte who chucked *you* out. ... Yes, and in a disgusting way too – with a kick on the backside!'

Nana went white.

'What's that?' she cried. 'A kick on the backside? ... No, that's going too far, that is! You see, it was me who threw him downstairs, the cuckold – because he's a cuckold, you know. His precious countess goes to bed with any man she can get, even that bastard Fauchery. ... And that Mignon, who walks the streets looking for customers for his bitch of a

wife, who's so skinny that nobody wants her ! ... What a filthy lot ! What a filthy lot !'

She was choking, and had to pause for breath.

'So, that's what they say, is it? ... Well, Francis, I'm going to have it out with them. ... Do you want to come along with me? ... Yes, I'll go and have it out with them, and we'll see if they'll have the nerve to go on talking about kicks on the backside. ... Kicks? Why, I've never taken a kick from anybody. And I never will, either, because I'd kill any man who laid so much as a finger on me.'

All the same, she eventually calmed down. After all, they could say what they liked, she regarded them as no better than the mud on her shoes. It was beneath her to bother about people like that. She had her conscience on her side. And Francis, seeing her unburden herself like that, dressed in an ordinary dressing-gown, turned familiar and allowed himself to give her a little advice as he took leave of her. She was making a mistake in sacrificing everything for the sake of an infatuation : infatuations like that spoiled everything. She listened to him with bowed head, while he spoke with a pained expression, as a connoisseur who was sorry to see such a lovely girl making such a mess of her life.

'Well, that's my business,' she said at last. 'Thanks all the same, Francis.'

She shook his hand, which in spite of his immaculate appearance was always a little greasy, and then went off to buy her fish. During the day that story about the kick on the backside occupied her thoughts. She even spoke about it to Fontan, and once again posed as a tough woman who wouldn't tolerate the smallest slap. Fontan, speaking as a person of superior intelligence, declared that all so-called gentlemen were boors whom it was one's duty to despise. And from that moment on, Nana regarded them with genuine disdain.

That same evening they went to the Bouffes to see a woman Fontan knew make her *début* in a tiny part. It was nearly one o'clock when they went back up the heights of Montmartre on foot. They had bought a coffee cake in the Rue de la Chaussée-d'Antin; and they ate it in bed, seeing that the

night was not warm and it was not worth while lighting a fire. Sitting side by side, with the bedclothes pulled up in front and the pillows piled up behind, they ate their supper and chatted about the woman at the Bouffes. Nana thought that she was ugly and common. Fontan, lying on his stomach, passed up the pieces of cake, which had been put between the candle and the matches on the edge of the bedside table. But they ended up by quarrelling.

'Oh, she's a real fright!' cried Nana. 'She's got eyes like gimlet holes and hair the colour of tow.'

'Shut up,' said Fontan. 'She's got a superb head of hair and fire in her eyes. . . . It's queer the way you women always tear each other to pieces.'

He looked annoyed.

'Come on, that's enough of that!' he snapped at last. 'You know I don't like that sort of nonsense. . . . Let's get a bit of sleep, or there'll be trouble.'

And he blew out the candle. Nana was furious, and went on talking : she wasn't going to be spoken to in that tone of voice; she was used to being treated with respect! As he made no reply, she had no alternative but to fall silent, but she could not go to sleep, and lay tossing to and fro.

'Bloody hell! Have you done moving about?' Fontan shouted all of a sudden, starting up.

'It isn't my fault if there are crumbs in the bed,' she snapped.

Sure enough, there were crumbs in the bed. She could feel them all over her, even under her thighs. A single crumb was enough to burn her skin and make her scratch herself till she bled. Besides, when you ate a cake, wasn't it common sense to shake out the bedclothes afterwards? Fontan, in a cold fury, had lit the candle again. The two of them got up, and barefoot and in their nightshirts, they pulled back the bedclothes and swept up the crumbs on the sheet with their hands. Fontan, who was shivering, went back to bed, telling her to go to the devil when she urged him to wipe his feet carefully. Finally she got back into bed too, but she had scarcely stretched herself out before she started up again. There were still some crumbs in the bed.

'That was bound to happen!' she cried. 'You brought them back into bed on your feet. ... I can't stand it, I tell you, I can't stand it!'

She made as if to step over him in order to jump out of bed. Then Fontan, wanting to sleep and driven to desperation, slapped her as hard as he could across the face. The blow was delivered with such force that Nana promptly found herself lying down again with her head on the pillow. She lay there in a daze.

'Oh,' she said simply, with the heavy sigh of a child.

For a moment or two he threatened her with a second slap, asking her if she was thinking of moving again. Then he blew out the candle, settled himself squarely on his back, and started snoring straight away. As for Nana, she lay with her face in the pillow, sobbing quietly to herself. It was cowardly of him to take advantage of his strength, but she had had a real fright, Fontan's comic mask had become so terrifying. And her anger began to disappear as if the slap had calmed her down. Full of respect for him, she squeezed up against the wall to leave him as much room as possible. She even ended up by falling asleep, her cheek tingling, her eyes full of tears, and feeling so deliciously exhausted, so weary and submissive, that she no longer felt the crumbs. When she woke up in the morning, she was holding Fontan in her bare arms and pressing him tightly against her breast. He'd never do that again, would he? Never again? She loved him too much. Why, it was even nice getting a slap, provided it came from him.

After that a new life began. For the slightest thing Fontan would slap her face. She grew accustomed to it, and took it lying down. Sometimes she screamed and threatened him, but then he would pin her against the wall and talk of strangling her, which had the effect of making her more amenable. More often than not, she would collapse on a chair and sob for five minutes on end. Then she would forget all about it, gaily singing and laughing, and bustling about so that she filled the little flat with the rustle of her skirts. The worst of it was that now Fontan used to disappear for the whole day and never return home before midnight, for he

had taken to going to cafés and meeting his old friends again. Nana put up with everything. She was fond and tremulous, her only fear being that she might never see him again if she levelled a single reproach at him. But on certain days, when she had neither Madame Maloir nor her aunt and little Louis with her, she was bored to tears. So one Sunday, when she was haggling over some pigeons at the La Rochefoucauld Market, she was delighted to meet Satin, who was buying a bunch of radishes. Since the evening when the Prince had drunk Fontan's champagne, they had lost sight of each other.

'Why, it's you! Do you live around here?' said Satin, astounded at seeing her in carpet-slippers in the street at that hour of the morning. 'You poor thing, you must be dead broke!'

Nana frowned at her to make her hold her tongue, because they were surrounded by other women who were still in their dressing-gowns, their dishevelled hair white with fluff. In the morning, as soon as they had got rid of the man they had picked up the previous night, all the local whores used to come marketing here, their eyes heavy with sleep, their feet in down-at-heel shoes, and themselves full of the bad-tempered weariness caused by a restless night. From every street in the crossroads they came down into the market, some of them still young, looking very pale and charming in their casual attire, and others hideous old women with bloated bellies and sagging jowls, who did not care in the least if they were seen like that outside their working hours. Not one of them deigned to smile when the passers-by on the pavement turned round to look at them, bustling about with the disdainful expression of housewives for whom men had ceased to exist. Satin, for instance, was paying for her bunch of radishes, when a young man, who looked like a clerk who was late for work, called out to her in passing :

'Evening, darling.'

She straightened up at once, and with the dignified air of an offended queen said :

'What does that little swine think he's up to?'

Then she fancied she recognized him. Three days before, about midnight, as she was coming home alone from the

boulevard, she had talked to him on the corner of the Rue La Bruyère for nearly half an hour, trying to persuade him to come home with her. But this recollection only made her angrier.

'The filthy bastards, calling out things like that to you in broad daylight!' she continued. 'When you're out on your own business, people ought to treat you with a bit of respect.'

Nana had ended up by buying her pigeons, although she had her doubts about their freshness. Then Satin offered to show her where she lived, just round the corner in the Rue La Rochefoucauld. The moment they were alone, Nana told her about her passion for Fontan, and the girl stopped outside her door, with her bundle of radishes under her arm, fascinated by a final detail in the other's story. For Nana, lying in her turn, swore that it was she who had thrown the Comte Muffat out, kicking him all the way downstairs.

'Oh, that's terrific!' said Satin. 'That's terrific! Kicked him downstairs, did you! And I bet he never said a word, did he? The bloody coward! I wish I'd been there to see his ugly mug! You did the right thing, love – and to hell with the money. It's the same with me: when I've got a crush on somebody, I don't care if it kills me. ... Now you'll come and see me, won't you? You promise? It's the door on the left. Knock three times, because there's a lot of bastards running after me.'

After that, whenever Nana felt bored, she went round to see Satin. She was always sure of finding her in, because the girl never went out before ten o'clock. Satin occupied a couple of rooms which a chemist had furnished for her in order to rescue her from the clutches of the police; but in little over a year she had broken the furniture, knocked in the chairs and dirtied the curtains in such a frenzy of filth and disorder that the two rooms looked as if they were inhabited by a pack of mad cats. On the mornings when she felt disgusted with herself and decided to clean up a bit, chair-rails and scraps of curtain would come away in her hands while she was struggling with the dirt. On those days the place was filthier than ever, and it was impossible to get in on account of objects which had fallen across the

doorways. The result was that she ended up by giving up all attempts at housework. In lamplight the mirror-fronted wardrobe, the clock and what remained of the curtains were still capable of creating an illusion of luxury for any man who came along. Besides, for six months past, her landlord had been threatening to evict her. Then why should she take care of the furniture? Just to please him? So whenever she got up in a merry mood, she would shout 'Gee up!' and kick the sides of the wardrobe and the chest of drawers until they creaked in protest.

Nana nearly always found her in bed. Even on the days when Satin went out to do her marketing she felt so tired when she got back upstairs that she flung herself down on the bed and went to sleep again. During the day she trailed around, dozing off on the chairs, and only emerging from this languid condition towards evening, when the gas was lit outside. Nana felt perfectly at home at Satin's, sitting doing nothing on the rumpled bed, among basins standing about on the floor and dirty petticoats which had been hung over the backs of armchairs the night before, staining them with mud. She would chat away for hours, pouring out endless confidences, while Satin lay on her bed in her chemise, with her feet higher than her head, smoking cigarettes as she listened. Sometimes, on afternoons when they were both in the dumps, they would treat themselves to absinthe, 'to help them to forget', as they put it. Satin did not go downstairs or even put on a petticoat, but simply went and leant over the banisters, to shout her order to the concierge's little girl, a kid of ten who, when she brought up the absinthe in a glass, would look furtively at the lady's bare legs. Every conversation led up to a single subject: the beastliness of men. Nana was deadly boring on the subject of Fontan; she could not say a dozen words without lapsing into endless repetitions of his sayings and doings. But Satin, good-natured as she was, would listen with tireless patience to these everlasting accounts of how Nana had watched for him at the window, how they had quarrelled over a dish of burnt stew, and how they had made it up in bed after hours of silent sulking. In her need to talk about these things, Nana had got to the point of telling of

254

every slap that she was given; the week before, he had given her a black eye, and only the previous evening he had sent her crashing across the bedside table, simply because he could not find his slippers. The other girl showed no astonishment, just blowing out cigarette smoke, and only breaking off to remark that, for her part, she always ducked, a move which sent the gentleman sprawling. Both of them revelled in these anecdotes about slaps and punches, and delighted in recounting the same stupid incidents a hundred times or more, abandoning themselves to the sort of languorous, pleasurable weariness which followed the thrashings they talked of. It was the pleasure of relating Fontan's blows, and of explaining everything about him down to the very way in which he took off his boots, that brought Nana back to Satin's every day, especially as the latter ended up by sympathizing with her, citing even worse cases, such as that of a pastrycook who used to leave her for dead on the floor, but whom she loved in spite of everything. Then came the days on which Nana cried, and declared that things could not go on as they were. Satin would accompany her back to her own door, and would linger outside in the street for an hour to see whether he murdered her. And the next day the two women would enjoy reliving the reconciliation all afternoon, though they secretly preferred the days when thrashings were in the air, for the prospect of a beating was more exciting.

They became inseparable. However, Satin never went to Nana's, Fontan having announced that he would have no sluts in his house. They used to go out together, and that was how Satin took her friend one day to see another woman, that Madame Robert who had occupied Nana's thoughts and inspired her with a certain respect ever since she had refused to come to her supper. Madame Robert lived in the Rue Mosnier, a silent new street in the Europe district, where there was not a single shop and where the handsome houses, with their small, constricted flats, were all inhabited by ladies. It was five o'clock; and alongside the deserted pavements the broughams of stockbrokers and merchants were drawn up in the aristocratic shelter of the tall white houses, while men were hurrying along, looking up at the windows,

where women in dressing-gowns seemed to be waiting. At first Nana refused to go up, saying huffily that she did not have the pleasure of the lady's acquaintance. But Satin insisted, saying that one could always bring along a friend on a visit. She was simply paying a courtesy call, for Madame Robert, whom she had met in a restaurant the day before, had been very charming to her, and had made her promise to come and see her. Finally Nana gave in. At the top of the stairs a drowsy little maid informed them that Madame had not come home yet, but she showed them into the drawing-room all the same, and left them there.

'Christ, it's smart!' murmured Satin.

It was a sombre middle-class room, hung with dark materials, and suggested the conventional taste of a Parisian shopkeeper who has retired after making his fortune. Nana was impressed, and tried to make a joke about it. But Satin showed annoyance, and swore that Madame Robert was a woman of impeccable virtue. She was always to be seen in the company of elderly, responsible-looking men, who offered her their arm. At present she had a retired chocolate-maker in tow, a serious soul. Whenever he came to see her he was so delighted with the general atmosphere of decorum that he had himself announced and addressed the lady of the house as 'dear child'.

'Look, this is her!' continued Satin, pointing to a photograph which stood in front of the clock.

Nana studied the portrait for a moment or two. It showed a very dark brunette, with a long face and lips pursed in a discreet smile. She looked every bit a society lady, though more reserved than most.

'That's funny,' murmured Nana at last. 'I'm certain I've seen that face before somewhere. Where I don't remember. But it can't have been anywhere respectable. . . . Oh, no, I'm sure it wasn't anywhere respectable.'

And turning to her friend, she added:

'So she made you promise to come and see her, did she? What does she want?'

'What does she want? Why, a chat, I suppose, a bit of company. . . . She's just being polite.'

Nana gave Satin a searching look, then clicked her tongue softly. Still, it was no business of hers. All the same, seeing that the lady was keeping them waiting, she declared that she was not going to stay any longer, and the two of them took their leave.

The next day Fontan informed Nana that he was not coming home to dinner, and she went round early to find Satin, with a view to treating her to a meal in a restaurant. The choice of restaurant posed a difficult problem. Satin proposed various brasseries which Nana considered appalling, and finally persuaded her to dine at Laure's. This was a *table d'hôte* in the Rue des Martyrs where dinner cost three francs.

Tired of waiting for the dinner-hour, and not knowing what to do out in the street, the pair went up to Laure's twenty minutes too early. The three dining-rooms were still empty, and they sat down at a table in the very room where Laure Piédefer was enthroned on a high bench behind a counter. This Laure was a lady of fifty whose swelling contours were tightly laced by belts and corsets. More women came in one after another, and each one craned up to reach over the saucers piled on the counter and kiss Laure on the mouth with tender familiarity, while the monstrous creature tried with tears in her eyes to divide her attentions in such a way as to make nobody jealous. In complete contrast, the waitress who served these ladies was a tall, lean woman, with a ravaged face, dark eyelids and eyes which glowed with sombre fire. The three rooms rapidly filled up. There were about a hundred women there, who had seated themselves wherever they could find a vacant place. Most of them were enormous creatures in their late thirties, with bloated flesh hanging in puffy folds over their flaccid lips, but in the midst of all these bulging bosoms and bellies there were a few slim, pretty girls to be seen. These still wore an innocent expression in spite of their immodest gestures, for they were just beginners in their profession, picked up in some dance-hall and brought along to Laure's by one of her female customers. Here the crowd of portly women, excited by the scent of their youth, jostled one another in order to treat them to

all kinds of dainties, paying court to them rather as a group of ardent old bachelors might have done. As for the men, there were very few of them – between ten and fifteen – and apart from four jolly fellows who had come to see the sight, and were cracking jokes, very much at ease, they were behaving very humbly in the midst of an overwhelming flood of petticoats.

'This grub of theirs is all right, eh?' said Satin.

Nana gave a satisfied nod. It was the old substantial dinner you get in a provincial hotel, and consisted of *vol-au-vent à la financière*, chicken and rice, kidney beans in gravy and *crème caramel*. The ladies fell with particular relish on the chicken and rice, almost bursting out of their bodices and wiping their lips with deliberate movements. At first Nana had been afraid of meeting some old friends who might have asked her stupid questions; but she was relieved to discover that there was nobody she knew in that motley throng, where faded dresses and lamentable hats mingled with expensive costumes in the fraternity of shared perversions. For a moment her attention was drawn by a young man with short curly hair and an insolent face, who was keeping a whole tableful of enormous women breathlessly attentive to his slightest caprice. But when the young man began to laugh, his chest swelled out.

'God, it's a woman!' she blurted out.

Satin, who was stuffing herself with chicken, looked up and murmured:

'Oh, yes, I know her.... A real good-looker, eh? You ought to see them fighting for her.'

Nana pouted in disgust. That was something she still could not understand. However, she remarked in her sensible tone of voice that there was no point in arguing about tastes or colours, because you could never tell what you might like yourself one day. So she ate her *crème caramel* with a philosophical air, well aware that Satin with her big blue innocent eyes was throwing the neighbouring tables into a state of great excitement. There was one woman in particular, a plump blonde sitting near her, who was making herself very

258

agreeable; she was so excited and attentive that Nana was on the point of intervening.

But at that moment a woman coming into the room gave her a shock of surprise, for she recognized her as Madame Robert. The latter, looking like a pretty brown mouse, gave a familiar nod to the tall thin waitress, and then came and leant on Laure's counter. The two women exchanged a lingering kiss. Nana thought that this was a very odd attention on the part of such a distinguished-looking woman, especially as Madame Robert's face no longer wore its modest expression. On the contrary, her eyes roved about the room as she chatted with the proprietress. Laure had just settled down once more with all the majesty of an old idol of vice, its face worn and polished by the kisses of the faithful. Behind the loaded plates she reigned over her bloated clientele of huge women, monstrous in comparison with even the largest among them, and enthroned in the opulence which was the reward for forty years as a hotel keeper.

But Madame Robert had caught sight of Satin. She left Laure and hurried over, full of charm, to tell her how sorry she was that she had not been at home the day before. But when Satin, utterly captivated, insisted on making room for her at the table, she swore that she had already dined : she had simply come along to have a look round. As she stood talking behind her new friend's chair, she leant lightly on her shoulders, smiling and asking her coaxingly :

'Now when shall I see you? If you were free ...'

Nana unfortunately failed to hear any more. The conversation was annoying her, and she was dying to tell this respectable lady a few home truths. But the sight of a troop of new arrivals paralysed her. It was a group of smart women in evening dress, wearing their diamonds. Under the influence of perverse curiosity they had come as a party to Laure's – whom they all treated with easy familiarity – to eat her three-franc dinner, while flashing a fortune in jewels in the jealous and astonished eyes of poor, shabbily-dressed prostitutes. The moment they came in, talking loudly, laughing merrily and seeming to bring in sunshine with them from the outside world, Nana turned her head away sharply. To her

intense annoyance she had recognized Lucy Stewart and Maria Blond among them, and for nearly five minutes – all the time the ladies chatted with Laure before passing into the next room – she kept her head down, and seemed busily engaged in rolling breadcrumbs into balls on the tablecloth. When at last she was able to look round, she was astonished to find the chair beside her empty. Satin had vanished.

'Where the devil has she gone?' she blurted out aloud.

The plump blonde who had been lavishing attentions on Satin laughed at her bad-tempered outburst; and when Nana, irritated by this laugh, scowled threateningly at her, she said in a languid drawl:

'It's not me, you know, that's pinched her from you – it's the other woman.'

Nana realized that she would be laughed at if she said any more, and made no reply. She even kept her seat for a little while, not wanting to show how angry she was. She could hear Lucy Stewart laughing at the far end of the next room, where she was treating a whole tableful of girls from the dance-halls of Montmartre and La Chapelle. It was very hot; the waitress was carrying away piles of dirty plates smelling of chicken and rice; while four gentlemen had ended up by treating half a dozen couples to choice wine in the hope of making them tipsy and hearing some juicy titbit. What was annoying Nana now was the thought of paying for Satin's dinner. What a little bitch she was, allowing somebody to buy her a meal, and then scarpering with the first bit of skirt that came along, without so much as a thank-you. Admittedly it was only a matter of three francs, but it annoyed her all the same, the way it had been done. Nevertheless she paid up, throwing the six francs at Laure, whom she despised more at that moment than the mud in the gutters.

In the Rue des Martyrs Nana felt her bitterness increasing. Naturally she wasn't going to run after Satin and go poking her nose into her filthy business. But her evening was spoilt, and she walked slowly back up towards Montmartre, raging against Madame Robert in particular. What cheek the woman had to go playing the lady – yes a lady of the

gutter! She felt sure now that she had met her at the Papillon, a low dance-hall in the Rue des Poissonniers, where men could buy her favours for thirty sous. And to think that a creature like that got her hooks into high civil servants with her modest looks, and to think that she refused suppers to which people did her the honour of inviting her, so that she could impress everybody with her virtue! She'd give her virtue! It was always prudes like that who let themselves go in low dives nobody knew anything about.

Meanwhile, thinking over these things, Nana had arrived at her home in the Rue Véron, and was taken aback to see a light in the flat. Fontan had come home in a sulky mood, for he too had been deserted by the friend who had taken him out to dinner. He listened coldly to the explanation she gave him, while she trembled for fear he might strike her, upset at finding him at home, when she had not been expecting him before one in the morning. She lied to him, admitting that she had spent six francs, but saying that it was with Madame Maloir. He showed no annoyance, however, and handed her a letter, which, although it was addressed to her, he had calmly opened. It was a letter from Georges, who was still a prisoner at Les Fondettes, relieving his feelings every week by sending her a passionate missive. Nana loved to be written to, especially when the letters were full of eloquent declarations of love and vows of passion. She used to read them to everybody. Fontan was familiar with Georges's style and appreciated it. But that evening she was so afraid of a scene that she affected indifference, skimming through the letter with a sulky expression and tossing it aside straight away. Fontan had begun drumming his fingers on a window-pane, unwilling to go to bed so early, but not knowing how to spend the rest of his evening. Suddenly he swung round.

'Let's answer that kid straight away,' he said.

Usually it was he who composed the replies, vying with Georges in the matter of style. He used to be delighted too when Nana, full of enthusiasm after hearing him read aloud his latest letter, would kiss him and swear that nobody but he could think up such things. This would fire their emotions, and they would end up in a frenzy of mutual adoration.

'Just as you like,' she replied. 'I'll make some tea, and we'll go to bed afterwards.'

Fontan accordingly installed himself at the table, after putting out pen, ink and paper. He rounded his arms and pulled a long face.

'My beloved,' he began aloud.

And for more than an hour he applied himself to his task, polishing his style here, and considering a phrase there, head in hands, and laughing to himself whenever he hit on a tender expression. Nana had already drunk two cups of tea in silence when he finally read out the letter as an actor reads on the stage, in a monotonous voice with a few sketchy gestures. It was five pages long, and in it he spoke of 'the delightful hours spent at La Mignotte, those hours whose memory lingered like a subtle perfume', swore 'eternal fidelity to that springtime of love', and ended up by declaring that his sole desire was 'to repeat those happy experiences, if happiness can be repeated'.

'I say all that out of politeness, you know,' he explained. 'Seeing that it's all for a laugh. ... I think that was a good one, don't you?'

He was triumphant. But Nana was still afraid of an outburst on his part, and made the mistake of failing to throw her arms round his neck while uttering cries of admiration. She thought the letter a respectable effort, but nothing more. He was extremely annoyed. If she didn't like his letter, she could write one herself. And so, instead of billing and cooing as they usually did, they sat coldly facing each other across the table. All the same Nana poured him a cup of tea.

'What filthy muck!' he cried, after dipping his lips in it. 'You've put salt in it!'

Nana was unlucky enough to shrug her shoulders, and he flew into a temper.

'Aha! I can see we're going to have trouble tonight!'

And with that the quarrel began. It was only ten o'clock, and that was as good a way of killing time as any. So he lashed himself into a rage, and threw in Nana's teeth a whole string of insults and all sorts of accusations, one after another, without giving her time to defend herself. She was

dirty, she was stupid, she had knocked about all over the place. Then he tackled the money question. Did *he* spend six francs when *he* dined out? No, somebody treated him to dinner; otherwise he'd have eaten at home. And to think of spending all that money on that old bawd Maloir! He'd chuck the old shrew out if she ever dared set foot in his place again. Oh, they'd get into a nice mess, the two of them, if they were going to chuck six francs out of the window every day like that!

'For a start, I want to see your accounts,' he shouted. 'Come on, hand over the money! Where do we stand?'

All his sordid avaricious instincts came to the surface. Cowed and scared, Nana hurriedly took their remaining cash out of the desk and brought it to him. Till then the key had been left in this common treasury of theirs, from which they had both drawn freely.

'What!' he exclaimed, when he had counted the money. 'There's scarcely seven thousand francs left out of seventeen thousand, and we've only been together three months. ... I don't believe it.'

He rushed over to the desk, pulled out the drawer, and brought it back to ransack it in the light of the lamp. But it did in fact contain only a little over six thousand eight hundred francs. At this a storm of fury burst forth.

'Ten thousand francs in three months!' he yelled. 'Bloody hell, what have you done with it all? Go on, answer! ... It all goes to your bitch of an aunt, doesn't it! Or else you're spending it on fancy men! ... Will you answer me!'

'Keep your hair on,' said Nana. 'It's easy to see where it's gone, if you'll only do your sums. ... You haven't allowed for the furniture, and then I've had to stock up with linen. Money goes fast when you're settling in a new place.'

But while insisting on explanations, he refused to listen to them.

'Yes, it goes a damn sight too fast,' he said more calmly. 'Listen here, my girl, I've had enough of this method of housekeeping. You know those seven thousand francs are mine. Well seeing that I've got them, I'm going to keep them : I don't want to be ruined. To each man his own.'

And he pocketed the money in a lordly manner, while Nana stared at him in amazement. He went on indulgently :

'You understand, I'm not such a fool as to keep other people's aunts and other people's kids. ... You decided to spend your own money, and that's your affair; but my money's sacred ! ... In future, when you cook a leg of mutton, I'll pay for half of it, and we'll settle up every night. There !'

Nana flared up indignantly, and could not help shouting :

'Look, it's you that's spent my ten thousand francs. ... Of all the dirty tricks !'

But he was in no mood to waste any more time on argument. Leaning across the table, he gave her a stinging slap in the face, saying :

'Say that again !'

She said it again, in spite of the slap, and he fell upon her, punching and kicking her for all he was worth. Soon he had reduced her to such a state that she ended up, as usual, by undressing and going to bed in a flood of tears. He was out of breath, and was going to bed in his turn, when he noticed the letter he had written to Georges lying on the table. He folded it carefully, and turning towards the bed, said in a threatening tone of voice :

'This is a bloody good letter, and I'm going to post it myself, because I don't like the tricks you women get up to. ... And now, stop moaning – you're getting on my nerves.'

Nana, who was giving little sobs and sighs, held her breath. When he was in bed she could bear it no longer and threw herself upon him in a burst of sobbing. Their fights always ended like that, for she trembled at the thought of losing him, and had a cowardly need to know that he belonged to her, in spite of everything. Twice he pushed her away with a disdainful gesture, but the warm embrace of this woman who was pleading with him with the great tearful eyes of a faithful animal finally roused his desire. He condescendingly let her have her way, but without lowering himself to making any advances; he simply allowed himself to be caressed and taken by force, as became a man whose forgiveness is worth

264

winning. Then he was seized with anxiety at the thought that Nana might be putting on an act with a view to regaining possession of the treasury key. The candle had already been blown out when he felt the need to reaffirm his decision.

'You know, my girl, I meant what I said. I'm keeping that money.'

Nana, who was falling asleep with her arms round his neck, made a reply that was little short of sublime.

'Don't worry. . . . I'll work for both of us.'

But from that evening onwards, their life together became more and more difficult. From one week's end to the other the noise of slaps filled the air, like the tick-tock of a clock which regulated their existence. By dint of being beaten, Nana became as supple as fine linen; her skin grew delicate, all pink and white, so soft to the touch and pleasing to the eye that she looked more beautiful than ever. The result was that Prullière began pestering her, coming to see her when Fontan was out, and pushing her into corners to kiss her. But she used to fight him off, full of indignation and blushing with shame; she thought it was disgusting of him to try to deceive a friend. Prullière would look angry and begin sneering at her. She must be out of her mind! How could she settle down with such an ape? Because there was no denying that Fontan was a regular ape with that great twitching nose of his. How could she stand an ugly brute who beat her up into the bargain!

'You may be right, but I love him the way he is,' she replied one day, in the calm manner of a woman admitting to an abominable taste.

Bosc contented himself with dining with them as often as possible. He shrugged his shoulders behind Prullière's back — a good-looking fellow all right, but with nothing much else to him. He had been present several times at quarrels between the couple, and at dessert, whenever Fontan slapped Nana, he would go on chewing solemnly, for the thing struck him as perfectly natural. To give some return for his dinner, he always used to go into ecstasies over their happiness. He declared himself a philosopher who had given up everything, even fame. Sometimes Prullière and Fontan lolled back in

their chairs, after the table had been cleared, losing count of time while with theatrical gestures and intonations they recalled their former successes till two in the morning. But he would sit lost in thought, finishing the brandy bottle in silence, and merely emitting a little contemptuous sniff from time to time. What was left of Talma? Nothing at all. In which case they ought to leave the poor devil alone instead of talking nonsense.

One evening he found Nana in tears. She took off her dressing-jacket to show him her back and arms which were all black and blue. He looked at her skin without being tempted to take advantage of the situation, as that fool Prullière would have been. Then he said sententiously :

'My dear girl, where there are women there are sure to be slaps. It was Napoleon who said that, I think. ... Wash yourself with salt water. Salt water's just the thing for those little bruises. You'll get plenty more like that, but don't complain as long as no bones are broken. ... I'm inviting myself to dinner, you know – I've spotted a leg of mutton.'

But Madame Lerat didn't see things that way. Every time Nana showed her a fresh bruise on her white skin she exploded with indignation. The man was killing her niece : things couldn't go on like that. As a matter of fact, Fontan had turned Madame Lerat out, saying that he didn't want to see her in his place again, and ever since that day, when he returned home and she happened to be there, she had to slip away through the kitchen, which she found horribly humiliating. Consequently she never stopped inveighing against the brute. She criticized his lack of breeding, pursing her lips like a highly respectable lady, whom nobody could teach anything on the subject of good manners.

'Oh, you can see straight away,' she used to tell Nana, 'he hasn't the slightest understanding of the proprieties. His mother must have been as common as dirt; no, don't deny it – it stands out a mile ! ... I'm not saying this for my own sake, although a person of my age is entitled to a little respect. ... But *you* – how can you possibly put up with his bad manners? Because without flattering myself, I've always taught you how to behave, and you've had the very best

advice at home. We were all very well bred in our family, weren't we now?'

Nana never demurred, but listened with bowed head.

'Then, too,' her aunt continued, 'you've only known perfect gentlemen till now. ... As a matter of fact, Zoé and I were talking about that very subject at my place last night. She can't understand it any more than I can. "How is it," she said, "that Madame, who used to have that perfect gentleman, Monsieur le Comte, at her beck and call – for between you and me, it seems he was simply crazy about her – how is it that Madame lets herself be beaten black and blue by that clown of a fellow?" I told her that a woman could put up with beatings at a pinch, but that I would never have stood for his rudeness. ... No, there isn't a word to be said for him. I wouldn't even have his picture in my room! And you're ruining yourself for a character like that, yes, ruining yourself, pet; you slave away for him when there are so many men – rich men too, and some of them in the government. ... Ah, well, it's not my place to say these things to you. All the same, the next time he tries any of his dirty tricks, I'd cut him short with a "Monsieur, who do you take me for?" said in that grand way of yours. That would stop the brute.'

At that Nana would burst out sobbing and stammer:

'Oh, Aunt, I love him.'

The fact of the matter was that Madame Lerat was beginning to feel anxious at seeing how hard her niece was finding it to give her the odd franc at long intervals to pay for little Louis's board and lodging. True, she was willing to make sacrifices, and to look after the child whatever might happen, while waiting for better times, but the thought that Fontan was preventing her and the kid, and its mother, from swimming in a sea of gold, made her so furious as to deny the very existence of love. So she would end up with the following stern remark:

'Now listen, one fine day, when he's taken the skin off your back, you'll come knocking at my door, and I'll open up to you.'

Soon money became Nana's chief preoccupation. Fontan had removed the seven thousand francs; they were doubtless

hidden away somewhere, and she would never have dared to ask him about them, for she was wary of offending that character, as Madame Lerat called him. She was terrified that he might think her capable of staying with him just for his money. Admittedly he had promised to pay the household expenses, and in the early days he had given her three francs every morning. But he insisted on his money's worth; for his three francs he wanted everything – butter, meat and early vegetables – and if she ventured to make an observation, if she hinted that you could not buy the whole market for three francs, he flew into a temper and called her a useless, extravagant, stupid cow, who could be taken in by any tradesman. Moreover, he was always ready to threaten to find board and lodging somewhere else. Then, at the end of the month, on certain mornings, he had forgotten to put three francs on the chest of drawers, and she had ventured to ask for them in a timid roundabout way. There had been such bitter quarrels as a result, and he had made her life so miserable on the slightest pretext, that she found it best not to count on him any more. On the other hand, when he had omitted to leave the three one-franc pieces, and found a meal waiting for him all the same, he was as happy as a sandboy, kissing Nana, paying her fulsome compliments, and waltzing around with a chair. She was so delighted at this that she got to the point of hoping that she would find nothing on the chest of drawers, in spite of all the trouble she experienced in making both ends meet. One day she even gave him back his three francs, telling him that she had some money left over from the previous day. As he had given her nothing then, he hesitated for a moment, thinking that she was trying to teach him a lesson. But she gazed at him with such loving eyes, and hugged him with such complete abandon, that he pocketed the coins with the trembling eagerness of a miser regaining possession of a sum of money he had resigned himself to losing.

From that day on he never troubled his head about money again, nor asked where it came from, looking black when there were only potatoes on the table, and laughing fit to burst at the sight of turkeys and legs of mutton, though this

268

did not prevent his giving Nana an occasional slap, even in a good mood, just to keep his hand in.

Nana had therefore found a means of satisfying all their needs, and on certain days the place was overflowing with food. Twice a week Bosc stuffed himself to the point of indigestion. One evening when Madame Lerat was leaving in a bad temper from having seen a copious dinner cooking that she was not destined to eat herself, she could not refrain from asking brutally who was paying for it all. Nana, taken by surprise, looked abashed and burst into tears.

'Well, that's a nice way to carry on,' said her aunt, who had understood straight away.

Nana had adopted this last resort for the sake of getting peace at home. Besides it was La Tricon who was really to blame. She had come across her in the Rue de Laval, one day when Fontan had gone off in a rage about a dish of cod. She had accordingly agreed to the proposals made her by La Tricon, who happened to be in a fix just then. As Fontan never came home before six o'clock, her afternoons were free, and she used to bring back forty francs, sixty francs, sometimes more. She could have talked in terms of ten or fifteen louis if she had kept her former position, but as matters stood, she was thankful to earn enough to keep the pot boiling. At night she used to forget all her troubles when Bosc sat there bursting with food, and Fontan, propping himself on his elbows, allowed her to kiss him on the eyelids with the lofty condescension of a man who is loved for his own sake.

As a result Nana's very adoration of her darling, her sweet pet, which was all the more blind and passionate because now she paid for everything, plunged her back into the squalor of her early days. She roamed the streets in the hope of earning a five-franc piece, just as when she had been a down-at-heel street-urchin years ago. One Sunday, at the La Rochefoucauld Market, she had made her peace with Satin, after flying at her with furious reproaches about Madame Robert. Satin had merely replied that, if you didn't like something, that was no reason why you should try to turn others against it. And Nana, who was broad-minded by nature, had accepted the philosophical argument that you can never tell

where your tastes will lead you, and forgiven her. Indeed her curiosity was aroused, and she began questioning her about obscure vices, astounded to find herself learning things at her time of life and with all her knowledge. She would burst out laughing, and utter cries of surprise, finding what Satin told her terribly funny, and yet she was a little shocked, for she basically disapproved of anything outside her own habits. So she went back to Laure's, eating there whenever Fontan dined out. She derived enormous amusement from the stories, love-affairs and jealousies which inflamed the female customers' passions without hindering their appetites in the slightest. Nevertheless, she still didn't belong, as she put it. Fat Laure often invited her, in her affectionate, motherly way, to spend a few days in her Asnières villa, a country house containing bedrooms for no less than seven ladies. But she was afraid, and always refused. Satin, however, swore that she was wrong, that gentlemen from Paris pushed you on swings and played *tonneau* with you, so that she promised to come some time in the future, when she could manage to leave town.

At that time Nana had a great deal on her mind and was in no mood for fun. She had to have money, and when La Tricon did not need her, which happened all too often, she did not know where to dispose of her charms. Then she and Satin would go on wild forays into the Paris streets, plunging into the sordid world of vice whose votaries prowled along muddy alleys in the flickering light of gas-lamps. Nana went back to the low dance-halls where she had kicked up her heels as a girl; and she revisited the dark corners on the outer boulevards where, when she was fifteen, men used to fondle her on corner-posts, while her father was looking for her to give her a hiding. The two women would scurry along, visiting all the dance-halls and cafés in a quarter, and climbing staircases, wet with spittle and spilt beer; or they would walk up and down streets, planting themselves in front of carriage gates. Satin, who had served her apprenticeship in the Latin Quarter, introduced Nana to Bullier's and the brasseries on the Boulevard Saint-Michel. But as the holidays began, the Latin Quarter took on an impoverished air, and they always

returned to the main boulevards, for it was there they had the best chance of finding custom. From the heights of Montmartre to the Observatory plateau, they scoured the whole city like this, on rainy evenings when their boots let in the water or hot evenings when their bodices clung to their skin, enduring long waits and endless walks, jostlings and quarrels, and the brutal caresses of a passer-by taken to some squalid furnished room, to come swearing down the greasy stairs afterwards.

The summer was drawing to a close, a stormy summer of burning nights. The pair used to set off together after dinner, about nine o'clock. Along the pavements of the Rue Notre-Dame de Lorette two files of women hurried towards the boulevards, their skirts hitched up and their heads bent, keeping close to the shops, but never once glancing at the window-displays. This was the frantic descent from the Bréda district which took place nightly when the gas-lamps had just been lit. Nana and Satin used to skirt the church and then go down the Rue Le Peletier. When they were about a hundred yards from the Café Riche, and had almost reached their parade-ground, they would drop the trains of their dresses, which until then they had been carefully holding up, and start walking with tiny steps and swaying hips, sweeping the pavements regardless of the dust, and slowing down even further when they crossed the bright patch of light in front of one of the big cafés. Strutting along, laughing loudly, and throwing backward glances at the men who turned to look at them, they were in their element. In the dusk their whitened faces, their rouged lips, and their darkened eyelids, took on the suggestive charm of an Oriental bazaar let out into the open street. Till eleven o'clock they wandered gaily among the jostling crowds, contenting themselves with an occasional 'filthy swine!' hurled after some clumsy man whose heel had ripped a flounce from their dresses. They exchanged familiar greetings with café waiters, stopped occasionally at a table for a chat, and accepted the odd drink, which they sipped very slowly, thankful for the chance to sit down while waiting for the theatres to empty. But, as the night advanced, if they had not made one or two trips to the Rue La Roche-

foucauld, they turned nasty, and their hunt for men grew more ferocious than ever. Under the trees along the darkening and emptying boulevards, fierce bargaining took place, accompanied by oaths and blows, while respectable family parties – fathers, mothers and daughters – who were used to such scenes, passed quietly by without quickening their pace. Then, when they had walked from the Opéra to the Gymnase a dozen times, and, in the deepening darkness, the men started breaking away and setting off for home, Nana and Satin kept to the pavements of the Rue du Faubourg-Montmartre. There, till two o'clock in the morning, restaurants, brasseries and butchers' shops blazed with light, while crowds of women clustered round the doors of the cafés, in this last living, lighted part of Paris, this last market open to nocturnal bargaining, where deals were being struck quite openly, group after group, from one end of the street to the other, as in the main corridor of a brothel. And on evenings when the two women came home without having had any success, they used to quarrel between themselves. The Rue Notre-Dame de Lorette stretched out dark and deserted in front of them, with shadowy women's figures discernible here and there. The district was straggling home, and poor whores exasperated at a night of fruitless soliciting, unwilling to admit defeat, went on arguing in hoarse voices with any stray drunkard they could catch at the corner of the Rue Bréda or the Rue Fontaine.

However, some windfalls came their way now and then, from gentlemen who slipped their decorations into their pockets as they went upstairs with them. Satin in particular had a good nose for this sort of customer. On rainy evenings, when the dripping city exhaled an insipid odour suggestive of a dirty bed, she knew that the wet weather and the fetid reek of the back streets sent men mad. Watching the best dressed among them, she could see that from the expression in their pale eyes. It was as if a fit of carnal madness were passing over Paris. She felt a little nervous, for the most distinguished-looking men were the most obscene. The varnish cracked, and the beast showed itself, exacting in its monstrous tastes, subtle in its perversions. The result was that Satin showed a

complete lack of respect, jeering at dignified gentlemen in carriages, and assuring them that their coachmen were better than they were, because they behaved properly to women and didn't kill them with diabolical ideas. The way in which smart people wallowed in the cesspools of vice still astonished Nana, for she had a few prejudices left, although Satin was rapidly ridding her of them.

Then there was no such thing as virtue left, was there, she used to say when she was talking seriously. From the top of the social ladder to the bottom, everybody was at it! Well, there must be some nice things going on in Paris between nine o'clock at night and three in the morning! And with that she would laugh and say that if you could have looked into every bedroom in the city, you would have seen some funny sights – the ordinary folk going at it hammer and tongs, and quite a few nobs, here and there, wallowing in the filth even deeper than the rest. This made her education complete.

One evening when she came to call for Satin she recognized the Marquis de Chouard coming unsteadily downstairs, white-faced and clinging to the banister-rail. She pretended to be blowing her nose. Upstairs she found Satin in the midst of indescribable filth : no cleaning had been done for a week, the bed was disgusting, and there were pots all over the place. Nana expressed surprise at her knowing the Marquis. Oh, yes, she knew him all right; in fact he'd made a real nuisance of himself to her and her pastrycook when they'd been living together. Now he came back from time to time, but he got on her nerves with his habit of sniffing in all the dirty corners, and even in her slippers.

'Yes, love, in my slippers. ... Oh, he's a filthy old man! And he's always asking for something special. ...'

What made Nana especially uneasy was the sincerity of this low debauchery. Remembering the comedy of pleasure she had taken part in at the height of her success, she was upset to see the whores around her slowly dying of it every day. Moreover, Satin inspired her with a terrible fear of the police. She was full of anecdotes about them. At one time she used to go to bed with a policeman in the public morals

273

brigade, to make sure they left her alone; and twice he had kept her from being listed as a prostitute. But now she was really frightened, for if she were caught again, she would be done for. According to her, the police arrested as many women as possible, in the hope of earning bonuses; they grabbed everybody and silenced you with a slap if you shouted, for they were sure of being defended and rewarded, even when they had taken a respectable girl among the rest. In the summer they would carry out raids on the boulevards in parties of twelve or fifteen, surrounding a long stretch of pavement and picking up as many as thirty women in an evening. Satin, however, knew the likely places, and the moment she caught a glimpse of a policeman, she took to her heels, in the midst of a panic-stricken stampede of long dresses fleeing through the crowd. This fear of the law, this dread of the police was such that some women would stand paralysed in the doorways of cafés, while the raid was sweeping down the avenue. But Satin was more afraid of being denounced; for her pastrycook had been blackguard enough to threaten to report her when she had left him. Yes, there were men who used that trick to live off their mistresses, not to mention the filthy bitches who handed you over out of sheer envy, if you were prettier than they were. Nana listened to these stories in growing terror. She had always been afraid of the Law, that unknown power, that instrument of male vegeance which could wipe her out without anybody in the world lifting a finger to defend her. She saw Saint-Lazare as a grave, a black hole in which they buried women alive after cutting off their hair. Admittedly she knew that she only had to leave Fontan to be able to find powerful protectors; and Satin told her of certain lists of women, accompanied by photographs, which the police had to consult, their instructions being that the women in question were on no account to be touched. Even so, Nana still trembled with fear as she imagined herself hustled and dragged away, and subjected the following day to a medical inspection; and the thought of the doctor's inspection chair filled her with shame and anguish, for all the times she had thrown modesty to the winds.

As it happened, one evening towards the end of September, as she was walking with Satin along the Boulevard Poissonnière, the latter suddenly broke into a frantic run. And when Nana asked her why, she panted :

'It's the police ! Come on ! Come on !'

There followed a wild stampede through the crowd. Skirts streamed out behind, and dresses were torn. There were blows and shrieks. A woman fell to the ground. The crowd stood laughing and watching the brutal tactics of the police as they rapidly closed in. Meanwhile, Nana had lost Satin. Her legs were failing her, and she would have been sure to be arrested if a man had not taken her arm and led her away under the noses of the angry police. It was Prullière, who had just recognized her. Without saying a word, he turned into the Rue Rougemont with her. The street was deserted just then, and she was able to stop and get her breath back, so faint and exhausted that he had to support her. She did not even thank him.

'Look here,' he said at last, 'you've got to give in. . . . Come up to my rooms.'

He lodged near by, in the Rue Bergère. But she bridled up straight away.

'No, I won't. . . .'

At that he retorted coarsely :

'Seeing that anybody can have you. . . . So why not me ?'

'Because.'

To her mind that explained everything. She was too fond of Fontan to deceive him with one of his friends. The other men didn't count because there was no pleasure involved, and she went with them out of sheer necessity. Faced with this mulish stubbornness, Prullière behaved with the spitefulness of a good-looking fellow whose vanity had been wounded.

'All right, just as you like,' he said. 'Only I'm not going your way, my dear. . . . So you'll have to look after yourself.'

And with that he left her. Terror took hold of her again, and she made a huge detour to return to Montmartre, running past the shops and turning white whenever a man approached her.

275

The next day, still shaken by the terrors of the previous night, Nana set off to call on her aunt, and, at the bottom of a quiet little street in Les Batignolles, came face to face with Labordette. At first both of them looked embarrassed, for he was on one of his usual secret errands. However, he was the first to regain his composure, expressing his delight at meeting her. Everybody, he said, was still dumbfounded at Nana's total eclipse. People kept asking for her, and old friends were pining away. And taking on a fatherly air, he ended up by giving her a regular talking-to.

'Frankly, dear, between you and me, the thing's getting ridiculous. Anybody can understand a crush, but to go as far as you've gone, getting bled white, with nothing in return but punches and kicks! ... Are you trying to win one of those prizes for virtue?'

She listened to him with an embarrassed look. But when he mentioned Rose, who was triumphantly enjoying her conquest of the Comte Muffat, a flame came into her eyes.

'Oh, if I wanted to . . .' she murmured.

As an obliging friend, he promptly offered to act as go-between. But she refused his help. He accordingly attacked her from a different direction, telling her that Bordenave was putting on a play of Fauchery's in which there was a splendid part for her.

'What! A play with a part for me!' she cried in amazement. 'But he's in it, and he never said anything to me!'

She did not mention Fontan by name. Moreover, she calmed down straight away, declaring that she would never go back on the stage. Labordette presumably remained unconvinced, for he continued with smiling insistence :

'You know you've got nothing to fear with me. I'll get your Muffat ready, you go back on the stage, and I'll bring him along to you.'

'No !' she cried.

And she left him. Her heroism made her feel quite proud of herself. No wretched man would ever have sacrificed himself like that without trumpeting the fact abroad. All the same, she was struck by one thing : Labordette had just given her exactly the same advice as Francis. That evening, when

Fontan came home, she questioned him about Fauchery's play. He had been back at the Variétés for the last two months. Why then hadn't he told her about the part?

'What part?' he said in his spiteful tone of voice. 'The great lady's part, maybe? ... Good God, so you think you've got some talent, do you? Why, that part would squash you, my girl. ... You really are a scream!'

She was terribly hurt. All that evening he made fun of her, calling her Mademoiselle Mars. And the more he jeered at her, the more she stood firm, deriving a bitter satisfaction from her heroic devotion, which rendered her very great and very loving in her own eyes. Since she had begun going with other men in order to supply his wants, her love for him had grown stronger, fanned by the fatigue and disgust she suffered in its cause. He had become a vice she paid for, a necessity she found it impossible to do without, for the blows he dealt her only stimulated her desire. He for his part, seeing her accept everything, ended up by taking undue advantage of her. She was getting on his nerves, and he began to feel such a ferocious hatred for her that he forgot where his interests lay. When Bosc gently remonstrated with him, he shouted angrily, no one knew why, that he had had enough of her and her good dinners, and that he was going to chuck her out, just for the pleasure of making another woman a present of his seven thousand francs. And that was how their liaison came to an end.

One evening, coming home about eleven o'clock, Nana found the door bolted. She knocked once – no answer: a second time – still no answer. Meanwhile, she saw a light under the door, and Fontan inside made no bones about walking up and down. Refusing to be deterred, she knocked again, calling out and beginning to lose her temper. At last Fontan's voice rose, slow and oily, uttering only the brief retort:

'Piss off!'

She beat on the door with both fists.

'Piss off!'

She banged hard enough to split the woodwork.

'Piss off!'

277

And for a quarter of an hour the same vulgar expression was hurled in her face, like a mocking echo to every blow she hammered on the door. At last, seeing that she was not giving up, he flung the door open, planted himself on the threshold, folded his arms, and said in the same cold, brutal voice :

'God Almighty, haven't you done yet? ... What do you want? ... Are you going to let us get a bit of sleep or aren't you? You can see for yourself that I've got company.'

Sure enough, he was not alone, for Nana saw the woman from the Bouffes, with her untidy tow hair and her gimlet-hole eyes, already stripped to her chemise and giggling among the furniture which she herself had paid for. But then Fontan stepped out on to the landing, a murderous look on his face, and his huge fingers curved like pincers.

'Clear off, or I'll wring your neck !'

At that, Nana burst into a nervous fit of sobbing. She was frightened, and took to her heels. This time she was the one who was being thrown out. In her fury the thought of Muffat suddenly occurred to her, and she raged inwardly at the idea that it should be Fontan of all men who had paid her out.

When she was out in the street, her first thought was to go and sleep with Satin, provided she had nobody with her. She found her standing outside her house, for she too had been turned out by her landlord, who had just had a padlock fastened to her door. This was illegal, of course, seeing that the furniture was her own; and cursing him roundly, she talked of hauling him in front of the local police commissioner. In the meantime, as midnight was striking, they had to begin thinking of finding a bed. And Satin, considering it inadvisable to involve the police in her affairs, ended up by taking Nana to a little hotel in the Rue Laval kept by a woman she knew. They were given a narrow room on the first floor, the window of which opened on to the yard.

'I'd rather have gone to Madame Robert's,' said Satin. 'There's always a corner there for me. ... But with you that's out of the question. She's getting so jealous it's quite ridiculous; she beat me the other night.'

When they had locked themselves in, Nana who had not

278

yet relieved her feelings, burst into tears and recounted over and over again the dirty trick Fontan had played on her. Satin listened indulgently, comforting her and railing against the male sex even more indignantly than her friend.

'Oh, the swine, the swine ! ... We'll have nothing more to do with them, that's what we'll do !'

Then she helped Nana undress with all the gentle attentions of an adoring and submissive lover. She kept saying coaxingly :

'Let's go straight to bed, pet. We'll be better off there. ... Oh, how silly you are to get all worked up ! I tell you, they're dirty swine ! Forget about them. ... I'm here, and I love you. Don't cry now – just to please your little darling.'

And, once in bed, she took Nana in her arms straight away to comfort her. She refused to hear Fontan's name mentioned again, and every time it returned to her friend's lips, she stopped it with a kiss, pouting in pretty indignation, her hair lying loosely on the pillow, and her face full of tender, childlike beauty. Little by little her gentle embrace persuaded Nana to dry her tears. She was touched, and returned Satin's caresses. When two o'clock struck the candle was still burning, and the sound of muffled laughter was mingling with words of love.

Suddenly a loud noise came up from the lower floors of the hotel, and Satin sat up, half-naked, listening hard.

'The police !' she said, turning pale. 'God, that's just our luck ! ... We haven't a chance.'

Time and again she had told Nana about the raids the police made on hotels; yet that night, when they had taken refuge in the Rue Laval, neither of them had given a thought to the danger they were running. At the word 'police', Nana lost her head. She jumped out of bed, ran across the room, and opened the window with the panic-stricken look of a lunatic on the point of jumping out. Fortunately, however, the little yard had a glass roof which was covered with a wire grating on a level with their bedroom. Without a moment's hesitation she swung her legs over the window-sill, and with her chemise flying and her thighs bared to the night air, she disappeared into the darkness.

'Come back!' Satin cried in alarm. 'You'll kill yourself.'

Then, as somebody started hammering at the door, she shut the window like a good friend, and threw Nana's clothes into the back of a wardrobe. She was already resigned to her fate, comforting herself with the thought that after all, if they registered her as a prostitute, she would never have this sort of stupid fright again. After pretending to be heavy with sleep, yawning and parleying, she finally opened the door to a big strapping fellow with a dirty beard, who said:

'Let's see your hands. ... You've got no needle pricks on your fingers, so you don't work for a living. Come on, get your clothes on.'

'But I'm not a dressmaker, I'm a polisher,' Satin retorted brazenly.

All the same, she obediently got dressed, knowing that it was no use arguing. Shouts could be heard all over the hotel; one girl was clinging to the doorposts, refusing to budge an inch; another, caught in bed with a lover who answered for her, was playing the respectable woman who has been grossly insulted, and talking of bringing an action against the Prefect of Police. For nearly an hour there could be heard the noise of heavy shoes on the stairs, of fists hammering on doors, of shrill arguments tailing off into sobs, of skirts brushing against the walls – all the sounds, in fact, attendant on the sudden awakening and frightened departure of a flock of women, as they were roughly packed off by three policemen under the command of an extremely polite, fair-haired commissioner. After they had gone, the hotel relapsed into complete silence.

Nobody had betrayed her: Nana was saved. Shivering and half-dead with fear, she groped her way back into the bedroom. Her bare feet were bleeding, for they had been cut on the grating. For a long time she remained sitting on the edge of the bed, listening all the time. Towards morning, however, she fell asleep, and at eight o'clock, when she woke up, she escaped from the hotel and ran to her aunt's. When Madame Lerat, who just then happened to be drinking her morning coffee with Zoé, saw her appear at such an early hour, be-

draggled and upset, she guessed what had happened straight away.

'So it's all over, is it?' she cried. 'I told you he'd take the skin off your back one of these days, didn't I? Well, come in; you'll always find a kind welcome here.'

Zoé stood up, murmuring with respectful familiarity:

'So Madame's come back to us. ... I was waiting for Madame.'

But Madame Lerat insisted on Nana's going and kissing little Louis at once, because, she said, his mother's return meant happiness for the child. Little Louis was still asleep, looking pale and sickly; and when Nana bent over his white, scrofulous face, the memory of all that she had suffered during the last few months brought a lump to her throat.

'Oh, my poor love, my poor love!' she stammered, bursting into a final fit of sobbing.

The Little Duchess was in rehearsal at the Variétés. The first act had just been worked out, and they were about to start on the second. Sitting in old armchairs on the proscenium, Fauchery and Bordenave were talking together, while the prompter, old Cossard, a little hunchback, perched on a straw-bottomed chair, was thumbing through the script, a pencil between his lips.

'Well, what are we waiting for?' Bordenave shouted all of a sudden, thumping the boards angrily with his thick cane. 'Barillot, why aren't we starting?'

'It's Monsieur Bosc – he's disappeared,' replied Barillot, who was acting as assistant stage-manager.

This reply unleashed a positive storm, with everybody shouting for Bosc, and Bordenave swearing and cursing.

'Hell and damnation, it's always the same. Whenever you ring for them, they're always somewhere they've no business to be. ... And then they grumble when they're kept after four o'clock.'

But just then Bosc came in looking completely unruffled.

'Eh? What? What do you want me for? Oh, it's my cue, is it? Why didn't you say so? ... All right! Simonne gives the cue, "Here come the guests", and I come in. ... Which way do I come?'

'Through the door, of course,' Fauchery snapped irritably.

'Yes, but where *is* the door?'

At this, Bordenave fell upon Barillot, cursing more than ever, and hammering the boards with his cane.

'God Almighty, I told you to put a chair there to stand for the door. Every day we've got to start all over again. ... Barillot? Where's Barillot? He's another one who disappears when you want him!'

However, Barillot came and put the chair in position himself, weathering the storm of Bordenave's wrath in silence. And the rehearsal began. Simonne, in her hat and

furs, began moving about like a maid arranging the furniture. She paused to say :

'It's freezing, you know, so I'll keep my hands in my muff.'

Then, changing her voice, she greeted Bosc with a little cry :

'Why, it's Monsieur le Comte! You're the first to arrive, Monsieur le Comte. Madame *will* be pleased.'

Bosc was wearing mud-stained trousers and a huge yellow overcoat, with a vast muffler wound round his neck. With his hands in his pockets, and an old hat on his head, he dragged himself across the stage, making no attempt to act, and saying in a dull voice :

'Don't disturb your mistress, Isabelle; I want to surprise her.'

The rehearsal continued. Bordenave slumped deep in his armchair, with a scowl on his face, and listened with an air of weariness. Fauchery was nervous, and kept shifting about in his seat. Every few minutes he felt an itch to interrupt, but he restrained himself. Then he heard whispering behind him in the dark, empty auditorium.

'Is she there?' he asked, leaning over towards Bordenave.

The latter nodded. Before accepting the part of Géraldine, which he had offered her, Nana had been anxious to see the play, for she hesitated to play the part of a courtesan a second time. What she dreamt of playing, in fact, was the part of a respectable woman. She was accordingly hiding in the shadows of a ground-floor box with Labordette, who was acting on her behalf in her negotiations. Fauchery glanced around to see if he could spot her, and then turned his attention to the rehearsal once more.

Only the front of the stage was lit up. A gas-jet on a support, fed by a pipe from the footlights, was burning in front of a reflector which was casting all its light on the proscenium. It looked like a big yellow eye staring through the gloom, in which it flared with a sort of sinister melancholy. Cossard was holding up the script next to the slender stem of the support, to see it clearly, and in the full glare of the light his hump stood out sharply. As for Bordenave and Fauchery, they were already drowned in shadow. It was only

in the middle of the huge building, over an area of a few square yards, that a faint glow suggested the light cast by a lantern nailed up in a railway station. It made the actors look like weird phantoms with their shadows dancing behind them. The rest of the stage was full of mist, and looked like a house in process of being demolished, or the gutted nave of a church littered with ladders and flats, on which the faded paintings suggested piles of ruins. Hanging high in the air the backdrops gave the impression of huge rags suspended from the rafters of some vast old-clothes shop, while far above them a ray of bright sunlight falling from a window clove the darkness of the rigging loft with a bar of gold.

Meanwhile some actors standing upstage were chatting together while waiting for their cues. Little by little they had raised their voices.

'Dammit, will you shut up!' howled Bordenave, furiously jumping up and down in his chair. 'I can't hear a word. . . . Go outside if you want to talk; the rest of us are working. . . . Barillot, if there's any more talking everybody's fined!'

They fell silent for a moment or two. They were sitting in a little group on a bench and some rustic chairs in the corner of a scenic garden, which was waiting to be put in position as the first setting that evening. Fontan and Prullière were listening to Rose Mignon, to whom the manager of the Folies-Dramatiques had just made a magnificent offer. Just then a voice shouted:

'The Duchess! . . . Saint-Firmin! . . . Hurry up, the Duchess and Saint-Firmin!'

Only when the call was repeated did Prullière remember that he was Saint-Firmin. Rose, who was playing the Duchesse Hélène, was already waiting to go with him, while old Bosc slowly returned to his seat, dragging his feet across the echoing, empty boards. Clarisse offered him a place on the bench beside her.

'What's he bawling like that for?' she said, referring to Bordenave. 'It's going to be marvellous here soon. . . . You can't put a play on nowadays without him throwing a fit.'

Bosc shrugged his shoulders. He was above that sort of thing. Fontan murmured:

'He can tell he's going to have a flop. And I must say the play strikes me as idiotic.'

Then, returning to what Rose had been telling them, he asked Clarisse :

'Do you really believe that story about the offer from the Folies? ... Three hundred francs a night for a hundred performances! Why not a country house into the bargain? ... If they gave his wife three hundred francs a night, Mignon would drop my good friend Bordenave like a hot brick!'

Clarisse did believe in the three hundred francs. That man Fontan was always running down his friends' successes! Just then Simonne interrupted her. She was shivering with cold. Buttoned up to the ears, with mufflers round their necks, they all looked at the ray of sunlight which shone brightly above them, without descending into the chill gloom of the stage. Outside it was freezing, under a clear November sky.

'And there's no fire in the green-room!' said Simonne. 'It's disgusting! He's becoming such a skinflint! ... I want to go – I don't want to catch my death of cold.'

'Silence!' Bordenave roared again.

After that there was nothing to be heard for a few minutes but the murmur of the actors' voices as they repeated their parts. They made only sketchy gestures, and they spoke in even tones so as not to tire themselves. All the same, when they wanted to stress some particular shade of meaning, they cast a glance at the auditorium, which lay before them like a gaping hole, full of vague shadows resembling the fine dust pent up in some high, windowless loft. The deserted auditorium, illuminated only by the half-light of the stage, was slumbering in a mysterious melancholy effacement. On the ceiling the frescoes were hidden in dense darkness. The stage-boxes on right and left were hung from top to bottom with huge lengths of grey canvas to protect the walls; and those coverings continued round the theatre, for strips of canvas had been draped along the velvet-covered ledges, lining the galleries with a double shroud, and staining the darkness with their pallid hue. In the general gloom only the dark recesses of the boxes were distinguishable, outlining the framework of

the various storeys, where the red velvet seats looked like so many black patches. The chandelier had been let down as far as it would go, so that it filled the stalls with its pendants, giving the impression that the audience had left on a journey from which it would never return.

Just then, in fact, Rose, playing the part of the little Duchess who had found her way into a courtesan's house, walked towards the footlights, raised her hands and pouted delightfully at the dark empty auditorium, which was as sad as a house of mourning.

'Heavens, what peculiar people!' she said, emphasizing the phrase, and sure that it would raise a laugh.

Far back in the ground-floor box in which she was hiding, Nana sat wrapped in a vast shawl, listening to the play and devouring Rose with her eyes. Turning to Labordette, she asked him in a whisper :

'You're sure he's going to come?'

'Certain. He'll probably turn up with Mignon, so as to have an excuse. ... As soon as he arrives, you'll go up to Mathilde's dressing-room and I'll bring him to you there.'

They were talking of the Comte Muffat. Labordette had arranged this meeting with him on neutral ground. He had had a serious talk with Bordenave, whose affairs had been gravely compromised by two failures in succession. The result was that Bordenave was eager to lend his theatre, and to offer Nana a part, for he was anxious to win the Count's favour, in the hope of getting a loan from him.

'And this part of Géraldine, what do you think of it?' continued Labordette.

But Nana sat motionless, and made no reply. After the first act, in which the author showed the Duc de Beaurivage deceiving his wife with the blonde Géraldine, a comic-opera star, the second act saw the Duchesse Hélène arriving at the actress's house for a masked ball, intent on finding out by what magical power ladies of that sort conquered and retained their husbands' affections. It was a cousin of hers, the handsome Oscar de Saint-Firmin, who had brought her along, in the hope of seducing her. As her first lesson, a lesson

which caused her tremendous surprise, she heard Géraldine swearing like a trooper at the Duke, who listened to her meekly with every appearance of delight, causing the Duchess to exclaim: 'So *that's* the way we ought to talk to men, is it!' This was virtually the only scene Géraldine had in this act. As for the Duchess, she was very soon punished for her curiosity, for an old buck, the Baron de Tardiveau, took her for a courtesan and became very attentive, while on the other side of the room, locked in an embrace on a chaise longue, the Duke made his peace with Géraldine. As this last part had not yet been given to anyone, old Cossard had got up to read it, and despite himself he was acting for all he was worth in Bosc's arms. The rehearsal had reached this point, with everyone in a grumpy mood, when Fauchery suddenly jumped up from his chair. He had restrained himself so far, but now his nerves had got the better of him.

'Not like that!' he shouted.

The actors paused, their arms hanging limply by their sides, while Fontan turned up his nose and asked with a sneer:

'What do you mean? What's not like that?'

'Nobody's getting it right! You're all hopelessly wrong!' continued Fauchery; and, gesticulating wildly and pacing up and down, he began miming the scene himself.

'You, Fontan – you've got to remember how excited Tardiveau is. You must lean forward like this to grab the Duchess. ... And it's then, Rose, that you've got to move away smartly, like that, but not too soon – only when you hear the kiss ...'

He broke off, and in the heat of his explanations called out to Cossard:

'Géraldine, let's have the kiss. ... A loud one, so we can all hear it!'

Old Cossard turned towards Bosc, and smacked his lips loudly.

'Good! There's the kiss,' said Fauchery triumphantly. 'Let's have it again. ... You see, Rose, I've had time to move, and then I give a little cry, like this: "Oh! She's kissed him!" But to allow you to do that, Tardiveau has to come upstage.

'... You hear that, Fontan? You come upstage. .... All right, try that, all together.'

The actors went through the scene again, but Fontan played with such bad grace that it was a complete failure. Twice Fauchery had to repeat his explanations, each time miming the scene with more warmth than before. The actors listened to him glumly, glanced at one another briefly as if he had asked them to walk on their heads, and then awkwardly tried the scene, only to stop short the moment it was over, looking as stiff as puppets whose strings had just been cut.

'No, it beats me : I don't understand,' Fontan said at last in his insolent tone of voice.

Bordenave had not uttered a word. He had slipped right down in his armchair, so that nothing could be seen of him now, in the sinister glow of the gas-lamp, but the top of his hat, which he had pulled down over his eyes, and his cane, which had slipped from his grasp and was lying across his stomach. Anyone would have thought he was asleep, but suddenly he sat up in his chair.

'It's idiotic, my boy,' he said calmly to Fauchery.

'What do you mean, idiotic?' cried the author, turning white. 'You're idiotic yourself !'

Bordenave promptly lost his temper. He repeated the word 'idiotic', racked his brains for something stronger and came up with 'imbecilic' and 'cretinous'. The audience would hiss them off the stage, and they'd never get to the end of the act. And when Fauchery, annoyed but not really hurt by these insults, which the two men always exchanged when they put on a new play, called the other a brute, Bordenave exploded. He brandished his cane in the air, snorted like a bull and shouted :

'God Almighty ! Shut your trap, will you ! ... You've wasted a quarter of an hour on a lot of nonsense. .... Yes, a lot of nonsense. And it's all so simple ! You, Fontan, you don't move. You, Rose, you make that little movement of yours, just that and no more, and you come downstage. .... Now then, let's get it right this time. Let's have the kiss, Cossard.'

The result was complete confusion, and the scene went no better than before. Bordenave, in his turn, mimed the differ-

ent parts with elephantine grace, while Fauchery sneered and shrugged his shoulders in pity. Then Fontan put his oar in, and even Bosc made so bold as to offer advice. Rose, worn out, had ended up by sitting on the chair which indicated the door. Nobody knew where they were any more, and to crown everything Simonne came on too soon, thinking she had heard her cue, and arrived in the midst of the confusion. This so enraged Bordenave that he whirled his stick around in a tremendous circle and caught her a resounding whack on her behind. At rehearsals he often used to beat women, provided he had slept with them before. Simonne ran away, followed by this furious shout :

'Take that ! And by God, if anybody else annoys me I'll shut up shop !'

Fauchery had just crammed his hat on his head, making as if to leave the theatre, but he came back downstage when he saw Bordenave sit down again, dripping with sweat. He too resumed his seat in the other armchair. For a little while they sat motionless side by side, while an oppressive silence fell upon the dark house. The actors waited for nearly two minutes. They all felt exhausted and dejected, as if they had just finished an overwhelming task.

'Well, let's go on,' Bordenave said at last, perfectly calm, and speaking in his usual voice.

'Yes, let's go on,' Fauchery repeated. 'We'll settle that scene tomorrow.'

And with that they stretched out in their chairs, while the rehearsal resumed its listless, indifferent course. During the quarrel between manager and author, Fontan and the others had been taking things easy on the bench and garden seats at the back of the stage, where they had been laughing, grumbling and making cutting remarks. But when Simonne came back, still smarting from her blow and choking with sobs, they turned serious, and declared that if they had been in her place, they would have strangled the swine. She dried her eyes and nodded. It was all over, she was dropping him, especially as Steiner had offered to launch her only the day before. Clarisse was astonished to hear this, for the banker was ruined : but Prullière began laughing and reminded

them of the trick that damned Jew had pulled off on the Stock Exchange with his Landes salt mines when he had been tied up with Rose. At the moment he was floating a new operation, a tunnel under the Bosphorus. Simonne listened in fascination. As for Clarisse, she had been in a fury for the past week at the thought that that little beast la Faloise, whom she had got rid of by throwing him into Gaga's venerable arms, was going to inherit the fortune of a very rich uncle! That was just her luck; she had always eased the way for other people. And now that pig Bordenave had given her another appalling part, a paltry fifty lines, as if she couldn't have played Géraldine! She longed for that role and was hoping against hope that Nana would refuse it.

'And what about me?' said Prullière bitterly. 'I haven't got more than two hundred lines. I wanted to give the part up. ... It's disgusting making me play that fellow Saint-Firmin: why it's a complete dud of a part. And then what a style the play's written in! It's going to be a flop, you can be sure of that!'

But just then Simonne, who had been chatting with old Barillot, came back out of breath to say:

'Talking of Nana, she's in the house.'

'Where?' Clarisse asked eagerly, getting up to look.

The news spread at once, and everybody craned forward. The rehearsal was interrupted for a moment. But Bordenave emerged from his immobility, shouting:

'What's happening? Go on, finish the act, and shut up, over there: it's insufferable!'

Nana was still following the play from the ground-floor box. Twice Labordette had tried to start chatting to her, but she had nudged him impatiently to stop him. The second act was drawing to a close when two shadows appeared at the back of the theatre. As they were tiptoeing down, trying not to make any noise, Nana recognized Mignon and the Comte Muffat. They came forward and silently shook hands with Bordenave.

'Ah, here they are,' she murmured with a sigh of relief.

Rose Mignon delivered the last lines of the act. Then Bordenave said they had to go through the second act again

before going on to the third. With that he left the rehearsal, and greeted the Count with exaggerated politeness, while Fauchery pretended to be entirely taken up with his actors, who had clustered around him. Mignon stood whistling softly, with his hands behind his back and his eyes fixed on his wife, who seemed rather nervous.

'Well, shall we go upstairs?' Labordette asked Nana. 'I'll install you in the dressing-room, and come back here to fetch him.'

Nana promptly left the ground-floor box. She had to grope her way along the passage outside the stalls, but Bordenave guessed where she was as she passed by in the dark, and caught up with her at the end of the passage behind the stage, a narrow tunnel where the gas burnt day and night. Here, in the hope of forcing a decision, he started enthusing over the courtesan's part.

'What a part, eh? What a splendid part! It's made for you. . . . Come to tomorrow's rehearsals.'

Nana remained unresponsive. She wanted to know what the third act was like.

'Oh, it's magnificent, the third act is! . . . The Duchess plays the courtesan in her own house, and this disgusts Beaurivage and makes him mend his ways. Then there's a very funny misunderstanding when Tardiveau arrives, under the impression that he's at a dancer's house.'

'And what does Géraldine do in that act?' interrupted Nana.

'Géraldine?' repeated Bordenave in some embarrassment. 'She has a scene which isn't very long, but very good. . . . It's made for you, I assure you! Will you sign?'

She looked steadily at him, and finally replied:

'We'll see about that later.'

And she rejoined Labordette, who was waiting for her on the stairs. Everybody in the theatre had recognized her, and they were all chattering away in whispers. Prullière was shocked at her return, and Clarisse was worried about the part. As for Fontan, he affected cool unconcern, for he did not consider it becoming to denigrate a woman he had loved. In his heart, however, his old love had turned to hate, and

he nursed the fiercest resentment against her for her devotion, her beauty and that life together of which his perverse and monstrous tastes had made him tire.

In the meantime, when Labordette reappeared and went up to the Count, Rose Mignon, whose suspicions had been aroused by Nana's presence, suddenly realized what was happening. Muffat bored her to tears, but she was beside herself at the thought of being dropped like this. She broke the silence she usually kept on such subjects in her husband's company, and said bluntly :

'You see what's going on? . . . By God, if she pulls off the Steiner trick again, I'll scratch her eyes out!'

Mignon, calm and haughty, shrugged his shoulders, with the air of a man from whom nothing can be hidden.

'Shut up,' he murmured. 'Do me the favour of shutting your trap.'

He knew what was what. He had drained Muffat dry, and he knew that at a sign from Nana the Count was ready to lie down and let her walk over him. It was hopeless trying to fight against passions like that. Accordingly, knowing what men were like, his only thought was how to turn the situation to the best possible account. He would have to wait for events – so he was waiting.

'Rose, you're on!' shouted Bordenave. 'They're starting Act Two again.'

'Off you go then,' said Mignon. 'Leave it to me to arrange things.'

Then, in a bantering mood in spite of everything, he thought it funny to congratulate Fauchery on his play. It was a very powerful piece of work. Only why was his great lady so respectable? It wasn't natural! With that he sniggered, and asked who had sat for the portrait of the Duc de Beaurivage, Géraldine's old dodderer. Far from getting annoyed, Fauchery smiled. But Bordenave glanced in Muffat's direction, with an annoyed expression on his face, and this struck Mignon, who became serious again.

'Let's start, for God's sake!' yelled the manager. 'Come along, Barillot! . . . What's that? Bosc isn't here? What the hell does he think he's up to?'

Bosc, however, came ambling forward, and the rehearsal began again just as Labordette was taking the Count away. The latter was trembling with excitement at the thought of seeing Nana once more. After the break between them he had felt a great sense of emptiness, and thinking that he might suffer from the sudden change in his habits, he had allowed himself to be taken to see Rose. Besides, in his dazed condition he wanted to forget everything, forbidding himself to go looking for Nana while avoiding an explanation with the Countess. It seemed to him that he owed it to his dignity to make this attempt to forget. But by a mysterious inner process Nana slowly began to reconquer him, first through memories of her, then through fleshly cravings and finally through a new, exclusive feeling of almost fatherly affection. His recollections of their last appalling meeting began to fade; he no longer saw Fontan, he no longer heard Nana taunting him about his wife's adultery as she threw him out. These things were just words which disappeared, whereas deep in his heart there remained a stinging hurt which caused him such ever-increasing pain that it almost choked him. Childish ideas occurred to him : he blamed himself for what had happened, telling himself that she would never have betrayed him if he had really loved her. His anguish became unbearable, and he felt utterly wretched. What he felt was like the ache of an old wound – no longer his previous blind desire, accepting anything and everything, but a jealous passion for that woman, an obsessive longing for her alone, her hair, her mouth, her body. When he remembered the sound of her voice, a shiver ran through his limbs; he lusted after her with greedy desires and aspirations of infinite delicacy. And this love had taken such a painful hold on him that when Labordette had broached the subject of an assignation, he had thrown himself into his arms on an irresistible impulse. The next moment he had felt ashamed of an act of self-abandonment which was so ridiculous on the part of a man of his position; but Labordette knew how to deal with any situation, and he gave a further proof of his tact when he left the Count at the foot of the stairs with these words, uttered in a casual tone of voice :

'The right-hand passage on the second floor. The door's ajar.'

Muffat was alone in that silent corner of the building. Passing the green-room, he had glanced through the open doors and noticed the utter dilapidation of the vast chamber, which looked shamefully stained and worn in broad daylight. But what surprised him most, as he emerged from the darkness and confusion of the stage, was the pure clear light and profound calm of the staircase well, which he had seen one evening smoky with gas-fumes and loud with the footsteps of women running from floor to floor. One could sense that the dressing-rooms were empty, the corridors deserted; there was not a soul to be seen, not a sound to be heard, while, through the square windows on a level with the stairs, the pale November sunlight poured in, casting yellow patches of light full of dancing dust, in the deathly peace which descended from above. He was glad of this calm and this silence, and he climbed the stairs slowly, trying to get his breath back as he went; his heart was beating wildly, and he was afraid that he might behave like a child and give way to sighs and tears. Accordingly, on the first-floor landing, he leant against the wall, certain that nobody could see him; and, pressing his handkerchief to his mouth, he gazed at the warped steps, the iron banister-rail polished by the friction of many hands, the peeling paint on the walls – all the squalor, in fact, of a brothel, crudely displayed at that pale afternoon hour when the inmates are asleep. When he reached the second floor he had to step over a big red cat, which was lying curled up on a step. Its eyes half-closed, this cat was keeping solitary watch over the theatre, drowsy from the close and now chilled smells which the women left behind them every night.

Sure enough, in the corridor on the right, the door of the dressing-room had been left ajar. Nana was waiting. Little Mathilde, a slut of a young actress, kept her dressing-room in a filthy condition, with chipped pots everywhere, a greasy dressing-table and a chair marked with a red stain, as if someone had bled on the straw. The paper pasted on the walls and ceiling was splashed from top to bottom with spots

294

of soapy water, and there was such an unpleasant smell of lavender water gone sour that Nana opened the window. She leant her elbows on the sill for a while, breathing the fresh air, and craning forward to catch sight of Madame Bron down below, whose broom she could hear energetically attacking the green flagstones of the narrow yard, which was buried in shadow. A canary, whose cage hung next to a shutter, was trilling away piercingly. The carriages on the boulevard and in the neighbouring streets were inaudible, and under the vast expanse of sleepy sunlight the city was as quiet as a country town. Raising her eyes, she caught sight of the small buildings and glass roofs of the galleries in the passage, and farther off, facing her, the tall houses of the Rue Vivienne, the backs of which stood silent and apparently deserted. A number of flat roofs rose in terraces, and on one of these a photographer had perched a big cage-like construction of blue glass. It was all very gay, and Nana was becoming absorbed in the scene when she suddenly had the impression that somebody had knocked on the door. She turned round and shouted:

'Come in.'

At the sight of the Count she shut the window. It was not warm in the room, and there was no need for the inquisitive Madame Bron to hear what was going to be said. The two of them gazed at one another gravely. Then, as the Count remained standing stiffly in front of her, looking as if he were choking with emotion, she burst out laughing, and said:

'Well, so here you are again, you big silly!'

He was so overcome that he seemed to have been turned to ice. He called Nana 'Madame', and esteemed himself happy to see her again. To shake things up, she accordingly spoke to him in even more familiar terms.

'Come on, get off your high horse! You wanted to see me, didn't you? Well it wasn't to stand looking at each other like a couple of china dogs. ... There was wrong on both sides – and I'm ready to forgive you!'

It was agreed to make no further mention of the affair, the Count nodding his assent. He was growing calmer, but as yet he could find nothing to say out of the flood of words

that rose tumultuously to his lips. Surprised at this coldness, Nana decided to make a bold approach.

'Come now,' she continued with a faint smile, 'you're a sensible man. Now that we've made our peace, let's shake hands on it and remain good friends in future.'

'What! Good friends?' he murmured with sudden disquiet.

'Yes, it may sound ridiculous, but I wanted you to think well of me. Now we've straightened things out, and if we meet again, at least we shan't look like a couple of boobies.'

He raised his hand as if to interrupt her.

'Let me finish. ... There isn't a man alive – not one, you hear me? – who can accuse me of doing the dirty on him. Well, it irked me to begin with you. ... We all have our sense of honour, you know.'

'I didn't mean that!' he shouted. 'Sit down and listen to me.'

And as if he were afraid of seeing her leave, he pushed her down on the only chair in the room. Then he paced up and down in growing agitation. The little dressing-room was snug and full of sunlight, and no sound from the outside world disturbed the pleasant, musty calm that reigned within. In the breaks in the conversation nothing could be heard but the shrill piping of the canary, like the trills of a distant flute.

'Listen,' he said, planting himself in front of her. 'I've come to take you back. ... Yes, I want to begin again. ... You know that perfectly well, so why do you talk to me like that? ... Answer me. Are you willing?'

She had bent her head, and was scratching at the blood-red straw of her chair. Seeing him so anxious, she did not hurry to answer. But at last she lifted up her face. It had assumed a grave expression, and she had succeeded in infusing a look of sadness into her beautiful eyes.

'Oh, that's impossible, my dear. I'll never take up with you again.'

'Why not?' he stammered, as an expression of unspeakable suffering passed across his face.

'Why not? Damn it all, because. ... It's impossible, that's all. I don't want to.'

He gazed ardently at her for a few seconds more. Then his

legs gave way under him, and he collapsed on to the floor. In a bored voice she merely added :

'Oh, don't behave like a baby !'

But it was too late. Falling at her feet, he had put his arms round her waist, and was hugging her tightly, pressing his face hard against her knees. When he felt her like that, and rediscovered her velvety limbs beneath the thin fabric of her dress, a shudder went through his body, and he started trembling feverishly, at the same time savagely pressing his face against her legs as if he wanted to force his way into her flesh. The old chair creaked, and beneath the low ceiling, in an atmosphere pungent with stale perfumes, there rose the sound of stifled sobs of desire.

'Well, and what next?' asked Nana, letting him do as he pleased. 'All this doesn't help you a bit, seeing that it's out of the question. God, what a child you are !'

He grew a little calmer, but he still remained on the floor, keeping hold of her, and saying in a broken voice :

'At least listen to what I came to offer you. . . . I've already seen a big house near the Parc Monceau. . . . I'd make your every wish come true. . . . To have you all to myself, I'd give my whole fortune. . . . Yes, that would be my only condition, that I should have you all to myself ! You understand? And if you agreed to be mine alone, why, then I'd want you to be the loveliest, richest woman on earth, with carriages, and diamonds, and dresses . . .'

At each offer Nana shook her head proudly. Then, as he went on, speaking of settling money on her, for he was at a loss as to what else to lay at her feet, she appeared to lose patience.

'Look, have you finished pawing me? . . . I'm a good sort, and I don't mind a bit of it, seeing that you're in such a terrible state; but that's enough now, isn't it? . . . So let me get up. You're making me tired.'

She extricated herself from his grasp, and once she was on her feet, she said :

'No, no, no. . . . I don't want to.'

At that he laboriously picked himself up and slumped on to the chair, resting his elbows on the back and burying his

face in his hands. Nana in her turn began pacing up and down. For a moment or two she looked at the stained wall-paper, the greasy dressing-table, the whole dirty room as it basked in the pale sunlight. Then, stopping in front of the Count, she spoke with quiet directness.

'It's funny how rich men fancy they can get anything with their money. . . . Well, and what if I say no? . . . I don't give a damn for your presents. You could give me Paris, and I'd still say no, no, no. . . . Look, it isn't exactly clean here, is it? Well, I'd think it was a lovely room if I wanted to live here with you. But a woman would die in one of your palaces, if she wasn't in love. . . . And as for money, you poor thing, I can get plenty of that when I want it! I don't give a damn for it! I spit on it!'

And with that she put on a disgusted expression. Then, changing her tone, she added in a melancholy voice:

'I know of something that's worth more than money. . . . Oh, if only somebody gave me what I longed for . . .'

He slowly raised his head, and a gleam of hope appeared in his eyes.

'Oh, you can't give it to me,' she continued; 'it doesn't depend on you, and that's why I'm telling you about it. . . . We're just having a chat, that's all. . . . What I'd like is to play the part of the respectable woman in that show of theirs.'

'What respectable woman?' he murmured in astonishment.

'Why, their Duchesse Hélène, of course! . . . If they think I'm going to play Géraldine, they can think again! A useless part – just one scene, and not much of a scene at that. Besides, that isn't the point. The fact is I've had enough of high-class tarts. Tarts, tarts – you'd think that's all I can play. When all's said and done, it's annoying, because I can see what they're thinking – they think I don't know how to be-have. Well, they're wrong, I tell you. I can be a lady when I want to, and no mistake! . . . Just look at this.'

She withdrew as far as the window, and then came strutting back, with the mincing gait and cautious air of a portly hen afraid of dirtying her claws. As for Muffat, he

followed her with his eyes still full of tears, baffled by this sudden scene of comedy in the midst of his anguish. She walked about for a while, to show her paces properly, smiling subtly, fluttering her eyelashes and swaying her hips, and then planted herself in front of him again.

'That's it, isn't it?'

'Yes, absolutely,' he stammered, his voice still unsteady and his eyes dimmed with tears.

'I tell you, I've got the respectable woman to a "t". I've tried it out at my place, and nobody's got my knack of looking like a duchess who doesn't give a damn for men. Did you notice when I passed you, looking at you through my lorgnette? It's in my blood, I tell you ... Besides, I want to play a respectable woman, I'm mad about it, I've got to have the part, you understand.'

She had grown serious, speaking in a hard voice and looking deeply moved, for her stupid longing was causing her real anguish. Muffat, still stunned by her refusals, sat there, not understanding. There was a silence, without even the buzzing of a fly to disturb the peace in the empty building.

'Now listen,' she continued bluntly. 'You're going to get me the part.'

He was dumbfounded, and with a despairing gesture he said :

'But that's impossible! You said yourself it doesn't depend on me.'

She interrupted him with a shrug of the shoulders.

'You just go down and tell Bordenave you want the part. ... Don't be such an innocent! Bordenave needs money badly. Well, you'll lend him some, seeing that you've got so much you can throw it around.'

And as he opened his mouth again to object, she lost her temper.

'All right, I understand : you're afraid of annoying Rose. I didn't mention that woman when you were crying on the floor – I'd have had too much to say about the two of you. ... Yes, when you've sworn to love a woman for ever, you don't pick up the first comer next day. Oh, I haven't forgotten that, I can tell you! ... Besides, I don't think I'd

fancy the Mignons' leftovers. You'd have done better to break it off with that filthy lot before coming slobbering at my knees.'

He tried to protest and finally managed to get a word in.

'I don't give a damn for Rose: I'll give her up straight away.'

Nana seemed satisfied on this point. She continued:

'Then what's bothering you? Bordenave's master here. . . . I suppose you're going to tell me there's Fauchery after Bordenave . . .'

She was speaking more slowly, for she had come to the delicate part of the matter. Muffat sat silent, with downcast eyes. He had remained deliberately ignorant of Fauchery's assiduous attentions to the Countess, reassuring himself in the long run, and hoping that he had been mistaken on that dreadful night spent in a doorway in the Rue Taitbout. But he still felt a silent, angry repugnance for the man.

'Come now, Fauchery isn't the devil!' said Nana, feeling her way cautiously and trying to find out how matters stood between husband and lover. 'You can get round him easily enough. At bottom he's quite a good sort, I assure you. . . . So it's agreed, eh? You'll tell him it's for my sake.'

The idea of taking such a step disgusted the Count.

'No, no, never!' he cried.

She waited a moment, on the verge of saying: 'Fauchery can't refuse you anything', but she felt that, as arguments went, that remark was a little too crude. However, she smiled a queer smile which spoke as plainly as words. Muffat had raised his eyes to look at her, and now lowered them again, looking pale and embarrassed.

'Oh, you're not very nice,' she murmured at last.

'I can't,' he said, in a voice full of anguish. 'I'll do anything you like, but not that, my love. Oh, please don't make me do that!'

She wasted no more time in argument. Taking his head between her small hands, she pushed it back a little, bent down, and pressed her mouth onto his in a long kiss. A shiver ran through his body, and he trembled beneath her, his eyes closed in ecstasy. She raised him to his feet.

300

'Go,' she said simply.

He started walking towards the door. But as he was leaving the room she took him in her arms again and turned meek and coaxing, looking up at him and rubbing her chin against his waistcoat like a cat.

'Where's the big house?' she whispered, with the laughing embarrassment of a little girl returning to the good things she had previously refused.

'In the Avenue de Villiers.'

'And there are carriages?'

'Yes.'

'Lace? Diamonds?'

'Yes.'

'Oh, how sweet you are, my pet. You know it was only out of jealousy just now. ... And this time I swear it won't be like the first time, because now you understand what a woman needs. You'll give me everything, won't you? So then I won't need anybody else.... It's all just for you now! That, and that, and that!'

When she had pushed him out of the room, after firing his blood with a rain of kisses on his hands and face, she stood panting for a while. God, what a smell there was in that slut Mathilde's dressing-room! It was warm enough, with that pleasant warmth of a room in the winter sunshine of Provence, but really it smelt far too strongly of stale lavender water, not to speak of other less mentionable things. She opened the window, and leaning on the sill again, started examining the glass roof of the passage below in order to kill time.

Muffat went staggering downstairs, his head swimming. What should he say? How should he broach this matter, which was none of his business? Just as he reached the stage, he heard sounds of quarrelling. They had nearly finished the second act, and Prullière was complaining angrily about an attempt on Fauchery's part to cut one of his speeches.

'Cut it all, then,' he shouted. 'I'd rather you did that! ... Dammit, I've got less than two hundred lines, and you want to cut some of those! No, I've had enough. You can give the part to somebody else.'

He took a little crumpled notebook out of his pocket, and twisted it feverishly in his hands, as if he were just about to throw it into Cossard's lap. His pale face was convulsed by outraged vanity, his lips drawn and his eyes inflamed; he was quite unable to conceal the turmoil of his emotions. To think of him, Prullière, the idol of the public, playing a part of only two hundred lines!

'Why not make me bring in letters on a tray?' he continued bitterly.

'Come, come, Prullière, be a good fellow,' said Bordenave, who was treating him gently because of his popularity with the public. 'Don't start one of your quarrels. ... We'll find you some good effects. That's right, isn't it, Fauchery? You'll put in some good effects. ... In the third act we might even be able to lengthen one scene.'

'In that case,' declared the actor, 'I want the last speech before the curtain. ... You owe me that at least.'

Fauchery's silence seemed to indicate consent, and Prullière, still very agitated, and dissatisfied in spite of everything, put his part back in his pocket. Bosc and Fontan had assumed expressions of profound indifference during this argument; considering that it was a case of every man for himself, and that this was no concern of theirs, they affected to take no interest in it. All the actors clustered round Fauchery, questioning him and fishing for compliments, while Mignon listened to the last of Prullière's complaints, without, however, losing sight of the Comte Muffat, whose return he had been watching for.

Coming back into the semi-darkness, the Count had paused at the back of the stage, hesitating to interrupt the quarrel. But Bordenave caught sight of him and rushed forward.

'What a bunch, eh?' he murmured. 'You can't imagine, Monsieur le Comte, how much trouble they give me. Every one of them's vainer than the next man, and they're shirkers into the bargain, a nasty lot, always mixed up in some shady business or other. Oh, they'd be delighted if I came a cropper. ... I'm sorry – I'm getting carried away.'

He stopped speaking and there was a silence while Muffat

tried to find some means of broaching the object of his errand. But he could not think of a way, and in order to have done with it all, he ended up by saying bluntly :

'Nana wants the part of the Duchess.'

Bordenave gave a start, and exclaimed :

'Oh, come now ! That's mad !'

Then, looking at the Count, he saw how pale and shaken he was, and promptly calmed down.

'Well, I'm damned !' he said simply.

And there followed a fresh silence. At bottom he didn't care. That buxom Nana playing the Duchess might be quite amusing. In any case, once it had happened, he would have Muffat firmly in his grasp. The result was that his decision was soon made. He turned and called out :

'Fauchery !'

The Count had been on the point of stopping him. But Fauchery did not hear. Pinned against the proscenium arch by Fontan, he was being compelled to listen to the actor's interpretation of the part of Tardiveau. Fontan saw Tardiveau as a native of Marseilles with a strong accent, and he gave a demonstration of what he meant. Whole speeches were reeled off with a southern accent. Was it good like that? Did it sound right? He appeared to be merely submitting to the author ideas of which he was himself uncertain. But when Fauchery seemed unenthusiastic and raised objections he lost his temper straight away. All right ! If the spirit of the part escaped him, it would be better for all concerned if he didn't play it at all.

'Fauchery !' Bordenave shouted again.

At that the young man ran off, delighted to escape from the actor, whom he left feeling hurt at such a hasty flight.

'Don't let's stay here,' said Bordenave. 'Come this way, gentlemen.'

To guard against eavesdroppers, he took them into the property room, behind the stage, while Mignon watched their disappearance in some surprise. They went down a few steps into a square room, whose two windows looked out on to the yard. A dingy light filtered in through the dirty panes, and hung wanly under the low ceiling. On shelves which

filled the whole room there was stacked a vast collection of all sorts of objects, which gave the impression of a clearance sale in a second-hand dealer's shop in the Rue de Lappe. It was an indescribable hotch-potch of plates, gilded cardboard goblets, old red umbrellas, Italian pitchers, clocks of all styles, trays and ink-pots, firearms and syringes, all lying chipped and broken, in unrecognizable piles, under a layer of dust an inch deep. An unbearable smell of old iron, rags and damp cardboard emanated from these heaps, in which the debris of forgotten plays had been collecting for half a century.

'Come in,' Bordenave repeated. 'We'll be alone at any rate.'

The Count was extremely embarrassed, and walked away a little distance to let the manager make the proposal for him. Fauchery was surprised.

'What is it?' he asked.

'Just this,' Bordenave said finally. 'An idea has occurred to us. ... Now don't jump when you hear it. It's perfectly serious. ... What do you think of Nana for the part of the Duchess?'

The author was taken aback for a moment. Then he exploded.

'Oh, no! You're joking, aren't you? ... People would laugh too much.'

'Well, what's so bad about people laughing? ... Think it over, my dear fellow. ... The idea appeals greatly to Monsieur le Comte.'

To keep himself in countenance Muffat had just taken off a dusty shelf an object which he did not seem to recognize. It was an egg-cup, the base of which had been mended with plaster. He kept hold of it unconsciously, and came forward murmuring:

'Yes, yes, it would be splendid.'

Fauchery turned towards him with an impatient gesture. The Count had nothing to do with his play, and he said bluntly:

'Never! ... Nana can play the courtesan as much as she likes, but a lady – no, never!'

'You're mistaken, I assure you,' replied the Count, grow-

ing bolder. 'As it happens, she has just been playing the part of a respectable woman for my benefit ...'

'Where?' asked Fauchery, with growing surprise.

'Upstairs in one of the dressing-rooms. ... Well, she was perfect. Such distinction! Above all, she has a way of looking at you as she goes by ... like this ...'

And, egg-cup in hand, he tried to imitate Nana, forgetting himself in his passionate desire to convince the others. Fauchery looked at him in amazement. He understood now, and his anger had abated. The Count became conscious of his gaze, in which mockery was mingled with pity, and stopped, blushing slightly.

'Heavens, it's a possibility,' the author murmured indulgently. 'She might even be quite good. ... The trouble is, the part has already been given. We can't take it away from Rose.'

'Oh, if that's the only obstacle,' said Bordenave, 'I can fix that.'

But then, seeing the other two against him, and realizing that Bordenave had some secret interest at stake, the young man tried to avoid defeat by rejecting the proposal more violently than before, in the hope of breaking off the conversation.

'Oh, no! Definitely not! Even if the part were still free, I'd never give it to her! ... Is that plain? Now leave me alone. ... I've no desire to kill my play!'

There was an awkward silence. Deciding that he was *de trop*, Bordenave walked away. The Count remained with his head bowed. He raised it with an effort, and said in a faltering voice:

'My dear fellow, what if I asked this of you as a favour?'

'I can't, I can't,' Fauchery repeated angrily.

Muffat's voice hardened.

'I beg you. ... I insist!'

And he fixed his eyes on him. The young man read a threat in that scowling gaze, and gave way all of a sudden, stammering incoherently:

'Do what you like. ... I don't care anyhow. ... You'll see ...'

At this the embarrassment of both increased. Fauchery was leaning against a set of shelves, and was nervously tapping the floor with his foot. Muffat seemed to be earnestly examining the egg-cup, which he was turning round and round between his fingers.

'It's an egg-cup,' Bordenave obligingly came and told him.

'Why, yes! It's an egg-cup,' the Count repeated.

'I'm sorry you've got yourself covered with dust,' continued the manager, putting the thing back on a shelf. 'If all this had to be dusted every day, there'd be no end to it, you understand. ... So it isn't very clean here. ... Whát a muddle, eh? But, believe it or not, there's even more for your money. Look here – look at all that.'

He walked Muffat along in front of the shelves, and in the greenish light coming in from the yard, identified the different properties for him, trying to interest him in his junk-shop stock-list, as he jokingly called it. Then, when they found themselves back with Fauchery, he said in a casual voice :

'Listen, since we're all agreed, let's settle the business straight away. ... Here's Mignon, just when he's wanted.'

For a while now Mignon had been prowling up and down the passage, and the moment Bordenave began talking of altering their agreement, he exploded angrily. It was infamous – they were trying to ruin his wife's career – he'd take the matter to court. Meanwhile Bordenave calmly expounded his reasons : he did not consider the part worthy of Rose, and he preferred to save her for an operetta he was going to put on after *The Little Duchess*. But when her husband went on shouting, he abruptly offered to cancel her contract in view of the offers the Folies-Dramatiques had made to the singer. Taken aback for a moment, Mignon did not deny these offers, but loudly professed a lofty disdain for money. His wife had been engaged to play the Duchesse Hélène, and she would play the part even if it cost him, Mignon, his whole fortune; his dignity, his honour, were at stake. Starting on this basis, the discussion grew interminable. The manager kept repeating the following argument : since the Folies were offering Rose three hundred francs a night for a hundred perform-

ances, while she only made a hundred and fifty with him, she would be the richer by fifteen thousand francs if he let her go. The husband, for his part, stuck to his artistic argument. What would people say if they saw his wife deprived of her part? Why, that she was not up to it, and that the theatre had been obliged to find a substitute for her; and this would do considerable harm to Rose's reputation. He could never allow that to happen; fame was more important than money. Then, all of a sudden, he suggested a compromise: Rose, according to her contract, was pledged to pay a forfeit of ten thousand francs if she gave up the part. Well then, let them give her ten thousand francs, and she would go to the Folies-Dramatiques. Bordenave was dumbfounded, while Mignon, who had not taken his eyes off the Count, waited calmly.

'In that case everything's settled,' Muffat murmured in relief. 'We can come to an understanding.'

'No, we can't, dammit all! That would be ridiculous!' cried Bordenave, carried away by his commercial instincts. 'Ten thousand francs to let Rose go! Why everybody would laugh at me!'

But the Count was nodding frantically to him to accept. He hesitated a little longer, and at last, grumbling regretfully over the ten thousand francs, even though they were not going to come out of his own pocket, he went on bluntly:

'All right, I agree. At least I'll have you off my hands.'

For a quarter of an hour Fontan had been listening in the yard. Intrigued by what was going on, he had gone downstairs and stationed himself in a place where he could hear everything. As soon as he had gathered what had been decided, he went back upstairs and treated himself to the pleasure of telling Rose. They had been arguing about her, he said, and she was being chucked out. Rose ran straight to the property-room. The four men fell silent as she came in. She looked at them. Muffat hung his head, while Fauchery answered her inquiring glance with a despairing shrug of the shoulders. As for Mignon, he was busy discussing the terms of the contract with Bordenave.

'What's up?' she asked curtly.

'Nothing,' said her husband. 'Bordenave is giving us ten thousand francs to get you to give up your part.'

She started trembling, looking very pale and clenching her little fists. For a few moments she stared at him, her whole nature in revolt, although usually in matters of business she meekly abdicated all responsibility to her husband, leaving him to sign agreements with her managers and her lovers. But all she did was utter this cry, which struck him like a whiplash:

'You're despicable!'

Then she made off. Mignon, utterly astonished, ran after her. What was the matter with her? Had she gone mad? He explained to her in a whisper that ten thousand francs from one party and fifteen thousand from the other came to twenty-five thousand. That was a wonderful deal! Muffat was dropping her in any case, and it was a pretty trick to have plucked him of this last feather. But Rose was so furious that she made no reply. Thereupon Mignon disdainfully left her to her feminine spite, and turning to Bordenave, who had come back on to the stage with Fauchery and Muffat, said:

'We'll sign tomorrow morning. Have the money with you.'

At that moment, Nana, to whom Labordette had told the news, appeared at the foot of the stairs. She was playing the respectable woman and putting on a distinguished air, to impress her colleagues and show the fools that when she chose to, she could be the smartest of them all. But she nearly spoilt the whole effect, for when Rose caught sight of her she rushed forward, choking with rage, and stammering:

'I'll pay you out for this. . . . The two of us have got to sort things out!'

Nana, forgetting herself in the face of this unexpected attack, was on the point of putting her hands on her hips and bawling her out. But she restrained herself, and drawing back like a marquise about to tread on an orange peel, said in a shriller voice than usual:

'What do you mean? You're mad, my dear!'

And with that she continued putting on airs and graces, while Rose stalked out, followed by Mignon, who could no longer recognize her. Clarisse was overjoyed, having just

obtained the part of Géraldine from Bordenave. Fauchery, on the other hand, was gloomily wandering around, unable to make up his mind to leave the theatre. His play was done for, and he was wondering how to save it. But Nana came up, took him by both wrists, and drawing him towards her, asked whether he really thought she was so very dreadful. She wasn't going to eat his play up, she said, making him laugh, and hinted that he would be foolish to cross her in view of his relationship with the Muffats. If her memory failed her, she would take her lines from the prompter, and there would be a full house every night. What was more, he was wrong about her abilities : she would show him what a good performance she could give. Then it was arranged that the author should make a few changes in the part of the Duchess so as to give more lines to Prullière, who was delighted. Indeed, amid all the joy which Nana instinctively spread about her, Fontan alone remained unmoved. In the middle of the ray of yellow light from the gas-jet, against which his goat-like profile was outlined in sharp relief, he stood affecting a casual pose. Nana went up to him calmly and shook hands with him.

'How are you getting on?'

'Not bad. How about you?'

'Very well, thank you.'

That was all. It was as if they had parted outside the theatre only the day before. Meanwhile the players were waiting for instructions; but Bordenave said that they wouldn't be rehearsing the third act. Turning up on time by accident, old Bosc went off grumbling that they were kept at the theatre for no reason and forced to waste whole afternoons. Everybody left. Out on the pavement they were blinded by the broad daylight, and stood blinking with the dazed expressions of people who had spent three hours with their nerves on edge, squabbling in the depths of a cellar. The Count, empty-headed and aching in every limb, got into a carriage with Nana, while Labordette took Fauchery off to console him.

A month later the first night of *The Little Duchess* was a disaster for Nana. She gave an appalling performance, displaying pretensions to high comedy which aroused the

audience's mirth. They did not hiss, they were so amused. Sitting in a stage-box, Rose Mignon greeted each of her rival's entrances with a shrill peal of laughter which set the whole house off. It was the beginning of her revenge. Accordingly, when Nana found herself alone with a downcast Muffat that night, she said in a fury :

'What a conspiracy, eh ! It's all jealousy, that's what it is. ... Oh, if only they knew how little I cared ! What do I need them for now? ... Listen, I'll bet you a hundred louis that I'll get all those who laughed at me tonight to lick the ground here at my feet ! Oh, yes, I'll teach your Paris what's what !'

THEREUPON Nana became a woman of fashion, a benefi-
ciary of male stupidity and lust, an aristocrat in the ranks of
her calling. Her success was sudden and decisive, a swift rise
to gallant fame, in the garish light of lunatic extravagance
and the wasteful follies of beauty. She at once became queen
among the most expensive of her kind. Her photographs were
displayed in shop-windows, and her remarks were quoted in
the papers. When she drove along the boulevards in her
carriage, people would turn round and tell one another who
she was, with all the emotion of a nation saluting its
sovereign, while she lolled back in her flimsy dresses, smiling
gaily under the rain of little golden curls which fell around
the blue of her made-up eyes and the red of her painted lips.
And the remarkable thing was that that buxom young
woman, who was so awkward on the stage, so comical when
she tried to play the respectable woman, was able to play
the enchantress in town without the slightest effort. She had
the supple grace of a serpent, a studied yet seemingly involuntary carelessness of dress which was exquisitely elegant,
the nervous distinction of a pedigree cat, an aristocratic re-
finement, proudly and rebelliously trampling Paris underfoot
like an all-powerful mistress. She set the fashion, and great
ladies imitated her.

Nana's house was in the Avenue de Villiers, on the corner
of the Rue Cardinet, in the luxurious quarter which was
springing up on the waste ground which had once been
the Monceau plain. Built in the Renaissance style by a
young painter intoxicated by his first success, who had been
forced to sell it as soon as it was ready, it was a palatial building designed on original lines, with modern facilities in a
deliberately eccentric setting. The Comte Muffat had bought
the house ready furnished, full of hosts of knick-knacks,
beautiful eastern hangings, old sideboards and big Louis XIII
chairs, so that Nana had come into a setting of the choicest

furniture from a wide variety of periods. But, as the studio which occupied the centre of the house could not be of any use to her, she had turned the existing arrangements upside down, installing a small drawing-room on the first floor, next to her bedroom and dressing-room, and leaving a conservatory, a large drawing-room and the dining-room on the ground floor. She astonished the architect with her ideas, for, as a Parisian working-girl with an instinctive feeling for elegance, she had developed at one stroke a taste for the refinements of luxury. In the event she did not spoil the house overmuch, and even added to the richness of the furniture, except here and there where traces of sentimental foolishness and vulgar splendour betrayed the former flower-girl who used to dream in front of shop-windows in the arcades.

In the courtyard a carpet was spread on the steps beneath the great awning over the front door, and the moment you entered the hall you were greeted by a smell of violets and a warm atmosphere enclosed in thick hangings. A stained-glass window, whose pink and yellow panes suggested the warm pallor of human flesh, lit the wide staircase, at the foot of which a Negro in carved wood held out a silver tray full of visiting cards, and four white marble women with bare breasts raised lamps in their uplifted hands. Bronzes and Chinese vases full of flowers, divans covered with old Persian rugs, and armchairs upholstered in old tapestry, furnished the entrance-hall, adorned the landings, and gave the first floor the appearance of an ante-room, where men's overcoats and hats were always lying around. Thick hangings deadened every sound, and there was a contemplative atmosphere; anybody coming in might have thought he was entering a chapel full of devout excitement, whose shuttered silence was fraught with mystery.

Nana only opened the large, somewhat too sumptuous Louis Seize drawing-room on gala evenings when she received society from the Tuileries or distinguished foreigners. Usually she only came downstairs at meal-times, feeling rather lost on days when she lunched by herself in the lofty dining-room, with its Gobelin tapestries and its monumental sideboard, adorned with old porcelain and marvellous pieces

of ancient plate. She used to go back upstairs as soon as possible, for she lived on the first floor, in three rooms, her bedroom, her dressing-room and the small drawing-room. Twice already she had redecorated the bedroom, the first time in mauve satin, the second in blue silk under lace; but she was not satisfied, considering the lace appliqué insipid and still looking in vain for something better. On the lavishly upholstered bed, which was as low as a sofa, there were twenty thousand francs' worth of Venetian point lace. The furniture was lacquered blue and white with silver filigree patterns; and everywhere there were scattered so many white bearskins that they completely covered the carpet – a luxurious caprice on Nana's part, for she had never been able to break herself of the habit of sitting on the floor to take off her stockings. Next door to the bedroom the little drawing-room was full of an amusing medley of exquisitely artistic objects. Against the pink silk hangings – a faded Turkish pink, embroidered with gold thread – were outlined a host of knick-knacks from every possible country and of every possible style : Italian cabinets, Spanish and Portuguese coffers, models of Chinese pagodas, a Japanese screen of delicate workmanship, together with china, bronzes, embroidered silks and needlepoint hangings, while armchairs as wide as beds, and sofas as deep as alcoves, suggested voluptuous idleness and the somnolent life of a seraglio. The keynote of the room was again old gold, blended with green and red, and nothing it contained indicated the courtesan too obviously, apart from the luxuriousness of the seats. Only two porcelain statuettes, a woman in her chemise hunting for fleas, and another stark naked, walking on her hands with her legs in the air, sufficed to sully the room with a note of basic stupidity.

Through a door which was nearly always open the dressing-room was visible, all in marble and glass, with a white bath, silver jugs and basins, and crystal and ivory appointments. A drawn curtain admitted a pale white light which seemed to slumber in a warm scent of violets, that disturbing perfume peculiar to Nana which filled the whole house from the attic to the courtyard.

The most difficult thing was getting the house going. Admittedly Nana had Zoé with her, that woman who had always been devoted to her fortunes and who, relying on her flair, had been calmly waiting for this success for months. Now Zoé was triumphant : as mistress of the house, she was making her pile while serving Madame as honestly as possible. But a lady's maid was no longer sufficient by herself : there had to be a butler, a coachman, a porter and a cook. Besides, it was necessary to fit out the stables. It was here that Labordette made himself extremely useful, undertaking all sorts of errands which bored the Count. He arranged the purchase of the horses, visited the coach-builders and guided the choice of the young woman, who was to be seen in the shops, leaning on his arm. Labordette even hired the servants – Charles, a big strapping coachman, who had been in service with the Duc de Corbreuse; Julien, a little smiling butler with curly hair; and a married couple, of whom the wife, Victorine, was a cook, while the husband, François, was taken on as porter and footman. The latter, wearing knee-breeches and a powdered wig, and dressed in Nana's livery – sky-blue with silver lace – received visitors in the hall. Everything was done with princely style and correctness.

By the end of the first month the house was running smoothly. It took over three hundred thousand francs a year to keep up. There were eight horses in the stables, and five carriages in the coach-houses, including a landau with silver appointments which were the talk of Paris for a while. And in the midst of this great wealth Nana began settling down and feathering her nest. After only the third performance of *The Little Duchess* she had abandoned the theatre, leaving Bordenave to struggle on under the threat of bankruptcy which, despite the Count's money, seemed imminent. All the same, she was still bitter about her failure. It added to the bitterness she felt over the lesson Fontan had given her, a shameful betrayal for which she held all men responsible. Accordingly she now claimed to be very strong-minded and proof against all infatuations. But thoughts of vengeance could not linger for long in her bird-brain. What did remain, except in hours of anger, was an ever-wakeful appetite for

spending, together with a natural contempt for the man who paid for her extravagant, wasteful whims and satisfied her pride in ruining her lovers.

To begin with, Nana put the Count on a proper footing, clearly laying down the conditions of their relationship. The Count gave twelve thousand francs a month, not counting presents, and asked for nothing in return save absolute fidelity. She swore fidelity, but insisted on being treated with consideration, on enjoying complete liberty as mistress of the house, and on having her every wish respected. For instance, she would receive her friends every day, while he was to come only at stated times; in short he was to put a blind trust in her in everything. And when he hesitated, seized with jealous anxiety, she stood on her dignity, threatening to return everything he had given her, or else swearing fidelity on little Louis's head. That had to be enough for him. There was no love where mutual esteem was lacking. By the end of the first month Muffat respected her.

But she wanted and obtained more than that. Soon she began to exert a good-natured influence on him. When he arrived in a grumpy mood, she would cheer him up, and after persuading him to tell her his troubles give him some advice. Little by little she took an interest in his domestic troubles, showing great sense, fairness and decency. Only on one occasion did she let anger get the better of her, and that was when he confided to her that Daguenet was probably going to ask for his daughter Estelle's hand in marriage. Since the Count had begun flaunting himself with Nana, Daguenet had thought it best to break with her and treat her like a whore, swearing to snatch his future father-in-law out of that creature's clutches. In return, Nana ran down her old Mimi eloquently. He was a rake who had squandered his fortune in the company of loose women; he had no moral sense, and if he didn't actually take money from other people he enjoyed what it bought, and only occasionally paid for flowers or a dinner himself. And when the Count seemed inclined to find excuses for these failings, she bluntly informed him that Daguenet had had her, and she added some disgusting details. Muffat went white, and after that there

315

was no further mention of the young man. That would teach him to show a lack of gratitude.

Meanwhile, before the house had been completely furnished, one evening after she had lavished the most fervent promises of fidelity on Muffat, Nana kept the Comte Xavier de Vandeuvres back for the night. For the past fortnight he had been paying her assiduous court, calling on her and sending her flowers, and now she gave way, not so much on a sudden impulse as to prove that she was free. The idea of gain came later, when next day Vandeuvres helped her to pay a bill which she did not wish to mention to the other man. From Vandeuvres she could count on between eight and ten thousand francs a month, which would prove very useful as pocket-money. At the time he was spending the last of his fortune in a fit of feverish folly. His horses and Lucy had eaten up three of his farms, and at one gulp Nana was going to swallow the last château, near Amiens. He seemed to be in a hurry to sweep everything away, down to the ruins of the old tower built by a Vandeuvres under Philip Augustus, maddened by a longing for ruin, and thinking it a great thing to leave the last golden bezants of his coat-of-arms in the clutches of this courtesan whom all Paris desired. He too accepted Nana's conditions, leaving her complete freedom of action in return for caresses on certain days, without even being sufficiently naïve in his passion to demand vows on her part. Muffat undoubtedly knew nothing. As for Vandeuvres, he knew what was happening, but he never made the slightest reference to it, and affected complete ignorance, smiling the subtle smile of the sceptical man of pleasure, who does not ask for the impossible provided he can have his hour and that Paris knows about it.

From then on, Nana's house was really fully appointed. The staff was complete in the stable, in the kitchen and in Madame's bedroom. Zoé organized everything, overcoming the most unexpected difficulties. The household ran like clockwork, organized like a big business concern, and working so well that during the first few months there were no hitches or breakdowns. Madame, however, gave Zoé a lot of trouble with her imprudent acts, her headstrong follies and

her fits of bravado. As a result the maid gradually became less watchful, having also noticed that she made more profit in times of trouble, when Madame had committed some folly which had to be covered up. At times like that presents rained upon her, and she fished a good many louis out of the troubled waters.

One morning, before Muffat had left the bedroom, Zoé ushered a gentleman who was trembling with emotion into the dressing-room, where Nana was changing her underwear.

'Why it's Zizi!' the young woman exclaimed in astonishment.

It was indeed Georges. Seeing her in her chemise, with her golden hair over her bare shoulders, he threw his arms around her neck, seized hold of her, and kissed her all over. She struggled to get free, frightened of being surprised, and stammering in a low voice:

'Stop it! He's here! Oh, you're such a silly. . . . And you, Zoé, are you out of your senses? Take him away, and keep him downstairs. I'll try and come down soon.'

Zoé had to push him in front of her. When Nana was able to rejoin them in the drawing-room downstairs, she gave both of them a scolding. Zoé pursed her lips and left the room with a vexed expression on her face, remarking that she had thought Madame would be pleased. Georges gazed at Nana with such obvious delight at seeing her again that his beautiful eyes began filling with tears. The bad days were over now; his mother thought that he had turned over a new leaf and had allowed him to leave Les Fondettes. But he had no sooner got off the train in Paris than he had taken a cab to come and kiss his sweet darling as soon as possible. He spoke of living at her side in future, as he had done in the country, when he had waited for her barefoot in the bedroom at La Mignotte. And as he told her about himself he stretched out his fingers, impatient to touch her after this cruel year of separation; he seized hold of her hands, felt about in the wide sleeves of her dressing-gown, travelled up as far as her shoulders.

'Do you still love your baby?' he asked in his childish voice.

'Of course I love him!' answered Nana, jerking away from

him. 'But you've come here without warning. . . . You know, my pet, I'm not my own mistress. You've got to be good.'

Getting out of his cab with the dazzling certainty that his desire was at last about to be satisfied, Georges had not even noticed what sort of house he was entering. But now he became conscious of his surroundings. He examined the sumptuous dining-room, with its lofty decorated ceiling, its Gobelin tapestries, its dresser ablaze with plate.

'Ah, yes,' he said sadly.

And she gave him to understand that he must never come in the morning, but only between four and six in the afternoon, if he cared to, because that was when she was at home to visitors. Then, as he looked at her with suppliant questioning eyes, without asking for anything, she, in her turn, kissed him on the forehead and spoke to him more kindly.

'Be good,' she murmured, 'and I'll do all I can.'

But the truth was that it meant nothing to her any more. She thought Georges very nice, and would have liked him as a companion, but nothing else. All the same, when he arrived every day at four o'clock he seemed so unhappy that she often gave way as in the old days, hiding him in cupboards and continually allowing him to pick up the crumbs of her beauty. He hardly ever left the house now, becoming as much one of its inmates as the little dog Bijou. Both of them were always nestling among their mistress's skirts, enjoying a little of her even when she was with another man, and collecting windfalls in the way of sugar and caresses in her hours of loneliness and boredom.

No doubt Madame Hugon found out that the boy had returned to that evil woman's arms, for she hurried to Paris to ask the help of her other son, Lieutenant Philippe, who was quartered at the time at Vincennes. Georges, who had been keeping out of the way of his elder brother, was filled with despair, for he was afraid that the latter might adopt violent methods, and as in his excitable passion for Nana he could not keep anything from her, he soon began talking of nothing else but his big brother, a strapping fellow who would stop at nothing.

'You see,' he explained, 'Mama won't come here as long as

she can send my brother. ... Oh, yes, she's sure to send Philippe to fetch me.'

The first time he said this Nana was deeply offended. She said curtly :

'I'd like to see him try ! He may be a lieutenant in the army, but François will chuck him out double quick !'

But then, as the boy kept returning to the subject of his brother, she ended up by taking a certain interest in Philippe. By the end of a week she knew him from head to foot, as a very tall, very strong fellow who was merry by nature but a little rough. She learnt intimate details about him too – that he had hair on his arms and a mole on his shoulder. The result was that one day, when she was full of a mental picture of the man she was supposed to throw out of her house, she exclaimed :

'I say, Zizi, there's still no sign of your brother. ... He's a deserter !'

The next day, when Georges and Nana were alone together, François came upstairs to ask whether Madame would receive Lieutenant Philippe Hugon. Georges went white and murmured :

'I thought this would happen : Mama warned me this morning.'

And he begged the young woman to send word that she could not receive his brother. But she was already on her feet, flushed with excitement, and she replied :

'Why shouldn't I see him? He'd think I was afraid. No, we're going to have a good laugh. ... François, leave the gentleman in the drawing-room for a quarter of an hour, and then bring him up to me.'

She did not sit down again, but began pacing feverishly up and down between the fireplace and a Venetian mirror hanging above an Italian chest. And each time she came to the mirror she glanced at her reflection and tried the effect of a smile, while Georges sat nervously on a sofa, trembling at the idea of the coming scene. As she walked up and down Nana kept coming out with brief staccato phrases :

'It'll calm the fellow down to wait a quarter of an hour. ... Besides, if he thinks he's come to see a tart, the drawing-

room will give him a shock. .... That's right, have a good look, laddie. There's nothing fake there. That'll teach you to respect the lady of the house. Because respect is all that matters to a man. .... Is the quarter of an hour up yet? No, barely ten minutes. Oh, we've got plenty of time.'

She could not stay in one place though. At the end of the quarter of an hour she sent Georges out of the room, after making him swear not to listen at the door, as that would look bad if the servants saw him. As he was going into the bedroom, Zizi ventured to say in a choking voice :

'He *is* my brother, you know ...'

'Have no fear,' she said with considerable dignity. 'If he's polite, I'll be polite.'

François showed in Philippe Hugon, who was in a frock-coat. At first Georges tiptoed to the far side of the bedroom, in obedience to the young woman's request. But the sound of voices stopped him, and he hesitated, in such anguish that his knees gave way under him. He began imagining some catastrophe, an exchange of blows, something terrible which would force him to break with Nana for good. The result was that he could not resist the temptation to come back and put his ear to the door. He could not hear at all well, for the thick door-curtains muffled every sound; but he managed to catch a few words spoken by Philippe, stern phrases in which the words 'children', 'family' and 'honour' were distinctly audible. He was so anxious about the answer his precious darling was going to make that his heart was pounding wildly, filling his head with a confused buzzing. She was sure to give vent to a 'dirty bastard' or a 'fuck off; this is my house'. But nothing happened, not so much as a whisper : it was as if Nana were dead in there ! Soon even his brother's voice grew softer, and he was puzzling over what was happening when a strange murmuring sound completed his stupefaction. Nana was sobbing ! For a moment he was torn between contending feelings, unable to decide whether to run away or to fall upon Philippe. But just then Zoé came into the bedroom, and he moved away from the door, ashamed at being caught out.

She began quietly putting away some linen in a wardrobe

320

while he stood mute and motionless, pressing his forehead against a windowpane, and eaten up with anxiety. After a short silence she asked:

'Is that your brother in there with Madame?'

'Yes,' the boy replied in a choking voice.

There was a fresh silence.

'And that's got you worried, has it, Monsieur Georges?'

'Yes,' he repeated in the same anguished tone.

Zoé was in no hurry. She folded up some lace and then said slowly:

'There's no need to worry.... Madame will fix it.'

And that was all: neither of them said another word. But she did not leave the room. For a good quarter of an hour she pottered around without seeming to notice the boy's exasperation, or the fact that his face was white with doubt and constraint. He kept casting sidelong glances in the direction of the drawing-room. What could they be doing in there that was taking so long? Maybe Nana was still crying. His brother, brute that he was, must have slapped her face. As a result, when Zoé finally left the room, he ran to the door, and once more pressed his ear against it. And he was amazed, utterly dumbfounded, to hear a sudden burst of laughter, tender whispering voices, and the stifled giggles of a woman who is being tickled. Then, almost immediately afterwards, Nana accompanied Philippe to the head of the stairs, and there was an exchange of cordial familiarities.

When Georges ventured to go into the drawing-room, the young woman was standing in front of the mirror, looking at herself.

'Well?' he asked in utter bewilderment.

'Well, what?' she said, without turning round. Then she added casually:

'What was all that nonsense you told me? Your brother's very nice!'

'So it's all right, is it?'

'Of course it's all right.... What's the matter with you? Anybody would think we were going to have a fight.'

Georges still failed to understand. He stammered:

'I thought I heard ... Weren't you crying?'

'Me crying!' she exclaimed, looking him in the eyes.
'You're dreaming! What makes you think I was crying?'

To his chagrin the boy was promptly given a scolding for
having disobeyed her and eavesdropped behind the door. She
refused to listen to him, but he returned to the subject, determined to find out what had happened.

'So my brother ...?'

'Your brother saw where he was straight away. ... You
see, I might have been a tart, in which case his intervention
would have been understandable, on account of your age
and the family honour. Oh, I understand that sort of feeling.
... But a single glance was enough for him, and he behaved
like a perfect gentleman. ... So don't worry any more.
It's all over, and he's going to set your mama's mind at
rest.'

And she added with a laugh :

'For that matter, you'll see your brother here. ... I've
invited him, and he's going to come back.'

'Oh, so he's going to come back,' said the boy, turning
white. He said no more, and there was no further mention
of Philippe. She began dressing to go out, and he watched her
with his big sad eyes. No doubt he was very glad that everything had been settled, for he would have preferred death to
a break with Nana, but deep in his heart there was a silent
anguish, a profound distress, which he had never felt before
and dared not talk about. He never found out how Philippe
reassured their mother, but three days later she returned to
Les Fondettes, apparently satisfied. That very evening, at
Nana's house, Georges gave a start when François announced the lieutenant, but the latter chaffed him merrily,
treating him like a young rascal whom he had helped out
of an unimportant scrape. The boy sat heavy-hearted, not
daring to move, and blushed girlishly at the least word that
was spoken to him. He had not spent much time in Philippe's
company, being ten years his junior; and he feared him as he
would a father, from whom love affairs had to be kept secret.
Accordingly he felt an uneasy sense of shame when he saw
him behaving so familiarly with Nana, and heard him
laughing uproariously like the healthy, pleasure-loving male

322

he was. However, as his brother soon took to calling every day, Georges ended up by getting used to it. Nana was radiant. This was the last appointment to her extravagant courtesan's household, an insolent housewarming in a mansion already overflowing with men and furniture.

One afternoon when the Hugon brothers were there, the Comte Muffat arrived outside his regular hours. On being told by Zoé that Madame was with some friends, he refused to go in and took his leave, making a great show of gentlemanly discretion. When he returned in the evening, Nana received him with the icy indignation of a woman who had been grossly offended.

'Monsieur,' she said, 'I have given you no cause to insult me. ... Let me make this clear : when I am at home to callers I expect you to come in just like other people.'

The Count gaped in astonishment.

'But, my dear ...' he tried to explain.

'Perhaps it was because I had visitors?' Yes, there were some men here, but what do you suppose I was doing with them? ... You give a woman a bad name when you play the discreet lover, and I don't want a bad name, thank you!'

He obtained his pardon with difficulty, but at bottom he was delighted. It was with scenes like this that she kept him in meek, unquestioning submission. She had long since succeeded in imposing Georges on him as a youngster who, she said, amused her. She made him dine with Philippe, and the Count behaved with great amiability; when they left the table, he took the young man on one side and asked after his mother. From then on, the Hugon brothers, Vandeuvres and Muffat were openly accepted as members of the household, and shook hands like close friends when they met. This was more convenient than the previous state of affairs. Muffat alone took care not to call too often, maintaining the ceremonious pretence of being an ordinary visitor. At night, while Nana sat on her bearskins taking off her stockings, he would talk amicably about the other gentlemen, especially Philippe, who was loyalty itself.

'Yes, it's true they're a nice lot,' Nana would say, remain-

ing on the floor to change her chemise. 'But you see, they know what I'm like. ... One word out of place, and I'd chuck them all out for you!'

However, in the midst of all this luxury, and surrounded by her courtiers, Nana was bored to tears. She had men for every minute of the night, and money all over the house, even among the brushes and combs in the drawers of her dressing-table. But all this had ceased to satisfy her; and she was conscious of a void in her existence, a gap which made her yawn. Her life dragged on devoid of occupation, each day bringing back the same monotonous hours. The next day did not exist : she lived like a bird, sure of having enough to eat, and ready to perch on the first branch she came to. This certainty of being fed left her to stretch out in languid ease all day, lulled to sleep in conventual idleness and submission as if she were the prisoner of her profession. Never going out except in her carriage, she began to lose the use of her legs. She reverted to her childish habits, kissing Bijou from morning to night and killing time with stupid pleasures, as she waited for some man or other whose caresses she would tolerate with weary indulgence. And in the midst of this self-abandonment she no longer thought of anything but her beauty, forever inspecting her body, and washing and scenting herself all over, in the proud knowledge that she could strip naked at any moment and in front of anyone without having any cause to blush.

Nana used to get up at ten in the morning. Bijou, the Scottish griffon dog, would wake her by licking her face; there would follow five minutes' play, with the dog running about over her arms and thighs, causing the Comte Muffat great distress. Bijou was the first male to arouse his jealousy. It wasn't decent, he thought, for an animal to go poking its nose under the bedclothes like that. Then Nana would go into her dressing-room and take a bath. About eleven o'clock Francis would come and put up her hair, pending the more elaborate hairdressing operation of the afternoon. At lunch, as she hated eating alone, she nearly always had Madame Maloir at table with her. The latter would arrive out of nowhere in the morning, wearing one of her eccentric hats,

and would return at night to that mysterious existence of hers in which, as it happened, nobody ever took any interest. But the hardest to bear were the two or three hours between lunch and dressing for the evening. Usually she challenged her old friend to a game of bezique; sometimes she would read the *Figaro*, in which the theatrical gossip and the society news interested her; and occasionally she even opened a book, for she fancied herself as a connoisseur of literature. Getting ready for the evening would occupy her till close on five o'clock, and only then would she awake from her lengthy doze, going for a drive or receiving a whole crowd of men at home, often dining out and always going to bed very late, only to get up the next morning as weary as before, and begin another day just like its predecessor.

Her great distraction was to go to Les Batignolles to see her little Louis at her aunt's. For a fortnight at a time she forgot all about him, but then she would be seized with a fit of maternal love and would hurry round on foot with all the modesty and tenderness of a good mother, bearing the sort of gifts one takes to patients in hospital – snuff for her aunt and oranges and biscuits for the child. Or else she would drive up in her landau on her way back from the Bois, dressed with a luxury which caused a sensation in the quiet street. Since her niece's rise in the world, Madame Lerat had been puffed up with vanity. She rarely went round to the Avenue de Villiers, saying that it wasn't her place to do so; but she triumphed over her own street, exultant when the young woman called in a dress worth four or five thousand francs, and spending the whole of the next day showing off her presents and quoting figures which astounded the neighbours. As often as not, Nana kept Sundays free for her family; and if Muffat invited her out on one of those days she would refuse with the smile of a good little housewife. Impossible, she would answer : she was dining at her aunt's; she was going to see baby. Besides, the poor little fellow was always ill. He was almost three years old, and quite a big boy. But he had an eczema on the back of his neck, and now matter was forming in his ears, which suggested that his skull was decaying. When she saw how pale he looked, with his bad blood and his flabby flesh

dotted with yellow patches, she would turn serious, but her chief feeling was one of astonishment. What could be the matter with the poor darling to grow so weakly, when his mother was so strong and healthy?

On the days when her child did not occupy her attention, Nana would sink back into the noisy monotony of her existence, with drives in the Bois, first nights at the theatre, dinners and suppers at the Maison-d'Or or the Café Anglais, not to mention visits to all the places and sights that drew the crowds – Mabille, the reviews, the races. But in spite of everything she still felt that stupid, idle void in her existence which gave her, so to speak, stomach cramps. And despite the ever-changing fancies that possessed her heart, she would stretch out her arms in a gesture of immense weariness the moment she was left alone. Solitude saddened her straight away, for it brought her face to face with the emptiness and boredom within her. Extremely gay by nature and profession, she became miserable once she was alone, and would sum up her life in the following complaint, which recurred incessantly between her yawns :

'Oh, what a bore men are !'

One afternoon, as she was returning home from a concert, Nana noticed a woman trotting along the pavement of the Rue Montmartre in down-at-heel boots, dirty skirts and a hat which had been ruined by the rain. All of a sudden she recognized her.

'Stop, Charles !' she shouted to the coachman.

And she called out : 'Satin, Satin !'

The passers-by turned their heads, and the whole street stared. Satin had come up, and was dirtying her clothes even more against the carriage wheels.

'Get in, girl,' Nana said calmly, ignoring the onlookers.

And with that she picked her up and carried her off, a disgusting sight in her light-blue landau, next to her dress of pearl-grey silk, trimmed with Chantilly : while the street smiled at the coachman's dignified demeanour.

From then on Nana had a passion to occupy her attention. Satin became her vice. Washed and dressed, and installed in the house in the Avenue de Villiers, she spent three days

326

talking about Saint-Lazare and the trouble the sisters had given her and the filthy police who had registered her as a prostitute. Nana expressed indignation, comforting her and promising to get her name taken off the official list, even if she had to go and see the Minister herself. Meanwhile there was no hurry : nobody would come looking for her at Nana's – that was certain. And the two women began to spend tender afternoons together, murmuring endearments to each other and mingling their kisses with laughter. The same little game which the arrival of the police had interrupted in the Rue de Laval was now resumed in a light-hearted spirit. One fine evening, however, it took a serious turn, and Nana, who had been so disgusted at Laure's, now understood. She was overwhelmed and excited by this new experience, the more so when on the morning of the fourth day Satin disappeared. Nobody had seen her go out. She had simply slipped out in her new dress, seized by a longing for a change of air, a nostalgic regret for her street-walker's beat.

That day there was such a terrible storm in the house that all the servants hung their heads in silence. Nana had come close to beating François for having failed to bar Satin's way. She did her best, however, to control herself, calling Satin a dirty little whore, and saying that this would teach her to pick filth like that out of the gutter. That afternoon, when Madame shut herself up in her room, Zoé heard her sobbing. In the evening she suddenly asked for her carriage and had herself driven to Laure's. It had occurred to her that she would probably find Satin at the *table d'hôte* in the Rue des Martyrs. She was not going there to see her again, but simply to slap her across the face. Sure enough, Satin was dining at a little table with Madame Robert. Catching sight of Nana, she started laughing; but Nana, though wounded to the quick, did not make a scene. On the contrary, she was very sweet and amiable. She ordered champagne, made five or six tablefuls tipsy, and then carried off Satin while Madame Robert was in the toilets. Not until they were in the carriage did she turn on her, biting her and threatening to kill her if she ran off again.

After that the same thing happened again and again. A

score of times Nana, a tragic figure filled with all the fury of a jilted woman, went off in pursuit of that slut, who kept running away on an impulse, bored by the comforts of the big house. Nana began talking of boxing Madame Robert's ears; one day she even thought of challenging her to a duel; there was one too many of them, she said. Now, whenever she dined at Laure's, she put on her diamonds, and occasionally took along with her Louise Violaine, Maria Blond and Tatan Néné, all of them ablaze with jewels. In the three grease-spattered dining-rooms, in the yellow glare of the gaslight, these four ladies would flaunt their luxury, delighting in the pleasure of dazzling the little whores of the district, whom they carried off when the meal was over. On those days Laure, as sleek and tight-laced as ever, would kiss everyone with an even more motherly air than usual. Yet in the midst of all these squabbles, Satin's blue eyes and pure virginal face remained perfectly calm; bitten, beaten and torn between the two women, she would simply remark that it was a funny business, and they would have done better to patch up their quarrel. It didn't do any good slapping her; she couldn't cut herself in two, however much she wanted to be nice to everybody. In the end it was Nana who won the day, she loaded Satin with so many favours and presents; and in revenge Madame Robert wrote some abominable anonymous letters to her rival's lovers.

For some time the Comte Muffat had seemed to have something on his mind. One morning, looking deeply moved, he laid before Nana an anonymous letter in which, in the first sentence, she read that she was accused of deceiving the Count with Vandeuvres and the Hugon brothers.

'It's a lie! It's a lie!' she cried in accents of extraordinary sincerity.

'You swear that?' asked Muffat, already greatly relieved.

'I'll swear it on anything you like. ... On ... the head of my child!'

But it was a long letter. Subsequently her relations with Satin were described in the crudest and lowest terms. When she had finished reading, she smiled.

'Now I know who it comes from,' she remarked simply.

And when Muffat demanded a denial of the allegations about Satin, she calmly replied :

'That's something which doesn't concern you, my pet. ....
What can it matter to you?'

She did not deny anything and he expressed horror and revulsion. At that she shrugged her shoulders. Where had he been all his life? Why, it was done everywhere! And she named her woman friends, and swore that society women did it too. In fact, to hear her speak, nothing could be commoner. What wasn't true wasn't true : he had just seen her explode with indignation over the accusation about Vandeuvres and the Hugon brothers. Oh, if there had been any truth in *that* story, he would have been justified in throttling her! But what was the good of lying to him about a matter of no consequence? And she repeated her previous question :

'Come now, what can it matter to you?'

Then as the scene dragged on, she cut him short in a peremptory tone of voice.

'Besides, my dear, if you don't like it, there's a very simple solution. .... The door's over there. .... Come now, you've got to take me as you find me !'

He bowed his head, for at bottom the young woman's protestations of fidelity had made him happy. And seeing the power she had over him, she gave up trying to spare his feelings. From then on, Satin was openly installed in the house, on the same footing as the gentlemen. Vandeuvres had not needed any anonymous letters to understand how matters stood; he teased Satin and tried to pick jealous quarrels with her, while Philippe and Georges treated her like an old friend, shaking hands with her and cracking dirty jokes.

Nana had had an adventure one evening when this slut of a girl had run out on her, and she had gone to dine in the Rue des Martyrs without being able to catch her. While she was eating by herself, Daguenet had appeared on the scene, for although he had turned over a new leaf, he occasionally dropped in, under the influence of his old vicious tendencies, hoping that nobody would meet him in this sinister haunt of the scum of Paris. Accordingly Nana's presence seemed to embarrass him at first. But he was not the man to run away,

and coming forward with a smile, he asked if Madame would be kind enough to allow him to dine at her table. Seeing that he was in a jocular mood, Nana assumed her magnificently frigid air and replied curtly:

'Sit down where you please, Monsieur. We are in a public place.'

Opening on this note, the conversation was anything but amusing. But over dessert, bored and impatient to show her power, Nana put her elbows on the table and asked him:

'Well, what about your marriage? Is it getting on all right?'

'Not really,' Daguenet admitted.

As a matter of fact, just when he had been about to venture his request at the Muffats', he had met with such a cold reception from the Count that he had prudently refrained. The whole thing struck him as a failure. Nana gazed at him with her bright eyes, her chin resting on one hand and her lip curling sarcastically.

'Oh, I'm a minx, I am,' she said in a drawl. 'Because anybody who wants the daughter will have to get the future father-in-law out of my clutches. ... You know, for a clever fellow you're pretty stupid. Fancy telling tales to a man who adores me and tells me everything! ... Listen – you'll get married if I want you to, laddie, and not otherwise.'

For the last few minutes he had become aware that this was the case, and he had already begun planning to make his submission. However, he went on joking, not wanting to let the matter take a serious turn, and after putting on his gloves, he asked with strict formality for the hand of Mademoiselle Estelle de Beuville. Nana ended up laughing as if she were being tickled. Oh, that Mimi! You couldn't hold a grudge against him. Daguenet's success with the ladies was due to the sweetness of his voice, a voice of such purity and musical fluidity as to have earned him the nickname 'Velvet-Mouth' from the courtesans. None of them could resist him when he enveloped them in that sonorous caress. He knew the power of his voice, and he lulled Nana to sleep with an endless flow of words, a long succession of pointless stories. When they left the *table d'hôte* she was hanging on

his arm, flushed and trembling; he had reconquered her. As it was very fine, she sent her carriage away, and walked with him as far as his own place, where she went upstairs with him without a word. Two hours later, as she was getting dressed again, she said:

'So you're still set on this marriage of yours, Mimi?'

'Dammit,' he murmured, 'it's the best thing I could do for myself. . . . I'm completely broke, you know.'

She called him to her to button her boots, and after a pause went on:

'Heavens, I've no objection. . . . I'll put in a word for you. . . . She's a dry stick, that girl, but seeing that that's what you all want. . . . I'm a kind-hearted soul; I'll fix it up for you.'

Then, her breasts still uncovered, she began laughing.

'Only, what will you give me in return?'

He caught her in his arms and started kissing her shoulders in a burst of gratitude, while she struggled playfully, leaning backwards and quivering with excitement.

'Oh, I know!' she cried, titillated by this game. 'Listen to what I want as a commission. . . . On your wedding day you'll make me a present of your innocence. . . . Before your wife, you understand!'

'That's it! That's it!' he said, laughing even louder than Nana.

This bargain amused them hugely. They thought it was a wonderful joke.

As it happened, there was a dinner-party at Nana's next day, the usual Thursday dinner-party with Muffat, Vandeuvres, the Hugon brothers and Satin. The Count arrived early. He needed eighty thousand francs to pay two or three of the young woman's debts, and to buy her a set of sapphires she was dying to possess. As he had already eaten deep into his capital, he was looking for somebody to lend him the money, for as yet he did not dare to sell one of his estates. On the advice of Nana herself he had approached Labordette, but the latter, considering it too big an undertaking for himself, had mentioned it to the hairdresser Francis, who was in the habit of arranging such matters to oblige his lady clients. By insisting on keeping his name out

331

of the affair, the Count put himself entirely in the hands of these two gentlemen, who both undertook to keep in hand the bill for a hundred thousand francs which he was to sign, apologizing at the same time for the interest charge of twenty thousand francs, and loudly denouncing the swindling usurers to whom, they said, they had been forced to apply. When Muffat was shown in, Francis was putting the last touches to Nana's coiffure, and Labordette was also in the dressing-room, behaving with the easy familiarity of a friend of no consequence. Seeing the Count, he discreetly placed a thick bundle of bank-notes among the powders and pomades, and the bill was signed on the marble-topped dressing-table. Nana pressed Labordette to stay to dinner, but he declined; he was showing a rich foreigner around Paris. However, when Muffat took him aside and begged him to go to Becker's, the jeweller's, and bring him back the set of sapphires, which he wanted to give the young woman as a surprise that very evening, Labordette gladly undertook the errand. Half an hour later Julien handed the jewel-case surreptitiously to the Count.

During dinner Nana was nervous. The sight of the eighty thousand francs had excited her. To think that all that money was going to go to tradespeople! The idea revolted her. As soon as the soup had been served, in that splendid dining-room, glittering with plate and crystal, she turned sentimental and waxed eloquent over the joys of poverty. The men were in evening dress; she herself wore a gown of white embroidered satin, while Satin was more simply dressed in black silk, with just a gold heart, a present from her friend, hanging round her neck. Julien and François were there waiting on the guests, assisted by Zoé, all three looking most dignified.

'I must say I had a lot more fun when I hadn't a sou,' said Nana.

She had placed Muffat on her right and Vandeuvres on her left, but she scarcely looked at them, she was so taken up with Satin, who sat in state between Philippe and Georges on the other side of the table.

'Isn't that right, love?' she kept saying at every turn. 'How

we used to laugh in those days, when we went to Ma Josse's school in the Rue Polonceau !'

While the roast was being served the two women plunged into an orgy of reminiscences. They used to have frequent fits of chattering of this kind when a sudden urge to stir up the mud of their childhood would take hold of them; and these fits always occurred when men were present, as if they were giving way to a burning desire to smear them with the dung on which they had grown to womanhood. The gentlemen turned pale visibly and exchanged embarrassed looks. The Hugon brothers tried to laugh, while Vandeuvres toyed nervously with his beard, and Muffat looked more serious than ever.

'You remember Victor?' said Nana. 'Now *he* was a dirty little devil and no mistake, taking little girls into cellars !'

'I remember him all right,' replied Satin. 'And the big yard at the building where you lived. There was a concierge, with a broom ...'

'Ma Boche; she's dead.'

'And I can picture your shop, too. . . . Your mum was a great fat thing. One night when we were playing, your dad came in stoned. God, was he stoned !'

At this point Vandeuvres broke into the ladies' reminiscences in an attempt to create a diversion.

'I say, my dear, I'd love to have more truffles. . . . They're delicious. I had some yesterday at the Duc de Corbreuse's, and they weren't anything like as good.'

'The truffles, Julien !' snapped Nana.

Then, returning to the subject, she went on :

'Yes, Dad was a great one for the drink. . . . And what a cropper he came ! You should have seen it ! And we went down with him. . . . Oh, I can tell you I had a hell of a time, and it's a miracle it didn't kill me like Mum and Dad.'

This time Muffat, who was toying irritably with a knife, made so bold as to intervene.

'What you're telling us isn't very cheerful.'

'What's that? Not very cheerful?' she cried, giving him a withering glance. 'I'll say it isn't cheerful ! . . . You ought to have been there to feed us, dear. . . . Oh, I'm the straight-

333

forward sort, I am; I call a spade a spade. Mum was a washerwoman and Dad died of drink. There! And if that doesn't suit you, if you're ashamed of my family ...'

They all protested. What on earth was she talking about? They had the greatest respect for her family. But she went on:

'If you're ashamed of my family, then get out of my house, because I'm not one of those women who deny their father and mother. ... You must take me and them together, you understand?'

They took her as requested; they accepted Mum, Dad, the past, anything she liked. Their eyes fixed on the table, the four men now sat in humble silence, while Nana, carried away by a feeling of omnipotence, trampled on them with the old muddy shoes she had worn years before in the Rue de la Goutte-d'Or. She went on and on: it was no use their bringing her fortunes or building her palaces, she would always look back nostalgically to the time when she used to munch apples in the street. Money was all a lot of rot, invented to keep the tradesmen happy. Finally her outburst petered out in the expression of a sentimental desire for a simple, open-hearted existence, spent in an atmosphere of universal kindness.

When she got to this point she noticed Julien waiting with his arms hanging limply by his sides.

'Well, what's the matter with you?' she said. 'Serve the champagne. Why are you standing there staring at me like a goose?'

During this scene the servants had never once smiled. They appeared to hear nothing, and the more their mistress let herself go, the more dignified they became. Without batting an eyelid, Julien started pouring out the champagne. Unfortunately François, who was handing round the fruit, tilted the fruit-dish too far, and the apples, pears and grapes rolled onto the table.

'You clumsy fool!' shouted Nana.

The footman made the mistake of trying to explain that the fruit was not firmly piled up. Zoé had disarranged it by taking out some oranges.

334

'Then it's Zoé who's the goose!' said Nana.

'But, Madame ...' murmured the maid in an injured tone of voice.

At this Madame rose to her feet, and in a sharp voice, with a gesture of queenly authority, said:

'That's enough of that! ... Leave the room, all of you! ... We don't need you any more.'

This summary action calmed her down, and she immediately became all sweetness and amiability. Dessert proved delightful, and the gentlemen found amusement in helping themselves. But Satin, having peeled a pear, came and ate it behind her darling, pressing against her shoulders and whispering remarks in her ear at which they roared with laughter. Then she decided to share her last piece of pear with Nana, and presented it to her between her teeth; the two women nibbled at each other's lips, finishing the pear in a kiss. At this there was a comic protest from the gentlemen, Philippe shouting to them to take no notice of anybody else, and Vandeuvres asking whether they were expected to leave the room. Georges, meanwhile, had come and put his arm around Satin's waist, and had led her back to her seat.

'You're a silly lot!' said Nana. 'You're making her blush, the poor darling. ... Never mind, sweetie, let them laugh, it's got nothing to do with them.'

And turning to Muffat, who was watching them with a serious expression, she added:

'Don't you agree, my dear?'

'Yes, of course,' he murmured with a slow nod of approval.

There were no more protests. In the midst of these fine gentlemen with their great names and their ancient traditions of respectability, the two women sat face to face, exchanging tender glances, triumphant and supreme in the tranquil abuse of their sex, and their open contempt for the male. And the gentlemen applauded them.

The company went upstairs to take coffee in the little drawing-room, where a couple of lamps shed a soft glow over the pink hangings and the lacquer and old gold of the knick-knacks. At that hour of the evening the light played discreetly over coffers, bronzes and china, lighting up silver and

335

ivory inlaid work, picking out the shining contours of a carved stick, and covering a panel with the shimmering gleams of watered silk. The fire, which had been burning since the afternoon, was dying out in glowing embers. It was very warm, and the air between the curtains and the door-hangings was hot and languid. The room was full of Nana's intimate life : a pair of her gloves, a fallen handkerchief, an open book lay scattered about, evoking an impression of their owner *en déshabillé*, in the midst of her scent of violets and that happy-go-lucky untidiness which created such a charming effect in these rich surroundings. As for the arm-chairs, which were as wide as beds, and the sofas, which were as deep as alcoves, they invited the visitor to slumbers oblivious of the flight of time, and to gay, affectionate, whis-pered conversations in shadowy corners.

Satin lit a cigarette and went and stretched out in the depths of a sofa near the fireplace. Vandeuvres began amus-ing himself by pretending to be ferociously jealous, threaten-ing to send her his seconds if she went on seducing Nana from her duty. Philippe and Georges joined in, teasing her and pestering her so mercilessly that she ended up by shout-ing :

'Darling! Darling! Please make them behave! They're still after me.'

'Now, then, leave her alone!' said Nana seriously. 'I won't have her annoyed, you know that perfectly well. . . . As for you, my pet, why do you always go and sit with them when they behave so badly?'

Satin, blushing scarlet and putting her tongue out, went into the dressing-room, whose wide-open door revealed a glimpse of pale marble surfaces gleaming in the milky light of a gas-jet in a globe of frosted glass. After that, Nana chatted with the four men like a charming hostess. During the day she had read a novel which was causing a sensation at the time. It was the story of a prostitute, and Nana in-veighed against it, declaring that it was all untrue, and ex-pressing an indignant revulsion against the sort of filthy literature which claimed to show life as it was – as if a writer could possibly describe everything, and as if novels weren't

supposed to be written just to while away the time! On the subject of books and plays Nana had very decided opinions: she liked tender, high-minded works which would set her dreaming and uplift her soul. Then, as the conversation turned to the troubles agitating Paris, the inflammatory articles in the papers, the incipient riots which followed the calls to arms issued nightly at public meetings, she launched into a wordy attack on the Republicans. What did they want, those dirty people who never washed from one year's end to the other? Wasn't everybody happy? Hadn't the Emperor done everything he could for the common people? A nice lot *they* were, and no mistake! She knew them and she could talk about them. And, forgetting the respect which she had just been insisting over dinner should be paid to her humble world of the Rue de la Goutte-d'Or, she began railing against her own class with all the fear and disgust of a woman who had risen above it. That very afternoon she had read in the *Figaro* an account of the proceedings at a public meeting which had taken a comical turn, and she was still chuckling about the slang words which had been used, and the angry reactions of a drunkard who had got himself chucked out.

'Oh, those drunks!' she said with a disgusted air. 'No, I tell you straight, their precious republic would be a disaster for everybody. .... Oh, may God preserve the Emperor for us as long as possible!'

'God will hear your prayer, my dear,' Muffat replied gravely. 'Have no fear, the Emperor's in no danger.'

He liked to hear her express such excellent views. The two of them, in fact, were in complete agreement on political matters. Vandeuvres and Captain Hugon likewise indulged in endless jokes about the 'hooligans', loud-mouthed brutes who took to their heels the moment they saw a bayonet. But Georges that evening remained pale and sombre.

'What's the matter with that baby?' asked Nana, noticing his troubled expression.

'With me? Nothing. I'm just listening,' he murmured.

But he was really suffering. Leaving the table, he had heard Philippe joking with the young woman; and now it

337

was Philippe, and not himself, who was sitting beside her. Without his knowing why, his heart was swelling fit to burst. He could not bear to see them so close together and such vile thoughts came crowding in on him that he felt shame mingling with his anguish. He, who laughed at Satin, who had accepted first Steiner and then Muffat, then all the rest, felt outraged and saw red at the thought that Philippe might one day touch that woman.

'Here, take Bijou,' she said to comfort him, and she passed him the little dog which had gone to sleep on her skirt.

And with that Georges grew happy again, for with the animal still warm from her lap in his arms, he was holding as it were a part of her.

The conversation had turned to a considerable loss which Vandeuvres had sustained the night before at the Imperial Club. Muffat, who was not a gambler, expressed his astonishment, but Vandeuvres alluded smilingly to his imminent ruin, about which Paris was already talking : the sort of death you died did not matter, he said – the important thing was to die well. For some time past, Nana had noticed that he was looking nervous, with a bitter twist to his mouth and a fitful gleam in the depths of his bright eyes. But he retained his haughty aristocratic air and the delicate elegance of his impoverished race; and as yet all that he revealed was an occasional fit of vertigo afflicting a mind already sapped by gambling and women. One night, lying beside her, he had frightened her by telling her a dreadful story : he was planning to shut himself up in his stables and burn himself to death with his horses once he had spent all his money. His only hope now was a horse called Lusignan which he was training for the Prix de Paris. He was living on this horse, which carried all his shaken credit, and, whenever Nana made some fresh demand, he would put off satisfying it till June, provided Lusignan won.

'Bah,' she said jokingly. 'He may just as well lose, since he's going to clean them all out at the races.'

By way of reply he merely gave a thin mysterious smile. Then he added casually :

'By the way, I've taken the liberty of giving your name to

338

my outsider, a filly ... Nana, Nana ... that sounds good. You aren't annoyed, are you?'

'Why should I be annoyed?' she said, secretly delighted.

The conversation continued, and the company was talking about a forthcoming execution which the young woman was longing to go and see, when Satin appeared at the dressing-room door, calling in her beseeching tones. She got up straight away, leaving the gentlemen lazily stretched out, finishing their cigars and discussing the grave question of the responsibility of a murderer suffering from chronic alcoholism. In the dressing-room Zoé was slumped on a chair, crying her heart out, while Satin was vainly trying to console her.

'What's the matter?' Nana asked in surprise.

'Oh, darling, do speak to her,' said Satin. 'I've been trying to make her listen to reason for the last twenty minutes. ... She's crying because you called her a goose.'

'Yes, Madame, it's very hard ... very hard,' stammered Zoé, choked by a fresh fit of sobbing.

This sight melted the young woman's heart at once. She spoke kindly to Zoé, and when the other woman refused to calm down, she squatted in front of her, and clasped her round the waist with affectionate familiarity.

'You silly thing, I said "goose" just as I might have said anything else. What shall I say? I was angry. ... There now, I was wrong. ... Now calm down.'

'And I love Madame so much,' stammered Zoé. 'After all I've done for Madame ...'

At that Nana kissed the maid, and, wanting to show that she wasn't vexed, gave her a dress she had worn three times. Their quarrels always ended with the giving of presents. Zoé dabbed her eyes with her handkerchief. She carried off the dress on her arm, adding that they were very upset in the kitchen and that Julien and François had been unable to eat, Madame's anger had taken away their appetites so completely. Whereupon Madame sent them a louis as a token of reconciliation. She suffered too much if people around her were unhappy.

Nana was returning to the drawing-room, happy at the

339

thought that she had patched up a quarrel which was making her dread the next day, when Satin whispered vehemently in her ear. She complained to Nana, threatening to go off if those men went on teasing her, and insisting that her darling should chuck them all out that night. That would teach them a lesson. And it would be so nice to be left on their own, the two of them! Nana, feeling worried again, swore that it was impossible. Whereupon the other shouted at her like a violent child trying to impose her authority:

'I insist, you hear? ... Send them away, or I'm off!'

And she went back into the drawing-room, stretched herself out on a divan tucked away near the window, and lay waiting, silent and deathlike, with her great eyes fixed on Nana.

The gentlemen were deciding against the new criminological theories, on the grounds that the splendid discovery of irresponsibility in certain pathological cases meant that there were no criminals left, but only sick people. The young woman, nodding her approval, was wondering how she could manage to get rid of the Count.

The others would soon be going, but he was certain to stay on. Sure enough, when Philippe got up to withdraw, Georges followed him straight away; his only concern was not to leave his brother behind. Vandeuvres lingered a few minutes longer, feeling his way, and waiting to find out if, by any chance, some important business might oblige Muffat to yield him his place. But when he saw the Count deliberately settling down for the night, he did not persist, but took his leave as became a man of tact. But as he was making for the door, he noticed Satin with her fixed stare; and realizing what was happening, he came over to her with an amused smile and shook hands with her.

'We're still friends, aren't we?' he murmured. 'Do forgive me. ... You're the nicer of the two, on my honour!'

Satin did not deign to reply. Nor did she take her eyes off Nana and the Count, who were now alone. Muffat, making himself at home, had sat down beside the young woman, taking her fingers and kissing them. Whereupon Nana, wishing to change the direction of his thoughts, asked him if his

340

daughter Estelle was better. The day before he had been complaining of the child's melancholy behaviour; he could not spend a single happy day at home, with his wife always out and his daughter locked in an icy silence. In family matters of this kind Nana was always full of good advice, and when Muffat abandoned his usual self-restraint, relaxing both body and mind, and launched out again into his plaints, she remembered the promise she had made.

'Why don't you marry her off?' she asked.

And with that she ventured to speak of Daguenet. At the mere mention of that name the Count flared up indignantly. Never, he said, after what she had told him!

She affected to be astonished and then burst out laughing. Putting her arms round his neck, she said:

'Oh, you jealous thing! But how ridiculous! ... Use your head. He'd told you something about me that wasn't true, and I was furious. ... But now I'd be sorry if ...'

Then, over Muffat's shoulder, she met Satin's gaze. Taken aback, she let go of him, and continued in a solemn voice:

'This marriage must take place, my dear; I don't want to prevent your daughter's happiness. That young man's a good sort; you couldn't possibly find a better match for your daughter.'

And she launched into an extraordinary eulogy of Daguenet. The Count had again taken her hands; he no longer said that the marriage was out of the question: he would see about it; they would talk the matter over. Then, when he talked of going to bed, she lowered her voice and excused herself. It was impossible; she was indisposed. If he loved her at all he would not insist. However, he stubbornly refused to go away, and she was beginning to give in when she met Satin's gaze once more. Then she grew inflexible. No, it was out of the question. The Count, deeply disturbed and looking very upset, had stood up and was looking for his hat. But at the door he felt the jewel-case in his pocket and remembered the set of sapphires. He had intended to hide them in the bed so that, when she went to bed before him, she would feel them against her legs; he had been planning this childish surprise ever since dinner-time. But now, in his anguish and distress at

being turned out of doors, he abruptly handed over the jewel-case.

'What is it?' she asked. 'Sapphires. . . . Oh, of course, it's that set. How sweet you are! . . . But I say, darling, do you think it's the same one? In the shop-window it looked more impressive.'

That was all the thanks he got before she let him go. He had just caught sight of Satin, stretched out in silent expectancy. He looked at the two women, and without further insistence accepted the inevitable and went downstairs. The hall door had not yet closed when Satin clasped Nana round the waist and started singing and dancing. Then she ran to the window.

'Oh, come and see how funny he looks down in the street!'

The two women leaned on their elbows on the wrought-iron window rail in the shadow of the curtains. One o'clock was striking. The Avenue de Villiers was deserted, and its double row of gas-lamps stretched away into the darkness of the damp March night, which was being swept by great gusts of wind laden with rain. Patches of waste land made gulfs of shadow, while the scaffolding round big houses under construction loomed upwards under the dark sky. And the two women rocked with helpless laughter as they saw Muffat's rounded back and watery shadow disappearing along the wet pavement, across the icy, empty plains of the new Paris. But Nana silenced Satin.

'Watch out – there's the police!'

They promptly stifled their laughter, and gazed in secret fear at two dark figures walking with measured tread along the opposite side of the Avenue. Amid her luxurious surroundings and the majestic splendour of a woman commanding absolute obedience, Nana had retained a terror of the police, and did not like to hear them mentioned any more than death. She felt distinctly uneasy when a policeman looked up at her house. You never knew how they might behave. They might easily take them for prostitutes if they heard them laughing at that hour of the night. Satin had given a little shudder and huddled up against Nana. Nevertheless the pair remained where they were, fascinated by the

342

approach of a lantern, the light of which was dancing among the puddles in the road. It was an old rag-and-bone woman who was raking about in the gutters. Satin recognized her.

'Why,' she exclaimed, 'it's Queen Pomaré with her wicker basket!'

And while a gust of wind lashed the fine rain in their faces she told her sweetheart the story of Queen Pomaré. Oh, she had been a splendid girl once, who had fascinated all Paris with her beauty. And such go, and such cheek – leading the men about by their noses, and leaving great notabilities blubbering on her staircase! Now she was always getting drunk, and the women of the district gave her absinthe for the sake of a laugh, after which the street urchins threw stones at her and chased her. Altogether it was a real come-down, a queen falling into the mud! Nana listened, feeling her blood freeze.

'You'll see,' added Satin.

She whistled like a man, and the rag-picker, who was directly below the window, raised her head and showed herself in the yellow glow of her lantern. Among that bundle of rags a blue, scarred face looked out from under a tattered kerchief, with a toothless hole of a mouth, and reddened bruises where the eyes should be. And Nana, faced with the hideous old age of this whore drowned in drink, had a sudden recollection, and saw passing in the darkness the vision of Chamont – Irma d'Anglars, that old harlot crowned with years and honours, climbing the steps of her château in the midst of reverential villagers. Then, as Satin whistled again, laughing at the old woman who could not see her, she murmured in a changed voice:

'Stop it – there are the police! Let's go back inside, pet.'

The measured steps were returning. They shut the window. Turning round, her hair all damp, and shivering with cold, Nana was taken aback for a moment by the sight of her drawing-room, as if she had forgotten it and were entering an unfamiliar place. The air in the room was so warm and scented that she experienced a sense of delighted surprise. The accumulated treasures, the antique furniture, the golden silk hangings, the ivories and bronzes, were slumbering in the rosy light of the lamps; while from the whole of the silent

house a rich feeling of great luxury emanated, the luxury of the solemn reception rooms, of the comfortable, spacious dining-room, of the vast, quiet staircase, of the soft carpets and seats. She felt a sudden blossoming of her nature, with its longing for domination and enjoyment and its desire to possess everything in order to destroy everything. Never before had she felt so profoundly the power of her sex. She gazed slowly around and remarked with a solemn philosophical air :

'Ah, well, in spite of everything, there's nothing like making hay while you're young !'

But already Satin was rolling on the bearskins in the bedroom and calling her.

'Come along ! Come along !'

Nana undressed in the dressing-room. To be quicker about it, she took her thick mass of blonde hair in both hands and began shaking it above the silver wash-basin, so that a shower of long hair-pins rang a chime on the shining metal.

THAT Sunday the race for the Grand Prix de Paris was being run in the Bois de Boulogne under a sky heavy with the first heat of June. The sun, that morning, had risen in a reddish mist, but towards eleven o'clock, just as the carriages were arriving at the Longchamp course, a southerly wind had swept away the clouds; long streamers of grey vapour drifted away and gaps of intense blue began spreading from one end of the horizon to the other. In the bright bursts of sunlight which alternated with the clouds the whole scene lit up, from the public enclosure, which was gradually filling with a crowd of carriages, riders and pedestrians, to the still vacant course, with the judge's box, the winning-post, and the poles of the telegraph, and thence on to the five symmetrical stands, rising in galleries of brickwork and timber in the middle of the weighing-enclosure opposite. Farther on, bathed in the noonday sunshine, lay the vast level plain, bordered with little trees, and shut in to the west by the wooded heights of Saint-Cloud and Suresnes, which, in their turn, were dominated by the grim silhouette of Mont-Valérien.

Nana was as excited as if the Grand Prix were going to determine her fortune, and decided to take up a position by the rail next to the winning-post. She had been one of the first to arrive, driving up in a landau with silver fittings, a present from the Comte Muffat, drawn *à la Daumont* by four splendid white horses. When she had made her appearance at the entrance to the public enclosures, with two postilions jogging along on the left-hand horses, and two footmen standing motionless behind the carriage, people had rushed to see her, as if a queen were passing. She was wearing the blue and white colours of the Vandeuvres stable in a remarkable outfit. This consisted of a little blue silk bodice and tunic, which fitted closely to her body and bulged out enormously over the small of her back, outlining her thighs in a very bold fashion

345

for this period of ballooning skirts. Then there was a white satin dress with white satin sleeves, and a white satin sash worn crosswise, the whole decorated with silver point-lace which shone in the sun. In addition to this, in order to be still more like a jockey, she had jauntily stuck a blue toque with a white feather on her chignon, from which her golden locks flowed down to the middle of her back like a huge russet horse's tail.

Twelve o'clock struck. The public had over three hours to wait for the Grand Prix to be run. When the landau had drawn up beside the rail, Nana settled down comfortably as if she were at home. She had taken it into her head to bring Bijou and little Louis with her, and the dog nestled among her skirts, shivering with cold in spite of the heat, while in his trappings of ribbon and laces, the child's poor little waxen face was pale and silent in the open air. Meanwhile the young woman, paying no attention to the people near her, talked at the top of her voice with Georges and Philippe Hugon, who were sitting in front of her on the other side in such a pile of bouquets of white roses and blue myosotis that they were buried up to their shoulders.

'So,' she was saying, 'as he was getting on my nerves ... I showed him the door. ... And now he's been sulking for two days.'

She was talking of Muffat, but she took care not to confess to the young men the real reason for this first quarrel, which was that one evening he had found a man's hat in her bed-room. It belonged to a passer-by she had picked up on a stupid impulse, out of sheer boredom.

'You've no idea how funny he is,' she continued, laughing herself at the details she was giving. 'He's a regular little bigot at bottom. Why, he even says his prayers every night. Yes, he does. He thinks I don't notice because I go to bed first so as not to embarrass him; but I watch him out of the corner of my eye. He jabbers away, and then he crosses him-self and turns round to climb over me and lie down by the wall.'

'Lord, that's clever,' murmured Philippe. 'So it's a case of before and after, is it?'

346

She laughed delightedly.

'Yes, that's it, before and after! When I'm going to sleep I can hear him jabbering away again. ... But the annoying thing is that we can't argue about anything now without him going pious on me. Now I've always been religious. Yes, you can laugh, but that won't prevent me believing what I believe. ... Only he's a bore about it : he's forever blubbering and talking about remorse. The day before yesterday, for instance, he had a regular fit of religion after our little row, and I was really worried about him afterwards ...'

But she broke off to say :

'Look, there are the Mignons arriving. Why, they've brought the children! ... Oh, look how the poor things are dolled up!'

The Mignons were in a landau painted in sombre colours, suggesting the comfort and luxury of a prosperous middle-class couple. Rose, dressed in a grey silk gown trimmed with red bows and puffs, was smiling happily at the high spirits of Henri and Charles, who were sitting on the front seat looking awkward in their ill-fitting schoolboys' suits. But, when the landau had drawn up by the rail, and she noticed Nana sitting in triumph among her bouquets, with her four horses and her livery, she pursed her lips, sat bolt upright and turned her head away. Mignon, on the contrary, looking the picture of freshness and gaiety, greeted her with a wave of the hand. He made it a principle to keep out of women's quarrels.

'By the way,' Nana continued, 'do you know a little old man who's very clean and neat but has bad teeth? ... A Monsieur Venot. ... He came to see me this morning.'

'Monsieur Venot!' said Georges in utter amazement. 'Why, that's impossible! He's a Jesuit!'

'I thought he was something of the sort. Oh, you've no idea what our conversation was like! It was hilarious! ... He spoke to me about the Count and his shattered marriage, and begged me to give a family back its happiness. ... He was very polite, and he smiled at me all the time. Well, I replied that I wanted nothing better, and I promised to bring the Count and his wife together again. ... And I wasn't joking,

you know : I'd be delighted to see them all happy again, the poor things! Besides it would be a relief to me, because honestly there are days when he bores me stiff.'

The weariness she had felt in the last few months escaped her in this heart-felt outburst. What was more, the Count appeared to be in considerable financial difficulties; he was very worried, and it seemed likely that the bill he had signed for Labordette would not be met.

'Talking of the Muffats, there's the Countess,' said Georges, whose gaze was wandering over the stands.

'Where?' cried Nana. 'What eyes our baby's got! ... Hold my parasol, Philippe.'

But with a quick movement Georges anticipated his brother, delighted at the chance to hold the blue silk parasol with its silver fringe. Nana scanned the scene with a huge pair of field-glasses.

'Ah, yes, I can see her,' she said at last. 'In the right-hand stand, near a pillar, eh? She's in mauve, with her daughter in white next to her. ... Ah, and there's Daguenet going to greet them.'

Thereupon Philippe talked of Daguenet's approaching marriage to that great gawk Estelle. It was all settled, and the banns were being called. At first the Countess had opposed the match but the Count, so they said, had insisted. Nana smiled.

'I know, I know,' she murmured. 'So much the better for Paul. He's a nice boy, and he deserves it.'

And leaning towards little Louis, she added :

'Are you enjoying yourself, love? What a serious face!'

Never smiling, and looking very old, the child was gazing at the crowds, as if the sight of them filled him with melancholy reflections. Bijou, banished from the skirts of the young woman, who was fidgeting a great deal, had gone and nestled against the little boy, still shivering with cold.

Meanwhile the enclosure was filling up. Carriages were continually arriving through the Porte de la Cascade in a thick, endless line. There were big charabancs such as the Pauline, from the Boulevard des Italiens, loaded with its fifty passengers, which went and drew up to the right of the

348

stands. Then there were dog-carts, victorias and immaculate landaus, mixed up with wretched cabs jolting along behind old hacks! Four-in-hands, pushing their four horses before them, and mail-coaches, in which the masters sat in the fresh air on the seats and left the servants to look after the hampers of champagne inside; spiders, whose huge wheels glittered with dazzling steel, and light tandems, as delicately formed as pieces of clockwork, which spun along amid a peal of little bells. Every now and then a rider went by, and a swarm of pedestrians ran frantically between the carriages. On the grass the distant rumbling which came from the avenues of the Bois suddenly gave place to a dull rustling sound; and now nothing could be heard but the hubbub of the swelling crowds, shouts, calls and the cracking of whips carrying loudly through the open air. When, amid gusts of wind, the sun reappeared at the edge of a cloud, a streak of gold ran across the racecourse, lighting up the harness and the varnished coach-panels, and touching the ladies' dresses with fire, while in this dusty radiance the coachmen high up on their boxes blazed brightly with their great whips.

Labordette was getting out of a barouche in which Gaga, Clarisse and Blanche de Sivry had kept a place for him. As he was hurrying across the course to enter the weighing-in enclosure, Nana got Georges to call him. Then, when he reached her, she asked laughingly:

'What's the betting on me?'

She was referring to Nana the filly, the Nana who had let herself be shamefully beaten in the Prix de Diane, and had not even been placed in April and May when she had run in the Prix Des Cars and the Grande Poule des Produits, both of which had been won by Lusignan, the other horse in the Vandeuvres stable. Lusignan had promptly become the favourite; and since the previous day he had been quoted at two to one.

'Still fifty to one against,' replied Labordette.

'Hell, I'm not worth much, am I?' said Nana, amused by this joke. 'In that case I'm not going to back myself. . . . No, dammit, I won't put a single louis on myself.'

Labordette went off again in a great hurry, but she called

him back. She wanted some advice. As he kept in touch with the world of trainers and jockeys, he had special information about the various stables. His forecasts had come true a score of times already, and people called him the King of the Tipsters.

'Tell me, what horse shall I pick?' asked the young woman. 'What's the betting on the English horse?'

'Spirit? Three to one against. . . . Valerio II the same. . . . As for the others, it's twenty-five to one against Cosinus, forty to one against Hasard, thirty to one against Boum, thirty-five to one against Pichenette, ten to one against Frangi-pane . . .'

'No, I refuse to bet on the English horse. I'm a patriot, I am. . . . Perhaps Valerio II, eh? The Duc de Corbreuse was looking radiant just now. . . . No, perhaps not. What do you say to fifty louis on Lusignan?'

Labordette gave her a peculiar look. She leant forward and questioned him in a low voice, for she knew that Vandeuvres commissioned him to deal with the bookmakers for him so as to be able to lay his bets more easily. If he had got to know something, he might as well tell her. But without entering into explanations Labordette persuaded her to trust to his flair; he would put on her fifty louis for her as he thought best, and she wouldn't regret leaving it to him.

'All the horses you like!' she cried gaily, letting him go. 'But not Nana – she's no good!'

There was a burst of uproarious laughter in the carriage. The young men thought her joke very amusing, while little Louis raised his pale eyes uncomprehendingly to his mother, surprised by her loud remarks. However, there was no escape for Labordette yet. Rose Mignon had beckoned to him, and was giving him instructions, while he wrote figures in a notebook. Then Clarisse and Gaga called him back, to change their bets; they had heard some comments in the crowd, and now wanted to bet on Lusignan instead of Valerio II. He scribbled away impassively and finally managed to escape, disappearing between two of the stands on the other side of the course.

Carriages were still arriving. By this time they were drawn up five rows deep, spreading out alongside the rail in a dense mass speckled with the light patches made by the white horses. Beyond them other carriages stood about separately in complete disorder, looking as if they had been stranded on the grass. Wheels and horses were pointing in all directions, side by side, askew, at right-angles or head to head. On such stretches of turf as remained unoccupied riders kept trotting, and dark clusters of pedestrians moved continually. Above this fairground scene and the confused motley of the crowd, the drinking-booths raised their grey canvas roofs, which gleamed white whenever the sun came out. But the real crush, full of surging bodies and eddying hats, was around the bookmakers, who stood in open carriages, gesticulating like dentists, with their odds pasted up on tall boards beside them.

'All the same, it's silly not knowing what horse to bet on,' Nana was saying. 'I really must risk a few louis on myself.'

She had stood up to pick out a bookmaker with a trust-worthy face, but forgot what she wanted as she caught sight of a whole crowd of people she knew. Besides the Mignons, and besides Gaga, Clarisse and Blanche, she could see to her right and left and behind her, among the mass of carriages now hemming in her landau, Tatan Néné and Maria Blond in a victoria, Caroline Héquet with her mother and two gentlemen in a barouche, Louise Violaine on her own, driving herself a little pony-carriage decked with orange and green ribbons, the colours of the Méchain stable, and finally Léa de Horn on the lofty seat of a mail-coach, with a bunch of noisy young men. Farther off, in an elegant underslung carriage, Lucy Stewart, in a very simple black dress, was putting on a distinguished air beside a tall young man in the uniform of a naval cadet. But what most astounded Nana was seeing Simonne arrive in a tandem which Steiner was driving, with a footman sitting motionless behind them with folded arms. She looked dazzling, dressed all in white satin striped with yellow, and covered with diamonds from waist to hat, while the banker was using a huge whip to urge on his two horses, which were harnessed in tandem – the leader

a little golden chestnut with a mouse-like trot, the other a big brown bay with a high-stepping action.

'Well, I'll be damned!' said Nana. 'So that thief Steiner has cleared out the Stock Exchange again, has he? ... I say, doesn't Simonne look good. She'd better watch out, or he'll get done by the law.'

All the same she exchanged greetings at a distance. Indeed she kept waving and smiling, turning round and forgetting nobody in her desire to be seen by all. And all the time she went on chatting.

'It's her son that Lucy's got in tow! Doesn't he look nice in uniform! That's why she's putting on airs! She's scared of him, you know, and passes herself off as an actress. ... Poor young man, I feel sorry for him. ... He looks as if he doesn't suspect a thing.'

'Bah!' Philippe murmured with a laugh. 'When she chooses to, she'll find him an heiress in the provinces.'

Nana was silent, for she had just caught sight of La Tricon in the thick of the carriages. Having arrived in a cab from which she could not see anything, La Tricon had calmly climbed up on to the coach-box, and there, with her noble face framed in ringlets, and holding her tall figure erect, she dominated the crowd like a queen enthroned among her feminine subjects. All the women smiled discreetly at her, while she haughtily pretended not to know them. She was not there on business; she went to the races for the love of the thing, as a fanatical gambler with a passion for horses.

'Why, there's that idiot la Faloise!' Georges said all of a sudden.

They were all taken aback. Nana could hardly recognize her la Faloise, for since he had come into his inheritance he had become terribly smart. He was wearing a wing-collar and a suit of light-coloured cloth which clung to his narrow shoulders. His hair was in little curls and he affected a weary sway of the body and a gentle drawl, with slang words and phrases which he did not take the trouble to finish.

'But he looks marvellous!' declared Nana, completely bowled over.

Gaga and Clarisse had called la Faloise, and were throw-

ing themselves at him in an attempt to win him back, but he left them straight away, sauntering off in a mocking, disdainful manner. Nana dazzled him, and he rushed over to stand on the step of her carriage. When she twitted him about Gaga, he murmured :

'Oh, no, I've finished with the old guard ! You mustn't try and land me with her any more ! Besides, you know, you're my sweetheart now ...'

He had put his hand to his heart. Nana roared with laughter at this sudden declaration out in the open. But she went on :

'I say, that's not all I'm after. You're making me forget I wanted to lay a bet. ... Georges, you see that bookmaker over there, the big red-faced fellow with the frizzy hair ? He's got a nasty common look that I like. ... Go and lay a bet on ... Oh, which horse should I back ?'

'I'm not patriotic – oh dear, no !' la Faloise stammered. 'I've put all my money on the English horse. ... It'll be simply ripping if the English horse wins ! And to hell with the French !'

Nana was shocked. They went on to discuss the merits of the various horses, and la Faloise, affecting to be very much in the know, dismissed them all as old screws. Frangipane, Baron Verdier's horse, was by The Truth out of Lenore : a big bay who would have had a good chance if they hadn't worn him out during training. As for Valerio II, from the Corbreuse stable, he wasn't ready yet, and he'd had the gripes in April; oh, yes, they were keeping it quiet, but he was sure of it, absolutely positive. And he ended up by advising Nana to choose Hasard, from the Méchain stable, the worst horse of the lot and one nobody had a good word for. Dammit, Hasard had wonderful form and a splendid action ! There was a horse that was going to surprise everybody !'

'No,' said Nana. 'I'm going to put ten louis on Lusignan and five on Boum.'

La Faloise burst out straight away :

'But, my dear girl, Boum's no good at all ! Don't choose him ! Gasc himself isn't backing his own horse. ... As for your Lusignan – never ! He hasn't a hope ! Think of it – he's

by Lamb out of Princess! By Lamb out of Princess! No, really! All too short in the legs!'

He was choking. Philippe pointed out that all the same Lusignan had won the Prix Des Cars and the Grande Poule des Produits. But the other started up again. What did that prove? Nothing at all. On the contrary, it was ground for suspicion. Besides Gresham was riding Lusignan, and that was enough for him! There was a jinx on Gresham, and he'd never get to the post.

The argument raging in Nana's landau seemed to spread from one end of the enclosure to the other. Yelping voices were raised as the passion for gambling swept the racecourse, setting faces alight and arms waving, while the bookmakers, perched on their carriages, shouted the odds and jotted figures down furiously. Their customers were just the small fry of the betting world, for the big bets were laid in the weighing-in enclosure; here there raged the frenzy of the small punters, who risked their five-franc pieces and displayed undisguised greed for the sake of a possible gain of a few louis. The great battle that day was going to be between Spirit and Lusignan. Englishmen, recognizable as such, were strolling about among the various groups, looking quite at home, their faces flushed and already triumphant. Bramah, a horse belonging to Lord Reading, had won the Grand Prix the previous year, and French hearts were still bleeding from that. This year it would be a disaster if France were beaten again. Accordingly all the ladies were frantic with national pride. The Vandeuvres stable became the rampart of French honour, and Lusignan was recommended and defended and acclaimed. Gaga, Blanche, Caroline and the others laid bets on him. Lucy Stewart abstained on account of her son, but it was rumoured that Rose Mignon had commissioned Labordette to place two hundred louis for her. Only La Tricon, sitting next to her driver, waited till the last minute. Very cool in the midst of all these arguments, and dominating the growing hubbub, in which the horses' names kept recurring in lively Parisian phrases mingled with guttural English exclamations, she sat listening and taking notes with a majestic air.

354

'And what about Nana?' said Georges. 'Isn't anybody betting on her?'

Not only was nobody betting on her; she was not even being mentioned. The outsider from the Vandeuvres stable had been eclipsed by Lusignan's popularity. But la Faloise flung his arms in the air and said:

'I've had an inspiration. ... I'm going to bet a louis on Nana.'

'Bravo! I'll bet a couple,' said Georges.

'And I'll bet three,' added Philippe.

And they went up and up, paying flattering court to Nana, and calling out figures as if they were bidding for her at an auction. La Faloise talked of covering her with gold. For that matter, everybody ought to lay bets on her; they would go and recruit some more backers. But as the three young men were going off to rally support, Nana shouted after them:

'I don't want anything to do with her, you know! Not for anything in the world! ... Georges, ten louis on Lusignan and five on Valerio II.'

Meanwhile they had set off, and she watched them in amusement as they slipped between wheels, ducked under horses' heads, and scoured the whole enclosure. As soon as they recognized somebody in a carriage they rushed up and pressed Nana's claims. And there were great bursts of laughter among the crowd when sometimes they turned round triumphantly signalling numbers with their fingers, while the young woman stood waving her parasol. However, they were not having much success. A few men let themselves be persuaded; Steiner, for instance, stirred by the sight of Nana, ventured three louis. But the women refused point-blank. 'What, to lose for certain?' they said. 'No thanks!' Besides they were in no hurry to work for the benefit of a filthy bitch who was lording it over them all with her four white horses, her postilions and her airs and graces. Gaga and Clarisse pursed their lips and asked la Faloise whether he was making fun of them. When Georges boldly presented himself at the Mignons' carriage, Rose turned her head away indignantly and made no reply. You had to be a

pretty low sort to let your name be given to a horse! Mignon, on the contrary, watched the young man go away with a look of amusement, and said that women always brought luck.

'Well?' asked Nana, when the young men returned after a prolonged visit to the bookmakers.

'The odds are forty to one against you,' said la Faloise.

'What's that? Forty to one!' she cried in astonishment. 'They were fifty to one before. . . . What's happening?'

Labordette had just reappeared. The course was being cleared, and the sound of a bell announced the first race. Amid the expectant murmur of the crowd, she questioned him about this sudden shortening of the odds. But he replied evasively; no doubt a few bets had been placed. She had to content herself with this explanation. Besides, Labordette added with a preoccupied expression that Vandeuvres was going to come along, if he could get away.

The race was coming to an end, almost unnoticed in the excited anticipation of the Grand Prix, when a cloud burst over the Hippodrome. A few minutes earlier the sun had disappeared, and a vivid light had cast a gloom over the crowd. The wind rose, and there followed a sudden deluge, with huge drops falling, and then sheets of water. There was a minute of confusion, with people shouting, joking and swearing, while those on foot rushed to take shelter under the canvas of the drinking-booths. In the carriages the women did their best to protect themselves, holding their parasols with both hands, while the startled footmen ran to the hoods. But the shower was already nearly over, and the sun began shining brightly through the drifting mist of fine rain. A blue cleft opened in the clouds as they were carried away over the Bois. And the skies seemed to smile again, setting the women laughing in a reassured way, while amid the snorting of the horses and the agitation of the drenched crowd that was shaking itself dry, a blaze of golden light lit up the enclosure, which was glittering with crystal drops.

'Oh, my poor little Louis!' said Nana. 'Are you terribly wet, darling?'

The little boy silently allowed his hands to be wiped. The

young woman had taken out her handkerchief. Next she
dabbed it over Bijou, who was trembling more violently than
ever. It was nothing; there were a few drops on the white
satin of her dress, but she didn't care. The flowers, refreshed
by the rain, had taken on a showy brilliance, and she smelt
one ecstatically, moistening her lips as if in dew.

Meanwhile this downpour had suddenly filled the stands.
Nana looked at them through her field-glasses. At that distance, she could only distinguish a compact, confused mass of
people, piled up in row upon row, a dark background relieved by pale patches which were human faces. The sunlight filtered in at the corners of the roof, flooding sections
of the seated crowd with a light which seemed to take the
colour out of the ladies' dresses. But Nana was especially
amused by the ladies whom the shower had driven from the
rows of chairs lined up on the sand below the stands. As
courtesans were strictly forbidden to enter the weighing-in
enclosure, she made some waspish remarks about the society
women there, whom she considered both ugly and hideously
dressed.

A murmur ran through the crowd as the Empress entered
the little central stand, a pavilion built like a chalet, with a
wide balcony furnished with red armchairs.

'Why, it's him!' said Georges. 'I didn't think he was on
duty this week.'

The stiff, solemn figure of the Comte Muffat had appeared
behind the Empress. The young men started joking about
him, expressing regret that Satin wasn't there to go and dig
him in the ribs. But Nana's field-glasses had focussed on the
head of the Prince of Scotland in the imperial stand.

'Heavens, it's Charles!' she cried.

She thought him stouter than before. In eighteen months
he had put on weight. She proceeded to enter into details;
oh, yes, he was a big, strapping fellow!

All round her, in the ladies' carriages, they were whispering that the Count had dropped her. It was quite a story.
Since he had been appearing in public with Nana, the Tuileries had taken exception to the Chamberlain's conduct. As a
result, in order to retain his position, he had just broken off

his liaison. La Faloise bluntly reported this story to the young woman, offering himself again, and calling her his sweetheart. But she laughed gaily, and said:

'That idiot. ... You don't know him; I've only to whistle and he'll drop everything to come running.'

For a few minutes she had been examining the Comtesse Sabine and Estelle. Daguenet was still with them. Fauchery had just arrived, and was pushing his way forward to greet them. He too stayed there with a smile on his face. At that Nana gestured scornfully at the stands, and continued:

'Besides, you know, those people don't impress me any more. ... I know them too well. You should see them when they're stripped! ... You wouldn't feel any respect for them then. Filth below stairs, filth above stairs, filth everywhere. ... That's why I don't want to be bothered any more.'

Her gestures took in everybody, from the grooms leading the horses onto the course, to the Empress chatting with Charles, who was a prince, but a bastard all the same.

'Bravo, Nana! ... Jolly good, Nana!' la Faloise cried enthusiastically.

The sound of a bell was lost in the wind as the races continued. The Prix d'Ispahan had just been run, and Berlingot, a horse from the Méchain stable, had won. Nana called Labordette back to ask for news of her hundred louis; but he burst out laughing, and refused to tell her which horses he had picked out for her, so as not to spoil her luck, as he put it. Her money was well placed, as she would find out later. And when she admitted that she had put ten louis on Lusignan and five on Valerio II, he shrugged his shoulders, as if to say that women did silly things whatever happened. This surprised her, and she looked nonplussed.

Just then the public enclosure grew livelier than ever, as open-air luncheon-parties were organized in the interval before the Grand Prix. There was much eating and even more drinking all over the place, on the grass, on the seats of the four-in-hands and the mail-coaches, and in the victorias, the broughams and the landaus. Cold meat was spread out everywhere, and footmen handed down dozens of champagne hampers out of the boots of carriages. Corks came out

with feeble pops, which were carried away on the wind. Jokes were exchanged, and the sound of breaking glasses added a note of discord to the nervous gaiety of the scene. Gaga and Clarisse were having a regular meal with Blanche, eating sandwiches on the carriage-rug with which they had been covering their knees. Louise Violaine had got down from her pony-carriage to join Caroline Héquet; and on the turf at their feet some gentlemen had installed a bar, to which Tatan, Maria, Simonne and the rest came to refresh themselves. Meanwhile, not far away, bottles were being emptied up in the air on Léa de Horn's mail-coach, where a whole bunch of posturing, gesticulating young men were getting tipsy above the heads of the crowd. Soon, however, the largest crowd had gathered around Nana's landau. She had risen to her feet, and had started pouring out glasses of champagne for the men who came to pay her their respects. François, one of the footmen, passed the bottles, while la Faloise, trying to put on a common accent, kept up a stream of patter.

'Roll up, gents, roll up ... it's all free, gratis and for nothing. ... There's plenty for everybody!'

'Do shut up, love,' Nana ended up by saying. 'We look like a fairground act.'

She thought he was very funny, and was enjoying herself hugely. For a moment she thought of sending Georges with a glass of champagne to Rose Mignon, who was making a great show of having nothing to drink. Henri and Charles were bored to tears; they would have loved to have some champagne. But Georges drank the glassful, fearing an argument. Then Nana remembered little Louis, whom she had forgotten behind her. Perhaps he was thirsty! And she forced him to take a few drops of wine, which made him cough dreadfully.

'Roll up, gents, roll up,' la Faloise repeated. 'It isn't two sous, it isn't one. ... We're giving it away ...'

But Nana broke in with an exclamation:

'Look, there's Bordenave over there! Call him. ... Oh, do run and fetch him, please!'

It was indeed Bordenave, strolling about with his hands

behind his back, wearing a hat that looked reddish in the sunlight, and a greasy frock-coat that was white at the seams. It was a Bordenave broken by bankruptcy, but irrepressible in spite of everything, flaunting his poverty before this fashionable crowd with the brashness of a man who was always ready to take fortune by force.

'Dammit, you're looking smart!' he said, when Nana held out her hand to him in a good-natured greeting.

Then, after emptying a glass of champagne, he made the following sorrowful comment:

'Ah, if only I were a woman!... Still, dammit all, it doesn't matter! Do you want to go back on the stage? I've had an idea: I'll hire the Gaîté, and the two of us will take Paris by storm.... You'll do that for me, won't you?'

And he lingered beside her, grumbling and growling, but glad to see her again; for that confounded Nana, he said, eased his heart just by being there in front of him. She was his daughter, blood of his blood!

The circle grew. Now la Faloise was filling glasses, and Georges and Philippe were picking up friends. A slow movement was gradually begun, bringing over the whole crowd in the enclosure. Nana favoured everybody with a laugh or a jest. The groups of tipplers drew nearer, and all the scattered champagne glasses moved in her direction. Soon there was only one noisy crowd, and that was round her landau, where she reigned above the outstretched glasses, her yellow hair floating in the breeze, and her snowy face bathed in sunshine. Then, at the summit of the multitude, to administer a final blow to the other women who were raging over her triumph, she lifted her brimming glass and assumed her famous pose as the victorious Venus.

But somebody touched her from behind, and on turning round she was surprised to see Mignon on the seat. She disappeared from view for a moment, and sat down beside him, for he had come to bring her a piece of serious news. Mignon kept telling everybody that it was ridiculous of his wife to bear Nana a grudge: he considered her attitude stupid and futile.

'Listen, my dear,' he murmured. 'Be careful: don't make

Rose too angry. . . . You understand, I'd rather warn you in time. . . . Yes, she's got a weapon she can use against you, and seeing that she's never forgiven you for the *Little Duchess* business . . .'

'A weapon?' said Nana. 'What the hell do I care about that?'

'Just listen : it's a letter she must have found in Fauchery's pocket, a letter written to that bastard Fauchery by the Comtesse Muffat. And, not to put too fine a point on it, it's all spelt out there. . . . Well, Rose wants to send the letter to the Count to take her revenge on him and you.'

'What the hell do I care?' Nana repeated. 'I think it's funny. . . . So it tells the truth about Fauchery, does it? Well, so much the better – the woman was getting on my nerves. We're going to have a good laugh!'

'No, I don't want that to happen,' Mignon retorted sharply. 'There'd be a terrible scandal! Besides, we've got nothing to gain by it . . .'

He paused, afraid of saying too much, while she declared that she certainly wasn't going to help a respectable woman to get out of trouble. But when he pressed the point she looked him straight in the eyes. Probably he was afraid of seeing Fauchery interfering in his life again if he broke with the Countess; and that was what Rose wanted, as well as revenge against Nana, for she still felt a certain affection for the journalist. Nana became thoughtful, recalling Monsieur Venot's call, and a plan began to take shape in her mind, while Mignon was trying to talk her over.

'Let's suppose that Rose sends the letter, shall we? There's a tremendous scandal. You're mixed up in it, and people say that you're the cause of it all. . . . First of all the Count leaves his wife . . .'

'Why should he?' she said. 'On the contrary . . .'

She broke off in her turn. There was no need for her to think aloud. Finally, to get rid of Mignon, she pretended to agree with him, and when he advised her to make her peace with Rose – possibly by paying her a brief visit on the race-course, in front of everybody else – she replied that she would see, that she would think it over.

361

A sudden hubbub made her stand up again. On the course a bunch of horses were thundering up to the winning-post. It was the end of the Prix de la Ville de Paris, and Cornemuse had won it. Now the Grand Prix was about to be run, and excitement was growing as the crowd, tortured by anxiety, stamped and swayed as if to hurry the minutes along. During these last few minutes the punters were astonished to see the odds against Nana, the outsider from the Vandeuvres stable, continuing to shorten. Gentlemen kept coming back every few moments with new odds : first the betting was thirty to one against Nana, next twenty-five to one, then twenty to one, then fifteen to one. Nobody could understand it. A filly that had been beaten on every race-course in the country. A filly that nobody had been willing to take at fifty to one that very morning! What did this sudden madness mean? Some laughed at it and maintained that the silly fools who were being taken in would be thoroughly cleaned out. Others looked serious and uneasy, sensing something suspicious behind it all. Perhaps somebody was pulling off a coup. Mention was made of swindles which had been winked at on racecourses; but on this occasion the great name of Vandeuvres put a stop to all such accusations, and altogether the sceptics carried the day when they prophesied that Nana would come in last of all.

'Who's riding Nana?' asked la Faloise.

Just then the real Nana reappeared, whereupon the gentlemen put an indecent construction on the question, and burst into uproarious laughter. Nana bowed.

'It's Price,' she replied.

And with that the discussion began again. Price was an English celebrity, unknown in France. Why had Vandeuvres brought this jockey over, seeing that Gresham usually rode Nana? Besides they were astonished to see him entrusting Lusignan to that fellow Gresham, who according to la Faloise never got a place. But all these remarks were swallowed up in jokes, denials and the noise of an extraordinary medley of opinions. People started draining bottles of champagne again to pass the time. Presently a whisper ran round

and the groups opened up. It was Vandeuvres. Nana affected to be annoyed with him.

'Well, you're a nice fellow arriving at this time of day. . . . And me longing to see the weighing-in enclosure.'

'Come along then,' he said; 'there's still time. You can take a turn with me. I happen to have a permit for a lady on me.'

And he led her away on his arm, while she enjoyed the jealous glances with which Lucy, Caroline and the others followed her. The Hugon brothers and la Faloise, left behind in the landau, continued to do the honours of her champagne. She shouted to them that she would be back in a moment.

But Vandeuvres caught sight of Labordette and called him over, and a few brief words were exchanged.

'You've picked everything up?'

'Yes.'

'For how much?'

'Fifteen hundred louis, spread all over the place.'

As Nana was obviously listening inquisitively, they stopped talking. Vandeuvres was very nervous, and he had those same bright eyes, shot with little flames, which frightened her at night when he spoke of burning himself to death with his horses. As they were crossing the course, she asked him in a low voice :

'I say, explain something to me. Why are the odds on your filly shortening? It's causing quite a stir !'

He gave a start, and blurted out :

'Ah, they're talking, are they? . . . What a bunch some of those punters are ! When I've got the favourite, they all make a rush for him, and there's nothing left for me. Then, when somebody starts backing an outsider, they yell for help as if they were being skinned alive.'

'But you really ought to have told me, because I've made my bets,' she went on. 'Has she got a chance?'

A sudden burst of unexpected anger overpowered him.

'Oh, leave me alone, will you? . . . Every horse has a chance. The odds are shortening because somebody's betting on her. Who, I don't know. . . . I'm leaving you if you're going to go on pestering me with your stupid questions.'

Such a tone was characteristic of neither his temperament nor his habits, and she was surprised rather than hurt. Besides he felt ashamed of himself straight away; and when she curtly asked him to behave politely, he apologized. For some time now he had suffered from sudden changes of mood like that. Nobody in the Paris of pleasure or society was ignorant of the fact that he was playing his last card that day. If his horses did not win, and if they lost him the considerable sums wagered on them, it would mean disaster and ruin for him; for the whole edifice of his credit and the lofty appearance he had kept up even though his existence was undermined, as if sapped by debt and debauchery, would come crashing down in a reverberating collapse. Moreover nobody was ignorant of the fact that Nana was the man-eating siren who had finished him off, the last to attack his crumbling fortune and to sweep up what little remained. Stories were told of crazy whims and fancies, of gold scattered to the four winds, of a visit to Baden-Baden on which she had not left him enough to pay the hotel bill, and of a handful of diamonds thrown on the fire during an evening's drunkenness in order to see whether they would burn like coal. Little by little, with her plump limbs and her coarse plebeian laughter, she had imposed herself on this elegant, effete scion of an ancient race. Now he was risking all, so completely possessed by his taste for vice and stupidity as to have lost even the vigour of his scepticism. A week before, Nana had made him promise her a château on the Normandy coast between Le Havre and Trouville; and now he was staking the last vestiges of his honour in order to keep his word. Only she irritated him, and he could have beaten her, he felt her to be so stupid.

The attendant at the gate, not daring to stop the woman on the Count's arm, had allowed them to enter the weighing-in enclosure. Nana, bursting with pride at the idea that at last she was setting foot on this forbidden ground, put on her best behaviour, and walked slowly past the ladies sitting at the foot of the stands. There was a dense mass of dresses covering ten rows of chairs, and their bright colours mingled gaily in the open air. As people recognized one another,

chairs were drawn apart or moved together to form friendly circles, as if the company were sitting under the trees in a public park. Children had been allowed to go free, and were running from one group to another, while, higher up, on the crowded rows of seats in the stands, the light-coloured dresses melted into the delicate shadows of the timberwork. Nana looked all the ladies in the face, and made a point of staring hard at the Comtesse Sabine. Then, as she was passing in front of the imperial stand, the sight of Muffat standing beside the Empress in all his official stiffness set her laughing.

'Oh, how silly he looks!' she said very loudly to Vandeuvres.

She insisted on seeing everything. This little patch of parkland with its green lawns and clumps of trees struck her as rather dull. An ice vendor had set up a large refreshment table near the entrance gates, and under a rustic thatched roof a dense throng of people were shouting and gesticulating; this was the ring. Close by were some empty stalls; and Nana was disappointed to find only a gendarme's horse there. Then there was the paddock, a small course about a hundred yards in circumference, where a stable-boy was walking Valerio II about in his hood. And there were a lot of men strolling along the gravel paths, all of them with their cards forming an orange patch in their button-holes, and a continual parade of people in the open galleries of the stands. All this interested her for a moment or two; but there really wasn't any reason to fret because they didn't let you in!

Daguenet and Fauchery, who were passing by, raised their hats to her. She beckoned to them, and they had to come over to listen to her make fun of the weighing-enclosure. But she broke off to say:

'Why, there's the Marquis de Chouard! How old he looks! The old boy's killing himself! Is he still leading the same wild life?'

Thereupon Daguenet recounted the latest story about the old man, something nobody knew about, because it had happened only two days before. After hanging about for months

he had just bought Gaga's daughter Amélie from her, for thirty thousand francs, so they said.

'God, what a filthy bit of business!' Nana exclaimed in disgust. 'Who'd have a daughter, I ask you! . . . But now I come to think of it, that must be Lili over there in the public enclosure, with a lady in a brougham. I recognized her face. . . . The old boy must have brought her along.'

Vandeuvres was not listening; he was impatient to get rid of her. But Fauchery having remarked as he left that if she hadn't seen the bookmakers she hadn't seen anything, the Count was obliged to take her to have a look in spite of his obvious repugnance. And she was promptly satisfied: this really was a curious sight.

Between lawns bordered by young chestnut trees, there was a round enclosure; and there, forming a vast circle in the shade of the pale green leaves, a thick line of bookmakers was waiting for the punters as if they were stall-holders at a fair. In order to overtop the crowd, they had taken up positions on wooden benches, and the odds they were offering were marked on boards on the trees beside them. Keeping a sharp look-out, they noted down bets in response to a gesture or a wink, so rapidly that some open-mouthed onlookers could not understand what was going on. Confusion reigned, as figures were called out and tumult greeted any unexpected change in the odds. Occasionally the uproar increased when a boy came running up, stopped at the entrance to the enclosure, and at the top of his voice announced the start or finish of a race, setting off a fresh hubbub in the midst of the gambling fever raging in the sunshine.

'Aren't they funny!' murmured Nana, who was vastly amused. 'They look as if they've got their faces inside out. . . . Look at that big fellow over there : I wouldn't like to meet him all alone on a dark night.'

Vandeuvres pointed out a bookmaker to her who had once been an assistant in a draper's shop, and who had made three million francs in two years. He was slight of build, fair-haired and delicate, and the people around him were treating

him with great respect, smiling as they spoke to him, or standing near by to catch a glimpse of him.

They were finally leaving the enclosure when Vandeuvres nodded slightly to another bookmaker, who thereupon ventured to call him. It was a former coachman of his, a huge fellow with the shoulders of an ox and a florid complexion. Since he had left to try his fortune at the races, with capital he had acquired by some shady means, the Count had tried to help him, entrusting him with his secret bets, and still treating him as a servant from whom there was no point in hiding anything. In spite of this patronage the man had lost very large sums in rapid succession, and now he too was playing his last card. His eyes were bloodshot, and he looked as if he were on the verge of an apoplectic fit.

'Well, Maréchal,' said the Count in a very low voice, 'how much have you laid bets for?'

'Five thousand louis, Monsieur le Comte,' replied the bookmaker, likewise lowering his voice. 'That's good, isn't it? ... I must admit I increased the odds; I've made them three to one.'

Vandeuvres looked annoyed.

'No, no, I don't want you to do that; put them back at two to one straight away. ... I shan't tell you anything again, Maréchal.'

'Oh, how can it hurt you now, Monsieur le Comte?' said the other, with a humble conspiratorial smile. 'I had to attract people so as to place your two thousand louis.'

At this Vandeuvres silenced him. But as he was going away Maréchal remembered something, and wished he had asked him about the shortening of the odds on his filly. He would be in a fine mess if the filly stood a chance, seeing that he had just taken a bet for two hundred louis at fifty to one.

Although Nana did not understand a word of what the Count was whispering, she did not dare to ask for fresh explanations. He seemed more nervous than ever, and abruptly handed her over to Labordette, whom they met in front of the weighing-in room.

'You take her back,' he said. 'I've got something to see to. ... Good-bye.'

And he went into the room, which was narrow and low ceilinged, and half filled with a huge pair of scales. It was like the left-luggage room in a suburban station, and Nana was once again deeply disappointed, for she had been picturing to herself something on a vast scale, a monumental machine for weighing horses. Discovering that they weighed only the jockeys, she declared that it wasn't worthwhile making such a fuss about their weighing. On the scales a jockey with an idiotic expression was waiting with his harness on his knees for a stout man in a frock-coat to check his weight; while outside the door a stable-boy was holding his horse, Cosinus, round which a silent, fascinated crowd was clustering.

The course was about to be cleared, and Labordette urged Nana to hurry up. But he turned back to show her a little man talking to Vandeuvres some distance away.

'Look, that's Price,' he said.

'Oh, yes, the man who's riding me,' she murmured with a laugh.

She found him terribly ugly. All the jockeys struck her as looking imbecilic – probably, she said, because they were prevented from growing bigger. This particular jockey was a man of forty, and with his long, thin face, hard, expressionless, and deeply furrowed, he looked like an old dried-up child. His body was so small and gnarled that his blue jacket with the white sleeves looked as if it had been thrown over a piece of wood.

'No,' she went on as she walked away, 'I don't think he could make me happy.'

A throng of people was still crowding the course, the turf of which had been wetted and trampled on till it had turned black. Another crowd was clustered in front of the two telegraph-boards, high up on their cast-iron pillars, looking up at them and greeting with a hum of voices the number of each horse as an electric wire connected with the weighing-in room made it appear. Gentlemen were checking their racecards : Pichenette had been scratched by her owner, and this caused a stir. However, Nana walked straight back on Labordette's arm, while the bell hanging on the

flag-staff rang steadily to warn people to clear the course.

'Oh, my dears,' she said, as she climbed into her landau again, 'their precious weighing-in enclosure's just a lot of humbug!'

All round her people cheered her and clapped their hands, shouting:

'Bravo, Nana!... Nana's come back to us!'

How silly they were! Did they think she was the sort to leave them in the lurch? She had come back just at the right time. Now quiet, everybody: the race was beginning! The champagne was forgotten, and everybody stopped drinking.

But Nana was astonished to find Gaga in her carriage, sitting with Bijou and little Louis on her lap. Gaga had in fact decided on this course of action to get closer to la Faloise, though she told Nana it was to kiss baby. She simply adored children, she said.

'By the way,' said Nana, 'isn't that Lili over there, in that old boy's brougham? ... Somebody's just told me a nice piece of news about her.'

Gaga put on a tearful expression.

'My dear, it's made me ill,' she said dolefully. 'Yesterday I had to stay in bed, I'd cried so much the day before, and today I didn't think I'd be able to come.... You know how I felt about it? I didn't want her to do it. I had her brought up in a convent in the hope that she'd make a good match. And I'd given her strict advice and kept a constant watch on her. ... Well, my dear, it was she who wanted to do it. We had a scene, with tears and insults, and it even got to the point where I slapped her face. She was bored, she said, and wanted a different sort of life.... And when she started saying: "You of all people haven't any right to stop me", I said to her: "You're a slut! You're bringing dishonour on us! Get out!" And I agreed to fix it up.... But that's my last hope gone, and, oh, I used to dream of such wonderful things!'

The sound of a quarrel brought them to their feet. It was Georges defending Vandeuvres against the vague rumours which were circulating among the various groups.

'Why should you say that he's dropping his own horse?'

the young man was shouting. 'Yesterday, at the Salon des Courses, he bet a thousand louis on Lusignan.'

'Yes, I was there,' said Philippe. 'And he didn't put a single louis on Nana. ... If the betting's ten to one against Nana, he's got nothing to do with it. It's ridiculous to imagine people are so calculating. Where would he stand to gain?'

Labordette was listening calmly. Shrugging his shoulders he said :

'Oh, drop it; people are bound to talk. ... The Count has just bet at least another hundred louis on Lusignan, and if he's laid a hundred louis on Nana, that's because an owner has always got to look as if he believes in his horses.'

'Oh, what the hell does it matter to us?' yelled la Faloise, waving his arms. 'It's Spirit that's going to win. ... Down with France ! Up with England !'

A long tremor ran through the crowd, while a fresh peal from the bell announced the arrival of the horses on the race-course. At this Nana climbed up on the seat of her landau to get a better view, trampling on the bouquets of roses and myosotis. With a sweeping glance she took in the whole vast horizon. At this last feverish moment the first thing she saw was the empty course, shut in by its grey rails, with a police-man standing at every other post; and the strip of grass, which was muddy in front of her, grew greener as it stretched away, and turned into a soft velvet carpet farther off. In the middle distance, as she lowered her eyes, she saw the public enclosure swarming with people, some on tiptoe, others hanging on to carriages. Horses were neighing and tent-canvases flapping, while riders urged their horses forward among the pedestrians rushing to get places along the rails. When Nana turned in the direction of the stands on the other side, the faces seemed to have shrunk, and the dense masses of heads were only a motley array, filling the gangways, the tiers of seats and the terraces on which ranks of dark profiles were outlined against the sky. Then she looked even farther, over the plain around the Hippodrome. Behind the ivy-covered windmill on the right, meadows interspersed with shady woods stretched away into the dis-tance; in front of her, as far as the Seine flowing at the foot

of the hill, parkland avenues intersected one another, lined just now with motionless files of waiting carriages; and in the direction of Boulogne, on the left, the landscape widened again, opening out towards the bluish shadows of Meudon through an avenue of paulonias, whose rosy, leafless tops formed a sheet of bright lake. People were still arriving, a trail of human ants kept coming across the distant fields along the narrow ribbon of road, while far away, in the direction of Paris, the non-paying public, like a flock of sheep in the woods, moved in a line of dark spots under the trees on the edge of the Bois.

Suddenly the hundred thousand souls covering this part of the plain, like insects swarming madly under the vast skies, had their spirits raised as the sun, which had been hidden for a quarter of an hour, reappeared, spreading out in a sea of light. And everything caught fire again, the women's parasols looking like countless golden bucklers above the heads of the crowd. The sun was greeted with cheers and bursts of laughter, and people stretched out their arms as if to brush aside the clouds.

Meanwhile a police officer advanced alone down the middle of the empty racecourse, while higher up, on the left, a man appeared with a red flag in his hand.

'That's the starter, the Baron de Mauriac,' said Labordette in reply to a question from Nana.

Around the young woman exclamations came from the men who were clustered about her carriage and even standing on the footboards. They kept up a disconnected conversation, tossing off words on the spur of the moment. Indeed Philippe and Georges, Bordenave and la Faloise found it impossible to keep quiet.

'Don't push . . . Let me see! . . . Ah, the judge is going into his box. . . . Did you say it was Monsieur de Souvigny? . . . He must have good eyesight if he can decide a close finish from a contraption like that! . . . Do be quiet – the flag's going up. . . . Look! Here they are! . . . It's Cosinus in front.'

A red and yellow banner was flapping in the air at the top of the mast. The horses came on to the course one by one, led by stable-boys, with the jockeys sitting in the saddle with

their arms at rest, the sunlight making them look like bright patches of colours. After Cosinus came Hasard and Boum. Then a murmur of voices greeted Spirit, a magnificent big brown bay, whose harsh colours, lemon and black, had a melancholy British quality. Valerio II scored a success as he came in; he was small and very lively in pale green bordered with pink. The two Vandeuvres horses were a long time coming, but at last the blue and white colours appeared behind Frangipane. However, Lusignan, a very dark bay, of irreproachable build, was almost forgotten in the astonishment caused by Nana. Nobody had seen her looking like this before, for the sudden sunlight lent the chestnut filly the golden sheen of a redhead's hair. She shone in the light like a new louis; her breast was deep, and her head and neck rose lightly from the delicate, sinewy line of her long back.

'Look, she's got my hair!' Nana shouted in delight. 'You know, I feel quite proud of her!'

As more people clambered on to the landau, Bordenave almost stepped on little Louis, whom his mother had forgotten. He picked him up with a fatherly growl and hoisted him on his shoulders, murmuring:

'The poor kid deserves to get a look-in too. ... Wait a minute and I'll show you Mama. ... Look at the gee-gee over there.'

As Bijou had started scratching his legs, he took charge of him too; while Nana, delighted by the animal bearing her name, glanced round at the other women to see how they were taking it. They were all fuming with rage. At that moment La Tricon, who till then had been sitting motionless on the top of her cab, began waving her hands about, giving a bookmaker instructions over the heads of the crowd. Her instinct had just spoken to her; she was backing Nana.

Meanwhile la Faloise was making an insufferable noise. He had taken a fancy to Frangipane.

'I've had an inspiration,' he kept shouting. 'Just look at Frangipane. What action, eh? ... I'll bet eight to one on Frangipane. Any takers?'

'Oh, pipe down,' Labordette said at last. 'You'll be sorry if you do.'

'Frangipane's a screw,' declared Philippe. 'He's sweating already.... You just watch the canter.'

The horses had gone up to the right, and now they set off for the preliminary canter, passing the stands in loose order. Immediately there was a passionate new burst of talk, with everybody speaking at once.

'Lusignan's too long in the back, but very fit. ... Not a penny, I tell you, on Valerio II; he's skittish and galloping with his head up – that's a bad sign.... Hey, it's Burne who's riding Spirit. ... I tell you he's got no shoulders. Well-made shoulders, that's the important thing. ... No, Spirit's definitely too quiet.... Listen, I saw Nana after the Grand Poule des Produits; she was dripping with sweat, her coat was deadly dull, and she was panting like mad. I'll bet you twenty louis she isn't placed! ... Oh, why doesn't he shut up? He's getting on our nerves with his precious Frangipane. It's too late – they're heading for the off.'

This was a reference to la Faloise, who was almost in tears and frantically trying to find a bookmaker. The others had to talk him out of it. Everybody was craning forward, but there was a false start, for the starter, who looked like a thin black line in the distance, had not lowered his flag. The horses came back to their places after galloping a little way. There were two more false starts, but at last the starter got the horses together and sent them off with a skill which elicited shouts of applause.

'Magnificent! ... No, he was just lucky! ... Never mind, they're off!'

The shouts died down, smothered by the anxiety filling every breast. The betting dropped now, as the battle was joined on the vast course. Silence reigned at first as if everybody were holding his breath. White faces were raised and bodies trembled. At first Hasard and Cosinus made the running, taking the lead; Valerio II came hard on their heels and the field followed in a confused mass. When they passed the stands, thundering over the ground like a sudden stormwind, they were already strung out over some fourteen lengths. Frangipane was last, and Nana was slightly behind Lusignan and Spirit.

'By God!' muttered Labordette. 'That English horse is moving fast out there!'

The whole company in the landau started talking and shouting again. Everybody stood on tiptoe to follow the bright splashes of colour which were the jockeys as they sped along in the sunshine. At the rise Valerio II took the lead and Cosinus and Hasard lost ground, while Lusignan and Spirit, running neck and neck, still had Nana behind them.

'Dammit, the English horse has won, that's obvious,' said Bordenave. 'Lusignan's tiring and Valerio II can't stay the course.'

'Well, it'll be a fine thing if the English horse wins!' exclaimed Philippe, in a burst of patriotic grief.

A feeling of anguish was beginning to take hold of the whole vast multitude. Another defeat! And an extraordinary prayer, almost religious in its intensity, went up for Lusignan, while people cursed Spirit and his funereal jockey. Among the crowd scattered over the grass, excitement sent groups of people running hell for leather. Horsemen crossed the grass at a furious gallop. And Nana, turning slowly, saw at her feet a surging mass of animals and men, a sea of heads swept round the course by the whirlwind of the race, which was streaking the horizon with the bright flash of the jockeys. She had followed the horses from behind, as their cruppers retreated and their legs gathered speed, diminishing in size until they looked like thin strands of hair. Now, at the far end of the course, they were speeding along in profile, tiny delicate creatures silhouetted against the distant green of the Bois. Then all of a sudden they disappeared behind a big clump of trees in the middle of the Hippodrome.

'Don't worry!' cried Georges, who was still full of hope. 'It isn't over yet. . . . The English horse is falling back.'

But la Faloise, seized again with contempt for his country, started cheering on Spirit in a quite outrageous fashion. Bravo! It served them right! France needed to be beaten! Spirit first and Frangipane second – that would teach his fellow countrymen! Labordette, exasperated beyond endurance, seriously threatened to throw him off the carriage.

'Let's see how many minutes they take,' said Bordenave

calmly, pulling out his watch while still holding up little
Louis.

One after another the horses reappeared from behind the
clump of trees. There was a long murmur of amazement
from the crowd. Valerio II was still in the lead, but Spirit
was gaining on him : and behind him, Lusignan had dropped
back, while another horse was taking his place. The crowd
could not make out what was happening straight away, for
they mixed up the colours. Then there was a chorus of
amazement.

'Why, it's Nana ! ... Nana ! ... Get along with you ! I tell
you Lusignan hasn't budged. ... Yes, it's Nana all right. You
can recognize her by her golden colour. ... Can you see her
now? She looks as if she's on fire. ... Bravo, Nana ! What a
minx she is. ... Nonsense, it doesn't make any difference.
She's making the running for Lusignan.'

For a few seconds that was everybody's opinion. But little
by little the filly went on steadily gaining. At that a wave of
feeling swept the crowd. The line of horses bringing up the
rear ceased to interest anybody as a supreme struggle began between Spirit, Nana, Lusignan and Valerio II. People
pointed them out, commenting on their performance as they
gained ground or fell back in stammering, disconnected
phrases. And Nana, who had just climbed up onto her coachman's seat, as if borne upwards by some unseen force, stood
there white-faced and trembling, so deeply moved that she
said nothing. Beside her, Labordette was smiling again.

'The English horse is in trouble,' said Philippe joyously.
'He's not doing well at all.'

'In any case it's all up with Lusignan,' shouted la Faloise.
'That's Valerio II coming up. ... Look, there are the four
of them bunched together.'

The same word was on every tongue.

'What a pace ! ... What a hell of a pace !'

The main body of horses was now arriving opposite them
like a flash of lightning. You could feel it coming, the breath
of it like a distant rumbling which grew louder every second.
The whole crowd had thrown themselves impetuously against
the rails, and preceding the horses a deep roar came from

countless breasts, drawing nearer and nearer like the sound of breakers on the shore. It was the brutal climax of a colossal game, with a hundred thousand spectators possessed by a single passion, burning with the same gambling fever, as they watched these animals whose galloping hooves were carrying off millions with them. The crowd jostled and pushed, fists clenched and mouths gaping, every man for himself, and every man whipping on the horse of his choice with voice and gesture. And the cry of the multitude, the cry of a wild beast reappearing in a frock-coat, grew more and more distinct :

'Here they come ! Here they come ! Here they come !'

Nana was still gaining ground, and as Valerio II fell back, she went into the lead, with Spirit two or three necks behind. The thunder of voices had increased. They were coming nearer and nearer, and a storm of oaths greeted them from the landau.

'Gee up, Lusignan, you great coward, you dirty screw ! ... Come on, Spirit ! Come on, old boy ! ... That Valerio's disgusting ! ... What a nag ! ... That's the end of my ten louis ! ... There's only Nana now ! Bravo, Nana ! Bravo, you bitch !'

And on the seat, without realizing what she was doing, Nana had started swaying her thighs and hips as if she were running the race herself. She kept jerking her belly forward, imagining that this was a help to the filly. With each jerk she gave a sigh of fatigue, saying in a low, anguished voice :

'Go on ... go on ... go on ...'

Then the crowd witnessed a splendid sight. Price, riding in the stirrups and brandishing his whip, flogged Nana with an arm of iron. The dried-up old child with his long, hard, dead face seemed to be breathing fire. And in a burst of furious audacity and triumphant will-power, he poured his heart into the filly, picked her up and carried her forward, drenched in foam, her eyes all bloodshot. The whole field went by with a roar of thunder, taking people's breath away and sweeping the air with it, while the judge sat waiting coldly, his eye fixed on his sighting-mark. Then there was a huge burst of cheering. With a supreme effort Price had just flung Nana past the post, beating Spirit by a head.

There came a sound like the roar of a rising tide : 'Nana !

Nana! Nana!' the cry rolled along, swelling with the violence of a storm, and gradually filling the horizon, from the depths of the Bois to Mont Valérien, and from the meadows of Longchamp to the plain of Boulogne. All over the public enclosure wild enthusiasm reigned, with cries of 'Long live Nana! Long live France! Down with England!' The women waved their parasols; men leapt and spun around, shouting and cheering; while others, with shouts of nervous laughter, threw their hats in the air. And from the other side of the course, the weighing-in enclosure responded, as emotion swept through the stands, although nothing was really visible but a trembling of the air, like the invisible flame of a brazier above that living mass of little disjointed figures, with waving arms and black dots which were eyes and open mouths. Far from dying down the noise swelled, beginning again at the end of the distant avenues, among the common people camping under the trees, and spreading until it reached its climax in the emotion of the imperial stand, where the Empress herself had applauded. 'Nana! Nana! Nana!' the cry rose in the glorious sunshine, whose golden rain beat down on the dizzy heads of the crowd.

At that, Nana, standing tall and erect on the seat of her landau, imagined that it was she whom they were applauding. For a moment she had stood motionless, stupefied by her triumph, gazing at the course as it was invaded by such a dense flood of people that the grass was hidden from sight beneath a sea of black hats. Then when all these people had come to a halt, leaving a lane as far as the exit, and applauding Nana again as she went off with Price lying exhausted and drained of energy on her neck, she slapped her thighs hard, forgetting herself completely, and triumphing in a succession of crude phrases.

'God, it's me, you know! ... God, what marvellous luck!'

And not knowing how to give expression to her overwhelming joy, she hugged and kissed little Louis, whom she had just discovered high in the air on Bordenave's shoulder.

'Three minutes and fourteen seconds,' said the latter, putting his watch again in his pocket.

Nana could still hear her name, which the whole plain was

echoing back to her. It was her people who were applauding her, while she towered above them, erect in the sunlight, with her golden hair and her white and sky-blue dress. Before slipping away, Labordette had just announced to her a win of two thousand louis, for he had put her fifty louis on Nana, at forty to one. But this money stirred her less than Nana's unexpected victory, the splendour of which had made her the queen of Paris. All the other ladies had lost. Rose Mignon had broken her parasol in a furious movement; Caroline Héquet, Clarisse, Simonne and even Lucy Stewart, in spite of her son's presence, were swearing under their breath in their exasperation at the plump courtesan's luck; while La Tricon, who had made the sign of the cross at both start and finish, drew herself up to her full height above them, delighted at the rightness of her instinct, and paying Nana the tribute of a woman of experience.

Meanwhile the crush of men around the landau was increasing. Nana's companions had set up a fierce clamour, and now Georges, choking with emotion, continued shouting all by himself in a broken voice. As the champagne had given out, Philippe, taking the footmen with him, had run to the refreshment bars. Nana's court was growing all the time, her triumph persuading the laggards to join her, so that the movement which had made her carriage the centre of the public enclosure was now ending in an apotheosis, with Queen Venus enthroned amid the enthusiasm of her subjects. Bordenave behind her was muttering oaths in an outburst of fatherly affection. Steiner himself had been reconquered, for he had deserted Simonne and was hoisting himself up on one of Nana's carriage steps. When the champagne had arrived, and she lifted up her brimming glass, there was such a storm of applause, and the shouts of 'Nana! Nana! Nana!' were so loudly repeated, that the crowd looked round in astonishment for the filly; and nobody could tell whether it was the horse or the woman that stirred every heart.

Mignon came running up in the meantime, in spite of Rose's black looks. He was lost in admiration for that confounded girl and had to kiss her at all costs. Then, after planting a fatherly kiss on both her cheeks, he said :

378

'What bothers me, is that now Rose is certain to send the letter.... She's beside herself with rage.'

'So much the better!' Nana retorted. 'That suits me down to the ground!'

But, noting his astonishment, she hurriedly corrected herself:

'No, no, what am I saying? ... Honestly, I don't know what I'm saying any more! ... I'm drunk.'

Drunk indeed, drunk with joy and sunshine, she stood with her glass still held high and toasted herself.

'To Nana! To Nana!' she shouted, amid a growing din of laughter and cheers which had gradually spread over the entire Hippodrome.

The races were coming to an end, and the Prix Vaublanc was being run. Carriages had begun driving off one by one. Meanwhile the name of Vandeuvres kept cropping up in arguments. It was obvious now that for the past two years Vandeuvres had been preparing his coup, instructing Gresham to hold Nana back, and bringing Lusignan forward only as a cover for the filly. The losers fumed with anger, while the winners shrugged their shoulders. What of it? Wasn't it allowed? An owner was free to run his stable as he thought fit. Plenty of others had done the same! Most people thought that Vandeuvres had been very clever laying all the bets he could on Nana through the agency of his friends, a procedure which explained the sudden shortening of the odds. There was talk of his having bet two thousand louis on the horse, which, at an average of thirty to one against, meant that he had won twelve hundred thousand francs, an amount so vast as to command respect and excuse everything.

But other rumours of a very serious nature were being whispered about, which had started in the weighing-in enclosure. The men coming back from there gave details, and voices rose as a terrible scandal was openly revealed. That poor fellow Vandeuvres was done for; he had spoilt his magnificent coup with a piece of utter stupidity, an idiotic theft, for he had commissioned Maréchal, a shady bookmaker, to lay two thousand louis on his behalf against Lusignan, in

order to get back the paltry thousand odd louis he had wagered in public – proof that his mind was giving way in the midst of the final collapse of his fortune. The bookmaker, warned that the favourite was not going to win, had made about sixty thousand francs on the horse. However, Labordette, for want of exact details and instructions, had gone to him to bet two hundred louis on Nana, which the bookmaker, in his ignorance of the real coup being planned, was still quoting at fifty to one against. Losing one hundred thousand francs on the filly, and consequently being forty thousand in the red, Maréchal, who felt the ground giving way under his feet, had suddenly understood everything when he saw Labordette and the Count talking together in front of the weighing-in room after the race was over. With the fury of a former coachman and the savagery of a man who has been robbed, he had just made a terrible scene in public, telling the whole story in the crudest terms, and stirring everybody up. It was said too that the stewards were going to meet.

Nana, whom Philippe and Georges had acquainted with the facts in a whisper, expressed her opinions without stopping laughing and drinking. When you came to think of it, it was quite likely; she remembered a few things which seemed to bear out what they said; besides that Maréchal looked a shifty character. All the same, she still had her doubts when Labordette appeared. He was very pale.

'Well?' she asked in a low voice.

'Done for!' he replied simply.

And he shrugged his shoulders. That Vandeuvres was just a child. She made a bored gesture.

That evening at Mabille Nana had a colossal success. When she appeared, about ten o'clock, the din was already tremendous. This traditional night of madness brought together all the pleasure-loving young people of Paris, a smart set bent on wallowing in the crudeness and imbecility of the servants' hall. There was a huge crush under the festoons of gas-lamps, and men in evening coats and women in outrageous low-necked gowns – old dresses which they did not mind getting dirty – were circling around and yelling at the

tops of their voices in an orgy of drunkenness. At a distance of thirty paces the brass section of the orchestra was inaudible. Nobody was dancing. Stupid jokes, none of them worth repeating, were going the rounds of the various groups, as people tried hard to be funny, without success. Seven women, locked in the cloakroom, were tearfully begging to be set free. A shallot was found, put up for auction, and knocked down at two louis. Just then Nana arrived, still wearing her blue and white racecourse outfit, and was presented with the shallot amid thunderous applause. She was grabbed willy-nilly, and three gentlemen bore her in triumph into the garden, across the ravaged flowerbeds and through the disembowelled shrubberies. As the orchestra was in their way, it was taken by storm, and the chairs and music-stands smashed. Fatherly police officers organized the disorder.

It was only on Tuesday that Nana recovered from the excitement of her victory. That morning she was chatting with Madame Lerat, the old lady having come to bring her news of little Louis, who had fallen ill from the effects of the fresh air. She was all agog about a story which was occupying the attention of all Paris. After being warned off all the racecourses in the country and expelled from the Cercle Impérial on the very evening after the race, Vandeuvres had burnt himself and his horses to death in his stable the next day.

'He told me he was going to,' the young woman kept saying. 'The man was a regular lunatic! ... It gave me quite a turn when they told me about it yesterday evening! You see, he could easily have murdered me one night. ... Besides, oughtn't he to have given a hint about his horse? At least I'd have made a fortune! ... He told Labordette that if I knew about it I'd tell my hairdresser straight away, and a lot of other men. Polite, wasn't he! ... Oh, no, I can't say I'll shed many tears over him.'

After thinking about it, she had grown very angry. Just then Labordette came in; he had settled his bets, and was bringing her about forty thousand francs. This only worsened her bad temper, for she ought to have won a million. Labordette, who had played the innocent throughout this affair,

washed his hands of Vandeuvres. These old families, he said, were worn out, and finished in a stupid way.

'Oh, no!' said Nana. 'It isn't stupid setting fire to yourself in a stable like that. Personally, I think he finished bloody well. . . . Oh, you know, I'm not defending that business of him and Maréchal. It's ridiculous. When I think that Blanche had the cheek to try and blame it on me! I said to her: "Did I tell him to steal?" Don't you think you can ask a man for money without driving him to crime? . . . If he'd said to me: "I've got nothing left", I'd have said to him: "All right, let's split up." And it wouldn't have gone any further than that.'

'Just so,' her aunt said gravely. 'When men get pig-headed about something, that's their fault!'

'But as for the way he went,' Nana went on, 'that really showed style. . . . They say it was awful, fit to give you the shudders. He'd sent everybody away, and he locked himself in the stables with a lot of paraffin oil. . . . And the way it blazed – you should have seen it! Just imagine a great big building, nearly all made of wood, and stuffed with hay and straw! . . . The flames went shooting up like church towers. . . . The best of it all was that the horses didn't want to be roasted. You could hear them lashing out, throwing themselves against the doors, and screaming just like human beings. Yes, the people who saw it still haven't got over it.'

Labordette let out a low murmur of incredulity. For his part he did not believe that Vandeuvres was dead. Somebody had sworn that he had seen him escaping through a window. He had set fire to his stables in a fit of madness, and as soon as it had started getting really hot it must have sobered him up. A man who had been such a fool about women, and so utterly worn out, couldn't possibly die as bravely as that.

Nana listened to him in disappointment. All she could think of to say was:

'Oh, the poor thing! It was so beautiful!'

ABOUT one in the morning, in the great bed with the Venetian point hangings, Nana and the Count were still awake. He had returned that evening after sulking for three days. The room, which was dimly lit by a lamp, was slumbering in the warm, damp odour of love, while the white lacquer furniture inlaid with silver shone with a vague pallor. A curtain had been drawn to, so that the bed lay deep in shadow. There was a sigh; then a kiss broke the silence, and Nana, slipping out of the covers, sat for a moment bare-legged on the edge of the bed. The Count let his head fall back on the pillow, and remained in darkness.

'Darling, do you believe in God?' she asked after thinking for a little while. Her face was serious, for she had been overcome by a feeling of pious terror on leaving her lover's arms.

Since the previous morning, in fact, she had complained of feeling unwell, and all her stupid ideas, as she called them, thoughts of death and hell, had been secretly tormenting her. Now and then she had nights like this, during which childish fears and horrible fantasies would come to her in waking nightmares. She went on :

'Tell me, do you think I'll go to heaven?'

And she gave a shudder, while the Count, surprised by these peculiar questions at such a moment, felt his old Catholic remorse reawakening in him. But then, with her night-gown slipping from her shoulders and her hair falling about her face, she threw herself on his chest, sobbing and clinging to him.

'I'm afraid of dying. ... I'm afraid of dying ...'

He had all the trouble in the world to disengage himself. Indeed he himself felt afraid of giving in to the sudden madness of this woman clinging to his body, and of being infected by her dread of the Invisible. He reasoned with her, telling her that she was perfectly healthy, and only had to behave well in order one day to deserve forgiveness. But she shook

her head. It was true that she never did any harm to anybody; and she even wore a medal of the Virgin all the time, which she showed to him hanging from a red thread between her breasts. Only it was laid down in advance that any unmarried woman who went with men would go to hell. Scraps of her catechism came back to her. Oh, if only you could tell for certain; but there it was – we didn't know; nobody ever came back to tell us the truth; and honestly it would be stupid to do without the good things of life if the priests were talking nonsense. All the same, she devoutly kissed her medal, which was still warm from contact with her skin, as if it were a charm against death, the idea of which filled her with icy horror.

Muffat was obliged to accompany her into the dressing-room, for she was terrified at the idea of being alone there for a minute, even leaving the door open. After he had gone back to bed she went on prowling around the room, inspecting every corner, and giving a start at the slightest noise. A mirror stopped her, and as of old she forgot herself in the contemplation of her nakedness. But the sight of her breasts, her hips and her thighs only increased her terror, and she ended up by slowly feeling the bones of her face with both hands.

'People are ugly when they're dead,' she said in a solemn tone of voice.

And she pressed her cheeks, widening her eyes and dropping her jaw, to see how she would look. Thus disfigured, she turned towards the Count :

'Look – my head will be quite small.'

At this he lost his temper.

'You're mad. Come to bed.'

He pictured her in the grave, emaciated by a century of sleep; and joining his hands he stammered a prayer. For some time now his religious beliefs had reconquered him; and every day his attack of faith assumed the same apoplectic intensity, which left him almost stunned. The joints of his fingers snapped, and he kept repeating the same two words over and over again : 'My God. ... My God. ... My God.' This was the cry of his weakness, the cry of that sin

which, though certain of being damned, he felt powerless to resist. When Nana returned, she found him hidden under the bedclothes; his face was haggard, his nails were digging into his chest, and his eyes were staring upwards as if in search of heaven. She started crying again, and the two of them embraced, their teeth chattering for no apparent reason as the same stupid obsession took hold of them. They had already spent a similar night together; but this time it was utterly idiotic, as Nana declared when she stopped feeling frightened. A sudden suspicion led her to question the Count cautiously : perhaps Rose Mignon had sent the famous letter. But that was not the case; it was fright and nothing more, for he was still unaware that he was a cuckold.

Two days later, after a fresh disappearance, Muffat presented himself in the morning, a time of day when he never came. He was ghastly pale, his eyes red, and his whole body still shaken by a great internal struggle. But Zoé, being in a fluster herself, did not notice his agitated state. She had run to meet him, shouting :

'Oh, Monsieur, do come in ! Madame nearly died last night.'

And when he asked for details, she answered :

'Something incredible. . . . A miscarriage, Monsieur !'

Nana had been pregnant for the past three months. For a long time she had thought that she was simply out of sorts, and Doctor Boutarel himself had been unsure. But when he finally made a definite diagnosis she was so annoyed that she did everything she could to conceal her condition. Her pregnancy struck her as a ridiculous accident, something which reflected unfavourably on her and would lead to her being chaffed if people found out. It was a bad joke in her view, a piece of really hard luck. She *would* have to get caught, when she thought that was all over. And she felt a perpetual sense of surprise, as if her sexual parts had been deranged; so they still made babies, even when you didn't want them to, and you used them for other purposes? Nature infuriated her, with this intervention of solemn motherhood in her career of pleasure – this gift of life in the midst of all the deaths she was spreading around her. Why could one not

dispose of one's self as fancy dictated? Shouldn't you be able to do what you like with yourself without all this trouble? And where had this brat come from? She couldn't even guess. Heavens, the man who had made the child would have done better to keep him for himself, for nobody wanted him, he was in everybody's way, and he certainly wouldn't have much happiness in life.

Meanwhile Zoé was describing the catastrophe.

'Madame had an attack of colic about four o' clock. When she didn't come back out of the dressing-room, I went in, and found her stretched out on the floor in a faint. Yes, Monsieur, on the floor, in a pool of blood, as if she'd been murdered.... Then I understood, you see. ... I was furious, because Madame might at least have told me she was in trouble. ... As it happened, Monsieur Georges was here, and he helped me to pick her up. But as soon as he heard the word "miscarriage" he fainted too. ... Oh, I tell you, I've been in a real state since yesterday.'

In fact the whole house seemed at sixes and sevens. All the servants kept rushing upstairs, downstairs, and through the rooms. Georges had spent the night in an armchair in the drawing-room. It was he who had announced the news to Madame's friends in the evening, at the hour when Madame was in the habit of receiving. He was still very pale, and he told his story in a voice full of emotion and amazement. Steiner, la Faloise, Philippe and others besides had called to see Nana, and at the first words they burst into exclamations; it was impossible ... he was joking. Then they turned serious, and gazed at her bedroom door, looking annoyed and shaking their heads; it was no laughing matter.

Till midnight a dozen gentlemen had sat chatting in low voices round the fire. They were all friends, and all deeply exercised by the same idea of paternity. They seemed to be apologizing to one another, and they looked as embarrassed as if they had done something clumsy. Finally, however, they straightened their shoulders, agreeing that it had nothing to do with them, and that it was all her doing. She was an amazing girl, wasn't she? Nobody could ever have believed

386

her capable of a joke like that! And they had gone off one by one, walking on tip-toe as if they were in a dead man's room where it would have been unseemly to laugh.

'Come upstairs, all the same, Monsieur,' Zoé said to Muffat. 'Madame will see you, because she's feeling much better. We're expecting the doctor, who promised to come back this morning.'

The maid had persuaded Georges to go back home to sleep, and upstairs in the drawing-room only Satin remained. She was stretched out on a divan, smoking a cigarette and looking at the ceiling. In the confusion which had followed the accident she had shown an icy fury, shrugging her shoulders and making ferocious remarks. Accordingly, when Zoé was passing in front of her and telling Monsieur again that poor Madame had suffered a great deal, she snapped:

'Serves her right! That'll teach her!'

They turned round in surprise. Satin had not moved a muscle; her eyes were still fixed on the ceiling, her cigarette was still pinched nervously between her lips.

'Well, that's nice of you, that is!' said Zoé.

Satin sat up, glared at the Count, and once more hurled her remark in his face:

'Serves her right! That'll teach her!'

And lying down again, she blew a thin jet of smoke into the air, as if to indicate that she had no interest in what was happening and was determined not to get involved. No, it was all too silly!

Zoé, however, introduced Muffat into the bedroom, where a scent of ether lingered in the warm silence, which was scarcely broken by the dull rumble of an occasional carriage in the Avenue de Villiers. Nana, looking very white on her pillow, was lying awake with wide-open, thoughtful eyes. She smiled when she saw the Count, but did not move.

'Ah, my pet,' she murmured in a drawn-out voice. 'I thought I would never see you again.'

Then, as he leant forward to kiss her on her hair, she was moved to tears and spoke to him in all sincerity as if he were its father.

'I didn't dare tell you.... I felt so happy! ... Oh, I used to

dream about him. ... I'd have liked him to be worthy of you. And now there's nothing left. ... Ah, well, perhaps it's better that way. I don't want to cause you any trouble.'

Astonished by this story of paternity, he began stammering incoherent phrases. He had drawn up a chair, and had sat down by the bed, leaning one arm on the covers. Then the young woman noticed his anguished expression, his bloodshot eyes, his lips trembling feverishly.

'What's the matter?' she asked. 'Are you ill too?'

'No,' he answered with some difficulty.

She gazed at him with grave eyes. Then she motioned to Zoé, who was hanging about arranging the medicine bottles, to leave the room. And when they were alone, she drew him close to her and asked again:

'What's the matter, darling? ... Your eyes are bursting with tears – I can see they are. ... Come on, speak up; you've come to tell me something.'

'No, no, I swear I haven't,' he stammered.

But, choking with anguish, and moved even more by this sickroom which he had entered unawares, he burst out sobbing, and buried his face in the sheets to smother the violence of his grief. Nana had realized what had happened. Obviously Rose Mignon had decided to send the letter. She let him cry for a little while, shaken by such violent spasms that the bed trembled under her. At last, in accents of motherly compassion, she asked:

'You've had trouble at home?'

He nodded. She paused again, and then said in a very low voice:

'So you know everything?'

He nodded. And a heavy silence fell once more in the grief-filled room. The night before, on his return from a party given by the Empress, he had received the letter Sabine had written to her lover. After a terrible night spent dreaming of revenge, he had gone out in the morning to resist a powerful urge to kill his wife. Outside, struck by the beauty of a fine June morning, he had lost the thread of his thoughts, and had come to see Nana as he always did in the dark hours of his life. It was only with her that he could abandon himself

to his misery, in the cowardly but joyful conviction that she would console him.

'Come now, calm down,' the young woman continued, trying to comfort him. 'I've known about it a long time, but I certainly wouldn't have opened your eyes. You remember you had your suspicions last year, but then, thanks to me, things sorted themselves out. Besides, you hadn't any proof. ... Well, you've got your proof now, and I know it's hard on you. All the same, you've got to make the best of it : what's happened is no disgrace to you.'

He had stopped crying. A sense of shame held him back, although he had long since slipped into the most intimate confessions about his marriage. She had to encourage him. Look, she was a woman : he could tell her anything. But he blurted out in a lifeless voice :

'You're ill, what's the good of tiring you? ... It was stupid of me to come. I'm going ...'

'No,' she said sharply. 'Stay. Perhaps I'll be able to give you some good advice. Only don't make me talk too much; the doctor says I mustn't.'

Finally he stood up and started walking around the room. She began questioning him.

'Now, what are you going to do?'

'I'm going to slap the man's face, dammit.'

She pursed her lips disapprovingly.

'That isn't very wise. ... And what about your wife?'

'I shall go to law; I've got evidence.'

'Not at all wise, dear. I'd even call it stupid. ... You know, I'll never let you do that.'

And in her weak voice she calmly explained the futility of a duel and a trial. For a week he would be the laughing-stock of the newspapers; he would be risking his whole existence, his peace of mind, his high situation at Court, the honour of his name, and all for what? Just to expose himself to mockery.

'What does that matter?' he cried. 'I'll have had my revenge.'

'My pet,' she said, 'in a case like that, if you don't get your revenge straight away, you never will.'

He paused, stammering incoherently. He was certainly no coward, but he felt she was right. An uneasy feeling was growing within him, a poor shameful feeling which had just taken all the force out of his anger. Moreover, in her determination to tell him everything, she dealt him a fresh blow.

'And do you know what's worrying you, darling? ... It's the fact that you're deceiving your wife yourself. You don't sleep away from home for nothing, do you? Your wife must have her suspicions. Well, then, how can you blame her? She'll tell you that you set her the example, and that'll shut your mouth. ... And that's why you're stamping around here instead of being at home murdering the two of them.'

Muffat had collapsed on the chair again, overwhelmed by these brutal remarks. She stopped to get her breath back, and then went on in a low voice :

'Oh, I'm tired out. Help me to sit up a bit, will you; I keep slipping down, and my head's too low.'

When he had helped her she heaved a sigh, feeling more comfortable. And she returned to the subject of an action for judicial separation. What a fine sight it would be! Couldn't he imagine the Countess's lawyer amusing Paris with his remarks about Nana? Everything would be trotted out – her fiasco at the Variétés, her house, her way of life. Oh no, she didn't want that sort of publicity. Some filthy bitches might perhaps have driven him to it in order to bang the big drum on his back; but she wanted his happiness before all else. She had put one arm round his neck and drawn him towards her, and was now holding him with his head close to hers, on the edge of the pillow. She whispered softly in his ear :

'Listen, pet, you must make it up with your wife.'

He rebelled at this. Never! He could not bear the thought, it was so shameful. All the same, she gently insisted.

'You must make it up with your wife. ... Come now, you don't want to hear everybody saying that I've broken up your marriage, do you? That would give me a horrible reputation. What would people think of me? ... Only promise that you'll always love me, because if you go with another woman ...'

Tears choked her, and he interrupted her with kisses, saying over and over again:

'You're crazy; it's impossible.'

'Yes,' she said, 'you must. . . . I'll make the best of it. After all, she *is* your wife. It isn't as if you were deceiving me with the first woman who came along.'

And she continued in this strain, giving him the best possible advice. She even spoke of God, and the Count thought he was listening to Monsieur Venot, when that old gentleman used to preach at him to save him from sin. However, Nana did not talk of breaking off their liaison; she advocated a complaisant arrangement, a good-natured division of his time between wife and mistress, a quiet life causing nobody any trouble, something like a pleasant sleep among the inevitable miseries of existence. Their life wouldn't be changed in any way. He would still be her special sweetheart, only he would come to see her a little less often and would give the Countess the nights he didn't spend with her. She was utterly exhausted by now, and concluded in a whisper:

'What's more, I'll feel that I've done a good deed, and you'll love me all the more for it.'

Silence reigned. She had closed her eyes, and lay on her pillow, looking paler than ever. The Count had listened to her patiently, under the pretext of not wanting her to tire herself. A good minute later she reopened her eyes, and murmured:

'Besides, what about the money? Where would you get the money from, if you quarrelled with her? Labordette came about the bill yesterday. . . . And I'm short of everything. I haven't got a thing to wear.'

Then she shut her eyes again, and looked dead. A shadow of profound anguish had passed over Muffat's face. Under the impact of the blow which had struck him the previous night, he had forgotten his financial difficulties, which were so serious that he did not know how to extricate himself from them. In spite of faithful promises to the contrary, the bill for a hundred thousand francs had just been put into circulation after being renewed only once, and Labordette, pretending to be in despair about it, had thrown all the blame on

Francis, declaring that never again would he get involved in a business deal with a man of so little breeding. The Count had to pay, for he could never allow his signature to be protested. Then, in addition to Nana's new demands, there was an extraordinary drain on his funds at home. On her return from Les Fondettes the Countess had suddenly displayed a taste for luxury, an appetite for worldly pleasures, which was eating up their fortune. People were beginning to talk about her numerous caprices, a whole new style of living, the squandering of five hundred thousand francs on a complete transformation of the old house in the Rue Miromesnil, the purchase of extravagantly magnificent gowns, and the disappearance of considerable sums, frittered away or perhaps given away, without her even thinking of accounting for them. Twice Muffat had ventured a few remarks, in his anxiety to know what was happening; but she had smiled and gazed at him with such a strange expression that he had not dared to question her any further for fear of getting too explicit an answer. If he was taking Daguenet as his son-in-law as a gift from Nana, it was chiefly in the hope of being able to reduce Estelle's dowry to two hundred thousand francs, and of then being free to come to an arrangement about the rest with a young man who was still delighted with this unexpected match.

Nevertheless, for the last week, under the pressing necessity of finding Labordette's hundred thousand francs, Muffat had been able to think of only one expedient, from which he recoiled. This was to sell Les Bordes, a magnificent property valued at half a million, which an uncle had recently left the Countess. However, her signature was necessary, and she herself, according to the terms of her marriage contract, could not part with the property without the Count's authorization. The previous day he had finally made up his mind to talk to his wife about this signature. And now everything was ruined; at present he would never accept such a compromise. This thought made the shock of the Countess's adultery doubly painful. He understood perfectly well what Nana was asking for, since in that growing self-abandonment which had led him to put her in possession of all his secrets, he

had complained of his position, and had confided to her the quandary he was in with regard to the Countess's signature.

Nana, however, did not seem to press the point. Her eyes remained closed; and seeing her so pale, he grew frightened and made her take a little ether. She gave a sigh, and without mentioning Daguenet started questioning him.

'When's the wedding going to be?'

'The contract is due to be signed on Tuesday, five days from now,' he answered.

Then, with her eyes still closed as if she were speaking in the darkness of her private thoughts, she murmured:

'Anyway, pet, see to what you've got to do. ... As far as I'm concerned, I want everybody to be happy.'

He took her hand and tried to soothe her. Yes, he would see about it; the important thing was for her to rest. And he no longer felt angry, for the warm, sleepy atmosphere of the sickroom, with its all-pervading scent of ether, had finally lulled him into a longing for happiness and peace. All his virility, outraged by the wrong he had suffered, had drained out of him in the warmth surrounding that bed, and the company of that ailing woman, under the exciting influence of her fever and the memory of shared delights. He bent over her and clasped her in his arms, while her motionless features wore a subtle smile of triumph. Just then Dr Boutarel appeared.

'Well, and how's this dear child?' he said familiarly to Muffat, treating him as her husband. 'Good Lord, we've been making her talk, haven't we?'

The doctor was a good-looking man, still quite young, who had a superb practice among the courtesans of Paris. A jovial fellow, always ready to laugh and joke with the ladies, but never going to bed with them, he charged very high fees and insisted on punctual payment. However, he would turn out in answer to the slightest call, and Nana, who was always trembling at the idea of death, would send for him two or three times a week, anxiously confiding to him childish ailments which he would cure while amusing her with items of gossip and tall stories. The ladies all adored him. But this time the childish ailment was serious.

Muffat withdrew deeply moved. Seeing his poor Nana so weak, all he felt was tender emotion. As he was leaving the room, she beckoned him back, and gave him her forehead to kiss. In a low voice, and with a playfully threatening look, she said :

'You know what I've allowed you to do. Go back to your wife, or it's all over between us and I'll get angry!'

The Comtesse Sabine had insisted that her daughter's marriage contract should be signed on a Tuesday, so that the renovated house, in which the paint was still scarcely dry, might be reopened with a grand reception. Five hundred invitations had been sent out to people in all spheres of society. On the morning of the great day the upholsterers were still nailing up hangings; and about nine in the evening, when the chandeliers were about to be lit, the architect, accompanied by the excited Countess, was giving his final orders.

It was one of those spring parties which have a peculiarly delicate charm. The warmth of the June evening had made it possible to open the two doors of the great drawing-room and to extend the dancing to the sanded paths of the garden. When the first guests arrived and were greeted at the door by the Count and Countess, they were positively dazzled. They only had to recall to mind the drawing-room of old, haunted by the icy memory of the Comtesse Muffat, that old-fashioned room full of an atmosphere of religious austerity, with its massive Empire furniture in mahogany, its yellow velvet hangings, and its greenish damp-stained ceiling. Now, from the very threshold of the entrance-hall, mosaics set off with gold could be seen shimmering in the light from lofty candelabra, while delicately chiselled banisters followed the curve of the marble staircase. The drawing-room looked no less splendid; it was hung with Genoa velvet, and the ceiling was covered with a vast Boucher tapestry for which the architect had paid a hundred thousand francs at the sale of the Château de Dampierre. The chandeliers and the crystal sconces lit up a luxurious display of mirrors and precious furniture. It was as if Sabine's chaise longue, that

solitary seat covered in red silk, whose soft contours had seemed so out of place in the old days, had grown and grown and multiplied until it filled the whole house with a voluptuous idleness and a keen love of pleasure which burned as fiercely as an autumn bonfire.

People were already dancing. The orchestra, which had been stationed in the garden, in front of one of the open windows, was playing a waltz, the supple rhythm of which was carried away on the night air, and could be heard only faintly in the house. And the garden seemed to spread out into the distance, bathed in transparent shadow and lit by Chinese lanterns, with a refreshment table installed in a crimson tent pitched on the edge of a lawn. The waltz, which happened to be the vulgar one from *The Blonde Venus*, with its naughty, laughing lilt, came rippling into the old house to send a warm thrill along the walls. It was as if some wind of sensuality had come in from the street and were sweeping a whole vanished epoch out of the proud mansion, carrying away the Muffats' past, a century of honour and religious faith which had fallen asleep beneath the lofty ceilings.

Meanwhile the old friends of the Count's mother had taken refuge in their accustomed place by the fireside. Dazzled and bewildered, they formed a little group in the midst of the crowd gradually invading the house. Madame Du Joncquoy, unable to recognize the various rooms, had come in through the dining-room. Madame Chantereau was gazing in astonishment at the garden, which struck her as immense. Soon, talking in low voices, the group in the corner began to give vent to all sorts of bitter reflections.

'I say,' murmured Madame Chantereau, 'just imagine if the Countess were to return to life. ... Can't you picture her coming in to find all these people in her house. ... And all this gilt, and this awful din. ... It's a scandal !'

'Sabine's out of her mind,' replied Madame Du Joncquoy. 'Did you see her at the door? Look, you can see her from here. ... She's wearing all her diamonds.'

For a moment or two they stood up to inspect the Count and Countess from a distance. Sabine, in a white dress trimmed with marvellous English point-lace, looked trium-

phantly beautiful, young and gay, and there was a touch of intoxication in her continual smile. Beside her stood Muffat, aged and a little pale, but likewise smiling in his calm, dignified way.

'And to think that he was once the master here,' continued Madame Chantereau, 'and that not even a footstool could have been brought in without his permission. ... Ah, well, she's changed all that; he's in *her* house now. ... Do you remember when she didn't want to do up her drawing-room? She's done up the whole house instead.'

But they fell silent as Madame de Chezelles came in, followed by a group of young men, going into ecstasies over the house and uttering little cries of approval.

'Oh, it's delicious! ... Exquisite! ... What marvellous taste!'

And she called out to the group by the fireside:

'What did I tell you? There's nothing like these old places when you take them in hand. ... They look so smart, don't you think? Too seventeenth century for words. ... At last she can receive in style.'

The two old ladies had sat down again, lowering their voices and chatting about the marriage, which was a subject of astonishment to a good many people. Estelle had just gone by, wearing a pink silk dress, as pale and flat-chested, silent and virginal as ever. She had accepted Daguenet uncomplainingly; and now she showed neither joy nor sadness, remaining as cold and white as on those winter evenings when she used to put logs on the fire. This whole party given in her honour, these lights, these flowers, this music left her quite unmoved.

'An adventurer,' Madame Du Joncquoy was saying. 'Speaking for myself, I've never seen him before.'

'Take care, here he is,' murmured Madame Chantereau.

Daguenet, who had caught sight of Madame Hugon with her sons, had hurried forward to offer his arm, laughing with her and behaving towards her with effusive affection, as if she had had a hand in his good fortune.

'Thank you,' she said, sitting down by the fireside. 'This is my old corner, you know.'

'Do you know him?' asked Madame Du Joncquoy, when Daguenet had gone.

'Certainly – a charming young man. Georges was very fond of him. .... Oh, they're a very respectable family.'

And the good lady defended him against an unspoken hostility which she could sense around her. His father, held in high regard by Louis-Philippe, had been a prefect up to the time of his death. The son had lead a rather wild life, perhaps, and people said he was ruined; but in any case, one of his uncles, a great landowner, was bound to leave him his fortune. The ladies, however, shook their heads, while Madame Hugon, herself somewhat embarrassed, kept harking back to the respectability of Daguenet's family. She was very tired, and complained of her legs. For the past month she had been staying in her house in the Rue de Richelieu, having a lot of things to see to, she said. Her motherly smile was tinged with sadness.

'All the same,' Madame Chantereau concluded, 'Estelle could have done much better for herself.'

There was a flourish of trumpets. A quadrille was about to begin and the crowd drew back to both sides of the drawing-room in order to leave the floor clear. Light-coloured gowns drifted by, mingling together among the dark dress-coats, while the bright light set jewels flashing, white plumes quivering and lilacs and roses flowering among the sea of heads. It was already very warm, and as the orchestra played its lively music a penetrating perfume rose from the light tulles and the rumpled silks and satins, in which bare shoulders gleamed wanly. In the distance, through the open doors of several rooms, the rows of seated ladies could be seen at the far end of the adjoining rooms, their smiles flashing discreetly, their eyes glowing, their mouths pouting as the breath of their fans caressed their faces. Guests still kept arriving, and a footman calling out their names, while gentlemen moved slowly through the groups of people, trying to find places for the ladies hanging on their arms, and standing on tiptoe to look for some vacant armchair in the distance. More and more people poured into the house, and skirts squeezed together with a rustling sound. There were corners

where a mass of lace, bows and bustles barred the way, while all the ladies showed polite resignation and remained imperturbably gracious, accustomed as they were to these dazzling throngs. Meanwhile, at the bottom of the garden, couples escaping from the stifling atmosphere of the great drawing-room, disappeared in the rosy glow of the Chinese lanterns, and shadowy dresses drifted along the edge of the lawn, as if in time with the music of the quadrille, which took on a sweet and distant quality behind the trees.

Steiner had just met Foucarmont and la Faloise there, drinking a glass of champagne outside the refreshment tent.

'It's frightfully smart,' said la Faloise, inspecting the crimson tent, which was supported by gilded lances. 'You might imagine you were at the gingerbread fair. . . . Yes, that's it – the gingerbread fair!'

Nowadays he continually affected a mocking tone, posing as the young man who has indulged in everything to excess and can no longer find anything worth taking seriously.

'How surprised poor Vandeuvres would be if he came back here,' murmured Foucarmont. 'You remember how he used to die of boredom over there by the fireside? God, it was more than your life was worth to laugh.'

'Vandeuvres? Oh, don't talk about him! He was a failure!' la Faloise said contemptuously. 'He made a mistake, he did, if he thought he'd impress us with his roasting! Nobody even mentions it any more. Dead, buried and forgotten – that's Vandeuvres! Here's to the next man!'

Then, as Steiner was shaking hands with him, he went on:

'You know, Nana's just arrived. . . . Oh, what an entrance she made! It was simply fantastic! . . . First of all she kissed the Countess. Then, when the children came up, she gave them her blessing, and said to Daguenet: "Listen, Paul, if you do her wrong, you'll have to answer for it to me . . ." What, you mean to say you missed that? Oh, it was amazing – a real success!'

The other two listened to him open-mouthed, and finally burst out laughing. He was delighted, and thought that he had been very clever.

'You thought that had really happened, didn't you? ...
And why shouldn't it, seeing that it's Nana who arranged the marriage. Besides, she's really one of the family.'

The Hugon brothers were passing, and Philippe silenced him. Then they all chatted about the marriage with the frankness of men on their own. Georges lost his temper with la Faloise for telling a story about it. It was true that Nana had landed Muffat with one of her old lovers as a son-in-law, but it wasn't true that she had slept with him as late as the previous night. Foucarmont shrugged his shoulders. Did anybody ever know when Nana slept with somebody? At which Georges angrily answered with an 'I know, Monsieur!' which set them all laughing. Anyway, as Steiner remarked, it was still a very funny business.

The refreshment tent was gradually being invaded by the crowd, so they retreated, though keeping together. La Faloise stared brazenly at the women, as if he thought that he was at Mabille. At the end of one of the paths the little group were surprised to find Monsieur Venot deep in conversation with Daguenet, and they indulged in some facile jokes which amused them hugely, asking one another whether he was hearing Daguenet's confession or giving him advice about the first night. Soon they reached one of the doors into the drawing-room, where a polka was sending couples swaying about so that they left a wake behind them among the men who were standing still. In the puffs of air which came from outside, the candle flames were burning very high; and when a dress went by, fluttering and rustling in time to the music, it caused a draught which cooled the scorching heat coming from the chandeliers.

'God, they're not exactly cold in there,' murmured la Faloise.

Blinking their eyes after emerging from the mysterious shadows of the garden, they pointed out to one another the Marquis de Chouard, a tall, isolated figure towering above the bare shoulders which surrounded him. His face was pale and very stern, and beneath its crown of sparse white hair it wore an expression of haughty dignity. Shocked by the Comte Muffat's behaviour, he had publicly broken off all

relations with him, and had declared his intention of never again setting foot in the house. If he had consented to put in an appearance that evening it was in response to his granddaughter's entreaties – although he disapproved of the match, and inveighed indignantly against the disintegration of the governing classes being brought about by the compromises of modern debauchery.

'Ah, this is the last straw,' Madame Du Joncquoy whispered in Madame Chantereau's ear as they sat by the fireside. 'That evil woman has bewitched the poor wretch. ... And to think we once knew him as a devout, upright man!'

'It seems that he's heading for ruin,' continued Madame Chantereau. 'My husband has had a bill of his in his hands. ... At present he's living in that house in the Avenue de Villiers. All Paris is talking about it. ... Heaven knows, I don't approve of Sabine's behaviour, but you must admit that he gives her plenty of causes for complaint, and, goodness me, if she decides to throw money away too ...'

'She isn't throwing just money away,' interrupted the other. 'Still, with both of them travelling the same way, they'll arrive there quicker. ... In the gutter, my dear, in the gutter.'

But just then a soft voice interrupted them. It was Monsieur Venot, who had come and sat down behind them, as if anxious to disappear from view. Bending forward, he murmured :

'Why despair? God manifests himself when all seems lost.'

He himself seemed undisturbed by the sight of the collapse of this house over which he had once ruled. Since his stay at Les Fondettes, he had been allowing the madness to increase, well aware that he was powerless to stop it. He had accepted everything – the Count's wild passion for Nana, Fauchery's attendance on the Countess, even Estelle's marriage to Daguenet. What did these things matter? He became more supple and mysterious than ever, nursing the hope of obtaining the same mastery over the young couple as over the estranged couple, for he knew that great depravity leads to great piety. God's hour would come.

'Our friend,' he continued in a low voice, 'is still prompted by the highest religious sentiments. . . . He has given me the sweetest proofs of this.'

'Well,' said Madame Du Juncquoy, 'he ought to come back and live with his wife for a start.'

'No doubt. . . . As it happens, I have hopes that this reconciliation will not be long delayed.'

At this the two old ladies started questioning him. But he grew very humble again. Heaven, he said, had to be left to carry out its designs. His only desire in bringing the Count and Countess together again was to avoid a public scandal. Religion tolerated many weaknesses, provided the proprieties were respected.

'Still,' continued Madame Du Joncquoy, 'you ought to have prevented this marriage to an adventurer.'

The little old gentleman assumed an expression of profound astonishment.

'You're mistaken. Monsieur Daguenet is a young man of the greatest merit. . . . I know his intentions. He is anxious to live down the errors of his youth. Estelle will bring him back to the path of virtue, you may be sure of that.'

'Oh, Estelle!' Madame Chantereau murmured disdainfully. 'I don't believe that that dear young thing is capable of doing anything : she's so insignificant.'

This opinion caused Monsieur Venot to smile. However, he went into no explanations about the young bride, and closing his eyes as if to indicate that he had abandoned all interest in the matter, he once again disappeared in his corner behind the ladies' skirts. Madame Hugon, though weary and absent-minded, had caught a few words of the conversation, and she now intervened, summing up in her tolerant way by remarking to the Marquis de Chouard, who had just come over to pay his respects :

'These ladies are too severe. Life is so hard for everybody. . . . Don't you agree, my dear friend, that we must forgive others a great deal if we wish to merit forgiveness ourselves?'

For a few seconds the Marquis looked embarrassed, afraid that this was a personal allusion. But the good lady wore such a sad smile that he recovered straight away, and said :

'No, there's no forgiveness for certain faults. It's that sort of indulgence that leads society to the abyss.'

The ball had grown even more animated. A fresh quadrille was imparting a slight swaying motion to the drawing-room floor, as if the old house had been thrown off balance by the dancing. Now and then, amid the pale confusion of heads, a woman's face with shining eyes and parted lips stood out sharply as it was whirled past by the dance, with the light from the chandeliers gleaming on the white skin. Madame Du Joncquoy declared that common sense was a thing of the past. It was madness to crowd five hundred people into a room which could scarcely contain two hundred : they might just as well sign the marriage contract on the Place du Carrousel. This was the result of the new ways, said Madame Chantereau : in the old days these solemnities took place in the bosom of the family, but nowadays one must have a mob of people, and the whole street must be allowed to enter freely in a tremendous crush, or else the evening would be a failure. If people advertised their luxury, and introduced the scum of Paris into their houses, it was only natural that such promiscuity should eventually poison their marriages. The ladies complained that they could not recognize more than fifty people. Where did all this crowd come from? Girls with low-necked dresses were making a great display of their shoulders. One woman had a golden dagger stuck in her chignon, while a bodice embroidered with jet beads clothed her in a coat of mail. Men were following another woman with meaning smiles, her clinging skirts were so strikingly bold. All the luxury of the departing winter was there – the sort of gathering a hostess can get together from casual acquaintances in a pleasure-loving, tolerant society, a company in which great names and shameful reputations rubbed shoulders in the same pursuit of pleasure. In the overcrowded rooms the quadrille unrolled the rhythmical symmetry of its figures.

'The Countess certainly has style,' la Faloise remarked at the garden door. 'She looks ten years younger than her daughter. ... By the way, Foucarmont, you can tell us some-

thing. Vandeuvres once wagered that she had no thighs to speak of.'

This affectation of cynicism was beginning to bore the others. Foucarmont contented himself with replying :

'Ask your cousin, my dear fellow. Here he comes.'

'I say, that's an idea !' cried la Faloise. 'I bet you ten louis she's got thighs.'

Sure enough, Fauchery was approaching. As a frequent visitor to the house, he had come round by way of the dining-room to avoid the crush in the doorways. Taken up again by Rose at the beginning of the winter, he now divided himself between the singer and the Countess, for although he was extremely weary he did not know how to abandon one of them. Sabine flattered his vanity, but Rose amused him more. Besides the passion Rose felt was a real one, a faithful, almost conjugal affection which was driving Mignon to despair.

'Listen, we want some information,' said la Faloise, seizing his cousin's arm. 'You see that lady in white silk?'

Ever since his inheritance had given him an insolent self-assurance, he had made a point of chaffing Fauchery, for he had an old grudge to satisfy, and wanted to take his revenge for the mockery he had endured when he had just arrived in Paris from the provinces.

'Yes, that lady wearing all the lace.'

The journalist stood on tiptoe, for as yet he did not understand.

'The Countess?' he said at last.

'Right, old chap. .... I've bet ten louis on her. Has she or hasn't she got thighs?'

And he burst out laughing, delighted to have scored off a fellow who had impressed him enormously when he had asked him whether the Countess slept with anybody. But Fauchery, without showing the slightest astonishment, stared him in the face.

'Go on, you idiot,' he said finally, shrugging his shoulders.

Then he shook hands with all the others, while la Faloise, in his discomfiture, no longer felt sure of having said something funny. The men chatted. Since the races the banker and

403

Foucarmont had formed part of the Avenue de Villiers set. Nana was much better, and every evening the Count called to ask after her. Meanwhile Fauchery, though listening to the others, seemed preoccupied, for during a quarrel that morning Rose had bluntly admitted sending the letter. Oh yes, he could present himself at his great lady's house: he would get a warm reception. After hesitating for a long time, he had come in spite of everything, out of bravado. But la Faloise's stupid joke had upset him in spite of his apparent calm.

'What's the matter?' asked Philippe. 'You look unwell.'

'I do? Not at all.... I've been working; that's why I'm so late.'

Then, coldly, in one of those unrecognized displays of heroism which solve the vulgar tragedies of existence, he said:

'All the same, I haven't paid my respects to our hosts. One must be polite.'

He even ventured a joke, for he turned to la Faloise and said:

'Don't you agree, you idiot?'

And with that he pushed his way through the crowd. The footman's full-throated voice was no longer calling out names, but near to the door the Count and Countess were still talking, detained by some ladies who had just arrived. At last he joined them, while the gentlemen who had remained on the garden steps stood on tiptoe to follow the scene. Nana, they thought, must have talked.

'The Count hasn't noticed him,' murmured Georges. 'Look out, he's turning round!... Here it comes!'

The band had just struck up the waltz from *The Blonde Venus* again. First Fauchery had bowed to the Countess, who went on smiling serenely. Then he had remained motionless for a moment, waiting very calmly behind the Count. That evening the Count had maintained an attitude of lofty gravity, holding his head high, as became a great dignitary. When at last he looked down at the journalist, he emphasized even further the majesty of his deportment. For a few seconds the two men looked at each other. It was Fauchery who first held out his hand; Muffat gave him his. Their

hands remained clasped, and the Comtesse Sabine stood smiling before them with downcast eyes, while the orchestra went on playing to the lilting roguish rhythm of the waltz.

'It couldn't be going better,' said Steiner.

'Are their hands glued together?' asked Foucarmont, surprised at this prolonged handclasp.

A memory he could not forget had brought a faint glow to Fauchery's pale cheeks. In his mind's eye he saw again the property-room bathed in a greenish light and filled with dusty bric-à-brac; and Muffat was there, egg-cup in hand, turning his suspicions to his advantage. Now Muffat's suspicions had all been confirmed, and the last vestiges of his dignity were crumbling in ruins. Fauchery's fears were allayed, and when he saw how merry and gay the Countess was he was seized with a desire to laugh. The whole thing struck him as terribly funny.

'Ah, here she is at last,' cried la Faloise, who did not drop a joke when he thought it was a good one. 'You see Nana coming in over there?'

'Shut up, you idiot,' muttered Philippe.

'But I tell you it's Nana! They're playing her waltz for her, dammit, because she's just arrived! ... What! Can't you see her? She's hugging all three of them – Cousin Fauchery, Cousin Sabine and her husband – and calling them her little darlings. Oh, these family scenes make me sick.'

Estelle had come up, and Fauchery complimented her, while she stood stiffly in her pink dress, gazing at him with the astonished look of a silent child, and darting glances at her father and mother. Daguenet, too, shook hands warmly with the journalist. They made a smiling group, and Monsieur Venot came stealing up behind them, beaming complacently at them and enveloping them in his sweet piety, delighted at these final acts of submission which were opening up the ways of Providence.

But the waltz still kept up its swaying, laughing, voluptuous rhythm, like a shriller expression of the pleasure beating against the old house like a rising tide. The flutes in the orchestra sent forth louder trills, the violins more languorous sighs. Beneath the Genoa velvet hangings, the gilding and the

paintings, the chandeliers exhaled a living heat, a glow of sunshine; while the crowd of guests, multiplied in the mirrors, seemed to grow larger as the murmur of its voices rose louder. The couples walking around the drawing-room with their arms round each other's waists, amid the smiles of the seated women, accentuated even further the quaking of the floors. In the garden a dull glow from the Chinese lanterns threw a distant, fiery reflection over the dark shadows of people looking for a breath of air at the far end of the paths. And this trembling of the walls, this red glow of light, seemed to mark the final conflagration in which the fabric of an ancient honour was cracking and burning on all sides. The timid, faltering gaiety which Fauchery one April evening had heard ring out with the sound of breaking crystal had gradually grown bolder and wilder, till it had burst forth in this party. Now the crack was growing; it was zigzagging through the house, foreshadowing approaching collapse. Among the drunkards in the slums it is utter poverty, empty cupboards, the madness of drink emptying every purse, which finish off tainted families. Here a waltz-tune was sounding the knell of an ancient family, in the sudden glare illuminating these accumulated riches, while Nana, an invisible presence, stretched her lithe limbs above the ball, to the vulgar lilt of the music, penetrating and corrupting this society with the ferment of her scent as if it hung in the warm air.

On the evening after the celebration of the marriage in church the Comte Muffat presented himself in his wife's bedroom, where he had not set foot for the last two years. At first the Countess recoiled in astonishment; but she went on smiling the intoxicated smile which was now always on her lips. He began stammering in great embarrassment; whereupon she gave him a short lecture. However, neither of them risked a clear explanation. It was religion which required them to forgive each other, and they tacitly agreed that they should both retain their freedom. Before going to bed, seeing that the Countess still appeared somewhat hesitant, they had a business conversation, and the Count was the first to speak of selling Les Bordes. She consented at once. They both needed considerable funds, and they agreed to share and

share alike. This completed the reconciliation, and Muffat felt a great alleviation of his remorse.

That very day, as Nana was dozing about two in the afternoon, Zoé made so bold as to knock on her bedroom door. The curtains were drawn, and a hot breath of air kept coming through the window into the cool twilight of the silent room. Recently the young woman had been getting up and about again, although she was still rather weak. She opened her eyes and asked :

'Who is it?'

Zoé was about to reply, but Daguenet pushed by her, and announced himself in person. Nana immediately propped herself up on her pillow, and dismissing her maid, cried :

'What! You! On your wedding day! ... What's the matter?'

Taken aback by the darkness, he remained in the middle of the room. However, getting used to it, he came forward after a while, wearing a dress-coat, a white tie and white gloves.

'Yes, it's me,' he said. 'Don't you remember?'

No, she remembered nothing, and he had to offer himself frankly to her, in his teasing way.

'Come now, here's your commission. ... I've brought you my innocence as a present.'

At that, as he was standing by the bed, she clasped him in her bare arms, shaking with laughter, and almost crying, she thought it so sweet of him.

'Oh, Mimi, how funny you are. ... You remembered after all! And to think I'd forgotten all about it! So you got away – you've come straight from church. Yes, it's true, you still smell of incense. ... Come on, fuck me then! Oh, harder than that, Mimi! Go on, it may be the last time.'

In the dark room, in which a vague odour of ether still lingered, their tender laughter suddenly died away. The heavy, warm breeze swelled the window-curtains, and children's voices could be heard out on the Avenue. Then they started joking again, for they were pressed for time. Daguenet was due to start off with his wife directly after the wedding breakfast.

407

TOWARDS the end of September the Comte Muffat, who was due to dine at Nana's that evening, came at dusk to tell her of a sudden summons he had received at the Tuileries. The lamps in the house had not yet been lit, and the servants were laughing uproariously in the kitchen, as he quietly mounted the stairs where the stained-glass windows gleamed in warm shadow. Upstairs the door of the drawing-room opened noiselessly. A faint pink glow was fading away on the ceiling of the room; and the red hangings, the deep divans, the lacquered furniture, and the medley of embroidered fabrics, bronzes and china, were already sleeping under a slowly advancing flood of shadows, which had submerged the corners of the room, leaving not a single gleam of ivory or glint of gold. And there in the darkness, on the only clearly visible surface, a white outspread petticoat, he saw Nana stretched out in Georges's arms. Any sort of denial was impossible. He gave a choking cry and stood gaping at them.

Nana had leapt to her feet, and she pushed him into the bedroom to give the boy time to escape.

'Go in there,' she murmured desperately, 'I'll explain . . .'

She was exasperated at being caught out in that way. Never before had she given way like that in her own house, in that drawing-room with the doors all open. To make her behave like that it had taken a row with Georges : maddened with jealousy of Philippe, he had sobbed so bitterly on her bosom that she had yielded to him, not knowing how to calm him, and at heart deeply troubled by his unhappiness. And on this one occasion when she had been stupid enough to forget herself like that, with a boy who could not even bring her a bunch of violets any more, his mother kept him on so tight a rein, the Count had to come along and catch them in the act. She really was unlucky. That was what happened to you if you showed a little kindness.

Meanwhile in the bedroom into which she had pushed Muffat it was pitch dark. Groping her way to the bell, she furiously rang and asked for a lamp. It was all Julien's fault. If there had been a lamp in the drawing-room, none of this would have happened. It was that stupid darkness that had softened her heart.

'Please be reasonable, darling,' she said, when Zoé had brought a lamp.

The Count, sitting with his hands on his knees, was gazing at the floor, stupefied by what he had just seen. He could not even summon up a cry of anger, simply trembling as if over-whelmed by a horror which had chilled his blood. This mute misery touched the young woman, and she tried to comfort him.

'All right, I've done wrong. . . . It's very bad what I did. . . . You see, I'm sorry I did it. I'm really terribly sorry, because I can see it's upset you. . . . Come now, be nice too, and forgive me.'

She had crouched down at his feet, trying to catch his eye with a look of tender submission, to find out whether he was very angry with her. Then, when he heaved a great sigh and seemed to be feeling better, she grew more coaxing, and with solemn kindness added a final excuse.

'You see, darling, you must try and understand. . . . I can't refuse that to my poor friends.'

The Count finally relented, only insisting that Georges should be sent away for good. But all his illusions were dead, and he no longer believed in her promise of fidelity. The next day Nana would deceive him again, and he only remained a prisoner of his passion in obedience to a cowardly obsession, to terror at the thought of living without her.

This was the period of her life when Nana lit up Paris with redoubled splendour. She rose higher than ever on the horizon of vice, dominating the city with her insolent display of luxury, and that contempt of money which made her openly squander fortunes. Her house had become a sort of glowing forge, where her continual desires burned fiercely and the slightest breath from her lips changed gold into fine ashes which the wind swept away every hour. Nobody had

ever seen such a passion for spending. The house seemed to have been built over an abyss in which men were swallowed up – their possessions, their bodies, their very names – without leaving even a trace of dust behind them. This woman, who had the tastes of a parrot, gobbling radishes and burnt almonds, but merely pecking at meat, had monthly table-bills amounting to five thousand francs. The kitchen was a scene of reckless expenditure, a river of wastefulness which emptied cask after cask of wine and swept along bills swollen by three or four hands in succession. Victorine and François reigned supreme in the kitchen, where they invited a host of friends, not to mention a tribe of cousins who were fed in their own homes with cold meats and beef tea. Julien insisted on commissions from the tradespeople, and the glaziers never replaced a pane of glass at a cost of thirty sous but he added twenty sous to the bill for himself. Charles devoured the horses' oats, doubling the amount charged for their provender and re-selling at the back gate what came in at the front; while in the midst of this general squandering, this sacking of a town taken by storm, Zoé skilfully succeeded in covering the thefts of everybody else the better to conceal her own. But what was stolen was nothing compared to what was wasted, with yesterday's food thrown away, such a huge stock of eatables in the house that it turned the servants' stomachs, the glasses sticky with sugar, the gas-burners blazing away till the walls were almost red-hot, instances of carelessness, cases of deliberate mischief and ordinary accidents – everything, in fact, which could hasten the ruin of a house devoured by so many mouths. Upstairs, in Madame's quarters, destruction raged even more fiercely, with ten-thousand-franc dresses which had been worn only twice sold by Zoé, jewels disappearing as if they had crumbled away at the bottom of drawers, and stupid purchases of novelties of the day which were left lying forgotten in some corner the next morning, or swept out into the street. She could not see any very expensive object without wanting to possess it, and consequently left a perpetual trail of flowers and costly knick-knacks behind her, all the happier the more her passing fancy cost. Nothing remained intact in her hands; everything

was broken or dirtied or withered between her little white fingers; a heap of nameless debris, twisted rags and muddy tatters followed her and marked her passage. Then, in the midst of this squandering of pocket-money, the big bills would fall due : twenty thousand francs owing to the milliner, thirty thousand to the linen-draper, twelve thousand to the bootmaker; her stable cost her fifty thousand, and in six months she ran up a bill of a hundred and twenty thousand francs at her dressmaker's. Although she had not enlarged her household establishment, which Labordette calculated as costing an average of four hundred thousand francs, she managed to spend a million that year, herself amazed at the figure, and incapable of saying where such a sum could have gone. Heaps of men piled on top of one another, and barrowfuls of gold, failed to fill the hole which, in the midst of this ruinous luxury, went on growing under the floors of her house.

Meanwhile Nana was cherishing a supreme caprice. Preoccupied once more with the idea of redecorating her bedroom, she thought that she had hit on the ideal scheme : the room was to be hung in tea-rose velvet, with little silver buttons and gold tassels and fringes, and the hangings were to be caught up at the ceiling to form a sort of tent. This decoration, she thought, was bound to look both luxurious and delicate, and would form a splendid background for her fair skin and rosy complexion. However, the bedroom was in any case only designed to serve as a setting for the bed, which was to be a dazzling marvel. Nana wanted a bed such as had never existed before, a throne, an altar, to which Paris would come in order to worship her sovereign nudity. It was to be all in chased gold and silver, like a great jewel, with golden roses scattered over a trellis-work of silver. On the bedhead a band of laughing Cupids would peep out from among the flowers, watching the voluptuous antics in the shadows of the bedcurtains. Nana had applied to Labordette, who had brought two goldsmiths to see her, and they were already busy with the designs. The bed would cost fifty thousand francs, and Muffat was to give it to her as a New Year's present.

What astonished the young woman was that in the midst

of this river of gold which flowed between her legs, she was constantly short of money. On certain days she found herself being pressed for ridiculously small sums of only a few louis. She was obliged to borrow from Zoé, or else she scraped up the money herself as best she could on her own account. But before resigning herself to adopting extreme measures, she would try her friends, jokingly persuading men to hand over all the money they had about them, even down to their coppers. For the last three months she had been emptying Philippe's pockets in particular, and now he never came to the house in moments of crisis without leaving his purse behind him when he left. Soon she grew bolder, and asked him for loans of two or three hundred francs – never more than that – in order to settle bills or pay pressing debts; and Philippe, who in July had been appointed paymaster to his regiment, would bring the money the next day, apologizing for not being rich, for good Mama Hugon now treated her sons with quite remarkable severity. After three months these little loans, which were often renewed, amounted to some ten thousand francs. The captain still laughed his fine, hearty laugh, but he was growing thinner; sometimes he seemed absent-minded, and a shadow of suffering would pass over his face. But one look from Nana's eyes would transfigure him in a sort of sensual ecstasy. She had a coaxing, caressing way with him, intoxicating him with furtive kisses, and giving herself to him in sudden fits of self-abandonment which had him dancing attendance on her as soon as he could escape from his military duties.

One evening, Nana having announced that she was also called Thérèse, and that her name-day fell on the fifteenth of October, the gentlemen all sent her presents. Captain Philippe brought his in person; it was an old comfit-dish in Dresden china with a gold mounting. He found her alone in her dressing-room. She had just emerged from the bath and had nothing on but a big red and white flannel dressing-gown, and was busy examining her presents, which were spread out on the table. She had already broken a rock-crystal bottle in her attempts to unstopper it.

'Oh, you're too sweet,' she said. 'What is it? Let's have a

look. . . . What a baby you are, spending your pennies on little thingummies like that.'

She scolded him, seeing that he wasn't rich, but at heart she was delighted to see him spending all his money on her, for that was the only proof of love which touched her. Meanwhile she was toying with the comfit-dish, opening and shutting it in an attempt to see how it was made.

'Be careful,' he murmured, 'it's very fragile.'

But she shrugged her shoulders. Did he think she was as clumsy as a street-porter? And all of a sudden the hinge came away in her fingers, and the lid fell and broke on the floor. She was stupefied and stood staring at the pieces, exclaiming :

'Oh, it's broken !'

Then she burst out laughing. The pieces lying on the floor struck her as funny. Her merriment was of the nervous kind, the stupid, spiteful laughter of a child amused by destruction. Philippe flared up angrily for a moment; the wretched girl did not know what anguish that knick-knack had cost him. Seeing how upset he was, she tried to contain herself.

'Look, it isn't my fault. . . . It was cracked. Those old things just don't last. . . . And it was that lid ! Didn't you see what a jump it gave?'

And once again she started roaring with laughter. But since, in spite of all his efforts, tears began coming to the young man's eyes, she flung her arms round his neck in a burst of affection.

'What a silly you are ! But I love you all the same. If nobody ever broke anything, all the shops would have to close down. That sort of thing's made to be broken. . . . Why, look at this fan – it's just held together with glue.'

She had picked up a fan, and as she pulled at the blades the silk tore in two. This seemed to excite her, and to show how little she cared for the other presents, once she had ruined his, she treated herself to a wholesale massacre, hitting each in turn and proving that not a single one was well made by destroying them all. A gleam appeared in her vacant eyes, and she drew back her lips to display her white teeth. Then, when all the presents were in pieces, she started laughing

again, looking very flushed, and beat on the table with the flat of her hands, lisping in a girlish voice :

'Finished ! All gone ! All gone !'

Then Philippe, infected by her excitement, pushed her backwards and gaily kissed her breasts. She abandoned herself to him, clinging to his shoulders, so happy that she could not remember having enjoyed herself so much for ages. Without letting go of him, she said caressingly :

'I say, darling, do bring me ten louis tomorrow. ... It's a bore, but there's a bill from my baker that is bothering me.'

He had turned pale. Then, giving her a final kiss on her forehead, he said simply :

'I'll try.'

Silence reigned for a moment. While she was dressing, he stood with his forehead pressed against the windowpane. After a minute had gone by, he turned round and said deliberately :

'Nana, you ought to marry me.'

The idea struck the young woman as so amusing that she was unable to finish tying her petticoats.

'My poor pet, you must be ill ! ... Are you offering me your hand because I asked you for ten louis? ... No, never, I'm too fond of you. Lord, what a silly idea !'

And, as Zoé came in just then to put her shoes on, they changed the subject. The maid had at once noticed the presents lying in pieces on the table. She asked if she could put them away, and when Madame told her to get rid of them, she carried the whole collection off in a fold of her skirt. In the kitchen Madame's debris was raked through and shared out among the servants.

That day Georges had stolen into the house in spite of Nana's orders to the contrary. François had seen him pass, but the servants had got to the point of laughing among themselves at their mistress's troubles. He had just slipped as far as the little drawing-room, when his brother's voice stopped him, and rooted to the spot behind the door, he overheard the whole scene, the kisses, the proposal of marriage. His blood froze, and he went off in a state of imbecilic horror, feeling as if there were a great void in his skull. It

414

was only in his own room, above his mother's flat in the Rue Richelieu, that his heart broke in a storm of wild sobs. This time there could be no doubt about the state of affairs. A horrible picture of Nana in Philippe's arms kept rising before his eyes, and this struck him as a sort of incest. Whenever he thought that he had calmed down, the memory of what had happened would return, and in a fresh fit of jealous rage he would throw himself on his bed, biting the sheets and shouting foul words which maddened him all the more. The whole day went by in this fashion. In order to stay shut up in his room, he complained of having a sick headache. But the night proved even worse, as a feverish urge to kill took hold of him in the midst of continual nightmares. If his brother had been living in the house, he would have gone and stabbed him to death. When day returned he tried to reason things out. It was he who ought to die, and he decided to throw himself out of the window the next time an omnibus went by. However, he went out about ten o'clock and roamed round Paris, walking up and down on the bridges, and finally feeling an irresistible urge to see Nana once more. With one word, perhaps, she would save him. And three o'clock was striking as he entered the house on the Avenue de Villiers.

About noon an appalling piece of news had crushed Madame Hugon. Philippe had been in prison since the previous evening, charged with having stolen twelve thousand francs from the funds of his regiment. For the last three months he had been abstracting small sums in the hope of being able to repay them, concealing the deficit with forged documents; and thanks to the inefficiency of the administrative services, this fraud had been repeatedly successful. The old lady, horror-stricken by her son's crime, promptly cried out in anger against Nana. She knew of Philippe's liaison, and her sadness had been due to this wretched state of affairs, which had kept her in Paris in constant fear of some catastrophe; but she had never expected such a shameful development as this, and now she blamed herself for refusing him money, seeing her behaviour as a form of complicity in his crime. She collapsed into an armchair, her legs paralysed, feeling useless, incapable of action, and doomed to stay

where she was till she died. But the sudden thought of
Georges consoled her; she still had Georges, and he would
be able to do something, perhaps even save them. Thereupon, without asking anybody for help, for she was anxious
to keep all these matters within the family, she dragged herself up to the next floor, clinging to the idea that she still had
somebody who loved her. But upstairs she found the bedroom
empty. The concierge told her that Monsieur Georges had
gone out early. The room was full of signs of a second
calamity; the bed with its gnawed sheets bore witness to
somebody's anguish; and a chair which had been thrown
on the floor among a heap of clothes looked like something
dead. Georges must be at that woman's house; and so, with
dry eyes and legs that had recovered their strength, Madame
Hugon went downstairs. She wanted her sons, and she set off
to reclaim them.

Since the morning Nana had been plagued with troubles.
First of all there was the baker, who as early as nine o'clock
had turned up with his bill, a demand for the paltry sum of a
hundred and thirty-three francs, which, in spite of the regal
establishment she maintained, she was unable to meet. In
his irritation at being abandoned for another baker the day
he had refused further credit, he had presented himself for
payment a score of times; and the servants were now espous-
ing his cause. François kept saying that Madame would
never pay him unless he made a tremendous scene; Charles
talked of going upstairs too, in order to get an outstanding
bill for straw settled; while Victorine advised them to wait
until some gentleman was present, and to get the money out
of her by suddenly asking for it in the middle of their conversation. Tempers rose in the kitchen, the tradesmen were
informed of the state of affairs, and there were gossiping
sessions lasting three or four hours on end, during which
Madame was stripped, plucked and talked about with the
ferocity peculiar to overpaid, underworked servants. Only
Julien, the butler, affected to defend his mistress : she was a
good sort, whatever they might say. And when the others
accused him of sleeping with her he gave a conceited laugh,
which made the cook frantic with rage; she would have liked

to be a man in order to spit on the backsides of women like that, she would have found them so disgusting. François had maliciously stationed the baker in the hall, without informing Madame, and when she came downstairs for lunch she found herself face to face with him. Taking the bill, she told him to come back about three o'clock. He left the house swearing like a trooper and vowing that he would be back on the stroke of three to get his money by hook or by crook.

Annoyed by this scene, Nana did not enjoy her lunch. This time she would have to get rid of the man. A dozen times she had put the money aside for him; but it had always melted away, one day being spent on some flowers, another day being given as a subscription to a fund in aid of an old gendarme. Besides she was counting on Philippe, and was astonished that he had not already turned up with his two hundred francs. She was really out of luck, seeing that two days before she had fitted out Satin again with a perfect trousseau, some twelve hundred francs' worth of dresses and lingerie; and now she had not a single louis left in the house.

About two o'clock, when Nana was beginning to feel anxious, Labordette arrived. He had brought with him the designs for the bed, and this created a diversion, a joyful interlude which made the young woman forget all her troubles. She clapped her hands and danced around. Then, bursting with curiosity, she bent over a table in the drawing-room and examined the designs, which Labordette proceeded to explain to her.

'You see,' he said, 'this is the body of the bed. In the middle there's a bunch of roses in full bloom, and then comes a garland of flowers and buds. The leaves will be in electrum and the roses in red gold. ... And here's the grand design for the bedhead, Cupids dancing in a ring on a silver trellis.'

But Nana interrupted him, beside herself with ecstasy.

'Oh, isn't he funny, that little one in the corner, with his bottom in the air! ... Just look at him! And what a sly laugh! They've all got such wicked eyes! ... You know, my dear, I'll never dare do anything naughty in front of them!'

Her pride was enormously flattered. The goldsmiths had

417

declared that no queen in the world slept on such a bed. However, a difficulty arose. Labordette showed her two designs for the footboard, one of which reproduced the pattern on the sides, while the other, a work of art in itself, depicted Night wrapped in her veils, with a faun uncovering her splendid nudity. He added, that if she chose this last design, the goldsmiths intended to make Night in her own likeness. This idea, which was in rather daring taste, made her turn pale with pleasure, and she pictured herself as a silver statuette symbolizing the warm voluptuous delights of darkness.

'Of course you'd only sit for the head and shoulders,' said Labordette.

She looked at him calmly.

'Why? ... If it's for a work of art, I don't care how much the sculptor sees of me.'

It went without saying that she had chosen the design depicting Night and the faun. But he interrupted her.

'Wait a minute. ... It's six thousand francs more.'

'Heavens above! What does that matter to me?' she exclaimed, bursting out laughing. 'Hasn't my little Muffer got the money?'

Nowadays, among her intimates, she always referred to the Comte Muffat in that way, and they no longer asked after him by any other name. 'Did you see your little Muffer last night? ... Well I'm blowed, I expected to find the little Muffer here.' It was just a harmless nickname, but one nevertheless which she did not as yet venture to use in his presence.

Labordette began rolling up the designs while he gave her some final details. The goldsmiths undertook to deliver the bed in two months' time, about 25 December, and the very next week a sculptor would come to make a clay model for the statuette of Night. As she was showing him out, Nana remembered the baker, and asked abruptly:

'By the way, you wouldn't have ten louis on you, would you?'

Labordette made it a strict rule, which stood him in good stead, never to lend women money. He always made the same reply.

'No, my girl, I'm broke. ... But would you like me to go and see your little Muffer?'

She refused. It was useless. Two days before she had succeeded in getting five thousand francs out of the Count. However, she soon regretted her discretion, for no sooner had Labordette gone than the baker reappeared, although it was barely half-past two, and swearing loudly sat himself down on a bench in the hall. Listening to him from the first floor, the young woman turned pale, upset most of all at hearing sounds of the servants' secret amusement rising from below. Down in the kitchen they were roaring with laughter; the coachman was staring across from the other side of the yard; and François crossed the hall for no apparent reason, then hurried off to report to the others after chuckling knowingly at the baker. They didn't give a damn for Madame; the house was echoing with their laughter; and she felt all alone, exposed to the servants' contemptuous surveillance and spattered with their obscene mockery. She had thought of borrowing the hundred and thirty-three francs from Zoé, but now she abandoned the idea; she already owed the maid some money, and she was too proud to risk a refusal. Such a wave of feeling swept over her that she went back into her bedroom, talking to herself.

'Come now, my girl, don't count on anyone but yourself. ... Your body's all your own, and it's better to make use of it than to let yourself be insulted.'

And without even calling Zoé, she dressed herself with feverish haste to hurry round to La Tricon's. At times of financial difficulty this was her last resort. Much sought after, and constantly solicited by the old lady, she would refuse or submit according to her needs; and on the increasingly frequent occasions when money was urgently needed for her princely establishment, she was sure to find twenty-five louis waiting for her at La Tricon's. She used to go to her house with an ease born of habit, just as poor people go to the pawn-shop.

But coming out of her bedroom, Nana bumped into Georges, who was standing in the middle of the drawing-

room. Not noticing his waxen pallor and the sombre fire in his wide eyes, she heaved a sigh of relief.

'Ah, you've come from your brother!'

'No,' said the boy, turning even paler.

At this she gave a gesture of despair. What did he want? Why was he barring her way? Look, she was in a hurry. Then, turning back, she asked:

'*You* haven't any money, have you?'

'No.'

'That's true. How silly of me! Never a penny, not even to pay your fare on the omnibus! ... Mama won't give you any money. And you call yourselves men!'

And she turned to go. But he held her back; he wanted to speak to her. She pushed him away, repeating that she was in too much of a hurry, but he stopped her by saying:

'Listen, I know you're going to marry my brother.'

Heavens, that was too funny for words. And she collapsed into a chair to have a good laugh.

'Yes,' the boy went on, 'and I don't want you to. ... It's me you're going to marry. ... That's why I've come.'

'What! You too?' she said. 'Why, it's a family disease. ... No, never! The very idea! Have I ever asked you to do anything nasty like that? No, neither you nor him! Never!'

Georges's face lit up. Perhaps he had made a mistake. He continued:

'Then swear to me that you don't go to bed with my brother.'

'Oh, you're beginning to get on my nerves,' said Nana, getting up and impatient to go. 'It's amusing for a minute, but when I tell you I'm in a hurry. ... I go to bed with your brother if I feel like it. What right have you to call me to account for what I do? Do you keep me? Do you pay for everything here? ... Yes, I go to bed with your brother ...'

He had caught hold of her arm, and squeezed it fit to break it, stammering:

'Don't say that. ... Don't say that ...'

With a sharp slap she freed herself from his grasp.

'Now he's taken to roughing me up! The little devil! ... Listen, dearie, out you go, and double quick! ... I used to

let you hang around out of kindness. Yes, that's right. And it's no use staring at me like that. ... Did you think I was going to be your mama all your life? I've got better things to do than bring up brats.'

He listened to her, rigid with anguish, yet without uttering a sound. Her every word pierced his heart so cruelly that he felt he was going to die. Not even noticing his suffering, she went on, delighted to have somebody on whom she could take her revenge for the annoyances she had suffered that morning.

'It's like your brother; he's another fine one, he is. He promised me two hundred francs, but does he turn up with them? Not likely! ... It isn't his money I care about. That isn't enough to pay for my pomade. ... But he's let me down at an awkward moment. ... Listen, do you want to know what's what? Well, because of your precious brother, I'm going out to earn twenty-five louis with another man.'

Losing his head, he barred her way, weeping, pleading, clasping his hands together, and stammering :

'Oh, no! Oh, no!'

'Just as you like,' she said. 'Have you got the money?'

No, he hadn't got the money. He would have given his life to have the money. Never before had he felt so wretched, so useless, such a little boy. His whole being, racked with sobs, expressed such utter misery that at last she noticed it and was touched. She gently pushed him away.

'Come, pet, let me pass : I've got to go. ... Be reasonable. You're just a baby, and it was nice for a week, but now I've got to look after myself. Think it over a bit. ... Now, your brother's a man. With him I don't say I wouldn't. ... Oh, do me a favour; there's no point in telling him all this. He needn't know where I'm going. I always let out too much when I'm in a hurry.'

She began laughing. Then, taking him in her arms, and kissing him on the forehead, she said :

'Good-bye, baby. It's over, all over between us, you understand. ... And now I'm off.'

And she left him. He stood in the middle of the drawing-room, with her last words ringing like a tocsin in his ears –

'It's over, all over' – and he thought that the ground was opening beneath his feet. In the emptiness of his mind, the man waiting for Nana had disappeared, and Philippe alone remained, clasped in the young woman's bare arms for ever. She didn't deny it; and she clearly loved him, since she wanted to spare him the pain of her infidelity. It was over, all over. He drew a deep breath and gazed round the room, suffocating beneath a crushing weight. Memories came back to him one after another – memories of merry nights at La Mignotte, of amorous hours during which he had thought of himself as her child, of pleasures stolen in this very room. And now these things would never happen again! He was too small; he had not grown up quickly enough; and Philippe had taken his place because he was a grown man. So this was the end : he couldn't go on living now. His passion had become steeped with an infinite tenderness, a sensual adoration, in which his whole being was involved. Besides how could he possibly forget if his brother was still there – his brother, blood of his blood, a second self, whose enjoyment of Nana drove him mad with jealousy? No, this was the end; he wanted to die.

All the doors remained open, as the servants wandered noisily round the house, after seeing Madame go out on foot. Downstairs on the bench in the hall the baker was laughing with Charles and François. Zoé came running across the drawing-room and looked surprised to see Georges there. She asked him if he was waiting for Madame. Yes, he was; he had forgotten to give her an answer to a question. And when he was alone, he started rummaging around. Finding nothing else to serve his purpose, he picked up a pair of sharply pointed scissors in the dressing-room, which Nana was forever using on her person to cut off hairs or dead skin. Then, for a whole hour, he waited patiently, his hand in his pocket, and his fingers nervously clasped around the scissors.

'Here's Madame,' said Zoé, coming back out of the bedroom, where she must have been watching for Nana from the window.

There was the sound of people running through the house, laughter dying away and doors shutting. Georges heard

422

Nana curtly paying off the baker. Then she came upstairs.

'What, you're still here?' she said when she saw him. 'We're going to fall out, you and I, young man!'

He followed her as she walked towards her bedroom.

'Nana, will you marry me?'

She shrugged her shoulders. It was too stupid; she refused to answer him any more. Her intention was to shut the door in his face.

'Nana, will you marry me?'

She slammed the door. He opened it with one hand, while he brought the other out of his pocket, holding the scissors. And, without a word, he plunged them into his chest.

Meanwhile, Nana had felt an instinctive premonition of disaster, and had swung round. When she saw him stab himself, she was seized with indignation.

'Oh, what an idiot! What an idiot! And with my scissors too! ... Stop it, you little fool! ... Oh, God! Oh, God!'

Panic seized her. Sinking on his knees, the boy had just given himself a second stab, which had stretched him out on the carpet, barring the threshold of the bedroom. At that Nana lost her head completely and screamed with all her might, not daring to step over this body which was shutting her in and preventing her from running for help.

'Zoé, Zoé! Come quick. . . . Make him stop it! ... It's just stupid – a child like that! ... Now he goes and kills himself! And in my house! Did you ever see the like of it?'

He frightened her. He was all white, with his eyes shut. There was scarcely any bleeding – only a little blood, a tiny stain disappearing under his waistcoat. She was just making up her mind to step over the body, when she saw something which made her recoil. Through the drawing-room door, which remained wide open facing her, an old lady was advancing. And in her terror, unable to understand what she was doing there, she recognized Madame Hugon. Still wearing her hat and gloves, Nana kept edging backwards. Her terror became so great that she tried to defend herself, stammering :

'Madame, it wasn't me, I swear it wasn't. . . . He wanted to marry me, and I said no, and he killed himself.'

Slowly Madame Hugon drew near, dressed in black, her face pale under her white hair. In the carriage the thought of Georges had vanished, and that of Philippe's crime had once more taken complete possession of her. Possibly this woman would be able to offer an explanation to the judges which would touch them : and she conceived the idea of begging her to testify in her son's favour. Downstairs the doors of the house stood open, and she started climbing the stairs on her ailing legs. She was hesitating as to which way to go when, all of a sudden, screams of horror guided her. Upstairs she found a man lying on the floor with blood on his shirt. It was Georges – it was her other child.

Nana kept repeating dully :

'He wanted to marry me, and I said no, and he killed himself.'

Without a sound Madame Hugon bent down. Yes, it was the other one, it was Georges. One of them disgraced, the other murdered. She felt no surprise, for her whole life was collapsing about her. Kneeling on the carpet, forgetting where she was, and seeing nobody else, she gazed fixedly at Georges's face and listened, with one hand on his heart. Then she gave a faint sigh. She had felt the heart beating. At that she raised her head, examined the room and the woman, and seemed to remember. A flame kindled in her vacant eyes, and she looked so tall and terrible in her silence that Nana trembled as she went on defending herself across the body that separated them.

'I swear to you, Madame. . . . If his brother were here, he could explain to you . . .'

'His brother has stolen some money – he is in prison,' the mother said harshly.

Nana felt as if she were choking. What was the meaning of all this? Now the other brother had turned thief. Were they all mad in that family? She stopped trying to justify herself, and allowed Madame Hugon to issue orders, as if she were no longer mistress in her own house. Some servants had finally come running upstairs, and the old lady insisted on their carrying the unconscious Georges down to her carriage. She preferred to risk killing him rather than let him

remain in that house. With dazed eyes Nana watched the servants as they carried poor Zizi by his legs and shoulders. His mother walked behind them, exhausted now and leaning on the furniture, as if almost destroyed by the ruin of all that she held dear. On the landing a sob came from her throat, and she turned round and said twice :

'Oh, you've done us so much harm ! ... Oh, you've done us so much harm !'

That was all. In her stupefaction Nana had sat down, still wearing her hat and gloves. The house relapsed into a heavy silence; the carriage had just driven away; and she sat motionless, not knowing what to think, her head buzzing after all that had happened. A quarter of an hour later, the Comte Muffat found her in the same place. When she saw him she relieved her feelings in a flood of words, telling him the whole dreadful story, repeating the same details a score of times, and picking up the blood-stained scissors to imitate Zizi's gesture when he had stabbed himself. Above all else she was intent on proving her own innocence.

'Look, darling, was it my fault? If you were the judge, would you condemn me? ... I certainly didn't tell Philippe to pinch the regimental funds any more than I urged that wretched boy to kill himself. ... I've suffered the most from the whole affair. They come and do stupid things in my house, they do their best to upset me, and they treat me like a hussy ...'

And she burst into tears. A nervous reaction made her languid and plaintive, tearful and miserable.

'You too, you look a bit peeved. ... If you don't believe me, ask Zoé if I had anything to do with it. ... Go on, Zoé, explain to Monsieur ...'

For the last few minutes the maid, who had brought a towel and a bowl of water out of the dressing-room, had been rubbing the carpet to remove the blood-stain before it dried.

'Oh, Monsieur,' she declared, 'Madame's terribly upset.'

Muffat was still benumbed and stupefied by the tragedy, his thoughts full of the mother weeping for her sons. He knew her greatness of heart, and pictured her in her widow's weeds, fading away all alone at Les Fondettes. But

meanwhile Nana was growing increasingly wretched, for the memory of Zizi lying on the floor, with a red hole in his shirt, was more than she could bear.

'He was such a darling, so sweet and caressing. . . . Oh, you know, pet, I'm sorry if it annoys you, but I loved that baby. I can't help it, I've got to say it. . . . Besides it can't matter to you now, he's not here any more. You've got what you wanted; you can be quite sure you'll never catch us again.'

And this last reflection caused her such overwhelming regret that he ended up by trying to console her. Come now, she must be brave; she was quite right, it wasn't her fault. But she stopped crying of her own accord to say:

'Listen, you must go over there and find out how he is for me. . . . Straight away! I insist!'

He picked up his hat and went off to get news of Georges. When he returned, three-quarters of an hour later, he saw Nana leaning anxiously out of a window; and he shouted up to her from the pavement that the boy wasn't dead, and that they even hoped to save his life. At this her mood promptly changed to one of extravagant joy: she started singing and dancing, and proclaimed that life was beautiful. Zoé in the meantime was far from satisfied with her cleaning. She kept looking at the stain, and every time she passed it she repeated:

'You know, Madame, it hasn't gone.'

Sure enough, the stain had reappeared, a pale red colour on the white roses in the carpet. It was like a splash of blood barring the way on the very threshold of the bedroom.

'Never mind,' said Nana, happy again. 'It'll wear off underfoot.'

By the following day the Comte Muffat had likewise forgotten the incident. For a moment, in the cab taking him to the Rue Richelieu, he had sworn never to return to that woman's house. Heaven was giving him a warning, and the misfortunes which had overtaken Philippe and Georges struck him as a portent of his own downfall. But neither the sight of Madame Hugon in tears, nor that of the boy burning with fever, had had the power to make him keep his vow; and nothing remained of the short-lived horror of the incident

but a sense of secret delight at being rid of a rival whose boyish charm had always exasperated him. His passion had by now become fiercely exclusive, the sort of passion peculiar to a man who has had no youth. His love for Nana involved an urgent need to know that she belonged to him alone, a need to hear her, to touch her, to feel her breath. It was a tenderness beyond sensual desire, and verging on pure sentiment, an uneasy affection, jealous of the past, and dreaming of redemption, of the two of them receiving forgiveness as they knelt before God the Father. Every day religion regained some of its former influence over him. He started practising it again, going to confession and communion, constantly struggling with temptation, and spicing the joys of sin and penance with pangs of remorse. Then, having received permission from his confessor to wear out his passion, he made a habit of this daily damnation, which he redeemed by means of ecstatic demonstrations of faith, full of pious humility. In all simplicity he offered Heaven the appalling torments afflicting him, as a form of expiatory suffering. These torments grew ever greater as he climbed his calvary with the profound anguish of a believer trapped in a courtesan's fierce sensuality. What hurt him most of all was the woman's continual infidelities, for he could not bear sharing her with the others, nor understand her stupid whims. Undying, unchanging love was what he longed for. However, she had sworn to be faithful and he paid her for that. But he sensed that she was a liar, incapable of controlling herself, giving herself to friends or passers-by, like a good-natured animal, born to live naked.

One morning when he saw Foucarmont leaving her house at an unusual hour, he made a scene about it. But she flared up angrily, tired of his jealousy. Previously, on several occasions, she had behaved kindly to him. Thus, on the evening when he had surprised her with Georges, she had been the first to recover her composure, admitting that she was in the wrong and showering sweet nothings on him to make him swallow her infidelity. But he had ended up by exasperating her with his stubborn refusal to understand women, and now she was brutal.

427

'All right, yes, I've been to bed with Foucarmont. What of it? ... That's taken the wind out of your sails, hasn't it, my little Muffer?'

It was the first time she had called him 'my little Muffer' to his face. The bluntness of her admission took his breath away; and as he clenched his fists, she marched up to him and looked him straight in the eyes.

'That's enough of that, eh? ... If you don't like it, you'll do me the pleasure of leaving. ... I don't want you yelling in my house. ... Just you get it into your head that I insist on being completely free. When I like the look of a man I go to bed with him. Yes, that's the way it is. ... And you've got to make up your mind straight away : yes or no. And if it's no, you can get out.'

She had gone and opened the door, but he did not leave. Now that was her way of binding him more closely to her. For the smallest thing, at the slightest sign of a quarrel, she would tell him he could take it or leave it, adding some disobliging reflections. She said she could always find somebody better than him; she had only too many to choose from; you could pick up as many men as you liked in the street, better-looking men too, with red blood in their veins. At this he would hang his head, and wait for better times when she needed money; then she would become affectionate and he would forget, one night of love making up for the tortures of the whole week. His reconciliation with his wife had made his home unbearable. Abandoned by Fauchery, who had once again fallen under Rose's influence, the Countess had plunged madly into other love affairs. Suffering from the restless feverishness of a woman in her forties, she was always hysterically nervous, filling the house with the maddening whirl of her life. Estelle, since her marriage, had seen nothing of her father; the flat-chested, insignificant girl had suddenly become a woman of iron will, so autocratic that Daguenet trembled in her presence. Nowadays he accompanied her to mass; a convert to religion, he was furious with his father-in-law, for ruining them with a courtesan. Monsieur Venot alone still behaved kindly towards the Count, for he was biding his time. He had even succeeded in

joining Nana's circle of intimates and was now a regular visitor to both houses, where his continual smile was to be seen behind every door. And Muffat, wretchedly unhappy at home, and driven out by boredom and shame, still preferred to live in the Avenue de Villiers, in spite of the insults to which he was subjected there.

Soon there was only one subject of dispute between Nana and the Count, and that was money. One day, after having faithfully promised to bring her ten thousand francs, he had dared to present himself at the appointed hour empty-handed. For two days she had been warming him up with caresses, and such a breach of faith, such a waste of affection, made her launch into a torrent of coarse abuse. She was white with fury.

'So, you haven't got the money, eh? ... Then go back where you came from, my little Muffer, and double quick. And the filthy bastard wanted to kiss me again! ... No money, no nothing, understand?'

He tried to explain, and said he would have the money in a couple of days, but she interrupted him violently.

'And what about my bills? They'll sell me up while Monsieur comes here on the nod. ... Go on, take a look at yourself! Do you think I love you for your looks? A man who's got a mug like yours has to pay the women who put up with him. ... By God, if you don't bring me the ten thousand francs tonight, you won't have even the tip of my little finger to suck. ... I'll send you back to your wife, that's what I'll do!'

That evening he brought the ten thousand francs. Nana offered him her lips, and he took a long kiss which consoled him for the whole day of anguish. What annoyed the young woman was having him forever hanging around her. She complained to Monsieur Venot, begging him to take her little Muffer back to the Countess. Hadn't their reconciliation served any useful purpose? She was sorry she had helped to bring it about, seeing that she still had him on her hands in spite of everything. On days when out of anger she forgot where her interests lay, she swore that she would play such a dirty trick on him that he would never again be able

to set foot in her house. But as she often complained, slapping her thighs in fury, even if she had spat in his face, he would have stayed on and even thanked her. Meanwhile the quarrels about money kept on recurring. She demanded money from him with coarse brutality, bawling him out over paltry sums, displaying an odious avidity every minute of the day, and cruelly informing him again and again that she slept with him for his money and nothing else; it gave her no pleasure at all, she said, for she loved another man, and she was the unluckiest of women to need an idiot like him. They did not even want him at Court any more, and there was talk of insisting on his resignation. The Empress had said: 'He is just too disgusting.' That was known for certain. Nana repeated the phrase to cut short all their quarrels.

'You know, you disgust me!'

Nowadays she no longer took any precautions; she had regained complete freedom. Every day she did her round of the lake, making acquaintances which ended up elsewhere. This was the happy hunting ground *par excellence*, where the leading courtesans hawked their wares in broad daylight, flaunting themselves amid the smiling tolerance and dazzling luxury of Paris. Duchesses pointed her out to one another with a glance, and rich merchants' wives copied her hats. Sometimes her landau, in order to get by, stopped a file of splendid carriages belonging to financiers who held the purse-strings of all Europe, or ministers whose plump fingers gripped France by the throat. She belonged to this society of the Bois de Boulogne, occupied a prominent place in it, was known in every capital and sought after by every foreigner, enhancing the splendours of this crowd with the madness of her debauchery, as if she were the supreme glory and sweetest pleasure of the nation. Then there were night-time liaisons, brief unions which she herself had forgotten the morning after, but which took her to all the great restaurants, and often on fine days to the Madrid. The staffs of all the embassies took her out, and she dined with Lucy Stewart, Caroline Héquet and Maria Blond in the company of gentlemen who murdered the French language and paid to be entertained, who engaged them by the evening to be amusing, and

were so worldly-wise and vacuous that they never even touched them. This the ladies called 'going on a spree', and they would go home, happy at having been despised, to finish the night in the arms of some lover of their choice.

When she did not actually throw her men in his teeth, the Comte Muffat pretended to know nothing of all this. He suffered enough in any case from the lesser indignities of their daily life. The house in the Avenue de Villiers had become a hell, a madhouse in which at every hour of the day some incident would produce an appalling crisis. Nana had got to the point of fighting with her servants. For a while she was very kind to Charles, the coachman; when she stopped at a restaurant she sent a waiter out with beer for him, and she talked to him from the inside of her landau, amused and delighted when he slanged the cabbies in a block of carriages. Then, for no reason at all, she called him an idiot. She was always quibbling over the straw, the bran or the oats; in spite of her love for animals, she thought that her horses ate too much. One day when she was settling up, she accused Charles of robbing her, and he flew into a rage and called her a whore to her face; of course his horses were better than she was, he said, because they didn't sleep with anybody and everybody. She answered him in the same vein, and the Count had to separate them and give the coachman the sack. This was the beginning of a general exodus on the part of the servants. Victorine and François left after the theft of some of her diamonds. Julien himself disappeared; and there was a rumour that it was Monsieur who had begged him to go, giving him a generous bribe, because he was sleeping with Madame. Every week there were new faces in the servants' hall. Never before had there been such a mess; the house was like a passage down which the scum of the employment agencies galloped, leaving chaos behind them. Zoé alone stayed on, looking as neat as ever, her only concern being how to organize this riot until she had got enough together to set up on her own account, a plan she had been hatching for a long time past.

These were just the anxieties he could admit to. The Count put up with the stupidity of Madame Maloir, playing

bezique with her in spite of the rancid smell she gave off; he
put up with Madame Lerat and her gossiping; and he put up
with little Louis and his mournful complaints, the complaints of a child eaten up by some disease inherited from
an unknown father. But he spent hours worse than these.
One evening, standing outside a door, he had heard Nana
furiously telling her maid that a man claiming to be rich had
just swindled her – a handsome man who said he was an
American with gold mines in his own country, a swine who
had gone off while she was asleep without leaving her a
single sou, and had even taken a packet of cigarette papers
with him. The Count had turned very pale, and had gone
back downstairs on tiptoe so as not to hear any more. But
on another occasion he was forced to hear everything. Nana,
infatuated with a music-hall baritone who had thrown her
over, decided to commit suicide in a fit of sentimental melan-
cholia; she drank a glass of water in which she had soaked a
handful of matches, which made her terribly sick, but failed
to kill her. The Count had to nurse her and listen to the
whole story of her passion, accompanied by tears and
promises never to get involved with men again. In her
contempt for those swine, as she called them, she could not,
however, remain emotionally unattached, for she always had
some sweetheart hanging around her, and was forever indulging in incomprehensible fancies and the perverse tastes
of a weary body. Since Zoé had deliberately relaxed her
efforts, service in the house deteriorated to such a degree that
Muffat no longer dared to push open a door, draw a curtain,
or open a cupboard; the old arrangements no longer worked,
and there were gentlemen all over the place, constantly
bumping into one another. Now he coughed before entering
a room, having almost caught the young woman hanging
around Francis's neck one evening when he had just gone out
of the dressing-room for two minutes to tell the coachman to
put the horses to, while her hairdresser was finishing her hair.
She gave herself to men suddenly, behind his back, taking
her pleasure hurriedly in every corner, with the first man
who came to hand, whether she was in her chemise or in full
evening dress. She would come back to the Count with her

face flushed, happy at having deceived him. With him it was just a bore, a tedious duty.

In his jealous anguish the unhappy man got to the point of feeling almost reassured when he left Nana and Satin alone together. He would have gladly encouraged her in this vice, to keep the men away from her. But here too everything started going wrong. Nana deceived Satin as she deceived the Count, abandoning herself to monstrous caprices, and picking up girls on street corners. Driving home, she would suddenly take a fancy to a little slut she saw on the pavement; her senses fired and her imagination excited, she would invite the girl into her carriage, pay her off, and send her away again. Then again, disguised as a man, she would go to infamous houses and watch scenes of debauchery to relieve her boredom. And Satin, angry at being continually spurned, would throw the house into uproar with appalling scenes. She had ended up by gaining complete ascendancy over Nana, who had come to respect her. Muffat even thought of forming an alliance with her. When he did not dare to say anything, he would let Satin loose on Nana. Twice she had forced her darling to take him back, while he for his part behaved obligingly to her, warning her and standing aside in her favour at the first sign of trouble. But this understanding did not last very long, for Satin too was a little cracked.

Some days she would go mad, smashing everything and wearing herself out in frenzies of love and anger, but looking irresistible all the same. Zoé was presumably putting ideas into her head, for the maid kept taking her into corners as if she wanted to recruit her for the grand design of which she had so far spoken to nobody.

At times, however, the Comte Muffat would still flare up unexpectedly in disgust. He who had put up with Satin for months, and who had ended up by tolerating the herd of strangers that went galloping through Nana's bedroom, would fly into a rage at the idea of being deceived by somebody of his own set, or even by somebody he knew. When she admitted her relations with Foucarmont, he suffered so acutely and considered the young man's treachery so base,

that he decided to challenge him to a duel. As he did not know where to find seconds for such an affair, he applied to Labordette for help. The latter, utterly taken aback, could not help bursting out laughing.

'A duel over Nana. ... But, my dear sir, all Paris would laugh at you. Nobody fights over Nana; it would be just too ridiculous.'

The Count turned very pale and made a violent gesture.

'Then I shall slap his face in the street.'

For a whole hour Labordette had to reason with him. A slap in the face would make things even worse; that evening everybody would know the real reason for the duel, and he would be the laughing-stock of all the papers. And Labordette kept returning to the same conclusion :

'Out of the question; it would be just too ridiculous.'

Every time Muffat heard this reply it cut into him like a sharp knife. He could not even fight for the woman he loved because people would burst out laughing. Never before had he felt more keenly the wretchedness of his love, the waste of his solemn devotion in this absurd life of pleasure. This was his last rebellion; he allowed Labordette to convince him, and henceforth he watched uncomplainingly the procession of his friends, of all the men who lived in Nana's house as if it were their home.

In a few months Nana gobbled them up, one after the other. The growing needs of her life of luxury sharpened her appetite, and she would clean a man out with one snap of her teeth. First she had Foucarmont, who lasted only a few days. He was dreaming of leaving the Navy, and during his ten years of service had saved about thirty thousand francs which he planned to invest in the United States; but his cautious and even miserly instincts were conquered; he spent everything, even signing promissory notes pledging his future. When Nana showed him the door, he was penniless. She was very kind to him, though, advising him to return to his ship. What was the good of being stubborn? Seeing that he had no money left, he could not stay with her any longer. He ought to understand that, and be reasonable. A ruined

man fell from her hands like a ripe fruit, to lie rotting on the ground.

Next Nana set to work on Steiner, without disgust but without affection. She called him a dirty Jew, and seemed to be paying back an old grudge, of which she was not really aware. He was fat and stupid, and she wasted no time on him, taking two bites at a time in order to finish the Prussian off more quickly. He had abandoned Simonne, and his Bosphorus scheme was in a bad way. Nana hastened its collapse by wild demands. For another month he struggled on, working financial miracles; he filled Europe with posters, advertisements and prospectuses in a colossal publicity campaign, obtaining money from the most distant countries. All these savings, from the pounds of speculators to the pence of the poor, were swallowed up in the Avenue de Villiers. Steiner was also a partner in an iron works in Alsace; and there, in a small provincial town, workmen black with coal-dust and soaked with sweat strained their sinews and heard their bones crack day and night to satisfy Nana's pleasures. Like a huge fire, she devoured everything, the profits from financial swindles no less than the fruits of labour. This time she did for Steiner, throwing him back into the gutter, sucked dry and so completely cleaned out that he was unable even to think up a new swindle. When his bank collapsed, he stammered and trembled at the thought of the police. He had just been declared bankrupt, and this man who had played with millions was flustered at the mere mention of money, and thrown into childish confusion. One evening at Nana's he burst into tears and asked her for a loan of a hundred francs, to pay his maidservant. And Nana, touched and amused at the end of this terrible old man, who had plundered Paris for twenty years, brought him the money, saying :

'You know, I'm giving you this because it's funny. . . . But listen, dear, you're too old for me to keep you. You've got to find something else to do.'

Then Nana went straight on to la Faloise. For some time he had been soliciting the honour of being ruined by her in order to complete his reputation as a man about town. He

needed a woman to launch him; that was the only thing still lacking. In two months all Paris would be talking of him, and he would see his name in the papers. In the event six weeks proved enough. His inheritance was in landed property, houses, fields, woods and farms. He had to sell quickly, one thing after another. At every mouthful Nana swallowed an acre. The leaves quivering in the sunshine, the vast fields of ripe corn, the golden September vineyards, the tall grass in which the cows stood knee-deep – everything was engulfed as if in an abyss; and there was even a water-course, a stone-quarry and three mills that disappeared. Nana passed by like an invading army, or one of those swarms of locusts whose fiery flight lays waste a whole province. She scorched the earth on which her little foot rested. Farm by farm, field by field, she ate up the inheritance in her charming way, without even noticing, just as she would have eaten a bag of burnt almonds on her lap between meals. It wasn't important; after all, they were only sweets. But at last, one evening, there only remained a little wood. She gulped it down disdainfully, for it was scarcely worth the trouble of opening one's mouth. La Faloise gave a foolish laugh as he sucked the knob of his cane. His debts were crushing him, all he had left was an income of a hundred francs a year, and he could see himself being compelled to go to the provinces to live with a finicky uncle; but that didn't matter, because he had made his mark – the *Figaro* had printed his name twice. And with his scraggy neck sticking out between the turn-down points of his collar, and his waist squeezed into an excessively short jacket, he would swagger about, uttering parrot-like exclamations and affecting the weariness of a puppet which has never felt a single emotion. He annoyed Nana so much that she ended up by giving him a thrashing.

Meanwhile Fauchery had returned, brought along by his cousin. Poor Fauchery was now quite the family man. After breaking with the Countess, he had fallen into Rose's hands, and she was treating him as if he were her lawful husband. Mignon acted simply as Madame's butler. Installed as master of the house, the journalist had lied to Rose, taking all sorts

of precautions when he deceived her, like a good husband who has finally decided to settle down. Nana's triumph consisted in possessing him and at the same time ruining a newspaper he had started with a friend's capital. She did not advertise their liaison; on the contrary, she took pleasure in treating him as a gentleman who had to be careful of his reputation, and when she spoke of Rose, it was as 'poor Rose'. The newspaper kept her in flowers for two months, and after the provincial subscriptions she took everything, from the gossip column to the theatre news. Then, after running down the editorial staff and disorganizing the management, she satisfied an expensive caprice and had a winter garden installed in a corner of her house; that did for the printing press. But all this was simply in fun. When Mignon, delighted at the progress of the affair, came to see if he could saddle her with Fauchery for good, she asked him if he took her for a fool. A penniless fellow who lived on his articles and his plays – not likely. That sort of idiocy was all very well for a talented woman like poor Rose, but not for her. Distrusting Mignon, and fearing some act of treachery on his part, for he was quite capable of denouncing them to his wife, she dismissed Fauchery, who in any case was no longer capable of paying her in anything but publicity. But she remembered him kindly, for the two of them had enjoyed themselves enormously at the expense of that fool la Faloise. They might never have thought of meeting each other again if the pleasure of making fun of such a perfect idiot had not appealed to them. It struck them as uproariously funny to kiss each other under his very nose, and to have a wild fling on his money. They would send him off on some errand to the other end of Paris, in order to be alone; and then, when he came back, they would crack jokes and make allusions he could not understand. One day, egged on by the journalist, she wagered she would slap la Faloise in the face; that evening she gave him a slap, and then went on hitting him, for she found it amusing and was delighted at the chance of showing what cowards men were. She called him her punch-bag, and would tell him to come forward and have his smack – smacks which made her hand red, because she was not used

to giving them yet. La Faloise would laugh in his idiotic way, with tears in his eyes. He was delighted at such familiarity, and thought it was simply marvellous.

One evening when he had received a good many slaps and was very excited, he said :

'You know, you ought to marry me. ... We'd make a funny couple, the two of us, don't you think?'

This was no empty suggestion. Seized with a desire to astonish Paris, he had slyly thought up this marriage. Nana's husband! Wouldn't that be smart! What a stunning apotheosis! But Nana put him sharply in his place.

'Me, marry you? ... No, thank you! If that idea had been tormenting me, I'd have found a husband long ago! And a man worth twenty of you, dearie. ... I've had heaps of proposals. Listen, count them up with me: Philippe, Georges, Foucarmont, Steiner – that makes four, not to mention the others you don't know. ... It's like a chorus they all trot out. The moment I'm nice to them, they start singing: "Will you marry me? Will you marry me?"'

Working herself up, she burst out indignantly :

'Oh, no, I won't! ... Do you think I'm made for that sort of thing? Just look at me. Why, I wouldn't be Nana any more if I saddled myself with a man. ... Besides it's too foul for words ...'

And she spat and hiccoughed with disgust, as if she had seen all the filth in the world spreading out beneath her.

One evening la Faloise vanished, and a week later it became known that he was in the provinces, staying with an uncle who was mad about botany. He was pasting up his specimens for him, in the hope of marrying a very plain and very pious cousin. Nana shed no tears for him. She simply said to the Count :

'Well, my little Muffer, that makes another rival less for you. You're gloating today. ... But he was getting serious! He wanted to marry me.'

He turned pale, and she flung her arms about his neck and hung there laughing, driving home every cruel remark with a caress.

'That's what narks you, isn't it? Knowing that you can't

438

marry Nana. . . . Well they're all pestering me with their proposals and you're fuming in your corner. . . . Well, it's no go – you've got to wait till your wife kicks the bucket. . . . Oh, if she died on us, you'd be round here double quick, wouldn't you, throwing yourself on the ground and offering me marriage with all the trimmings – sighs and tears and promises. Wouldn't that be nice, darling, eh?'

Her voice had grown gentle, and she was teasing him in a ferociously wheedling manner. He was deeply moved, and started blushing, as he returned her kisses. Suddenly she exclaimed :

'Good God, to think I guessed ! He's thought about it; he's waiting for his wife to snuff it. . . . Well, that's the ruddy limit ! Why he's even worse than the others !'

Muffat had accepted the others. Nowadays he put the last shreds of his dignity into remaining 'Monsieur' for the servants and intimates of the house, the man who, giving the most, was the official lover. And his passion grew fiercer. He maintained his position by paying for it, buying even smiles at a high price. He was often robbed, and he never got his money's worth : but it was like a disease gnawing at his vitals, from which he could not prevent himself from suffering. Whenever he entered Nana's bedroom he contented himself with opening the windows for a moment, to get rid of the odours the others had left behind them, the body smells of fair-haired men and dark, and cigar-smoke whose pungency choked him. This bedroom had become a veritable public place, so many boots were wiped on its threshold; and not a single man was stopped by the blood-stain barring the way. Zoé was still preoccupied by this stain; it had become something of an obsession with her, for it offended her sense of cleanliness to see it always there. In spite of everything her eyes would constantly turn in its direction, and nowadays she never entered Madame's room without saying :

'It's funny how it doesn't go. . . . And heaven knows there's enough people come in here.'

Nana, who had had reassuring news of Georges, now convalescing in his mother's care at Les Fondettes, always made the same reply :

'Dammit, it needs time. . . . It's getting paler as people walk on it.'

In fact, each of the gentlemen, Foucarmont, Steiner, la Faloise and Fauchery, had carried away a little of the stain on the soles of his shoes. And Muffat, whom the blood-stain preoccupied as much as it did Zoé, kept studying it in spite of himself, as if to discover from the degree to which it had faded, how many men had passed that way. He secretly dreaded it, and always stepped over it out of a sudden fear of crushing some live thing, some naked member lying on the floor.

Then in the bedroom he would become intoxicated with passion and forget everything, from the mob of men who were forever crossing it to the sign of mourning which barred the doorway. Outside in the open he would sometimes weep in the street out of sheer disgust, swearing never to go back. And the moment the door-curtain fell behind him, he was completely reconquered; he felt himself melting in the warm air of the room, felt his flesh being steeped in perfume, felt himself being overcome by a voluptuous yearning for anni-hilation. A pious churchgoer, accustomed to ecstatic ex-periences in sumptuous chapels, he encountered here exactly the same mystical sensations as when he knelt beneath some stained-glass window and surrendered to the intoxication of the organ music and incense. Woman dominated him with the jealous tyranny of a God of wrath, terrifying him but granting him moments of joy as keen as spasms, in return for hours of hideous torments, visions of hell and eternal tor-tures. He stammered out the same despairing prayers as in church, and above all suffered the same fits of humility peculiar to an accursed creature crushed under the mud from which he has sprung. His carnal desires and his spiritual needs merged together, and seemed to spring from the dark depths of his being like a single blossom on the tree of his existence. He abandoned himself to the power of love and faith, those twin levers which move the world. And in spite of all the struggles of his reason, this bedroom of Nana's filled him with madness, and he would submit shudderingly to the omnipotence of sex, just as he would swoon before the mysterious power of heaven.

Then, when she felt how humble he was, Nana was tyrannical in her triumph. The passion for defiling things was inborn in her. It was not enough for her to destroy them, she had to soil them too. Her delicate hands left abominable traces, corrupting with their touch whatever they had broken. And he submissively lent himself to this game, remembering the stories of saints eaten up by lice, who in turn ate their own excrement. Once she held him captive in her room behind locked doors, she treated herself to the spectacle of a man's infamy. At first they simply indulged in playful antics; she would give him little slaps and impose comical tasks on him, making him lisp like a child and repeat sentences after her.

'Say like me : "Shan't ! Coco doethn't want to !"'

He would meekly obey her, even copying her accent.

'Shan't ! Coco doethn't want to !'

Or else she would play the bear, walking about on all fours on her fur rugs, wearing only her chemise, and growling as she circled round him, as if she wanted to eat him. She would even nibble his calves for the fun of the thing. Then, getting to her feet, she would say :

'It's your turn now; go on. . . . I bet you don't play the bear half as well as me.'

So far it was all very charming. As a bear she amused him with her white skin and her mane of red hair. He would laugh and go down on all fours too, growling and biting her calves, while she ran away, pretending to be terrified.

'Aren't we silly !' she would say after a while. 'You've no idea how ugly you are, pet. If only they could see you like this at the Tuileries !'

But before long these little games went wrong. The trouble was not cruelty on her part, for she remained as good-natured as ever; it was as if a wind of madness were blowing ever more strongly through the closed bedroom. Lust deranged their brains and plunged them into the delirious fantasies of the flesh. The old pious terrors of their sleepless nights now turned into a thirst for bestiality, a mania for walking on all fours, growling and biting.

One day, when he was playing the bear, she pushed him

so hard that he fell against a piece of furniture, and when she saw the lump on his forehead she could not help bursting out laughing. After that, her appetite whetted by experiments with la Faloise, she treated him like an animal, thrashing him and kicking him around.

'Gee up! Gee up! . . . You're the horse. . . . Gee up, now! . . . Get a move on, you dirty screw!'

At other times he was a dog. She would throw her scented handkerchief to the far end of the room, and he had to run and pick it up with his teeth, dragging himself along on his hands and knees.

'Fetch it, Caesar! . . . You must wait, I'll give you what for if you don't get a move on! . . . Well done, Caesar! Good dog! Nice dog! . . . Sit up and beg!'

And he loved his degradation, enjoying the pleasure of being an animal. He longed to sink even further, and would cry —

'Hit harder. . . . Woof, woof! I'm a mad dog! Hit away!'

Taken by a whim, she insisted on his coming one evening dressed in his superb uniform of court chamberlain. She roared with laughter and poked merciless fun at him when she had him there in all his glory, with his sword, cocked hat and white breeches, and his dress-coat of red cloth trimmed with gold, with the symbolic key hanging on its left-hand skirt. This key amused her more than anything else, inspiring her with a wildly fanciful series of obscene explanations. Laughing all the time, and carried away by her irreverence for pomp and grandeur, and by the joy of humiliating him in the official dignity of his uniform, she shook him and pinched him, shouting: 'Get a move on, chamberlain!' and finally kicking him in the behind. Every kick was a heartfelt insult to the Tuileries and the majesty of the imperial court, dominating an abject and frightened people. That was what she thought of society. She was taking her revenge, settling an unconscious family grudge, bequeathed to her in her blood. Then, once the chamberlain was undressed and his uniform spread out on the floor, she shouted at him to jump, and he jumped; she shouted at him to spit, and he spat; she shouted at him to trample on the gold, the eagles and the decorations,

442

and he trampled on them. Abracadabra, and nothing was left; everything was swept away. She smashed a chamberlain just as she smashed a bottle or a comfit-box, turning him into filth, and reducing him to a heap of mud in the gutter.

Meanwhile the goldsmiths had failed to keep their promise, and the bed was not delivered until about the middle of January. Muffat happened to be in Normandy, where he had gone to sell a last scrap of property, because Nana was insisting on four thousand francs straight away. He was not due in Paris for another two days; but once his business was finished, he hurried back to the capital, and without even dropping in at the Rue Miromesnil, went straight to the Avenue de Villiers. Ten o'clock was striking. As he had a key to a side door opening on the Rue Cardinet, he went up unhindered. In the drawing-room upstairs Zoé, who was dusting the bronzes, stood dumbfounded at the sight of him; and, not knowing how to stop him, she started telling him in long, rambling sentences that Monsieur Venot, looking terribly upset, had been searching for him since the previous day, and that he had already called twice to beg her to send Monsieur round to his house, if Monsieur arrived at Madame's before going home. Muffat listened to her without being able to make head or tale of her story; then he noticed her agitation, and was seized by a sudden fit of jealousy of which he no longer believed himself capable. Hearing the sound of laughter in the bedroom, he threw himself against the door, and it gave way, the two flaps flying open, while Zoé withdrew with a shrug of her shoulders. So much the worse for Madame! Seeing that Madame had lost her senses, Madame could sort things out for herself.

And on the threshold Muffat uttered a cry at the sight that met his eyes.

'God! ... Oh, God!'

The newly decorated bedroom was resplendent in all its royal luxury. Silver buttons shone like bright stars on the tea-rose velvet of the hangings, which were of that pink flesh-tint which the sky assumes on fine evenings when Venus lights up on the horizon, against the clear background of the fading daylight. The golden cords hanging from the corners,

and the gold lace-work framing the panels, were like delicate flames or flowing locks of red hair, half-covering the nakedness of the room and setting off its voluptuous pallor. Then, facing him, there was the gold and silver bed, shining in all the fresh splendour of its chasing, a throne wide enough for Nana to stretch out the glory of her naked limbs, an altar of Byzantine luxury, worthy of the omnipotence of her sex, which at that very moment lay openly displayed in the religious immodesty of an awe-inspiring idol. And beside her, beneath the snowy gleam of her bosom, amid her godlike triumph, there wallowed a shameful, decrepit thing, a comic and lamentable ruin, the Marquis de Chouard in his nightshirt.

The Count had clasped his hands together and, shuddering from head to foot, kept repeating :

'God ! Oh, God !'

It was for the Marquis de Chouard that the golden roses were blossoming on the side-panels, bunches of golden roses blooming among the golden leaves; it was for him that the Cupids in their topsy-turvy round were leaning down from the silver trellis-work with loving, roguish laughter. And it was for him that the faun at his feet was uncovering the sleeping nymph worn out by voluptuous pleasure, that figure of Night copied from Nana's celebrated nudity, even down to the heavy thighs by which everyone could recognize her. Cast there like a human rag, rotted and perished by sixty years of debauchery, he brought a touch of the charnelhouse to the glory of the woman's dazzling flesh. Seeing the door open, he had sat up, seized with the sudden terror of an old dotard. This last night of love had rendered him imbecile and plunged him into his second childhood; speech failing him, he remained in an attitude of flight, half-paralysed, stammering and shivering, his night-shirt hitched up over his skeletal body and one leg sticking out of the bedclothes, a poor, pallid leg, covered with grey hairs. In spite of her annoyance Nana could not help laughing.

'Lie down and get under the bedclothes,' she said, turning him over and burying him under the sheet, as if he were some filthy thing she could not show anyone.

Then she jumped out of bed to shut the door again. She was unlucky with her little Muffer, and no mistake. He always turned up when he wasn't wanted. And why had he gone to look for money in Normandy? The old man had brought her the four thousand francs she needed, and she had let him have his way with her. She pushed the door shut and shouted:

'So much the worse for you! It's your own fault. Is that the way to come into a room? Good-bye and good riddance!'

Muffat remained standing before the closed door, thunderstruck by what he had just seen. His shuddering grew more violent, mounting from his feet to his chest and skull. Then, like a tree shaken by a high wind, he swayed forward and fell on his knees, with all his bones creaking. And stretching his hands out in despair, he stammered:

'God, this is too much! This is too much!'

He had accepted everything so far, but he could do so no longer. He felt that he had come to the end of his tether, that he was lost in that darkness where man's reason fails him. In an extraordinary outburst of faith, raising his hands higher and higher, he searched for heaven and called upon God.

'Oh, no, I don't want to! ... Oh, come to me, God! Help me! Let me die sooner! ... Oh, no, not that man, God. It's all over: take me, carry me away, so that I won't see any more, so that I won't feel any more. ... Oh, I belong to you, God. Our Father which art in heaven ...'

And he went on, burning with faith, an ardent prayer escaping from his lips. But then someone touched him on the shoulder. He looked up; it was Monsieur Venot, surprised to find him praying outside that closed door. Then, as if God himself had answered his appeal, he flung his arms round the little old man's neck. At last he could weep, and he burst into sobs, repeating over and over again:

'Brother ... brother ...'

All his suffering humanity found relief in that cry. He soaked Monsieur Venot's face with tears; he kissed it, uttering disjointed phrases.

'Oh, my dear brother, how I am suffering! ... Only you

are left to me, brother. . . . Take me away for ever — for pity's sake, take me away . . .'

Then Monsieur Venot clasped him in his arms and called him brother too. But he had a fresh blow in store for him. Since the previous day he had been looking for him to inform him that the Comtesse Sabine, in a supreme fit of aberration, had just eloped with a buyer from a large draper's shop; this had caused a terrible scandal, and all Paris was already talking about it. Seeing him in a state of such religious fervour, Monsieur Venot felt the opportunity to be favourable, and immediately told him of the commonplace tragedy on which his marriage had foundered. The Count was unmoved. His wife had gone. That meant nothing to him; he would see about it later on. And seized with anguish once more, he gazed in terror at the door, the walls, the ceiling, repeating this single supplication :

'Take me away. . . . I can't bear it any longer. Take me away.'

Monsieur Venot led him away as if he had been a child. From that day on, Muffat was entirely in his power, and returned to the strict observance of the duties of religion. His life lay in ruins about him. First he had resigned his position as chamberlain in deference to the outraged modesty of the Tuileries, and then his daughter Estelle had brought an action against him for the recovery of a sum of sixty thousand francs, a legacy left her by an aunt which she ought to have received at the time of her marriage. Ruined, and eking out a living on the remains of his vast fortune, he allowed himself to be gradually finished off by the Countess, who ate up the leavings Nana had scorned. Corrupted by the courtesan's promiscuity, and driven to every excess, Sabine put the finishing touches to his ruin. After a succession of affairs, she had returned home, and he had taken her back in a spirit of Christian resignation and forgiveness. She accompanied him as his living disgrace, but he grew increasingly indifferent, and eventually ceased to suffer from such considerations. Heaven had taken him out of the hands of Woman to restore him to the arms of God. The voluptuous pleasures he had enjoyed with Nana were prolonged in religious ecstasies

accompanied by the same stammered pleas, the same despairing prayers, the same fits of humility peculiar to an accursed creature crushed under the mud from which he has sprung. In the gloomy interiors of churches, his knees chilled by the flagstones, he would experience once more the delights of the past, feeling his muscles contract and his head spin in the same delicious satisfaction of the obscure needs of his being.

On the evening of the final break Mignon presented himself at the house in the Avenue de Villiers. He was growing accustomed to Faucherv, and was beginning to discover countless advantages in his wife's acquisition of a second husband. He left all the little domestic matters to the journalist, entrusted him with the active supervision of the household and spent the money earned by his theatrical successes on the household's everyday expenses. Since, for his part, Fauchery behaved very reasonably, without any ridiculous jealousy, and proving just as accommodating as Mignon himself about Rose's incidental activities, the two men got on better and better, delighting in a partnership which was so fertile in all sorts of benefits, and settling down side by side in an association in which they no longer caused each other any embarrassment or inconvenience. The whole thing was well organized and admirably run, with each man vying with the other in the cause of the common good. That very evening, indeed, Mignon had come along, on Fauchery's advice, to see if he could entice Nana's maid from her, for the journalist had formed a high opinion of the woman's exceptional intelligence. Rose was in despair, because for the past month she had had to make do with inexperienced girls who caused her constant trouble. When Zoé opened the door to him he pushed her straight away into the dining-room. At his opening remark she smiled : it was impossible, she said, for she was leaving Madame to set up on her own account. And she added with quiet vanity that she was receiving offers of employment every day, ladies were fighting over her, and that Madame Blanche would give anything to have her back. Zoé was taking over La Tricon's establishment, in fulfilment of an old plan she had been meditating on for a long time. Ambitious to make her fortune, she was investing all her

savings in it, full of grandiose ideas of enlarging the business, renting a great house, combining every amenity within its walls. In fact, it was with this in view that she had tried to recruit Satin, who at the time was dying in hospital, she had ruined her health so completely.

When Mignon persisted with his offer, speaking of the risks involved in business, Zoé, without explaining the exact nature of her establishment, gave a tight-lipped smile, as if she had just put a sweet in her mouth, and merely replied :

'Oh, the luxury trade always pays. . . . You see, I've worked for other people long enough, and now I want other people to work for me.'

And her lip curled ferociously. At last she was going to be 'Madame', and, for the sake of a few louis, all those women whose slops she had emptied for the past fifteen years were going to grovel at her feet.

Mignon asked to be announced, and Zoé left him for a moment, after remarking that Madame had had a very bad day. He had only been there once before, and he did not know the house at all. The dining-room, with its Gobelin tapestries, its sideboard and its plate, struck him with astonishment, and opening the doors, he inspected the drawing-room and the winter garden, before returning to the hall. The oppressive luxury, the gilded furniture, the silks and velvets, gradually filled him with such a feeling of admiration that it set his heart pounding. When Zoé came to fetch him, she offered to show him the other rooms, the dressing-room and the bedroom. In the latter Mignon's heart almost burst; and he was carried away by a feeling of tender enthusiasm. That confounded Nana amazed him, and he was no mean judge. In the midst of the disintegration of the household and the servants' wild orgy of waste, there was still a mass of riches stopping up the holes and overflowing the ruins. And Mignon, confronted with this magnificent monument, recalled some of the great works he had seen. Near Marseilles he had been shown an aqueduct whose stone arches straddled an abyss, a gigantic work which had cost millions of francs and ten years of struggle. At Cherbourg he had seen the enormous new port under construction, with

hundreds of men sweating in the sun, while cranes filled the sea with huge lumps of rock, building a wall on which workmen were occasionally crushed into a bloody pulp. But all that now struck him as insignificant, and Nana excited him much more. Viewing the fruit of her labours, he felt once more the sensation of respect he had experienced on a festive evening in a sugar-refiner's château. This château had been built for the refiner, a palatial edifice of royal splendour which had been paid for by a single material – sugar. It was with something else, a tiny thing that people laughed at, a little of her delicate nudity – it was with this shameful trifle, so powerful that it could move the world, that all alone, without workmen, and without the aid of machines invented by engineers, she had shaken Paris to its foundations, and had built up this fortune on the bodies of dead men.

'God, what an implement!' Mignon exclaimed in his ecstasy, feeling a new surge of personal gratitude.

Nana had gradually lapsed into a state of deep depression. To begin with, the encounter between the Marquis and the Count had given her a fit of feverish nervousness, into which there entered an element of laughter. Then the thought of that old man going away in a cab half-dead, and of her poor Muffer, whom she would never see again, now that she had driven him so wild, brought on a mood of sentimental melancholy. After that she had flown into a temper on learning that Satin, who had disappeared about a fortnight before, was ill in Lariboisière and at the point of death, Madame Robert had reduced her to such a pitiful condition. While she was having the horses put to in order to go and take a last look at the little slut, Zoé had come up to her and calmly given her a week's notice. She was plunged into despair; it was as if she were losing a member of her own family. Heavens above, what was to become of her all alone? She begged Zoé to stay, and the latter, highly flattered by Madame's despair, ended up by kissing her to show that she was not leaving in anger; she simply had to go, and business came before personal feelings.

But that was not the end of the shocks Nana was to receive that day. Thoroughly upset, she had given up the idea of

going out, and was moping in her little drawing-room, when Labordette arrived to tell her of an opportunity of buying some magnificent lace, and in the course of his remarks casually let out the information that Georges was dead. Her blood froze.

'Zizi dead!' she cried.

And her eyes involuntarily looked for the pink stain on the carpet; but it had disappeared at last, worn away by people's feet. Meanwhile Labordette had begun giving her details. It was not known for certain how he had died; some said that his wound had reopened, while others claimed that he had committed suicide by throwing himself into one of the pools at Les Fondettes. Nana kept repeating:

'Dead! Dead!'

She had had a lump in her throat all day, and now she relieved her feelings by bursting out sobbing. She had a sensation of infinite sadness, overwhelming in its depth and immensity. Labordette tried to comfort her over Georges, but she silenced him with a gesture, and stammered:

'It isn't just him; it's everything, everything.... I'm so unhappy.... Oh, I know what's going to happen. They'll start saying again what a bitch I am, what with that mother mourning her son, and that poor man who was groaning outside my door this morning, and all the other people who are ruined now after spending all they had with me. ... That's it, lay into Nana; lay into the bitch. Oh, I've got a broad back. I can hear them as if they were here. "That filthy whore who goes to bed with everybody, cleans out some of them, drives others to death, and causes grief to lots of people ..."'

She was obliged to break off, choked by her tears, and in her anguish she flung herself across the divan, burying her face in a cushion. The consciousness of the catastrophes around her, the disasters she had caused, overwhelmed her with a warm continuous flood of emotion, and her voice broke into the pathetic plaint of a little girl:

'Oh, I'm so miserable! I'm so miserable! ... I can't go on like this – it's choking me. ... It's horrible being misunderstood, and seeing everybody siding against you because

they're stronger than you. All the same, when you've got nothing to feel guilty about and your conscience is clear ... why then, no, dammit, no ...'

Her anger began to turn to rebellion. Getting up, she dried her eyes, and walked about in great agitation.

'No, dammit, they can say what they like; it isn't my fault. Am I a bad sort? I give away everything I've got, and I wouldn't kill a fly. ... It's their fault – yes, it's all their fault! ... I never wanted to hurt them. But they came running after me, and now they're kicking the bucket, or begging in the street, or crying their eyes out ...'

Then, stopping in front of Labordette, she slapped him on the shoulders, saying:

'Come on, you were there – tell the truth. ... Was it me that egged them on? Weren't there always a dozen of them fighting to see who could invent the dirtiest trick? They used to disgust me, they did! I did all I could not to copy them, they scared me that much. Look here, I'll give you an example: they all wanted to marry me. Now, that's a nice idea, isn't it! Yes, dearie, I could have been a countess or a baroness a dozen times over, if I'd agreed. Well now, I refused, because I was a decent sort. ... Oh, when I think of all the crimes and all the dirty deeds I've spared them! ... They'd have stolen, murdered, killed their fathers and mothers for me. I had only to say the word, and I didn't say it. ... And now you see what I've got for it. ... Take Daguenet, for instance; I married him off, that down-and-out, and got him into society, after keeping him gratis for weeks. And when I met him yesterday he looked the other way. Well, to hell with you, you bastard! I'm not half as bad as you are!'

She had begun pacing up and down again, and now she smashed her fist down on a table.

'By God, it isn't fair! Society's all wrong. They come down on the women, when it's the men who insist on you doing things. ... Listen – I can tell you this now: when I used to go with them, well, I didn't enjoy it, no, I didn't enjoy it one little bit. It was a bore, honest it was. ... Well then, how can it be my fault, I ask you? ... Yes, they bored me to tears. If it hadn't been for them and what they made of me, I'd be in

451

a convent now saying my prayers, because I've always been religious. .... And after all, if they've kicked the bucket or lost all their money, they've only themselves to blame. I'd got nothing to do with it.'

'Of course not,' said Labordette, thoroughly convinced.

Zoé showed in Mignon, and Nana received him smilingly; she had had a good cry, and it was all over now. Still glowing with enthusiasm, he complimented her on her house; but she told him that she had had enough of the place, that she had other plans now, and that she would sell everything up one of these days. Then, as he gave a pretext for his call, saying that he had come about a benefit performance in aid of old Bosc, who was tied to his armchair by paralysis, she expressed deep sympathy, and took two boxes. When Zoé announced that Madame's carriage was waiting, she asked for her hat; and while she was tying the strings she told the two men about poor Satin, adding :

'I'm going to the hospital. .... Nobody's ever loved me as much as her. Oh, they're right when they say that men are heartless. .... Perhaps she'll be dead by the time I get there – who knows? Never mind, I'll ask to see her. I want to give her a kiss.'

Labordette and Mignon smiled, and, as Nana had shaken off her sadness, she smiled too. Those two didn't count : they could understand. And they admired her in respectful silence, while she finished buttoning her gloves. She alone was left standing, amid the accumulated riches of her mansion, while a host of men lay stricken at her feet. Like those monsters of ancient times whose fearful domains were covered with skeletons, she rested her feet on human skulls and was surrounded by catastrophes. There was the raging holocaust in which Vandeuvres had died, the melancholy which had taken Foucarmont to the China seas, the financial disaster which had reduced Steiner to living like an honest man, the satisfied imbecility of la Faloise, the tragic ruin of the Muffats, and the white corpse of Georges, over which Philippe was now watching, for he had come out of prison the day before. She had finished her labour of ruin and death. The fly that had come from the dungheap of the slums, carry-

ing the ferment of social decay, had poisoned all these men simply by alighting on them. It was fitting and just. She had avenged the beggars and outcasts of her world. And while, as it were, her sex rose in a halo of glory and blazed down on her prostrate victims like a rising sun shining down on a field of carnage, she remained as unconscious of her actions as a splendid animal, ignorant of the havoc she had wreaked, and as good-natured as ever. She was still big and plump, splendidly healthy and splendidly gay. But this no longer counted for anything, because she was tired of her house; it struck her as ridiculously small, and full of furniture which got in her way. Still, it had just been a beginning; and she was already planning something better. She set off to kiss Satin for the last time, dressed in all her finery, and looking clean and wholesome and brand-new as if she had never been used.

14

SUDDENLY Nana disappeared, vanishing from sight again in a fresh flight, this time a journey to exotic foreign parts. Before her departure she had treated herself to the experience of a sale, making a clean sweep of everything she possessed – house, furniture, jewellery and even dresses and linen. Figures were bandied about, it was said that the five days' sale had produced more than six hundred thousand francs. One last time Paris had seen her in a spectacular theatrical production. It was called *Mélusine*, and it was put on at the Théâtre de la Gaîté, which the penniless Bordenave had bluffed the owners into leasing to him. Here she found herself appearing once more with Prullière and Fontan. She had only a walking-on part, but it was the great attraction of the show, consisting as it did of three poses representing a silent fairy queen. Then one fine morning, in the midst of this great success, when Bordenave, in his passion for advertising, was exciting the interest of all Paris with colossal posters, it became known that she had left for Cairo the previous day. She had simply had a few words with her manager, something had been said which had vexed her, and she had gone off on the impulse of a woman too rich to put up with any annoyance. Besides she was satisfying an old ambition, for she had long dreamt of visiting the Turkish Empire.

Months went by, and she began to be forgotten. When her name was mentioned in her old haunts, the strangest stories were told, and everybody gave the most contradictory and far-fetched information. She had conquered the heart of the Viceroy, and was reigning, in the innermost precincts of a palace, over two hundred slaves, having one or two of them beheaded now and then, for the sake of a little amusement. Not a bit of it : she had ruined herself with a huge Negro, satisfying a filthy passion which had left her without a penny to her name, wallowing in the crapulous debauchery of Cairo. A fortnight later there was much astonishment when

somebody swore to having met her in Russia. A legend started to take shape in which she was the mistress of a foreign prince, and people began talking about her diamonds. Soon every woman in Paris was acquainted with them from the current descriptions, but nobody could cite a precise source of information. There were rings, bracelets, ear-rings, a necklace an inch wide, and a royal diadem surmounted by a central diamond the size of a thumb. Pictured in imagination in those far-away countries, she took on the mysterious radiance of an idol laden with precious stones. People now spoke of her without laughing, full of a dreamy respect for this fortune she had acquired among the barbarians.

One evening in July, about eight o'clock, while driving down the Rue du Faubourg-Saint-Honoré, Lucy caught sight of Caroline Héquet, who had come out on foot to place an order at a local shop. Lucy called to her, and immediately asked her :

'Have you had dinner? Are you free? ... Then come with me, my dear.... Nana's back in town.'

The other got in at once, and Lucy went on :

'And you know, my dear, she may be dead while we're chatting.'

'Dead? What an idea !' cried Caroline in astonishment. 'But where? And what of?'

'At the Grand Hôtel ... of smallpox.... Oh, it's a fantastic story !'

Lucy told her coachman to drive fast, and while the horses trotted rapidly along the Rue Royale and the boulevards, she told Caroline what had happened to Nana in jerky breathless phrases.

'Just imagine, Nana arrives here from Russia – I don't know why she left – a quarrel with her prince, I suppose.... She leaves her bags at the station, and goes to her aunt's – you remember that old woman.... Well, there she finds her baby ill with smallpox, the baby dies the next day, and she has a row with the aunt about some money she was supposed to send her, not a penny of which the aunt had ever seen.... It seems that's what the child died of, because it had been neglected and badly cared for.... Right, Nana clears off and

goes to a hotel, and she's beginning to think about her bags when she runs into Mignon. . . . She comes over queer, starts having the shivers, and wants to be sick, and Mignon takes her back to her hotel, promising to see to her things. . . . Isn't it funny how it all works out?' But this is the best part of the story : Rose finds out about Nana's illness, and gets indignant at the idea of her being alone in a furnished room. So she rushes round, crying like a baby, to look after her. . . . You remember how they used to loathe each other, like a couple of regular furies. Well, my dear, Rosie had Nana moved to the Grand Hôtel, so that at least she'd die in a decent place, and she's already spent three nights there, even if she does kick the bucket in the end. It's Labordette who told me all about it. And I wanted to see for myself . . .'

'Yes, yes,' Caroline broke in excitedly. 'Let's go up to see her.'

They had arrived at the hotel. On the boulevard the coachman had had to rein in the horses in the midst of a mass of carriages and pedestrians. During the day the Legislative Body had voted for war; and now a crowd was streaming down all the side-streets, flowing along the pavements, and invading the roadway. Beyond the Madeleine the sun had set behind a blood-red cloud, casting a reflection like a great fire which set the lofty windows ablaze. Dusk was falling, and it was an oppressive, melancholy hour, for the avenues were already fading into the darkness, and they were not yet studded with the bright dots of the gas-lamps. And among the moving crowds distant voices grew ever louder, and eyes gleamed in pale faces, while a great wind of anguish and amazement set every head spinning.

'Here's Mignon,' said Lucy. 'He'll tell us if there's any news.'

Mignon was standing under the vast porch of the Grand Hôtel. He looked nervous, and was gazing at the crowd. At Lucy's first question, he exclaimed angrily :

'How should I know? I've spent the last two days trying to get Rose to leave that room up there. . . . After all, it's idiotic, taking a risk like that ! She'll look marvellous if she catches it, with holes in her face ! That's all we need !'

The idea that Rose might lose her beauty was driving him to distraction. He had abandoned Nana completely and could not understand the stupid devotion women showed one another. But then he saw Fauchery crossing the boulevard, and when the journalist joined them, anxiously asking for news, the two men egged each other on. By now they were on the most familiar terms.

'Everything's just the same, old chap,' declared Mignon. 'You ought to go up and force her to come with you.'

'Thank you for nothing,' said the journalist. 'Why don't you go up yourself?'

Then, when Lucy asked them for the number of Nana's room, they begged her to make Rose come down; otherwise they would end up by getting very angry. However, Lucy and Caroline did not go up straight away. They had caught sight of Fontan strolling along with his hands in his pockets, greatly amused by the faces of the crowd. When he learnt that Nana was lying ill upstairs, he put on a great show of sympathy and said :

'Poor girl ! ... I'll go and have a word with her. ... What's the matter with her anyway?'

'Smallpox,' replied Mignon.

The actor had already taken a step in the direction of the courtyard, but now he turned back, muttering with a shudder :

'Good Lord !'

The smallpox was no joke. Fontan had nearly had it when he was five years old, and Mignon told the story of one of his nieces who had died of it. As for Fauchery, he could speak of it from personal experience, for he still bore traces of it in the shape of three little pock-marks which he pointed out to them at the base of his nose. And when Mignon again urged him to go up under the pretext that nobody ever had it twice he angrily rejected that theory, citing various cases and calling the medical profession a set of brutes. But Lucy and Caroline interrupted them, surprised at the growing crowd.

'Look what a lot of people !'

The darkness was deepening, and in the distance gas-lamps were lighting up one by one. Meanwhile curious faces

could be seen at the windows, while under the trees, the human flood swelled from one minute to the next, till it ran in one enormous stream from the Madeleine to the Bastille. The carriages in its midst rolled along slowly. A dull murmuring came from this dense mass of people, silent as yet, who had left their homes out of a desire to form a crowd, and were now shuffling along, their blood stirred by the same fever. But suddenly a strong movement divided the throng. Among the jostling, scattering groups, a band of men in workmen's caps and white smocks had appeared, uttering a regular cry which had the rhythmical beat of hammers on an anvil.

'To Berlin! To Berlin! To Berlin!'

And the crowd stared in gloomy distrust, yet already won over and moved by heroic visions, as if a military band were passing by.

'That's right, go and get your throats cut,' muttered Mignon, in a bitter philosophical mood.

But Fontan thought it all very fine, and spoke of enlisting. When the enemy was at the frontiers, every citizen ought to rise up to defend his country. And with that he assumed the pose of Bonaparte at Austerlitz.

'Look, are you coming upstairs with us?' Lucy asked him.

'To catch the smallpox?' he said. 'No thanks!'

On a bench in front of the Grand Hôtel, a man sat hiding his face in his handkerchief. On arriving, Fauchery had indicated him to Mignon with a wink of the eye. He was still there; yes, he was still there. And the journalist detained the two women in order to point him out to them. When the man raised his head they recognized him, and let out an exclamation. It was the Comte Muffat, glancing up at one of the windows.

'You know, he's been waiting there since this morning,' Mignon told them. 'I saw him at six o'clock, and he hasn't budged. ... The moment Labordette started spreading the news, he came here with his handkerchief hiding his face.... Every half hour he drags himself over to where we are to ask if the person upstairs is any better, and then he goes back and sits down.... But dammit all, that room isn't healthy.... It's

all very well being fond of people, but nobody wants to die.'

The Count sat with raised eyes, and did not seem conscious of what was going on around him. No doubt he was ignorant of the declaration of war, and he neither saw nor heard the crowd.

'Look, here he comes,' said Fauchery. 'Now you'll see.'

Sure enough, the Count had left the bench and was going in through the lofty doorway. But the porter, who had come to know his face, did not give him time to put his question. He said in a sharp tone of voice :

'Monsieur, she died just a minute ago.'

Nana dead! It was a blow for them all. Without a word Muffat had gone back to the bench, his face buried in his handkerchief. The others burst into exclamations, but they were cut short by another group that passed by howling :

'To Berlin! To Berlin! To Berlin!'

Nana dead! A lovely girl like her! Mignon sighed and looked relieved; at last Rose was going to come downstairs. A chill fell on the company. Fontan, whose dream in life was a tragic role, had put on a grief-stricken expression, pulling down the corners of his mouth and rolling his eyes, while Fauchery chewed his cigar nervously, for despite his professional cynicism he was genuinely touched. However, the two women continued to express their astonishment. The last time Lucy had seen her was at the Gaîté : Blanche too had seen her in *Mélusine*. Oh, how marvellous she looked, my dear, when she appeared at the back of the crystal grotto! The gentlemen also remembered her very well. Fontan had played Prince Cocorico. And now their memories had been awakened they launched into interminable details. What an effect she created with that splendid figure of hers in the crystal grotto! She didn't say a word; the authors had even cut the line or two they had given her, because they were superfluous. No, not a single word : it was more impressive that way, and she took the audience's breath away by simply showing herself. You wouldn't find another body like that. Those shoulders, those legs, and that waist! Funny to think that she was dead. You know, over her tights, she had nothing on but a golden girdle which hardly concealed her behind

and in front. Around her the grotto, all made of glass, was as bright as day. Cascades of diamonds flowed down; strings of white pearls streamed along the stalactites hanging from the ceiling; and amid the transparent atmosphere and flowing spring-water, which was crossed by a broad ray of electric light, she shone like a sun with that rosy skin and fiery hair of hers. Paris would always see her like that, shining high up in the midst of all that glittering crystal, like the Blessed Sacrament. No, it was just stupid to let yourself die when you'd reached a position like that. Now she must be looking a pretty sight in that room upstairs!

'And all that pleasure gone for good!' said Mignon in a melancholy voice, as became a man who did not like to see something good and useful wasted.

He sounded Lucy and Caroline to find out whether they were going upstairs after all. Of course they were; their curiosity had increased. Just then Blanche arrived, out of breath and cursing the crowds blocking the pavements. When she heard the news there was a fresh outburst of exclamations, and with a great rustling of skirts the ladies moved towards the staircase. Mignon followed them, calling out:

'Tell Rose I'm waiting for her. ... And tell her to hurry up.'

'Nobody really knows whether the danger of infection is greater at the beginning or near the end,' Fontan was explaining to Fauchery. 'A young doctor I know actually told me that the hours immediately following death are particularly dangerous. ... There's something in the air. ... Ah, but I'm sorry she went off suddenly like this. ... I'd have been so glad to shake hands with her one last time.'

'But what's the use of going up now?' said the journalist.

'Yes, what's the use?' the two others repeated.

The crowd was growing all the time. In the bright light cast by the shop-windows and the flickering glare of the gas-lamps, two streams of people could be distinguished flowing along the pavements, with countless hats bobbing on the surface. A fever of excitement was now rapidly gaining ground, and people were rushing to follow the bands of men in smocks. A continuous forward movement seemed to be

sweeping the roadway, and from thousands of throats the stubborn, staccato cry kept recurring :

'To Berlin ! To Berlin ! To Berlin !'

The room up on the fourth floor cost twelve francs a day, since Rose had wanted something decent and yet not luxurious, for luxury is unnecessary when a person is suffering. Hung with Louis XIII cretonne printed with a bold floral pattern, it contained the mahogany furniture found in all hotels, and on the floor there was a red carpet adorned with black foliage. The oppressive silence, relieved only by an occasional whisper, was suddenly broken by voices in the corridor.

'I tell you we're lost. The porter told us to turn to the right. . . . What a barracks the place is !'

'Wait a bit, let's have a look. Room 401, room 401 . . .'

'Look – over here . . . 405, 403. . . . We must be there. . . . Ah, at last, 401 ! . . . Hurry up ! Hush now, hush !'

The voices fell silent. There was a cough and a moment's pause. Then the door opened slowly, and Lucy came in, followed by Caroline and Blanche. They stopped short; there were already five women in the room. Gaga was lying back in the solitary armchair, a red velvet Voltaire. In front of the fireplace Simonne and Clarisse were standing chatting with Léa de Horn, who was seated on a chair; while by the bed, to the left of the door, Rose Mignon, perched on the edge of the log-bin, sat staring at the body, hidden in the shadow of the curtains. All the others had their hats and gloves on, and looked as if they were paying a call; she alone sat there with bare hands and untidy hair, pale with fatigue after three sleepless nights, stunned and heart-broken by this sudden death. A shaded lamp standing on the corner of the chest of drawers cast a bright pool of light over Gaga.

'What a dreadful shame !' murmured Lucy, as she shook hands with Rose. 'We wanted to say good-bye to her.'

And she turned her head to try and see her, but the lamp was too far off, and she did not dare bring it nearer. On the bed a grey mass lay stretched out, but only the red chignon was distinguishable and a pale patch which was presumably the face. Lucy added :

461

'I hadn't seen her since the Gaîté, at the back of the grotto ...'

At this Rose emerged from her stupor, and smiled as she said :

'Ah, she's changed, she's changed ...'

Then she lapsed into more contemplation, neither moving nor speaking. Deciding that perhaps they would be able to look at her a little later, the three women joined the others in front of the fireplace. Simonne and Clarisse were discussing the dead woman's diamonds in low tones. Did they really exist after all? Nobody had set eyes on them; the whole thing must be a hoax, but Léa de Horn knew somebody who had seen them, and they were enormous stones. Besides that wasn't all; she had brought back lots of other treasures from Russia – embroidered stuffs, valuable curios, a gold dinner service, even pieces of furniture. Yes, my dear, fifty-two boxes, huge packing-cases some of them, enough to fill three waggons. And it had all been left at the station. Hard luck, wasn't it, dying without even having time to unpack your bags. And she had a tidy bit of cash besides – something like a million. Lucy asked who was going to inherit it all. Oh, distant relations – probably the aunt. It would be a pleasant surprise for the old woman. She knew nothing about it yet, for the sick woman had stubbornly refused to let her know that she was ill, harbouring a grudge against her over her little boy's death. At that all the women exchanged sorrowful remarks about the little boy, whom they remembered seeing at the races – a sickly child who looked so old and sad, one of those poor brats, in fact, who had never asked to be born.

'He's better off under the ground,' said Blanche.

'So's she for that matter,' added Caroline. 'Life's no joke.'

In that gloomy room melancholy ideas began to take hold of them, and they felt a little frightened. It was silly staying there chatting so long, but a desire to see her kept them rooted to the spot. It was very hot, and in the humid gloom of the room, the lamp-glass cast a moon-like patch of light on the ceiling. Under the bed, a dish full of carbolic acid gave off an insipid smell. Every now and then a breath of air

462

filled out the curtains over the open window, and a dull roaring sound could be heard coming from the boulevard below.

'Did she suffer much?' asked Lucy, who was absorbed in contemplation of the clock, which was adorned with nude statuettes of the three Graces smiling like opera-dancers.

Gaga seemed to wake up.

'Heavens, yes!' she said. 'I was here and I can tell you it wasn't a pretty sight. . . . Why, she suddenly had a shuddering fit . . .'

But she was unable to continue her story, for a shout arose outside :

'To Berlin ! To Berlin ! To Berlin !'

And Lucy, who was suffocating, flung the window wide open and leant her elbows on the sill. It was pleasant there, with the cool air falling from the starry sky. Across the way there were windows ablaze with light, and reflections of gaslight were dancing in the gilt lettering of the shop-signs. Then down below there was a fascinating sight. The crowds could be seen flowing like a torrent along the pavements and in the roadway, in the midst of a medley of carriages, among vast moving shadows in which lanterns and gas-lamps gleamed like sparks. But the group which was approaching, shouting and yelling, carried torches, and a red glow was coming from the Madeleine, cutting a trail of fire through the crowds, and spreading far and wide over the people's heads like a sheet of flame. Lucy called Blanche and Caroline, forgetting where she was, and shouting :

'Come and look. . . . You've got a marvellous view from up here.'

All three leant out, fascinated. The trees obscured their view, and occasionally the torches disappeared under the foliage. They tried to catch a glimpse of their men, waiting down below, but a protruding balcony hid the door; and they could only make out the Comte Muffat, huddled on the bench like a dark parcel, with his face buried in his handkerchief. A carriage had drawn up, and Lucy recognized another of Nana's acquaintances getting out : Maria Blond. She was not alone; a stout man got out after her.

'It's that crook Steiner,' said Caroline. 'What, haven't

they sent him back to Cologne yet? ... I want to see his face when he comes in.'

They turned round, but when Maria Blond appeared ten minutes later, after taking the wrong staircase twice, she was alone. And when Lucy, in some astonishment, asked her where Steiner was, she retorted:

'What, him? My dear, you don't think he's going to come up here, do you? ... It's a wonder he's brought me as far as the door. ... There are about a dozen of them down there, smoking cigars.'

Sure enough, all the gentlemen of their acquaintance seemed to have gathered together outside. They had come out to see what was happening on the boulevards, had hailed one another outside the Grand Hôtel, and after expressing shocked surprise at the poor girl's death had gone on to discuss politics and strategy. Bordenave, Prullière, Daguenet, Labordette and others besides had swollen the group, and now they were listening to Fontan, who was explaining his plan for taking Berlin within a week.

Meanwhile, Maria Blond, moved to tears as she stood by the bedside, was murmuring like the others before her:

'Poor pet! ... The last time I saw her was at the Gaîté, in the grotto ...'

'Ah, she's changed, she's changed,' Rose Mignon repeated with her mournful smile.

Two more women arrived: Tatan Néné and Louise Violaine. They had been wandering around the Grand Hôtel for twenty minutes, passed on from one waiter to the next, and had gone up and down more than thirty flights of stairs, amid a stampede of travellers hurrying to leave Paris in the panic caused by the war and the excitement on the boulevards. Accordingly, when they came in, they simply collapsed on a couple of chairs, too tired to take any interest in the dead woman. Just then a loud noise came from the next room, where people were pushing trunks about and bumping into furniture to an accompaniment of outlandish syllables. It was a young Austrian couple. Gaga told how, during Nana's death-agony, the neighbours had played tag together, and how, as only a locked door separated the two

464

rooms, they heard them laughing and kissing whenever one of them caught the other.

'Come along, it's time we were off,' said Clarisse. 'We shan't bring her to life again. ... Coming, Simonne?'

They all looked at the bed out of the corners of their eyes, but nobody budged. All the same, they began getting ready, giving little pats to their skirts. Lucy was leaning on the window-sill again. She was alone this time, and a feeling of sadness gradually took her by the throat, as if a wave of melancholy were rising from that howling mob. Torches were still passing by, shedding showers of sparks; and the crowds stretching away into the distance were surging along like flocks of sheep being driven to the slaughter-house at night. These shadowy masses rolling by in a dizzying human flood exhaled a sense of terror, a pitiful premonition of future massacres. Broken cries came from their throats as they rushed in a fever of excitement towards the unknown, out of sight beyond the dark wall of the horizon.

'To Berlin! To Berlin! To Berlin!'

Lucy turned round and stood, her back to the window, her face very pale.

'Heavens, what's going to become of us?'

The women shook their heads. They were in a serious mood, very uneasy about the turn events were taking.

'Speaking for myself,' said Caroline Héquet in her deliberate way, 'I'm leaving for London the day after tomorrow. ... Mama's already over there getting a house ready for me. ... I'm certainly not going to stay here in Paris to be killed.'

Her mother, cautious woman that she was, had persuaded her to invest all her money abroad. After all you never knew how a war might end. But Maria Blond expressed disgust at this attitude. She was a patriot, and spoke of following the army.

'What a coward! ... Yes, if they wanted me, I'd put on a man's clothes to take a pot-shot at those Prussian pigs. ... And what would it matter if we all snuffed it afterwards? Our skins aren't as precious as all that!'

Blanche de Sivry flared up angrily.

'Don't you dare say anything against the Prussians!. ... They're men like all the rest, and they aren't always pestering us women like your precious Frenchmen. ... They've just expelled the little Prussian who was with me, a terribly rich fellow, and such a gentle soul he couldn't hurt a fly. It's disgraceful the way they've treated him, and it's ruined me. ... And if anybody starts annoying me, I'll go and join him in Germany.'

Then, while the two of them were squabbling together, Gaga murmured sadly :

'It's all up with me; I never have any luck. It's only a week since I finished paying for my little house at Juvisy, and God knows the trouble it cost me. Lili had to help me. ... And now war's been declared, and the Prussians'll come, and they'll burn everything. ... How can I begin all over again at my time of life, I'd like to know?'

'Bah!' said Clarisse. 'I don't give a damn for the war. I'll always get by.'

'That's right,' said Simonne. 'It'll be a bit queer at first. ... But we may do quite well out of it.'

Her smile explained what she meant. Tatan Néné and Louise Violaine agreed with her. The former told them that she had had some marvellous times with the military; they were good sorts, and would do anything to please a woman. But as the ladies had raised their voices, Rose Mignon, still sitting on the log-bin by the bed, silenced them with a whispered 'Hush!'

They all froze, and glanced towards the dead woman, as if this request for silence had emanated from the shadows inside the curtains. In the oppressive silence which followed, a deathly hush which made them conscious of the rigid corpse stretched out near them, the shouts of the mob burst out :

'To Berlin! To Berlin! To Berlin!'

But soon they forgot again. Léa de Horn, who had a political *salon* where former ministers of Louis-Philippe were in the habit of coining subtle epigrams, shrugged her shoulders and continued in a low voice :

'What utter folly this war is! What bloodthirsty stupidity!'

At this Lucy promptly took up the cudgels for the Empire. She had slept with a Prince of the Imperial Blood, and the war was a point of family honour for her.

'Nonsense, my dear. We couldn't let ourselves be insulted any more. This war is for France's honour. . . . Oh, you know, I'm not saying that because of the Prince. He was an old miser. Just imagine, at night, when he was going to bed, he used to hide his louis in his boots, and when we played bezique, he used beans, because one day I'd grabbed the stake-money for fun. . . . But that doesn't prevent me from being fair. The Emperor was right.'

Léa shook her head with an air of superiority, as became a woman who was repeating the opinion of important people. And raising her voice, she said :

'This is the end. They're out of their minds at the Tuileries. France ought to have driven them out yesterday . . .'

They all interrupted her angrily. What was the matter with her? She must be mad attacking the Emperor like that. Were people unhappy? Was business doing badly? Paris would never enjoy itself so much again.

Gaga was beside herself with rage, wide awake now and very indignant.

'Shut up ! I've never heard such nonsense. You don't know what you're saying. . . . I lived through Louis-Philippe's reign, and it was a time of beggars and misers, my dear. And then came 48. Oh, that was a pretty disgusting thing, their Republic ! After the February Revolution I nearly starved to death – yes, me, Gaga ! . . . Oh, if you'd been through all that, you'd go down on your knees before the Emperor, because he's been a regular father to us, yes, a regular father . . .'

They had to calm her down, but she continued with pious fervour :

'Oh, Lord, try to make the Emperor victorious. And save the Empire for us !'

They all echoed this prayer. Blanche admitted that she burnt candles in church for the Emperor. Caroline had fallen for him, and for two months had hung around wherever he was likely to pass, but without managing to attract his attention. And the others burst into furious denunciations of the

Republicans, and talked of exterminating them at the frontier, so that Napoleon III, after beating the enemy, should reign peacefully in the midst of universal enjoyment.

'That horrid Bismarck – now there's another swine for you!' said Maria Blond.

'To think that I knew him!' cried Simonne. 'If only I'd known what he was going to do, I'd have put some poison in his glass.'

But Blanche, with whom the expulsion of her Prussian still rankled, ventured to defend Bismarck. Perhaps he wasn't so bad as all that. Every man to his trade.

'You know,' she added, 'he adores women.'

'What the hell do we care?' said Clarisse. 'We don't want to pick him up, do we?'

'There's always too many men like that,' Louise Violaine declared solemnly. 'It's better to do without them than get mixed up with such monsters.'

And the discussion continued. Bismarck was torn to pieces, and each woman, in her Bonapartist zeal, gave him a good kick, while Tatan Néné kept saying:

'Bismarck! They've driven me crazy talking about that fellow! ... Oh, I hate him! ... I've never met him, mind.... You can't know everybody.'

'Never mind,' said Léa de Horn, by way of conclusion. 'That Bismarck's going to give us a damned good hiding ...'

But she could not continue. The ladies all pounced on her at once. What? A hiding? It was Bismarck they were going to send home, thumping him with their rifle-butts all the way. What a thing for a Frenchwoman to say!

'Hush,' whispered Rose, offended by all the noise.

Reminded of the chill presence of the corpse, they all stopped together. They felt ill-at-ease, confronted once more with death, and filled with a vague fear of disease. On the boulevard the hoarse, broken shouting continued:

'To Berlin! To Berlin! To Berlin!'

Then, just as they were making up their minds to go, a voice was heard calling from the corridor:

'Rose! Rose!'

468

Gaga opened the door in astonishment, and disappeared for a moment. When she returned, she said:

'My dear, it's Fauchery. He's out there at the end of the corridor. . . . He won't come any further, and he's beside himself because you're staying near that body.'

Mignon had at last succeeded in persuading the journalist to go upstairs. Lucy, who was still at the window, leant out, and caught sight of the gentlemen on the pavement, looking up and signalling to her. Mignon was shaking his fists in exasperation; Steiner, Fontan, Bordenave and the others were stretching out their arms with an air of anxious reproach, while Daguenet was simply standing smoking a cigar, with his hands behind his back, so as not to compromise himself.

'That's right, dear,' said Lucy, leaving the window open. 'I promised to make you go down. . . . They're all calling us now.'

Rose slowly got up from the log-bin.

'I'm coming, I'm coming,' she murmured. 'She doesn't need me any more. . . . They're going to send along a nurse.'

And she started hunting around for her hat and shawl. Mechanically she poured some water into a basin on the dressing-table, and while washing her hands and face, continued:

'You know, it's been a great blow to me. . . . We were never nice to each other in the old days. And yet this has driven me out of my senses. . . . I've got all sorts of strange ideas, wanting to die myself, and feeling the end of the world coming. . . . Yes, I need some fresh air.'

The corpse was beginning to poison the atmosphere of the room. Casual insouciance gave place to sudden panic.

'Let's be off, darlings,' Gaga kept saying. 'It isn't healthy here.'

They hurried out, glancing at the bed as they went. But while Lucy, Blanche and Caroline were still there, Rose gave a last look round, to make sure that the room was tidy. She drew one of the curtains across the window; and then it occurred to her that the lamp did not look right, and that what was needed was a candle. She lit one of the brass

candelabra on the mantelpiece and placed it on the bedside table next to the corpse. A bright light suddenly lit up the dead woman's face. Horror-stricken they all shuddered and took flight.

'Ah, she's changed, she's changed,' murmured Rose Mignon, the last to leave.

She went out and shut the door. Nana was left alone, her face upturned in the light from the candle. What lay on the pillow was a charnel-house, a heap of pus and blood, a shovelful of putrid flesh. The pustules had invaded the whole face, so that one pock touched the next. Withered and sunken, they had taken on the greyish colour of mud, and on that shapeless pulp, in which the features had ceased to be discernible, they already looked like mould from the grave. One eye, the left eye, had completely foundered in the bubbling purulence, and the other, which remained half open, looked like a dark, decaying hole. The nose was still suppurating. A large reddish crust starting on one of the cheeks was invading the mouth, twisting it into a terrible grin. And around this grotesque and horrible mask of death, the hair, the beautiful hair, still blazed like sunlight and flowed in a stream of gold. Venus was decomposing. It was as if the poison she had picked up in the gutters, from the carcases left there by the roadside, that ferment with which she had poisoned a whole people, had now risen to her face and rotted it.

The room was empty. A great breath of despair came up from the boulevard and filled out the curtains.

'To Berlin ! To Berlin ! To Berlin !'

MORE ABOUT PENGUINS, PELICANS, PEREGRINES AND PUFFINS

For further information about books available from Penguins please write to Dept EP, Penguin Books Ltd, Harmondsworth, Middlesex UB7 0DA.

In the U.S.A.: For a complete list of books available from Penguins in the United States write to Dept DG, Penguin Books, 299 Murray Hill Parkway, East Rutherford, New Jersey 07073.

In Canada: For a complete list of books available from Penguins in Canada write to Penguin Books Canada Ltd, 2801 John Street, Markham, Ontario L3R 1B4.

In Australia: For a complete list of books available from Penguins in Australia write to the Marketing Department, Penguin Books Australia Ltd, P.O. Box 257, Ringwood, Victoria 3134.

In New Zealand: For a complete list of books available from Penguins in New Zealand write to the Marketing Department, Penguin Books (N.Z.) Ltd, Private Bag, Takapuna, Auckland 9.

In India: For a complete list of books available from Penguins in India write to Penguin Overseas Ltd, 706 Eros Apartments, 56 Nehru Place, New Delhi 110019.